# Aye, I am a Fairy

Second book in The Fairies Saga

*USA Today Bestselling author*

# Dani Haviland

Copyright 2014 by Dani Haviland
Published by Chill Out!
All rights reserved

~ The Fairies Saga ~
By Dani Haviland

In chronological order:
Naked in the Winter Wind
Ha'penny Jenny
Aye, I am a Fairy
Dances Naked
Little Bear and the Ladies
The Great Big Fairy
Chasing Christmas
Little Drummer Boy
Never Too Young
Time in a Little Blue Bottle

ISBN 978-0-9840308-2-8

(Book cover by www.TheKillionGroupInc.com)

## SOMETHING SPECIAL

Just so you won't get confused about who's who, I put a CAST OF CHARACTERS on the last page of the book. I figured that was the easiest place to find it.

And if while reading, you find that someone is narrating the story—that it's in the first person—that's just Evie taking over. Sometimes that old lady in a young person's body just won't shush!

(If you want to know more about Evie and her experience with time travel and rejuvenation, read NAKED IN THE WINTER WIND, the first book in the series)

Quickie lesson in Scots: "I dinna ken ye cut yer heid with the dirk," means, "I didn't know you cut your head with the knife."

# Contents

# *Part One — Are You My Mama?

## *Preface

*August 12, 1781*
*Pomeroys' Place, North Carolina*

"Dang, I wish there was a way I could call Leah; tell her I was sorry I had to leave, that I loved her so much, but that she had three infant siblings in the 18th century who I had to go back and take care of, that she was an adult now and could manage just fine, and, that…that…" I was exasperated and couldn't finish my explanation, but I knew Sarah understood.

"I know what you're going through, and I think there might be a way to let her know. I mean, it's how I keep my sanity with having my daughter in the 20th century." Sarah reached into the cupboard and pulled out a sheet of paper, a small wooden box, and a goose feather.

"What? Write to her?" I asked, stunned at her suggestion.

Sarah nodded silently, lips pulled taut in a painful grimace. She set the items on the kitchen table and picked up the paring knife. She scored the end of the feather, creating a reservoir in the end of the quill, and then offered it to me. "I write her about our life, the day to day things mostly, then put the dated letters in the box and let them accumulate. Eventually, I'll send them overseas to Barden Hall with a note for Jody's family to hold them, unopened, until the year 1980." Sarah opened the inlaid topped box, took out the small inkwell, and set it next to the paper and quill.

"If, I mean, I'm *sure* Ramona and Gregg will have contacted Sam Eastman, my best friend and former professor, by then. He was the only one I trusted to tell that I was going back, coming back here to this time. I'm certain he already figured out that's what happened to Mona when she disappeared—that she followed me to the 18th century. And now she has returned to his time, back to the 20th century, with a husband and two children."

Sarah sighed, shrugged her shoulders, and then relaxed into a smile. "Call me a romantic," she said as she played with the nib on the quill, running her finger over the fresh cut to make sure it was smooth. "In 1980, I went back to Barden Hall in Scotland—that's the estate where Jody was born. I worked up the nerve to talk to the current owners. Of course, they didn't know who I was, and I wasn't going to tell them that I was the wife of the man who owned their place 200 years earlier!"

Sarah regained her composure quickly. "I just said I was intrigued by the location, and had heard a bit of its history when I was in town. They told me times were tough and that they were going to have to sell the property. I could hear the heartbreak in their voices. I decided right then and there to do what I could to help Jody's family, even if they were about seven generations removed from him. I bought the estate and let them stay on as caretakers. I...I didn't know what the future held, but didn't want the ancestral land and buildings to go to just anyone. I thought Mona might want to live there after she got out of school and was ready to settle down. Sam had the deed and was to give it to her when she graduated or got married or whenever. I left it up to him to determine when she would be receptive to the idea of living in Scotland. I told him just to make sure he gave the current occupants at least six months' notice before they had to move out. And well, I didn't even know if they wanted to live there after they got the money."

"So, you're saying I should write a letter, or letters, now, and put them in your little box there, then your daughter can give it, them, to Leah?"

"Well, that could work, but you might want to establish another destination—sort of an alternate backup site—for your letters, in case mine don't make it. You know what they say about putting all your eggs in one basket..." she joked.

I frowned as I realized what she had said. "Twentieth century, you said. But I came from the 21st century, 2012. Well, at least the first time. I just came back from 2013 last week. You're writing to, what, 1980?"

"It doesn't matter which decade it is. And it probably won't make a difference to them whether or not they even get these." She sighed and stroked the top of the inlaid wooden box. "I mean, it's not as if they know we're writing them. I'm doing it for Jody and me. He writes, too. It helps us feel connected with them. I *hope* they get the letters, but I doubt that they'll make a dramatic difference in their lives." She shrugged her shoulders. "I can't take photographs, so they're getting written snapshots of our lives instead."

"So you think I could write a letter now, today, and ask for someone to get in touch with my daughter two hundred and thirty years from now? That then—in our future, their present—they could let her know why I had to leave and that I'm okay?" I was starting to feel better already.

"Well, continuity is the key; it has to be successfully passed down through the generations. You can write a letter and I'll put it in with mine, and maybe the 21st century Barden Hall group will forward it to her or, or..."

*If I only knew who I could send a letter to...even a card...a business card...*

*My eyes opened wide with a clear, distinct memory—bright, shining, and sparkled with hope. Sarah's treasure box of letters had ignited a memory for me. The business card Wallace had found in my backpack two months ago, just after the babies were born, was from a James Melbourne. I*

2

*suddenly knew who he was! New memories were tumbling over each other—like a movie preview—an interesting clip, but not enough words or images to tell the whole story. I recalled meeting a charming young Englishman, a James Melbourne, and an odd little man, a Master Simon. That's when I first encountered Simon! It was in a café in Greensboro. I figured out a map, an ancient map... I shook my head. That wasn't important. What I needed to know was if James was from the same Melbourne line as those who were now living in London. Wallace's Uncle Tony, Julian's brother, was a Melbourne. And he was possibly—probably, hopefully—James Melbourne's ancestor. Well, I knew they shared the same coat of arms, and maybe, if they shared the same residence—hmm...*

"Sarah," I said, bringing myself out of my own reverie, "I know of someone now whose family will still be around in the 21st century." I inhaled deeply and elaborated. "You said it would be best to have two sources of delivery, right? So I'll leave my originals with yours, and then send copies to...hmm. I need to talk to Wallace. Excuse me; I'll be write back. Get it? W.R.I.T.E. Oh, never mind."

Wallace was bringing out Aries for his daily ride. The high-strung stallion didn't like being cooped up and was easier to handle if ridden daily. I ran outside, my arms flailing in the air, signaling for Wallace to stop before he rode out. "Whoa, whoa, wait," I blurted out breathlessly.

"Is there something wrong?" he asked, and pulled back the reins, ready to dismount.

"No, no. I just have to ask you a quick question. What are the chances your Uncle Tony would ever sell his place in England?"

"Which one?" he replied.

I'm sure my shocked look wasn't what he expected. His shy grin at my reaction wasn't the least bit rude, but still made me feel silly.

"Well, I'm certain the last place he'd ever sell or relinquish would be his home in London. Country estates can come and go, but that house is as much a part of him as his right hand. He could go on without it, but wouldn't like it." He scowled in concern and repositioned himself in the saddle, ready again for his boot soles to touch the soil. "Are you sure you're all right? Should I put off the ride?"

"Oh, no, please don't. It's just that I think I found a way to tell Leah what happened—or will happen—so maybe she won't feel so bad that I left. I'll explain when you get back. Have a nice ride, okay?" I said, and blew him a kiss.

Wallace reached out and gently retrieved the imaginary buss in the palm of his hand as if it were a butterfly, brought it to his lips, kissed it, and blew it back to me. "Share this with the children. We won't be too long." He reined the horse back toward the road and was off like his boots were on fire and his trousers were catching.

3

I skipped back to the house, unable to hold back my elation at finding a way to contact Leah. I could let her know about her new family, what had happened to me, and that I hadn't left her on purpose…at least, the first time. I would be able to 'talk' to her, even across more than two centuries.

*Last year, I had awakened here—in what was the past for me—with amnesia. Sometime before that—probably no more than a day or two earlier and in the 21st century—I became acquainted with a descendent of Wallace's Uncle Tony: James Melbourne. I was sure he'd help me out if I wrote to him and ask that he contact Leah and pass on my information. I grinned as I recalled our little meeting with the curious map owner and (unbeknownst to us) time traveler, Master Simon. James knew right away that there was more to the map than Simon was telling us. Well, I'd explain that to him, too, in the letter.*

"Mommy, Mommy; both boys want you real bad," Jenny hollered, almost running into me, unaware that I was moving so quickly in her direction. "And Leo has a poopy clout. Do you want me to change it while you feed Judah?"

I held onto Jenny's shoulders, steadying the two of us after our minor collision. "That would be wonderful. I don't know what I did to get such a great helper, but if I couldn't feel you under my hands right now, I'd swear you were an angel. Come on; I'll race you to the house."

I bent forward, dropped my hands to the ground, and crouched into a starting position. "Ready, set…hey! You were supposed to wait until I said go," I carped, as I picked up my skirt to chase after my ten-year-old adopted daughter. It was a great day.

# *1 Blasted Alarm Clock

*Monday, August 5, 2013*
*Greensboro, North Carolina*

*Good morning, good morning, good morninnnnngggg guhh guhh!*
*Nothing to do...*

Slam, thump, "Ouch! Son-a-bitchin' thing!" Leah finally got the alarm shut off on the fourth smack. She must have moved it when she got into bed last night. Or was that this morning?

"Ugh," she groaned as she turned over. She grabbed the gray stuffed hippopotamus and plopped it over her throbbing head, effectively shutting out the world with the loftiness of the velour and polyester water-horse pillow.

*In the town, where I was born, lived a ma'a'aan...*thump.

"Hah! Gotcha on the first try!" Leah exclaimed with pride, then fell back and moaned, "Oh, no," the pain of her class one hangover trumping her momentary elation at winning the whack-the-alarm-clock contest. She rolled over and looked at it. It was 5:15. If she had to work today, she only had 15 minutes to get dressed and slug down a cup of coffee before it was time to head out the door. If she had the day off, she could roll over and sleep until noon if she wanted. It would be easy enough to check. She made sure she entered her work schedule into her smartphone every week as soon as it was posted.

"Okay, where did I leave you this time?" Leah was forever misplacing her phone. She was so notorious that she even customized a message for the opening screen page that said, "Tell Leah you found her phone. You can contact her at work at Moses H. Cone Hospital...." So far, every one of the three people who had found it had returned it. "Mom was worse than me," she said softly, "she lost and found hers five times."

Then she saw them: the two identical solar-powered smartphones. "Oh, crap." Traces of talcum powder were still visible on one. She had dusted it the night before, looking for the engraved initials to verify what she already knew: it was her mother's.

*Her mother disappeared from Greensboro ten months ago, apparently falling off the earth without a trace. Yesterday she reappeared at her hospital's emergency room with a musket ball in her shoulder, looking forty years younger, fifty pounds thinner, and as a nursing mother. Before they had a chance for explanations, Leah was knocked out by the phony attending doctor. He then kidnapped Mom and shuffled her out the door in a wheelchair. He forced her to drive away—drugged and still recovering—in a stolen car, leading the hospital personnel and police on a chaotic chase to a vacant lot at the edge of town. The police found the car within minutes, but not its occupants.*

*Leah, still stunned at her mother's sudden appearance then re-disappearance, had told her supervisor that she was related to the kidnapped woman. Nurse Gata, not wanting to be burdened with paperwork or inquiries, gave Leah the left-behind personal belongings bag. It's only contents: the colonial-style dress her mother had been wearing when she came into the emergency room and the prototype smartphone.*

"I guess it wasn't a dream after all," she said as she softly touched the phone with the white disclosed initials DUM: Danielle Ursula Madigan.

Leah picked up her own phone, the one without the powder, and scanned her calendar. Cool, she had today off. She stumbled into the kitchen, opened the refrigerator door, and saw the carton of orange juice. "I don't think so," she groaned, "What I need is the hair of the dog that bit me." She shoved the juice aside. "Ooh, there's an idea," she said and grabbed the carton of vanilla-flavored soymilk coffee creamer. She took her dirty coffee cup out of the sink, gave it a fast rinse, shook off the water, and then poured a healthy slug of the sweetened coffee creamer in it.

"Ah, my little friend," she said to the bottle of Glenturret whisky on the counter and tipped a shot into the mug. She swished the cup, dipped her finger in it, and swirled the mix. She lifted the cup to her lips and sniffed. "Smells pretty good, but I'm sure it'd be better warmed."

She put the cup in the microwave, nuked it half a minute, then pulled it out and did the swish, finger dip, and swirl routine again to make sure the hot and cold spots were blended. "Ah, that's too good," she said as she finished sipping down half the concoction with her first taste. "That should take the edge off the hangover."

*Ding dong.*

Leah took her cup of homemade crème liqueur to the table and sat down in front of the two phones. The notification tone wasn't from hers—she had disabled the audio email and text message alerts long ago. She picked up her mother's phone and slid her finger across the face of it. The little animated letter was dancing all over the screen. Her mother's email address was still valid, although there hadn't been any real activity on it for the last six months. The Alchemy spam blocker had virtually blocked all of the junk mail; this one must be legitimate. Leah took another sip of her liquid courage and double-clicked the letter.

*'Remember meeting me in that little café in Greensboro last Halloween? Did that strange little man—Simon was it?—ever figure out his map? Hopefully you were able to finish your little Revolutionary War sightsee and had a safe journey home to Alaska. I will be returning to North Carolina 5th August. After I take care of some business, I would like to visit your state. Is your offer for a three-hour tour still open? Please let me know so I can schedule flights on this end. Yours sincerely,, James Melbourne'*

"What the fu..." Leah looked at the properties of the email. The

6

origination was a UK internet provider and the name was 'Lord' James Melbourne, MP. Last Halloween—that was when her mother had first disappeared. Maybe this man could shed some light on what happened.

Leah quickly typed in her reply. *'Please contact me as soon as possible. This is in regards to my mother, Dani Madigan. Thank you, Leah Madigan.'*

She hit send, then wondered if she should have included her phone number. "Nope. I doubt I'd be coherent over the phone. If he's going to be here today, maybe we can meet face to face." Leah touched her hair and realized she was a mess. She'd better clean up if she was going to meet the man—a British Lord, no less—who might have a clue about what happened to her mother last year. She wouldn't tell him about yesterday unless… No, don't anticipate, she admonished herself. Just take a shower and go from there. One small step at a time. Baby steps, lady, baby steps.

## *2 To Go or Not to Go

*Two days earlier: Saturday, August 3, 2013*
*London, England*

There was nothing physically wrong with him, but James was miserable. He was emotionally exhausted, and felt as if he had just endured six months of intestinal flu, with boils and a case of jock itch thrown in just to make sure he was as worn down as much as humanly possible.

By all that was sane or usual, he should still be in honeymoon mode—frisky and fondling the blonde beauty he had married after a whirlwind courtship—not protecting himself both physically and financially from her. Thefts, graft, slander. She never seemed to run out of ammunition for her assaults on everything he had or was.

He realized now that the marriage had been a sham from the beginning. As soon as the 'I do's' were exchanged, she began shunning him. Although she eventually allowed him to consummate the marriage, he never had a decent wedding night with her, or even an adequate afternoon quickie.

All aspects of his existence were a mess because of her. He had done all he could to reclaim his former wonderfully-boring-but-financially-secure-life, and now it was time for the professionals to take over. His solicitor's office was doing everything legally possible to protect him from further virtual assaults, and hopefully they could reverse the recent damages. She had contrived to empty all of their joint accounts, and now her fleet of hired vultures was seeking every last asset he had or hoped to have.

James needed distraction, any task would suffice, but a potentially profitable one in a foreign country, far away from the carrion-consuming crew's prying eyes, would be best.

The owner of the small American company had pursued him for three months now. For some reason he—or would that be she?—really wanted him to buy the historic mill near Greensboro, North Carolina. By the numbers, this would be an easy, 'Thank you for the offer, but we are not interested at this time,' response for purchase of the modest American textile company. He had left a message for the owner two months ago, tactfully explaining that this venture really wasn't what he was looking for. That hadn't slowed down the communiqués, though. Every other week, he received more pictures and the latest figures, always with a personal note attached. He should have been firmer with his refusal, and request that the proposals cease, but now he was glad that there was a diversion for him. Yes, it looked like America was calling louder all the time, and now was a good time to answer.

*Numbers don't show everything of value here. Just come by and visit the mill. I'm sure you will then agree that this would be a great*

*investment/acquisition for you.*
        *Regards, Bibb*

Bibb. What kind of name was that? He had never been able to speak with Bibb on the phone. All correspondence had been via post or email. His request for a videoconference had been gently rejected in such a way that further appeals would have been discourteous. Was Bibb a man or a woman? The handwriting was firm and open, not sloppy or inconsistent. That in itself showed honesty and self-assuredness. You can't judge a book by its cover, or a company by the hard numbers from what this note was saying. However, a strong hand meant something, he rationalized. It sounded like a trip to America was in order.

His passport was still valid, at least he was fairly certain it was. "Better check it out. That's all I need," James said to the portrait on the wall, "to show up at Heathrow with expired papers."

He swung the oil painting of great-grandpa-so-many-times-over Lord Anthony 'Tony' Melbourne away from the wall to reveal the safe. He dialed in the combination: 1-8-5, his IQ on the Mensa entrance exam. Clotilde would never figure out that one. She was so dim that she had to be prompted on how to address a dinner invitation. "I guess that's why she's so fond of credit cards. She needs help to write a check, but can manage to scrawl a 'C' with a curlicue tail on a slip of paper."

And there it was. The passport was still in its plastic bag, right on top of the bundle of mysterious old letters that were still tied together with a faded blue ribbon.

Those letters. Grandpa said they weren't to be opened until when? He remembered it was the 21st century, but couldn't recall which year. It seemed like forever when he heard about them as a child. He thought he'd be an old man before he was allowed to read them. He had agreed not to snoop, though. It was the principle of honor involved, after all. The Melbourne family valued honor more than any other concept. I guess it could be said that they prided themselves on how honorable they were. Obviously, having a lot of, or too much, pride was not a problem for them. All that mattered was honor.

"Do the honorable deed, and it will come back to bless you—repay you, if you will—many times over, but only if done selflessly. A good deed done with greed as motivation is null and void, or worse," Grandpa would lecture. Then he'd add his own take on the family rule: "'Twill come back to bite ye on the arse, sure as sin," he'd mimic in a broad Scots accent.

He never tired of hearing Grandpa's stories, even though they seemed to get a bit more colorful with every retelling. The tale of the fairies who helped draft the Magna Carta had to be out and out fabrication, but Grandpa had such a way with words, blending facts James had learned in

9

school and knew to be true with fantasies worthy of a Hugo Award.

The stories of Great-grandpa Lord Anthony Melbourne and his heroics in the Second Uprising were admirable but boring. He didn't have the excitement and mystery that surrounded his younger brother, Lord Julian Hart, who had disappeared in America during the Revolutionary War. Maybe that's why James always kept Uncle Julian's portrait with him wherever he lived or went to school: he was fascinated by the rumors, mystery, and intrigue.

"Speaking of intrigue, what's the status of that passport? I'd better check before I get distracted again," he said to the portrait.

James had ADD, attention deficit disorder, or so he had been told. "Nah," he replied to his own unspoken thought. "I just don't want to focus on only one project at a time. I'd miss out on too much that way," he rationalized aloud.

However, that was not how his teachers felt. "He'll never accomplish anything," they'd say. "A straight path is the shortest route to one's goal." They suggested, almost insisted, that he be medicated, but Grandpa refused.

"Don't worry about it," Grandpa would soothe. "Don't live your life to please them or anyone else. It's your life to live, and you should choose, or better still, make your own road, no matter how meandering or long it may be. When I was young, the saying was, 'If it feels good, do it.' I would say the same to you with the caveat that 'do it' as long as it doesn't hurt others, or yourself."

James turned the bag over in his hand. He kept the passport in a zip top plastic bag just in case something spilled in his travel bag or he got caught in a downpour or "I fall in a lake," he joked to Grandpa.

"Can you imagine these bags two hundred, even one hundred, years ago?" Grandpa asked. "People would think they were magic, maybe conjured up by a witch. Right handy, though, aye?" Grandfather was always putting a spin on the common items in their lives, encouraging James to appreciate all the simple, modern-day treasures most people took for granted.

*Focus, man: what's the date!* James pulled out the passport. Great, it didn't expire until 2016; three more years left on it. "Hey! Here's that little Greek coin from my trip to North Carolina last year." The man at the rare coin store had only offered him £100 for it. The online rate was a little more or less, depending on the buyer. He had decided he'd rather keep the token that had come with the purchase of the stolen Revolutionary War document than admit the financial blunder.

"Another poor investment," his father had chided. "When will you learn?" James had disappointed him again.

James removed the rose-themed business card from inside the

passport book. "Dani Madigan," he said aloud. "Sweet little old lady. Hey, I wonder if she knows that her first name is scrambled into her last. Probably does—she seemed pretty bright."

There was no telling how that fiasco with the map, the coin, and that strange little old man—Simon without a second name—would have turned out last autumn if she hadn't interceded. She was from Alaska, visiting Greensboro, and had no interest in the matter, but had stepped in and acted as mediator for the two men.

James soon found out that the 'historical document' he had purchased earlier that day from a shaggy-haired man in period dress, just outside the Gilford Courthouse, was not a record of soldiers or regiments involved in a Revolutionary War battle with Great Uncle Julian as the homespun-clan man had alluded to. What the velvet bag actually contained was a parchment map. It appeared old, and made no sense. It was hand drawn in black ink with exotic—or encrypted—symbols, and had no reference key.

Evidently the document had been stolen from Simon—the uptight old coot in a black frock coat that Dani had rescued from the side of the road earlier that same day. The odd-looking man was passionate about the chart with the strange writing, and probably would have done anything to get it back. Thank goodness, he didn't have a gun or knife. Since there was nothing on the map that James was interested in, he negotiated a deal. Simon could have the map, and he would keep the silver coin that had been hidden, threaded on a cord, tucked inside the velvet sheath.

James set the card down and picked up the Athena and Pegasus struck silver coin with the two small holes drilled in it. *Well, it may not be worth much, but it would make a sweet little pendant. I'd better hide it before Clotilde finds it and makes off with it, too.* He stuffed the coin deep into the corner of his hemp fabric wallet. "Stay put—I might need you later," he said aloud to the silver token.

He picked up the card again. "I wonder how Dani's doing. If I'm going all the way to America to check out that mill, I might as well take a side trip to see her in Alaska. Beautiful summers, great fishing…maybe she knows of a charter service that lands on glaciers. What's the name of that tall mountain—McKinley is it?—or do they call it by its native name now, Denali? Either way, a trip with good company, fresh air, and lots of frozen blue water would be a great distraction.

And now was a great time for a holiday. There might not be much left of the Melbourne family fortune after Clotilde was done suing him for divorce. He might as well enjoy it until the judgment was decided. If her solicitors got their way, she'd have it all. Well, maybe she wouldn't get it all, but she was sure to get at least half, if not more, of the property and monies. She had a fleet of solicitors working on commission, and now there

11

was the sudden absence of their prenup.

Even though there had been a pre-nuptial agreement, all the copies had mysteriously disappeared. He couldn't believe there wasn't a record of it, so went to the registrar to look for it himself. As it turned out, Clotilde had been there first. It wouldn't have been so bad if the clerk had just said, "Nope, nothing here. Sorry you made the trip," but that smirk! And the snide remark that went with it, "Are you sure there was a prenuptial? Clotilde, er, Lady Melbourne, came by earlier, and we couldn't find it for her either."

Well, between her insincere 'sorry,' and the way the woman was twisting the pearl and diamond pendant he had given Clotilde months earlier as a gift, rather an enticement, he was sure there was complicity. Price for filing a pre-nuptial agreement: £10. Price for absconding with the duly-filed copy of same agreement: one diamond and pearl necklace.

Maybe not all was lost. He couldn't prove Clotilde had stolen the document, but the agreement was referred to in their marriage contract. Hopefully that would hold sway in court, even if the original couldn't be found.

Grandpa had warned him about her, but he had been 'truly, deeply, madly in love' with Clotilde. He should have believed Grandpa when he told him that he was only 'truly, deeply, madly in lust' with the hot little blonde.

James shuddered at the thought of her and the impact she had made on his life. "It's only stuff and money," he reminded himself aloud, trying to rationalize the additional losses he was sure to incur. "She can't take my breath away—at least, not anymore—now that my eyes are truly open. And she can't steal my joy. I can still find happiness in the larks, roses, and butterflies that enhance the beauty of a warm summer's day. She has to live with herself, not me. Thank You, Lord, for that!"

Roses, rose card, remember to contact Dani… It's probably oh-my-gawd-thirty in Alaska right now. So, send an email—fast and unobtrusive—and there for her to read when she's ready. *Remember Grandpa used to say, 'Two hundred, even one hundred, years ago, who would have believed we could communicate so quickly? Sending pictures over the airwaves and bouncing invisible information—letters, pictures, even movies—off of artificial moons? It would be considered magic or, even worse, diabolical.'*

*Yes, I appreciate the speed of life, Grandpa—at least parts of life. If the electronic age hadn't been so fast, though, I wouldn't be missing all the money from our joint checking account.*

Clotilde wasn't supposed to have his password. Grandpa's idea of making sure two passwords were used to access their personal funds was great. It's just that neither one of them suspected that Clotilde was a thief, or that she had a brother who was a computer guru. For a brother, though, he sure didn't look like her.

James shook his head, trying to erase the bad thought that was creeping in. Brother or boyfriend—what difference did it make? The divorce would be final on Monday, and she could do—er, rather be with—whomever she wanted. At least she hadn't given him an STD. Actually, after they were legally married, she had had a perpetual headache. Ugh, the thought of being intimate with that two-faced gold digger literally made him sick to his stomach.

James went to the bathroom cabinet and moved the bottles around, looking for the pink stuff he had bought for indigestion. And, there it was under the bottle—a little slip of paper in Clotilde's writing—and on it was the combination to the wall safe.

He grabbed the note and the antacid, gulping the bellyache medicine right from the bottle, not bothering with the little plastic cup. He went to his desk and got his note pad and all the pens he could find. He methodically wrote the number eight with each pen, setting each writing implement next to its written numeral, then compared the colors of the inks on the tablet to the one on the scrap of paper. Which pen had she used? Of course, she used the engraved Lamy 2000 pen that Grandpa had given him for Christmas. He smoothed out her little crib note. *Let's see. A stroke here and a curve there, and that's now a four and not a one, a six instead of a five. 1-8-5 was now modified to a combination of 4-8-6. Let's see her try and open it with those numbers!*

Before he closed the safe, he wanted to make sure there wasn't anything else he needed in there. Those mysterious letters—they didn't need to spend any more time in there. Whether they were valuable or not made no difference to him. He just didn't want Clotilde's slimy paws on the decades old—no, make that centuries old—documents.

He took out the bundle and turned it over. Yup, they hadn't been disturbed. It didn't appear that the thin blue ribbon had ever been removed or retied. No creases were visible, and the ends were frayed and bent in the same odd directions. Evidently she hadn't seen any value in his family's history.

He reached further back and found it. The long, fat manila envelope was still there. Okay, looks weren't everything. James removed the envelope and unwound the dark red string that secured the flap. He blew into the slot, popped it open, and dumped out the cash. Only it wasn't currency inside anymore. It was the Sunday comics, cut up into pound-sized notes. He laughed aloud. He hadn't realized that Clotilde had a sense of humor. He had been wrong about that, too. *The funny papers for making the funny money. Not bad, Clotilde, not bad.*

He carefully replaced the phony money in the envelope and returned it to the safe in the same spot. He reached further back and found the old

13

wooden cigar box. He set it on the desk, flipped open the lid, and sniffed the fat Cuban cigars, wrinkling his nose at the musty scent that still lingered. He never understood why people smoked—tobacco or anything else—but Grandpa's ruse was beneficial. Clotilde had had no interest in the contents of the stinky carton.

He removed all the desiccated and flaky rolls of tobacco leaves, lifted up the corrugated cream-colored paper divider, and took out the three old hard packs of Marlboro 'cigarettes.' He flipped open the top of the first one and dumped the contents into his hand. The flag jewels: rubies, sapphires, and diamonds. Well, only a few diamonds were left, but there were still quite a few rubies and sapphires, and they were all of high quality. The second box, for menthol cigarettes, held what he called the forest jewels: emeralds and yellow topazes of three-carat-plus size. Topazes weren't as valuable per se, but their large size would fetch a good price from a reputable dealer. Last, but not least, the box for unfiltered cigarettes. This is where Grandpa kept what he called his babies. They were decent-sized and, although there were only three of each, they were perfect—flawless baby blue and soft pink-hued diamonds. The family jewels were kept in old cigarette packs in a vintage cigar box, stashed in the back of the family vault.

She really was dumb. Didn't she know that cigars were supposed to be kept at room temperature in a humidor, not in a flimsy box in a cold safe? She must have actually believed Grandpa when he said that he kept his tobacco locked up so he wouldn't start smoking again. Well, James thought, he might have to pretend to take up that bad habit himself.

He combined the contents of all the cigarette packs into the menthol box and put it in his inside jacket pocket. *Hmm...I guess I'll consider this my smoking jacket.* He placed the two empty packs of cigarettes, paper divider, and the flaky cigars back into the box and returned it to the safe. The bundle of ribbon-tied letters fit perfectly in his outer jacket pocket. Sweet little old Dani's rosy business card went into his wallet, next to the Greek coin, and then it and the passport went into his pocket. He was almost ready to roll.

"And back you go," he said to the strip of paper with the altered safe combination. "How profound." The combination had been written on the back of a Chinese fortune cookie insert. "'You will reap what you sow.' I can only hope." He replaced the paper in the bathroom cabinet underneath the bellyache medicine. "And here, you might need this, too."

Yes, an extended trip to America sounded very appealing. James went to his desk and opened up the laptop. He signed into his email account and typed in Dani's email address. *Remember meeting me in that little café in Greensboro last Halloween? Did that strange little man, Simon was it, ever figure out his map? Hopefully, you were able to finish your little*

*Revolutionary War sightsee and had a safe journey home to Alaska. I will be returning to North Carolina 5th August. After I take care of some business, I would like to visit your state. Is your offer for a three-hour tour still open? Please let me know so I can schedule flights on this end. Regards, Lord James Melbourne*

James looked over the short note, grinned, then erased the title 'Lord,' and pressed send. *Email: I wonder how the war with the Colonies would have turned out if we had instant messaging and satellite imaging back then. Oh well, I'm sure it turned out like it was supposed to. It's not as if we could go back in time and change history or anything.*

James looked around his den—his office—with an unbiased eye. What was the most valuable thing in here? Okay, rewind, most important and valuable to him. Right now, it was the laptop, or at least what was on it. She'd want his computer even though she had her own. She'd only want it because she wouldn't want him to have anything. That would be easy enough. *All files remotely backed up, so here little red PC, have a cup of cold coffee.*

James held the computer sideways over the rubbish bin and poured the cold java into the USB ports, turned it around 90 degrees and doused the power port, internal networking hub, and all those other rectangular holes with metal pins and tangs inside. A quick flip to wash all the coffee around and, oh yeah, the mini slots on the other side. "How about a little coffee syrup, Sweetie? You always liked the sugar-free almond flavor now, didn't you? I'll make sure I mix it up just right for you. Here," he said as he grabbed a paper towel from the bottom desk drawer, "we don't want to look messy or have any dribbles now, do we? Let me wipe you down, polish you up, turn you around, and *voila!* You look like a brand new portal to online shopping!

"Online shopping. That reminds me…oh, here it is." James scanned the phone numbers in his smartphone until he found RCCR—Royal Credit Card Registry—and pressed call. "Yes ma'am, I would like to report a theft. Yes, this is Lord James Melbourne, and my credit cards have been stolen. It seems that all my private financial information has been compromised. My authorization code is 1781. Please stop access to all accounts immediately."

"Yes, sir, right away, sir. Will there be anything else, sir?" replied the excited young lady on the other end of the line.

"Yes, yes there is. If anyone should call about this, I would like to remind you of the confidentiality clause. No one is to discuss these accounts, or why they were closed, unless they have the authorization code. And that includes a court order. The House of Lords does have its privileges. Do I make myself clear?" James bluffed.

"Yes, sir. Will there be anything else, sir?" asked the now squeaky-voiced agent on the other end of the line, her excitement rising with each mention of who he was.

"Yes, please don't ask me again if there will be anything else, sir," James said with a smile in his voice.

"Yes, sir, will…er…yes, sir. I hope the rest of your day, rest of your week and month, go better for you, sir. You seem to be having a rough day."

"That's an understatement. Thank you for the good wishes. Good-bye."

And that was that. A cup of cold coffee and a phone call to start the road to freedom. "Come on, Uncle Julian, let's go," he said, and took the portrait of Lord Julian Hart off the wall. "Let's see if you had the right idea about making a fresh start in America."

# *3 Pre-flight Preparations

*August 4, 2013,*
*England*

The Club had been a tradition for the Melbourne men for centuries. James patted the brown-paper-wrapped portrait of Lord Julian Hart. "How about if you stay at the Club until I find us a new home?" he asked the painting. He didn't expect an audible answer, but did get an ethereal feeling of satisfaction from his many times over great-uncle. "Yeah, I think it's a good idea, too," he said.

The Club had resisted change for decades. The addition of electricity in the mid-20th century was accepted begrudgingly by many of the older patrons, but the younger generation had won over the old coots when they promised brighter reading lights than fireplaces, candles, or oil lamps could provide. The latest change—and hopefully the last for a long time—was the addition of wireless internet access. Cell phones and laptops were still *verboten* in the main rooms, but the former coal room had been converted into a communications parlor. Old-fashioned phone booths had been brought in to insure both privacy for the info seeker and lack of intrusion on the other members. No one wanted to hear about hair appointments, football bets or ugh, a *tête-à-tête* with a mistress.

James took his glass of Glenturret into a corner booth. He had altered the interior design of the phone booths to make them more marketable: padded the seat, and added a high intensity reading light and a pull-down shelf. The instant desk was a convenient place to set a glass and a mini laptop, or in his case, what he referred to as his cell phone on steroids: his smartphone. He could listen to Vivaldi in private while cruising the internet to check his email and book the flight for his overseas trip.

He clicked and deleted his way through the junk email. No matter how many filters, encryptions, and restrictions he put on his account, he still got requests to buy male enhancement products and knock-off Rolex watches. He smiled and looked down at his genuine Rolex and saw that he had plenty of time to get to the airport.

A few more clicks and deletions, and he was down to the legitimate correspondences. *'We would be happy to have you visit. Come at your earliest convenience. Saturday, August 10th is the annual company picnic and celebration at the mill. We'd be honored to share our little carnival and fireworks show with you (and yours, if applicable). Regards, Bibb Stephens'*

There was still no clue as to whether Bibb was a man or a woman. It wasn't important either way. Unless the mill and surrounding property were absolute disasters, he was going to buy the whole works. If all else failed, he could raze the buildings and breed horses. He still had the funds at the bank that weren't under the family name. The Pomeroy-Hart fortune was a long-held family secret: 'to be used only in extreme circumstances' was the rule. The family had never had to use it before, and it would be nice if he didn't have to either. Clotilde had no idea that the Pomeroy-Hart fortune even existed. It had always been a secret, only to be shared with the first-born male offspring. Well, that wasn't going to happen since his marriage to Clotilde would soon be null and void.

Null and void—that would be preferable to his present situation. Right now, the marriage was a power vacuum, a black hole trying to suck the life, money, and spirit out of him. '*Nope. Ain't gonna let it happen in this lifetime,' as Grandpa would say.* James sniggered and shook his head. If he didn't find someone worthy to love, who would love him back and be happy to provide him with an heir, the fortune would be left to charity. He was the last in the long line of Melbournes. The Harts had died out years before—at least as far as the direct line went—and nobody knew what happened to the Pomeroys.

'Click on Buy Now to proceed to check out,' and ten seconds later, the ticket purchase to North Carolina via New York City was complete. "See you in a few days, Bibb," James said to no one in particular as he closed out the screen on his smartphone.

The time had come to put a padlock on his life in England. He still needed to make two stops before the airport: the post office and the garage. He could leave the Corniche in the Club's parking garage. 'No women allowed' still had it merits. There was no way Clotilde could get in there and drive off in his car.

He knew how much she loved the Bentley. He remembered the first day he had seen her. She sauntered into the restaurant and asked the *maître d'* who owned the car. That should have been his first clue that she was a gold digger. She had coveted the car so much that she had come after it, willing to seduce whoever owned it in order to make it hers. He doubted that it would have made a difference to her whether it was a man or a woman. Yes, he was just the person attached to the name on the car's title.

He shook his head, hoping he didn't look like a wet dog when he did it. Physically moving his skull side to side really was the only way to clear her out of his brain at times. Ugh, a shiver ran down the back of his legs. He had actually wanted to have children with that woman. It was probably the only good thing she had done for him, although he didn't realize it at the time. She had said no to children.

Ж

Before he got too carried away, James needed to make arrangements for his snail mail. He pulled up to the little postal outlet. It was empty except for him and the middle-aged clerk. "Sir, I would like to forward all my mail to my club," he said. "Here's the form with the address and my signature. Is there anything else you require?"

18

The clerk with the nostalgic green visor and gold-rimmed bifocals used his ink-stained index finger to scan over all the blanks on the change of address form. "I'll just need to see some identification, sir."

James pulled his passport out of the baggie. "Safe and dry," he said under his breath, and put it in the open hand of the stern-faced postal worker.

The clerk looked at the picture, up at James, and then back down again. "Hmph," he snorted. "If this is you, then you have an expert forger one step ahead of you." He took a paper from the wire basket on the counter behind him. "Here, someone has beaten you to this."

James's eyes widened, his cheeks reddened, his jaws clenched. Apparently Clotilde's brother/boyfriend person—her accomplice in the theft and attempted destruction of the Melbourne family fortune—was now trying to, or was, intercepting his mail.

"Don't worry, sir. Sir?" The agent tapped James on the sleeve of his wool jacket. He repeated himself to make sure he had James's attention. "Don't worry, sir. I smelled a rat. I told the two of them that there was a 48-hour waiting period for all of this to take effect. The Lady Melbourne was right put off, she was. She looked a bit too eager to get her hands on the post. I told her she couldn't get it even if it was addressed to you, er, her husband. That's when she changed the address. Then she came back an hour later with a man she claimed was you: Lord James Melbourne. I told the two of them that I couldn't release the letter because it had already been sent to the forwarding department. They would be able to get their mail at the new address in 48-hours. When they said they wanted to change it back to the original address, I told them then it would be an additional 48-hours. She just about blew her eyebrows off at that point. I just grinned and told her she could either wait 48-hours or 96-hours plus the weekend, her choice. That's when she squealed, stomped her feet, and stormed out of here with the mister following right behind her. Yes, it was magnificent. Best case of customer irritation I've ever caused."

The clerk—his nametag read Richard Smith—had a dreamy look of recollection. He took off his readers to wipe away a tear. "It was truly beautiful." He sniffed and wiped the corners of his eyes again.

"I'm sorry, sir," he said, and came out of his reverie. He looked at Lord James Melbourne's consternate frown and smiled. "Shall I just 'lose' the application that Lady Melbourne submitted?"

James sighed deeply with relief and smiled. "Yes, I'd appreciate it very much."

"Consider it done. Oh, here's your mail." The clerk handed him a long, thin manila envelope.

"Hmm." James read the short, one-page handwritten note—it didn't make any sense. *I need to talk to you about Leah. And watch out for the*

*MacLeods! ~ Benji MacKay'* A USA phone number was listed beneath it.

He checked inside the envelope again—nothing else inside. Then he noticed the postage and North Carolina return address, and felt inspired. "Richard, do you drive?" he asked, as he took out his pen. He scribbled a comment on the bottom of the note that read, *Sorry—I don't know a Leah or any MacLeods. JIM.* James stuck the note back in the envelope. Yes, and he didn't recall knowing a Benji MacKay in England, much less in the United States.

"You can call me Ric. Oh, yes, sir. I have a 1976 Ford Fiesta. I drove it to work every day until the transmission failed last March. It's still in the garage at home. I can't afford the repairs right now. I was offered £300 for it, but I really don't want to get rid of it. It doesn't bother me to walk to work, and the wife and I can stay home instead of going on holiday this year. I'm sure something will turn up; maybe I'll win the lottery!"

James pulled the keys to the Bentley out of his pocket. "Here," he said, and laid the keys on the counter. "I'll make you a deal. If you take me to the airport this afternoon, you can keep that," he nodded to the black sedan parked outside, "free and clear. Consider it compensation for a job well done."

Ric's jaw dropped. He slowly pulled the green visor off his head with one hand, the glasses off his bulbous nose with the other. He walked over to the window and gazed at the car. "But that's a Bentley Corniche," he said softly. He took a quick breath and returned to chilly civic clerk mode. "It's not nice to tease people like that, sir," he said sharply.

"No tease, it's not a trick, and I have the title. I can, and will, sign it over to you once you get me to the airport. Can you get me there by four o'clock today?"

"If you can be here by three o'clock, I'll have you there by four. I'm supposed to stay until five, but I can manage to get a bit of a bellyache around three in order to get you to Heathrow by four. Is there anything else I can do for you, sir?"

"Yes. Would you return this to the sender?" He handed the envelope back to Ric. "Is there anything due for postage?"

The clerk shook his head and held up his hand, smiling—he'd been well compensated with the gift of the car. "I got this."

"And please make sure my mail gets to my club, and that those two…two," James pursed his lips, trying to think of a civil noun to call the thieves, but drew a blank. "That those *two*," he repeated with disgust, "don't try to bamboozle anyone else."

"No worries, sir. I'm the only one who works this branch." He accepted the envelope from James, taped it closed, put it in the out box, then grinned broadly and said, "And I know their faces."

Ж

20

The airline agent was most accommodating. "Sir, since this flight is overbooked, and you paid full fare for your ticket, would you like to have a seat in first class? Sir? Sir?"

"Uh, yes, thank you," he replied sheepishly. If he had been looking for a sign that he was doing the right thing, this would definitely qualify. Life was right on track. First class track, he thought as he patted the cigarette pack in his right pocket, the bundle of letters tied with the blue ribbon, in his left.

Going through security was no problem, although the tiny Indian woman with the red dot between her eyes did look at him strangely. "No bags or computers; just shoes, sir?"

"Well, I can walk much further in shoes. Laptops give me blisters," he said with a smile. She gave him a blank look, then grinned when she realized what he was inferring. "Have a nice trip, sir, and here are your shoes."

James sat down on the hard plastic bench and tied his Kenmoors. "Loosen up, James," he mumbled. He sat up straight and frowned, pursed his lips, then sighed, frustrated at the noises he was making. *Okay, mumbling is acceptable—nothing to worry about. Just keep the volume down, the words short, and it'll be okay.* He slapped his knees with both hands, ready to start the tour of the airport shops.

The longhaired, middle-aged woman at the bank reminded him of Dani Madigan. Dani. He hadn't received an email reply from her yet, but the time zones were nine hours apart. Hopefully all was well with that perky, off-center older American lady. Now why couldn't he meet someone like her, only younger? Maybe she had a daughter... Now that was an interesting thought. He'd save that one for later. Right now, he needed to—ugh—go shopping.

James walked into a bathroom stall at the airport and removed the American dollars from the white bank envelope. He put half of the bills into the wallet and returned it to his breast pocket. He pulled out a few hundreds, folded them, put them in his front trousers pocket, and zipped the rest into his money belt.

He came out to wash his hands, looked at himself in the mirror, and shook his head. He looked like an old man without the gray hair or wrinkles. It was time he treated himself to a new look and dressed his age. He had been attired like an older gentleman for too long. Three-piece suits, a tie, and Florsheim shoes were the mandatory uniform for members of the House of Lords.

*Oh, my God! Am I even considering losing the title? Am I letting that little bleached-blond harlot force me into ending the generations long heritage, even if I don't have an heir? Change in plans—find the airport post office.*

21

The microscopic suite was not easy to find. Even the 'you are here' maps at the airport only had an asterisk for the postal outlet location. Airport security was actually helpful. They did have a function other than bumping up add-on charges to airfare ticket prices and patting down—or was that feeling up?—random passengers. James finally found the kiosk and the clerk who had the required forms.

*'The Right Honourable the Lords Spiritual and Temporal of the United Kingdom of Great Britain and Northern Ireland in Parliament assembled- Be it known that due to unforeseen circumstances, I, Lord James Ignatius Melbourne, request leave of absence until further notice. Please be advised that I have not deserted my position and am in full possession of my faculties. Any urgent correspondence can be forwarded to my club, Mrs. White's House of Chocolates, but do not expect an immediate answer. I prefer to remain incommunicado at this time. Your humble servant, Lord James I. Melbourne'*

"There, that should do it," he said as he reread the handwritten note. "Can you send this Royal Mail with Recorded Delivery Service and have a copy made for me?"

"Yes, sir, I happen to have a copier right under here." The teenaged young man was a diligent public servant, even if he didn't look the part. He was dressed appropriately, but unfortunately, his purple Mohawk haircut brought out the maroon tones of his acne-pocked face. "Here you go," he said, and presented the copy of the letter to James. "Is this good enough for your needs?"

James examined the duplicate made on the little nine-inch long by two-inch wide scanner. "Hmm, I guess size really doesn't matter." He glanced up, and they both grinned at the sexual innuendo, "At least in printers," he added.

"Ahem."

James turned around and saw it was a woman—her age hard to determine under her exotic, cat-like make up—who had cleared her throat.

"Lad, isn't it almost time for you to close?" Technically, it was a question, but by her tone, she was actually telling him what to do.

*Lad: that must be his name. James looked at the nametag: 'Vladimir Chekov.' A fine Irish name, he thought and smiled. He resisted the urge to make the smart aleck remark, but his grin remained.* "Would you make sure this gets sent to this address? Here," James turned the copied letter around on the little square foot area of counter space. He scribbled 'certified original copy' and signed, dated, and printed out his full name and title. "This is to go to my club at this address," he scribbled the address on the back of the document. "The original goes to the Clerk of the Parliaments."

"Got it! Oh, here—I accidentally made two copies. Would you like this one, too? No charge," Lad added lightly.

"Tell you what," James took it, and signed and dated it, too. "You keep this," he pulled out a £10 note and held it up to him, "and this, and I'll take this." He took one of Vladimir's business cards. "I'd appreciate it if you kept it in a safe place. If both the original and first copy are compromised, I'll give you a call. Sometimes it's wise to have two insurance policies," he said and winked.

"Sounds like a plan," said the female with the feline makeup, as she plucked the money out of James's hand. "Ready?" she asked Lad.

"Ready." He nodded to James and folded up the extra document. "Have a nice holiday, Lord James," his voice lowered, "or whatever."

"Thanks, and I hope you have a good evening, Lad," James lowered his tone, mimicking the youth's, "or whatever."

Ж

James felt out of place in the youth-oriented store. This boutique was for the younger generation was his first thought. His second thought was that that was who he was, or should be. Either way, he liked the idea of supporting the smaller shops. *Chill out, dude! You're going to America. Think like an American, dress like an American, sleep like an American. Sleep like an American?*

He shook his head and started pawing the odd-looking goods in the oversized bin. "What are these?" he asked the young nerdy clerk.

"Oh, those're buckwheat pillows. They conform to your neck and head. They're really quite comfy. We also have them filled with rice or beans. If you don't like 'em, you can always rip 'em open, throw the bits and pieces into a pot of boiling water, and eat 'em," he added with a smile.

"They're especially comfortable on airplanes," commented a woman behind him.

James turned around to see who had spoken and gasped. "Uh, yes. It is difficult to get comfortable on those long flights," he said, quickly composing himself. *The female salesperson who spoke looked just like Dani Madigan, although she didn't sound a thing like her. This was eerie: it seemed like Ms. Madigan was everywhere around him today.* "Thanks, I'll take one," he told her.

"Buckwheat, beans, or rice, sir?" the Dani-looking clerk asked.

"Um, rice will be fine," he replied, giving her what he hoped she saw as a smile, not the grimace of insecurity.

*'And maybe some chicken broth for a foot soak,' he felt like adding. These extemporaneous puns never popped into his head before. Weird. Is this what happened when he didn't have any stress in his life—or maybe now he had more? Hmm, let me see. No wife, no stock portfolio, no household, no personal obligations to satisfy, no hobnobbing, nor wheels to grease. Yes, he definitely had less stress, not more.*

What he needed now was to buy clothes—laid-back, comfortable

23

togs—and something to carry them in. He had been dressed as a middle-aged businessman since his mid-teens. Keeping up with business suits that fit him had been a challenge. He was called 'shrimp' and 'midget' while in middle school. "Don't worry, you'll reach your height eventually," Grandpa had told him. "Work on what's in here," he said, tapping him on the left temple, "before you get carried away with life and women, your head in the clouds up here," indicating a tallish six feet height.

And he was right. Grandpa was always right. He listened to Grandpa and studied hard. He was a whiz with math, and economics just seemed so logical. Statistics: why was that supposed to be a hard course? The bump from middle school straight to university was awkward because of his youth and short stature, but it turned out to be a blessing. He spent his time on studies and breezed through university in three years. By his last year, he was secure in his grades and had garnered the attention of four of the top securities and stock agencies in the United Kingdom.

Grandpa pulled a few strings and got him a position at a prominent financial firm, working the phones in the back office. His deep voice fooled the business partner who hired him. Although he had been granted the position on the merit of his grades, telephonic presence, and composure, Otis, the senior partner, had balked and tried to take back the job offer when he met James face to face. James wasn't sure, but he could just about swear that Otis paled when Grandpa pulled him aside and spoke with him in private. Blackmail or a verbal arm twist; either way, he was glad Grandpa had gone to bat for him.

The money and position, along with the seat in the House of Lords at the age of majority, had turned his life around. It could have gotten out of hand, but he had told Grandpa that he would spend at least one evening a week at the club. Grandpa told him, "Keep yourself grounded, and don't believe everything that's said about you. You're still a steed whether they call you a jackass or a magical Pegasus. Come to pasture with the rest of the old stallions. They'll help you keep life in perspective."

The company was good, and the advice even better, but he was still young, flawed, and frisky. He didn't want to ask for their counsel when it came to women and, in retrospect, he should have. His mentors would have warned him against taking the advice of an unschooled woman, especially when she was urging him to cash in his investment portfolio. He was fortunate to discover her deception before it was too late and was able to save the family fortune before it wound up in her Swiss bank account.

She was furious when he responded to her ploy by cutting off her access to their joint bank accounts. He put her on a monthly allowance and, even though it was a generous one, she still whined that it wasn't enough. So, since she couldn't get her hands on his stocks or monies while married, she went another route and trumped up an outlandish reason for a divorce.

"He's a flaming faggot," she declared to the tabloids. "If it doesn't have a beard, he can't get it up." She was merciless. He was almost disassociated from his club when the story first came out. His only saving grace was that she had taken one step beyond propriety and declared that all members of The Club were gay. After that bloated accusation, The Club members—his fellow political and business associates and their friends—realized that the stories she was spreading were bogus. The good old boys pulled some strings, and the tabloid tales stopped like a boot on a football.

The media stories may have stopped, but the stares and double-takes didn't. His face was well-known now, and in a negative way. Yes, a long holiday to America or 'wherever' would not be questioned and would be most welcomed.

Ж

"Are these supposed to be this way?" he asked the prickle-faced sales associate.

"Too right! You get air-conditioned and are supporting the poor boys and girls on Camperdown Street at the same time. You see, they custom rip, tear, and stain these, special like. They're well dapper, these are. You get to have the latest in fashion *and* give the lads and girls gainful employment at the same time." The clerk with the metal studs and clips peppering his face and ears puffed out his chest. "Me little brother did these hisself. See, he signed them right here with his mark." He pointed to a modified happy face with a tongue sticking out, a la Hot Licks by The Rolling Stones. *Not very original, James thought.*

"See, it's almost a self-portrait," the clerk added. "Oh, wait; someone took out the pin. Here," he said, and took a safety pin off of his lip ring, "now this looks just like Snake Bones. Weel, his real name is Pierce, but he gets a bit put off when you call 'im that. Mum was the one that give 'im that moniker. He had three piercings before he was able to walk, she said. The social workers threatened to take her off the dole if she didn't stop punching holes in 'im, but the name stuck. He still has only the three holes. He never did want any more, but he do have quite a few tats, he do."

"Tats? Oh, tattoos. Uh, yes, I'd be glad to help the Camperdown Street entrepreneurs," James said, and held up the trousers up to his waist to check the fit. "I'll just try them on and wear them out, if you don't mind."

James came out of the modified phone booth dressing room wearing the custom ripped and stained jeans. *Everyone had scoffed at him when he bought all the old British Telecom phone booths. He made a killing on reselling them all over the United Kingdom and the USA. He got more money for selling them used than they garnered new.* He patted the phone booth door. "Thanks for paying for the trip, the mill, and the new lease on life," he said softly. He stopped and looked at the clerk who was oblivious to his presence. He clenched his jaws and pulled back a grin. He didn't

25

know whether he'd been talking out loud to himself or was speaking so softly that he hadn't been heard.

Pierce's brother turned to him and asked, "How about some shirts to go with 'em? We have 'em from bland and conservative, to wild and torn, to just slightly modified for the folks who aren't quite ready to take the starch out of their shorts."

"Are these more from the Camperdown Street crew?" James asked, holding up a pale blue Oxford pre-washed shirt with rolled up cuffs.

"The shirts are from Carnaby Street. The ladies say that a businessman with his sleeves pushed up is 'bout as sexy as they come—with the clothes on, that it is."

James rifled through a few Polos and Oxfords, and even found a genuine Levi snap-up shirt. He checked the neck sizes and told his personal dresser, "Here, I'll take the lot of them. Do you have any cargo trousers that are less holey?"

"Genuine Levi 501's, prewashed, worn, and then washed again for that American look. Is that where yer goin'?"

"Is this what I'd wear if it were?"

"You'd look just like a Yank on the ranch in these...or on the road."

James had seen the look of recognition in the clerk's eye early on. He probably would have been helpful regardless, but the lad knew he was helping the notorious 'gay' Lord James Melbourne, the man who broke the heart of Clotilde, the darling of the jet set.

"Thanks, this will be all. No, wait, I'll take those sunglasses, too. Gets bright on the beaches, you know." James hadn't told him where he was going. If he believed that he was going to the Bahamas, well, that was fine. A little misdirection every now and then kept the tabloids on their toes.

James left with his old three-piece suit and his other 'new' clothes in an oversized shopping bag, heading right to the leather store. He felt odd in worn out jeans and high-shine Florsheims, but his stop at the shoe store would have to wait a few minutes. He needed a carry-on bag for the trip.

"State-of-the-art valise with tuck-away handle, combination or thumbprint lock—or both—your choice," the sales rep tugged at the bottom of the leather satchel, "and hidden compartment. It's guaranteed to fit under an airplane seat so you don't have to check it as luggage."

James turned the bag over and saw the inflated price. He looked up at the clerk with an 'are you sure about this price?' look in his eyes, then back at the tag. The older salesman stuttered, "Oh, if you're a subject of the Crown, then there's a 25% discount."

James looked back up again without saying a word. The old man blushed and stammered, "Of course, that includes your initials engraved in two places—while you wait. I can do more than just initials if you would like, my lord...er...sir."

James winced slightly at his title. He was still recognized, even in his casual costume—that is, attire. "Here, just put J.I.M. on this blank, and how about if you stamp inside the hidden compartment, too? It won't show through on the bottom, will it?"

"Oh, no, sir, I'll make sure it's discreet. So, you want J dot I dot M dot, correct?"

"Yes," James said, then changed his mind. "No, on second thought, leave out the dots."

His mother had had a sense of humor, according to Grandpa. James didn't like his middle name, Ignatius, but Immaculata or Innocencia would have been far worse. Isaac wouldn't have been too bad, but all he ever used was the initial, so it didn't make a difference. He disliked being called Jim—too rural—but he might loosen up and change his attitude in America. The name James sounded fine for an Earl or a Duke—or a butler, he recalled, thinking of 'the other James.' Well, whichever name felt more comfortable, that's the one he'd wear.

He completed the cash transaction and checked his Rolex for the time. It was a very fine timepiece, and maybe too flashy for travel, but with all the imitation ones on the market, it probably wouldn't draw attention to his status. Hmm…boarding was in less than an hour.

Next, the shoe store. The clerk was sharp, knew his trade, and could tell James's shoe size just by looking. Jok, a forty-something Brad Pitt look-alike, picked out a very comfortable cross trainer shoe for him to try on. It fit perfectly. He also talked him into a pair of Birkenstock sandals, and that's when James's stomach turned. The salesman stroked the bottom of his foot in what could have been—must have been—a suggestive manner. James looked him in the eye and saw that he was indeed being suggestive. "No, thanks," James said, grimacing, "but I'll take the sandals," and changed up to a sincere smile.

The 'phew' look on the flirting clerk's face was priceless. It was a good sales commission for him, even if he didn't get lucky. At least, and probably most important, he wouldn't get in trouble for making a pass. The man who had just walked in was evidently the big boss.

"Jok's a great salesman," James commented to the sweating, obese man with the manager nametag pinned askew on the pocket of his stained sports coat. "Brad, er, Jok got me set up with just the right size and style of shoes for my needs. Give the man a raise. Good help is hard to find."

James looked back and saw the clerk's pouty lips mouth the words, 'thank you.' Then Jok smiled and said aloud with sincerity, "Have a safe flight."

James went into the men's room and repacked his new old clothes and shoes into his new leather carry-on bag. He came out feeling empowered, as if he could tackle anyone, solve any problem, or win any hand of cards. His vision was clear and he was devoid of stress. As he headed to his departure gate, he saw a little kiosk that sold toiletries. He grabbed toothpaste and brush, floss, deodorant, comb, and shampoo. He started to grab the razor, then pulled his hand back. *Nope, not in this new lifetime—at least, not for a while. I may change my mind after a couple of days, but I've always wondered what color my beard is.* He ran his right hand across his chin. *I guess I'll find out now, won't I?*

The first-class passengers were being called to board when he reached his gate. He flashed his passport and smiled at the gate attendant, then followed the snaky portable hallway to the jet doorway. He had been given a window seat and was grateful. He wouldn't be getting elbows to the head or shoulders when the other passengers boarded.

"Would you like a pillow, sir?"

He bolted at the voice. Dani Madigan? He looked up and saw a twenty-something flight attendant with bleached blond hair and too much Revlon. "Ah, yes, please." He accepted the pillow and tried to calm down, but his heart still raced.

Dani Madigan. He had sent her an email several hours ago, but with all of his last minute posting and purchasing, he hadn't checked his smartphone for any replies. The plane was still boarding so he could connect to the internet.

*Voila*—a reply!

He opened the email. 'This is an automated reply. The mailbox of Dani Madigan is no longer being monitored.' *Oh, crap!* He finished reading the rest of the auto-reply, even though he was sure it was just legalese jargon meant to protect the email server. 'If you would like to contact the administrator of the Dani Madigan estate, please email...'

"She's dead?" James whispered. "Oh, shit..." He quickly typed in and saved the address for Leah Madigan. 'My condolences on the loss of your mother, or was she your sister? Sorry, I don't know your relationship to Dani. I only met her once, last Halloween, but she was a very smart, charming, and compassionate woman. If I can be of any assistance, please let me know. Regards, Lord,' he backspaced four times to delete the title then signed off, 'James Melbourne.' She probably had no idea who he was and wouldn't care if he was titled or not, so to hell with the paranoia. Besides, her email address was in America. And Americans didn't give a rip about anyone but themselves. Plain old James Melbourne was good enough for her—and for him, too.

James shifted around in his nice, oversized first class seat and found just the right spot for the small pillow the flight attendant had given him. It was then that he realized the one thing he hadn't purchased: a book to read.

As if someone had been reading his mind, the flight attendant—he looked up and saw her name was Barbie, how appropriate—walked by him

28

with a wicker basket of books and magazines. "Would you care for something to read, sir?"

He grinned as he realized that there was no sense of recognition in her voice. "Let's see," he said, and picked through the periodicals and paperbacks. He scanned the headlines of the pulps and saw that they were all current; his face wasn't visible anywhere.

"This looks like someone has read it quite a few times." The upper corner was torn off the book and there were about thirty pages dog-eared. "*Through the Stones*," he read aloud. "Never heard of it, but I'll give it a shot. Looks like somebody sure liked it, though," he added, as he flipped through the book, making sure it had all of the pages.

Barbie was bumped from behind and her ribcage pushed right into James's face. "Oh, my. Sorry, sir," she said, then quickly regained her composure and got back to the subject of the book. "It's a time travel, romance, and history novel, all in one. I think I've read that one about six, no seven, times. It's the first in a series, and I read them all again in sequence whenever a new one comes out. Lots of stand-by time, you know," she added, almost as an excuse.

"Lisa Sinclaire—never heard of her—but I'll take your word for it, and that of whoever read this before."

He turned over the well-worn book, glanced at the reviews, read the prologue, and scanned a few of the dog-eared pages. *Ooh, lusty story. I can handle some diversion. At least it doesn't have naked ladies or pirates on the cover.'*

The thought of a plain cover reminded James of his bundle of antique letters wrapped with the simple 'do not read before' paper. Well, now was as good a time as any to check on the date. He quickly retrieved his carry-on, pulled out his 'smoking jacket,' and was able to extract the letters and re-roll the coat before Barbie started her in-flight safety spiel. He covertly put his tray table down and placed the letters on top, carefully untying the bundle to verify once again that Clotilde hadn't been into them.

After a bit of fingernail picking to get the primary bow untied, the rest of the unwrapping was easy. As he pulled away the last bit of blue satin, he noticed some fading. The bundle had been accessed, but not recently. The faded ribbon looked like that on an old Christmas ornament he had received when he was six years old.

*"I got you a bike," Great Aunt Mary Jane had whispered a few days before Christmas. He was so excited; he had his heart set on a retro-style bicycle. Then Christmas morning came and he was presented with an acrylic globe enclosing a thumb-sized version of the Sting Ray bike that he wanted so much. "You're too young for a bike like that," she chided. She held him close and kissed him on top of his head. "Maybe when you're ten or twelve," she soothed when she saw the tear that had sneaked out.*

*The ornament was even more painful because he was forced to have it on the tree for the next four years, until he was old enough to have the real bike. The next year, the ornament wasn't in the box of decorations. "I didn't throw it away, honest, Grandpa," he said when Aunt Mary Jane noticed that it wasn't in the carton at the tree decorating party.*

*"I believe you. I know you'd never lie to me. No worries," Grandpa said.*

*And there it was on Christmas morning: the full-sized, bronze-hued Sting Ray bike with the glittery-gold vinyl banana seat and extended sissy bar on the back. The 'To James, From Grandpa' note was tied on with the same faded blue ribbon that used to hang the miniature bicycle ornament that had mysteriously disappeared.*

*Grandpa whispered in his ear, "I put that sorry excuse for a bike ornament in the dust bin. You can retrieve it, if you'd like," he added with a chuckle.*

*"No, thanks!" James had proclaimed a little too loudly. He gave Grandpa a big hug and Aunt Mary Jane a little grin. "Looks like the little bike you gave me grew up. Thank you," he said to her graciously, and gave her a peck on the cheek. It wasn't her fault that she was so protective of him.*

James held the ribbon out full length. Yup, there it was—the mustard stain. The ornament had been sitting on the dinner table when brats were the main course. He had flipped the mustard spoon a little too hard, and it had splashed the little bike insult…er…ornament. Someone had been into these letters at some point, and it was most likely Grandpa.

*Yeah, right, Grandpa. We have to wait, you said.* James looked at the cover letter. *Do not open before November 1, 2012. Okay, I'm playing by the rules. That was almost a year ago.*

'Read me First' was written on the top paper. *Alice in Wonderland. Okay, I'm game.*

James blanked out his surroundings as he began reading the letter, disappearing into his own personal world.

"Sir? Sir? You have to put your tray up and stow your bag under the seat." It was Barbie shaking him on the shoulder, trying to bring him out of his stupor, but it sounded like it was that sweet little old lady, Dani Madigan, who was trying to get his attention.

"What? What? Oh, yes, sorry. Some deep reading here," he said as an excuse. He flipped up the tray and stashed his leather bag under the seat in front of him with his left hand, his right holding the ancient letters close to his heart.

*Dear James,*

*I know it seems like you saw me only yesterday, but if all has gone according to instructions, you will be getting this 230 years after I have*

30

*written it. I think you can verify this if you have the paper dated. Remember that strange man, Simon? He does have something to do with us, or rather me. I followed him into the park, and I accidentally fell through time. Right now, I am living with your ancestors. I actually married your great—I don't know how many times over—uncle's son. I think I found the Revolutionary War relative you were looking for. That is, if you were looking for Lord Julian Wallace Hart, brother of Lord Anthony Melbourne. Julian's a wonderful man, and his (step) son and I have three children (triplets!).*

*The reason for my letter is that I want you to contact my daughter, Leah Madigan. Please, share this:*

*Leah,*

*I am alive and well in 1781. All the stories by Lisa Sinclaire are pretty much true. I will show up again on August 4, 2013 at the hospital you work in, but you will have to let me return home to my new family. You are bright and grown up now, and can live life on your own, but my babies and my new husband, Wallace Pomeroy-Hart, need me. Sarah and Jody Pomeroy are as wonderful as you told me and as the history (not science fiction or fantasy) books say. It is possible to change history on a small scale or I wouldn't be here with your siblings who are nearly 200 years older than you.*

*James, as of August 4, 2013, Leah is working at the Moses H. Cone Memorial Hospital in Greensboro, not far from our little cafe. She was, will be, my recovery room nurse. So, if you have a chance to talk to her in person, would you please explain what happened and let her read this letter? I love her very much and don't want her to worry about me. Oh, and I have a new first name: Evie. I'll write more as time goes by, but please do not read any other letters (I hope to get a journal started for you/her) until you get a chance to speak with her and let this settle in for both of you.*

*Hugs and kisses from me and your great-many-times-over uncles and love from,*
*Mom*

James turned the paper over, sniffed it, and then looked at it again. Something was wrong with this document. There were three other letters in the bundle. He glanced at them, and then realized what was different about this one: it was written with a ballpoint pen. The script width was consistent, not the thick-and-thin flow of the characters on the other letters. "She must have had one with her." He looked up quickly and saw that if he had been speaking out loud, no one had heard him.

Barbie was still checking the overhead lockers, walking down the aisles, and smiling. He had time to check emails. He clicked on the in box and didn't see any new messages. He was sure that he had sent the message to Bibb. He/she was generally quick at responding, no matter what time the notes were sent. He opened up the sent messages file. "Oh, crap." James looked up and around. He knew he had said that out loud, but the ambient aircraft noise had sucked up the sounds.

*Flight arrives at noon today, Flt 3923, Greensboro. Let me know if we can get together. James Melbourne*

Oops! James had sent the same message to both Leah and Bibb. It was meant for Bibb only, but he had typed in the address for Leah earlier, meaning to send her a personal letter of condolences. Hopefully, she didn't take it wrong. Maybe he would get an answer from one of them by the time he got into New York. He scrolled down and saw that he *had* sent the condolences to Leah. He reread the message. Ugh, how ugly and impersonal. It would have been better if he hadn't sent anything. But he had, and if she replied, at least now he knew her relationship to Dani. It had also created an opportunity to meet and share the letter with her. And now it was imperative that he do so, too. Her mother had asked him to.

"Sir? Sir?" the woman called.

James shuddered at the voice. He knew it was Barbie, but she still sounded like Dani. He started powering off his smartphone before she could ask, then glanced up and gave her a smile.

The book! He grabbed the book out of the seat pocket in front of him and looked again. '*Through the Stones*' by Lisa Sinclaire, the same author Dani—or Evie, as she said she was called now—referred to. He reread the back cover. '*Through the Stones*, released in the USA and rest of the world as *Lost*—The story of Sarah and Jody Pomeroy, and their adventures in the 18th century.'

James heard the pilot's greeting, shut his eyes, and closed out the real world. It would take seven hours to get to New York. He'd better read his 'history' book right away. He opened his eyes, then the book, and started reading.

"The picnic spot looked harmless enough. Who would have thought that it was an ancient portal to another time? Not a likely place..." *Yeah, well, neither was North Carolina.* He sighed and kept reading. *Neither was North Carolina.*

# *4 Let's Get Together

*August 5, 2013*
*Greensboro, NC, USA*

Leah crawled back into bed after her little 'hair of the dog' cocktail, still not ready to face the day. She snuggled up to Harry the stuffed hippo and let him lead her into sleep's sweet oblivion. Seconds, hours—maybe it was only minutes later—she was rudely awakened by her polyester pellet-filled buddy blowing raspberries in her ear. "Hmph." Her phone had fallen onto her pillow and was vibrating, signaling the hour. She picked it up and squinted: ten o'clock. She blinked and refocused: the little pigeon icon was fluttering across the screen. She had mail.

*Flight arrives at noon today, Flt 3923, Greensboro. Let me know if we can get together. James Melbourne*

First the condolences—and he didn't even know whether I was her sister or her daughter—and now he wants to meet me? "Ho-kay." Leah snorted, "Time to Google the name." She searched the full name listed in the email's return address properties. "Right…a British lord, and a randy one at that, according to the tabloids. Not bad looking, though… Why are all the cute ones gay?"

Leah had time for a shower, a quick breakfast, and then maybe, just maybe, she'd drive to the airport and see what this Lord James Melbourne dude was all about. "Yeah, right, as if I don't have anything better to do." She looked around her tiny, white-walled apartment and realized that she really didn't have anything better to do. "Shower for one, coming up!"

The long hot shower cleared her head. The chilly rinse afterwards made sure her inner core was cool so she could handle the hot summer day outside. Rather than use the blow dryer and add to the Greensboro heat, she ran her brush through her hair the one hundred strokes her mother had told her was necessary for healthy hair. She twisted her thick locks up into a rope, wrapped it into a knot on top of her head, and secured the bun with a chopstick.

Whether the man she was going to meet was a British lord or not, she wasn't going to get dressed up to meet *any* new person on her day off. A tank top, a lightweight shirt, and skirts were acceptable wear just about anywhere this time of year. The style of shoes she wore would dress up or down the outfit. She looked at the pile of footwear by the door and made an easy decision. Slip-on sandals were comfortable, she didn't have to bend over to tie them, and they didn't remind her of work. She wiggled her hips in imaginary flirtation, visualizing herself as 'classy casual,' and slid her toes in.

Leah reached for her oversized keyring on the table and saw the two smartphones next to it. She took a deep breath and grabbed the works.

Maybe she'd find the courage to check out the files on her mother's phone if someone else was with her. She certainly didn't have the strength—or rather nerve—to do it alone. It also might be easier to do it alongside someone she didn't know, but who was acquainted with—or at least had met—her mother.

The purple Prius was right where she left it in the parking lot outside her apartment. "Nice car," she said, as she patted the side mirror, "you've learned to stay where I put you. Yeah, well, if only people were as dependable."

She shuddered as she recalled that moment ten months ago. The Park Service had called and said her car had been left in their parking lot overnight; was there a problem?

*"My car is where?" she asked, dumbfounded. "Hanging Rock Park? Where's my mother? She's the one who had it last."*

*"No one was with the car, ma'am, and there were no signs of foul play. We just thought maybe you left it here because you had run out of gas or something. Can you get a ride out here so you can drive it home, or do you need to call a tow truck?"*

*Billy, her next-door neighbor, had given her a ride to the park. She had been so stressed over the ordeal that she had forgotten to bring her spare key. No, she was more than stressed—she was irate—pissed way off the Richter scale at her mother for leaving the car, and then taking off to God only knew where. Before she totally freaked out about not remembering to bring a spare key, though, Leah checked under the right rear bumper. The key was there. She remembered thinking, 'Well, at least Mom did something right and left the key where I told her to.'*

*Then there was the waiting. That was the worst part of the ordeal. The first day she was nothing but mad. By the second morning—she had to go to work that day, too—the rage had subsided, and concern took its place. She made a call to the police and filed a missing persons report. "Why did you wait so long to call?" the condescending dispatcher accused, rather than asked.*

*"Because she's a sane adult woman who's on vacation, and she doesn't have to answer to her daughter, that's why...if it's any of your blankety, blank, blank business!" she screamed, swallowing the curse words that she knew would haunt her if she loosed them on the recorded phone line.*

*Her furor must have worked: a police officer was at her door within an hour. She shared the voice mail she had received two days before and gave him a copy of a ten-year-old picture, embarrassed that she didn't have a current one. However, whether the photo was ten minutes old or ten years old didn't make a difference. No ransom demands were made, no body found, nor were there any signs of foul play.*

*Billy Burke, the neighbor who had taken her to the park to retrieve her car, was also a Greensboro police detective, and although missing persons was not his department, he helped search on his own time. He took a copy of her mother's photo and sent it to InterPol—or whatever it was he called it. He said if her mother went through any airline, bus, marine, or railroad terminal, this new-fangled technology would detect her as soon as she was in view of the security cameras. Ten months had passed, and not even a false alarm had been triggered.*

Well, she hadn't had much but straws to grasp at before, so anything this 'Lord' James Melbourne person remembered about meeting her disappearing mama last Halloween would be appreciated. Yes, any clues would be welcome, especially after seeing her mother—or her mother's younger clone—yesterday in the recovery room at the hospital.

Ж

Leah rolled all the car windows down, letting the hot air blow out before she turned on the air conditioning. She pulled into the little 'Cuppa Joe' drive-through coffee shop for her cup of iced fortitude. "Triple shot iced vanilla soy latte, please," she said to the young orange-haired barista. The perky teenager quickly produced the drink and handed her the sealed cup with a couple of chocolate-covered coffee beans settled into the lid's recess. Leah gave the efficient carrot-top girl a ten-dollar bill and told her to keep the change. She was feeling generous today. Maybe the energy of the world would feel like giving back. She could only hope.

It was only 11:00 a.m. and flight 3923 wasn't due in until 12:05. No worries—the airport parking lot was covered and the inside bars were air-conditioned. At least she wasn't traveling, so she wouldn't have to deal with the long lines for security. Leah strolled leisurely down the wide concourse, grateful for the abundance of cool, dry air, and spotted a little bar that wasn't totally crowded. It looked like lots of other Greensboro sweat-heads had the same idea about how to handle a hot August day.

All the tables were either full or hadn't been bussed and were cluttered with dirty glasses. Leah wanted a table, but didn't feel like clearing off a place to sit. The bar was empty, though, brilliantly clean, and very inviting. The bartender looked to be in good spirits, too. *Right. Good spirits, as in spirit dispenser, as in bartender. Punny lady—your mudder would be proud of you.*

Leah ordered a Baileys on the rocks, and as discretely as she could, dumped the works into the white and brown striped Cuppa Joe coffee cup. The bartender hadn't missed her custom brew and smiled at her. She grinned weakly in return, sipped her drink, and looked down, twirling her cocktail napkin in circles with her index finger. She wasn't ready to engage in conversation, nor did she care to watch the TV above her with the latest in Hollywood scandals.

Sniff, sniff, gulp, sniff.

Leah turned around to see if someone behind her really was crying, or if someone had changed the channel to a noontime soap opera. Over in the corner, half-hidden by a silk and plastic dieffenbachia, was an attractive gray-haired lady sitting at a table littered with dirty dishes. She had pushed the empty glasses aside, and was using one of the used cocktail napkins as a dust broom to move the tortilla chip crumbs away from her. Evidently the small noises caught the bartender's attention, too, because he was on his way to the table with a bar towel and a fresh bowl of chips for her.

The woman turned around and said sincerely, "Thanks, how sweet of you." She set three photographs on the table in front of her and sighed.

Leah wasn't a snoop, but she couldn't help but look over Ms. Sniffle's shoulder to see her display. The first picture was a black and white studio photo of a dark-haired toddler with a big smile, maybe two-years-old. The second was a class picture of a pre-adolescent scholar, complete with sash across his shoulders, almost like an honors vestment. The last one was familiar to her—the stock photo she had seen in her Google search: Lord James Melbourne.

It was obvious by the way the woman smiled at and touched her photos that she was fond of the men, or rather, man. They looked like shots of Lord James at different times in his life. And, it appeared as if he and she might be related. There was a definite family resemblance with their high cheekbones, full mouths, and beautiful brown eyes. It was possible that this woman was either his mother or his very young grandmother.

Leah realized she was staring, and turned back to face the bottles beneath the mirror at the back of the bar. The friendly bartender came over to her, holding a carafe of coffee. "Would you like me to freshen that up for you?" he asked.

She pulled off the lid and let him pour in some fresh coffee. "Not too much now; you need to leave room for the *crème*," she said.

He smiled and dumped in a scoop of ice. He had anticipated her drink, and already had a shot of Bailey's ready. He poured it right from the shot glass into the coffee cup. She went for her purse to pay the drink, but he put up his hand in a 'stop' gesture. He wiped an imaginary spill off the counter with his bar rag, leaned over and asked, "Are you waiting for someone special?"

"Uh, yes, sort of," she replied lamely. She really wasn't in the mood to engage in a conversation with a stranger, even if he did seem like a decent sort.

"Oh, sorry," he apologized, and then noticed the lady with the tabletop montage had come up to the bar and was standing a few feet away. He excused himself to Leah with a nod, and walked over to the older woman. "What can I get for you, ma'am?"

36

"An iced tea, please," she replied politely. "And do you have a blank piece of paper? I need to make a sign."

He looked under the counter, shoved a few items aside, "Let me see..." then pulled out a football schedule. The backside was blank, a perfect canvas for a small poster. "Will this do?"

"Yes, thank you." She took the sheet to her table, gathered up her photos, placed a soft kiss on the top of the pack, and put it back into the side pocket of her beige designer bag. She unzipped the middle part of her purse and pawed through it. By her scowl of frustration, she didn't find what she was searching for. She looked back to the bartender and asked, "Do you happen to have a black felt-tipped marker?"

He rummaged under the counter again and replied, "Sorry."

Leah took pity on the frustrated woman. "Here, I have a marker. It's dark purple, but wide, and should make letters that are easy to read."

"Oh, thank you so much." The older lady accepted the marker, then moved her basket of chips to the next table and spread out the repurposed poster. She started with a large 'L' then changed it into a triangle. She continued on with 'James' on the first line and 'Melbourne' on the second line, ending with a mirror image of the first accidental triangle at the end, effectively making a decorative panel around his name.

She returned the marker to Leah. "Thanks again," she said, then went back to her table to watch the next onslaught of passengers coming through.

*Looks like we're waiting for the same man. Maybe he really hadn't meant to send me that email, after all. Oh, well, it's cool in here, the drink is just right, and I might have a first-class drama developing right in front of me. It beats the heck out of staying at home and doing laundry.*

And, there he was. 'Wow! What a stud,' was all Leah could think. She bowed her head down and made the snap decision to play invisible. She glanced over at the lady in coral, clutching her bag nervously as she stood up to walk out into the corridor with her little handmade sign.

*I guess I was wrong about them being related. A man would surely know his own mother. She wouldn't—shouldn't—have needed a sign with his name on it for him to recognize her. But then again, she didn't have an English accent, and he's an English lord. But why was she so passionate about his pictures?* Leah realized that either she had an overactive imagination from reading too many romance novels or she had stumbled onto a long-kept international secret.

# *5 Bibb

Well, one thing was obvious: the two of them had never met. James was stunned, but still composed. Elbows close at his side, shallow breathing—his body language practically screamed, 'Oh, so that's who you are?' The older lady was almost comical—giddy and schoolgirlish—as if she was finally meeting the movie star she had had a crush on for years. She was positively gaga over the good-looking man, hands up, barely holding in check the urge to paw him to make sure he was real.

He certainly didn't look the way Leah had imagined an English lord would look. The facial features were definitely the man from the photographs and internet stories, but that's where the similarity to 'Lord James Melbourne' ended. He sported a two-day-old beard, had a casual, 'I haven't a care in the world and I'm on vacation' attitude, and was wearing clothes that looked as if they belonged on a male model hawking macho colognes in a glamour magazine. He was also able to pull off the 'happy hunk' aura without seeming proud or vain—he was simply a man meeting a long lost relative in an airport. And his mother, or grandmother, had eyes only for him. Leah couldn't hear what they were saying, but he seemed surprised about something. The older lady was glowing with delight, but was managing to contain her earlier excitement.

And then the two of them walked into the bar. Ho boy! The lady looked over at Leah, smiled, and said proudly, "I got him!"

"Glad I could help," Leah said, and saluted her with her cup of joe.

Lord James's eyes widened at her gesture. "Ms. Madigan?" he asked, and looked right at her.

*Good Grief. Where's a Harry Potter cloak of invisibility when you need it? So much for taking a low profile.* Leah smiled weakly, "Yes, that's me. James Melbourne, I presume."

"Do you two know each other?" the lady asked. She was genuinely confused, but regained her composure quickly. "Come sit down," she continued, not waiting for an answer, moving chairs around in order to make a place for Leah to join them at their little round table. "I'm Bibb Stephens, his m…, er, the mill owner who…well, just call me Bibb."

The Freudian slip of nearly saying 'mother' was missed by James, but Leah heard it and filed it away, deciding that it was best to try and forget it. That was Bibb's secret to share or keep hidden away.

"Would you like more tea, ma'am?" the barkeeper asked, a pitcher of tea in one hand, a fresh basket of tortilla chips in the other.

"Yes, please." She changed her focus from the waiter to the object of her adoration. "James, would you like to try one of these, or maybe you'd rather have a cold beer?"

"Thank you. I'll try the tea on ice. And you, Ms. Madigan?"

"I'm good, I still have my Irish coffee." Leah lifted her cup and took a long drink, trying to hide her discomfort at being the third person in a two-person reunion.

The waiter brought the glass of iced tea to the table. Bibb put down a $20 bill, and momentarily glanced away from James to be sure the server saw the money. Leah looked over at Bibb, saw her new acquaintance's head pull back in shock, and followed her gaze. Bibb was staring at the bartender. Leah could see that the man who had moments earlier given her a free spike to her iced coffee, was watching her anxiously. As soon as he saw Leah return his stare, he looked guilty, grabbed the cash, and went back behind the bar. He popped open the till, took out some ones, rushed back to the table, put down the change, and was back behind the bar in seconds. Head bent towards his belly, he fumbled with the knot in his little bar towel apron, mumbling curses until he got it off, and then threw it into the mini laundry basket. He dashed out of the establishment awkwardly, all elbows and feet, bumping into a young man who was evidently his shift relief.

"Hey, Harry, what's your hurry? You're supposed to wait until I clock in before you take off. Is there anything going on that I should know about? Harry? Harry!"

But Harry the bartender was now sprinting down the concourse, getting distance between himself and the bar as quickly as possible. He took one last nervous glance back over his shoulder at Leah, and then was gone.

Leah lifted her cup to take another sip, then realized her lips were tingling. "Oh, shit," she mumbled, "I think I've been drugged. Shit, shit, shit." She lay her head down on the table, turned it sideways, and saw James bend forward to look into her eyes.

"Do you need to go to the hospital?" he asked. "Bibb, where's the nearest hospital, and how close is your car? Would an ambulance be faster?"

Leah managed to lift one finger to indicate 'wait.' She knew what she had to do. She opened her mouth and poked her index finger down her throat as far as she could. Her gag reflex made her cough, but she continued jabbing.

Bibb picked up on what was happening. She rushed behind the bar, grabbed first a trashcan and then the laundry basket, and passed them over the counter to the new barkeeper, who handed them to James. Leah hacked and choked, then started vomiting, bringing up the drug-laced coffee and whiskey blend. James handed her a fistful of napkins to wipe her mouth. The replacement bartender came over with a glass of water and handed it to Bibb, the obvious mother in the little sick-child scenario.

Leah put her head back onto the table and turned to look at her small audience one by one. "Why?" she asked the new bartender.

"Did he ask you if you were waiting for someone?"

Leah managed a slight nod in reply. "I think he wanted to take you home with him. He was getting off shift, and well, there's a new date rape drug out there, and he just broke up with his girlfriend. I think he wanted you to, um, be with him. Don't think I'm condoning his action—he's going to get canned for sure. If you want his name and contact information, I'll help you fill out the police report. He's been in trouble before, but nothing like this; just some petty theft."

Bibb still had the glass of water in her hand. "Do you think you can handle this now?" she asked, offering it to her.

"Thanks," Leah said. She gulped a mouthful, performed a quick swish swish, and spit into the trash can. "Do you have any sugar and saltine crackers?" she asked the bartender.

The bartender answered, "Sure," looked at Bibb and James like, 'Is she nuts?' then went behind the bar and brought out the sugar dispenser and a basket of cellophane-wrapped saltine crackers.

Leah poured a few hearty shakes of salt and a stream of sugar into the water. "May I?" she asked as she reached for the spoon at the side of James's glass of iced tea. He nodded and watched as she stirred her little concoction. She cautiously sipped, and then without setting the glass down, finished drinking her brew. "More water, please," she asked the bartender. She turned her attention to a packet of saltines. She tugged at the easy-tear strip, first from one side, and then the other, but only managed to crush the still-wrapped crackers.

"Here, allow me," said James. He picked up another package and used his teeth to start the tear needed to open it.

"Thanks," Leah said, smiling as she accepted the crackers. *He certainly isn't a stuffy Brit; too bad he's gay.*

She noticed her new acquaintances' stares and explained. "You see, the salt and sugar in the water make a saline and dextrose solution to help rehydrate my body and balance my electrolytes, just in case I lost too much fluid—which I doubt I did—but better to err on the side of caution. It's the same principle as drinking Gatorade or Pedi-a-lyte when you or a child has the stomach flu. And the soda crackers will help absorb any residual poison." Leah saw the shocked looks of her two new friends. "Oh, I'm a nurse, and no, I do *not* want to go to the hospital on my day off, thank you very much! I'm sure I'll be fine."

The bartender approached the table with trepidation, a glass of water in one hand and a napkin with scribbling on it in the other. "Here you are. This is all the information he gave when he was hired last week. Normally we would have done a thorough background check, but he admitted to the petty theft, and we were shorthanded. Of course, we're *really* going to be short now. I doubt he'll be back."

"No loss there," said Bibb. James nodded in agreement. Leah took the slip of paper, stuffed it into her shirt pocket, and then returned her head

40

to the tabletop. Bibb saw the bartender was still standing by, making sure that Leah was okay. "Next time, try the union hall," she advised. "They'll do the screening for you. Ready everyone?"

"Yes, Mom," Leah said, reaching down to pick up her purse. James bent over at the same time.

The two of them shared one of those moments frozen in time. They were linked eye-to-eye, simple spirits, naked souls in a world where no one else existed. They shared a stare, a blink, another stare, then they both returned to the world that contained other people.

"I mean, Bibb," Leah corrected absently.

"Yes, let's get out of here. Do you want to go to the constable's station first?" James asked Leah.

James turned and looked across the table at Bibb, trying to visualize her in another light. 'Mom?' he thought. Blink, blink. *I have to get this done in the right order. First, alert the authorities, then talk to Leah about her mother, and then confer with Bibb about the mill purchase.*

"No, I don't." Leah's reply brought him back from his introspection. "I doubt they'd be able to catch him anyway. He's probably on his way to…to…oh, crap." Leah snorted with disgust and returned to her slumped-over position on the table, her head on her forearms.

"I think she needs to go home," James said to Bibb. He turned his attention to his newfound lady in distress, "Do you think you can drive?"

"I'll make it," she answered, bringing her head up. "I certainly didn't want this to be your first impression of me." She grunted and corrected herself. "*Anyone's* first impression of me. Maybe we ought to do this another day? The last twenty-four hours have been pretty rough for me."

"I know," James said.

Leah glared at James. *How do you know how my day has been?*

"I have to talk to you right away about your mother," he said, his tone letting her know that delay was not an option for him.

At the mention of her mother, Leah's spine tensed. She slowly pulled herself together—physically and emotionally—into a straight-backed, Mother Superior bearing, complete with scowl. She didn't like anyone telling her what to do, especially on her day off.

"It is *very* important," he stressed, ignoring her glare. He turned to Bibb. "I think our business will have to wait until later."

Bibb looked disappointed, but nodded and stood up, apparently getting ready to leave the two young people to their serious discussion about Leah's mother. James arose in response, his English gentlemanly behavior showing his appreciation of her gracious parting after their confused and awkward initial meeting.

As he reached out to shake Bibb's hand, his arm brushed up against the outside pocket of the valise next to him, dislodging his secreted bundle of ancient letters. Bibb's eyes went to the source of the crinkly noise. James saw her flash of recognition of the blue ribbon-wrapped package. She looked up at him—wide-eyed, but mute. He could tell by her stare that she knew what was in the letters. She might even know more than he did if she had read beyond the first one, the only letter he had opened.

Time stopped for the two of them as they sized each other up, neither one of them wanting to speak first.

It was Leah, though, who broke the uncomfortable silence. "Are you sure that you two don't need a moment, or a few hours, before we talk, James?" *She didn't know what was going on with these two, but did remember how Bibb had looked over the pictures of him. Maybe the truth would be revealed, which might not be what she wanted.*

Something quickly passed between James and Bibb—a spark of recognition? James shook it off, and Bibb changed her focus to Leah, "Is this meeting about your mother, Evie?"

Leah answered slowly, moving her head side to side in confusion. "No, my mother's name is Dani," she said, almost as a question. "James met her last year before she…uh…left."

Leah looked at Bibb, then James, and then back to Bibb again. She could tell that they both knew something about her mother's disappearance. Why else would the two of them pale at the word *left*? "Okay, I think all three of us need to talk. But not here," Leah said with a shudder of disgust at the fresh memory of being drugged.

James spoke to both of them, looking hard at each one in turn. "I agree, but I have to stop and pick up my vehicle. Could one of you drop me off at the Duck Inn Diner?"

"Sure," Bibb answered enthusiastically, before Leah even had a chance to reflect on where the Duck Inn Diner was. Bibb saw the look of confusion on Leah's face. "It's that little café that has a statue of a hound with a dead duck in its mouth out front. It's right before you get to the Guilford Courthouse Museum." Leah nodded her head in recognition. "We'll meet you there. James, did you have luggage to claim?"

James was still stunned, trying to figure out where Bibb fit into all of this and how she could possibly know about those letters. They were a long held Melbourne family secret, and she wasn't a Melbourne.

"James? James?" Bibb called softly, trying to get his attention without tapping him. "Lord James Melbourne?"

"Sorry, what were you saying?"

"Luggage, do you have any?" she repeated.

"No, just this," he said vacantly, lifting up the leather bag and setting it back down on the table. He bit his lip, looked at the bag again, and snatched the letters from the side pocket. He took a deep breath of resolution, unzipped the center section, and stashed the papers inside. "Let's go."

Leah was way ahead of them in the corridor, making her way to the parking garage and her car. Bibb escorted James, looking sideways every few moments to make sure he was keeping up with her fast pace. He smiled in automated response, then sank back into his private little bubble of bewilderment. An awkward silence kept pace with the odd couple as they wove their way through the crowd, past the baggage claim, and through the automated exit doors that opened into a heat rated at blast furnace level—Lord James Melbourne's welcome-back greeting to North Carolina.

Bibb's deli mustard-colored vintage Volvo was pristine, waxed to brilliance, but squealed when the air conditioning kicked in. James looked at her with the unexpected noise, but she just smiled, tilted her head, shrugged one shoulder, and said, "Hey, it works."

James returned her smile, and then retreated into his own realm of reflection, uncomfortable with the prospect of polite, meaningless conversation. He looked out the side window and saw Leah at the stop light in a purple Prius. He flashed recognition: that was the same car Dani was driving last autumn. October 31. Halloween, the waitress called it.

*That seemed a lifetime ago. Back then, he was free, although he didn't think so at the time. He had felt burdened with the inherited family responsibilities. The trip to the States had been a lark and a gift to himself. He came to check out Lord Julian Hart's involvement with the Revolutionary War, and maybe find out what had really happened to him and his stepson, Lord Wallace Urquhart, Ninth Earl of Cavendish. Were they kidnapped, then murdered when their families refused to pay ransom, or did they become mysterious secret agents, covertly helping the young, colonial-era America win her freedom? The British citizen in James hoped the two had died honorably, but the visceral man wanted to believe that the two men had done what they believed was right, and followed their hearts, no matter what the political implications.*

*Focus, James, focus! You made the trip, purchased the 'historical document' that was really a boner of a map and not the registry of British soldiers involved in the North Carolina colony during the uprising, met that strange pickle-puss of a man, Simon, and the colorful, perky and just a bit plump, Dani Madigan. Then you went back to England, met and married the body-beautiful Clotilde, and life rapidly crumbled into biscuit crumbs and glass shards.*

*And now full circle back to America. A divorce, a cryptic bundle of centuries-old correspondences, and a cigarette pack full of precious jewels. Yeah, right. Now add to that the mysterious mill owner/businesswoman Bibb who knows about the very secret Melbourne letters. And let's not forget the recently recovered from date-rape-poisoning, Leah Madigan. Yesterday she was the hospital nurse to her AWOL mother who returned for a one-day reappearance after traveling back in time 230 years. Phew! And he didn't even want to bring into the game of guess who, when, where, and why of Grandpa and his disappearance last year. To hell with full circle: his life was a never-ending, enigmatic, Möbius loop!*

"Are you getting out now, or do you want to wait for...oh, she's here already." Bibb turned off the ignition, but the car kept sputtering. A wheeze, a couple of knocks, a long, low whistle, and then the engine finally shut down. "What can I say?" Bibb shrugged, "It gets me where I want to go, even if it does complain afterwards."

The two of them chuckled as they walked into the little café, the mood of the day elevated by the singing of the veteran Volvo.

"Hey, there! Welcome back!" Frankie, the waitress who had served him pot roast and hot rolls last Halloween, was there with two of the same, old tattered menus. "Pick a table; there're still a few left," she joked.

Only two of the tables had patrons seated at them, and one of them was Leah. She was in the back of the room, running her finger across the rim of a sweaty glass of fresh lemonade. She looked up and smiled as they approached, then instinctively moved her glass to the side, making more room for the two of them.

Frankie followed the two newcomers to the table and set down the menus. "Special of the day is a chef's salad—too hot to cook, as far as I'm concerned. But we have a long list of sandwiches, too," she said, and pointed to the highlighted area inside the menu.

"Cherry pie a la mode," Leah announced with a confidant attitude that screamed, 'Don't mess with me. I'll eat dessert first if I want to!'

"Make that two; I didn't get mine last time. Mo...er, Bibb, what would you like?" James asked, a little chagrined at almost calling her mother.

"I'll follow suit. Now, if you'll excuse me a moment, I'd like to freshen up," she said, bringing her hand up to the tip of her nose, covering her mouth and whatever expression she was hiding.

James stood up as Bibb left the table. She nodded, smiled, and then rushed to the ladies room, sniffing loudly as the door shut behind her.

James didn't even want to think what that was all about. He was glad that she was gone, though. He needed to talk to Leah right away and figure out a time and place where the two of them could speak privately and at length. He looked at her and was direct, "I have to show you something. But first, I know you saw your mother yesterday." *It was cold and quick, and hopefully less painful this way.*

"Ho-kay," Leah drawled. "How did you know? I hardly recognized her, and I didn't think that there were very many people who did see her."

"She told me," he said, "rather, she wrote to me about it. It's all here in her letter. Actually, there are several letters, but she left a note to 'read me first' on this one. In it, she asked me not to read the others until I had spoken with you. She said she had to go back to her husband and her babies, your siblings. She had triplets, she said."

Leah was stone-faced, but listening. "Did she say how come she looked forty years younger? And triplets? How?"

"Well, no, she didn't say anything about aging, at least there's nothing in the first letter. We can read the others together—if it's okay with you—after we read the first one. As far as having three babies, triplets are a naturally occurring phenomenon, and if she is married, well, you know," he said, eyes downcast, then cleared his throat, embarrassed at the familiarity he had just shown.

Leah smiled at his blush. "Yes, after lunch we can go to my apartment and read the letter, or letters. I have something to show you, too. Or maybe I do. I'm confused. I wish I had something stronger than this lemonade. But I'll put any enhancements in it myself, thank you very much!"

Just then, Bibb returned from the ladies room. She sniffled, then smiled weakly. "Anything interesting going on?"

Something snapped in James. "Yes, something very interesting. Evie. You asked Leah if her mother's name was Evie. Why did you ask that?"

"Oh, shit," Bibb replied succinctly.

"Who's Evie?" asked Leah. "My mother's name is Dani, and why, 'oh, shit'? Do you know my mother or where she is?"

Bibb let out a long sigh. "No," she said, waiting for inspiration, "but I know where she was yesterday. Does that count?"

"Is everyone ready for pie?" asked Frankie, her hands full of bowls containing cherries, crust, and ice cream.

"Yes," said Leah, ignoring for the moment all of the excitement of the last three minutes. "My mother always said, 'When you don't know what to do, eat.' She said you could think better on a full stomach. And Lord knows, we need all the help we can get."

# *6 Pie

The three strangers ate their pie in segregated silence. James was pensive—busy with calculations and theories about whatever. Bibb looked stern—like a mother trying to decide if she should put her wayward child in the corner or swat his bottom. And Leah—well, she was content, at peace for the first time in nearly a year. She didn't know if these two people, new to her life, would believe her wild story, but she knew they were willing to listen. There was a slim but real possibility that they would even believe her when she told them what had happened at the hospital yesterday.

Explaining her crazy story would certainly be easier because they *were* strangers. After she related it, she would never have to face them again. This Lord James fellow wasn't a local, and the gray-haired woman, Bibb, who hung onto his every word, might be from North Carolina, but they had never met before today and probably wouldn't again. Anonymity was a place of comfort in this situation. Unloading on anyone—especially someone she wouldn't have to face again—would make her feel better. She had to tell her story to someone before she became a raving alcoholic. Who cared what they thought about her after she talked to them? They'd be out of her life in hours, maybe even minutes.

On the other hand, they might have answers about what had happened. Ah, yes, for now—at least for the next few minutes—she could bask in the warmth of the hearth of hope. She might even have an assistant or two in solving the enigma of her mother's reappearance and re-disappearance yesterday.

*It was a class AAA mystery: Two days ago, her sixty-year-old mother, who had been missing for ten months, showed up in the emergency room as a young Jane Doe, a musket ball lodged near her heart.*

*The surgeons successfully removed the lead ball, and the next morning, Leah found her mother—in a much younger body—as her patient in recovery. The two of them spent a few awkward minutes together—her mother said she didn't remember anything, although she did know that Leah was her daughter—and then her mother re-disappeared, this time abducted by a weird little man pretending to be her doctor. The stolen car used in the kidnapping was found a short time later, but her rejuvenated mother and the phony physician had vanished into the woods.*

"Ah, that was good," sighed Leah, as she returned to her company, leaving her musing behind. She pushed her dish away and pulled the lemonade closer. "What? Don't you like pie?" she asked her two fellow diners, an engaging grin on her face and just a touch of sarcasm in her tone.

James had eaten all of the cherries and ice cream, leaving the crust untouched, and Bibb had just pushed her food around to make it look like she had eaten. They all knew the subject of their little get together wasn't the food, but how they figured in each other's lives with respect to the disappearance of Leah's mother.

*James felt an honest smile come to his face. It could have been an awkward situation, but Leah was putting a bright spin on the gathering, lightening the mood, and taking over as moderator of the meeting, preempting the chance of bruised egos. She was definitely the daughter of that off-center old lady, Dani. She, too, was a take-charge type of person and not mousey at all. The young woman had a dry wit and seemed a decent sort. Leah was also easy on the eyes and seemed to have received a lion's share of intelligence. James's smile increased—she was also young enough to reproduce.*

"Hello? Hello? Anyone home in there?" asked Leah, as she mimed knocking on his head.

James blushed like a schoolboy. "Sorry, ma'am. I guess I'm still on London time. What did you say?"

"Don't call me ma'am," Leah said with mock indignation. "I'm not *that* old! I just wanted to know if you wanted to get set up at your motel or whatever, and then we could meet back at my place."

"Um," stalled James. He looked out into the parking lot and saw the old red pickup pull in. "I have to take care of something first. Excuse me, I'll be right back," he said, and left the table.

James exited the restaurant into the noonday sun. He was out of earshot of the two women, but didn't miss any of their conversation. The ladies were rapt, silently watching his proceedings in the parking lot. James handed a thick envelope to the pudgy, middle-aged man in dirty jeans and a baseball cap. The slightly greasy, but obviously happy man opened it. He looked inside, grinned, and gave James a keyring with a mini blue metallic flashlight and several keys on it. They shook hands, spoke a few more words, and then walked away from each other. The man wearing the stained Charlie Daniels tee shirt was grinning and singing as he stuffed the envelope into the hip pocket of his sagging jeans.

*It looked like James just made his day. Maybe he could do the same for me, Leah thought.*

James came back into the cafe with an equally large smile. "Now I have a vehicle and won't have to beg a ride. And, as to your question, Ms. Madigan: no and yes. No, I don't need to get set up at a motel or whatever yet, and yes, I'd be more than happy to meet at your place, preferably right away. Are we ready?"

"Well, since we'll be in separate vehicles, it might help to know where you're going. Here, I'll draw you a map." Leah dug into her purse for a pen with one hand and grabbed a couple of napkins with the other.

"Let me help with that," James said. "Excuse me just a moment." He stood up and walked over to Frankie who was seated at the counter, working a crossword puzzle. "Frankie, do you still have those maps?"

"Well, here's the city map," she said, and reached towards the end of the counter to retrieve one of the yellow-edged advertisement street maps, "and the maps to Hanging Rock Park are in the back."

"Hanging Rock Park?" he asked.

"Yes, Hanging Rock State Park. That's where you went with your two friends last Halloween, isn't it? Oh, you didn't go with them, did you? I thought the three of you left together. Hey, is that your mother over there? It looks like you got a family reunion going with her and the other lady. Is she your girlfriend?" she asked, one eyebrow raised

James just smiled at Frankie's nosiness and said, "Thanks for the maps."

He noticed the awkward silence between the two women as he returned to the table. Evidently, the rapport they had established at the airport bar had evaporated. Either that or they hadn't found anything in common to talk about. *That'll come soon enough.*

"Here you are, ladies," James said cheerily, waving the two city maps like a fan. "Did you find a pen?" he asked Leah.

"Sure did," she said, and held up her purple marker. She accepted the maps from him and opened out the first one, found the café's location on it, and drew an 'X'. She found her street, traced the route to her apartment with her finger, then went back and highlighted the way with the purple pen. "Not exactly a straight route, but easy enough to find. Just follow behind me and use the map if we get separated. Sound good?"

"I think I can manage that," answered James with the same upbeat tone.

"What's the address?" Bibb asked, frowning, as if she felt left out of their mini road trip.

Leah grabbed the second map, drew a quick line indicating the route, made an 'X' at the café and a 'Y' at her home, and then wrote her address in clear, bold letters above the 'Y'. Almost as an afterthought, she added her cell phone number, looked up at the older woman, and smiled.

Bibb returned the smile. She had felt alienated. Her two new friends were enjoying a youthful rapport, and she was the odd—rather the old—one out. But no matter what else happened today, this Leah had shown herself to be a lady. She may not be of noble birth, but she did have the ability to make others feel at ease. She had also been there to help when assistance was needed, even if it was only to offer a purple marker to a stranger in an airport. Yes, Bibb had a gut feeling that this was Evie's daughter, even if she had said that her mother's name was Dani.

Frankie came by with the check and a pitcher of ice water. "Will there be anything else?" she asked, looking intently at James's, then Leah's hands, checking to see if they showed signs of being married or engaged.

She smiled and sighed in relief at seeing bare fingers on both of them.

The perusal wasn't missed by either Bibb or James. Leah was looking into her purse for her wallet, and was oblivious of the inferred relationship, or lack of same. Bibb grabbed the check, said, "I've got this," got up, and walked over to the cash register.

"One more thing before we leave," James said. "Excuse me, for a moment."

James went to the wall of maps and flyers for local points of interest and found the one for Hanging Rock State Park. He took it, then went to the cashier's station and waited while Frankie gave Bibb her change for their light lunch. At the end of the transaction, Bibb smiled and stood back, letting him come forward to talk with their server.

"Frankie, remember that old parchment map Ms. Madigan and that crazy old man were studying last autumn?" She nodded and waited for him to continue. "Did you give them this map to identify the points on the old one, that is, to use as a reference?"

"Yeah," she replied slowly. "That's when I told them that the symbol they were pointing to was for the monadnock, you know, that tall, clumpy chunk of rock there at the park. I gave them that same map," she tapped the map in his hand, "and Ms. Madigan took him where he wanted to go, I guess. Here," she said as she opened up the map, "they were talking about trails, and well, bless me, it was nearly a year ago. I can't remember everything now, can I? Oh, but wait, I told them that where they were going was supposed to be sacred Indian ground. That must have been right there," she pointed to an area off center of the map.

"Thank you, Ms. Frankie, you have been most helpful." James gave her a short bow, and then picked up her hand, bringing it to his lips. He gave her the briefest and lightest kiss possible, and said, "I hope our paths cross again. Have a pleasant day."

Frankie brought her hand up to her chest and said softly, "You're welcome. I hope you find what you're looking for."

"Me, too," he said with a grin and a nod.

Leah had come over and joined Bibb on the sidelines of the little display of British comportment. They looked at each other and shared a tender smile at his generosity. The act meant so much to the waitress, and took little effort on his part. He looked over to his two new lady friends, shifted his eyes from them to the cars outside, and held the door open for them.

"Good-bye," the two of them said to Frankie at the same time. "You've got great cherry pie," added Leah. "I'll be back."

"Sure," replied Frankie, cradling her recently bussed paw to her breast, "sure."

The odd trio—the nurse on her day off, the older businesswoman, and the English lord on hiatus—gathered in the parking lot next to James's 'new' acquisition. Bibb looked at the front of the old red truck, and then peered into the rolled down driver's window. "'64 Dodge with push button automatic transmission: sweet! Does it have a 318 in it?"

"Yes, it does. The only thing it needs is a new paint job and an upgrade from its 2-55 air conditioner."

"Two fifty-five?" asked Leah.

Bibb had picked up on the joke, and answered her, "Two windows down at fifty-five miles an hour. Ready to lead the way?" she asked Leah.

"Let's roll," she replied with a hopeful tone. "Yeah, let's roll," she echoed softly as she got into her car, remembering what the little conference was going to entail. "How in the hell am I going to get them to believe what happened? Shit."

# *7 The White Knight

"Drive on the right side. Just follow behind her, and drive on the right," James said out loud to help him concentrate on driving on the wrong—for him—side of the road.

Leah was correct; it was an easy place to find. He drove into the parking lot, and Bibb pulled into the space next to him. The two of them walked past the apartment complex's fenced-in swimming pool. "Sweet," remarked James at the sparkling, clear water. He pulled out his white handkerchief and wiped his sweat-beaded brow. Hopefully he could find a motel with a pool. Summer in North Carolina was hotter than he could ever have imagined.

James and Bibb strolled side by side, a business-friendly two feet apart, toward the little four-plex building that held Leah's apartment unit. They knew they were at the right place. They could see Leah up ahead, sorting through her large bundle of keys, searching for the right one to open the door.

It happened so quickly, it seemed as if time had jumped forward a few seconds while they watched. Someone was suddenly behind Leah, grabbing and pulling her towards him. The young, ponytailed punk with jeans slung so low that six inches of his plaid boxers showed, must have been stalking her, hiding in the bushes.

Leah's attacker wasn't aware of his audience—he was focused on subduing her. He yanked Leah towards his chest and slammed his body up against hers. His sweaty forearm wrapped around her neck in that same split second, making sure she didn't get a chance to yell. Her hand reflexively unclenched with the shock of impact, and her keys dropped to the ground.

"Go ahead and scream," he whispered hoarsely in her ear. "I'll cut the noise outta you right quick, I will."

She tried to gulp in fear at his words, but his arm cut off her ability to swallow. She could, however, still smell. He reeked of alcohol and fear, sweat and stale cigar smoke.

"Open the damned door, and don't try no funny stuff," he growled.

Leah tried to tell him that she had dropped her keys, but couldn't breathe a word because of his stranglehold. She cautiously lifted her right hand and pointed to the lock with her finger, made a twisting movement, as if she was unlocking it, then pointed to the ground.

The odiferous assailant realized what she was trying to say and loosened his hold, just enough for her to bend sideways to pick up the keys. He kept shadowing her body, though, so close that when she moved, he was like her second spine.

He hadn't left her any room for a self-defense move, and Leah definitely didn't want to be breathing out of a second hole in her throat. She looked down for her keys and saw movement behind her. She didn't dare turn her head to focus, though. She'd have to trust the man she had just met to help her out of this predicament.

She straightened up slowly, the mugger still molded to her back. She used the wrong key on purpose, fumbling first, trying hard to get it into the keyhole. She wanted her attacker to try to unlock the door himself; that might give her enough slack to slip away.

"Just give me the damned keys," he huffed. "And which one is for the meds cabinet at the hospital?"

Leah slid the keys up the doorframe, up high so he would have to reach with his knife-holding hand to grab them. As soon as she felt the blade back off, she twisted out of his grasp and darted away, her head ducked down as if she were in a low overhead tunnel, sprinting to the opening and daylight.

James had sneaked up behind the assailant without a sound. As soon as Leah was free, he kicked the legs out from underneath him.

"Oof." Thunk! The punk's head smacked the ground. "Oh, bollocks," he groaned, as he looked up at the sky from the hard concrete walkway.

James stomped his cross-trainer sneaker on the wrist of the tweaked-out mugger, popping the switchblade knife out of the sweaty, dirty palm.

"I'm calling 911 right now," Bibb hollered.

James pulled the skinny drug seeker up by his unharmed left hand, twisting it up behind his back until he stopped resisting. "Okay, okay, already," the punk whined, almost in tears.

"What's going on here?" thundered Billy. Leah's neighbor was in his doorway, his left hand clutching the towel wrapped around his waist, his service revolver in his right.

Leah was several yards away, in the middle of the commons area, clinging to the metal upright pole of the communal mailbox, frozen in terror, hyperventilating. Billy looked at her, then back to James, the apparent white knight in Leah's rescue.

"This rogue just put a knife to Ms. Madigan's neck and was forcing her to let him into her apartment. Apparently he also wanted to know which key opened the pharmaceutical cabinet at the hospital," James said, as he craned his neck, looking to make sure Leah was safe. He turned his attention back to the man holding the revolver and asked, "Are you a police officer or does everyone have a gun here in America?"

Billy's mouth twitched. He didn't know whether to scowl or grin at the Englishman's question. Instead, he settled into police detective mode. "I'm a police officer, but I fear you have me at a disadvantage." A sheepish grin crept up his face as he looked down at his towel. "Do you have him under control?"

James opened his mouth to say, "Yes," then changed it to a loud and forceful, "NO!" and pushed the mugger forward into the locked front door, slamming his face into it, momentarily incapacitating him. Not caring if he had inflicted severe damage on him or not, James sprinted across the freshly mowed lawn toward Leah, still crouched behind the island of mailboxes. Harry, the bartender who had slipped the date rape drug into her iced coffee, was sneaking toward her from the blind side of the apartment building, holding an object in his hand.

Harry saw his former customer running at him, his eyes black with vengeance. He switched directions, like a running back avoiding the defensive end, but the young man's fleet feet weren't fast enough. James, the former rugby player, had a few moves of his own. He faked right then moved left, cutting off his opponents retreat. Harry screamed out in his own defense, "She was coming on to me, then backed out. She's a prick tease, she…"

The whining ex-bartender didn't get a chance to finish. James tackled him in the midsection and knocked the wind out of him, causing the cowardly liar to drop his blackjack at the same time. James kicked the weapon out of the way, then squatted down and picked it up. "Get up," he snarled, "then move over there with the other one."

James heard the sirens in the background as Harry stumbled forward. Leah's attentive neighbor had the first man laid out on the grass, spread-eagled. "You get down there, too; you know the drill," the cop barked, motioning to the ground with his gun. The nearly naked police officer turned his focus to James, "Thanks for the help, buddy. I'm Billy Burke."

James didn't take the time to introduce himself, but nodded quickly to acknowledge that he had heard him, then dashed over to Leah. "Are you okay?" he asked, biting off and swallowing the endearing term 'sweetie' he wanted to call her.

She looked up at him blankly, the shock of the afternoon attacks stealing the color and emotion from her face. "I don't know—am I?" she asked, confused. She put her hands out in front of her face and turned them over one at a time, looking for cuts or abrasions in a detached, distant manner.

"Here, let me help," James offered. He neared her cautiously and lifted her chin to check her neck, briefly touched her shoulders to knock off some grassy bits, and then walked around her. He pulled up her hair that had come undone to check underneath it. She bent her chin to her chest to help with the inspection. "No, no cuts on your neck; just greasy marks from his hands and arm." He stepped back and looked further down, noticing how beautiful her legs were, accentuated by the simple sandals she wore. "And everything else looks fine down…well…" he stammered, "I can't see any bleeding. But how do you *feel*?"

Leah looked over at Billy, talking to the newly arrived police officers. By his stance, he was still the officer in charge, even if the towel was his only uniform. Bibb was talking to another officer, evidently giving him her report since she was the one who had called 911. Leah looked to James and said dejectedly, "I feel…I feel like I need a hug." She moved cautiously into his arms, arms that had automatically opened up for her.

Just as gingerly as she had moved into meet him, he enveloped her. He sighed at the scent of her hair, an aroma of violets and woman sweat, slightly salty and with just the right amount of musk. He closed his eyes and let her relax into his chest, finding his comfort and composure with her, too, his forearms subconsciously crossing her back in a gesture of protection.

"Hey! What's going on there?" Billy yelled at the young couple locked in a familiar embrace. *He didn't know the man who was hugging his girl. Even if he had just physically protected her from the two assailants, he didn't want this stranger—or anyone else—hurting her emotionally. She was his to protect.*

"I'm okay now, Billy," Leah said with complete confidence as she looked up at James, letting him know with a nod that he could let go of her now. She added, "He took care of everything." She walked towards Billy slowly and asked apprehensively, "We don't need to talk to them about it right now, do we?" She nodded to the police officers who were either writing reports or escorting the bandits into the backseats of the squad cars. She looked back at James to make sure he felt the same way she did.

He nodded in reply—he would rather talk to them later, too. He was still enjoying the afterglow from the best hug he had ever had from a woman and didn't want it to be tainted with words and reflections about the recent violence. He embraced the inner peace and comfort, the first he could remember as an adult. He felt his sense of satisfaction grow, and then inhaled sharply when he noticed Billy's scowl. He turned away. He didn't want to share this feeling with anyone.

Billy's mustache twitched before he answered Leah. He was unsure about his gut feeling that this Brit was a decent man. He had never before been wrong about his first impressions of people, but there was always a first time. "No, I'll get the report started," he said to her, "then I'll bring it home for you. He can come down to the station now, or drop by here later, and look it over with you. Are you sure you're okay?"

Leah still felt shaky, although her white knight's embrace had calmed her. "Yeah, I'm fine, really." Leah turned her attention to Bibb and James. "Are you two ready to come in now?"

*She knew what she wanted to do. It was mystery-sharing time. Whether she could solve it or just expose it further, she didn't know.*

*However, she did know that these two people—strangers she had just met at the airport—were the crayons needed to help scribble and add color to her blank page of explanation about what had happened to her mother.*

# *8 Mother

James followed Leah to the front doorstep, surreptitiously scanning the premises while broadly using his white handkerchief to mop the sweat from his brow and the back of his neck. He tucked the cloth into his back pocket, and then squatted down to retrieve her oversized brass keyring. He stood up and offered it to her with a big smirk, then backed away, giving her a wide berth, making sure she had plenty of room to unlock the door.

"Yeah, right," Leah said, grinning. She had picked up on his little joke that he wouldn't crowd her as the bandit had while she opened the door.

James looked back and saw Bibb finishing up with her attending police officer. The man tipped his hat at her, and said, "Thank you very much, ma'am. It's been a pleasure. If you remember anything else, you still have my number, right?"

"Oh, yes, yes, Officer Daily. And if I have any more problems with break-ins, you'll be the first person I call. You and your men have been so helpful and understanding with the mess at the mill. I hope it will all be resolved shortly. Have a nice afternoon now," she said, dismissing him with an abbreviated wave.

James waited for her outside the apartment door. She greeted him with a smile, then looked up at him and asked in a light conversational tone, as if the scrambling, knockdown incident had never happened, "Are you ready to go inside? I'm sure the heat here is insufferable compared to England."

"Yes, the *atmosphere* here is quite different from what I am used to. Here, allow me," he said, as he opened the door for her.

Leah was waiting with three glasses of ice water. "Sorry, I don't have much in the way of refreshments. My life has been a mess lately. I, uh…" Leah suddenly remembered their little *tête-à-tête* in the café. Her face and heart turned to clay, her mood suddenly tense and chilly. She had to ask, or risk her chest bursting. "Bibb, why did you ask if my mother's name was Evie?"

A small groan escaped from Bibb as she slid into a kitchen chair. She swallowed hard, sat up straight, and glanced at Leah sheepishly. "I talk too much," she said, and then looked down at pile of shoes on the floor beside her.

*Well, it looks like she's going to be mum for a while, Leah thought. By the flinches and short, sharp breaths Bibb was now making, it appeared she was trying to conjure up her own disappearance. It was time for another approach.*

Leah didn't know what her guests had planned for the afternoon, but she didn't have to return to work until tomorrow. She wanted some answers and would rather have them sooner than later. She canted her head to the side and looked hard at James, not letting go of his attention with her piercing, soul-grasping gaze. "Now, what's this about a letter from my mother?"

James shifted his position in the softness of the couch. *She sure didn't dance around, but sprinted right to where she wanted to be. He could, and did, respect that.* He quickly stole a glance at Bibb to see her reaction to the query. There was nothing. She was guarded. Her eyes were focused on the items scattered across the kitchen counter, as if by staring at them, she could clean up and rearrange the clutter.

James cleared his throat. "For generations—actually, for over two hundred years—the Melbourne family have been guardians of a bundle of letters that were to remain sealed until 1st November, 2012. There was a note on the bundle that said to read *only* the first letter on that date. Well, I read it, almost a year late, but..." James looked hard at Bibb to see if she leaked any signs of shame or knowledge of the letters, "someone looked at them early."

*There, Bibb made a gesture. Whether consciously or not, she had dipped her head and shut her eyes in shame.*

"If I—or anyone who was supposed to—had read them," he said, cleared his throat, and stared at Bibb again, "on the assigned date, you would have been spared the last ten months of not knowing where your mother was. As it turned out, well..." James cleared his throat again. "Hopefully you and I can read the letter together, and maybe you'll find solace in the explanation given to you in your mother's own words."

*Leah bit her bottom lip, grateful that she had been prepared for the shock with James's quick blast of information at the café. Lord knows what she would have done if she hadn't been given a heads-up.* "But did the letter say anything about how she, what would you call it, went back?"

Since she was looking at him, James answered the question. "No. All she knew was that she 'fell' when she went back in time last year. Now, how she returned to then—which was 1781, by the way—I don't know. It could have been the same way, but last year, didn't they find her car—your car—way out of town?"

Leah nodded. "Yesterday that phony doctor kidnapped her and forced her to drive to an empty lot, just east of town. The cops found the stolen car, but not them. That was nowhere near Hanging Rock Park—more than an hour away and northwest of here—which is where they found my car last November. However she traveled, I doubt she started off in the same place both times."

James shrugged his shoulders and let a soft, "hmph," escape. He didn't know what to say, nor did Leah. He stared at Bibb, willing her to add to the conversation. He would bet the biggest diamond in the cigarette pack that she had read more than just the first letter. He stole a glance over at Leah, and saw that she, too, was staring at Bibb.

Bibb finally spoke up, softly at first, and then with resolve. "It was the coin. That was how she came back here two days ago, then returned to her husband and the babies the next day. You saw her pendant, didn't you?" she asked Leah.

Leah nodded slowly, not knowing where this strange story was headed. She glanced over and saw the bottle of whisky. No, she had better stay completely sober for this revelation.

"Your grandfather, Marty, read the letters before he was supposed to. He was, is, a great man, even if he is a bit impetuous at times. How she traveled—Lord, it was only yesterday and the day before, but it was also 230 years ago—is revealed in the second letter. I...well, Marty and I read them all. She never did find out how she wound up there in the first place, but she definitely did go back."

Bibb shifted in her seat. "You see, Marty didn't know what kind of coin had been used. The letters just referred to a coin that James had inadvertently received with the purchase of a map on Halloween, 2012. Since you were only a toddler when he read the letters, he would have to wait until you grew up and went to America to find out more. He couldn't do anything...well, not anything. I think he did a great job of making sure you were well-mannered and got a proper education. He also tried to protect you from the wrong kind of woman, but I see that didn't go well."

James shrugged his shoulder, ignored the dig, and stonily waited for her to continue.

"When you came back last year, told him your story, and showed him the coin, he studied it and went out and got one just like it, all the way down to the little drilled holes." Bibb sighed heavily. "Then he left, and I never heard from him again. I think he went back to be with them." Bibb turned to James. "What did he tell you before he left?"

"He told me he had a terminal disease and wanted to die like a man. He was insistent that I not know what he had, although he did assure me it wasn't hereditary or contagious. He said he had three cases of Glenturret, a waterproof GPS, and a good used sailboat. He wanted to sail around the world and 'discover' who he really was before he died."

James stopped for a moment, obviously thinking about something. "He never did let me see his boat nor tell me which port he was sailing from. I was concerned about his supplies. Glenturret is a mighty fine whisky, but I wanted to make sure he had other provisions. The thought of him wasting away at sea, drunk out of his mind, was not how I wanted to remember him. You see, he may have been my grandfather, but he was the one who reared me. He was more like a father to me."

"I know. Tell me about your family," Bibb asked, suddenly very interested in the new topic.

James paused at her remark. Now was as good a time as any. "Why?" he asked, watching her for any emotional reaction.

And he got it. Bibb sputtered, cleared her throat as if to speak, and then finally said, "Oh, never mind," stood up, and walked toward the door.

He got up from the couch and sidled over to the door, blocking it with an outstretched arm. "You don't need to leave. I know. It's just I don't know why."

Bibb took a deep breath and looked at him, as if he was holding a knife to her throat. "Tell me what you know," she said dryly.

"No," he replied slowly, turning his head from one side to the other, and then back again to center, "You tell me, *mother*."

Bibb sighed deeply in resignation. "It was a dilemma that actually solved itself and one other problem. You see, the man you knew as your father, the adventurer who never wanted to sit still for his duty in the House of Lords, or even for a civil dinner with friends, was, shall we say, not attracted to the opposite sex. As long as Bruce was climbing mountains in Nepal or scouting buried treasure in the Negev, he could be with whomever he chose. And he chose Siegfried, a very rich man who shared many of his own tastes.

"Marty only had him, the one son. You see, Bruce's mother had died in childbirth. He never remarried, never really got over losing Teighlor." Bibb shrugged her shoulders in defeat. "He never stopped loving her; she was a tough act to follow. Still, an heir was needed for the House of Lords, and it didn't look like Bruce was going to reproduce."

Bibb paused, then regained her determination to relate the story. "Marty, Martin—that's his grandfather's name," Bibb said to Leah to involve her in the story, "had once been quite an adventurer, too. After Teighlor's death, he came to America to…well, he said to see if he could ever feel passion again. He planned to visit the last place his great-uncle many times over, Lord Julian Hart, was stationed during the Revolutionary War. You see, since he was a child, he had always wanted to know what had become of Julian. That mystery was the closest thing he ever had to an obsession, and he wanted to see if the research would revive the *spunk* in him."

Bibb started giggling, then proceeded to laugh out loud. "Oh, his *spunk* was fine all right. He met me, one thing led to another, and well," she paused, took a long deep breath, closed her eyes, and said with gentle gratitude, "we began a wonderful winter romance. He left, but came back again a year later, and then, nine months later, you were born."

Bibb looked at James to see his reaction to the story. She didn't get what she expected, though. "Did he ever find out anything about Uncle Julian?" he asked.

Bibb blinked hard a couple of times, sputtered, then replied, "Gee, I don't know. I forgot to ask. I had other concerns by then. You see, I was nearly forty years old, trying to make enough money to keep my little fabric mill ahead of the bankers, and twelve people gainfully employed. Having a baby really hadn't been in my plans, nor had marriage. So Marty and I worked it out. He wanted, needed, an heir for Bruce. I needed some financial help, and..." Bibb faded out her commentary with another shrug and a hard gaze down at her hands in her lap, turning them over as if they were going to reveal the answer as to why everyone was here.

It was an awkward moment for everyone, especially Leah, although she wasn't personally involved. "But you never stopped caring, did you?" she asked in a valiant effort to rescue the embarrassed, estranged parent. "You kept those pictures with you, and followed his actions with the media after Marty left and you no longer had an insider to tell you what was going on in his life."

Bibb brightened at her words. If she had said them herself, it would have sounded like an excuse, or even bragging. But having heard someone else—a veritable stranger—speak on her behalf was bliss. She looked at James and smiled, "I got as close as I could without getting near you physically. It would have ruined everything."

Bibb turned her attention back to her hostess. "You see, the story was that Bruce had married a young lady from a well-to-do family in Caracas. The two both loved adventure, so decided to take a one-year honeymoon in South America, where they would climb the tallest peaks in each country. There she conceived, gave birth, and then conveniently died. Bruce was distraught, of course, and asked his father to help him rear the child. He was the absent parent who couldn't bear the sight of his own child because he reminded him so much of his deceased wife. Well, it was a believable story. The wife was total fabrication, of course. At the time, there was so much going on with the Prince Charles and Princess Diana drama that no one cared about minor earls and dukes, what they were up to, or with whom.

"Bruce died just before your father—your real father, Marty—left. His demise was unfortunate, but he told your father—his father, too—that he had no regrets. He was proud of his little brother, even if he did wind up with a loser for a wife." Bibb smiled at this. "I never met Bruce, but he seemed to be a likable fellow, even if he was a bit self-indulgent. I guess he got a kick out of Clotilde—was that her name?"

James winced at the mention of her and nodded. He had momentarily forgotten about that smear on his life's history. "What do you mean?" he asked, only because it was apparent Bibb wanted to tell him about it.

"Oh, she and her 'brother' go way back. I guess one of Bruce's friends, Roy, went to school with her. Bruce said she had gone to Roy's father, saying that she was pregnant, and it was Roy's child. She wanted £1000 per month maintenance for the bastard. Roy's father knew about his son's sexual orientation, and just laughed in her face. When that didn't work, her 'brother' went to the father, said that Roy had promised to support him for the rest of his life, and then dumped him, leaving him heartbroken and penniless. He wanted £1000 a month spousal support. Those two were a real crock of spoiled turnips. Not only were they asking the same amount, when the erstwhile 'brother,' Roy's supposed ex-boyfriend, showed up with his demands, Clotilde was waiting for him in the car. Can you imagine that?"

James rubbed his forehead with his thumb and index finger, trying to erase the memory of Clotilde and her 'brother.' "Yes, I can imagine that, but would rather not. Let's just leave the topics of conversation at fake marriages, illegitimate children, and disappearing parents," he said flatly, trying hard not to be rude. "No, one more topic: why were you trying to get me to buy the mill?"

Bibb flushed as she realized that she had overstepped the bounds of propriety with bringing up the subject of skanky Clotilde, who was probably legally still his wife. Bibb said, 'sorry,' with her eyes, not wanting to apologize verbally for the *faux pas,* thus continuing the uneasiness. "I didn't know how else to get you to come to America and talk to me. I wanted to see you. I didn't know how I would broach the subject of me and your real father, but I guess you can say I just had faith that it would come out."

Leah watched James as he sneaked glances at Bibb. His lips, puckered and tight, showed that he was fed up with her deceptions. Leah picked up on his unspoken need to be away from this intense older woman. Yes, Leah had plenty of sympathy for the man who had just OD'd on too much information and emotion. She also knew he was too much of a gentleman to say anything. His eyes shifted to her, and his whole demeanor softened. She smiled back at him, and then turned to her female guest.

"Bibb, didn't you say you had to go check in with your office?" Leah put her suggestion to leave in a gentle and tactful manner; Bibb had never mentioned her office or business.

"Oh, yes; I do think that would be wise of me. If you don't mind, I think I'll excuse myself." Bibb reached into her purse and pulled out a little silver-plated embossed box. She flipped it open and took out a business card. "Please, call me after you get a chance to…um…get caught up with James. I might have answers to questions that you haven't even thought of asking yet."

Leah slowly bobbed her head up and down, said, "Thanks, I might just do that," and then put the card down on the cluttered kitchen counter. "You've got my number, too; it's on the map. I hope you understand," she

61

said gently, still wanting the woman to leave before the civil tone of the meeting evaporated completely.

Too much had happened too soon. Her mother's sudden reappearance yesterday as a very young nursing mother with a musket ball wound in her shoulder was still fresh on her mind. Now it looked as if that was just the feather poking out of the pillow. There was a lot more to learn, and she didn't know if she was ready for that much information right now. She glanced over at the bottle of whisky on the counter. "Shut up," she said. "Not you," she added with a smile at the perplexed James. *Hmm, such a fine looking, nice man...*

## *9 A Dip and an Explosion

Bibb had left, and it was just the two of them now. Leah breathed a huge sigh of relief. She looked over at the uptight and befuddled man sitting on her overstuffed sofa, his head in his hands. James turned his face to her as if to ask, 'Now, what?'

"Do you want to go swimming," Leah replied to his unspoken question.

It wasn't what James had expected to hear, but sounded like a great idea. "Hmph," escaped his throat. He realized that the only thing better to clear his mind than a dip in that crystal clear swimming pool with his bright and foxy new female friend, would be to have a nice glass of whisky to go with it.

But, it was time for reality. The last twenty-four hours had been crammed with about as many new emotions and stresses as his mere mortal body could handle. The disposal of his life—or at least putting it on hold—before he left England; the long transatlantic flight; the historic letters he had just read that seemed like they were a lost chapter out of that Lisa Sinclaire book—that was unbelievably weird; the near poisoning of this new friend; a short but tense drive on American roads in a vintage, un-air-conditioned pickup truck with the steering wheel on the wrong side—at least for him; the sweaty tackle and wrestle into the grass of two stinky drug-addicted assailants, one of whom had held a knife on his new friend; and finally, and most certainly not least, the revelation that his grandfather was really his father, and that the mother who he thought had died in childbirth was a complete fabrication. His real mother was still alive—a feisty American businesswoman who had contrived to bring him across the Atlantic Ocean to meet her under false pretenses! James shook his head as he thought of the gall of that woman.

"I mean, I'd love to go, but I didn't think to bring swimming trunks," he said. *Damn, he really did want to get cooled off, but he doubted her neighbors would appreciate him skinny-dipping.*

"No worries," Leah said brightly. "I think I can get you covered. Here, do you like whisky?" She handed him a cup with what appeared to be a cartoon dinosaur on it.

"Oh, my, you do know how to take a man's breath away. Thank you." He lifted the charming, cast-glass mug to his nose and inhaled the bouquet of the premium Scotch whisky.

"You're welcome. I'll be right back."

Leah rushed next door to Billy's apartment, quickly rapped on the door, then burst in. "Hey, Billy, do you have an extra pair of swimming trunks for my new buddy?"

"Sure, come on in. I have loads in here," he called from his

63

bedroom. "Hey, he seems like a keeper," he remarked, as he rummaged through the closet.

"Yeah, well, he looks nice, and he's certainly a sweetheart, but I think he's more your type as far as a keeper goes." Leah added glumly, "He's gay."

"Oh, no, no, no he's not!" Billy sang. "He's straight as a telephone pole. I guarantee it."

"Okay, whatever you say," Leah agreed half-heartedly, and accepted the pair of bright orange Hawaiian print shorts from him. She didn't tell him that her new friend's sexual orientation had been prime fodder for the British tabloids just a couple of months ago. "Thanks," she called back, as she let herself out.

Ж

Leah cleared her throat as she came in, just to make sure she didn't catch James off guard. "Flintstones?" he asked, as he held up the cup. "I remember them." He put down the cup, took the shorts from Leah, and held them up to his hips, "Great, these look like they'll fit. Where should I change?"

"Just a sec." Leah opened up the bathroom door, looked around, grabbed the box of tampons from the back of the toilet and threw it into the cabinet, wiped the counters quickly with a used facecloth, then threw it and the other assorted dirty clothes on the floor into the hamper. "You can get dressed in here," she said. "Just don't open the other door; I'll be in there changing."

"Okay," James said. "But don't change too much. I like you just as you are, and besides, I don't think I could handle any more surprises. Oh, sorry…am I being too familiar?"

"Not if you stay on that side of the bathroom door, you're not," Leah replied lightly. "I'll be out in a sec."

The two came out of their respective rooms at the same time. "Oh, I thought you Brits were supposed to be as white as a fish's belly," Leah said.

"Well, I used to claim the olive skin-tone was from my South American Indian mother. Since she was a total fabrication, it must be from somewhere else," James said with an eye roll and a snort.

"Sorry, I didn't mean to stir up old shi…stuff. Here, let me grab a few towels and the phone."

Leah's phone was where she had left it on the table. Her mother's phone, still smudged white on the side with talc, was next to it. She set down the stack of towels next to the phones and decided to indulge. At least she wasn't drinking alone. She grabbed her Flintstone cup and poured in a healthy splash of Glenturret, swirled the dark amber fluid around, and inhaled. Peace. For the first time in ten months, she felt it. Her whole face brightened. She took a long, slow sip, letting it cool her lips first, flood her

64

tongue, then allowing it to slip back, to warm her throat and belly.

James watched as she savored her drink. *Wow, such a sensual woman, went through his head, but he restrained himself from voicing it aloud.* Instead, he said, "You have good taste in whisky. That's a fine trait in a woman."

"It's a fine trait in anyone. Come on," she picked up her mother's phone and tilted it back and forth playfully, "I'll show you mine if you show me yours. Bring those letters, would you?"

James picked up the valise with his clothes hanging on the outside. His shirt and trousers, still damp with sweat, were flopped over the top, his shoes tied together at the handle in a futile attempt at letting everything dry out. Yes, the humidity was stifling, but the outlook for the day was promising. He followed Leah out the door, his bag in one hand, his drink in the other. "Do you have your keys, and should I lock it?"

"Yes and yes. You'd better walk on the grass, though—the sidewalk's hot."

James obediently followed behind Leah, enjoying the coolness of the springy, well-manicured lawn as it crushed beneath his feet. He tried not to stare as her bathing suit cover-up swished back and forth across her legs. He glanced up. The bright yellow cotton was barely long enough to cover her bottom which wiggled in the most mesmerizing rhythm... *Eyes up, Melbourne!*

Leah's voice brought him out of his fanny-watching trance. "The fence is to keep out non-residents and little kids without adult supervision, not to keep ducks and geese in," she deadpanned, looking back to make sure he was still with her.

He chuckled politely and did a quick, two-step run to catch up with her.

"Now this is the rough part. Ow, ow, ouch, ouch, ow," she sang as she dashed across the textured concrete to the shade of the umbrella table and lawn chairs. James followed—and tried to be stoic—but wound up doing the same hot-foot dance right behind her, proud that he hadn't copied her sing-song exclamations. He plopped down in the overstuffed cushioned patio chair, brought his feet up off the ground, and set his drink down next to hers. He noticed that she hadn't spilled any of hers either.

"Normally I like mine naked," he said, and paused for her reaction.

And he got it. Leah looked at him like, 'What are you talking about?'

"But on a day like today, I think it's better to have it on the rocks," and lifted his drink.

"Uh, oh...yes," Flushed with embarrassment, she answered his toast. "Cheers!" She took a lingering drink and sighed in satisfaction as she set her cup down. The tone had been set. "Now, you can tell a lot about a

65

person by the way he—or she—gets into the water." Leah pulled her yellow cotton print cover-up off over her head and looked at James, grinning as if she knew a secret, and then dove into the deep end of the pool.

James set his drink on the table, the valise on the chair, and followed her in. He came up for air at the shallow end of the pool, having swum the whole length with one breath. He shook his head like a shaggy dog. *I should have gotten a haircut before I left,* went through his mind as he dipped back into the water to get his dark, thick hair out of his face.

"No, I think it looks good long," Leah said.

"Am I that easy to read?" James asked, feeling a little giddy from the whisky and cold-water shock.

"Yes, no, I mean, don't you know you aren't supposed to drink and dive?" Leah replied quickly, smiling lamely at her own weak pun.

*It wasn't nice to read someone's mind, and she probably wouldn't have 'peeked' if she hadn't had the drink. Oh, well; it was an obvious conclusion to him re-dipping his head in the water to get the hair out of his eyes. Quick, change the subject.* "Did you know you can get the same effect as an isolation tank, pretty much, by floating in a swimming pool and closing your eyes?"

Leah lay back in the cool comfort of the chlorine-enhanced water and relaxed, trying hard not to squeeze her eyes shut too tightly. The water splashed against her face, making her flinch, but she willed herself to loosen every muscle in her body. First, relax the back, then the shoulders, elbows, hands, and fingers. Next phase, top of head, face, neck, and down: concentrate on a separate portion of the anatomy with each slow breath in and controlled exhale out. She had just about achieved her swimming pool nirvana when she felt a bump. Her hand jerked away as she balled up reflexively, turning around to see who or what she had collided into. It was James. He was in the same sedate pose as she had been, but evidently hadn't been disturbed by their encounter.

*Wow, he's so perfect,* she thought as she returned to her back-floating serenity. *Oh, well. It's probably a good thing he is gay. Life is so much less complicated when sex isn't involved. Friends with benefits tend to be less friends and more benefit seekers. And guy friends aren't bitchy, don't get jealous, and... Crap, Leah, just lie back and relax. At least he isn't afraid of a man with a knife. There's something to be said about having a white knight from England on your side. I wonder if I should order a pizza...*

Leah couldn't keep her mind still, but James could. He had fallen into a deep, peaceful sleep. He dreamt of flying—flying without an airplane—more like floating with a purpose. His thoughts were of greens and blues, living and breathing elements of the earth moving around below him. He saw two old trees down an old dusty road. There were two sets of footprints leading to the trees. One set stopped at the tree and turned back to the road. The other looked like slipper prints. Those went right through the trees, then disappeared. A flash of a pink gown appeared momentarily, then a noise, like an electrical short, and then nothing. No, not nothing—he smelled bananas. Now it was just the trees, their branches hanging nearly to the ground, as if they were mourning…

KABAAM! The explosion literally rattled the doors and windows of the apartments near to the pool. James's body curled up immediately into 'protect the vital organs' mode. He sank briefly, then rebounded with arms flailing, mouth spitting and sputtering, totally disoriented at being awakened from a deep dream state into a large body of water.

Leah had been relaxed, but was not asleep. She flipped over, swam to the edge, scrambled out, and ran to the fence. "My apartment! It's on fire!" she screamed. She struggled with the gate latch, realized it had to be unlocked with her key, and then panicked. Rather than get her keys, she grabbed the hot tubular steel and tried to climb over the fence.

James realized some of what was going on. "Freeze!" he ordered.

Leah instinctively obeyed, but let loose of the fence railing. She turned around and glared at him, "But my apartment's on fire and, and…"

"Call the fire department from here. Your phone's on the table. Your life isn't worth anything that could possibly be inside. Now! Call them!" he shouted.

Leah grabbed the phone, dialed 911, and shouted, "My apartment's on fire!"

The operator answered, "Yes, ma'am, we have units on the way. We've already received a call. Do NOT go into the building, and stay back at least 500 feet. Let the men do their job. Now, are you or anyone else injured?"

"No, not me; I was away when, oh my God! Billy was right next door! Billy Burke lives next door, and he was inside just a few minutes ago!"

"Ma'am, calm down. Detective Burke was the one who called in the explosion. He's fine. Now, if you're okay, I'd like to get off the line. Are you sure you're okay?" The dispatcher was firm, but concerned, and Leah could tell.

"Yeah, I guess I'm fine. Thanks." She pushed the end button, yelped, "Shit!" then, "Ouch, ouch, ouch, ouch!" She had been so stunned by all that was going on, she hadn't realized that her feet were burning. She walked awkwardly but quickly on the outside edges of her soles to the first step at the shallow end of the pool, a perplexed penguin finding relief.

James stood on the metal cross bar of the fence, straining to see what was transpiring at the scene of excitement. He got down and hop-stepped across the burning deck into the water next to Leah, the two of them still contained in the once peaceful realm of the swimming pool zone. He put his arm around her shoulder and squeezed it tightly. She turned into him and buried her face into his fuzzy chest, and sobbed quietly, no tears coming from her eyes. She stopped all movement suddenly, as if someone had once again told her to freeze. She pulled back from James, placed her hands on his biceps to steady herself, and said, "Your hair tickles my nose," wrinkling it like a rabbit testing the air.

"Well, that's a good thing. It means you're still alive and," he tipped her chin up to look into her eyes, "*that* is a very good thing. Everything else is just stuff. Now, shall we let the professionals take care of their job, and you and I, well, how about we go out to dinner?"

Leah walked into the water further, then turned around and sat on the top step, immersing her bottom in the warmer, upper region of the pool. "No shirt, no shoes, no service is the rule at just about every restaurant I know of. I have a shirt, but damn, I don't even have any shoes. And I don't have any money, or a debit card, or...or..."

James sat down next to her, urging her to scoot sideways so they would both fit. "Well, what do you have?"

"Well...well," she stuttered, searching for an answer.

"That was a rhetorical question. You have a car, keys, two smartphones, and last, but not least," he finished with a smile, "me. I have some money, but my vehicle doesn't have air conditioning, so if you wouldn't mind, could we take yours to maybe an air-conditioned motel with room service? After dinner, I can go out and get you a few clothes so you're decent enough that you can go buy yourself whatever you need. You see, today I have money. It looks like I won't be buying the mill from Bibb, after all. Luring me to America under false pretenses..." James shook his head as if saying, 'shame, shame.'

"Okay, I guess that will work. As long as Billy is okay," Leah said glumly. All of a sudden, she brightened up, "Hey, that means I probably won't have to go to work tomorrow! There's always a bright side to everything. It's just that sometimes you have to look harder."

Leah stood up out of the water, the wet bottom half of her red one-piece bathing suit darker than the now completely dry top half. "Let's roll, Daddy-O. I'm hungry," she said, and reached out to help James stand up.

"I'm not *that* old," he replied as he took her hand, "and definitely not anybody's daddy."

He flinched as he let go of her hand. Hopefully she hadn't misinterpreted the little squeak that had come at the end of his statement, that it was actually him biting off the word 'yet' that made his sentence end oddly. The truth was that he wasn't anybody's daddy, but he'd like to be somebody's daddy. But, you don't reveal that to someone you've just invited to a motel, dinner, and a new wardrobe.

## *10 Bad Reception and Pizza

Leah hated to make left hand turns, so drove to the first motel that was on her side of the street. "This should be an easy place to get in and out of," she said. "I'll wait in the car for you. I'd make a lousy first impression with the way I'm dressed. They'd probably kick me out for hooking if I tried to get a room."

"Hooking?"

"Soliciting; selling sex…" Leah explained awkwardly.

"Oh. I'll be just a minute then," James said, quickly regaining his composure. "At least they have air conditioning. I don't see how anyone could live here without it," he added with a shudder.

James opened the car door into the oppressive heat and humidity, leaving Leah and the air-conditioned car in the shade of the ramada. He entered the stuffy and stale lobby through the double set of glass doors. He was still wearing the borrowed swimming trunk shorts, but had thrown on his newly acquired vintage U2 tee shirt.

"James Melbourne, and I'll be paying cash," he said as he wiped the sweat off his forehead with the back of his hand. "I'm not sure how long I'll be staying, so please give me a room that isn't promised for the next few nights," he added politely, and put down a hundred dollar bill.

"Will it be just you, sir?" asked the indifferent young man behind the counter.

"No, there are two of us," he replied tersely, hoping the longhaired clerk wasn't going to be too nosy.

"Well, I'll need his name, too, and both of your drivers licenses." The clerk paused at seeing James's stubborn stare. "It's the law. I personally don't care who you are or who you take up to your room."

"Well, you'll just have to be satisfied with this," James pulled out his wallet and thrust down his British driver's license, "and this," he threw down a second hundred dollar bill and growled, "because her apartment and everything in it—including her driver's license—just burned to the ground. And you can verify that on your evening news if you don't believe me."

The clerk was wide-eyed at the sound of menace in James's voice. He quickly gave him the key. "It's out back. It has a discreet entrance, and it doesn't have any reservations pending."

James glared at him, uttered a short grunt of disgust, then slapped his hand down on top of the second hundred dollar bill, palming it back into his fist. "Call the police department. They'll verify the recent apartment fire and that a woman just lost her home because of it. Tell your boss he can speak with me if he has a problem with it."

James turned his back to leave and heard the clerk say softly under his breath, "Asshole."

James had a keen sense of hearing, and almost ignored it, but he had had a rough day and was tired of people taking advantage of his good humor. "Asshole?" he repeated loudly as he spun around, embarrassing the clerk in front of the old couple who had come in after him and were now waiting their turn to get a room. "Asshole? You bet I am, or can be. Just don't do anything stupid, rude, or illegal around me—my temper is getting rather short these days." He finished his mini tirade with, "Americans, hah!"

James huffed out the front doors, shoving them hard to release some of his pent up anger. He suddenly realized that he was being followed. It was the little old man who had been in the lobby with the frail-looking woman. It was obvious the man wanted to speak with him.

"We're not all bad, Americans, that is," he said as he gently touched James's arm. "I'm sorry your friend lost her home. It happened to us, too. The policeman said there have been three in the last twenty-four hours. They suspect the arsonists were looking for drugs. My wife has cancer, and we have, or rather had, some very powerful painkillers. The sickos hang around the cancer wards in hospitals and follow the terminally ill patients to their homes. They snatch the drugs, then torch the houses to hide any evidence." The man shrugged his shoulders and nodded toward his wife. "I lost everything, but I still have her. I hope they'll let us refill the prescription. They're real picky about refills. That and they cost so darned much." He shook his head with disgust, "As if we look like drug addicts... No, it looks like you and your lady friend got lucky. No one was hurt, were they? Oh, I'm sorry; I'm rambling. Don't let people like him bother you. I'm sure his type are all over the world, and aren't limited to just the United States."

James nodded in acknowledgment. "Thanks for reminding me. Yes, idiots plague the globe. It's been a rough day for me all around, but neither my friend nor I were hurt, so I guess I shouldn't complain. I hope it all works out for you, your wife, and her medicine. Good afternoon to you both," James said, giving him a weak smile in farewell.

Leah sat in the car and watched her new friend chat with the old man, the back of her head leaned against the side window, a smile radiant on her sun-warmed face. She was content, despite her new and dire—but not hopeless—situation.

As James got nearer, he saw and returned her smile. It grew to a big grin when he realized how fortunate it was that they were able to share the day's dramas and surprises with each other. He got in the car and pointed the way. "The room's just over there, number 123, a basic sequential number... Oh, never mind, I babble when I'm fatigued."

Leah pulled up to the parking spot in front of the room and started giggling. "If you carry in your bag, I'll get everything else, okay?"

"What? Oh, right. You don't have anything, do you? Would you like me to carry you? The tarmac has to be hot. If you grab my bag, I think I can handle you."

*James was enjoying their little repartee. When was the last time he had fun? He couldn't remember, which brought a serious frown to his brow. Then his smile returned.* "Today is the first day of the rest of your life, madam. Would you care to start it by being carried over a threshold?"

"Oh, my white knight, however should I thank you? I have no more gold or jewels." Leah batted her eyelashes in an exaggerated coquettish fashion. "Maybe there is something else I can offer?" She burst out laughing at the thought of her overt offer of her body to a gay man. "Yeah, right," she added. "No, just unlock and open the door. I'll make a mad dash inside. Here's your bag."

James accepted the valise, walked to the door, and swiped the magnetic keycard. He pushed the handle down, opened the door, and held it back with his outstretched arm. "On your mark, get set, GO!" he called playfully.

Leah was ready. She opened the car door, dashed across the short span of asphalt and concrete, and pushed past James, clutching her two smartphones and keys next to her chest. She jumped into the middle of the king-sized bed. "Ooh, nice," she said.

James stepped in and let go of the door, allowing it to shut behind him. He set the bag down, and looked around for the reason for her excitement. A pained groan escaped as he stared wide-eyed at the huge bed, the only bed in the room.

Leah didn't have to be psychic to see what was going on inside James's head. "Don't worry, its fine," she said.

His face fell. He knew it did—he didn't have the energy to mask his feelings. Now he was going to have to go back to that rude desk clerk and either get a different room—one with two beds—or 'pack up' and go to another motel.

She patted the red floral bedspread next to her. "See, it's fine because as hot as it is today, it won't make any difference if you hog all the covers. I won't mind because I won't need them!"

James couldn't help but smile at her lame joke. "But what if I snore?" he asked, continuing the levity with this spunky brunette who for some reason, had graced his life.

"Why," she drawled, "don't you see? That's why they gave us extra pillows? If you snore just a little loud, I'll cover my head with my extra pillow. If you snore *real* loud, I'll put yours over *your* head!" She grabbed one of the pillows, threw it at him, and then rolled over, grabbing another polyester-filled projectile.

James clutched the pillow she had just popped him with, feigned left with it, then right, made a tight spin, and then threw it at her at the end of his little pirouette. Leah batted it away with hers and scooted up next to the headboard. She fluffed it up and put it behind her head, stopping the pillow fight and changing the mood from frivolity to light-hearted practicality. "I want pizza for dinner, if that's okay with you. I was dreaming of pizza while we were in the pool, and now that's about all I can think about. Thin crust pizza with tons of pepperoni and a beer. I can get the pizza delivered, but I don't think they deliver beer. So, do you want pepperoni, or are you a sausage man?" she asked with an impish grin.

*Sausage man? What in the hell is she grinning about? It's doubtful she's ever read any of those made up stories in the British tabloids about me being gay. She's an American and Americans don't care about anyone but themselves.* He paused before answering carefully. "I like sausage, but pepperoni is good, too. I saw a liquor store across the street. You go ahead and order the pizza, and I'll get a couple of pints of beer. Do you need some money?"

Leah winced. "Yes, please. Oh, God, I hate to ask anyone for money. As soon as we get something to eat and a few... Oh, shit. We have a lot to talk about, don't we? Crap. I have to call work and tell them I won't be in tomorrow. Damn, I don't even have scrubs much less a pair of work shoes. I can probably go to the bank, and hopefully, they'll let me have some of my money, even if I don't have my ID or wallet. Shit, I don't even have a pair of shoes so I can walk into a store to *buy* a pair of shoes or clothes or, or..." Leah started sobbing uncontrollably. She rolled over and buried her face into the pillow next to her, embarrassed at her loss of emotional control.

"Hey, you," James said, shaking her shoulder. "One thing at a time, okay? Now, we have a place to clean up and spend the night. You have a phone and can call in for food. I told you, I have money, and it doesn't bother me to share it. While you're waiting for the pizza, I'll get some liquid refreshments." He gently rocked her shoulder again with the mention of beer. "*Then*, after we eat, we can take on the rest of the world, okay?"

"Okay." She sniffed and pulled her face out of her percale-covered hiding place. "I'm just so embarrassed and confused, and don't know what to do."

"I heard a wise woman once say that when you don't know what to do, eat. It makes the brain work better. Besides, you can consider dinner a thank you for giving me my first pillow fight. That was fun. So, make your call, and I'll be back before you can miss me."

James got off the bed and had his hand on the door to leave when Leah spoke. "You haven't even left yet, and I miss you already." She paused to reflect on what she had just said. "How can that be? I just met you a few hours ago?"

He thought for a moment before opening the door, then turned back to face her. "I don't know. Weird, huh?" was all he could manage to say before he left.

Ж

James saw the old man who he had met earlier outside the lobby. He took a few quick running steps to catch up with him. "Sir, do you know where I could buy some sandals? All of my friend's clothes burned in the apartment fire. She doesn't even have a pair of shoes to wear shopping."

"Come here," said the man, once again holding James by the arm. "See that big building? It's called a Wal-Mart. We have lots of them here in the USA. You can get just about everything from food and drink, to clothes and shoes, to video cameras to...well, just about everything but a kitchen sink. But you *can* get towels for the kitchen sink," he added with a chuckle.

"And beer?" asked James.

"And beer," he replied. "I'm going there now. Do you want a lift?"

"Thanks. I'd appreciate it."

James followed the man to an older, dark-green Jeep Cherokee parked a couple of cars away. He stood outside the left hand door, looked down, and saw the steering wheel. "Oops," he said, and walked around to the other side of the car. "I think it'll take a while for me to get used to the steering wheel and driving being on the wrong side."

"No, we drive on the *right* side. You drive on the *left* side overseas. England?"

"Yes, I'm sorry, I didn't introduce myself. My name is James Melbourne. I just got in at noon today, so I'm still a bit punchy."

"Mike, Mike Skupnieweitz, a fine Irish name," the old man giggled as he nodded to the Irish rock band tee shirt James was wearing. "But you can call me Skup. There are quite a few Mikes around, but I'm the only Skup I've ever met; except for my father, of course, but he's gone now, so I'm the only one."

The drive took a short three minutes. "Okay, here we are. I'll let you out here while I go park. I hope everything turns out okay for you and your lady friend."

"Thanks, Skup. Hope it turns out better than okay for you, and your wife, too. Give her my best," James said, and exited the car.

Ж

"Wow!" James gasped involuntarily when he saw how vast the inside of the store was. "Where's the map?"

"Welcome to Wal-Mart, sir," said a smiling, gray-haired woman with a white and blue nametag that read Rwanda. "May I help you find anything?"

"Yes, I've come for beer and sandals."

She pointed out the two areas, and said, "Have a nice day now, sir."

James accepted the shopping cart and nodded farewell. *How polite these people seem to be, even if they do have strange names. Does she even*

73

*know that Rwanda is a country in Africa?*

After a quick five-minute shopping trip, James was on his way to the exit, ready to take the short walk back to his motel in the broiling afternoon heat. He noticed Skup at the pharmacy counter, arguing with the clerk. He didn't want to be snoopy, but his new friend was involved in a major confrontation.

"Sir, your insurance won't cover this duplication," the woman said. "You have to pay for it out of pocket. If you don't have the money, we can't let you have the pills. That's all there is to it. I can't help it if it's wrong—it's just the way it is." She looked over his head, ending their eye contact and the conversation. She huffed, and then looked back at him. "Life isn't always fair," she said with exasperation.

James walked up to the woman and asked, "How much is it?"

She looked at Skup as if to ask, 'Do you know this weirdo?'

Skup said, "It's $130," then blinked back the tears and looked down at the tiled floor, embarrassed about the brouhaha he had caused.

James pulled the cash out of his pocket, peeled off two one-hundred dollar bills, and handed them to the woman. He turned to Skup and asked, "Do you have more shopping to do?"

The clerk took the money, stapled the receipt to the bag, and pushed both the medicine and the change to the edge of the counter, not knowing who got which.

"No, this is all I needed," Skup said, staring incredulously at his benefactor, shaking his head back and forth in amazement.

James took the $70 and the bag of pills, smiled, and said a quick, "Thanks," to the clerk. He folded the bills, put them back into his pocket, handed Skup the bag, and asked, "Do you think you could give me a ride back to the motel? It's hotter out there than I'm used to."

"Be glad to, mate," replied Skup brightly, placing his hand on James's arm, leading the way, the two of them strolling out of the store like an elderly father guiding his reticent son.

The Jeep wasn't too far from the door. James noticed a little blue and white handicapped tag hanging from the rear view mirror. Skup took it down and placed it into the pocket on the inside of his door. "Thank you. You know you didn't have to do that."

"You're right. And you didn't have to offer me a ride to the store." James grinned and continued, "Life is sure strange—wonderful, at times—giving you people you need when you need them the most. And if those people just happen to have something you require at the same time, whether it be a ride to the store or money for pain killers, all the better."

By the end of the conversation, they were back at the motel. James saw a man with a red pizza bag outside the door of his room. He and Leah were arguing about something. "Thanks again, Skup," he said, and rushed out of the car, the bag of beer and sandals tucked under his arm.

James quietly stood behind the pizza delivery teen, listening to the frustrated exchange. "I told you, I can't accept $100 bills. Even if you told me I could keep the change, there've been so many fake ones floating around, the boss'd kill me."

Leah looked at James in exasperation. James spoke up. "How much is it?"

The pimply-faced young man with the ball cap on backwards said, "$12.50, not including the tip."

"Would you take $20, and I get to keep the hat?"

Time stood still as the kid worked the math in his head. He didn't appear to be too bright, and was actually mouthing the computation, finally coming to the conclusion that it was a good bargain. "Okay, but don't expect me to make change. We don't take $50 bills either."

James reached into his pocket and pulled out the change from Wal-Mart, gave the delivery boy the $20 bill, then reached over and snatched the hat off his head. Leah took the pizza inside and left the door open for him.

"Thanks," said the teen, as he walked back to his little white Ford Focus, hand combing his hair, trying to urge his wayward mop down over his high forehead.

James approached the threshold, the doubled white plastic bag in one hand, his new black and gold mesh Caterpillar hat in the other. He bent over into a deep bow, then popped up and placed the hat on his head to make his grand, lampooned entrance into the room. "Do I look American now?" he asked with a sly smile, waiting for her response.

Leah snorted a quick laugh at his exaggerated performance. James placed his bounty from the store on the combination writing desk and dinner table, and used his body to hide the bag's contents. With a southern accent worthy of any of the Beverly Hillbillies, he announced, "And now, for the greatest woman since Lo-retta Lynn, I got you a present from the Wal-Mart: shoes for my little barefoot princess!"

He reverted to his normal British accent to add, "Well, actually they're sandals because I didn't know your shoe size. I figured these would at least get you into a store where you could do your own purchasing." He knelt down at her feet and saw that the sandals in his hands were tied together by a plastic cord. He bit it in two, urged one of her feet up, and placed a sandal on it.

Leah's eyes rolled back into her head, savoring, appreciating the romantic gesture. He had to be gay! No straight man was this wonderful, and fun, and sensitive, and well, perfect! "Thank you, milord," she said in an affected British accent.

James winced at hearing 'milord,' but quickly corrected his facial composure. "No, you're supposed to say, 'Thanks, darlin', or something like that. I'm not very good at this."

"Oh, no; you're wonderful. I'm just glad I took a quick shower while you were gone and that my feet are clean." Leah changed to a hillbilly accent, "Now I'm not barefoot and pregnant like all them other girls. They'd be so jealous of me havin' shoes."

He heard someone say, "I think you'd look beautiful pregnant," then realized that it was *his* voice who had just spoken aloud the words he had been thinking.

"Well, I don't know if I'll ever get that way," she said in a serious tone. "All the good ones out there are either dead, married, or gay." She quickly changed to a lighter tone, "Hey, the pizza's getting cold and the beer's getting hot. You did get beer, too, didn't you?"

"Of course I did, girlfriend," he replied with a lisp and a swish of his wrist.

*Evidently, she had heard or read the fabricated stories spread by Clotilde that he was homosexual. Well, if thinking that he was gay would make her feel more comfortable with him, he wouldn't correct her misconception. Besides, he didn't know if she could handle any more shocks to her system. Better save that one for another day.*

# *11 The Slumber Party

Leah grabbed two beers from the six-pack and put the rest in the mini-fridge under the bathroom sink. She and James settled down at the table and ate their pizza in a comfortable silence, washing down the excitement of the day with the cold beer. James picked up a slice of pepperoni that had fallen off his third piece of pizza. He held the disc up to the light coming through the curtain gap and suddenly flashed understanding.

The coin. His grandfather—father, he reminded himself—had to wait until he grew up, came to America, and got suckered into buying that 'historical document' before he could find out what kind of coin was needed for time travel. And now he, James Ignatius Melbourne, had that same ancient silver time travel ticket in his wallet.

"Are you okay?" Leah asked, apparently for the second or third time. He hadn't heard her speak, but came out of his daze when he felt her cool hand on his arm.

"I don't know…well, yes, probably. I think we've been putting this off long enough. Are you finished with your meal?" He noticed that she had been playing with, not eating, the last piece of pizza she had taken, and was twisting the aluminum ring on the top of her can of beer rather than drinking it.

"Yes, and done drinking, too. I want to be clear headed when we look at the smartphone. I don't know if my mother took any pictures, shot videos, or made voice recordings while gone for those ten months, but I *do* know that I don't want to look for them by myself. Are *you* ready?"

James shifted his body a bit, then admitted, "I will be in just a moment. Excuse me, please," and got up to use the bathroom.

Leah chuckled. It was obvious what he was doing. The bathroom door was closed, but the walls were thin. She could hear what sounded like a garden hose filling the commode. The sound was strange to her. She had had boyfriends in the past, but never lived with another man. Spending the night with Billy a couple of times in the last ten months didn't count as sleepovers, did they? Nah, neither did this. Gay men were just good girlfriends with extra plumbing.

"Don't come out yet," Leah hollered through the closed door. She still had her one-piece bathing suit on under her shirt and it was getting uncomfortable. She pulled the mid-thigh length cover-up off over her head, slipped her arms out of the straps of the swimsuit, pulled it down, wriggled and tugged to get it off, and then tossed the wad of red Lycra onto the chair. She grabbed the shirt and put it back on, still feeling naked since she was now bottomless. She stood in front of the mirror on the dresser and did a quick turn to make sure her butt cheeks weren't hanging out. Still firm, she thought to herself. Lots of walking everyday assured that. She put both arms straight out to the side and twisted her wrists, loosening her stiff muscles, then looked again. Nope, no pubes showing either—she was dressed decently enough for a gay man. She drew the quilted coverlet down, jumped into bed, called out, "Okay, you can come out now," sat up, cross-legged, and pulled the sheet into her lap.

James looked around as he came out of the bathroom. "What's going on?"

Leah pointed to her bathing suit lying on the seat of the straight-backed chair. "Just getting comfortable. Here," she patted the bed next to her, "and bring your letters and those smartphones with you, would you?"

Leah fluffed and rearranged her pillows, then set the other two against the headboard for him. James, his hands full of papers and phones, put one knee on the bed, then suddenly yelped, "Aagh!"

Leah started giggling. She recognized the barely audible sound: her smartphone had vibrated and startled James. He tossed and caught, then re-tossed the buzzing phone several times with one hand, like it was a hot potato, before finally lobbing it into Leah's lap.

She quickly picked it up, held it to her ear, and snickered, trying to keep a full-blown laugh from escaping. "Hello? Oh, okay," she said, suddenly somber. "Yes, I'd appreciate it. Okay, I'll see you on the 20th. Bye."

Leah put down the phone and looked at James, still standing with one knee on the bed, wide-eyed, waiting to find out what the phone call was about, his letters and the other smartphone clutched to his chest.

"That was my supervisor," she said in a monotone, staring through him as if he were a window. "She said I could have two weeks off to get everything back together again, if I wanted. She heard the story about the fire on the radio." Leah set the phone down in her lap. "Wow," she added, her voice flat, low, and totally without enthusiasm.

"Here," James said, and handed her the other phone and letters.

Leah accepted them dispassionately, not aware of what she was doing. Her eyes were staring forward, unblinking.

He waved his hand in front of her face, but got no reaction. "Hey, am I supposed to take off my pants, too?" he asked, curious to see if she was even aware of what he was saying.

"Sure, whatever," she answered mechanically, waving her free hand, as if she were shooing away a slow moth.

"Okay, you asked for it." James stood at the foot of the bed, right in her line of sight—if she had been focusing. He tucked in his chin and started fumbling with the knotted cord in the swim shorts. He glanced up and saw that she was still off in la-la land. "Come on now," he pled, "You really don't want me to bring out the monster now, do you?"

Leah snorted, and laughed, then kept laughing out loud until she was rolling on her side, tears squeezing out from both eyes. "Thanks," she giggled, "I needed that. Would you grab me a couple of tissues, please?"

James brought the box from the sink, grabbed a fistful of tissues, and handed them to her. A few swipes to her eyes, a hearty honking of her nose, and Leah was back to reality. "James? James?" she called. She looked around and saw that she was suddenly alone. "James," she cried in terror, "where did you go?"

"Hold on," he answered from the bathroom. "Now *I'm* changing."

"Well, don't change too much. I like you just as you are," she replied, suddenly very grateful that he was with her and hadn't left.

James came out of the bathroom wearing the John Deere tractor boxer shorts the salesman had talked him into buying before he left Heathrow. He grabbed the Caterpillar cap he had bought from the pizza delivery boy. "Now do I look like I'm from America?" he drawled.

"You're getting there," she said brightly, then took a clinical tone. "So, which do we do first: the smartphone search or the letters?"

James took off the hat and reached into his carry-on bag for his wallet. He pulled out the silver ancient Greek coin he had found hidden inside the sheath of the old map, that 'historical document' he bought last Halloween that had set this mystery in motion. He twisted the shiny drachma back and forth, showing it to her quickly. "Heads or tails?"

"Heads. Hey, is that the coin you had to grow up to get, so your grandfather—or father or whatever he was back then—could go back in time?" asked Leah.

James flipped the coin. "Heads for the smartphone, tails for the letters. It's tails. Here," he said and handed her the bundle of letters. He pushed down the quilt, scooted under the sheet, and made sure it was tucked in his lap. He looked down, patted the sheet, and commented, "Gap insurance: this fly doesn't have buttons. Yes, this is *the* coin—here."

Leah took it gingerly. "Oh, shit! This is just like the one my mother had on when she was in the hospital. Hers was on a piece of black ribbon. She wore it like a necklace. If your," she nodded as if to ask a question, "father?" James returned the nod, "had one of these, and he disappeared, and my mother had one, and she disappeared...whoa!" She set the coin down in James's hand. "Do you have any idea how it works?"

"Yes, I have an idea, but only an idea. Let's read. Maybe this will help explain it."

Leah cuddled up to James and looked over his shoulder as he read aloud.

*Dear James,*

*I know it seems like you saw me only yesterday, but if all has gone according to instructions, you will be getting this 230 years after I have* written it. *I think you can verify this if you have the paper dated. Remember that strange man, Simon? He does have something to do with us, or rather me. I followed him into the park, and I accidentally fell through time. Right now, I am living with your ancestors. I actually married your great—I don't know how many times over—uncle's son. I think I found the Revolutionary War relative you were looking for. That is, if you were looking for Lord Julian Wallace Hart, brother of Lord Anthony Melbourne. Julian's a wonderful man, and his (step) son and I have three children (triplets!).*

*The reason for my letter is that I want you to contact my daughter, Leah Madigan. Please, share this:*

*Leah,*

*I am alive and well in 1781. All the stories by Lisa Sinclaire are pretty much true. I will show up again on August 4, 2013 at the hospital you work in, but you will have to let me return home to my new family. You are bright and grown up now, and can live life on your own, but my babies and my new husband, Wallace Pomeroy-Hart, need me. Sarah and Jody Pomeroy are as wonderful as you told me and as the history (not science fiction or fantasy) books say. It is possible to change history on a small scale or I wouldn't be here with your siblings who are nearly 200 years older than you.*

*James, as of August 4, 2013, Leah is working at the Moses H. Cone Memorial Hospital in Greensboro, not far from our little cafe. She was, will be, my recovery room nurse. So, if you have a chance to talk to her in person, would you please explain what happened and let her read this letter? I love her very much and don't want her to worry about me. Oh, and I have a new first name: Evie. I'll write more as time goes by, but please do not read any other letters (I hope to get a journal started for you/her) until you get a chance to speak with her and let this settle in for both of you.*

*Hugs and kisses from me and your great-many-times-over uncles and love from, Mom*

Leah pulled away from him after he had finished reading. "So that's why you knew Bibb was familiar with the letters—she asked about my mother, Evie? And she had triplets, so that means I'm not an only child anymore." She paused, then asked, "Hey, have you ever heard of Lisa Sinclaire?"

"Yes, and this is the very strange part. Actually, all of this is very strange, so let's just say that this is another hugely odd factor. Just as I realized that I hadn't brought anything, other than this," he said as he tapped the pile of letters, "to read on the plane from London, the flight attendant came through the cabin with a basket of books and magazines for perusal. She suggested I read '*Through the Stones*' by Lisa Sinclaire. I had that book in my hands for the first time just moments before I read your mother's letter. Well, I read the letter—which you know is a big shock in itself—and then there it was, on my lap, all ready for me to do the historical research. My grandfather, er, father, never had her books around, as far as I know. But since he had read and probably studied these," James fanned the letters, "he probably had her books hidden, not wanting to influence me with her stories. Someone other than Bibb apparently knows something, possibly a," James laughed menacingly and shook his face in front of Leah's, "secret agent or," he returned his normal tone, "Perhaps it was fate that had a hand in all of this."

"Let's put that fate idea of yours on hold for a moment. I personally don't subscribe to that theory, but I've never been one to stomp on another's beliefs, either. I want to—well, I really don't want to, but I think I'm ready to—see what's on this." Leah picked up the white-smudged smartphone with her thumb and index finger and held it away from her, as if it were a poopy diaper. "Would you do the honors? I'm not brave enough." She dropped the phone into his open hand and returned to her comfort spot, snuggled against his shoulder.

"Okay, here goes," he said, and powered on the phone.

"Hello, there. Would you tell Dani you found her phone? I guess I've lost it again. You can call..."

Leah reached across James and tapped the menu icon on the phone's screen. She had found her nerve. "Excuse me, I can drive now."

James nodded and handed her the phone. Leah sat up straight and pulled her body away from his, feeling braver. "It's just like my phone, an Almost Alchemy prototype. I just want to bypass this, this old stuff," she said sniffling.

James reached over and grabbed a wad of fresh tissues for her. She nodded thanks, and used one hand to wipe her nose, the other to navigate to the audio recordings menu. Click, tap, tap. The file contained only prerecorded music files and the voice mail greeting. Leah could tell by the details column that they were all from early 2012, months before her mother disappeared.

Click, tap, tap. Photo files. Leah scanned the files without blinking, her face empty of emotions. "Phew," she huffed, as she closed the folder. "No new pictures, just old stuff. All of the file dates are pre October 31, 2012. She didn't even take pictures on the day she left. One more folder, and then I can breathe right again."

She tapped on the video folder icon. "Oh, crap. Here, you open it. Oh, no...wait..." Leah bolted into the bathroom, slammed the toilet seat up, and heaved.

James didn't ask if she was okay. To him, there was nothing worse than someone trying to talk to you while you were vomiting. And, if she was tossing her pizza and beer, there was something obviously wrong. He stood behind her and helped hold her hair out of her face, gently pulling back the stray strands that had fallen away from her one-handed grasp. She finally finished, but didn't bring her head up. James grabbed a washcloth for her from the overhead tubular metal towel shelf while he kept hold of her hair with the other.

"Thanks," she mumbled, as she used it to wipe her mouth.

James stepped back to the sink, unwrapped a glass tumbler, and filled it halfway with cool water. She accepted it with a grimace of embarrassment, shut the door, and turned back to the commode to rinse and spit.

Palm out like a butler with a tray of *hors d'oeuvres*, he was ready for her when she came out.

Leah accepted his gift—a warm, damp washcloth—and moved to the sink to perform a more thorough job of washing her face, hopefully removing some of her terror at the same time.

James wanted to hold her to him, comfort her, but realized that she was going to have to make the first move. Instead, he walked over to the bed, picked up the used tissues, threw them in the garbage, and rearranged the sheets and pillows. He folded back the quilt, and then sat at the end of the bed, waiting for her to make that move.

Leah looked over at him and tried to smile. Embarrassed that her weak stomach had betrayed her, she turned away briefly, still shaky, then came back around, her eyes fixed with steely determination—she would follow through with looking at that smartphone, no matter what. Just as she began to declare her resolve, he looked into her eyes. She averted his gaze and looked down, down to his lap.

"Mph!" She managed to transform her outburst of laughter, converting it to a noise halfway between a cough and a strangled snort. She turned around, went back into the bathroom, and came back out. "Here," she said, and threw a hand towel at him. "It looks like the monster's trying to come out."

James looked down and blushed at the sight of his limp penis poking through the gap of his yellow and green boxer shorts. He quickly grabbed the white towel and covered himself. "Sorry about that," he said, still blushing red. "I think I'll go back and apply the gap insurance." He stood up with the impromptu apron covering the front of his skivvies, pulled back the sheets, and slid in. "So, now that I've both distracted *and* entertained you—are you ready for the main show?"

"You know, you talk about fate. Well, I believe that God has all of this," she waved her hand towards the door and the little pile composed of old letters and the smartphone, "under control. I think that how we deal with everything is what makes us who we are. There are mysteries to be solved, and mysteries to be accepted. Wisdom is knowing which is which. Let's watch the video that was made on March tenth of this year."

James pulled back the sheets so Leah could slide in next to him. *What a bright and sensitive woman! Why hadn't he met someone like her sooner? A smile crept across his face. If what she had just said was true, God wanted her in his life now, not earlier, not later. And now was a good time for him.* "Ready?" he asked, grateful all over again for her presence.

Leah snuggled up close to him, clutched his arm, and nodded. She was warm and fragrant, and he was very glad that the sheet was in his lap. The stressful situation they shared hadn't been relayed to his maleness—'it' had a mind of its own. He bit his lip and double-clicked the newest video file.

*"A cell phone is a communications device. It often has a GPS in it, that's global positioning system, which uses satellites to pinpoint its location. This smartphone version can take pictures, cruise the internet, do calculations, play music, and much, much more."*

"That's my mother," Leah said, half as a question, half as a statement.

"Yeah, I know, but who's that?" James said, then decided to be mum and watch the rest of the show.

Dani/Evie continued, *"Oh, when I remember 21st century stuff, I forget that you don't know what I'm talking about. That probably sounded Greek to you, didn't it?"*

*"No,"* the man in the video started off slowly, *"I ken how to speak a bit of Greek, and that is no Greek. The only words I recognized were pictures and music. Are ye tellin' me that this wee box can make music and all those other things ye were talkin' about?"*

*"Yes, but I don't know if I want to turn it on. I'm afraid it'll be like Pandora's Box. I don't know if there are any evils in there, but I'll bet there is information about my past life in it. I don't want to know about who I was and where I came from—at least not yet. I like it here and now in 1781."*

*"Are ye sayin' that ye canna miss what ye dinna ken ye had?"* the very big red-haired man asked.

Dani/Evie paused. She started to speak, then stopped, started, and then stopped again. Finally she said, *"How do you say it, 'better the devil you know than the devil you don't'?"*

*"Aye, that's it, and true it is. What do ye want to do with this? Ye could use it as a mirror. It has a wee light on it. It would be easy to find in the dark."*

*"And why would I need a mirror in the dark?"* Dani/Evie asked with a chuckle. *"Thanks, Jody, you always seem to make me feel better. Just put it in a safe place, and if I get curious about it, I'll come to you. We can look at it together."*

*"I'll put it back in here,"* the man who was evidently named Jody said as he put it into his sporran. *"It's unlikely anyone will take it without me kennin' about it if it's in here. Now, since it's jest the two of us, how about an early dinner? I'll chase down some eggs if ye wouldna mind fixin' some of those egg burritos. José sent along some more of those long keepin' tomatoes fer ye."*

*"Sounds like a good plan. I'll get right on it."*

There was nothing but darkness—black screen—on the video portion of the little movie, but they could still hear incidental sounds of movement. Obviously, Jody's sporran was moving when he walked and bent over looking for eggs, but there wasn't any video. James and Leah shifted their positions, but never took their eyes off the smartphone's little monitor. A few moments later, there was dialogue:

*"Ho, there, Jessie."* The voice was Jody's, and the clanking of leather and metal made it sound as if he was grabbing reins or a halter. *"Sarah, what are ye doin' home now? I thought ye had a bairn to bring into the world. And why are ye ridin' so late in the day? Ye ken it isna always safe."*

*"Hello, Jody; glad to see you, too,"* a woman with a thick English, not Scottish, accent replied coldly. Evidently her name was Sarah.

*"Sorry, ye gave me a fright,"* Jody's voice sounded apologetic. *"Are ye ailin'?"* There was no reply, but it sounded as if she was dismounting. *"Then why did ye come back so soon and so close to mirk?"*

There was the sound of two bodies close—by the squish and thunk noises, probably hugging with the sporran in between them—and then the swish, swish of walking. After a moment, there were stifled sounds of animals in a barn, then the conversation began anew:

*"Now dinna be givin' her a sair wame with too many oats,"* Jody's voice scolded, then he murmured in Gaelic to the nag. *"Yes, yer a good mare, and I thank ye, but dinna be lettin' well-meanin' women knot up yer wame."*

Sounds of movement began again, then wood smacking on wood—evidently the woman was returning the second helping of oats back to a lidded wooden box.

*"What happened out there today? Are Mrs. Donaldson and her bairn awright? And where's Hannah? Did she stay with her?"* Jody asked.

*"Mrs. Donaldson is fine. I think she miscalculated her due date by a month. She is plenty big all right, but not ready for delivery. I'm not positive, but I'm pretty sure I heard two heartbeats when I checked her. I left Hannah with her, just in case. She'll be a big help as a babysitter, cook, and housekeeper. Those four little Donaldson girls sure have a lot of energy. If Mrs. Donaldson is having twins, she should be on bed rest for the*

next few weeks. I don't think Mac can handle his chores, the cooking, cleaning, and all those little girls without an extra hand. Hannah was more than willing. Girls would rather do anyone else's chores but their own. That, I think, will never change. Mona was the same way," said Sarah.

"Then why did ye come home tonight? Ye could have waited fer the morn and not afeart me," Jody said.

"Oh, that isn't why I came back early. I know it sounds crazy, but I felt like Ian was here. I wanted to get back here and give him a piece of my mind. Now that I'm here, though, I wonder why I acted so impulsively. He's not here, is he?" Sarah asked sheepishly.

"Nooo," Jody answered slowly, "but he was."

"I knew it!" exclaimed Sarah. There was silence and then a snort. "What happened? Did he see Evie, and did she see him?"

"Nae, they dinna see each other. He dinna want to see me either, but I came up behind him—and he dinna get a chance to run and hide, the coward. He dinna even ask about the bairns, or bairn. I dinna think he kens there's more than one. He lied to me, sayin' that he'd been castrated, that Evie should go on with her life and get marrit to someone else."

"The bastard," Sarah huffed. There was a moment of silence. "Sorry, no disrespect meant to your sister."

"Aye, the word may be wrong, but I feel the same. By the way, he did say to say 'hallo' to you."

There was another pause, this one longer, then Sarah said, "Hmph."

"I agree with that," said Jody. "Come on in. We're havin' egg burritos for supper, a la Evie. By the way, she dinna ask about Ian, and I dinna offer up what he said. She's in a good mood now, and I dinna want to spoil it."

There was the sound of more walking then a new voice. "Sarah!" was voiced loudly and excitedly.

James and Leah looked at each other. "Mom," Leah said just as James said, "Your Mom."

They turned their attention back to the smartphone screen. It was still dark, but now there were kitchen noises—pans clanking, dishes banging, chairs moving. "Are you sure you wouldn't rather sit down and take a load off?" It was Dani/Evie again. "You must have ridden all day today, or at least I'll bet it feels like it."

"That's for sure. By the way, it looks like Mrs. Donaldson is going to be the first to have twins in the neighborhood. It turns out she isn't due for a month or so. I left Hannah with her to watch the girls and take care of the house so she could get some rest. You are putting your feet up several times a day, aren't you?" Sarah asked in a clinical tone.

Dani/Evie replied, "Yes, ma'am, I am! Hey, I have some news— unless Jody already told you."

85

There was a long pause, as if everyone was looking at each other. Dani/Evie continued, *"Ian came back. And get this, he didn't come back for me—big surprise."* She sounded very sarcastic with the remark. She continued, *"He came back for my old cell phone!"*

*"Cell phone,"* asked Sarah, *"as in cellular phone?"* There was another pause before Sarah continued. *"Where did you have a cellular phone hidden? I never saw you take one out of your bag."*

Dani/Evie replied, *"It was in one of my coat pockets. I didn't even know I had one. Jody, show it to her."*

All of a sudden, the screen was bright. There on the screen was a good-looking, middle-aged woman with curly light brown hair streaked with gray. Coming around the side of her was the huge, red-haired man, Jody. The smartphone was being turned around so Leah and James were getting a jumbled view of the room, but not on purpose—the phone was being examined by Sarah. *"Well, I'll be. They sure got small, didn't they? Too bad there aren't any signals, you could... Oh, sorry."*

Dani/Evie's face was on the screen and she looked sad. *"Sarah, cell phones do more than just make phone calls. Like I was telling Jody, you can type notes to people—they call it texting—and they get the message immediately. You can also record and play music, take pictures and look at them right away, even make movies with that little thing in your hand. It has a bunch of different types of calculators and language translators in it, and a radio—which wouldn't work here and now, of course, since there aren't any radio signals. Neither would the phone..."*

The image on the screen was moving all around again. It was obvious that it was in stealth mode and no one knew that the record button had been pushed. Suddenly, the image of Jody filled the screen, but it was Dani/Evie who was speaking. *"It's real scary how fast technology is moving—or rather will move. It's all so quick and disposable in my time, my former time. Sarah, I don't want to go back!"*

The screen turned toward Dani/Evie again as she came closer to the camera and continued speaking. *"Good grief, I don't even know how I got here, so how 'could' I go back? And, as I was telling Jody, I don't want to know about the old me—who I was—before all 'this' happened,"* she gestured to the room around her. *"I'm fine just as I am,"* she said with pride and sadness at the same time.

*"Hey,"* she said with shock. The image zig-zagged all around the room again. *"When did this happen? When did the light go from green to red?"* The image stabilized on Jody's face.

He spoke carefully, *"I first noticed it when I tried to give it to ye when ye were sittin' at the table. Why? Is there somethin' wrong?"* The image became a close up of a fearful Jody as he grabbed the phone.

*"No, not wrong,"* said Dani/Evie. Her face came in close, then the

86

edge of her hand appeared, and the little documentary was over.

"She turned off the smartphone. She didn't know it was recording, and as soon as she saw that it was, she turned it off. I'm not crazy, that woman really was my mother, and she really is *younger than me?*" Leah said, ending her stoic explanation with a squeak of uncertainty.

James took the phone from her and powered it off. "Hey, you," he said, and turned to face her. He put his hand on her cheek and made sure she was looking into his eyes before he spoke. "You're the one who just told me about mysteries. 'There are mysteries to be solved and mysteries to be accepted,' you said. And wisdom is knowing which is which. I don't think anyone can explain how your mother got younger. Maybe there is something to witchcraft and magic. No, just magic. I don't believe your mother could ever be involved with witchcraft. Now, we accept that she came back to you yesterday as a younger person, okay?"

Leah sniffed and nodded, glad that she had someone to offer her clarity.

"Now, we know—or think we know—that it's possible to go back to the 18th century. She said 1781. She was here last year, traveled into the past somehow or other, ten months ago; came back here two days ago, and then went back there, to 1781, I hope, yesterday."

Leah responded thoughtfully, "Yes, she went back to 1781, for sure." She saw the puzzled look on his face. "For sure, because she wrote the letters, see?"

James rolled his eyes, took a deep breath, and moved the letters and the smartphones to the bedside table. He turned sideways, pulled the pillows away from the headboard, fluffed one, then put the other to the side of him. He scooted down, then lay his head on the pillow, turning to face Leah. "That's it. I'm spent. I started on this trip yesterday, and haven't slept in 36 hours, at least. I'm not trying to be rude, but I don't...don't think I could...could...say anything rational so, so..." James's eyes fluttered as he spoke, and then closed as he fell asleep in mid-sentence.

Leah went through the same motions of pillow fluffing, scooting, and lying down, then faced her new friend. "It's been a rough 36 hours for me, too. Thanks for being my white knight, Lord James Melbourne. I sure wish you weren't a fairy." She put her hand an inch above his lightly bearded cheek and traced the air above the strong jaw line. "Otherwise you'd be perfect." She pulled back her hand, tucked it into her chest next to her other hand, and fell into a deep sleep.

## *12 New Roommates
*August 6, 2013, 5:15 AM*

Leah awoke at 5:15 a.m. and stared at the ceiling. She didn't want to get up and face the day, much less the world, but her body had been waking at this same hour, except in the instance of extreme hangovers, for five years. There was no chance of a hangover from yesterday, though, that was for sure. She had drunk alcohol twice and puked it up both times. True, she was either drugged or severely stressed in both instances, but maybe it was time to quit using the chemical numbing agents. At least now she knew what happened to her mother, and whether it was a rational explanation or not, it made her feel better.

Snort, rumble, and loud exhale…what? Leah turned over and saw the very handsome man lying next to her. She smiled with recollection of the day before. He was so nice, kind, and had a sharp wit. She remembered thinking that he was practically perfect. She saw his mouth hanging lax, the tongue hanging to the side a little. Okay, slight flaw; nobody sleeps with his mouth closed all the time. And then there was that other imperfection. Her eyes glanced down and saw what most men had first thing in the morning. Well, he made a decent pup tent, but he might as well be a eunuch. Why did he have to be gay?

*Bzzz, Bzzz*. The noise startled Leah. She realized what it was, jumped up, and reached across James to grab her smartphone. The alarm was always set 'just in case' she didn't wake up in time for work. With all of the excitement last night, she had forgotten to deactivate it. If she could shut it off in time, the loud cyber-rooster-crowing MP3 file wouldn't play and wake James. Oops, too late—the pre-alarm vibration alone had been enough to rouse him. His eyes were still shut, but now his mouth was, too. He was faking it. "I get the bathroom first," she sang, as she bounded out of bed.

James rolled over just in time to see her grab the bottom of her shirt and pull it down over her butt cheeks. He rolled back over onto his back and started chuckling. He knew she thought that he was gay. She was treating him like a person, not as a jerk who was after her body, or a piece of man meat to be used to get her own jollies. Well, he would neither confirm nor deny his sexual orientation, and hopefully she wouldn't ask. He liked her too much to lose her.

Leah came out of the bathroom right away. "Well, that was quick," she said. "It's amazing how fast you can get ready in the morning if you don't have a toothbrush, comb, clothes or, or…"

*She looked over at James—he wasn't leering, but his relaxed smile was unsettling. 'Could he be straight?' she thought. He wasn't being rude in any way, it was just that he was letting her babble which, now that she thought about it, must be a generalized male thing, not a tolerant, straight boyfriend thing.*

"Well, then it looks like I won't have to fight for counter space, either," James said. "If you're done in there…" He turned away from her to get out of bed, put his feet on the floor, and looked down to see his happy male member playing peek-a-boo out of the fly in his shorts. He shoved it back in and stood up, looking behind him to see if he could make a discreet entrance into the bathroom.

Leah was standing in front of the chair, turning her bathing suit right side out. He edged around the bed and saw her trying to hide a smirk. Right, she had awakened before he had, and had seen what he was now trying to hide in his skivvies. Oh, well, it just proved that he was a healthy human male. Just what type of male he truly was would have to remain a secret, at least for a while.

James grabbed his bag on the way into the bathroom. A shower was in order. He didn't stink from all of the sweating the day before—the swim in the pool had taken care of that—but he still felt polluted.

The water temperature was just right, the pressure more than he was used to, the soap extra slippery, and well, he couldn't help but do himself a favor. She'd never know, and he might be more relaxed as a result. And heaven knew, he needed every helping hand he could get. He snorted a short laugh at his own pun. Maybe he wouldn't have to be his own best friend after the two of them got all this sorted out. He could only hope.

The long, sudsy shower took care of all his discomforts. "What time is it?" he asked as he came out of the bathroom, his Rolex in his hand.

Leah smiled at the screen on her smartphone. "It's 5:55, make a wish," she said brightly. She saw his confusion and explained. "It's a kid thing that I never grew out of. Every hour has one of them, you know: 1:11, 2:22, and so on? You're supposed to make a wish when you see all the same digits on the time display."

"Do I have to say the wish out loud?" he said before thinking. Duh! He knew what he had just been wishing, but he certainly wasn't going to share that…at least not yet.

"I wish we could—'I' could—be with my mother again," Leah said, her voice squeaking with mock bravery.

"'We could' is good for me, too," he said, and gave her a one-armed hug. "There, I got the time set and here, try these on." James handed her a pair of his custom torn jeans and a pale blue Oxford shirt with long sleeves. "And I got some sandals for you from the store yesterday. I forgot, did I show them to you already or…"

"Yeah, well yesterday was a little exciting, and yes, you did—they fit fine. Hey, is that a real Rolex?"

"Yes," he said, waiting for the punchline he felt was sure to follow.

"Sweet," she grinned, "looks just like the clones. I'll be right back."

89

She grabbed the clothes and went into the bathroom.

And right back she was, rolling up the shirtsleeves as she emerged. "It's faster getting dressed when I don't have to mess with, um, undergarments. This isn't too revealing, is it?"

"Well, it reveals that you're definitely a woman, but no, you are quite presentable. How about coffee and breakfast first, then we can go on a shopping spree, my treat," he bowed shortly before her and winked.

She rolled her eyes at his mini display of gallantry. "Only if I can drive—I have to be of some use. Let me get my shoes on."

Leah sat down on the edge of the bed and bent over to latch the Velcro bindings on her sandals. James glanced at her and realized he could see down the front of her shirt. He quickly averted his eyes by gentlemanly reflex, and turned away, giving her privacy. *'You're a gay man, you're a gay man,' the little angel on his right shoulder kept chanting over and over in his head. 'For a while, just for a while,' answered the devil on the left.*

He picked up the room key and his bag, and opened the door. "I'll wait out here for you," he said over his shoulder on the way out. Once outside, he leaned against the exterior wall and let out a long sigh of contentment. *She had said 'we could be with my mother' before she changed it to 'I could be with my mother.' She likes me! What a wonderful thought to start the day.*

Ж

"Fast food or sit down?" Leah asked as she held the door open behind her. He flashed the room key at her so she knew to go ahead and close the door. She replied by picking up her bundle of keys, shaking them at him—she had her keys, too—and double clicked the key to unlock the little purple Prius.

He opened the car door for her. "Sit down," he said, as if he was telling a dog to behave himself. He walked around to the other side of the car, got in, then looked over at her to make sure she understood what he meant.

She rolled her eyes, said "Woof," and panted like a happy puppy.

"Actually, I'd prefer sit down because I'd like fresh fruit and porridge for breakfast—and I don't think we can get that at a drive through. At least, the oatmeal would be a little messy to eat wrapped in paper."

Leah laughed at his joke. "I thought you English lords were supposed to be all stuffy and somber. You're fun."

*James stifled his impulse to invite her to find out just how much fun he could be.* Instead, he sighed in resignation, and said, "Well, I was born both human and an heir to a title. Sometimes I'm able to keep the two in balance, but since I've been here—with you—I've enjoyed squelching the 'stuffy and somber' aspect. I may be un-balanced this way, but it is so much more…well, you said it, fun."

90

Leah pulled up to a little cafeteria-style café. He held the car door open for her, then she reciprocated at the front door, sweeping her arm out wide to introduce him to the eatery. "Best of both worlds here: grab a tray and fill 'er up."

The two enjoyed a quick, cool, and comfortable breakfast. After they finished, Leah stacked their dirty dishes on the cafeteria tray and took it to the conveyor belt that led to the dishwasher behind the hole in the wall. James stood as she left, feeling awkward. She looked back at him and smiled. "You don't have this at home, do you?"

"Well, we probably do somewhere, but not where I'm used to dining. And I'm certainly not used to my breakfast date clearing the dishes. But I'm sure that life would be different for you, too, if you came over to my part of the world."

James suddenly became uncomfortable, speaking of the home and life he might not ever have again. In emotional self-defense, he switched gears and attitudes. "So are you ready to go shopping, girlfriend," he said broadly, hands on hips, mimicking a drag queen.

"Wally World, here we come," she replied.

Ж

"Oops, wrong one," she said when she saw that he was opening the door on the passenger's side for her.

"That has been the most difficult adjustment I've had to make here. I cringe as you drive sometimes, afraid that an oncoming vehicle will smash right into us. Or that would be smash 'left' into us, wouldn't it?"

Leah laughed. "You know, I don't know how I ever survived without you. I'm going to miss you when you leave. How long were—are—you going to stay?"

*He wanted to say, 'As long as you'll have me, sweetheart,' but shoved his fantasy response back to savor at a later time.* "I don't know. Really, I don't know." James turned around, and found it easier to unload his burden while facing away from her. "This was supposed to be a short business trip—at least, that was my thought up to about three days ago. Then my whole world pretty much fell apart. I'd tell you about it, but then I'd have to relive it as I explained it, so please don't ask me now. Before I left, I pretty much said to hell with everything, tied up my life with little notes to put my 'position' on hold indefinitely, and forwarded my mail to my club. I said 'piss off' to some legal matters I was tired of dealing with, went to the airport, bought a new bag and filled it with new—well, new to me—clothes, hopped on a plane, and here I am. You know everything that's happened to me since I hit Greensboro. Actually, not having to deal with worldly possessions is quite refreshing."

James suddenly realized that Leah had far less in worldly possessions than he did. Embarrassed, he turned to face her, ready to

91

apologize, but she was smiling.

"You know, it's all just *stuff*. Having a good friend to talk to and be with is so much more important than having an apartment full of clothes, a good paying, respectable job, rooms full of the latest electronics, money in the bank. Ooh, money in the bank. I still have that, but I digress. Yesterday, I lost probably everything I owned except the shirt and bathing suit on my back. But I got a new friend who has helped me with my mysteries…" She glanced up at him to see how he had reacted to the word 'mysteries,' "and I feel better and more fulfilled than…well…ever as an adult. Does that sound too sappy?"

"No, I was thinking along the same lines except all my 'stuff' will probably go away with the legal problems instead of with a house fire. The result is the same, though. We're a happy, unencumbered-by-material-goods couple."

"Practically perfect pair," escaped Leah's lips before she could think. Rather than retract or explain her remark, she said, "And…we have arrived!"

"Oh, I was here yesterday. Now, should I get a trolley? That seems to be what everyone does." James was looking confused on the outside in order to try and hide his elation at Leah's remark about them being a 'practically perfect pair.' He could only hope that the limitation of the word 'practically' was because of his supposed homosexuality. *Be patient, James. Don't let lust ruin the friendship. If she's as worthy a woman as you think, she'll understand the reason for your deception. After all, you never claimed to be gay—that was her assumption.*

"James, oh, James," Leah called out in a lilting, sing-song manner, but didn't get a response from her introspective friend. "Come on, sweetheart," she said decidedly, and grabbed him by the inner elbow, pulling him and the cart along with her. "I don't want to lose you–this is a big store."

"Oh, sorry," James said, as he tagged along beside her, happy all over again to be with her.

"Now, I don't want much, at least for now," she explained, as she led the way into the heart of the shopping emporium. "Actually, I'm not sure what I want to do in the long run. For the short run, though, I think we better go see Billy at the police station. I want to make sure he knows I'm okay. I also want to try again to see if he'll let me have a copy of the police report about the kidnapping. I want to know where they found the car Mom was in when she disappeared. Then I want to go to the last place I know she visited last year, the Guilford County Courthouse Museum. It's taken me ten months to get the nerve to even think about going there. I still wouldn't even think about it if I didn't have you here with me. I want to get some insight on what was going through her head that day. Here," she added, changing the subject, "are these too skimpy?" she asked, and held up a pair of red lace thong panties.

James hadn't been paying attention to which department they were in. He looked up and saw that they were in the lingerie area. He gulped, then got back into the game. "These, dear? It looks like there's only one hair ribbon!" He put his hand to his mouth in mock shock, "Panties, you say? Oh, my, my. No, dear. You'd lose those in the laundry, for sure."

Leah laughed at his silliness, then went over to the wall of plastic packages, pulled down a multi-pack of cotton briefs, then turned her attention to the tiers of bras. He knew he shouldn't be, but he was embarrassed about where they were, so rounded the corner so he wasn't watching her.

The next department was where he wanted to be anyway. He looked through the racks of ladies nightshirts and pajamas, found one he liked, and threw it in the cart. He paused a moment, took it out again, and looked at the tag. *Nope, XL doesn't look like my lady.* He put it back and found the same item in size M, then did his best to hide it under the pack of panties.

While Leah was at the clearance rack, shuffling through assorted styles and sizes, involved with saving him a few dollars, he pushed the cart around until he found what he was looking for: men's pajama pants. He pawed through the hangers, and checked all the flies, until he found a pair of sleep shorts in his size with buttons on the flap. He breathed a sigh of relief as he put them in the cart—his part of the shopping was done. He looked up and saw Leah.

"Did you get lost?" She looked at what he had just put in the cart, straightened out the folded over shorts, fingered the two buttons on the fly, and said, "Good choice. Now let's go get me a hairbrush and a toothbrush. My mouth feels like the bottom of a birdcage."

It didn't take long to check out, pay, and get back on the road. "I'll change clothes at the police station. I want to get there before Billy's shift is over. We're cutting it close as it is." Leah found a parking place. "Sweet, he's still here," she said, when she spotted Billy's classic '85 blue Corvette convertible.

The two of them walked into the station where Leah was personally greeted by the female officer at the information desk. "Hi, Leah. Billy's still here. Let me buzz him. He wanted to see you as soon as you got in."

James wandered around the lobby, looking at the historical pictures on the walls, while Leah made small talk with the lady at the desk. Many of the paintings depicted the Revolutionary War battles that had taken place practically under his feet over 230 years ago. He knew little about the conflict, except where it related to his ancestors. They hadn't made a big deal out of it in his school studies—it was merely a bump in his country's effort to make sure the sun always shone on the British Empire. Around here, though, the shadows of the war were still cast on the community. He hadn't realized that Greensboro was such an important historical region when he considered the mill purchase. Hopefully, nobody held grudges against the British after all these years.

Leah walked up beside James to look at the painting on the wall with him. "We'll see more of this later at the museum. Come on, Billy's waiting for us."

James didn't know if she had been calling him and he hadn't heard her, or if she just wanted to be more personal in bringing him in to Billy's office with her. He definitely had a case of jet lag to go with the shocks of the last twenty-four hours.

"Hi there, I'm Billy Burke, Leah's neighbor," Billy said, as he thrust his hand out in greeting. "You probably don't recognize me with my clothes on," he teased, referring to meeting him the day before wearing nothing but a towel. "Sorry, bad joke. Here, please sit down."

James and Leah sat down. Leah was anxious, literally perched on the edge of her seat, her teeth biting her lower lip in anticipation of whatever was coming next.

"Here's the report on the assault. I'd appreciate it if you'd check it out and make sure I didn't miss anything. And here," he placed another thin pile of paper next to the first one, "is the report on the arson. Bottom line, Leah, someone wants your keys. I think we need to get with the hospital and have them change their policy on pharmaceutical cabinets. Then, we can do a public interest story on TV about the recent attacks and fire bombings and how—hopefully this will come to fruition—doctors, nurses, and supervisors will no longer have keys to access controlled medications. I know the technology is out there for thumbprint recognition. It would be pricey to implement, but I don't believe we ought to set a price on the lives of people, especially those helping others, like doctors and nurses."

James picked up the arson report, scanned it, and then looked up at Billy. Leah was still reading the report on the assault. He had been there on both occasions and didn't remember Leah giving out any information to anyone, much less a police officer. That was supposed to come later. "Officer Burke," he began.

"Please, just call me Billy," he replied.

"Okay, Billy, how did you know who I was? I don't remember seeing Leah talk to you, and I know I didn't get a chance to introduce myself."

Billy picked up the nameplate off his desk and pointed to his title. "Detective is my job. It wasn't too hard to figure out, though. As a matter of course, I checked out the new, or rather unfamiliar, vehicle in the parking lot. I ran the plates, called the last registered owner, and he told me that he had just sold—or rather, that he had re-sold—the truck to you. I ran your name, found out that you were a decent enough fellow to accompany Leah overnight, and left a message for you to call."

"Message? I never received a message. Oh, bother." James opened up the side of his valise and pulled out his smartphone. "I forgot to turn it back on after I landed. Wow, looks like six messages. How many were yours?"

"Just the one, I wasn't worried. You two seemed fully capable of taking care of each other," Billy winked, as he whispered the last part.

James quickly looked over at Leah and saw that she was still involved with the first report. He turned back to Billy, gave a weak smile, and shook his head slightly. Billy gave him the 'ah ha!' nod, then grinned broadly, making a covert finger over finger jester of 'shame, shame on you' as he silently mouthed those words. James shook his head again. No wonder Leah liked Billy so much. The officer was a likable sort and seemed to have the same great sense of humor that she did.

Leah looked up at the two men communicating without words. "Do you two need a moment in private?" she asked coyly.

"No, no, strictly business," Billy mocked in a stern voice, then returned to police officer mode and asked, "Do you want to add anything to, or take anything away from, the reports? The rats are still in our custody now. There were warrants out for both of them from Virginia. It seems as if they just moved here to go after fresh meat. They didn't count on England's finest being around to take them down."

Leah glanced over at James, gave a weak, nervous smile, and then turned back to Billy. "Will I have to testify? I want them to be convicted, but I really don't want to see them again." Her mouth was producing flat, unemotional tones, but her eyes were begging, 'Please, don't make me do it.'

"We'll see how it goes. We're going to file charges, then extradite them to Virginia and let the VA boys have their way with the two of them first. If you do have to testify, it won't be for quite a while. And then there's always the possibility that they'll plead guilty, or maybe even no contest, so they can get leniency. Yeah, right—at least on the leniency part," Billy joked, but with a serious edge in his voice.

James saw that Billy was sensitive to Leah's situation and had her best interests in mind in dealing with the situation. Now he saw her friend the cop in a different light. Yes, if he really *were* a gay man, then Billy would be quite attractive to him. But then again, there were plenty of others out there for the good-looking detective. James had never believed that there was someone for everyone, at least not until yesterday and Leah. So today really did feel like the first day of the rest of his life. At least now he had a life full of great possibilities. And someone worthy of sharing them with.

James heard Billy's chair scoot out from under the desk. He stood up and they shook hands again. "Thanks for taking care of my girl for me. Here's my card," Billy said, and handed him the official Greensboro Police Department business card, "and I wrote my personal cell number on the back. Leah, may I speak with James alone for a moment, please?"

Leah looked from Billy to James and back again, and then smiled in a knowing manner. "Sure, I'll be right outside," she drawled smoothly, and sauntered out into the lobby.

Billy started in on James as soon as the door was shut. "Look, she thinks you're gay. You're not, are you?" James shook his head briskly. "Right, I knew that, but I wanted to make sure you weren't going to lie to me. That's a biggie for me and for her. She thinks I might have a thing for you, and I'll let her keep thinking that if it helps her 'heal,' shall we say. She's been through a lot in the last year, losing her mother and now this—those creeps and her apartment practically burned to the ground. She needs a friend, not a lover."

James nodded in agreement and looked Billy hard in the eyes. "Oh, like that is it?" Billy asked. "You'd rather keep her as a friend and have her believe a lie than get a little? I like you more all the time. Keep me posted as to her mental health.

"And I'm not supposed to do this," Billy held out an envelope to James, "and I told her I wasn't going to be able to get this for her, but I don't think there's a problem with you having it. You aren't from around here, aren't likely to stir up any shit, and I'll bet you have the discretion to keep the information to yourself. Leah's very fragile, whether she knows it or not. I'd hate for this," he tapped the envelope now in James's hand, "to get out to any of the tabloids. They'd have a field day with alien abduction theories with what's in here.

"In a nutshell, the woman—a Jane Doe who Leah had in her charge at the hospital three days ago—was kidnapped by a strange little man posing as a doctor. He coerced the patient into a stolen car and had her drive the two of them out to a deserted area. We found the car two hours later. There were two sets of footprints leaving it, one of his small Colonial-style boots, the others were of the woman's slippers. The man's set of prints walked up to a point near two trees, then turned around and disappeared. The slipper prints, the Jane Doe who was Leah's patient, led right between the trees, and then *they* disappeared.

"I think Leah feels guilty about not stopping the man before he kidnapped the woman. She tried, but wound up drugged or knocked out or something. We still can't figure out how she lost consciousness. I know she didn't just pass out, but there were no marks on her, nor traces of chemicals. She stood up to him, though, and did what she could to try to prevent the kidnapping. And then yesterday's double whammy." Billy walked around to the front of the desk and opened the door. He put his hand on James's shoulder. "Just be there for her, okay?"

James looked him in the eye and smiled. "Gladly. She's one helluva woman, and I won't let anything happen to her, I promise."

Billy's hand was still on James's shoulder. He had left it there just a tad too long for comfort. James shifted his eyes and Billy realized what he was doing. "Looks like she's getting a helluva man, too," he said softly, then winked and patted James's shoulder in dismissal. "Keep in touch."

Ж

Leah looked back from the front desk and saw her two men in the doorway. It looked like Billy had a new friend, she thought. "Keep in touch," Billy was saying to James while patting him on the shoulder. Leah's heart sank. It wasn't jealousy—it was sadness. She felt like she had just lost part of her new friend to her old friend.

# *13 Guilford Courthouse Museum

James set his bag down on the chair in the waiting room and discreetly slipped the envelope Billy had given him inside it. He would have to check it out when he was alone. Evidently Leah hadn't told Billy about her suspicion that the kidnapped woman who disappeared was her mother in a younger body. Of course not—who would believe that story, even her best friend?

*Former best friend, he thought proudly.* He gulped in embarrassment. Pride—that cursed Melbourne pride—he didn't want to succumb to it. No, he would let Billy remain her best friend: her best gay friend. He would, however, lay claim that he had now become a 'great' friend to her.

"Don't forget to check your emails," Leah said, breaking his reverie. She grabbed him by the arm. "Come on, but let's go somewhere a bit more private. How about the parking lot of the museum? I'd like to get in and out of there before it gets too hot. It's mostly just walking the grounds, but I hear they also have some great displays of the tools and stuff that people used back in the old days."

"And that your mother is using today," said James. "Ironic, but if she was here three days ago and went back, then she's using items like they have in the museum today, right?"

Leah gulped. "Hell if I know," she said flatly.

The silence that followed was uncomfortable for both of them. "Sorry," James said, "I was just thinking out loud. I'll try to keep my thoughts to myself."

Leah didn't say anything, but raised her eyebrows and nodded, indicating a 'Well, okay' reply. The silence remained, but wasn't uncomfortable.

A few minutes later, they pulled into the museum parking lot. Leah found a place near the entrance, under a tree. "Shaded parking is always at a premium in the summer," she remarked absently. "I'll go see when they open and how much it costs while you check your messages."

Leah got out of the car without waiting for his reply. James watched her as she left. He couldn't see her face, but by the way she had her hand up to her eyes and nose, she was crying. "She's fragile," Billy had said. *No, she's tough, he thought to himself, very tough, but still a woman. They're allowed to grieve in their own way, and that usually involves tears.*

James did the taps and slides on his smartphone screen to open his voice mail. "You son of a bitch…." It was Clotilde. He didn't want to know what that was about, so deleted it without even listening to it.

"Hi, this is Billy, Leah's friend. Can you come down to the station in the morning? I want to give you something. I also want both of you to look over the reports on yesterday's 'incidents.' Thanks and welcome to America. It isn't always this crazy."

James saved the phone number in his address book, then deleted the message. He wanted to make sure his possession of the report was kept as discreet as Billy had wanted it to be. James changed menus to view the missed calls. Three more were from Clotilde's phone, but he didn't recognize the other one, other than that it was from the UK. He opened it.

"Hi, Lord James, this is Ric Smith. You gave me the car, remember? Well, that crazy woman is trying to say that I stole it. I have the title, and the police here are okay, but is there some way you can get her off my back? And she tried to get your mail again, but I took care of that. You had an important looking parcel that came in just after you left. I took it over to your club rather than forward it through the system. I thought it would be safer that way. Also, since it's there now, if you have someone there who you trust, he can open it for you. The package was marked urgent. Just thought you'd want to know, and thanks again for the car. The missus says she owes you a chocolate cake and a big kiss. Oh, and if you need me, the number is…."

James saved that phone number to the address book, too. He slid the cursor to 'W,' opened the file for the name 'White, Mrs. Coco,' and hit call.

"Mrs. White's Chocolate House; how may I help you, sir?" The man on the other end of the phone always answered the same way. If it was a wrong number, the name of the 'company' would throw the callers off, and they would recheck the number they had dialed. If a valid call, the person would be male. All members of The Club—originally called Mrs. White's Chocolate House, but now referred to as 'White's' by outsiders and The Club by members—were male.

"James? James Bradford?" asked James Melbourne.

"Yes, sir. Is this who I think it is?" asked the man on the other end of the call in England.

"Well, if you think that this is the other James, then yes, it is. There should have been a package delivered there for me. It would have arrived yesterday, possibly today. Do you know of it?"

"Yes, sir, I put it in the back with all of your other correspondence." There was a pause as neither person spoke. "Sir, would you like me to open it for you? It was marked urgent, and it would be no problem."

"Yes, please do. I'll hold if you don't mind." James picked up his bag and took out the envelope Billy had given him earlier. It contained a typewritten report and a hand drawn map. He glanced over the map while the other James in England was opening the parcel. He heard the sound of paper being ripped, and then a voice.

"It looks like a map, sir. It's on parchment and has a note attached, on a smaller piece of parchment. The note says, 'I am returning the map to you. Please keep it safe. I hope to see you two weeks after your 28th birthday. I'll meet you at the double X. Have Leah send plenty of IV tubing and various sizes of trocars. Also any other medical supplies that she deems appropriate for the conditions. Love.'"

"Love who?" asked James, stunned at what he had just heard.

"It doesn't say a name, just 'love,' a comma, and then a...a...a happy face. It doesn't make much sense to me, sir."

"Well," James in America replied, "compared to what's been happening here in the last few days, this is pretty tame. I'll tell you what I'd like you to do. Scan and email me a copy of the map and the note. Then take the originals, put them into a different envelope, and put it in the safe there at the club. Write something like 'recipes for eel pie' and your name on the outside, so no one will bother it. Do you need my email address?"

"No, sir; I still have it. Oh, and your solicitor came in just a bit ago. He thought you were here. He said if I heard from you that you were to call him right away. However, I think he's still here. Would you like me to patch you through?"

"Yes, please do, and thank you."

While James waited for the call to go through, he put the map back inside the envelope and wrote '17/8/2013, double X, trocars, and IV tubing' on the back of it, then added LEAH in bold letters.

James in England came back on the line, "Lord James, could you wait just a moment longer? He is, um, indisposed, but wanted to speak with you."

"Fine, I'll hold." James leaned back into the seat and relaxed, eyes closed as he wondered about the note, and what it could mean. As he sat, his pen moved by itself across the back of the envelope, like a planchette over a ouija board.

"Hello, hello, are you there?"

"Yes, I'm here. What's going on?" James asked anxiously, as he sat up to speak with Alfred Schofield, his lawyer. He looked out and saw Leah walking slowly, head down, toward the car.

"It's final, the divorce is final. But get this—she perjured herself so many times, the judge threw out her half of the community property award. She doesn't get a penny! Now I guess she's running around, trying to take back all of the donations you gave to various charities and organizations in the past. What she's doing borders on extortion. I didn't know if you wanted me to do something about it or not. I would suggest a letter to all of the institutions, explaining the status of your marriage to her, and that you do not condone her actions. I'd be more than happy to take care of this for you. Good Lord, I'd do it for free just to see that...that...tramp gets knocked back down into the gutter from whence she came. Oh, sorry—I get carried away when it comes to her."

"No, don't do it for free, but definitely do it, and do it quickly. Just take your usual fee from the legal expenses account. And one other thing: I did a bit of bartering with the clerk at the auxiliary postal outlet just south of Westminster. His name is Richard Smith. He now owns the Corniche, free and clear. Clotilde's been threatening him. What I'd like you to do is make sure she knows that if she tries to talk to him about *anything*, she'll be jailed for assault. He's a good man, so if he needs anything else, take care of those needs, too. Now, it looks like I'll be gone longer than I had planned. I'll be checking in with James Bradford, there at the club, so if you have a message for me, give it to him. Look, I have to go now. Thanks for all that you've done. Good-bye for now."

Leah leaned over and looked in through her opened driver's side window to see if he was done with his phone calls. James saluted her with the phone, then put it in his shirt pocket. "You forgot to change clothes at the police station," he said with a grin as he looked down at her clutching her—rather his—trousers.

Leah smiled back, the weight of her dilemma now lighter since she had someone to share it with. "No worries. Here, scoot over into the driver's seat. I'll change in the car."

James looked over at the limited area between the seats, then down to his long—well, longer than hers—legs, opened his door, and got out.

Leah saw the 'look,' and followed his visual suggestion to walk around to the other side. He held the door open for her and grinned. She reached in behind the seat, pawed through the big white shopping bag, found the orange sundress she had selected from the clearance rack, tossed it over her head, and unbuttoned the shirt underneath it. She pushed her hands through the armholes of the sleeveless dress, then tugged off the shirt, all while under cover of cotton. She then plopped down into the passenger seat, and gave him a rebellious scowl that seemed to say, 'Hey, I'm sure I could have done it in the driver's seat, but I'll do it your way.' She kicked off her sandals, placed her bare feet on the dashboard, and lifted her bottom. She wiggled and tugged, but with no success. Even though the jeans she had borrowed from him were too big for her, she still couldn't get them off. She wouldn't stop trying, though, and grunted and cursed, as if that would help. Her brow beaded up with sweat, as did other parts of her body, which made her frustrated struggle even harder—the pants were stuck to her body.

James waited outside the car, arms crossed in front of his chest, right index finger tapping a silent tattoo on his elbow. He didn't say a word until it became obvious that she wasn't going to give up, even though there was no way she could win the battle of de-pantsing herself while crammed into the front seat of a summer-heated sub-compact car.

"Here, get out and stand up to take them off. I'll play dressing room wall," he said, and opened the door, keeping his back turned to her, providing a privacy barrier, in case other visitors drove into the parking lot.

Thirty seconds later, she said, "There, done," and sat back in the passenger's seat to put her sandals back on. She looked up at him and said, "Yes, I could have taken the clothes inside and changed in the ladies room, but then I would have had to either carry them around or bring them back here."

"I didn't say anything," James said. He didn't tell her that he had been thinking it hard enough, though.

"Well, you were thinking it hard enough, though," she said, echoing verbally the words he had just been thinking.

James didn't say anything—just smiled.

"I know, I know, I shouldn't read people's minds without their permission. Sorry, I'll try not to do it again," she said with mild sarcasm, batting her eyes, her bottom lip puffed out as if looking for forgiveness.

James could see she was trying to make a joke out of something he felt was probably the truth. "Apology accepted," he said, wondering what he could do to mess with her, and see if she really could read minds. "Give me a number between one and ten," he asked, and began concentrating on the number one hundred.

"One hundred, er ten," she replied.

"Close enough," he said. He'd have to start doing mathematical equations in his head if he felt a personal thought about her come around. Cloud her with calculus—that was the solution to the predicament. It was the non-mathematical problem of his feelings about her that was the real poser.

"Let's start outside and look around the grounds first before it gets too hot," she suggested, as she fanned herself with the flyer. It was already warm.

She got back behind the wheel and drove down the paved loop byway, stopping at the numbered pullouts, following the documented trail suggested by the flyer. They got out and viewed the large monuments, walking side by side silently, taking in the words cast and etched into the memorials, then got back into the air-conditioned car. A few pullouts later, they took the small hike down the crushed granite trail to the tall white monolith marking the third line.

It was there, halfway to the monument that looked like it belonged in Washington, D.C., that they stopped and stared at each other. James could tell by her startled look that she, too, could hear the spine-tingling whispers of the ghosts who seemed to be hovering nearby. The trees seemed to exude the essence of the pain and determination of those who had fallen so many years before.

Leah squeezed his arm, letting him know wordlessly that she wanted to go back to the museum.

"It's too much for me," she said when they got back to the car. "I'm glad they made the sacrifice—the Continental Patriots, that is—but I wish so many people hadn't died, from both countries. This is awkward because you were on the other side, if you know what I mean."

"I'm sorry. I didn't mean to ruin the experience for you. I was touched by it, too, if that makes a difference. If you recall, my family fought over here, too. Remember the letter?"

Leah snorted and looked at him sternly.

*Duh, of course she remembered it! He swallowed and started again.* "It was a cold, calculated, and merciless war on the part of England, who wanted to keep control over her asset across the water, but," he stressed, "America was also the new home to immigrants from there and other European countries, many of whom died trying to help establish it. My ancestor, Lord Julian Hart, a great British soldier with extensive military experience, made the change, and I know many others transferred allegiances, too. Right here, right now, I am British because of where my father was born, and you are American because of where your mother was born. Now, Lord Julian Hart went against 'geographic genetics,' if you will, and went with his heart. Who is to say that I couldn't—or wouldn't—do the same?"

Leah shook her head, confused. "I didn't bring you here to change your nationality. I came here to see what my mother saw—and maybe experience what she did—just before she *left*. I know she was very patriotic, and after walking through here, I'm sure she was...well, distraught." She pulled into the parking lot, turned off the engine, and looked over at James. "You see, besides being patriotic, she was also very emotional. Come on, let's go inside."

"I met her, remember?" James quickly got out of the car and opened the door for Leah before she could do it herself. "You mother was also bright, compassionate, had a great sense of humor, and could handle a volatile situation with a finesse that would make a professional negotiator envious. Whoa!" James's flat palm suddenly smacked his forehead in a classic 'I coulda had a V-8' gesture, and then he froze, his eyes wide-open in shock.

"What happened? Are you okay?" Leah asked.

James remained mum, staring into the trees, his eyes unfocused.

"Come sit down inside where it's cooler." Leah put her hand on his elbow to guide him into the building. He shook his head and remained on the sidewalk outside the museum entrance, stunned. Back into nurse-mode, Leah took charge, hooked her arm in his, and led him to a bench in the shade. She checked his pulse, using his Rolex to time the rate. It was fast, but within limits. James was hyperventilating and glassy-eyed, but snapped out of it after a minute of her patting his hand and offering soothing assurances.

*He started coming out of his mini-trance as soon as she held his hand. When he felt her skin on his, he relaxed, but remembered to make sure to begin thinking about multiplication tables in order to keep an unreadable mind. This way, he could enjoy her touch and be calculating at the same time.*

"What just happened?" she asked, still clutching his hand, her eyebrows pinched together in concern.

"Describe the doctor who took your mother away," he said, frowning.

"Well, he was real short, not dwarfish, but not petite either. He had thinning hair, was maybe fifty-ish, looked like...well, do you know who E.T. the Exterrestrial is, the alien from the movie? He kind of reminded me of him—almost, but not quite, toad-ish. And he had an accent. Not quite British, but definitely not Scottish or French or Italian. Do you know what I mean when I say continental?"

James watched Leah intently as she explained. He let her finish her description, then asked, "Was he very confident? How should I say..."

"Full of himself? Yes, that's him, all right. Do you know him?" she asked, eyes wide in surprise.

"Are we done here? I really would like to go somewhere private. We have a lot to talk about. Same motel, or should we find another?"

Leah closed her eyes and blocked out everything except 'same motel.' If they got another place, they might wind up with two beds. Well, tonight she didn't want to sleep by herself. She wanted to be held, even if by a gay man. No, tonight she wanted to be held, but *especially* by a gay man. She needed comfort and compassion, not groping or sex.

"Same motel," she said decisively. "I'm more than ready to go now."

The ride back to the motel was quiet, too quiet, and just a bit spooky. But they were still content in each other's company. Leah reached over and patted his hand at the stop sign. "Check-out time is noon. We still have a few minutes before they go in and toss the beer. Are you thirsty?"

"Are you sure you want to drink more beer after yesterday?" he asked, remembering her reaction to having a link to her mother's past through a mini-movie on her smartphone.

"Maybe I'll use the beer to wash my hair and drink water. It's healthier for me, for sure. I think I need to start taking better care of myself. I've been a little lax lately."

"Well, you've had a lot to contend with," he said, and patted her leg absently, "I'll help share the load in any way I can."

Leah looked down at his hand and smiled. He immediately started figuring the square root of all of the prime numbers starting with two. He grinned back at her, and said, "Well, the broad shoulders I inherited from my father have to be good for something, now don't they?"

She evaded the answer with the announcement, "We're home! Why don't you settle up with the front desk, and I'll bring in the clothes and stuff."

James gave her the room key in answer and said, "I'll be back before you can miss me," blew her a kiss, and wondered why in the hell did he just say and do that?

## *14 The Other James

*August 6, 2013, 9:30 AM*
*London*

James Bradford hung up the phone and studied the note and map in his hand again. None of it made sense. Maybe he should call Eight about it. No, he *definitely* should call Eight about it.

Damn! He had already read the note to Clotilde's sappy—and soon-to-be-ex—husband, James Melbourne. How in the hell was he supposed to know that the contents had to do with the treasure? It appeared to be just an ordinary business envelope, like dozens of others that passed through his hands every week. Well, it didn't say gold or gems on it anywhere, but sure as the sun set in the west, this was a treasure map he was holding. Why else would there be such a cryptic note attached to it? Didn't X always mark the spot? And this one had a double X on it, so it must be twice as valuable.

He put the map on the table and called the cell phone number Eight had given him. "Shit, no answer," he mumbled, "and the effin' voice mailbox is full. Doesn't that asshole know how to delete old messages?" He snorted with disgust. Probably not. Well, if *he* was in charge of this mission—which for the moment, it looked like he was—he'd change the coordinates of the map, at least temporarily for the scan, before emailing it to Melbourne.

Bradford went into the little alcove that was the back office. This was still a club for the enjoyment of its members, and business was never supposed to take place within its walls, but the members had agreed that a multipurpose fax/scanner/copier machine installed for 'recreational' purposes—or at least to facilitate the same—would benefit its members. If one needed directions to, or information about, an event, a quick scan of a hand-drawn map with added details could be copied or sent electronically to a smartphone or computer. Members could quickly and easily share information on their favorite hunting lodges, taverns, or fishing spots.

Or hookers, JB theorized. He had never overheard a comment like that, but these lords and upper class businessmen were males, after all. Names and numbers of women who were a good poke were sure to be shared amongst best mates. After all, that's how he and Eight first got involved. *Hmm, I wonder if that pink-haired tart is still around.*

He shook his head, trying to move the memory of that wild weekend to an empty spot in his brain where he could enjoy it in private at a later time. "Okay, we'll think about her later," he mumbled as he stuck his hand down the front of his trousers to rearrange his stinky bit that had swelled with excitement at the thought of Pinkie.

The map was old parchment. He couldn't just scratch the ink off with his bone-handled penknife or use that white paint-y stuff on the existing X's to cover them up. He'd have to find a way to mask them temporarily, at least long enough for the scan.

He opened up the cabinet of paper stock and looked through it for some of that fancy caramel-colored writing paper. Nope, there were different sizes and thicknesses, but all the paper was white. What he needed was…was a brainstorm.

And then there it was. Poking out of the rubbish can next to him was a football schedule, 'edged' in parchment. Somebody had spilled coffee on their copy and thrown it away.

JB took out a fresh piece of paper, crumpled it up, and dunked it into the half-empty cup of cold coffee on the counter. He squeezed the excess fluid back into the cup and grabbed a fistful of paper from the recycle bin. He placed the coffee-soaked paper between a short stack of misprints and overruns, then used the palm of his hand to express as much as he could into, or onto, the other sheets. It worked, sort of, but his colored copy was still too wet to work with.

Aha! He gathered up his treasure map and note, packaging, and forgery project, and scurried across the hall into the men's room. An iron and ironing board were always on hand for last minute wardrobe touch ups.

He set the temperature to linen and impatiently pressed the sandwiched papers, forcing and cooking out most of the coffee from of the non-absorbent sheet. He was making a mess, but he didn't care—let the butler take care of it. He flipped the stack of pages over and worked the sheets until his crafty little deception material was dry. Voila—artificial parchment! He clutched his precious fabrication and documents close to him, looked up and down the hall to make sure he was alone, and then slithered back to the multipurpose machine.

He held the three sheets of coffee-stained paper next to the map until he found a portion of it that was the right hue. As it turned out, it was the edge of the blotting sheet that was perfect for his patch. He grabbed the shears out of the pencil cup and carefully cut out a rectangle large enough to cover the two original penned X's on the map. He clipped a corner off a strip of cellophane tape and used it to hold the patch in place for the scan. Then it was time to use his true genius: deception.

He grabbed the black felt-tipped marker and made two more X's on the edge of his patch. He had to put them somewhere; he had already read the note to the other James referring to them. Well, they were still on the map, but now they were a whole inch and a half away from where they should be. And since he was the caretaker of the original document, Melbourne would never know the difference.

A couple of clicks and a double fistful of numbers pushed, and the doctored scan was on its way to James Melbourne's smartphone.

JB grinned, proud of his initiative. When he finally got in touch with Eight, he would send *him* the right information. That was if the dolt could ever figure out how to open an attached document on his phone.

JB reached into the supply cabinet and grabbed a fresh manila envelope. He wrote 'Eel Pie Recipes by James Bradford' across the face. Melbourne probably wouldn't be back to retrieve these, and with his name on the envelope, no one else would bother them. Yup, James Melbourne was a genius, all right. He just didn't know that he, JB, James Bradford, 'the other James,' was a bigger one—one big enough to use Melbourne and all his monies and title for his own needs. Baby sister Clotilde would be so proud of him.

# *15 The Letter
*August 6, 2013, Noon*

The same rude clerk from the day before was behind the front desk again today. There was something different about him, though. He looked the same—was wearing the same Ozzy Osborne tee-shirt, still hadn't shaved, and his frayed elastic band still couldn't contain his overabundant hair into a queue—but there was something else. That was it! He had lost his snide, 'why don't you go to hell' attitude. The young man's eyes were shifting, racing back and forth under his uni-brow. Something must be wrong. Yes, Clerk was definitely uncomfortable.

"Good morning, sir; are you checking out now?" he asked in a very professional but stilted manner.

James turned and looked behind him. Clerk had to be speaking to someone else. But there wasn't anyone. Then he saw the reason for the change in character. No one was behind him, but there *was* someone else in the room. A portly gentleman in a dark blue pinstriped suit was sitting on the padded bench near the lamp table in the corner. The bespectacled man with a bad comb-over looked very out of place wearing a jacket and tie. It was another hot and muggy day, and tees and shorts or torn jeans seemed to be the summer uniform of this laid-back southern town. Mr. Pinstripe looked more like he belonged in an oversized leather chair at a board meeting than in a motel lobby.

The stern-faced man had a magazine in his lap, but James saw the clipboard sitting on top of it, his pen ready in hand. The apparent inspector was looking down and just about to write something, when he caught James's gaze. James put on a beatific smile and nodded once as if to say, 'Good day to you,' then turned his attention back to the once-snotty desk clerk.

"No, I will not be checking out today. I'll be here at least until tomorrow." James put the hundred-dollar bill on the counter for the one night's stay and waited for his change. He hadn't noticed it the day before, but now saw the undersized refrigerator with a glass door—like the ones in the markets that held soda and beer for sale—at the end of the counter. There wasn't any beer or soda in this one, though, but it did have small cartons of milks and juices. The display shelf next to it was loaded with mini boxes of cereals and cellophane-wrapped sweet rolls, muffins, and bagels. "How much for the milk, juice, and cereals?" he asked.

"A buck each," the clerk replied mindlessly, then winced as his eyes shifted to the man in the corner, hoping he hadn't been heard.

James smirked at him. He had picked up on the little deception, but didn't make a remark. He'd rather have the clerk owe him one. He took his change and the receipt, turned to leave, then came back around and put both hands on the counter, leaning forward to make his point. "The sign says free continental breakfast, but it doesn't say I have to eat it here in the lobby or lounge, or at any certain time. I think I'll take my breakfast now. Hand me a couple of those milks, orange juices, yellow boxes of cereal, a couple of bagels, and are those cream cheese and jams in there? Yes, I'll take those, too," he said assertively.

A great sense of satisfaction washed over James as he realized that he was being waited on by the man who had been so boorish the day before. His tone changed as he added coolly, "And will you put them in a bag for me?"

The Ozzy devotee grabbed one of the empty bags next to the cereal and started filling James's breakfast order. He brought it to the counter and set it down just a little too hard. James looked over to the man in the suit, and then back to the clerk who was now gulping hard in mortification at his own impetuousness. He choked back his anger at being manipulated by James. "Will there be anything else, sir," he said through clenched teeth.

"Yes, please put in some of those paper napkins, bowls, plates, and plastic service-ware, too. That is, if it's not too much trouble," James whispered, grinning from ear to ear. *Wasn't this what they called instant karma?*

The clerk started to throw the utensils into the bag, then at the last moment, very precisely and with an exaggerated gentleness, placed them in the brown paper sack. "Anything else, *sir*?" he asked, dragging out the last word and giving James a scrunched up, full-face glare, eyebrows touching and chin pinched up to nearly meet his nose.

"Yes," replied James brightly, "have a *nice* day." He picked up the bag with one hand and slapped the counter with the other, intentionally making a loud smack. The clerk and the examiner both jumped at the unexpected noise. "You have a nice day, too," James said, as he nodded to the flustered man in the cheap suit. He pushed the glass door open with a stiff arm, exiting into the noonday sun, the blast of hot summer air setting the smile of satisfaction deep into his face.

James whistled random notes as he tapped on the door for Leah to let him in. "What got into you?" she asked as she stuck her head out the opened door.

"Oh, I was just out—how do you say?—*scoring* lunch. I think this will be easier on your stomach than the pizza and beer." James's attitude suddenly dropped as he remembered the message he had just received from England. "Full or empty?" he asked flatly.

"Full or empty what?" Leah asked, wondering why his mood had once again changed so quickly and dramatically.

"Stomach. Do you want shocking news on a full or an empty stomach? However, with the little history I have with you, I would suggest an empty stomach." James set the bag on the table and started pulling out the fare.

Leah didn't answer with words, but instead grabbed a box of milk and tugged at the top, trying unsuccessfully to open the 'easy open' carton. She pulled and squished, and was getting ready to pull it apart with her teeth, when James said, "Here, let me."

He took a plastic knife, wedged it between the layers of compressed paper, and popped out the pour spout. He handed it to her, and then sat on the end of the bed, hands folded in his lap, jaws clenched, wondering how this was going to play out.

"Thanks," she took a long gulp, "I needed that." She took another slug, and then set the carton down as if it was a stein of beer. She wiped her mouth with an exaggerated flourish and grinned. "Okay, so what's the latest and greatest shocking news in our mystery series?" she asked brightly.

He didn't want to, but needed to, take care of this now. There was no reason to wait to share the information with her—it wouldn't change or become less cryptic with time. He let out a deep sigh, placed his hands on his knees, stood up, and brought the desk chair over to sit at the table beside her. It would help if he could see her face when he showed it to her. He pulled the white envelope out and set it down with his doodles right side up. "What does this mean to you?" he asked.

"Well, my name, that's me." She looked up and laughed at him. "Right, I always try to do the easy ones first. It makes people think I'm smarter than I am. Okay, the date is a week and a half from now. Double XX, that could be extra, extra large size or a very dirty movie, I guess. Trocars and IV tubing are what are used for blood transfusions, and that's a little map. What's all this about?"

"Well, that's the mystery, isn't it?" James asked with a wink and a double eyebrow pop a la Groucho Marx. "Seriously, though, I retrieved one of the messages on the smartphone. It ultimately led to information about an old map that was just sent to me in England."

Leah looked at him like, 'Yeah? So what?'

"Well, the map had a note on it which said that I was to meet *him* at the double X two weeks after my 28th birthday, which would make it this 17th August, and to make sure to have Leah send plenty of IV tubing and various sizes of trocars. Oh, and any other medical supplies as you deem appropriate for the conditions."

Leah grabbed her mouth and ran to the bathroom, barely managing to get the toilet seat up in time to vomit the milk she had just drunk.

James unwrapped a glass tumbler, filled it with water, then grabbed a clean washcloth and wet it. "Here," he said, as he handed it to her, "next time I won't give you a choice."

Leah wiped her mouth. "I hope there isn't a next time. I don't know

111

if my stomach can handle any more of this." She paused for a moment, then looked at James with narrowed eyes. "And no, I am *not* pregnant."

"I didn't say anything!" he said, although the thought had crossed his mind.

"No way, Jose, absolutely no chance of it. I haven't been exposed in ages!" Leah paused and added, "As if it was any business of yours," then snorted, "Hmph!"

James didn't say anything, but went back to the table, sat down, and pulled his smartphone from his pocket. Leah stomped over to the bed, yanked open the Wal-Mart bag with more force than necessary, and pulled out the new toothbrush and travel-sized tube of toothpaste. She threw the plastic and cardboard wrappers at the garbage and missed. "Erggh!" she exclaimed, bent over and picked up her mess, and put it into the trash can. She went to the sink and scrubbed her teeth vigorously, rinsed and spat, then smacked the toothbrush way too hard on the edge the basin to knock off the excess water. She grabbed at the bag again and started flinging clothes out of it, searching for her hairbrush. She finally found it and began tearing at the packaging. "Erggh!" she screeched again as she fought the stiff plastic.

James ignored her temper tantrum. He knew he hadn't done anything wrong—that she was just mad at herself. It wasn't her fault that she had a weak stomach when it came to stress. It was obvious she was trying to be strong, but was frustrated at her body's involuntary reactions. He'd let her calm down at her own rate while he checked to see if he'd received the scanned copy of the map and note.

And there it was. He looked over the map as a whole, then zoomed in on different areas, looking for the XX zone.

He gasped audibly and flushed scarlet as he realized that he'd seen this map before. It was the same map, the 'historical document' he had bought last year. With the help of Leah's mother, the sweet little old lady, Dani Madigan, who was now the time traveling young mother of triplets, Evie—wound up 'returning' to that weird Master Simon fellow.

He was deep in thought, trying to figure out how the map could have come back to him, when he felt the kiss on the back of his neck. Gulp.

"I'm so sorry I flew off the handle. You didn't do anything wrong. I was just so mad that I threw up again. I know you weren't insinuating that I was pregnant. Damn, that seems to be the only thing I can control—whether I get pregnant or not!"

James was listening to her, but was also trying to isolate and hide away that blissful feeling of her lips on his neck. Half a blink later, at the words 'I get pregnant,' the sensation of her kiss returned in full. *Two squared is four. Four squared is sixteen. Sixteen squared is, shoot; I'd better go slower. Three squared is nine. Ah, hell. You don't have time for this. Just talk to her.*

112

He took a deep breath for composure. It had nothing to do with sharing this new, shocking information—it was a physical movement to stifle his effervescent feelings for her, but he didn't want her to know that. "Here, this is a copy of the map that started it all," he said before he lost focus. "I had just bought this map from a stranger outside the museum when I met your mother last year. You did know I met her at that same diner where we had pie, right?"

Leah nodded her head sadly. He continued, "I knew even back then that I had something to do with this map and your mother—sort of a premonition, I suppose."

He felt a slight blush rise with his need to explain himself. He didn't want her to think he was insinuating there was anything inappropriate going on between her mother and him, but Leah nodded—she understood—so he continued.

"I remember telling her that Simon was not revealing everything. I felt that the map, somehow, was important to me. At the time, I was just looking to see if my great-uncle, Lord Julian Hart, fought as a British soldier or turned coat...er...rather, began fighting with the Continental Army. That's how I attained the coin—the coin I showed you yesterday—it was tucked inside the map sheath. And now the map has returned to me, or at least a copy of it has. I...I...I think I'm supposed to go *back*."

# *16 We Need a Plan

"So what are we going to do?" she asked.

"I would suggest that we make a plan. Would you see if there's any stationery in the nightstand over there?" James took out his wallet, pulled out the little silver Greek coin, and examined it closely once again as she brought the paper and pen to the table.

She grinned as she handed him the pen and announced, "Here, I always wanted a secretary."

He smiled back and took the cheap plastic ballpoint pen from her. *Those fingers are so long, beautiful, graceful, and sensibly manicured. Concentrate, man!* "Number one," he said as he wrote the Roman numeral one in the upper left corner. "Take care of old business. That's what you have to do. I put all my affairs in order before I left England. Well, almost. I think I'll have to call my solicitor and review my will. I'm pretty sure I cut out Clotilde two months after... Oh, excuse me; I'm babbling. I'll help you clean out your apartment if you'd like. I'm sure it's going to be very emotional and..."

"And dirty," Leah interrupted. "Here, start another page. We need a shopping list. I could care less about cleaning up the place, but I do want to go through it and see if I have anything left. Write down latex—no, nitrile— disposable gloves and masks."

James looked at her sideways.

"Not Halloween masks, you silly—dust masks. I don't want to get black lung disease from digging through that crap, I mean, my belongings. And we might want some big trash bags and..."

Leah dropped her head onto the tabletop in a controlled flop, pressing her forehead into the Formica. She rolled her head sideways, back and forth a couple of times, then said, "I don't think there's anything there that I care about except my photos. Believe it or not, I was paranoid and put all the old ones in a fireproof safe. All my recent ones are backed up online."

Leah was suddenly quiet. She wanted to be back with her mother, but hadn't thought about much more than that. The how's and why's of getting there made no difference to her. If there was a way, she was going to do it. But now she wanted James to go, too. She popped up and looked at James with a frown of doubt on her face. "So, you're pretty sure you know how to go back, and you'll take me with you, right?"

"Well, I'm not sure that you're supposed to go back with me." He saw the look of terror mixed with anger on her face. He fumbled for a quick response to *the look*. "The note said 'I hope to meet *you* and I'll meet *you*,' but that could mean the plural you. It didn't say that you *weren't* supposed to come along with me, so I guess it would be okay. Why? Do you want to go back?"

"Duh? Yeah! I thought that was what we were going to do. You and me, go back together to see my mother and your great uncle."

"Well, if I'm going back—which it looks like I am predestined to do—then yes, I would like to have you with me. And I certainly wouldn't want you to try to go back by yourself. A single woman back then, traveling alone... No, it would not be a good idea."

Leah pursed her lips in thought, a sly smile creeping in to change her steely, determined expression. Now there was someone in her life who believed her story and who was willing to protect her in this crazy venture. No, she corrected herself, feeling her smile grow into a full-fledged grin— he wanted to protect her. "Hey, are we going to *stay* back?" she asked before thinking.

"To tell you the truth, I hadn't given it a lot of thought. I am shell shocked. I know what I'm supposed to do—what I was asked to do—which is go back with those IV supplies, but I don't know if I'm supposed to go back just to accomplish a deed and then return here, or to stay there. And if you're coming with me, then... I don't know. How do you feel?"

James winced, groaned, shook his head, and said curtly, "Ugh, I mean that is such a female remark, 'How do you feel,' 'Tell me your feelings'?" James saw the quizzical look on Leah's face. "Oh, sorry, I meant no disrespect."

"None taken," she said with just a hint of a giggle. *He's so cute when he acts straight.* She realized that she'd just been asked a question. "Oh, how do I feel? Let's see, hmm, I have a job. That could be a plus, but is actually a neutral. There's the fact that my home just burned down, probably to the ground—that's another neutral. At least there isn't much to pack, or rather dispose of, which would actually make it a slight plus. I have a car, which I can sell it, so that's another neutral. My family? All I have is my mother, and she's back *there*, so that's a big plus for going back and staying back. As far as friends go, I have lots of acquaintances and buddies, but the only one here—other than you, of course—is Billy. He's gay, though, and it's not as if I could settle down and start a family with him. So, since you'll be with me if I go back, and the long-range future here with Billy is chummy and not romantic, I'd say staying here for friends is another neutral. Geez, I don't have even one reason to stay here—or should I say, stay *now*? We didn't even have to tally that one up. How about you? What do you have to come back to?"

James let out a deep sigh. "Pretty much what you said, except my house didn't burn down. I just found out—actually, it was with the same phone call as the news about the map and the note—that I'm a single man again. That was the legal mess I had referred to earlier. I thought I was going to lose everything in the divorce, but the justice system performed just

115

that: justice. I took hiatus from my *position* before I left, the household is set up to take care of itself, trusts are in place for all my assets, and other than verifying that the beneficiary of my will and estate is not *her*, there aren't any other incumbencies. I have no next of kin to worry about. My father—or that would be my older brother, wouldn't it?—is dead."

James frowned in recollection. The man really had seemed like a belligerent older brother rather than a parent. He continued, "My real father—the man I grew up loving as my grandfather—is missing, and I presume is back in the 18th century. I think he's the one who sent the note and map. Lord only knows how he managed that. I know the original letters—remember, we still have to read those—were held in trust and were to be passed down from generation to generation. I believe..."

James stopped talking, leaned back in the chair, and frowned. "I have to figure out what to call everyone now. Martin, his friends called him Marty, is my father. Bruce, who I thought was my father, was really my brother, actually my half-brother. Okay, from now on, fu...forget fathers and grandfathers: it's Bruce and Marty, okay?"

Leah shrugged, trying to hide her uncomfortable grin. "That's fine with me. I didn't know them anyway. Using their first names is a lot less confusing to me. At least Bibb is Bibb since you never called her mother."

"Well, that's another kettle of rotten fish, isn't it?" James said with disgust.

"I won't go there, and you shouldn't either. It doesn't look like she fits into any of this, so let's just drop it, okay? I'm a little sensitive about mother-bashing right now. I'm sorry I even brought her up."

"Oh, Leah, I'm so sorry. God, it's just that I never had a mother. How could I ever miss or be sensitive about someone I never knew?"

Leah held her hand up with the gesture to stop, so he did. She continued, "What about your truck? And how did you get it so quickly? You weren't even in North Carolina for two hours and had a classic Dodge pickup."

"Oh, that. I have an arrangement with Jess Rogers. He lives here in Greensboro. Since I prefer not to use credit cards, I can't rent a car from the usual rental companies. I buy the truck when I get here, then resell it back to him when I'm ready to leave. Of course, he makes a profit, but I also have reliable transportation as long as I care to stay. However, I didn't even think about air conditioning and hadn't realized it got so hot here in the summer. It was quite pleasant last October. So, since you brought it up, do you think Billy would like to have the Dodge? No charge, of course. I like the beast— the truck, that is," James said with a dip of his brow, making sure with eye contact that she understood that he wasn't referring to Billy in a romantic way. "I'd like it to have a good home."

"I'm sure he'd love that. He's into classic muscle vehicles and groans every time he has to rent a truck or RV to go camping. He can't even fit a small tent and ice chest into the back of the 'Vette. Oh, yeah, lists—I want to start another one. What should we take with us? I don't know the whole story of Mom, but I know she didn't go back on purpose, and probably didn't have anything but the clothes on her back. Oh, and her smartphone, but I digress. What should we take back?"

James turned the pen over in his hand thoughtfully. "Technology— not necessarily stuff, but the knowledge of how to fabricate needful things."

"Ooh, ooh," Leah exclaimed, bouncing up and down like a five-year-old trying to get the kindergarten teacher's attention. "I had this book in grade school. Actually, Mom got it for me, and she liked to read it, too. I think it was 'The Way Things Work' or something like that. If I still had it, it probably burned up, but I'm sure we can get another one at a bookstore. Hey!" she added, as if she was having rapid-fire brainstorms, "I'll bet I can download it, too. We can download all sorts of books, and if we have too many, well, memory cards are small and can be discreet. We can even put them in a wallet and have a whole library of information in a little card holder the size of my palm."

James tilted his head and winched. "I don't know about that. I think that's cheating and messing with the whole great scheme of things...or God's Plan, or whatever you want to call it. The letter just said to bring the IV tools—if that's what you would call them—and any other medical items that *you* deemed fit."

"Okay, but how about duct tape? Mom said you could fix anything with duct tape and WD40, but I don't think I want to take an aerosol can. Did you know you can remove warts with duct tape?"

"No, and I'm glad I never needed to find out. I'll concede to the duct tape," James started writing out his list, "and maybe the one book. But remember, that could be dangerous. People back then were still very superstitious. They were burning witches just a few years earlier. Hey, how about you make a copy of the book with pen and ink so it doesn't have photographs and color illustrations? It would look like da Vinci's Codex. That way it wouldn't be suspicious if it did fall into the wrong hands." He bent over the list and wrote: pen, ink, paper for Codex copy of Works book.

James felt Leah's eyes on him and brought up his head to stare back. It was almost as if she was putting thoughts into his head. "You don't think," he asked, his head turning slowly side to side, "that Leonardo da Vinci was a time traveler, do you?"

"Leonard Vincent was the name of a 20th century time traveling genius according to some theories I've heard. I think there are a few science fiction novels out there about him, too. Well, I guess we'll just have to be more discreet so *our* Codex is never found. Hmm, what else do we need to take? Food: I have a great recipe for granola. I can throw together a batch with or without an oven. Mom always made it for long trips. It won't need refrigeration and... Oh, my God, do you know how to hunt? We can't possibly take enough food for the two of us for even a week."

"Yes, I do. Grandpa—I mean, Marty—made sure I knew how to use and maintain rifles and handguns, that I could call and track game, and that I also knew how to clean and prepare what I shot. That was the rule for fishing and hunting: you kill it, you clean it. Of course, we considered it an honor to cook the meat ourselves. It was a good thing, too. Our cook didn't want to touch it—no way, no how. 'How disgusting,' she said. 'You don't even know what it's been eating'. 'Well, no, I don't, grand...er, Marty...would reply, but I do know who'll be eating it!" James paused, then added. "But I don't have a rifle *or* a gun. How hard is it to get either one or both of them?"

"Actually, pretty easy, but I don't know what the waiting period is, so that's probably something we should do today. Hey, I'm feeling better. Hand me a bagel and some of that cream cheese, please. It looks like we're going to have a long afternoon."

# *17 Apartment Clean Up

James pushed aside the paperwork and set the table for a light lunch.

"I think we should go to the apartment and see what state it's in before we get too carried away," Leah said between bites of bagel, cream cheese, and strawberry jam. "I know it makes more sense to go get the cleaning supplies first, but I want to go check it out right away. Hey, would you share the last milk with me? I'm not afraid of your germs."

James choked back his thoughts before they became full visuals about how he'd rather swap spit with her in another way. He cleared his throat, pushed the carton towards her, and concentrated on what caliber of gun he should buy. A handgun would be the easiest to carry and conceal. Ammunition would be needed, too. Black powder was available in the late 18th century, as was shot, but he needed to make sure he took plenty of brass shell casings and a portable reloading kit. Great, thinking about guns and ammo was the distraction he needed. She was so sexy, provocative, and desirable, without even trying. Good grief! What would he do if she ever decided to 'turn it on'? *Stifle that thought, Melbourne! Get back to distracting yourself with caliber size and should the gun have a clip or be a revolver.*

Their light lunch finished, the two were ready to take care of old business: Leah's apartment clean up. Once that was done, they could devote all of their time and energies into preparing for their journey into the past and the semi-known. It wasn't totally unknown, after all. They did know much about what had happened—or was going to happen—thanks to history books and museums. Optimistically, they would find her mother and whoever—hopefully it was Marty—had sent James the map and the note.

Ж

The two of them pulled into the apartment complex parking lot and saw several large black plastic bags on Leah's front porch and her burned-beyond-salvage couch lying sideways on the lawn. Her front door was open, and rock and roll music was blaring from within so loudly that the windows were shuddering. Leah showed no fear as she led the way inside, James following closely behind her. He didn't know what they were walking into, but robbers didn't bag up messes and leave them on the lawn, nor did they have loud party music playing as they rousted a place.

"Hey, there!" Billy called out to them from behind a pile of burned and singed bedding and towels, his hand waving broadly overhead. "Here, let me turn this down."

Leah's bare-chested neighbor slid the volume bar down on the oversized boom box that sat on the floor under the window. "They don't make them like this anymore, do they? Man, you can actually *feel* the bass tones!" Billy wiped his hands on the red rag that was stuffed into the front pocket of his cutoff blue jeans. "Hey, how's it goin', man?" he said to James.

James nodded a tacit 'okay,' and Billy continued in his hyper, happy mode, "And how's my sweetheart? Here, give me some sugar."

Leah leaned in and gave him a quick kiss on his exaggerated puckered lips, then took a step back to see what he had been up to in her burned-out abode.

James turned away from the little show and rolled his eyes, not knowing whether he was disgusted, jealous, or amused. It was probably more jealousy, so he decided to give himself a break on the math facts and study the damage to the apartment. That would take just as much concentration.

The bedroom seemed to have been the first site of attack. All her clothes had been pulled out of the closet and drawers, and thrown onto the bed. The covers were pulled back, and the mattress turned halfway around, as if someone had looked underneath it. Evidently, the thieves had brought a propane torch and can of lighter fluid with them. The clothes were burned where they had been thrown. The bed was charred in places, and had smoldered, but the bedding and clothes were burnt beyond use. The plastic-laminated dresser hadn't burned, but the arsonists had smashed the drawers and broken the mirror. Too bad for them—they were sure to have at least seven years bad luck for their felonious caper.

"The kitchen was actually worse," Billy said, bringing James out of his shock at seeing the wanton destruction. "They were probably mad that they'd gone to all that effort then didn't find what they wanted. Your car was here, Leah, and you were out of the apartment. That meant to them that it was easy pickings. They didn't realize that it was a secure pool area, so you would have taken your keys with you. Look, they didn't even want your jewelry. Here, I bagged it." Billy handed her a plastic baggie containing earrings, bracelets, and necklaces. "The jewelry box was smashed, probably because they didn't have your keys. They also did a number on the bathroom. Be careful in those sandals. The mirror broke into a million pieces. Apparently you didn't have much in there—all they left were some OTC pain killers, ointments, and Band-Aids."

Leah ignored the comment, went into the bathroom, opened the linen closet, and peered inside, staring as if she couldn't remember what she was looking for.

Billy led James into the combined kitchen/dining/living room area. "Your table is intact," he called back to Leah. "I guess they didn't see a need to smash it to see if anything was hidden inside."

James looked up and yes, Billy was grinning at his own little nonsense joke. He grinned back. *Billy was a nice cop and a nice man—silly, but nice.*

Billy nodded towards Leah as he looked at James, raising his eyebrows, asking wordlessly, 'Well, did you?'

James answered him with a scowl and a sharp head shake.

Billy mouthed, 'Oh, poor baby.'

James's nonverbal reply was a glare and a wide head shake. He wasn't going to ruin his relationship with her. They were on the right, but narrow, path. The two of them had a chance at a great life ahead of them. He didn't want to blow it by moving too fast. James kept shaking his head side to side as Billy chortled without noise at the frustration he knew the British import must be experiencing.

James couldn't help but return the sentiment, and inadvertently slipped, letting out an audible chuckle.

A bathroom cabinet door shut with a clap. "What's going on in there, you two?"

"Nothing, dear," they replied in unison, then looked at each other, and laughed out loud.

"I don't believe it," she said dryly, and came into the kitchen, "but I don't think I want to know, either," then grinned.

"That's for sure," James said, before he could stop himself. *Fool! Quick—change the subject! She probably thinks you meant there 'was' something going on that she wouldn't want to know about.*

"How much of this do you want to keep, Leah?" James asked as he turned to look away from her. *Don't let her see your face. You might be transparent. She might see that there really wasn't anything going on, that there isn't—and couldn't be—any attraction between you and Billy. You don't want to have to explain, 'No, I'm not gay—you're the one who I think is sexy.' That would ruin this wonderful, blossoming-into-a-field-of-lilies platonic relationship. Okay, so the decimal equivalent of pi is 3.1415926535...*

Billy cleared his throat to get Leah's attention and spare more embarrassment for James. "Oh, and by the way, sweetie, I called the insurance company for you. Remember that you told me I needed to get renters insurance? Well, I got it last year, and from the same place you got yours. Well, I kind of fibbed and told them that you had asked me to call for you. Since they had to come out and assess the smoke damage to my unit, would they please check on yours at the same time? They're due here any minute. All they need is a quick look-see and a signature. They said they'd hand us checks on the spot." Billy's babbling stopped and his voice turned to one of concern. "Are you okay, honey?"

James had been listening to their conversation from the other side of the room and rushed to her when he heard the question. He grabbed Leah by the shoulders, turned her to him, and looked deep into her eyes to see what was wrong. They were wide and unblinking, her breathing shallow. She looked as if she was in shock.

"Come outside with me," he said, and gathered her close, walking beside her as if they were in a three-legged race without a leg band. He led her into the muggy but fresh noontime air.

"Billy, would you get her a wet washcloth, please?" he hollered, and then turned his full attention back to Leah. He put his hands on her cheeks and brought her face towards his, locking his eyes onto hers. "Look, you are mine, and I am going to take care of you, no matter what, do you understand?"

Leah nodded. James wanted to talk to her subconscious before she snapped out of whatever momentary shock she had slipped into and before Billy came out with the cloth. "You are not allowed to freak out or panic or worry about anything. You are mine, and I am going to take care of you. Now, say it."

"I am yours, and you will take care of me," she said, still in a daze. "I am yours, and you will..." The last part of her mantra was muffled into James's chest as he grabbed her to him when Billy came outside with the washcloth.

"It took a minute to find one that wasn't all sooty. Is she going to be okay?" he asked, as he placed the cloth into James's hand.

"She'll be fine. She is mine, and I am going to take care of her," he declared to himself and to Billy. He smiled as he pulled away from her, gently pushing aside her hair so he could place the damp white terrycloth on her brow.

Billy grinned. He knew it was true—his gut told him so. He was happy about it, too. "Can I be the best man?" he asked lightheartedly.

"Sure," Leah said dreamily. "You can be the maid of honor, too."

"No, I'll settle for best man, but I just might wear pink lace panties for the occasion," he joked. "Now, on a serious note..." Billy looked at James to see if they should continue on the serious note. James nodded his head. The two of them weren't psychic, but when it came to taking care of her needs, they were both on the same wavelength.

Before Billy could say anything else, though, Leah started in, her slow-witted, stalled speech quickly accelerating with each new thought, finally ending with a fast-paced repartee. "Everything material I care about is in the safe. I'd like to take it back to the motel and look through it there. After I do that, Billy, would you keep it for me? Oh, and I'll need another drivers license since my purse probably burned in the fire. And I want to get a gun—no, two guns. I don't think James can have one, but I can have two, can't I? And when is that insurance person coming? I'm thirsty, can I get a drink?"

Leah was now spewing questions and comments rapidly, almost on top of one another. She paused when she saw the two men staring at her.

"Why are you two looking at me like that? I'm fine, really I am," she said, finally back to her normal tone and pace.

Billy pulled his shoulders back, glanced at James, and then answered only one of her questions. "Uh, yeah, a drink. I have cold water, tea, and beer in the fridge. What's your poison?" Billy asked, looking first at Leah, then at James, and then back at her.

"Well, if I marry an Englishman, I'd better start getting used to drinking tea, right, dear?" she whispered as she batted her eyelashes at James and grinned. Then she poked him in the belly with her index finger, taking him by surprise, and announced in a perky voice, "Let's drink over there in the shade, though. It stinks inside."

Billy went into his apartment and quickly came out with two beers and a bottle of lemon tea. James hadn't indicated his preference of liquid refreshment, but Billy was sure that after Leah's little surprise remark about marriage, a beer—or six—was in order for his new friend.

# *18 Peter Anthony

The three of them drank their brews in the shade, enjoying the comfortable silence—the men lying sideways on the lawn, peeling the labels from their bottles of beer, and Leah, back against the Sumac tree, an all-knowing grin spread across her face—a little she-Buddha without the belly. Letting out long, contented sighs, she looked to be at peace, nothing like the panicked little girl in the kitchen ten minutes earlier. She gazed out, not looking at anything, but instead looking *beyond* everything—beyond the buildings, the parking lot, up through the clouds, to the emptiness out further still.

The men had finished their beers, and Billy was just about to ask James if he wanted—or needed—another one, when he saw a man in a straw hat carrying a briefcase approach the front door of Leah's apartment. He jumped up and shouted, "We'll be right there," to the man in the lightweight, pale blue seersucker suit.

"Looks like we had a little barbecue that got out of control," the stranger joked as Billy approached him. He was young, blonde, and had an athletic build. The suit fit him well as far as cut went, but he looked as if he should be barefoot, in a Speedo on a swimming team, rather than shod, in a three-piece suit, carrying an attaché case.

"Hi, Peter Anthony, and I'm here to do the on-site assessment and," he patted the side of his briefcase, "disbursement of funds for the losses and inconvenience. Is that Ms. Madigan?" he asked, as he looked at Leah coming up the concrete sidewalk. James was walking one step behind her, looking intently at, and sizing up, the new man in the neighborhood.

"Peter Anthony, at your service," he said, and took a step forward, offering his hand. Leah shook hands with him, then pulled back, moving softly and securely into James's body, her new comfort zone. "Now, was there a police report on this? What I have in my notes is that this was a case of arson and incidental damage to your," he looked at Billy and bit his bottom lip, "apartment. William Burke, is it?"

"No," grinned Billy, "just Billy Burke. No Billy Bob or Billy Jo, just Billy Burke."

The insurance man chuckled. "Okay, just Billy Burke, do you happen to have a copy of the police report?"

"Yes, I do. Let's go inside. It still stinks in there, but at least it's cool. Would you like a beer? We have iced tea and cold water, too." Billy, excited at meeting the new, good-looking blonde, practically bounced as he led the way into his apartment.

It was obvious to Leah and James that the attraction was shared between the two men. "Oh, you're a police officer," Peter had drawled when he saw that Billy was the one who had filed the report. "That's such a dangerous and exciting job. I'll bet you have lots of interesting stories to tell," he said, actually batting his eyelashes at Billy with his last remark.

"Yes, there's somebody for everyone," James said softly under his breath at seeing the giddiness that was overwhelming the two new acquaintances. It also appeared that Leah was getting a contact high from the friskiness the two men were barely holding in check. She looked up and smiled at James, then turned into his chest and rubbed her nose into it. His flesh tingled in response. *Oh, to hell with math problems—let her look.*

Leah and Billy got checks, business cards, and a hearty handshake out of Peter before he left. "If there is anything else you need, don't hesitate to call. I think we found everything, but if there are any other losses that weren't itemized, let me know. I'll be glad to rectify any oversights."

Leah snorted at the word 'rectify,' and James elbowed her to get her to hush. But Peter hadn't noticed. He had eyes only for Billy. James noticed that the business card Peter had given Billy had handwriting on the back. He sighed at the righteousness of the situation. He was taking Leah from Billy, but the way of the world had put Peter in his life. It looked like Billy wouldn't be lonely.

Leah reflected his feelings verbally—evidently she had been thinking the same thing. "You know, God has a way of making everything right. I'll be leaving with you and, up until an hour ago, it looked as if Billy would be left alone. But see, God has it all under control. Peter seems like a nice man. It's not often you meet a nice man who's a hunk, too." Leah looked up at James, reached up and felt his biceps, and cooed, "Ooh, nice," then put her hand on his shoulder and placed a soft—almost, but not quite sisterly—kiss on his shocked lips, "Nice." She knocked some soot off of the front of her sundress and returned to the business at hand: clean up.

"You know, I'll bet I can take some of this money," she said, and waved the check in the air, "and hire someone to take care of this mess. The carpet, walls, cabinets, and all of that are the responsibility of that greedy so and so landlord. Doesn't the Salvation Army have a list of people looking for odd jobs? Billy...hey, Billy, I'm talking to *you*. James doesn't know anyone around here 'cept you and me."

"Oh, don't worry; I'll take care of it. I know the man who's in charge of the halfway house. Those guys need work and like getting out, even if it is to a hot, smoky apartment." Billy sighed at what appeared to be nothing, but James and Leah knew what it was: he was in lust.

All of a sudden, Billy frowned. "Leah, why do you want two guns? You're not going to go out and do something stupid, are you?"

"No, nothing stupid; but if I said it was for protection, you'd tell me no, that I'd just be asking for trouble. James and I are going...um...on a camping trip, and I want something in case a bear or mountain lion or something attacks us. I think we should both have one, but he isn't a citizen.

Hey, when we're married, he'll be a citizen by default because I am, right?"

"You weren't joking were you?" asked Billy.

"Um, about what? I don't recall making any jokes, dumb or otherwise, at least in the last hour or two." Leah said with a mischievous smile.

Billy looked over at James who was beaming as if it had just been confirmed that he had both won the lottery and found the cure for cancer. Billy shook his head at Leah. "You have known this man for what, 24 hours, and you're going to marry him?" James lost his smile at the remark. Billy continued, "Well, if it was anyone other than this Limey here, I'd arrest him on something just to keep him away from you, then tie *you* up and stash you in the closet until you came to your senses. But," he dragged out the anticipation, "I think you two will do fine together. If ever two people just seemed right for each other from the get go, it's you two. Oh, and yes, he'll be an American citizen, or at least have dual citizenship, *if* he marries you. Now, tell me you aren't going to marry him just so he can have a gun permit."

"Nope, not for the gun permit and not for all the money he has—which from what I understand, there's quite a bit of—but no," Leah said, shaking her head and grinning, "that's not why."

James squirmed with discomfort at the mention of money—he'd been that route with a woman. Leah didn't seem the type, but he could be wrong. He'd been wrong before.

"I had an epiphany," Leah said with pride. "I was freaked out, and then all of a sudden, it was clear. I didn't need to worry about anything, James will take care of me and any problems that come my, our, way. It was as if my life had been fuzzy, like I had had Vaseline in my eyes. Now all is clear and fresh and bright and, well, just wonderful. Any *problems* we may have being married can be overcome, I'm sure."

James and Billy shared a look when she stressed the word 'problems' with just a bit of irony. Evidently, she still wanted James even if he was gay. James stayed stoic for the rest of the revelation, but Billy had to cover his mouth and pretend to cough in order to hide a chuckle. Oh, she had a big surprise coming if she—when she—decided to consummate the marriage. A big, happy surprise.

## *19 Safe, I Do's, and a Truck

"Now where's that safe?" Billy asked, as he made his way toward the bedroom. "I'll load it into the back of your car for you." He kicked aside a pile of molten no-longer-identifiable plastic. "Man, there's sure a lot of crap around here. Sorry 'bout that Leah, but I swear you didn't have this much stuff before the fire. If I didn't know better, I'd swear that someone came in and dropped off their garbage in here. There's more trash than the dumpster can handle, that's for sure."

Leah grabbed the broom out of the closet and used it to knock around some of the piles of burnt clothing and shoes. The thieves had actually yanked out all the cleaning supplies and the vacuum, looking for their treasure. The broom hit the once tan, but now smoke-streaked gray, fireproof safe. "Here it is," she called out.

Billy squatted down in front of the blackened and blistered box, and inspected the lock. He rubbed his thumb across the stark flash marks at the keyhole where the bandits had used a torch to try to open it. "They didn't hurt it. These were built to be fire resistant, so the propane torch didn't faze it." Billy tilted it forward to get his hands under it, then it fell back on his fingers. "Dang! That sucker's heavy!"

"Here, let me show you a trick," James said. "Hand me the broom, would you, Leah?" He tipped the top of the safe back, then shoved the broom handle under the front of it, making room for his fingers underneath. He was crouched in front of it, ready to pull it to him and lift, when she screeched.

"Wait!" She snatched the rag from Billy's pants pocket. "Get up," she ordered.

James stood up and stepped back, and Leah moved in to wipe the heavy soot and peeled paint from the safe. "We don't want you to get filthy, now, do we? We still have lots to do. I don't want to have to wash laundry, too." She stepped back, then nodded to let him know he could proceed.

"Do you need some help there?" Billy asked, a bit chagrined that James had hefted the safe with such ease.

"You can make sure nothing's in my way and open the boot. I can't see my feet."

Leah sang out, "I'll get the trunk," and rushed ahead to the car. She fidgeted with her keyring to find the right button to unlock the trunk, popped it open, and froze.

"Excuse me," James said, standing behind her, holding the safe, which seemed to be getting heavier by the second. He repeated himself, but Leah still didn't move out of the way. "Is there a problem?" he asked loudly. "Hello? Hello?"

"Oh, oh," she stammered, coming to her senses. She huffed as she tried to compose herself, but stayed where she was, facing the contents of the trunk. "No, no problem, it's just this." She picked up the little beige plastic bin and turned around to show it to James. It held the green calico dress and ivory-colored silk handkerchief her mother had left behind when she was kidnapped from the hospital. Leah moved aside as if in a trance, allowing James to put the safe down.

"What is it?" James asked, as he brushed the ashy dust off of his hands.

Leah looked up at him, then around and behind him. She wanted to make sure they were alone. Billy hadn't followed them; he was still back at the apartment.

"This is the dress my mother was wearing when she came *back*. And the hankie she had. I was going to have Abby down at the crime lab test it to see if she could match it with the DNA from my mother's hairbrush, the one she had left here last fall. Except the hairbrush was still in the apartment, and I think it's too crispy to check now."

"Well…" He sighed loudly, paused, then spoke softly, "We don't need to prove anything to anyone now, do we? We—you and I—know it was her, and no one else needs to be in on it. Besides, anyone else would just think we'd sniffed or smoked something illegal, or gone completely insane. Now, are *you* going to be okay?"

"Yes," she said proudly, suddenly snapping out of her momentary funk. "I just remembered, I am not allowed to freak out, panic, or worry about anything. I have someone to take care of me—and everything or anything that comes my way. And the good news is, my purse is back here, too. I won't have to get another drivers license. I also have my debit card, so I won't have to ask you for any more money."

Leah placed her hand on the back of James's arm, "Come on. Let's go back inside. Billy's probably wondering what happened to us. I'll leave everything in the car for now. It looks like I have my traveling outfit and won't have to go shopping for a dress to wear. That's something else to add to our list, Mister Secretary: clothing for you and shoes for us. Man, I *love* having a secretary!"

"And I *love* having a chauffeur," James added in the same bright tone.

Billy came out of his apartment with two huge bags of trash and added them to the existing pile of rubbish. "Looks like you could use a truck there, Billy," suggested James. He reached into his pocket and took out his two-part keyring with the truck keys. He pulled back on the coupler, separating his half with the little LED flashlight and one set of keys. He held up the other half to Billy. Billy's hand opened automatically and caught the keys as James dropped them. "The round one is to the door lock and the square-ish one is for the ignition. Do you think you can figure out a push button gearbox, or do you want me to show you?"

"Whoa, really? That would be awesome! I mean, I'm sure I can figure out how to shift with push buttons." He let out a low whistle. "That is a *fine* truck," and turned around to appreciate the vintage Dodge muscle truck again. "Hey, why don't you two just go do...um...whatever. I have this," he used his head to point to Leah's torn-apart apartment, "under control. Actually, I am getting paid for this. It's still an arson investigation. Those two creeps who attacked you yesterday knew about the fire, but wouldn't give us the names of their cohorts. Too bad I couldn't use a little of this on them," he said, and lifted the end of the rubber water hose on the grass with his foot.

"Uh," Leah's eyes widened at the suggestion of violence and coerced information. James looked at Billy and shook his head rapidly, but Billy had already seen the result of his gaffe.

"Just kidding," he said, hoping she would believe him. "Hey, I think you'd better get out of the sun. You're looking a little ragged. James, why don't you take her to a nice, cool restaurant for an early dinner?"

"Come on, sweetheart," James said, as he put his arm around her shoulders, "I'll treat and you drive." He gave her a big-brotherly kiss on the top of her head, then looked up to see Billy grinning at the two of them. "Thanks for everything, Billy. I don't know how she—we—could have handled it without you."

"I'm glad I could help. You know, to protect and to serve... Just go have a nice evening, and have a piece of pie for me, hear?" he said and waved them good-bye.

## *20 A Birth Certificate Needed

James held the car door open for Leah, then walked around and got in. He took his pen and the folded up motel stationery notebook from his shirt pocket and rattled off his notes, transcribing on his thigh-top desk as he enumerated, "Shoes-Leah, me; clothes-me; backpack-Leah, IV stuff-Leah, guns-me…"

Leah cut in excitedly. "Hey, you forgot to put down that we have to get married! I'm pretty sure there's a waiting period for both that and the guns. We should probably get hitched first, though, because I don't think it takes as long. It's still early; maybe we can make it to the courthouse before they close." She took a breath, then continued rapidly, "Let's see; my birth certificate is in the safe; I'll need that. I'm sure you'll need your divorce papers, too. Hmm, I don't know how the rest of this'll work since you're not a US citizen. Maybe I should call first and see what we need. They might get kind of fussy about that part."

"Slow down a bit," James said. Leah took her foot off the gas and lightly touched the brake. "No, not literally," he clarified, and she came back up to speed. "Let's go back to the motel first and get your birth certificate and anything else you need out of the safe. I'll call my solicitor and have him fax a copy of the divorce papers there. I'm sure the motel has a fax machine. This way we can have everything we need *before* we go, okay?"

"Yes, dear," she replied contentedly. "I'll let you take care of everything. Just let me know what you want me to do."

James didn't say a word, only nodded. *Could he have really hypnotized her when she was in that stunned state less than an hour ago? She was certainly agreeable to anything he said or wanted, both voiced and tacit. Time would tell if the power of suggestion wore off or not. He was willing to wait and see. They still had a journey to make. A journey back in time sounded crazy, but doing it with her as his wife seemed a lot more logical. She was cute, smart, and perky, and now he'd have someone to list as beneficiary and heir to his estate if they did decide to come back.*

The two returned to the motel room and its cool but stale air in a comfortable silence. James set the safe on the floor, not sure that the motel's flimsy, general-purpose table would support its weight. The lock hadn't been damaged by the fire, and its key was still on her big brass keyring. It was time for the lady to investigate.

Leah sat cross-legged in front of her treasure trove of history, thumbing through the salvaged documents, pausing briefly to share a photo of herself and her mother on her first birthday. Leah had been a bald-headed baby, but already had big, beautiful, hazel eyes. Both mother and daughter's faces were covered with chocolate icing and smiles.

James gasped, shocked at how much Leah looked like her mother, Dani, as she was known in the 20th and 21st centuries. A sudden wonderful thought caused his mouth to curl up into a full smile. If all went as planned, he and Leah would make beautiful babies, too.

While his fiancée was blissfully reminiscing with her pictorial history, James made his phone call to England. The solicitor's secretary was working late, congratulated him on the outcome of the divorce, and said she was more than happy to help him, assuring him that the copies would be faxed immediately.

James stepped out into the hot afternoon sun and strolled through the parking lot toward the lobby, pausing to examine the dried up blossoms on the gardenia bush outside the entryway, allowing an extra minute or two for the documents to be sent. He'd have to get used to the intense heat. August in Greensboro was certainly nothing like summers in London, or even in the country. He had found the last two days tolerable with air conditioning, but they wouldn't have that comfort where they were going— or rather 'when' they were going.

The clerk was still behind the counter when he walked in, but the examiner was gone. So was the lad's bad attitude. "Sorry about being such a dick the past two days," he said, eyes cast down in shame. "You wouldn't believe the crap that's been going on. My brother got busted and is in jail on assault charges. He's such an idiot! It's not your problem, and I shouldn't have been so rude. And this morning, well, I could have lost my job if you'd complained. I'm trying to get back on track, and it hasn't been easy. *Pax?*" he asked with a slight grimace, eyes wide in hope.

"*Pax,*" James replied, and shook his hand, giving him total forgiveness. "Life's too short for grudges. Now, did I just receive a facsimile?" He nodded to the machine in the back that was making the screeches and flat tones of one fax machine talking to another.

The clerk went back and grabbed the short pile of papers. "Are you Lord James Melbourne?" he asked sheepishly.

James nodded and said, "That I am," and accepted the documents. "Thank you, and I hope everything works out for you and your brother."

The clerk gave him a nod from the shoulders, as if he was deciding whether he was supposed to bow to royalty or not. James put up his hand to stop him and shook his head, turned around, and then pushed open the glass door, back into the hot muggy summer air.

James had the copies of his divorce papers in hand as he walked into the room. "Oh, aren't I doing a good enough job as secretary?" he asked when he saw what she was doing.

Leah had another piece of paper on the table. This one was a reclaimed sheet of yellow legal pad paper, probably from the safe. "I was thinking about all the *stuff* we should take back and what my mother would want. I mean, if she had known she was going back, what would she have wanted to take with her? Well, she loves two things, not counting me because I'm not a thing. Anyway, she loves gardening and sewing. I can't bring her back bolts of fabric because of the weight, but from what I can see of this dress, the thread is irregular. I can throw in some spools of thread or maybe just one of those jumbo ones. And gardening; there are so many food plants she could grow. Seeds would be easy to take back and would give the biggest return. I've got my debit card and, shoot, I might as well spend my money.

"I—we—can go to the library and use the computers there," she continued. "I can order online and get everything rushed here to the motel. I know of one company that packs their seeds in hermetically sealed foil envelopes. Even if I fell in a creek carrying them, they'd be fine. And before you scold me, I'll make sure I only get heirloom varieties. I wouldn't want to upset the natural timeline. However, I *would* like to throw in some seedless watermelon seeds. Spontaneous mutations happen all the time, and I believe something like that would be okay, don't you?"

"How do you get seeds for a seedless watermelon? No, never mind; I don't need to know. Just make sure you fabricate a little bag of some kind to stash them in. I know it's important that they be sealed, and foil packets are lighter weight and safer than putting the seeds in glass bottles, but I still feel funny about taking back current technology. We need to make sure we're discreet."

"Revolutionary War era clothing reproductions would be easier to find online, too," Leah said. "Well, maybe. There are a lot of re-enactors in this area, but I don't know if they'd give up or sell the shirts off their backs. The library will be a great place for us to work. First off, it's cool and bright. There's lots of desk space, too, so I can do the copying of the 'Works' codex, and you can create your maps. There's only so much research you can do on the internet, too. So much is still only in books. I don't think the written word will ever disappear. At least, I hope not."

Leah bent over the yellow paper on the table, focused on her work, her eyes and mouth moving along with her thoughts and penned lines. James stood by the doorway, holding the fax papers he had just received. He looked them over, not comprehending what he was reading. "Hey," he asked suddenly, "you said your mother liked to sew. Can *you* sew?"

"Sure, simple stuff—like bags or pillow cases." Leah looked over at James, grinned, and shook her head slowly. "I don't think I'll be making my own wedding dress, though," she added, and watched for his reaction.

Shocked and befuddled, James tossed the papers in the air, as if he'd just been goosed. Leah laughed as he grabbed and slapped wildly, trying to retrieve the flying documents before they hit the floor. He bent over, red-faced in embarrassment, and gathered the rest of them from the carpet. He bit his bottom lip as he brought the slippery mess to the table, and concentrated on arranging the papers, trying to compose himself, shifting them around so they all faced the same direction, not worrying if they were in order or not. He wasn't ready to read them—that was obvious. Maybe he'd just hand them to the clerk as they were.

Leah stopped giggling; he had suffered enough humiliation. "Why did you want to know if I could sew?" she asked, still smirking.

"I was just wondering if you needed help in that area. I've done a little stitching in my time. I might be able to help with that task."

Leah's urge to giggle returned at the thought of this hunky man sitting on a settee with an embroidery sampler in his lap, a wicker basket full of colored flosses, a pair of stork-shaped scissors at his side.

"I guess I'd better make a note for us to go to the fabric store." James said, ignoring her tittering. He picked up the green calico fabric from the beige tub. "So this is the dress your mother wore?" he asked, although he knew that it was.

Leah nodded. "I guess I'd better try it on in case it needs altering. She used to be big...what am I saying? You met her last year. But she looked to be my size now. Here, let me go change."

James took the dress out of the bin and held it up for inspection. "Uh, I think this will need a little work," he said, sticking his finger through the hole in the bodice over the heart area.

"Eww! I'll have to make a little patch. I didn't notice it the other night." She started to recall that first night, when she had sung 'Some Enchanted Evening' while dancing around her cluttered living room with her mother's dress as her partner. "Not now," she mumbled softly, then continued aloud, "It looks like someone at the hospital went ahead and washed the blood out of it. I'm not squeamish, but that would have really sent me over the edge. But that hole—the dress would be perfect except for that. Damn! This calico print is over 200 years old. What are the chances I'll be able to find fabric just like it for a patch?"

"I'd say pretty good," James answered, even though he knew it was a rhetorical question, that she had just been rambling, and hadn't expected an answer.

"Huh—what the...?" Leah bit off the words of chastisement that were trying to break past her lips. Who was he, trying to tell her that finding 200-year-old fabric was a breeze?

"Look at the hem. See, there's about a three-inch hem in the dress. Just cut out a matching swatch, make your patch with some of that iron-on sticky stuff, and no one but you and your laundress will know that a musket ball went through."

Leah winced when she heard the word 'musket ball.' "Sorry," James said. "We know she's okay, though, right?"

"Yeah, Mom's a tough old broad. Whether she's in the body of a sixty year old or a seventeen year old, she can handle just about anything that comes her way, whether it be musket balls or strange little men with magic potions that knock you—rather me—on my butt."

Leah took the dress from him with a sincere smile—Mom was still alive and she was going to go see her very soon. Rather than try on the garment in the cramped little bathroom, though, she pulled her sundress off over her head right where she stood. At least now she had panties and a bra. Besides, he was gay—it wouldn't bother him.

James picked up the yellow note sheet of seeds to buy and checked to see if she had included muskmelons. Whether they were called cantaloupes, *casabas,* or muskmelons, he wanted to make sure they brought back seeds for them. He glanced over at the movement behind him. He quickly turned back to the paper. She was practically naked, wearing nothing but her underclothes! Why didn't she change in the bathroom?

*Because she thinks you're a gay man, Melbourne! At least she's partially clothed. Her underthings aren't much more revealing than her bathing suit. Count backwards, man; from a thousand—and in Latin. Don't let her know...*

"See, perfect fit," Leah declared, as she walked over to the table, sashaying the skirts back and forth, ending with a dip reminiscent of a curtsey.

"Very nice, the green brings out the color in your eyes," James said, then quickly changed the subject, unsure if he could conceal his awe at how beautiful she was. "Now, do you want to finish up here before we go shopping again?" *Cool, shopping was such an unpleasant task, he didn't need any mind-masking thoughts; it was its own.* "And what are you doing here?" he asked, pointing to her diagram.

Leah contained her chuckle. She knew she had embarrassed him, and he was just changing the subject. "Let's make it later for the shopping, if that's okay with you. I was just designing my little stash bags. I want to have hidden compartments in them. I can hide the packs of seeds—or whatever else needs to be discreet—between the lining and the bag itself. But I don't know how well I can put together a backpack. I still might try, though. Your leather bag there looks plain and simple enough for you to use. Maybe I'll just make a duffle bag, sew some straps on the sides, and whip together a bunch of smaller cloth bags for the medical supplies. I can keep them and the secret-liner-stash-bag inside of it. I want to keep the plastic down to a minimum," she remarked, then returned to her sketches.

James took the pile of divorce papers, tapped them into alignment again, and got up to put them in his satchel. He looked back over at Leah, bent over her scrap of paper, drawing designs on one side, flipping it over to continue the list of seeds she wanted to bring on the reverse, and then back again to her bag pattern. All of a sudden, she would mutter, 'Oh, yeah,' or sit up straight with a new idea, then bend forward and jot it down. He realized that he was supposed to be doing something—anything—rather than leaning against the bathroom doorway enjoying the view of the woman who was to become his wife. He remembered the papers in his hand. Later, he thought, and stuffed them into the leather bag.

James came back to the table and sat across from her. He watched her face as she muttered to herself, noticed the way her eyebrows arched in excitement, and how she rolled her eyes whenever she mumbled, 'Well, maybe.' He recalled how her whole attitude had slowed to near disappointment with the thought that books might go away forever. *Damn!* He was falling in love with her. He smiled at that comforting thought. It was a first for him. It couldn't be that he was falling in 'lust' with her, because as he was admiring her, her sexuality never crossed his mind.

"Are you okay?" she asked, as she leaned into his face, her nose practically touching his.

"Oh, more than okay—I'm just admiring my future. Did you find your birth certificate?" he asked, hoping she would remember that they still needed to go to wherever it was you went—the courthouse maybe?—to get a marriage license.

"Oh, yeah. I stuffed it in my purse already. Do you have yours?"

"Uh, no, I have my passport, though. Will that do?"

*He blanched at the thought of the birth certificate. He had never seen his, and now he knew why. He had most likely been born in America. Because of his family's status, the official document was never required. A member of the House of Lord's word was good enough for the schools, and even for getting a passport, although that was probably a gray area. He seemed to remember a little bit of discussion when he went in with his father to get his when he was 14. Or that would be when he went with big brother Bruce to get the passport. Bruce and the clerk took their conference into the supervisor's office behind closed doors. It was the supervisor who came out to finish the paperwork, the clerk standing in the corner—mute, glaring at the men.*

*The passport was needed for a trip to Nepal. Bruce wanted to see how James would do at mountain climbing, his passion. That was a joke. It was like putting an adolescent in a Ferrari in the Grand Prix to see if he would like driving.*

*Bruce had him outfitted with state of the art climbing gear. James felt both ridiculous and humiliated. The outfitter kept making comments about how petite and cute he was. He also took too much time adjusting the fit around his crotch. The whole episode was one he didn't want to recall. He didn't make it past base camp, and Bruce never let him live it down.*

*"You went and spoiled the whole trip for me and my mates. And*

*embarrassed me, too! Who ever heard of getting altitude sickness at base camp? I should have left you there with the Sherpa women, but your grandfather would have killed me if I had."*

He had been a disappointment to Bruce his whole life, but now it didn't matter. He had been his grandfather's pride and joy, and now that he knew who the real parent was, he was aglow with recollection.

"Are you sure you're okay?" Leah repeated, breaking his reverie. "You look like you're daydreaming again. Save that for this evening. We have places to go, people to see, and a wedding license to buy!"

James grinned with satisfaction and picked up his bag. Leah grabbed her purse and a bottle of water, then they went outside, *al fresco,* to the Guilford County Grille, also known as daytime in a Greensboro summer.

James did the tap and grab of the car door handle to open it, certain he'd receive second-degree burns if he touched it for more than a full second. At this time of year, and this time of day, it was an unwelcome challenge to get car doors opened without blistering fingers. The internal temperature of the car was at least 134 degrees—or at least that's what the little digital thermometer read as Leah turned on the ignition.

Out of habit, she turned on the air conditioning. James reached over and shut it off. "What the…" she protested. "It's hot in here!"

"Yes, it is, and we both have to get used to the heat. Now, roll down the windows and tough it out. And if you think *you* feel miserable, remember, I'm from England where it seldom reaches 80 degrees, much less this 99 degrees with 99 per cent humidity nonsense."

"Okay, but when we get back, I'm going to take a long, cold shower," she said between clenched teeth.

James had a quick visual of how nice it would be to climb into the shower with her, but choked it off. *Shoes, I need to get shoes. Where can I get shoes?*

"And no, you don't get to come in the shower with me. You'll have to wait your turn. Oh, remind me to look in the phonebook for a shoe repair shop. They might have a line on someone in the area who does cobbler work for the re-enactors. It'll take a while to get two pairs of shoes made. I don't want to wait until the last minute, and then have to go barefooted." Leah paused, then asked, "Is it hot enough for you?"

"Yes, it is," he sighed in resignation, "I'll have to remember to grab a water bottle every time we go out. People really lived here without air conditioning 200 years ago?"

"People *still* live here without air conditioning. Put that on your list: find alternative ways to stay cool in hot climates. I think some of Frank Lloyd Wright's architectural designs used prevailing air currents and shade to facilitate cooling for his school in Tucson. At least, that's what I remember from high school. Hey, did you know that I went to school in

136

Arizona? I actually saw it, or rather felt it, get to 123 degrees! But it was a dry heat. I swear this heat here, right now, is worse. And are you sure you don't want to work into this gradually?" Leah grabbed the water bottle, set it between her legs, and twisted off the cap.

James watched her drink half the bottle in one long gulp. She was radiant with sweat, provocative without trying, but also uncomfortable. He realized they would be wise to make use of what they had while they had it.

"I'm sure," he said, and turned the air conditioning to full power with his left hand, powering up his window with his right. "I'm sure I want to do this *gradually*. Can I have some of that water? I promise not to drink it all."

Leah took the water bottle from between her thighs and handed it to him, grabbed the steering wheel, and rolled up her window. "I was pretty sure you were a smart man, even beyond those fancy honors sashes. Smart in school doesn't mean smart in life. Good living skills will get you further than knowing the value of pi to the tenth decimal point."

James gawked at her. *Did she even know she was reading his mind all the time? Doubtful. She probably believed those purposely-distracting computations he employed were her random thoughts. Well, that was okay. He was more than happy to share his thoughts with her. And anything else of his she wanted to access, too.*

# *21 Necessary Documents

The clerk at the courthouse was as polite as she could be, but she was also resolute. A passport would not work for getting a marriage license.

"Now, let me get this straight," James said. "It's $60 for the document. I can take it right out that door, stop at any church and get any preacher to stand in front of us and ask 'Do you?' and 'Do you?,' have all of us sign it, bring it back here, and then we're married?"

"Yes," she drawled, talking slowly to him, as if he was mentally challenged and she wanted to make sure he understood, "but you have to have a US birth certificate to get married here. Now, if you were born in America, and can provide me with that very necessary document, then I'd be happy to take your money, and let you find a preacher. Even a magistrate can do the officiating—that means ask the words—and he's even closer; he's just down the hall. But I can't let you marry the lady with just a passport. Now, is there something else I can do for you, or can I take care of the next person in line?"

James exhaled sharply. "Thank you for the information. I'll see what I can do." He turned to Leah, put his arm around her shoulder, and headed for the door. He stopped just short of leaving, delaying the inevitable while enjoying the coolness of the refrigeration, and the nearness of his fiancée. "You know what I have to do, don't you?" Before she had a chance to answer, he said, "Of course you do, you always know what I'm thinking."

Leah frowned. "I don't do it on purpose. Yes, I know what needs to be done, but let's stay in here to make the call. I don't want to go out into that heat again until we have to." She sat on the slatted bench by the exit and looked up at him, waiting for him to sit down.

James resigned himself to the task. He had to call Bibb and see if she had a birth certificate for him. He was still angry at being deceived about his parentage, but he'd have to get over it. After all, it was as much his father's fault as hers. They were both in on it. And Bruce—he had to have known about it, too.

Suddenly, he felt like such a dupe, as if he was the only one in the world left out of the inside joke. He could feel his face flare with anger—red-hot rage, barely contained. He sat down hard on the bench, his chin on his knuckles like Rodin's statue of The Thinker. He snorted with disgust as he looked at the highlighted phone number on the smartphone clutched in his other hand. He would rather do anything—even change a flat tire in this heat—than call *her*.

"Here, let me," Leah said, as she put her hand on top of his and the phone.

He relinquished the phone to her, then leaned back against the cool wall, and stared up at the ceiling. *Why was this so hard for him?*

Leah answered his unspoken question. "I think it's one, you're mad at her for being your mother, and then shocked or disturbed or whatever, at finding out that you're an American, or at least a dual citizen. Hey, things happen for a reason. At least now we can be married when we go back." Leah's voice changed—someone was on the phone. "Hi, I was looking for Bibb, Bibb Stephens?" *Yeah, right, as if there was more than one Bibb at this phone number.* "When do you think she'll be back? Oh, is there any way to contact her? Hmm. Well, have her call Leah back at this number...."

Leah gave the man on the other end of the conversation her phone number. She didn't mind if Bibb called her. On the contrary, she was going to have a mother-in-law! She beamed at the thought of having more family.

"What?" James wanted to know what Leah had been told, but he also wanted to know why she was suddenly so radiant.

"Oh, she went out of the country for a few days. She'll be back Monday or Tuesday. We'll still have plenty of time to get the license," she replied absently. She knew he wanted to know why she was so happy all of a sudden. Well, she would leave the unspoken question of her contentment unexplained for now. She sighed deeply. Her mother would have liked Bibb. She always did admire strong women.

## *22 Preparing to Blast

Leah took the debit card out of her wallet, wrapped her yellow one-paged seed order/tote-bag pattern/to-do-list around it, and slipped it into her back pocket for easy access. She was ready to go shopping online. She had finished the list of seeds she wanted to get for her mother, the former Alaskan gardener.

"Mom could grow monster cabbages, arm-long carrots, and the most magnificent roses in Alaska, but it frustrated her that she couldn't get watermelons or okra to do worth a darn. She did okay with tomatoes, but only because she had a greenhouse. In Arizona, it was just the opposite. Not much, other than squash and melons, grew in the summer. The sun was so bright and hot, it actually burned the plants. When that happened, her compost pile grew, but so did her frustration. I think that's one reason she moved to Alaska—she got fed up with the heat. So where is she now? Back in the heat!"

"Didn't you say it was a different kind of heat—and that it seldom got truly cold in Arizona?"

Leah nodded. "Yeah, at least where we lived. The heat was bad, but the worst part was being cooped up inside all day. It was too hot to go anywhere when the sun was out, at least if you had to park your car anywhere in the open. We always did the grocery shopping at about nine at night. Even then, it was still warm, but at least the car didn't turn into an oven during the hour or so you were in the store. Refrigeration for a home or a car wasn't a luxury—it was a necessity. Then there was the 'fed up with the dirt and sand' syndrome. Anyone who lived in the desert as long as she had—and me, too—got tired of seeing burnt out, barren, vacant lots, and crushed granite landscaping. It was too expensive to have a grass lawn. You see, there wasn't enough rainfall to support one without irrigation, and water cost a fortune. We never got much of a break, either. No autumn. Summer lasted from March until November. Spring was nice enough—both weeks," she looked at him to make sure he had caught her little joke. He had and chuckled with her. "Except when those Palo Verde trees exploded with yellow blossoms. The pollen was so thick, you couldn't breathe or see."

"Really?" James asked, "You had pollen so heavy you couldn't see?"

"Well, not that way. It wasn't the density of the pollen that made it hard to see—it was the hay fever that came with it. Allergies were so bad that, damn, I wish I had a nickel for every box of tissues and bottle of antihistamines that were sold in the Valley of the Sun for one year...hell, even for the month of March. It makes my nose tickle just thinking about it. Hey, that's something I think I'll put in my medical kit. Antihistamines are good to have on hand if someone has an allergic reaction, not just for hay

140

fever." Leah pulled her mini yellow notebook from her back pocket and scribbled her latest stock suggestion in the margin.

"Don't you think we should get you a real notebook for your list? It looks like you're about to run out of room."

"When I run out of room that means we have enough stuff. And by the way, how's *your* list doing?"

James scooted closer to Leah. "I think I'll get a revolver. I can get the shells, reloading kit, and supplies at this store," he said, pointing to the name of a sporting goods store in the opened yellow page section of the phone directory. "We have to do something about the guns, though. When we're done here, we should see if you can buy one here," he pointed to his list, "and then go to Wal-Mart and get the other."

Leah thought about it before replying. "I think I'll take Billy's advice. He told me to go ahead and use the pawn shops. We'd get a better deal, possibly, but there wouldn't be so many people watching us buy them. It's not illegal or anything. It's just that it's been known to happen that an honest, upright citizen buys a gun and is tailed after the sale by a no-goodnik who robs him, so he can use the weapon in a crime. If the original owner doesn't get the theft reported in time, then he's accused of the offense because the gun was registered to him. We can be both discreet and safe in this. Do you know what kind of gun you want?"

James grinned. She knew he knew, or that he'd been considering it a lot lately. He'd been distracting himself with thoughts of guns to keep her from *seeing* him think about her. "Take a guess," he asked.

"Well, the first one that comes to my mind is Dirty Harry and his .44 magnum pistol. But I don't think you'd want to bring a handgun with a barrel that long. Is that the caliber, though?"

"Yes, very astute of you, my dear. Give the lady a gold star. Yes, .44 magnum, but with a 4" barrel. A Smith & Wesson model 629 Mountain Gun would work for anything and everything. It might have too much of a kick for you, but we can go to the shooting range. You can get acquainted with it there, and we can sight both of them in at the same time. Have you ever fired a gun?"

"Billy took me shooting last winter. I hit the targets every time and even got a few bullseyes. He said I was a natural. I guess that's a good thing. Anyway, it didn't scare me, and the revolver felt comfortable in my hand. But I suppose the gun manufacturers design them that way on purpose. Come on, let's go."

Ж

Three pawnshops and two handguns later, they were back in the car. "I'm bushed," Leah said. "I'm more tired than if I'd just worked a twelve-hour shift with a full floor."

"I'm a bit spent myself. I think it's the heat as much as any other one thing. Although we have had—or rather, you have had—a lot more to deal with than usual. So much for having the day off, eh?" James said with a chuckle.

"I'm tired, but you know what I'd like to do? I know, I know, rhetorical question—I'm not looking for an answer. I want to go swimming. I really liked floating in the pool with you. At least this time, I'm sure I won't be awakened by my apartment being blown up. They can't do that two days in a row now, can they?"

James snorted at her joke. He was glad she could laugh about it now. "Okay, let's pull up to the motel. I'll run in and get the suits. We can change at Billy's, right? Or should we change in the room first?"

"You know, I don't even care if I'm wearing a bathing suit. I'd jump in with what I have on now, although I don't suggest you do it in long pants." Leah looked at the clock in the dashboard. "Rats. It's past Billy's bedtime. He's probably asleep already. I don't want to disturb him. Yes, let's change clothes first. After we're done swimming, we can grab a burger at a drive-through and bring it home for dinner."

James started laughing, apparently for no reason at all.

"What's so funny?" Leah asked. "I don't remember making a joke or farting."

James laughed even harder, barely able to breathe. "Farting?" he chortled, as he finally settled downed enough to form the word.

"Slapstick, potty humor, whatever—you know. You laugh when someone falls down, accidentally farts… Geez, it's not funny if you have to explain it." She huffed in exasperation, then turned to him and asked indignantly, "So, what *is* so damned funny?"

He sighed and relaxed back into the seat, shaking his head slightly in amazement. "I guess it's not really *comical*. It's just that I—that is, we—are considering the motel our home. I never, ever, in my wildest dreams thought I would consider an oversized bedroom with a shower and a toilet—which I paid for by the day—to be my home. But you know, home is where you're with someone you lu..," James choked on the word love, cleared his throat in embarrassment, and continued, "with someone you care about. Right?"

"Right.…" Leah drawled. She knew what he had almost said. It was probably better that he hadn't said the 'L' word. She could wait. He was smart, kind, had a hot body, but she wasn't sure that she was ready to hear *that* word from any man yet. Even if they were getting married in a few days.

She pulled into the parking spot in front of their 'home' and left the engine—and air conditioning—running. James ran in and donned the bright green John Deere boxer shorts he had slept in. He made sure that he kept on his 'tighty whitey' underwear underneath, though. Any gaps that occurred would only reveal good old American cotton briefs. He chuckled at his little ploy as he walked out the door, waving for Leah to come in and change clothes while he babysat the car.

Leah saw James come out in his 'gap' shorts, but didn't say a word. *It's his body, and if he wants to show it off, that's his prerogative. True, it is a nice body, but I really can't tell the man how to dress—at least not until he's my husband. Then I'll definitely have a word or two to say about him going out in public with his tallywhacker popping out of his shorts.* Instead, she kept her mouth shut, grinned, and raised one eyebrow as in 'uh huh,' then took the room key from him.

It took her a full minute to strip off her dress, tug on the red one-piece swimsuit, and throw the dress back over it. "Ooh, towels," she said aloud, and grabbed all the big ones. One last look around the room—oops, grab the key—and she was outside the door, waving the little white and green keycard like it was a winning lottery ticket.

Leah got back behind the wheel and placed the keycard in James's hand. "You know, this is like a winning lottery ticket." She didn't look for his reaction, but knew she should explain herself. "Well, kind of. I mean, I feel like I won you because, Lord knows, I didn't buy you, never asked for you, or even felt like I did anything to deserve you."

"Wow!" James replied, totally stunned. He remained silent for a moment, letting her words sink in. "You know," he said, tentatively placing his hand on her bare thigh, "I do believe that is *the* nicest thing anyone has ever said to me—and I mean *ever*. Wow! Thank you."

"Well…" Leah said, and paused, unsure of what to say or do next. She hadn't meant to be all mushy, but it *was* true. She felt that if she hadn't verbalized it, she would always regret not taking the opportunity. "You were past due."

She cleared her throat and changed her attitude, "Are you sure you should wear those underpants in public, I mean, at least without the 'gap insurance' towel?" She hadn't intended to say anything about his revealing wardrobe, but now needed to say something—anything—to change the subject.

"What? You think that little old thing might pop out again?" He laughed and watched for her reaction.

Leah just shook her head and blushed, trying to pretend that this conversation really wasn't happening. "Don't worry," he said after a moment of watching her discomfort, "I kept on my—what do the sailors call them, 'skivvies'?—you know, cotton briefs."

Leah took a deep breath, partly from relief, mostly from exasperation. If she couldn't change the subject, she'd just ignore it. "Ho-kay," she drawled, "we're almost there. Grab the phones and the towels, and we'll make a mad dash to the pool."

Leah pulled her car in next to 'the beast' in the parking lot. "Looks like Billy did a bit of wax and polish on the old Dodge. Man, it looks good!"

James gave it a cursory once over after he got out of the car. He stopped as he got to the back end of the truck, bent over, and exclaimed, "He even polished the exhaust pipe!" He shook his head in amazement. "I guess he didn't have time to go out and get it chromed. Good grief, if he keeps treating it this nice, what's he going to do to it after he owns it?"

"Owns it?" Leah asked.

"Yes, didn't you get the memo? It's going to be my thank-you gift to him." He wasn't going to elaborate on why he was thanking him. If Leah was 'peeking,' she'd know.

"'Thank you' for suggesting that you and I get married?" Leah asked coyly.

"Yes." James walked around to her side of the car and took her hand. He brought it up to his lips and gave it a gentle kiss, pulled back, and looked into her eyes. "And to thank him for being the way he is. If he was trying to put on an act and, shall we say, be 'someone he wasn't,' he might marry you for show, and then, where would I be?"

Leah rolled her eyes, not knowing how she should react. She was beginning to feel the same way. Rather than swoon and get romantic, though, she simply said, "Hell, if I know," and pulled him alongside her as she walked briskly toward the pool area. Suddenly, hearing the word 'love' was both scary and exciting.

# *23 Sneaking Out
*August 7, 2013, 1:11 AM*

James was glad his internal clock hadn't reset to North Carolina time. He wanted to wake up early so he could sneak out while Leah slept. He needed to be clear-headed, too. His body was still on London time, which made his secret sortie easier. He looked at his watch. It was 1:11 a.m.

Quick, make a wish, he thought, as he remembered Leah's little superstitious habit. *Okay, I wish this would go off without a hitch, and that Leah and I can go back in time and live happily ever after.* He chuckled softly. *Well, I don't have to short-change myself on the wishes now, do I? Okay, here's a couple more. And I wish we catch up to our missing parents, and that we have many beautiful, healthy children.* He swung his feet out of bed. *Yeah, well, if they're her offspring, they'll definitely be beautiful. I'll simply wish for healthy.*

He looked over at the sleeping lady who he hoped would be the mother of his children. Her face was animated, grinning, even letting out a little laugh, but ended with a frown. She was obviously dreaming. Hopefully she was a sound sleeper.

He grabbed his trousers and shirt from the back of the chair and put his hand completely around her large bundle of keys, muffling any jingling noises. He threw his clothing over his arm, clenched the keys tight in his fist, and put his other hand on the doorknob. He looked around behind him. Something was wrong. He took a quick, startled breath as he realized that he didn't have the room key. There wasn't any use in sneaking out in the wee hours if he had to knock on the door to get back in!

He tip-toed back to the table, grabbed the keycard, and then realized that he didn't have any shoes. Darn, he must be half-asleep—he wasn't as clever as he thought he was. He grabbed her sandals. They were closer and would work for the quick trip to the edge of town. He opened the door, took one more look back into the room—still feeling like there was something missing—and saw it. The map and police report Billy had given him was inside his bag, which was on the chair, scooted under the table. He propped opened the door with one foot and reached in. He tipped the back of the chair toward him with his fingertips and caught it, just before it fell to the floor. Hmph. He might have a career as a cat burglar—if he made a checklist of items needed before setting to work!

He eased the door shut and performed the same awkward clubfooted dance to the car that he had used at the pool—the asphalt was still hot, even at night. Leaning against the warm metal of the Prius, he pulled his pants on over his sleep shorts, dropped the sandals to the ground, and inched his toes in far enough that they'd stay on his feet. A quick tug and wiggle into his shirt, and he was dressed.

Ready to roll, James opened the door, put one foot inside, and groaned. *Hmph! Wrong side of the car, Melbourne!*

Operation Deception, take number two. James winced as the engine turned over. Hopefully she hadn't heard it. He checked the gauge to make sure he had enough fuel, backed up, and drove into a parking space on the other side of the motel. He turned on the car's interior lights and dug into the valise until he found the map and the official police report Billy had given him. He looked again at the back of the envelope and the markings he had made while talking with James Bradford—JB as the gentleman's gentleman liked to be called—at the Club. Besides his list of what to bring and when to leave, he had also subconsciously drawn a map on the envelope. Hmm, it was strange, yet familiar. And maybe something worth keeping, too.

He looked over the police report and map again. The location was pretty straightforward. It should be easy to find, even if he wasn't familiar with Greensboro. He'd better head out and get it done quickly, though. Leah was an early riser, and he wanted to at least look like he was asleep before she got up.

Ж

It had only taken 45 minutes to get to the highway exit, but from that point on, he was lost. Was he supposed to take a right turn before or after the house with the windmill lawn ornament? Didn't these people believe in street signs? And how could he tell which was the third road on the left when the streets and driveways all looked the same size? It didn't help that it was a new moon tonight and there weren't any streetlights. It was as dark as the inside of a black bear's gullet at midnight.

After twenty minutes of dead ends, u-turns, and curse words, James pulled onto the shoulder of the latest wrong road, and put the car in park. Crap, no doubt about it, he was lost. Not only was he unable to find his destination, it was beginning to look as if he'd have to wait until daylight to find his way back to the highway. How could he have been so stupid! Why did he feel the need to keep this a secret? He could have waited until morning, told Leah about his plan, and let her come with him. This was her town. She definitely knew her way around it better than he did. It would have been so simple, both of them working together, one driving, the other navigating—and in the daylight. It was doubtful they would have got lost.

James reclined the seat and shut his eyes. Okay, a little inspiration here would be appreciated, whoever is in charge of conniving, lost, and misplaced bastards. Surely, the way of the world—or spirits of the forest, or whatever—would help him. Or God. Leah said He was the One who would help.

"Okay, here goes. Lord, I'd appreciate a little direction here," James beseeched, both nervous and humble. He hadn't prayed in ages, but knew that an insincere heart was worthless, no matter what the situation. He opened his eyes again and looked at the almost empty passenger seat next to him. The envelope with his scribbling on it was facing him. He looked down at it, out the window, and then chuckled in relief.

He knew where he was now. What he had 'doodled' the day before—the drawing his 'subconscious' had sketched—was the map he had really needed. "Okay, thank You, Lord," he said, half-wondering, half-certain that—but one-hundred percent grateful to—the superior power who had shown him the way. He wasn't at his destination yet, but James now knew the right route to take.

Leah's little car drove directly to the site without James hesitating or making even one more wrong turn. His autopilot was the 'Superior Being' who had guided his hand in drawing the map the day before. The former Doubting Thomas was beyond happy, enveloped in a full-body smile—if there was such an anatomical possibility. The warm, contented feeling assured him that he was doing the right thing—that everything was going to be just fine. "Thanks again," he said, at peace in his cocoon of confidence.

James drove a quarter mile down the road, turned at a big billboard, and then a few hundred yards more to the spot. The police report's very detailed description of the area verified that he was at the site of the disappearance. He really didn't need it to confirm what he already knew, though. Dani, aka Evie, Leah's mother, had been through here recently. He could feel her emotional traces—almost smell her. Hmm. Would a bloodhound be able to track her back in time by her scent? Nah...well...maybe, but he didn't need to get distracted right now. He'd have to remember to ask Leah about that later.

He left the motor running. Remnants of the 'do not cross' tapes the police had set up several days earlier, caught the car's headlights and seemed to glow—brilliant yellow stripes slicing through the otherwise nighttime-darkened landscape.

It appeared that high winds had come through and completely blown away one side of the taped perimeter. James wanted to ensure that no one—other than he and Leah—went between *those* trees. He wasn't being selfish, either. Passing through the time portal might kill someone if he didn't know what he was doing. Well, maybe, maybe not, but a child with an active imagination playing Revolutionary War hero in this 'hot zone' could inadvertently travel back in time, and then where would he be? Totally confused and out of his own era. No, he would take precautionary measures for everyone's safety *and* for his and Leah's personal needs.

James stood across from the tree adorned with streamers of lemon-pudding-yellow tape, studying the scene of the disappearance. Suddenly, a full body shiver rattled him. It felt as if he was looking at an old photograph. No, it was more than that. He could swear that he had seen this place—*been* here before—but how could that be? This was the first time he had ever traveled this far out of Greensboro proper.

He looked across to the other tree, its bright ribbon no longer tied on, but tangled amid the low-growing shrubs beneath it. He had no way to verify it, but he felt in his gut that it had once marked the other side of the time portal. He grabbed at the tape with a forked stick, then tugged it toward him, gathering it around his bent arm like a coil of rope. He wasn't going near that spot until it was time.

What he knew to be the real time portal was directly across from the area cordoned off for the stolen car. There were plenty of similar old trees in the area, but he knew they weren't the same. He counted over six trees to the left, then walked over to the sixth one, making sure he stepped on grassy patches, avoiding the dusty areas. He wasn't stealing anything, and the police were probably done with their investigation, but he didn't want to attract attention, either. The shoes he was wearing, Leah's sandals, would make a definite, distinct impression in the soft ground. True, there were dozens, maybe hundreds of shoe treads just like them, but he didn't need to be careless.

"You look like a good candidate for most mysterious tree of the year. Allow me to dress you for the occasion," he proclaimed with mock pomp and a quick bow to the tired old magnolia, thick in the middle with its multi-trunked base. He strung the other end of the tape to its sister tree fifteen feet away and stood back to appreciate his deception.

"One possibility assured, some—maybe many—tragedies averted. See you in ten days," he said, and saluted his adorned trees. "And you, too," he added, and saluted the two true—and plain-looking—portal bastions. "My lady and I will be here at daybreak on the 17th. In the meantime, don't let anyone chop you down for firewood or toothpicks, okay?"

James walked back to the grassy knoll where he had parked the car. Six trees to the right of the taped trees: that would be easy to remember. "Right, I want six kids," he said. He started the engine and put it in gear. "Time to go home to the future missus, little purple Prius. Maybe I can get a little nap before it's time to get up."

James pulled into the motel parking lot and turned off the headlights. He didn't need them to find his parking space, and the light shining in the window might wake her. It was still dark, thankfully, and no one was stirring. He leaned against the car, took off his day clothes and her sandals, and gathered everything together. He paused, looked back, and then had another, 'Ah, crap' moment as he realized that he had forgotten his bag again. He opened the car door with the key rather than the button so the lights didn't flash, then grabbed the bag and the map. "I can't let her find you, little one," he said as he stuffed the envelope back into the zippered pocket, "at least, not until it's time."

148

James swiped the keycard in the door and heard Leah snort. Crap, was she up? He opened the door slowly in case she was still asleep. No use being noisy and awakening her if she wasn't already.

Phew! She was still asleep, but looked restless. He set down his armload of clothes and goodies, and stood next to the bed, stepping out of her shoes right where he had found them. Hopefully they weren't dusty. It was too dark to see, and he didn't want to chance waking her with a quick cleaning.

After he said his silent prayer of thanks, his mind was at peace. His muscles, however, were still tight and tired from his furtive middle-of-the-night foray. He stepped around the bed, pulled back the sheets, and lay on his back, letting the coolness of the bedding take away the tension. His hope that it wouldn't take long to fall asleep was the last thought he had.

# *24 A Bad Morning

*August 7, 2013, 7:00 AM*

"Aaaahhh!"

The sudden noise—louder than a cherry bomb exploding at the end of his nose—sky-rocketed James out of bed. His heart pumped with an exaggerated force, his breathing as rapid as if he'd just run a four-minute-mile. He stood resolute, wide-stanced, fists raised in anticipation of a battle. His adrenaline-fueled reaction to fight had overridden the ancient run and hide reflex, but he was still disoriented,

He sucked in a lungful of air. It slowed his heart rate and cleared his head. He realized now where he was: in a motel room with Leah. His eyes darted back and forth across the room, searching for clues as to what could have happened to cause her to scream so loud and long.

And then he saw it.

*Leah* was the upheaval. She was still asleep, though—unaware of her actions—and experiencing a category five nightmare.

James stared as she thrashed on her side of the bed—his hands lax at his side, helpless. He didn't know what he should do. Should he try to restrain her so she didn't hurt herself? Shout at her to wake up? Shake her?

She suddenly stopped screaming, but had not awakened. Her body was tense, arms held close to her side, rigid, as if bound to a plank. But her head remained active, tossing side to side sharply, resisting the unseen assailant, her eyes squeezed tight in fear. Her chin, with jaws clenched tight, was tucked into her chest, as if trying to avoid opening her mouth. Her hands jerked up suddenly, crossing in front of her face in a classic gesture of self-defense.

Should he waken a person in a bad dream or not? James didn't know. He'd never read about it, nor did he have any personal experience with it. He had shared a bed with Leah longer than he had anyone. Even when he was married, Clotilde had insisted on separate bedrooms. He had to do something, though, so stayed low, away from her erratic wild punches, and reached over to shake her arm.

"Aaaahhh," she shrieked at his touch, then added kicking to her physically active dream. Now she was chaos personified. Her body was contorted, twisted upon itself, a pile of pajamas, limbs, and long brown hair thrown together in a haphazard manner. She was miserable in her unconscious state, and he didn't know how to help her. It was as if she were on fire…

Fire. That's what he could do—he'd treat her as if she was literally on fire. He sidled around the bed, grabbed the ice bucket, popped the top to make sure the cubes had melted, then stood above her and poured a steady stream of the chilly water onto the top of her head, hoping to douse her burning rage and fear.

"What the fu..." she screamed as she bolted out of the bed and out of her nightmare. "What'd you do that for?"

Leah was angry, but free of her terrors. And that was a good thing. Her being victimized by the nightmare demons was scary, even for him. He could only imagine what it was like for her on the inside of those hallucinations.

"You were having a bad dream..." he started to explain.

"Then why didn't you just pinch my arm or something," she snapped.

She wasn't yelling, but he could tell by the hostility in her eyes that she wanted to. He shrugged his shoulders and stayed mute. She'd figure it out as soon as her rage subsided. Right now, she was probably still half-asleep. Never argue with a drunk or someone who just woke up. That was common sense, and it didn't take a psychology degree to understand that.

Leah grabbed the wet pillow and threw it across the small room, hitting the mirror on the dresser. She stomped her bare feet on the way to the bathroom, then slammed the door behind her.

*Oh, well, he thought. At least she's not fighting off the bogeyman or whoever it was.*

"Crap! James, would you hand me my purse, please," Leah called in frustration from the bathroom. The door opened up a crack, and she thrust out an arm.

He picked up her little bag and put the strap in her hand. "Here."

"Thanks," she said curtly, and shut the door hard.

He heard the sink running, toilet flushing, and then the shower started. It looked as if he would have to wait for his turn at the toilet. *How rude, he thought.*

As it turned out, it was a very quick shower. Leah came out wrapped in the undersized bath towel, clutching another towel—wadded into a bundle—close to her chest. "It's all yours," she said, nodding to the opened bathroom door, almost urging him with her eyes to leave the little sanctuary that was both their bedroom and living room.

He picked out clean clothes from his bag and went into the bathroom, hoping that their life would be back to normal after he was done.

The shower felt good, just as good as it had the day before, good. He let the stress of the last few minutes wash down the drain with the suds from his shampoo. The little bar of soap felt like a palm-held lubricant. He wiped it under his armpit, foregoing a washcloth, then across his chest to the other side. As his hand slid past, his thumb bumped his nipple, giving him a small jolt.

*That's* what he needed: a jolt. But he wanted more than a small one. She was done in the bathroom, at least for now. He'd take his time and his

151

pleasure in the shower. A few more swipes across his body for cleanliness, then it was time for sudsing for happiness.

He was a fast responder, even if he did say so himself. He didn't know about other men, and frankly didn't care. He knew what felt good to his body and, although he normally didn't pleasure himself more than once or twice a month, he now had stimulation—at least, mental and visual stimulation—with the lovely lady, Leah. Every time she touched him, he got little quickenings of electricity up his arms, down his spine, then up between his legs. She had kissed him—albeit as a friend and not a lover, or even as a boyfriend—a couple of times. He took those little memories and compounded them, multiplied them in his emotional database, until they were passionate kisses and caresses. In his mind, it was her hands stroking between his legs, up and around his cock. He leaned his chin over his shoulder, opened his mouth wide, and made oral love to his own flesh-substitute for her breast, rolling his tongue in wide circles, lips gently gliding across, resisting the urge to suck hard. It would be difficult to explain a love bite suddenly appearing on his upper arm. He couldn't—rather, didn't want to—stop the compulsion for a quick nip to his own skin, though, so went ahead and clenched a bit of flesh between his teeth. It was all that was needed to send him over the edge with the spasms and spurts of self-induced ecstasy.

At least clean-up in the shower was easy. He turned the water temperature to cool, inhaled in a few slow, deep breaths to compose himself, then shut off the water. A brisk drying off, quick tooth brushing, and a second swipe of the towel through his hair, and he was ready to face his fantasy female in the flesh. "Down boy," he said softly as he looked down and rearranged his privates. "You'll have to wait until tomorrow. Same time, same station."

"Are you going to be in there all day?" Leah asked, not even trying to hide her irritation.

James pulled the door open quickly, startling her. "Nope, we got places to go and maybe people to see. Ready for breakfast? I'm starved."

They left the motel room in silence. Her face was blank, but he knew she'd be back to normal soon—or at least he hoped she would. He wasn't going to let anything bother him this morning. He was still enjoying the afterglow of his liaison in the shower with Lady Fingers.

Leah pulled into a different Mom and Pop café for breakfast. The sign said 'seat yourself,' so that's what they almost did.

"I want red meat," Leah said abruptly, as they made their way to the back for a table out of the morning sun. James sat down, but Leah remained standing. "Steak and eggs; rare on the steak and well-done on the fried eggs. And lots of black coffee. Would you order for me," she said, rather than asked, her eyes averting his. She turned to leave. "I'll be right back," she added over her shoulder, almost managing to break a smile before she left.

James scooted into the booth, nodded that he had heard her request, but didn't know or care whether she had seen it. He was still grinning on the inside and didn't feel chatty. He was content in his own body, but could tell that she wasn't. It must be that her bad dream was still bothering her. He went ahead and ordered a lighter breakfast of oatmeal, cottage cheese, and juice for himself.

Leah was still in the bathroom, or at least that's where he thought she was, when the food came out. "No, the meat and eggs are for the lady," he explained to the waitress who tried to put the heartier fare in front of him.

Fifteen minutes later, Leah was still not back. *This is ridiculous!* He didn't feel as if he should go back to the restroom and call out to see if she was okay. How tacky was that? He certainly wouldn't want her checking on him if the tables were turned. He took a bite of his oatmeal. It was cold. Well, he would wait a while longer for her. It was her food that was getting cold. His was already there.

Ten more minutes and two more cups of coffee later, and he decided to go to the restroom, but not for her. His bladder couldn't hold much more. He walked into the men's room, did his thing, and came out. The door to the ladies room was blocked open with a 'closed for cleaning' pop-up cone placed in the doorway. He leaned inside, looked around, and saw someone in the stall.

"Hallo," he called out.

"Hey, it's closed for cleaning. You can either hold it or use the men's room. Oh," said the matronly woman with the toilet bowl brush in her hand as she looked out from behind the partition, "Use the men's room. This is the ladies room, sir."

"Oh, sorry." James didn't want to explain to a stranger—or to anyone—that he had lost his girlfriend when she went to the restroom. The Beatle's tune, 'She Came In Through the Bathroom Window' went through his head. On second thought, he'd take one more look. He glanced back in the ladies room and saw that it didn't have any windows. Now this was a mystery that needed to be solved. How in the hell did she just disappear, and what could he do about it?

He walked back to the table, sat down, picked up a little plastic container of strawberry jam, peeled back the covering, and used his coffee spoon to scoop the red glob into his oatmeal. He stirred mindlessly, then looked up and saw Leah walk through the front door. He bit back the urge to ask, 'Where in the hell have you been?' and 'Don't you know it's rude to ditch your breakfast date?' Instead, he found more power in saying nothing. He took a bite of his sweetened cold mush, and realized he had lost his appetite. He forced himself to swallow the gruel and quickly washed it down with the now lukewarm coffee. What a crappy morning this was turning out

153

to be!

He didn't look up at her. He was afraid he'd reveal a strong negative emotion if she saw his eyes. It was better to keep his head down and ponder the strings of scarlet swirls in the gray mass of once-hot breakfast cereal. He felt her hand on his and looked up.

"I am so sorry," she said. "I thought I'd be back before you missed me. I, um, had to go get some," she rolled her eyes, "personal hygiene products. I didn't want to make a special trip to the store and, God, call attention to the situation. I just ran across the street to the gas station. I thought I'd be in and out before the food got here. As it was, they had a power failure, the pumps stopped, and they couldn't ring up any sales on the cash registers. They kept telling me that it would be just one more minute and…"

James put his hand on top of hers. "Don't be embarrassed about that. I mean, if it had happened to me, you would have understood, I'm sure. Not that I'd start a period or anything, but…" James began stammering, and Leah started giggling. *He knew she had a visual of him going in to buy himself tampons or winged pads or whatever it was that women used. He had no idea what they were beyond what he had seen in commercials.* "Sorry," he said with an affected lisp, a twist of his wrist, and a big smirk, "it's just that when it's my time of the month, I get so bitchy…"

He thought he was being funny, but at the word 'bitchy,' she froze. "Hey," she said with complete honesty and no bitterness, "I can be quite the bitch, but that's not who I am normally. True, I get a bit cranky a day or two before and on 'day one,' but it was the nightmare that sent me over the edge this morning. And then I messed my pants, and well…I woke up with someone pouring cold water on my head after a very realistic nightmare, and then found out that I had to deal with a period on top of that. Sorry, I shouldn't have taken it out on you. I usually just stomp around the house, and since I live alone and there's nobody there, no one's feelings get hurt."

"Well, apology accepted. I'll just mark my little calendar so I can do the eggshell-walk starting, what, 26 days from now?" Leah nodded and grimaced. "Because you are not going to be alone anymore, okay?" Leah nodded again, but this time smiled. "I'm glad you smiled at that one. I really like being around you. But please, don't take off again without telling me. I didn't know whether to be scared or mad. Hey, is that steak still a little warm? This oatmeal is cold."

"Okay, here," she said, as she cut a piece of meat from the middle of the steak. "Open wide and chew your food well, sweetie. Is it okay?" she asked, as if she was talking to a two-year-old. James nodded, exaggerated his chewing, and played the part of the toddler, eliciting a giggle from Leah. "Good, you take the meat, and I'll take the oatmeal. I like it better cold and with a little milk on it." She poured the cream from the little steel pitcher

154

onto the pinkish mass, stirred it in, and took a big bite. "Um, um, good," she declared. They were back to normal.

# *25 Family Values

He opened her car door. "Okay, where do we go first?"

Leah waited until he was inside to answer. "I don't know. What did you have down on your list?" She looked over and saw that he had pulled out his motel stationery 'notebook' and was looking through it. "Oh, and don't forget to buckle up; click it or ticket, you know?"

"Yes, Mommy," he replied, and reached across and buckled in. *He settled back into the seat and rolled the word 'Mommy' around in his head like a ball of warm clay, squeezing it, rolling it between his palms into a snake, wrapping it around his fingers. Mommy: he was going to make her a mommy one day.*

"Hello! Hello!" Leah finally reached over and smacked him on the arm to pull him out of his daydream. He jerked his head back and realized that he had been fantasizing. "What's the matter?" she asked jokingly. "Didn't you get a good night's sleep last night?"

James tipped his head, squinted his eyes, and looked at her with a smirk. "Well, it started out fine, but, no. I'm okay." *Quick, recover! Don't let her in your head! She can't know about you sneaking out.* "Hey, how about if we do the pen and paper shopping first, then go to the library? If we have those, I can do the maps, and you can at least get started on your codex this morning. Then maybe we can do a little research and see where we can get colonial-era clothes and shoes. Sound like a plan?"

*James didn't wait for her answer, instead, he turned toward the window—he didn't want her to look at him. He still had a little ball of that 'Mommy clay' he wanted to play with.*

"Even if you really weren't an only child, you were reared as one, weren't you?" Leah asked, seemingly out of the blue.

*Uh-oh. If Leah wasn't peeking into his mind intentionally, she was at least thinking along the same lines as he was: children and parents.* "Um, yeah; an only child reared by his doting grandfather. He adored me and gave me lots of attention, but made sure that I was neither spoiled nor a brat. I was given chores to do, and good manners and good marks were mandatory. How about you? Did you have any siblings? I mean, did you have any when growing up?" he corrected, remembering the 18th century triplets her mother had just had.

"Mom always wanted more kids, but Dad didn't. I mean, I wasn't an accident or anything. Mom didn't go poking holes in his condoms or go off the pill without telling him. I mean, when one person's dream was to live the fast life in NYC, and the other wanted a big garden and babies, where's the middle ground? Well, I guess that would be me. He'd do anything to make her happy. He loved me dearly, but one kid was enough. He said that he already had the perfect child, so why should they have more? Dad didn't get

156

to have the high profile position in LA or New York City that he always wanted, but did fine lowering his goals, establishing his own video production business in Phoenix. So, Mom put up with the heat in Arizona and well, they stayed married for me, which made me feel like I had compromised two lives. But they didn't try to make me feel like that—really, they didn't. I was loved and the only thing that would have been better would be if they loved each other like they had when they were newlyweds. But I guess fairy tales don't always come true, do they?"

"We'll see," he said. "I mean, I think we have it planned out well. I don't see what could possibly go wrong with us and what we're doing."

As soon as the words were out, he knew they were poorly chosen. Fairy tales were meant to be happy and fun, and his explanation of their journey to the past was of a calculated procedure, with no romance or passion involved. He didn't know how to fix what he had just said, so stayed mum. Hopefully, she realized that he was just a tongue-tied Brit who had a hard time expressing his feelings about her and their future together.

They rode the rest of the way to the crafts store in an uncomfortable silence. Leah pulled into a parking place—she had found a prime spot, under a tree, so they were in the shade—and turned off the ignition. She didn't get out or even unbuckle. She breathed out with a snort of resolve. "You said you wanted children. You didn't change your mind or anything, did you?"

"Hell, no! I mean, heavens no. And as far as any career interference goes, I doubt we'll have a problem with that. I mean, since we both pretty much want to stay 'back,'" he nodded his head to make sure that she was still agreeable; she returned the nod. "I think we'll have our hands full with living off the land or whatever you want to call it. I mean, I doubt that I could make it as a blacksmith, but I would try if I had to. I would prefer to be a farmer rather than a banker, ugh, or a trapper or…well, just about anything else. I want to be with my family at all times. How about you?"

"Well, duh? Women didn't work outside the home unless they were maids, whores, or whatever. Even schoolteachers were mostly men. And I sure as hell don't want to clean up anyone else's messes or, or…well, you know what I mean. No, I do *not* intend to work outside of the home. Hmph!"

James chuckled at her little exclamation of intent to be a stay-at-home wife. The silent treatment was over. "Yes, I'm sure you'll have your hands full with helping your mother with your siblings until we have children of our own…"

Leah shared a blush with James at his presumption. He didn't even try to continue the sentence. They were both still shy when it came to *that* topic.

"Well, I don't think we'll be starting on a family for at least four and a half more days. Hopefully by then, Bibb will be back, and we can get married." Leah looked askance at her last remark, avoiding his face. Whether or not he was gay, he still had great curbside appeal.

James didn't say a word. He couldn't have if he tried. His grin was stretched so big that his mouth wouldn't open. He was going to have a real wedding night soon!

# *26 Clark Kent

"Here you go," he said, and put down a hundred-dollar bill.

"Thank you, Lord Melbourne," the clerk said with an all-knowing grin.

James could see that he wasn't being mean or teasing when he called him by his title. He had a look on his face like he—and only he—knew the secret that he was really 'Lord' James Melbourne.

"Please, just call me James," he said, trying not to grimace. "I'm in America, and it doesn't sound right over here." James suddenly realized that he had just told a full-blown lie. 'Lord' had *never* sounded right in front of his name. Well, no, he admitted to himself; it didn't bother him when he was surrounded by his long-time friends and peers at his club. There it felt like it was part of his connection to his extended family, the other members. They were comfortable with their titles and so was he when he was with them.

"And I never got your name," he asked to be polite, although it would be nice to call him something besides 'clerk' when referring to him.

"Clark," the clerk replied.

"Like Clark Kent?" asked Leah, as she walked in the door. "Hi," she said, acknowledging James, "I just came in to get our late breakfast."

"Well, actually," the clerk began indecisively. He didn't know whether they would make fun of him or not—probably not since the dude was some sort of British royalty, and the woman was a decent sort. "Actually," he repeated, "that is my name, or my first two names. My full name is Clark Kent MacLeod."

"Scottish then, aye?" James asked with a brogue.

"Originally; I still have lots of cousins over there, and that's where my two older brothers were born, but my parents came over here when Mom was pregnant with me." Clark looked over and saw Leah pawing through the little refrigerator. "Here," he said, and offered her a plastic bag, "Go ahead and fill 'er up. No one else has been eating those. I'll have to throw them out if they go beyond the expiration dates."

Leah accepted the bag and started her little 'free breakfast' shopping trip. "Did your mother know that Clark Kent was the alias of Superman?" she asked innocently.

"Yeah, actually she did. I half think she did it to piss off—excuse me—make Dad mad. Every one of the firstborn males in my father's family since the mid 1700's has had the same name. She thought it was bad enough having a husband and a first son with the name Atholl Grant MacLeod, but Dad didn't. He was Atholl the 7th and my eldest brother was Atholl the 8th. When she had another son, she wanted to name him something plain and simple, like Bill or George, but not Dad. He went in and signed the birth certificate of his second son with the name Atholl the 9th. Man, was she mad! I think she almost divorced him over that one. And then when she got pregnant with me, well, she wouldn't even let him know when it was time to go to the hospital. She had her girlfriend drive her in when her water leaked or broke or whatever that's called.

"Anyhow, she wasn't home that night to make his dinner. She called him and said to phone in an order or pizza. She wouldn't be home for a while, that she had to help a friend do something or whatever. It was a lame excuse and he was suspicious, but he wasn't the type to care much about anything. He found out where she was by accident, though. The neighbor lady came over to get pajamas for my brothers. She said they were spending the night with her because Mom was at the hospital, having her baby. He was so mad when he found out that he went to the bar and got shit-faced—I mean, he got real drunk.

"Mom called him from the hospital the next day and said she hoped he wasn't too disappointed. This time they had a daughter. He didn't care about no stinkin' girl, so she was happy. She had me dressed and bundled in pink for over a month before he found out. He never changed the diapers, so he wouldn't have known. But my oldest brother, Eight, he was watching her give me a bath and asked how come his little sister had a dick. Dad heard him and was so mad that, well, he left. He went home to Scotland—took my brothers with him, too—and never came back."

Clark shrugged his shoulders at the revelation. "His loss, I guess. Mom had called me 'Sissy' up until that time. Since he was gone—and she said 'good riddance to bad rubbish' about him—then she could tell everybody my real name. She said she called me Clark Kent because I started out with a secret identity, just like Superman. Well, my secret identity was that I was a 'young' man not a 'super' man, but it was fun. At least, I'm not Atholl the 10th!"

"Gee, and I thought the middle name Ignatius was tough," James said. "Thanks for brunch. I'll see you tomorrow, about the same time unless you want me to pay for a couple more days right now?"

"Nah, I'll see you tomorrow. I'll try to get some new pastries in or at least more varieties of yogurt. Those are pretty good if you freeze them first. Almost as good as ice cream."

# *27 We Should Read

"I think it's about time we read at least the second letter," James suggested pensively. "I mean, right now we're acting on the information just from the first one, which was really just a way for me to, um, get in touch with you..."

All of a sudden, James felt embarrassed. He cleared his throat a couple of times, hoping that it would also clear his head, but that didn't work. Maybe it was the phrase, 'get in touch with you,' that was tripping him up. He looked over at Leah to see if she had picked up on his discomfort and the reason for it. He had forgotten to keep his thoughts guarded.

Leah hadn't responded to his proposition about moving forward with the histories because she evidently hadn't heard him. She was still deeply involved with modifying her sketches and adding to her lists. There was no telling which one she was working on now. She was as bad as he was about bouncing all over the place with her thoughts and activities.

I wonder if she has ADD, too, he thought. Two parents with the same genetic trait would probably pass it on to their children. He released a long sigh, then realized it was very loud, and probably sounded wistful. Gulp. That wasn't what he should be thinking of—change of thought time. Shirts, shirts; he needed to find someone to make a shirt for him or do it himself. No, he didn't have time to sew since it would all have to be done by hand, and he had already volunteered to help her make her backpack and...

"You know, it may seem like I'm a bit hyper," she said suddenly. "I mean, look at me; I've got at least five different projects going on here. But it's okay. When I get bored or stumped with one, I just move on to the next one. Mom told me it was because I was 'highly intelligent.' She didn't believe in all that attention deficit disorder stuff. She had the same thing going on when she was in school. She'd finish her work early, get bored and start doodling or daydreaming, and then miss what the teacher had just said. *Her* mother told those teachers that they weren't going fast enough for her daughter, and if they wanted to really help her, they would give her something else to do when she was finished with the assignments. So, they let her go to the music room and play the piano. The music teacher showed her the basics. Mom took off from there with just a stack of music books to guide her. Man, she was motivated. She'd rip right through her schoolwork just so she could go do her thing in the music room. Her grades went up and, even though she never did anything with it, she learned how to play piano pretty well. Me, I just drew and doodled until high school. Then, once I started being home-schooled, I dropped the doodling and blasted through everything so I could go to college early, get my degree, and make enough money that I didn't have to worry about bills."

James had moved over to sit on the bed when she started her little dissertation on the ways the women of her family handled their high intelligence. "It must be a dominant gene in your family," he said out loud before he could bite his tongue. "I mean, you and your mother both are, well, from what little I have seen of both of you, very smart women." *Phew, compliment them both, and maybe she won't know that you were thinking about the succeeding generation and your chance of having a bright daughter with her.*

Leah turned around in her chair to answer him. "Yeah, the dominant traits in our line includes hazel eyes, thick, dark hair, above average intelligence and," she got up from her chair and put her head down, as if she were a lioness, stalking her next meal, "we're all a bunch of alpha females... So watch out!" She suddenly jumped onto the bed next to him, grabbed a pillow, and rose up on her knees as if to attack him with it.

James lay back dramatically, playing the part of the petrified prey, but also kept a sharp eye on her, waiting to see if she was going to launch her pillow projectile or not.

Someone walked past the door, and she changed focus at the noise. He took advantage of her distraction and rushed in for a mid-belly tackle, bringing her down beside him. Her shirt had come up a couple inches, showing her smooth, latte-colored belly. He rolled his head over her perfect 'innie' belly button and blew a raspberry into it, sending her into cataclysms of giggles, laughs, and snorts. He pulled back to do it again, ignoring her half-hearted pleas to stop. He approached to within two inches of her belly, and her laughs and snorts started anew—and he hadn't even touched her. He pulled back as if to stop their little game, let her compose herself, and then leaned toward her with nothing but 'the look' of intent to start again.

Her roars and snorts of laughter began again—just the thought of more belly-blowing had sent her into giddy hysterics.

"Okay, okay, I give up, you win. Oh, please," she begged, the words tumbling out between panted breaths from her full-blown laugh overload, "don't even look at my tummy. I'm about ready to pee my pants as it is."

"So who's the alpha now?" he asked with a self-confident grin. He leaned backed, rested on one elbow, looked her hard in the eye, and then glanced down to her belly in defiance of her instructions, proving his dominance over her emotions and giggle reflexes with a mere squint at her midriff.

"You are!" she proclaimed, and tossed the pillow at his head. She jumped off the bed and ran into the bathroom, turning to peek out at him before she shut the door completely. "But you're only the alpha 'cause I said so!"

James rolled all the way over onto his back and looked up at the ceiling. *Yup, she's mine because she said so. I wouldn't want it any other way. She's mine.*

## *28 One on the Books

*August 8, 2013, 5:30 AM*

"What are you doing?" Leah asked when she came out of the bathroom and saw James lying on the floor.

"Isn't it obvious?" he asked. *Ah-ha! He had inadvertently pulled one over on her, hidden a part of himself without trying.* "Um, I'm checking the carpet for fleas."

"What?" she asked, then realized he was joking. "No...really? Oh, I get it," she said, as she realized what he was doing. "You're getting buff, doing pushups to impress the ladies."

"Well, yes and no," he drawled, trying to mimic the local accent. "I'm *keepin'* in shape for my health. And if it just so happens to impress *my* lady, all the better."

Leah walked over to him. He was crouched on the floor, legs tucked underneath him, ready to stand up. She smacked him on the back of the head with her opened hand and turned away.

"What was that for?" he asked, automatically bringing his hand up to the now stinging spot.

"That's one on the books. I'm sure you'll deserve it one day, when I won't be able to reach you," she said with a grin, then added a shoulder wiggle of sassiness. *She didn't want to tell him that he was just so darned cute that she couldn't keep her hands off him.*

"Okay, fair's fair." He straightened up, pulled his white and blue op-art Beatles tee-shirt back down over his hips, took the two steps forward to stand directly in front of her, swiftly grabbed her by the shoulders, and pulled her to him fast and hard, not giving her a chance to resist. He gave her a long, passionate kiss, complete with tongue and shoulder caress. When he felt her relax in his arms and lean into him, wanting more, he stopped. He stood up straight again, watched her until she came out of her reverie enough to open her eyes, then said, "That's one on the books for me. Come on; let's go to breakfast and then the library. We've got lots to do."

## *29 Brothers MacLeod

Even though he was the youngest of the three MacLeod brothers, Clark was once again assuming the role of father and guidance counselor to Eight. "Remember. If you're going to stay here, you can't get in trouble. This is the only job that we have between the three of us. Niner's off somewhere—says he thinks he's found something and promised to stay outta trouble—so that leaves you. I'll see if I can get a little side work for you. Maybe the boss'll let you clean the carpets or something. We have money to pay back."

"I don't want to clean no stinkin' carpets. Just set me up with a TV and a suitcase of brewskies, and I'll be fine," Eight said, and kicked back in the boss's black vinyl office chair, planting his filthy, loose-laced sneakers on the pile of file folders.

"And get your 'effin' shoes off that desk! What—are you trying to get me fired? Don't you realize, asshole, that if I don't have a job, then I can't be your guardian? And if I'm not you're guardian, you're back in jail? That bail bondsman will snap back his money from the court in a heartbeat and you'll be back in the slammer. Those guys have their own rules, and I signed papers saying that I would—and you would, too—follow them."

Eight didn't say anything, just glared at his younger brother, then started picking boogers out of his nose, examining them one by one before popping them into his mouth.

Clark ignored the scowl and the disgusting manners. He turned away, intending to go back to the front counter to distract himself with his job, something he actually had some control over. But he couldn't stand it. Whether he was a vicious criminal or simply a moronic creep, the man was still his brother, his family. He turned back to the slovenly array of dirty clothes and stinky hair that was his own flesh and blood. He shook his head and snorted at the sorry excuse for a man. He was ashamed that anyone—especially his own brother—could be so ignorant, and not care that in just a short time, he would be behind bars.

He couldn't hold back the compulsion to talk to him like their long absent father should have years ago. The words rushed up from his churning gut and burst forth in a sinister growl, as if he was possessed by an angry paternal spirit. "What, do you want to eat gray meat and mush for the rest of your life? Do you like wearing bright orange jammies everywhere? Does it trip your trigger to have nothing but men in the shower with you? Huh? Don't they make you work in there, too? Get up at the butt crack of dawn to slave away in the laundry, trying to get shit stains out of the other inmate's underwear for twenty cents an hour, getting white bread and peanut butter sandwiches for lunch and a plop of grape jelly for dessert. Damn, dude, why don't you just do what you're told to do on the outside, so you don't have to go back to the slammer?"

Eight kept his glower, but decided he'd go ahead and answer him. This wasn't the first time he had to explain it to his baby brother, but hopefully, it would be the last. "Because I told Grandpa I'd do it," he said bluntly, as if that answer should be enough. But, he knew it wouldn't be, so he continued. "I told him I'd get rid of every last one of them, including the girl. Niner almost got her, too. Shit, we didn't think she'd go out to the swimmin' pool with that effin' Limey. Niner sure took care of her place, though. Hey, that reminds me, have you seen him? He was supposed to catch up with me at the Fish Shack, but I got a little distracted. You know how it is; the chick offered me a trick I couldn't refuse. Hey, isn't that called encampment or something if you pay for a blow job and she won't put out?"

"It's call entrapment, asshole, and she was an undercover cop. And no, you're not supposed to be out soliciting when you're out on bail."

"Hey, I ain't no effin' solicitor. That reminds me, that effin' solicitor or lawyer—or whatever it is they call themselves over here—owes me change. I gave him a fistful of money and it couldn't 'a cost over five grand for him just to stand up in front of the judge and say not guilty. Shit, I coulda done that myself!"

"Eight, what part of bail don't you understand? You paid the fee to the lawyer—that's what they call them here—and then he took the rest of the money and gave it to the court for bail. There still wasn't enough so I had to go to a bail bondsman. I had to sign papers for the rest of the money and promise him that you'd be with me day and night, and if you took off, I'd let him know about it right away."

Clark saw that his brother didn't comprehend what he had just said, so tried again. "Hey, if you take off, and I don't tell him about it, then he'll come and find your ass and throw it in jail—no more bond possible—and then they send me to jail, too. So no disappearing acts, okay?"

"Yeah, well, okay. Thanks, I guess. But what about my money; when do I get it back?"

"Well, if they find you not guilty, and you haven't screwed up before the court date..." Clark looked at his wayward older brother to see if he was following his train of thought. It appeared he was. "Then," he continued, "You'll get what's left of your money back after the bail bondsman gets his. If you're found guilty, they'll probably keep most of it as a fine, plus you'll have to serve time in prison. Hey, where'd you get that much money anyhow? No, wait, I don't want to know. Don't tell me anything. Crap. How come you and Niner are so screwed up?"

"You may think that we're screwed up, but if Niner comes through, then we'll have a bag full of jewels and the deed to that old mill. That old lady wouldn't sell to the Rancho Diablo guys, but she'll *give* it to us, and then we can name our price to Diablo. Not bad for just readin' some old letters, eh?"

"What are you talking about? Grandpa never knew what was in those old letters."

"Well, maybe he did and maybe he didn't. He was told by *his* great-grandpa that in one letter, there was a young girl named Leah who was working at a Moses Hospital in Greensboro on a certain day. You see, I'm not as dumb as you think. I asked around and, well, I didn't find any Leah working there, but I did know the *day* all the excitement was supposed to happen," he bragged.

"Grandpa was also told that there'd be an unknown broad who'd come in, shot in the shoulder, and that this nurse Leah would be the one to tend to her. Well, I just sort of hung around, waiting for that day to come. When it did, I went to the emergency room and waited. Sure enough, some fine-lookin' woman in a old-fashioned dress come in, half-dead it looked like. I had to wait for her to come out of the surgery, then I kind of followed her to her room. I hid in the laundry closet 'cause they kept tellin' me that if I didn't have business there that I had to go somewheres else.

"Well, when I was hid, I sawed the shot lady's one nurse get knocked out by this freaky little man in a long, black frock coat. He run away, pushing that hurt woman in a wheelchair out of the hospital. I guess they stole a car and got away. So, no matter what her name was, this nurse had to be the one Grandpa had heard about.

"I followed the nurse home to see where she lived, then tailed her from there to the airport the next day. I gave the bartender, Harry, a c-note to drug her so I could take her back to her place and get the letters that told where the treasure was. Well, at least I thought that she was the one who'd have them. Then I saw the Limey there at the airport bar with her, and I'll be damned if *he* didn't have them in his carry-on bag. He had them sittin' right there in the side pocket, just waitin' for me to snag 'em. Well, I almost got 'em, but he shoved them inside when that nurse woman started puking all over the place. Harry split, but I had promised him another c-note if he'd help get those papers for me. He went to her place first, but I didn't know that. I was hiding out until I could get her to open the door. I would have had her, too, if that Limey hadn't knocked me down. She ran and Harry went after her to...um...to try and convince her to give us the letters, but the Limey got him, too. Hey," Eight exclaimed, seeing the look of disgust in his little brother's eyes, "he was a big dude. I mean not tall, but that guy was built like a coal train locomotive."

"That's not what I mean. Why don't you just get a job and give up on those old fairy tales?" Clark asked. "There's no bag of jewels, and everyone who's ever went after them has wound up dead, missing, or in prison."

"What? Do you want me to wind up like you—lickin' boots and kissin' arse for minimum wage?" Eight scoffed, and put his dirty shoes back up on the desk, daring his brother with the sneer on his face to tell him to move his feet again.

Clark reached over and knocked the shoes off the desk, grabbed the folders and replaced them in the basket before they fell on the floor, and then sat in the other chair. "Well," he said, drawing out the word for effect. "At least I can have the comfort of a *real* woman when I want and can eat steak every once in a while. And if I decide to go for a walk, I don't have to worry that some sniper is going to take me out if I wander past a fence."

Clark watched as Eight pulled up his grimy, once-white tank top to inspect his navel and see if he had any good globs of belly button lint that needed picking. He shook his head in disgust and continued his lecture. "That might not seem like much to you now, but if they nail you on the assault charge—and they probably will—then my boot-lickin' job might just start lookin' real nice." Clark leaned back in the straight-backed chair and laced his fingers behind his head. "Yup, nice, curvy *real* women, and ice cream, any time I want it..."

"Well, we'll see," Eight said with self-assurance as he pulled his shirt back over his hairy gut, then sat up straight. "I still think I have a shot at getting those letters. They should tell me where the jewels are. That old lady who was with those two at the airport is the one who's on the news all the time. She's the one who owns the mill, and I know where she lives. All I have to do is go up and *talk* to her, real nice like, and ask her to get the letters for us." Eight had a dreamy look in his eyes. "Yup, me and Niner will talk to her *real* nice like."

"Well, I don't want to know about it, and I don't want to hear about letters or old ladies or mills or anything else that sounds like a plan that might get you—no, that *will* get you—into trouble. And you can't go anywhere without me, and I say stay put! Now, get up off your hairy ass and grab that broom. Someone broke a bottle by the front door, and you need to clean it up before someone steps on it and the motel gets sued."

Eight leaned forward, groaned and stood up, arching his back in an exaggerated stretch. Physical labor just wasn't his thing. He was the brains behind their plans and sometimes the muscle. But he'd sweep a bit of floor just to shut up little brother. He was such a wimp. Mother must have screwed around on Pa because he certainly didn't act like a MacLeod, even if he did look like one. He gave Clark a fake smile, grabbed the broom and dustpan, and opened the door to go outside.

"That's him!" he hissed, then popped back inside and hid behind the door.

"Who?" Clark asked.

"Uh, nobody," Eight replied a little too quickly, trying to recover from the shock. He didn't want to involve Clark in any of this. If he did, then he and Niner would have to split the money three ways. As it was, Harry thought he should get something besides the $200 for his effort, and the brothers should at least help him make bail. "Piss on 'im," he whispered, talking to himself.

"What?" asked Clark, "Piss on who?"

"Nothing. Nobody. I'm just having a rough day."

But it wasn't a rough day for him. It had just brightened up considerably. The dark-haired Limey with the letters in his bag was staying at his brother's motel. It would be no trouble to get the master key from Clark when he wasn't looking, sneak into the room, and grab the letters. They even had a copy machine in the office, so if he could figure out how to use it, he'd make copies, and return the originals. The Brit would never know he'd been robbed. And the MacLeods would finally have the treasure.

## **Part Two — Chasing Mama

## **30 Clean the Carpet
*August 8, 2013, 10:30 AM*

Clark opened the door to his room and there he was. Eight was still snoring, sound asleep. He loosened his grasp and dropped the carpet shampooer, letting it fall a noisy, hose-and-attachments-rattling ten inches to the floor. Eight snorted, rolled over, and pulled a second pillow over his head; it was too early for him to wake up.

Clark didn't like sharing his tiny room with the ingrate, but he had told the bail bondsman that he'd be his big brother's custodian and would keep an eye on him twenty-four hours a day while he was out on bail. That didn't mean he'd share his king-sized bed with the fetid fellow, though. He had managed to wedge the motel's rollaway cot into the economy-sized room by shoving it under the bathroom counter. It was either that or Eight would have to sleep in the tub. And that wasn't likely. Eight hated baths—he thought they were for girls only.

"Wake up, dude!" Clark kicked his brother's foot to punctuate his request, then walked over and opened the window another couple inches. Eight's stench was overpowering. Until he was done with his instructions and could leave the room, those erratic breezes would have to do to make the air quality tolerable.

"Today you start your new job—cleaning carpets—so get out of bed."

Eight grunted, scratched his crotch, and rolled over to the edge of the cot. He started to sit up and smacked the side of his head on the underside of the bathroom counter. "Damn!" He flopped back onto the thin foam mattress, dropped one holey sock-covered foot over the edge, scooted the other leg over to join it, and then paused to figure out his next move. He finally slithered over the edge, following his feet to the floor, where he sat, glassy-eyed and panting, legs splayed apart, wondering why he even bothered to listen to his brother.

Clark waited for Eight to extricate himself from under the counter before he continued. "Listen, I'll show you how to do the first one, but then you'll have to do the rest of the rooms yourself. I can't be with you the whole time you're working, but I'll never be more than a few hundred feet away. Now, can I trust you not to run away?"

"No worries about that." Eight grinned, remembering that his quarry was just a few rooms away. "No worries." He grabbed the mini coffee pot on the counter and poured out two cups of coffee, one only half-full. He reached into his pocket, slyly opened a little paper envelope, and dumped its contents into the full cup. He glanced back, saw that his brother was looking at a sheet of paper, and then went back to preparing the coffee. He made a big show of pouring sugar into both cups, stirring them with a flourish, pinkie held out.

Clark waited until his brother was done with the barista duties, and then gave him the list of empty rooms to clean along with a master keycard.

"Sweet," Eight said when Clark told him what it was, "I mean, thanks." He held up the keycard as if it was the Jewel of the Nile—he wouldn't even have to steal it from him.

He watched—well, sort of—as Clark showed him how to operate the carpet cleaner. "Do this room first," Clark said. "I'll come back and check on you in half an hour or so. I have some people checking out real soon, so you're on your own. Don't disappoint me, eh?"

"No worries," he repeated, then gloated, "No worries. Oh, and thanks for starting the coffee. Here, I fixed one for you, too," he said with a wink. "I hope you like lots of sugar."

## **31 Mickey and Minnie Mouse
*August 8, 2013, 11:00 AM*

James picked up a used plastic bag for trash and saw there was still something in it: the nightshirt he had bought for Leah on their first shopping trip together. "Hey," he called out.

"Yesss," Leah said slowly, anticipating a joke or a prank. *Why am I so comfortable with him? He always seems to be able to please and surprise me. He certainly seems like Mr. Right. And so far, he hasn't given me any reason to regret my snap decision to marry him and go on the long—lifelong—trip back to the 18th century and Mom.*

James squinted as he tried to read her face, confused and unsure of her suspicious reaction. *'Why is she grinning like that? Did I say something funny, or fart? Oh, good grief! She really is getting under my skin...and what a wonderful place for her to be... Stop that, Melbourne! Pay attention to the conversation you started!* "I purchased something for you, but forgot to give it to you. You've been sleeping in your shirt and I…um…thought that this might be a little more…" He gulped as he searched for a better word—couldn't think of one—and so just spit it out, "modest."

"Oh, you don't like looking at my butt cheeks when I get up in the morning?" She raised one eyebrow, as if waiting for a reply—but really didn't want or expect one—and then laughed out loud. She knew he had watched her perform discrete tugs at her shirttail when she got out of bed. At least now she had panties, though.

Rather than answer her awkward question, James shook his head, ignoring it. He took the red, white, and black nightshirt out of the bag, unfolded it, and shook it out, as if it were a toreador's cape.

"Mickey and Minnie Mouse!" she squealed, "a practically perfect pair." Leah suddenly remembered the last time she had said those words—their first full day together. She had referred to the two of them as such after spending their first platonic night together in the motel's king-sized bed. Well, she had been right about the designation, even if she hadn't known much about him at the time. And he was getting more and more desirable every day, every hour.

*James remembered when he had heard her use that phrase and could tell by the look of nostalgia on her face that she was thinking about that day, too.* "So how come Minnie gets to wear a skirt, but Mickey goes around with nothing on but shoes and gloves? Do you think we could get away with that? I mean, with this heat, it almost sounds like a good idea, except for the gloves part."

"Well, maybe," she paused and added, "but only *after* we're married." Leah felt a blush bloom instantly, racing from her cheeks to her shoulders. *Damn, why was this happening?*

172

She quickly changed the subject, trying to quench her body's sudden warmth. "How did you know I wore a size medium?" she asked coolly. She knew it was a dumb question, but had to change the subject from running around with her soon to be husband, both of them naked... *Damn, I'm blushing again!*

James could see how embarrassed she was with the topic of nudity. He smirked at her and said, "Oh, does the 'M' mean medium? I thought if I gave it to you, then that 'M' meant you would be *mine.*"

"Oh, so if *you* wear this, then *you're* mine?" she asked coyly. Any lingering doubts about marrying him were evaporating with each blush. Now she was definitely glad she had decided to marry him—he was absolutely charming!

James performed a fast one-handed grab, pulled off his tee shirt, and donned the new nightshirt in four seconds flat. He straightened out the seams of the snug-fitting garment, brought his face up to look at her, and said, "If that's all it takes, then I'm all yours, *darlin'.*"

"Here," she approached him cautiously. She wanted to be frisky, but besides the fact that she wasn't sure how much he was just playing the hetero sexy hunk, and how much was real appeal—she was beginning to doubt those tabloid stories that he was gay—she was still on her period and didn't want to get too carried away. She knew the first time with him probably wouldn't be perfect, but she at least wanted it less messy. "I get the shirt tonight. You can wear it tomorrow," she cooed, "if you're a good boy."

Leah reached down and fingered the hem of the nightshirt, gently lifting it above his hips, keeping her eyes away from his face, but unable to keep her hands off his skin. His flesh felt so good under her hands. She wanted to savor every nuance of his firm and slightly furry form.

James let her take the shirt, only giving her a token amount of assistance in its removal. *Her hands were cool on his belly, ribs, then up and across his shoulders and arms, as she gently tugged the soft cotton over his head. Yes, they were cool and inspiring. He'd have to turn the temperature down on the shower in the morning and remember how her hands had been all over his upper torso. It wouldn't take too much to stretch this memory into one of 'her hands all over his lower body.'*

"If you don't mind," she said, breaking his reverie, "I want to take a shower. I feel kind of icky, and really, I want to enjoy every luxury I can before we leave. I think I'll miss showers more than anything else."

"You do that," James said, then sucked in air at the thought that maybe she pleasured herself in the shower like he did. "You do that," he repeated. Hopefully, she took images and memories of him in there with her. At least, he thought women did the same thing in private that men did...

## **\*\*32 Call 911**
*August 8, 2013, 11:00 AM*

Eight had watched the Brit and Leah—yeah, that was her name—
leave an hour earlier. They were probably renting the room on a daily basis.
That meant they'd have to be back by noon to pay for the next day. He'd
have to do something fast. One thing he had learned from Grandpa was to
strike now—today's lucky break might be a stone wall tomorrow.

He hid in the empty room next to theirs and waited for them to
return. It was 11:00. Check-out time was noon. He was pretty sure he hadn't
missed them. Nope, there they were. The Limey always let the woman
drive. He was either very brave or really lazy. Gee, he probably even had
her wipe his butt. He chuckled at his own crude thought. Well, he'd let her
wipe his ass anytime. She was kinda cute, but a little young for his tastes.

*James thought he saw someone in the empty room next to theirs.*
*Well, maybe it was rented out now. The season was slow, and there weren't*
*any new cars in the parking lot, but maybe someone had taken a taxi here.*
*Hopefully, they wouldn't be too noisy. He and Leah were keeping early*
*hours and certainly didn't want to have party animals in the room next door,*
*staying up until the wee hours of the morning, drinking, and carousing. The*
*wee hours were when they got up for their walk, breakfast, and to complete*
*the tasks on their to-do checklist.*

Eight pulled back quickly. Damn! The man had seen him, or at least
had seen that there was someone in the room. Damn, damn, damn!

He listened at the door, waiting for what seemed like an hour for
them to leave. What was taking them so long? Didn't they know that they
had to pay for the room in the next fifteen minutes?

Finally, the door was shutting. Eight peaked out and saw the Brit
walking towards the office. He also heard the shower running. Evidently,
the woman was still in the room, taking a midday shower. Hmm, maybe he'd
get a free show. Nope, concentrate on getting the letters. Once he had them,
he could have all the hookers and shower shows that money could buy.

Ж✕Ж

The lobby was empty when James came in. The ever-present Clark
was nowhere to be seen or heard. James called out, "Hallo" several times,
both inside and out. As he stepped behind the Formica counter in the tiny
office, he heard odd noises, almost like grunts, then suddenly, *crash!*

James pushed open the 'employees only' door and saw Clark on the
floor, his body twisted like a drunken yogi, nearly buried under rolls of toilet
paper and boxes of tissues.

"Are you okay?" he asked, as he tossed aside paper products to
make room so he could help the fallen man get to his feet.

Clark reached out and accepted the assistance. "Uh, I think so. I'm

174

sure glad I grabbed for that shelf and not the one with the glasses and ice buckets. Thanks."

Clark nudged aside the cartons of toilet paper and tissues with his feet, trying to create order out of chaos, when he suddenly looked up at James. "Oh, is it check-out time already? Sorry, I think I passed out there for a few minutes. Uh, am I bleeding?" Clark took a quick inventory as he patted himself down. "Not that I'm afraid of blood or anything—I just don't want to make a mess on the carpet. Oh, shit! Eight's supposed to be cleaning the carpets and…oh, excuse me."

Clark scurried over to his position behind the counter and stood up straight, shoulders back, chin out, as if he were acting the part of a storekeeper in a high school play. He watched James with unblinking eyes, waiting for him to proceed to the other side and take on his role as customer. "Was everything to your satisfaction, sir?" he asked, as if nothing had happened.

James dipped his head and looked into Clark's eyes, shook his head slowly side to side and asked, "Are you sure you didn't hit your head a little too hard? If you'd like, we can take you to the emergency room. Your eyes don't look quite right." James didn't want to say it looked like he was high, that his pupils were dilated, but that was what he saw.

"I'm fine, uh…I think…" Clark's last words trailed off to a whisper. He grabbed the counter and slid to the floor in a controlled fall. "Oh, shit," he mumbled, as he rolled forward, his body bent in half. And then he was out cold.

James ran back around to Clark's side of the counter and straightened out his slumped-over body. He put his ear to his chest. He was still breathing, but his heart was racing. He didn't want to leave him alone and run back to get Leah. Well, when in doubt, call 911.

James reached up and grabbed the cordless phone from the counter. He dialed 911, but there was no answer. "Shit!" He stood up and looked around. The desk phone was a multi-line model. He picked up the receiver, dialed 911 again, and got the same response: nothing but a click and a return to the dial tone. He looked at the phone' again and saw the little sticker: Dial 9 for an outside line. "Well, fuck!" he exclaimed. He pushed another line, dialed 9, waited for the tone, and then dialed 911.

"You're not supposed to say fuck," mumbled Clark, as he tried to open his eyes. He managed to get a peek of daylight, then his eyeballs rolled back into his head, and he was unconscious again.

James crouched down; one hand holding the phone, the other on Clark's wrist, making sure he was alive, his heart still beating.

"Is this an emergency?" asked the woman on the other end of the line.

"Yes, yes, um, I don't know what's going on here, but the desk

175

clerk fell. I thought he was going to be okay, but now his pupils are dilated, and he can't even sit up. I think he hit his head pretty hard. Um…can you send an ambulance…um…right away?"

"Calm down, sir. I already have a unit dispatched. Can the man breathe and is he bleeding?"

James always thought that he'd be able to handle an emergency in a cool, calm, collected manner. Even excitable would be better than this. He was panicking, and that was making him even more frazzled. *Focus, man, this isn't about you and how you're handling the situation. Just answer her questions!* "Um, bleeding, no; breathing, yes. And his heart seems to be racing. How soon until they get here?"

"They're on their way now, sir," the iron-willed voice on the other end replied.

*You're worthless, Melbourne, a babbling idiot. She's holding this situation together by the strength of her tone while you're falling apart.*

The piercing whine of the sirens brought James out of his pity party. "I can hear them now, ma'am. Please tell them we're in the main lobby, not in one of the rooms." He hung up the phone, then realized that neither of them had said good-bye. Well, he didn't have anything else to say, so she could just call back if she forgot to ask him something.

The sirens were getting closer. He didn't want Leah to be frightened. *Shoot, she'd be fine in this situation. This was what she was trained for.* He swallowed hard. Now he was glad that she wasn't here. He didn't want her to see his ineptitude. *Buck up, Melbourne!* He looked down at Clark. He was still alive and breathing, but his pasty-white complexion was now tinged green. He lifted the man's right shoulder and turned him onto his side. Hopefully it was just a little gas.

Braat!

"I guess not," James said, and turned away from the pukey, coffee-colored mess Clark had just regurgitated.

Sirens, flashing lights, and a sense of charged excitement filled the air outside the front door. Three assorted-sized medics tumbled out of the gleaming white and blue ambulance and pushed through the glass doors, ready to remedy any situation.

James stood up from behind the counter to make his presence known. "He's back here, but watch out—he just lost his cookies and everything else." James moved away and made way for the professionals and their paraphernalia.

"What do you know about him?" asked the square-jawed lady medic with the aluminum clipboard.

"Um, his name is Clark Kent MacLeod and when I came in, he was in the back room. Evidently, a shelf of supplies fell on top of him. It was only rolls of toilet paper and boxes of tissues, and I thought he'd be okay, but then he started acting strange, and his eyes were dilated..." James paused and bit his bottom lip. He didn't want to suggest anything that might get the lad in trouble, but they should probably know.

"Yes?" the lady asked, "You wanted to say more about his eyes?"

"Well, it looked like he was stoned, but I don't think he's the type, despite his long hair. He's a pretty straightforward and dependable kid. He practically runs this place, from what I've seen. I think he lives here, too. And no, before you ask, I don't know about any next of kin." He paused as he watched the medics check Clark's vitals, and then noticed one of them scraping the remains of the vomit into a plastic bag.

He turned away and asked the medic, "Which hospital are you taking him to?"

"Moses H. Cohn," she said. "But give us a few minutes to get there and for the doctors to check him out."

James would make sure he and Leah went to see him. There were worse feelings than being alone in a hospital with no one to care about you, but not many. In this case, he had control over it. He knew he'd want someone to be concerned if their places were switched.

Ж☦Ж

Eight stepped out from the room and watched to make sure that the Brit had gone into the lobby. It would take him a while to find Clark. That date rape drug he got from Harry would be just the ticket to put baby brother out of commission for a while. He couldn't possibly have tasted it in the coffee after all the sugar he had put into it for him. "Sweet!" he said, then chuckled at the irony of his remark.

And now that JB had the map, he had the letters, and Niner had the old broad, they were sure to find out where the treasure was hidden.

## **33 Leah's Shower
*August 8, 2013, 11:15 AM*

"I don't care if it *is* the middle of the day," Leah said aloud, as if trying to convince herself. "A cool shower taken when the sun's still shining never hurt anyone, and it's fat-free and environmentally friendly. Well, at least it is when you live in a town with a capable water treatment plant, adequate rainfall, and plenty of reservoirs."

She wasn't in the desert anymore, where she had always felt guilty about taking long showers. "Yeah, guilty and poor," she grumbled. She started the shower and remembered how her Dad had almost hit the roof the first time the water bill hit $200.

*"What the hell is this?" he bellowed. "I'm going to call the City right now and have them read that meter again."*

*She had heard his side of the conversation, but it didn't really mean anything to her until later. His emotions were high—that part she recalled. He was generally a very mellow person, but when he felt that he had been wronged, watch out!*

*"No, I don't have a pool or a lawn, and the garden is dormant now. You'd better get someone out here right away. If you read the meter correctly like you claim, then I'll bet there's a leak in the water main or hose or whatever it is that goes up to the house. Okay, water line, whatever. Just get someone out here right away. I'm not going to pay for what I didn't use."*

*Well, the utility man came to the house and checked the meter on site. No, they hadn't estimated this residence in months. He checked the integrity of the line to the house with some sort of metal detector apparatus, and that came up negative too; no breaks or leaks. It was at that very moment—the two men figuratively scratching their heads, trying to solve the dilemma—when she came outside with the towel wrapped around her head, fresh out of the shower. She walked nonchalantly up to the mailbox, retrieved a bundle of letters and the latest issue of her favorite fashion magazine, waved to the two slack-jawed men, and went back inside the house.*

*"How old is she?" asked the meter man.*

*Dad gritted his teeth and said, "Fifteen," huffed in disgust, then apologized to the man.*

*"Yeah, mine's sixteen now, and male. If she's anything like he is, you'd better put a timer on her or start making her pay the bills herself. I doubt that it'll get any better unless you find some way to curtail it, I mean her."*

*She remembered how excited she was when Dad told her that he was increasing her allowance from $20 a week to $200 a month. She gave* *him a big hug, did a little 'money dance,' then stopped when she saw his face. "Okay, what's the catch?" she asked, realizing that if it sounded too good to be true, then it probably was.*

*"You have to pay the water bill. Anything left after that is yours. I'll go ahead and pay this month's bill—it was $200—but you'd better time your showers if you don't want to start owing me your allowances for the next six months."*

Leah stuck her hand behind the shower curtain to test the water. It was just right. If she had a thermometer, it would probably read two degrees cooler than body temperature. If she got it too warm, it was uncomfortable, and if it was too cool, her body would overcompensate and her core temperature would rise in self-protection. Yes, tepid was just right.

The guilt-free, unrestricted stream of water running down her warm, sweaty body—overheated from the late morning run—felt extra sweet. She leaned into the high-pressure water stream and felt its coolness penetrate her thick hair. She ran her fingers through her silky, saturated tresses, indulging her tactile senses, then stepped out of the flow and poured the entire bottle of motel-provided shampoo-conditioner blend onto the top of her head, working the pearly matrix into thick suds from her scalp to the ends. Her whole body tingled at the sensual richness of the foamy bubble cascade as it slipped down her wet curves. Back under the shower nozzle, the water pushed the lather off her head. The mass slid down between her breasts, forming a little eddy at her bellybutton, then flowed over and around her belly mound to the juncture of her thighs. She crouched forward just a bit and spread her legs to let the sudsy water wash away the muskiness of her period. She snorted. Mom had told her the best part about being pregnant was not having a monthly—that and not having to worry about getting pregnant! Well, pregnancy would come later—she hoped. First, she had to get exposed!

Leah turned around and rinsed the rest of the shampoo out of her hair. As the water raced down her back, she bent forward and presented her backside to the main force of the water spray. She spread her legs further until the rapid river of water raced down her butt crack forward to tickle her pleasure spot. She gasped at the intensity, and recalled the first time she had experienced the quick elation of gentle water pressure down there. She grinned; no stinky fingers this way. She bent over further still, accelerating the rate of water flow with her splayed position, her head on the opposite wall for stability. She crossed her arms and gently fondled her water-slickened nipples, circling each one, gently working up to mild tugging and twisting. She wasn't completely ambidextrous, but was able to excite both sides at the same time.

Now it was time for dessert: the mental image. She could almost feel James's soft hair beneath her hands as he suckled her, his tongue working the rosy brown erectile tissue in his mouth. She gasped at the reality of her shower fantasy. *Phew!* It probably wasn't as good as the real thing, but it was what she had, and the sensation it produced was real enough.

She stood up straight and turned the water temperature down just a tad to recover. *He couldn't be gay, he just couldn't be. He was such a good kisser! Well, maybe men kissed each other, but that wasn't the only thing. There was something else... Oh, to hell with it.* She could stand two in a row. If he got back before she was done with her second dessert, he'd just have to wait for her to be finished with the bathroom.

Leah enhanced her memory of leaning up against him as she removed the shirt. He had only put it on because he wanted to belong to her, and it wasn't just for the journey back in time. Mmm. She recalled how firm and muscular his arms were, his skin soft with the downy covering of fine hair. She touched herself again and visualized his body next to hers. She had taken her time in removing his shirt on purpose, so she could memorize the nuances of his muscle groups, the exact firmness of his biceps, the sharpness of his elbow, his musky aroma. And it wasn't sweat that she had smelled; it was male readiness musk.

Her eyes popped open as concrete certainty landed in front of her like a hundred ton boulder—immovable and hard to miss. *He had been in such an all-fired-up hurry to strip off his shirt, to don mine as a cotton polyester claim that he belonged to me. I can't image Billy doing that... Well, yes, I can, but he'd have the look of a court jester in his eyes, waiting for me to laugh. James wasn't waiting for appreciation or applause, though; he had the look of lust. No, more than just the look. I could feel it when I leaned into him to take off his shirt. He was firm and wanted me!*

She rubbed herself faster now, more vigorously, getting closer to a second orgasm with the thought that he was truly a gentleman, *her* gentleman. He had not taken advantage of her sleeping next to him, had let her touch and tease him without returning the pawing. And that 'one on the books' kiss. It was fantastic! He wanted her, had agreed to marry and take care of her, but it was because of how he *really* felt about her, and not from guilt or obligation to be her escort back in time to visit her mother. He had money and a title, but s*he* was who, and what, he wanted.

And she wanted him, too.

She spurted with the image of consummating their wedding night, the night he would admit his sexuality. She sighed deeply as she relaxed into her joy and the tub, the cool water raining down on her head, dribbling past her closed eyes. *Yes, I'm certain he's straight, but I won't let him know I'm onto his secret yet; at least until my period's over. Hmm, countdown number two—only three more days...*

Knock, knock, knock. Leah was brought out of her afterglow by the rapid, insistent knocking on the door. Shoot! She had the key and James was locked out. "Coming," she hollered loudly. "I've already come," she sang softly, "Twice." She wrapped one towel around her head and grabbed another one to hold in front of her. She'd treat him to a butt shot, at least.

She opened the door with a sly grin, nothing but the barely decent hand towel in front of her. "Come on in," she trilled when she saw James's shocked face. She turned around, flashed her bare fanny at him, and bounced back into the bathroom.

"Um…um…" James mumbled, shocked and stunned, unable to compose a coherent sentence. "Crap." He stared at the bathroom door. She was standing on the other side, just inches away—naked and apparently frisky. He slowly started banging his head on the door's molding. "Why? Or why now?" he groaned.

He took a deep breath to compose himself, then called through the door. "Leah, we have a problem. Could you throw on something quick? We have to go to the hospital."

"What?" she screeched, and poked her head out the door. She couldn't believe what she'd heard, but just the tone of his voice was enough to tell her that there was an emergency.

"I said we have to go to the hospital. The ambulance just took Clark to the emergency room. I found him on the floor when I went to pay the rent. I…I…I think he was drugged."

Leah popped out of the bathroom, her hair a tangle worthy of Medusa, clad only in her sports bra and white cotton panties. James turned his head back to the wooden doorframe and continued his head banging, ultimately rolling his forehead side to side in disbelief and frustration. He couldn't even appreciate her near-nude appearance!

Leah had thrown on a dress and was calling him, probably for the second time since her voice was loud and adamant. "Come on! I've got all the keys. Tell me what happened on the way. They're taking him to my hospital, aren't they?"

James nodded as he held open the room door for her, remembering at the last moment to grab a couple of water bottles and his bag. *Poor Clark. First Leah, then him. Why all these attacks? Modern day chemicals, pfft! I wonder if they had poisonings back in the old days. Of course, dummy— remember Socrates and hemlock? It's just that back then they didn't have 911, ambulances, and stomach pumps.*

Leah quickly opened the car door for herself rather than wait for his gentlemanly deed. He saw that she had, nodded that he understood, and walked around just in time to catch the passenger door as she pushed it open from the inside, sparing his fingers the solar-heated door handle.

She sped out of the parking lot, got onto the highway, then turned to him and gave him the 'look' to start the story now.

181

He began without preamble. "I walked in to pay Clark, but he—nobody—was around. I called out and heard a moan. Clark was on the floor, covered with toilet paper and tissues." Leah frowned in disbelief. He clarified his statement, "I mean, rolls of toilet paper and boxes of tissues—the supply shelf had collapsed on top of him. He was disoriented, but let me help him up and guide him to the front counter. I noticed his eyes were dilated and well…just not right. I don't think he does drugs; at least not while working. He looked sick, collapsed again to the floor, and started puking. I turned him on his side so he didn't choke on his own vomit. That's when it hit me: the smell. It was the same as when you and I first met at the airport. But why him?"

"Yeah, and why me?" Leah echoed his unspoken question. "I think there was more to that bartender wanting me than just for a good time. Hey," she popped up like a sharp spring in her seat cushion had just poked her. "Your bag—is everything in it? Do you think someone could be after the letters? I mean, they were nearby in both instances."

"And so were you. I don't think I want to leave you alone again, ever, even for a quick shower. I can live without the letters, but I couldn't live without you. Oh, that sounded sappy, but damn it, I don't *need* the letters. Hell, they survived for 230 years without me, but what I'm trying to say is now that you're here with me, well, you're flesh and blood, and joy and hope, and sass…"

"And ass," Leah finished. "Thank you…really, thanks. I think I get the picture, because I feel the same way about you. Although, I haven't seen *your* ass…"

"Well, you've seen my... Hey, we're here," he said, glad for the opportunity to change the subject about her seeing his boxer short's 'pop out' the first day they had shared the motel room.

"Saved by the emergency room sign," Leah crowed. She knew what he meant, though, and that was enough.

## **\*\*34 After 911**

"We're here for Clark MacLeod," James told the woman at the admissions window. "No, I'm not next of kin, but I am the one who found him and maybe saved his life." Since he didn't get even a blink of acknowledgment, he asked, "Doesn't that count?" not really expecting an answer. He looked up and saw that Leah was attempting an end run, standing by the big potted plant beside the security door, waiting to sneak in with the next person with this week's access code.

"I'm sorry, sir. You'll have to wait out here until they call you. Please have a seat."

But James stood resolute, his feet planted like a Doberman pinscher protecting his home. He had grown fond of the mop-headed kid, and if it was him all alone in an emergency room, he'd want someone, anyone, to come check on him.

A doctor—or intern or whoever—in green scrubs approached the door and punched in his pass code. Leah smiled familiarly and followed in behind him like she belonged. James saw that his family proxy had been admitted, so backed off in his stare-down with the receptionist, retreating to a front row seat in the waiting room. She smirked at him; she had won the confrontation. Although she was sporting the victor's grin, he had his person in behind the lines, checking on their friend. He may have lost the eye to eye contest, but had won the territorial battle. The bossy administrator just didn't know it yet.

While he was waiting for Leah's report on Clark, James decided to check out her theory about his bag and the letters it contained being the ultimate target of the attacks. He opened up the leather satchel and looked for them.

All of the letters were missing!

*Stop stressing, Melbourne, breathe. They have to be in here somewhere. You must have moved them from the side pocket to another section.*

He pressed on the innocuous black thumbprint-lock button and the bag 'click-clicked.' The steel bar that secured the rods released, and the center section opened up. He pawed through the limited contents. The divorce papers, his little motel stationery notebook, passport, and the cigarette pack of jewels were still in there, but not the blue ribbon-tied bundle of letters.

He clutched the bag to his chest and sank back into the padded waiting room chair. His heart dropped to his stomach, and his stomach rose to his throat. Now *he* felt like he was going to puke. "How and where?" he asked aloud softly, as if some ethereal being was going to answer his question.

He was sure the letters had been there this morning. He closed his eyes and went back over when he had last seen them. No, he didn't remember locking them away. They were going to read them this afternoon. They weren't even hidden, just shoved into the side pocket. Someone knew what he was looking for.

"Yeah, or they fell out onto the floor, Mr. Paranoia," James mumbled. He pulled back from the situation emotionally to assess it like Billy would. *Okay, letters verified in bag before breakfast. The bag was in my possession the entire meal and at the shopping trip to the fabric store and at the library. Check. It was locked in the car when we went on our spontaneous late morning run at the park. Check. Bag was in Leah's hand when she went into our room by herself. Yes, but… Hmm, she was in the shower while I was tending to Clark in the lobby. Hmm, hmm. Clark couldn't be the culprit, but could he have faked an incident and had an accomplice sneak into the room and grab the letters while Leah was in the shower? Well, yes, but most likely, no. Clark wouldn't poison or drug himself in order to…well, in order to do anything. And he definitely wasn't faking the dilated eyes, puking, and passed out position under the supply shelf. The motel was pretty much empty. Someone would need either our key or a pass key to get into the room.*

No, the motel wasn't empty he recalled with a flash. He had seen, or thought that he had seen, someone in the room next to theirs just before he went to pay the bill. It was possible, probable, that the mystery person did something—gave Clark a spiked drink, perhaps—then took his pass key. That person could have sneaked into their room while he was tending to the fallen clerk and calling 911. And if the culprit had been hiding out next door, he would have seen him leave, heard the water running, and known that Leah was occupied and therefore out of the picture. He then could have let himself in, grabbed the letters, and sneaked back out while she was still in the shower.

He sighed heavily with gratitude. The letters were gone—who cared, not him—not really. But the thief had been decent enough—no, wrong word; smart enough—to listen for the shower, so he wasn't caught in the act. He paled at the thought. Leah catching a thief in her all-together or dressed as she was when he came into the room to get her: nothing but a bath towel on her head and a hand towel over her breasts and…oh, crap!

James raced to the water fountain, closed his eyes, held his breath, and put his face in the stream of chilled water. Hopefully, the cold face wash would keep his fear-fueled bile from coming up. He brought up his head and swiped his forearm across his face, squeegee-ing the excess droplets with the back of his forearm. Terror induced regurgitation averted. Now what?

He had to call Billy was what. This was his specialty. But what could he tell him had been stolen? The truth: old, priceless, antique family

184

heirlooms, historical documents maybe? But he knew it wouldn't matter to Billy what was stolen. What would matter to him too, he realized, was that Leah had been in the bathroom, one unlocked door away, naked and vulnerable, when the unforced break-in occurred. They were no longer safe where they were.

James went back to the waiting area and debated on whether to call Billy right away—he was probably just going to bed—or should he wait until later. *What good would later be? Call now, Melbourne. It's no different than you going to bed at midnight rather than 9 PM.* James took out his phone and dialed before he could rationalize, argue, or doubt his convictions for calling.

"Yo, bro," Billy answered sprightly, "What's happenin' with you and my favorite lady, Lady Leah?"

James's first reaction was pride that Leah's best friend was happy that he was going to marry her. Second and now most urgent reaction: ask for help.

"Billy, we've been robbed," he said. As soon as the words were out of his mouth, he realized that he considered the letters hers as much as his. Duh! Her mother wrote them or at least she had written the first one.

"Robbed? Of what? When? Is Leah okay? Where are you right now?" Billy fired off his questions, not even taking a breath between them or pausing for James to answer.

"Letters; she's okay, but we're at the hospital," James replied just as rapidly. He suddenly realized how lame 'letters' must have sounded. "They were historical family papers, over 200 years old, Revolutionary War documents, probably worth a fortune, but they were my family's and Leah's, too. Her..." James stopped his compulsion to tell him that her mother had written the letters to her 230 years ago. *Damn! I must be stressed. Shut up, Melbourne, and let Billy come over and take care of this before he changes his mind about you and letting you marry his pride and joy.* James realized Billy was talking and he hadn't been listening.

"Sorry, mate, I'm a little stressed here. We're at Leah's ER and seeing to the motel clerk, Clark. Shoot, I'm sorry. No, Leah wasn't hurt and neither was I. I think the lad was doped with the same stuff used on Leah at the airport."

"What? Leah was doped at the airport? When? Shit, no, wait a minute. Let me get my clothes on, and I'll be right there."

James got a flash image: Billy in nothing but his towel again. Thankfully he never got an image of him without the towel. Now that would be very disturbing...

James looked over and saw Leah exiting the big double doors from the ER ward. The scowl on her face was three layers deep. "What?" he asked, as she walked toward him, looking in both directions, as if to make sure they didn't have any witnesses.

"Clark's a little dopey, but he'll be okay. He doesn't remember anything except his arms and mouth going numb, and then clutching for the shelf to break his fall. Oh, and you helping him get up. He said to tell you thanks. I told him you stayed with him and called 911. His eyes really popped open at that. I got the gut feeling that he's not used to people being nice to him or helping him out. Uh, do you think we ought to call Billy?" she added, not as an afterthought, but with just a bit of guilt or shame for not suggesting it earlier.

"*We* already did; he's on his way."

Just then, a male nurse came out from behind the closed doors to greet them. "Leah and James?" he asked to make sure he had the right people. James glared at him with mild disgust. *Of course, he was James,* and then he backed off. The man was only being cautious, which was part of his job. "Yes," Leah replied. "This is James and I'm Leah."

"The patient, I mean Mr. MacLeod, asked to speak with you two." The man in green didn't wait for them to accept his invitation, but turned and pressed in his code to admit them into the inner sanctum of healing. Leah shrugged at James, then the two of them followed through the doors, the valise clutched tightly under James's arm.

"Hey, thanks, mate," Clark called out cheerily when he saw James come around the drawn curtains. "I'm sure glad I grabbed for the TP and not the glasses and ice buckets..."

"That was my first thought, too," said James. He was glad the kid was feeling better. At least, he sure looked better.

"Um, I need to ask you both a favor. I could be in big trouble. I don't want you to lie for me or anything, but just swear that, well, tell him what happened. You see, as soon as they bring me a phone, I have to call the bail bondsman and tell him that my twenty-four/seven supervision got compromised, but not on purpose. Damn! I don't know what happened. One minute everything's fine, and the next minute...well, you know, you were there."

"What's twenty-four/seven supervision?" James asked. Just then, an aide appeared with a cordless phone. "Dial 9 to get out," she said. James inhaled deeply, recalling his frustration with that little idiosyncrasy of the American phone system.

"Nurse! Ma'am?" Clark called to the aide. The frumpy woman turned and scowled as if he was interrupting her dinner. "Ma'am," he repeated when he was sure he had her attention, "can you hand me my pants? I need my wallet out of them."

The aide grunted and left the area to reappear a few seconds later with a white drawstring plastic bag. She set it down hard at his side. "Here," she said gruffly, then shuffled away.

"Thank you," he called after her with complete sincerity. James was glad to see that he didn't repay her rudeness in kind. He really had caught him at a bad time when they first met. The lad had better manners than most young men his age.

Clark took his wallet from his pants, dialed the phone, and then held up one finger to make sure they knew he wanted them to wait.

"Yes, this is Clark MacLeod, and due to circumstances beyond my control, I have lost contact with my brother, Atholl MacLeod the Eighth. I was, am, his twenty-four/seven custodian. I am currently at the emergency room at the hospital, and the last time I saw him was at the motel where I worked. Yes, yes, that's the right address. He might be in the office or in room 122. Yes, I understand that you have to pick him up. Hopefully, my ride in the ambulance to the ER is validation enough that I didn't plan something. Yes, I have witnesses, and they're willing to give statements. I just don't want to pay a huge fine because I passed out!"

Leah and James looked at each other with wide eyes. Leah mouthed the words, "Are the letters safe?"

James turned his head slowly, side to side, and saw her blanch. Now it was his turn. He put up one finger and asked her to wait. He needed to talk to Clark about his brother.

Clark hung up the phone. "Well, it looks like I'm off the hook. I don't know if they'll keep Eight in there for good or let him come back to the motel with me when I get out of here. I need to call them once I'm back up to snuff and at home, er, work. Well, same difference since I live there. Is there something wrong, *James*?" he asked, stressing the use of his Christian name as opposed to his titled name.

Leah looked over and saw that James did look off. "You'd better sit down," she said. "What's wrong?" she whispered to him once her back was turned to Clark.

James took a deep breath to compose himself, then told a bold-faced lie, "I guess I'm just a bit hungry. If you're okay here, Clark, I think we'll go get our belated lunch. Are you going to need a ride back to the motel?"

"Nah, the bus comes right by both places. I'll probably be back there before you are. Not much is going on. I had them call my boss when I was still in the ambulance. He should be there by now. It'll do him good to put in an hour or so. You know how some of those salary workers are." Clark grinned. He was feeling better, and if he didn't have to watch out for his brother, he'd feel even better. He still didn't trust the man, even if they were related.

Leah stood next to James, waiting for him to say good-bye so they could leave. She was in a hurry to find out what the big mystery was, but didn't want Clark to know something was amiss.

"I'm ready if you are, ma'am," James said, offering his elbow.

"Take care, Clark. We'll see you soon, I'm sure."

Just then, the grumpy nurse-type person came in with a lunch platter. "Ciao!" Clark proclaimed with a broad wave of his hand to his two friends. "Ooh, chow," he said as a light joke to Ms. Grumpy.

The aide couldn't help but let a smile escape at his pun. She put down the food on the swing-out tray beside him, then patted him on the head, "*Manga!*" she said sweetly, and waddled away, chuckling at the silly man-child who had just made her smile.

ЖЖ

"So, what's going on?" Leah asked as soon as they were out of earshot.

"I got a letter last week just before I left England. It was from a…um," James closed his eyes, trying to recall the writing on the hastily scribbled note. "It was from a Benji MacKay. It said to watch out for the MacLeods and…um, 'I need to talk to you about Leah.' Crap, Leah, I didn't know you or anyone else with your name when I got the note. And I certainly didn't know any MacLeods to look out for. It was postmarked North Carolina and had a phone number. I wrote on the bottom of the letter that I didn't know a Leah or any MacLeods, and gave it back to the postal clerk to return to the sender."

"Do you happen to remember the phone number?" she asked hopefully.

"No, it's a miracle that I even remember the names." James shook his head. "Well, I guess if it was meant to be, we'll catch up with this Benji MacKay. I guess we could look up the name in the phone book or Google it, but I don't even recall what town in North Carolina it was from."

"Well, you've already met *Leah*," she said, batting her eyes at him playfully, "and we found out the hard way to watch out for the MacLeods—at least, for one of them."

She sighed, then grabbed James by the inner elbow, ready to escort him away from the drama and trauma of the hospital ER area. "So, life goes on, even if you didn't get the message like you were supposed to. Maybe that was all there was to it. And, like you said, if it was meant to be, then he'll catch up to you or us." Leah stopped suddenly and turned to James. "Do you think we'd better call Billy and tell him that he doesn't need to come down here?"

"Yes, that would be a good idea. He'll want to conduct a thorough investigation, though, no matter what. You see, I…um…kinda let him know you were poisoned at the airport, but that you're okay. Shoot."

"Don't worry about it. I got this." Leah pulled out her phone, speed dialed Billy, and started right into her diatribe, bright as a kindergarten teacher on the first day of school. "Hey, Billy. James said he called you about the fiasco at the motel that ended up with a trip to the ER. It turns out

188

it was no big deal. Please, go ahead and go back to bed. I promise we'll talk about it later. You need your sleep, and James wants to eat out." Leah grinned as she listened to Billy's reply. "No, not that way. Clean up your act, mister. We'll see you later."

Leah turned to James. "See, no further explanations needed. Now, we have lots of work to do and…" She shook her head quickly. "I don't want to have anything else to consider—my plate is full. As it is, I feel like I have to eat with my fingers because there isn't even enough room on the dish for the knife and fork!"

James grinned and visualized fancy Rogers sterling silverware, Waterford crystal, and fine Haviland china, then decided he had better push back the thought of her licking her fingers after a fried chicken dinner. Hurry up, seventeenth of August!

## **35 Interim and Waiting

It was still relatively early—three in the afternoon—but Leah was done for the day. Four long days in a row, hunched over projects on the wide tables under the bright lights of the library, had taken its toll. Her shoulders ached from the unaccustomed posture, and her eyes were teary from the constant focusing and refocusing required for her research and transcription.

Leah got up and walked away from her pile of tomes on 18th century etiquette and grooming, and stood behind James. He was totally involved in his drafting and hadn't heard her move. She didn't want to disturb him—he was making good progress—but she was done, at least for now. She watched as he traced the lines of the library's original map with his fingertip, then use the same finger to mark an invisible trail on his own 'old' parchment paper. Next, he'd pick up his pen, look at the nib each time to make sure he wasn't going to start a stroke with a blob of ink, then scribe his memorized finger-traced trail. She watched for several minutes, how long she didn't know. Time seemed to be standing still for her right now, but he must have recreated over a half dozen paths on his masterpiece while she stood behind him. She hated to interrupt his work, but she was starting to sway, and her head felt too heavy for her neck.

"Is it okay with you if we leave the library early? My eyes won't focus, and I'm afraid that if I keep pushing myself, I'll make more mistakes than progress. How about you? How are you feeling?"

James pushed his papers away and let out a big sigh. "I'm getting a bit bleary-eyed myself. How about just a break, though? If we give our eyes a rest, maybe we can come back here later or, then again, there's no reason why I can't finish this at *home*."

She smiled at the word *home*. "Yeah, I'd appreciate that," she said, grateful that she didn't have to be pushy. She helped him gather their works and let him pack everything into his leather valise.

"You know—well, you probably do—lying down in the middle of the afternoon is a luxury we may not be able to indulge in next month, or even next week. Well, at least on a bed with a comfortable mattress. Did you know that they stuffed mattresses with corn husks and/or straw?"

"Or feathers," he reminded her, as they walked out of the library into the afternoon sun. "Maybe we ought to see if we can invest in a gaggle of geese. Goose down is both soft and warm. I really don't think straw can be that comfortable, no matter how much it's romanticized."

"Besides, it's dusty and mice brood, pee, and poop in it. Gee, that motel bed is sounding more enticing all the time. Come on, do you want to drive this time?" she asked, partly out of courtesy, but mostly with a perverse sense of humor. She knew he hated to drive in America.

James opened the driver's side door for her, "Sure, if everyone drives on the 'correct' side of the road. No, thanks, I'll just balance the load in the car by sitting in the passenger seat." He got in and reclined the seat back, closed his eyes, and pasted a fake—well, sort of fake—smile of bliss on his face in an exaggerated parody of a pampered commuter.

"You did drive in England, right?" she asked. James nodded, then realized she couldn't hear him nod—she was concentrating on negotiating the exit from the parking lot onto the highway. He brought the seat back up. "Yes, I did, and I'm proud to say I was never in an accident nor received any driving citations."

"So what kind of car did you drive?"

"A black sedan." He didn't want to sound boastful, so left out the fact that it was a classic Bentley Corniche, and that he had given it away to a near stranger—a nice public works employee—rather than risk it going back to his ex-wife. *Quick, change the subject.* "Morning or evening?" he asked.

"What?"

"What is not an option," he said sassily, "morning or evening?"

"Both!" she said with a bold self-assuredness.

"Ooh, what a greedy one, you are, aren't you?" he said with the same playfulness. She smiled and nodded briskly, as if she had won this round of rock, paper, scissors.

"Okay, five o'clock tomorrow morning we're going for a run, or maybe just a walk, depending on what shape we're in. And then, since you said both, we can take another one after the afternoon traffic has died down, and the air isn't so smoggy."

Leah groaned. "Yeah, well, you're right. Walking and riding horses are the most common modes of transportation there—I mean here, back then—or riding in a wagon or a coach. And," she added with exaggerated exasperation, "Since we *can't* take horses back with us, and a wagon would be *extremely* awkward to carry in our backpacks..."

She looked over to see if he was listening. He was and didn't even try to stifle his chortle at the mental image of a buckboard wagon poking out of the top of a hiker's backpack. "Well, I guess you're right about working out. But since our shoes aren't finished, I'm going to insist on buying a pair of cross trainers, so I can at least be comfortable getting my legs and lungs into shape. Are you game?"

"Oh, very game," he replied, squeezing back the image of her legs and what covered her lungs getting into shape. *Shoes, shoes, think of shoes: colors, tread designs, lace the shoes, pull out the tongue, no, no, wrong tongue image. Put in a sock-covered foot, tie the laces...*

"We'll have to have lace-up shoes, for sure," Leah added, for no apparent reason.

"Why?" he asked. He knew the real reason why she had spoken of laces, but now wanted to continue the mental game of ping pong that bounced the invisible ball of a thought back and forth, using only their own wits as paddles. "I mean, if we're going to leave the shoes here, what difference does it make? Velcro closures are faster to get on and off, right?"

"Well, yeah, but, gee, I don't know. I keep trying to be era correct in everything we do, and I guess I got carried away."

*Round one to Leah. She was fast with her excuse. Even if he knew the real reason for her train of thought, it was still possible she didn't realize she was sharing his mental images and feelings.*

"Hey, do you think that we can stop at the mall and get the shoes now?" she asked. "We can put off the afternoon nap until the shopping's done. I really don't want to get into a hot car one more time than I have to. This shouldn't take too long. They have lots of shoe stores to choose from."

*Afternoon nap, snuggled down...* "Yes, let's do that," he said quickly before the thought of lying next to her in the middle of the day for no reason other than their shared relaxation, blossomed into a size he couldn't contain. He should have taken a longer time in the shower this morning. He had a bad—or at least an overwhelming—case of Leah overload.

She had asked him about whether he wanted to go shopping or not, but it was just a courtesy query and she knew he knew it. She had already pulled into the mall. She was looking for a place to park, trying to remember which side of the huge complex had the most shoe stores, when it hit her. She shook her head in mild self-disgust. The whole idea of the trip was to get shoes so they could exercise at least once a day, and here she was, prowling the parking lot so she could get closer to her stores of choice. Bad Leah, she scolded herself.

There, a tree at the end of the lot without a car underneath. Shade would be better in the long run—ha ha, she thought—than a shorter trek to the air conditioning inside. That brought up another concern.

"This sounds ridiculous, but the air is so smoggy and nasty in town late in the day that maybe we ought to drive out of town to do our walking, at least for the evening walk."

James paused to think about what she had said before he replied. "Normally, I would agree with you, but this will only be for a few days. I would assume that when we do *go back,* the air will be considerably cleaner." Leah snorted at his remark, but he ignored it and continued, "Our lungs will be able to recover from any potential damage that a week of smog could incur. They will also be stronger when they have fresh air to process. Hence, breathe the crud now, and we'll have more energy from breathing the cleaner, more oxygenated-air later, right?"

"Right," she said. He came around to open her door for her, but once again, she was already out before he could get there.

"You know, you're going to have to practice being a lady," he said in exasperation.

Leah didn't say a word, but glared a 'what are you talkin about?' scowl at him.

"I mean, letting a man open the door for you, expecting a man to rise when you leave the table: common, for me, courtesies that Americans used to have, or so I would expect. I know not everyone in that era was from England—or Great Britain, as it were—but other countries in Europe had the same respect for women that seems to have disappeared with the women's lib movement in the late twentieth century."

Leah started to make a smart aleck remark, but instead said, "You're right. I'm sorry, sir, and I will do my best to keep that mindset in place. I would appreciate it," she looked over at him as he held open the door at the mall entrance for her, "if you would *gently* remind me when I am being— how shall we say?—inappropriate in my actions?"

"Yes, my Lady Leah, and since you *are* a lady, I will strive to always be gentle with you." James gave her a short bow, raised her hand to his lips, and gave a brief, soft kiss. He glanced up and saw her smile. She was blushing which made him grin with pride. He reached over to take her elbow, then saw one of the reasons for her blushing. The two of them and their little display of elegant manners had attracted a small covey of teenaged girls. They were all huddled together, bumping shoulders with each other, grinning, giggling, and 'ahh-ing' at the sight of an attentive gentleman. Just beyond them was a group—well, it almost looked like a gang—of young men tsk-ing and snorting.

James shook his head at them. *There still may be hope for the lads. Maybe they'd see that having one fine lady to appreciate was better than hanging about with their mates. A pack of lonely males lolling about, wishing for—but not brave enough to seek out—female companionship could be taught.*

James nodded at the ladies as he passed, aware of—but ignoring— their tittering and blushing. He then winked at the young men, tipped his head, and looked back to the ladies with a visual suggestion that they go see to the fair damsels. *If the lads didn't have a man in their lives to show them how to make a woman feel like a lady, the least he could do was let them see how his woman appreciated it.*

ЖЖ

Leah had ushered him into three different shoe stores before settling into one that satisfied her. James had heard stories of women and their shoes. Wasn't it Imelda Marcos who had rooms and rooms loaded with thousands of pairs of black dress shoes? Well, at least Leah had moved quickly through the first two stores. She had evaluated their styles with a two-minute tour, then walked with him arm in arm to the next venue.

The third emporium apparently suited her needs. She picked up two similar pairs of tan-colored high top sports shoes and carried them to the checkout counter, patiently waiting for the bald, slightly heavy set and mustached older man to finish his transaction with the mother of three youngsters.

"You're monsters!" the woman screamed at her young school-aged children. "And you," she scolded the youngest, the only girl, "you're as bad as or worse than your brothers! If you don't settle down, I won't take you to McDonald's, d'you hear me?"

*Well, they certainly heard her, as did everyone else in a fifty-yard radius. He wasn't an expert on children—actually knew nothing of child-rearing except to recall how he had been treated—but he was certain that this woman had lost control over these children years ago. He couldn't imagine Marty behaving like her. Child care and discipline theories—he and Leah could talk about that this afternoon maybe. When they were lying down in that comfortable bed together, resting....*

"Hey, you," Leah said in a hoarse whisper as she shook his arm, "what size shoe do you wear?"

A red blush of embarrassment flashed across his face; she had caught him daydreaming again. "Um, eleven," he answered. "Regular width," he added. *Ho boy...*

"Look at these," she said and handed him the pair of size eleven shoes she had already selected. "For me, these might just pass as the real thing, at least from a distance. See." Leah modeled the shoes she had on, turning her ankle to show him the sides and back, then the waffle pattern on the bottom. "I mean, they look like leather, and they'll be good enough just like they are, except for maybe the stripes on the sides. Those'll come off easily enough, though. They're probably too light in color, but under a long dress, hey, I might be able to get by with these cool, comfortable shoes. Do you want to try a pair? They're unisex or whatever they call it. See, size 11 men's or 13 women's," she added, pointing to the back of the box.

"These are the latest in shoe fabric technology," said the shoe salesman—his tag read Walter. "Actually, I think we were only supposed to test market them for the manufacturer. I read about them in the trades, but I didn't know they were in production yet. These got here in the last shipment, but didn't have a bar code, so I'm not sure what they cost. This lady sure knew what she was looking for, though. Those," he said, pointing to the other pair of tan high-top running shoes on the checkout counter, "are almost the same, but these are more versatile. They feel like a cross trainer with the heavy duty insoles, arch and ankle supports, but look more like a dress boot. Well, except for those stupid diagonal accent pieces that shoe manufacturers insist on putting on the sides. The fabric is micro-porous so your foot can breathe out, but water and mud can't get in. They look like leather, but are synthetic, and can actually sustain more wear and tear than the finest calf hide."

James tried on a pair, then noticed that the laces would have to be changed. "Can I dye the fabric?—I assume that's what you call it—so it looks like a darker leather?"

"I don't see why not," Walter said. "We have a wide range of dyes, although most of them are in the pastel and neon ranges—bridesmaid's and prom shoes, you know."

James didn't know, but accepted his word for it. "Do you have real leather laces that are long enough for these?" he asked, hoping that this would be a one-stop shop for the shoes they needed.

"It just so happens that I have some over here in the clearance area. Lumberjacks and construction workers prefer the leather laces over the nylon ones because of the spark factor." Walter could tell his customer didn't know what he was talking about. "Nylon, static electricity, working in a spark-free environment—well, it's a safety issue. One stray spark could cause an explosion. So, anyway, these should work for you if you want to go with the 'war era' look. You must not be re-enactors, though. They only go with the real deal. You see, the tread pattern in these shoes would cause all sorts of protests."

Walter looked up and saw James look concerned. "However, you just go down to the hardware store, pick up a cheap little electric grinder, and grind down all the ridges. The shoe's traction will suck afterwards, and you won't get the wear life, but your buds out there in the field won't give you any guff."

James gave a sigh of relief. He could do that. Tomorrow. Right now, he would pay the man. Then he and Leah could go take a siesta…

James pulled out his smaller money roll, peeled back four one-hundred-dollar bills, and looked up at Walter. "How much do you think they should be?" he asked since Walter had already told him they didn't carry a price tag.

"Well," Walter stroked his chin and looked around. He grabbed two pair of long leather boot laces and pushed them next to the bottle of shoe dye. "Just a minute." He left then came back with two different styles of shoe brushes and a small, non-descript bottle of whitish fluid. "Here, dye the shoes, then grind down the soles. Rough up the fabric with the brushes, re-dye a second time using a very light coat mixed in with some of this stuff, then grind out any traces of dye on the soles. Make sure you give them a coarse brushing a few times while they're drying to give them some depth and aging. Use your own discretion on how much of the sole to grind down, though. Hopefully there aren't too many purists in your re-enactment group. If so, just try and stay on grassy or rocky areas and keep away from mud and fine dust. They'll never know the difference. Here," he pulled out a business card from his shirt pocket protector, "let me give you my cell number. If you need anything else, I might be able to help you. I've been doing events since I was in clouts."

He wrote his number on the back of the card then looked up and saw the puzzled look on James's face, "That's diapers, mate. I'm a second generation re-enactor."

"Oh, really? I have a lady who is supposed to be making some pants and a shirt for me, but I can't seem to get her motivated. Do you happen to have a spare set that you'd be willing to sell?"

"Let's see, I have a shirt that I was going to put on eBay that should fit you, but my spare pair of pants would probably be too big in the waist. But if you want them, I could make you a deal on the set. If it works out for you, I could meet you after I get off work. I'd need to go home to get them. I don't get off until 7, so how about 8:30 or 9 and say, $100 for the set?"

"That sounds great! Hmm, do you happen have access to a shift that will fit my lady?" James asked, dipping his head in acknowledgement to Leah who, he was glad to notice, was blushing again.

"I don't, but my sister just might. Let's get done here, and then I'll give her a call. That is, after I get these other folks taken care of." James turned around and saw there were two other couples browsing in the store now. "How about $400 for the two pairs of shoes...er, boots...the dye, brushes, laces, and goop? No charge for the hints."

James pulled out the bills, and said, "Don't worry; I don't need a receipt. I'll call you later."

James waved good-bye and joined Leah outside the store in the mall corridor. She was holding the oversized bag of shoe boxes and assorted paraphernalia close to her chest. "You look like you're carrying a very big baby," he said before he could stop himself. Rather than wince—which is what he would have done three days ago—he added to the comment, bravely saying, "You're going to be a beautiful mommy, and do you know how I know that?"

Leah was both flustered and flattered, but not at all embarrassed. She tilted her head to the side, trying to think of a quick, sharp retort. *Oops, too late for the quick part—better just go for the vanilla reply.* "Okay, how do you know?" she paused, adding dramatically, "my good Sir James Melbourne."

"Because you are already the most beautiful woman in the world, and pregnancy could only enhance your inner and outer beauty. Come on; let's go back *home*, Lady Leah." James took the large bag and offered her his elbow, ready to escort her outside.

They passed the same youths they had seen earlier. This time, he was glad to see, the boys and girls had changed social structures and were now congealed into a large group with clusters of paired-off couples. They were learning to interact, and he had helped.

*Cupid can take all forms; who would have thunk it?*

## **36 An Afternoon Nap

When they arrived at the motel, their same convenient parking place was still available. It appeared that not much was going on for tourism in mid-August Greensboro. James got out and opened the car door for Leah. She gave him a big smile; she had remembered to wait for him. He grabbed the big bag of shoes from the back with one hand, his leather bag with the other.

"Let me have the key," Leah asked, "my hands aren't full." He turned around and let her fish the key card out of his back pocket. He couldn't help but enjoy the proximity of her hand and managed to keep quiet, foregoing any sassy remarks. *Soon enough, man, soon enough.*

She let him into the room, then took the sack of shoes from him and set it under the refrigeration unit. They could do the cobbler tasks later…it was time for a break. She went to the sink and splashed cold water on her face. She reached up for a hand towel and found his hand attached to the other end.

"Next," he said. "Even with refrigeration in both the car and room, I still feel like I've been bathed in sweat and dust. I guess we'll have to get used to each other's body odor, too. I never read about anyone using deodorant in the 18th century."

"I don't think people stank as much back then—but you're right, except that I don't think you ever stink."

"Thank you and back at you. What do you mean people didn't stink as much? I mean, body odor is body odor, right?"

"Well, yes and no," Leah explained as she took her smartphone out of her purse and put it on the table, plugging it into the charger. She didn't want to open the curtains to use the solar charger. "It's all the crud and poisons we put in our bodies that come out through our pores that makes us stink so badly. American spies in Vietnam couldn't eat chocolate or other American food, or they would be smelled for miles, or at least detected by the locals. I don't think we'll have to worry about getting sniffed out as aliens or spies or anything, though. So, that being said, I'm going to enjoy myself and make sure I get lots of chocolate before we leave. Too bad I can't get cacao trees to grow in North Carolina. Hmm, but maybe I could find some carob beans…"

"Hey, you," James said, after he finished washing his face and neck. He accepted the towel she gave him with a thank you nod, "stop thinking for a little while and give that brain and body a rest." He finished drying off and hung up the towel. "We're going on a run, or at least a walk, tonight, and I don't want to carry you back; now lie down," he ordered with a grin.

James kicked off his shoes, tugged at his sweaty socks until they came loose, then stepped on the heels to pull them off. He walked around to his side of the bed, fluffed his pillows, then lay back with an exhalation of contentment—mid-afternoon mattress-enhanced bliss.

Leah crawled onto the bed next to him and lay flat on her back, her pose mimicking his. She reached over and moved her hand next to his until they were touching, pinkie to pinkie. She sighed contentedly, then held her breath and squeezed her eyes closed. She wanted to know—had to know. She took a deep breath, then asked the question all at once before she lost her nerve, "If we got married, I mean *when* we get married, do you think you could *do it*?"

"What? Yes, I could *do it*. I've done it before." He started to add 'you know' to the sentence—she knew he had been married—but thought that by adding that remark, he'd sound arrogant. Instead, he looked up at the ceiling, feeling just a bit insulted, and asked, "How about you? Do you know how to *do it*?" He turned to look at her, not sure if he should see her expression when she replied, but curious just the same.

She turned to face him, "If you're asking if I'm a virgin or not," she glared at him, then backed off in resignation, "I'm not. I don't want you to think that I've been promiscuous or anything, because I haven't."

Leah took a deep breath, then decided he should know more about her. She got up from the bed and moved to the table, patting the chair next to her as an invitation for him to sit with her. This was too personal to talk about while lying next to each other. He rolled out of bed quietly and sat down, facing her.

"I had a big crush on the second string quarterback—that's a football player—in high school," she said, looking at his chin rather than his eyes. She was embarrassed, but determined to tell him the story. "I was truly, deeply, madly in love with him. After a couple of months, just after football season was over, he finally noticed me. He said I was the most beautiful girl in the world and asked me to go steady with him. I was in seventh heaven, the happiest girl on campus. After a while—shoot, maybe a week—he said that if I really loved him, I would, you know." Leah glanced up at James to make sure he knew what she was talking about. He briefly closed his eyes then nodded, letting her know that he knew it was painful, and she could continue uninterrupted.

"Well, I resisted, I really did. I wanted to make sure that he loved me first, before I would, well, *do it*. So, we went down to the river and parked and messed around, you know, kissing and stuff. Well, he said that he loved me and then we, you know… Shoot, it was over so quickly that I wondered what the big deal was supposed to be. I mean, really, there wasn't any pleasure in it for me, that's for sure.

"Then the next day at school, he was standing there by the lockers with his buddies. They were all slapping him on the back and he was grinning, and then the way they all looked at me… Well, I have never, ever felt that bad in my life. I didn't tell my mother about it, and she was nice enough not to ask. I think she hoped *it* hadn't happened, and that I was just upset because my boyfriend had dumped me. Well, I refused to go back to that school. So, she let me finish high school at home. It was actually better for me; I was more motivated that way. I didn't have the distraction of all the guys and those girls—they were just as bad as the guys—talking about me behind my back.

"Then I went to college. It was a whole different group of people, but unfortunately, many of the same self-absorbed types were there, too. I almost fell for it again, the same old line. The man was an Adonis. He had dark hair, broad shoulders, and an infectious smile," she turned to James, dipped her head, looked him in the eye, and grinned. *Yes, she'd let him know without words that she had a history of weakness for his body type.*

"Anyhow, I went out with him a few times and he was gracious enough. I wasn't close to any other female students, so I hadn't heard the stories about him. He took me to a nice restaurant, then asked me to his apartment to show me his artwork. Really, I fell for that. He gave me a glass of wine, and well, let's just say that I didn't know to poke my finger down my throat when I felt my mouth tingling and my hands start to go numb. He, well, pretty much had his way with me. I woke up the next morning in the back seat of my car. I was sore—physically sore you know where and also where you don't want to know where—and had a headache that I hoped, really hoped, was going to kill me.

"I didn't know how to go about having him arrested. I didn't think I could prove anything anyhow. But, I didn't want him to rule me by intimidation, either. I wasn't going to quit college or give up on getting my degree because of him. I went on to graduate with honors. And him… Well, let's just say that I wore out three felt-tipped markers warning women about him in every bathroom stall within a five-mile radius of that campus. If he ever scored again, it was with someone from out of town and with a very strong bladder."

"Oh, I am so sorry," James said, and reached up to brush the hair from her forehead. "No one should have to go through that alone. Is that why you haven't let a man get close to you?"

"I'm close to Billy, and he's a man. And I'm close to you, and you're a man," she said. "So, now that I've told you about my experiences, what about you? Are you a 'Joe Stud' in England?"

Leah was grinning, but not in a happy way. James could see that after her painful revelation, she had subconsciously become aggressive, and was trying to put him on the defensive.

"Well," he began, "I was always the youngest and the shortest in school, so staying a virgin until college was not only possible, but losing my virginity—other than to my right or left hand—was an impossibility."

"Improbability," Leah corrected.

"Improbability," James said, accepting the correction. "When I got to college, I was still very young and very short. But, I grew taller at about the same time as the fact that my family had money was disclosed. I had lots of older women chasing me. The younger ones, the ones my age, were still in upper school. I received lots of warnings about women from both my father and my grandfather; that is, Bruce and Marty. I took it under advisement, but still managed to have an awkward, shall we say collision, with a much older and richer woman. You see, because she had more money than me, I figured that she wasn't after the family fortune. That type of woman came later. Anyhow, this older woman was a collector. After we had our encounter, she told me that I was her 212$^{th}$ virgin. Believe me when I say that I was quite put off with women for quite a while."

Leah tried to control the growing smirk on her face, but couldn't. James saw it, and knew it for what it was—she thought she had just found out why he was gay. Let her think it. At least that would be a non-biological reason.

She managed to get her grin under control and asked, truly curious, "But why did you get married if you didn't like women?"

"My father—Bruce, who was actually my older brother—insisted. He said I had to get married and provide an heir for the Melbourne line. I didn't see what the hurry was. I had just turned 27, but he was insistent. He wanted to make sure all was in order before he left. He had another one of his year-long mountain climbing expeditions to start. 'I'm certainly not going to have any more children—you were enough of a hassle,' he said. I don't see how I could have been a problem for him since he was never around. Ugh, he really was a mean older brother. But I shouldn't speak ill of the dead. At least he died doing what he enjoyed."

"That still doesn't explain your wife, or ex-wife. Did you love her?"

"No," James replied quickly and flatly. "Sorry, she's a painful subject." Leah started to say something, but he stopped her. "No, you told me about yours, so I'll tell you about my horrible incident. Sorry, I don't mean to belittle yours—they were far worse. It's just that for me, this turned me inside out and literally ended a dynasty."

James took in a deep, settling breath, and began. "One night, a nice looking woman came into the restaurant where I was dining and sat down and started a conversation with me. Her flattery was well spent on my naiveté. I had no upper school or college romances to learn from and never had married parents. Or rather, I should say, I never had both a mother and a father living with me who I could see interact. I was a sucker. She was a pro and knew how to, how do you say, get me hot and bothered? Well, she did that a few times, then said that she wouldn't have sex with me until we were married. I was okay with that. Shoot, I would have danced on top of

201

Buckingham Palace bare-assed naked in order to get her into the sack. When Bruce found out that there was a woman in my life, he was so excited. Excited, but never even bothered to meet her. He pulled all sorts of strings so I could get married in a hurry—before I changed my mind, I suppose.

"The wedding date was only two weeks after I had met her. Grandpa—Marty—was out of the country at the time. I told him about her on the phone. He warned me that I was not in love, but in lust, and suggested I go to a whorehouse and spend a couple grand to get it out of my system. In retrospect, it would have been money well spent. But, no, I listened to Bruce and got married.

"We were to honeymoon on a cruise. She said she wanted to wait until we were in international waters to consummate the marriage. She spent those first few days in the cruise ship's casinos, playing the slots. She had quite a love affair going with this one bank of one-armed bandits, but I digress. We were headed to Greece. It seemed like days—I guess it was days—before I found out that we were, and had been since our first day out, in international waters.  You see, I finally insisted on asking the captain myself. She had always volunteered to find out 'if it was time yet,' as if she was happy or excited about it.

"Anyhow, we were officially in international waters, and I was going to get laid by someone who wasn't more than twice my age. Of course, she wanted a big dinner first with lots of champagne, and well, from what you tell me, you've never had sex with someone who was drunk on her, or his, butt. Well, it's disgusting. And then she got sick and was puking all over the place from eating bad shrimp. Needless to say, her food poisoning ails continued the rest of the cruise.

"When we got home, she always had a headache or was on the rag—sorry, that was crude—but regardless, she always had an excuse. I finally had to resort to bribery with jewelry. So, we had sex two more times. But, damn, I don't know why I even tried after the second time. She always had to have 'just a wee dram to help her get in the mood.' Her wee dram was half a bottle of whisky. She had to be slobbering drunk before I was allowed to touch her. Do you know what that did to my masculinity?"

"Uh, I could only guess," Leah said hesitantly. "So, how come you're willing to marry me?"

"I am not *willing* to marry you, I *want* to marry you." He shrugged his shoulders, unsure of what to do or say next. Finally, he blurted out, "I just know it's the *right* thing to do. And I don't want us to be two single people traveling back in time together. That could be dangerous for you."

"Okay," Leah conceded. It wasn't what she had hoped her fiancé would give as the reason he wanted to marry her. Maybe he was just a tongue-tied Limey. Hopefully, he would get more romantic with time. At least he was a decent man, and a good marriage could grow into a great marriage with that as a start.

Leah stood up and groaned as she stretched. "I'm tired. Let's get that nap and then have some dinner." She stumbled back to bed. "Don't let me sleep too late," she smashed a pillow over her head, "because then I won't be able to sleep tonight...."

And then she was out.

## **37 Wardrobe Master
*August 11, 2013, 9:00 PM*

James was glad they had taken time out for a nap, but now she was cutting z's and he couldn't sleep. He had almost hoped—well, really *had* hoped—that the two of them were going to get a little frisky before sleeping. Their little lady and gentleman show at the mall had them both wound up. Unfortunately, their revelations about past experiences had made them both uncomfortable and put the kibosh on that possibility.

*Give it time, Melbourne. You two haven't even known each other a week, and you're already engaged to be married and sleeping in the same bed.*

*Yeah, and that's the extent of it—just sleeping and a marriage of convenience.*

*Who are you trying to tell the marriage is just for convenience, Melbourne? You know better and have known it since the first time you locked eyes with her in the bar. Five minutes after meeting her, she was yours!*

*Yeah, but don't you think that she's just using you? She admitted she knew you had money, and she doesn't care that you're gay. Is that going to be her excuse for not wanting to have sex with you?*

*No! She only accepted the money for necessities, and that was with reservations and tears about not being able to fend for herself. She's had bad experiences with men and is comfortable with a gay—or supposedly gay—man, so just let her fall for the real me without the sexuality. The animal instincts for both of us will kick in when the time is right.*

*Yeah, right, if she isn't so pissed off at you for deceiving her by then that she never wants to speak to you again.*

*No, no, no—that was her supposition, her belief in those tabloid stories. She never asked if I was gay. And I'm not a cad, have never taken liberties with her, and have treated her with nothing but the respect that she or any other woman deserves.*

*Yeah, well, well…*

James's body wasn't tossing or turning, but the opposing passions of doubt and confidence were waging a cutthroat game of clay court tennis in his brain, knocking about the ball of his relationship with Leah—first with the racket of self-assurance, returned with the paddle of enflamed distrust, then back again, self-assurance finally winning out. The defining moment came when he realized that Billy was on his side. No, Billy was on *their* side. Her best friend Billy had given the two of them his blessing. That should erase any lingering doubts she had. She trusted him more than anyone, or had trusted him…

James was also the only other person who knew the real secret of what had happened to her mother, Dani Madigan—that she had traveled back to the 18<sup>th</sup> century, was suddenly youthful, and was the author of at least one of those mysterious, much sought after letters. And in just a few days, he would be escorting Leah back in time to see her mom. Now, if only there was someone staying behind in this era whom he could trust…

*Bzzz! Bzzz!*

The vibration of the smartphone woke him up. He must have fallen asleep, at least for a short time. He put his hand beside him, automatically reaching for Leah. He had a moment of panic—she was gone. He heard the toilet flush and breathed a sigh of relief. Then it hit him. He was going to be waking up next to her, or very close to her, for the rest of his life.

"What are you purring about?" Leah asked, and threw a hand towel at his head. "You look too happy."

James grinned at her question, then produced a mock frown at her statement. "How can you be too happy?" he asked, as he grabbed the towel and scooted up into a seated position. He'd wait until her head was turned to *give* it back to her.

Her face pinched, twisted, and then grinned as she sported a series of exaggerated emotional masks, searching for an answer. "Well, I guess it would depend on what you were happy about. I mean, if you're happy about someone else's misfortunes, then any happy—including too happy—would be wrong."

"Nope, this definitely was not a negative issue. Remind me about it tonight when we get back from dinner and our visit with Walter. Right now, I want to get going. I feel like eating Chinese food tonight. How about you? It'll be a long time before we can have General Tso's chicken again."

"Sounds good to me. Maybe when we go back, I'll make my own version, General Cornwallis's chicken—chopped and skewered and roasted over a slow-burning flame."

James shook his head at the mental image she had evoked. How ironic that this soft-hearted woman who had recoiled, even shuddered, at the inference of using heavy-handed interrogation methods on the man who had attacked her, was now suggesting cooking a chicken in effigy of the British general who had, or would, wreak havoc on early-American patriots.

"Okay," he said, "but I want to see you chase down a chicken, chop off its head, and pluck it first. Come on, let's go before you spoil my appetite. We won't have too many more chances at easy meals. Oh, and we need to make sure we take salt with us."

"And a pan, too. We can roast a chicken or squirrel or whatever, but it's hard to skewer oatmeal," she said dryly, then turned to the door.

James wadded up the towel and tossed it at her head as he rolled out of bed. She turned around and caught it, her hand popping up in front of her face just in time to intercept the terrycloth ball.

"So, I'll remember the oatmeal; don't you forget to bring a pan," he said. "And dishcloths, too," he added, as he waved the small towel, "because I doubt there'll be automatic dishwashers available to us."

ЖЖ

After they finished dinner, James called Walter and got the address and directions to his house; he would be home in fifteen minutes, he said. That left them just enough time for a little chat and to let their supper settle.

The sun had set and the warm, sultry air actually felt good after being inside the air-conditioned restaurant for an hour. James inhaled deeply. He didn't know if he was psyching himself up to feeling better about 'natural' air, or was it that non-Freon-modified air was just fresher? Well, whichever it was, this evening the atmosphere was pleasant, almost invigorating.

Leah walked out a couple minutes later, came over to the car, and leaned against the side of it with him, wearing a frown so intense, it almost looked painful.

"What's wrong?" he asked.

"I have to sell this car. It's going to be a pain to get it done at the last minute, and then what do I do with the money? I don't have any family—here and now, that is." If possible, her frown deepened. "And it's not just the money, either. What if it doesn't sell before we leave? I don't want to just give it away. Well, I can't do that because I still owe money on it, and if I let the bank take it back, it will ruin my credit and... What's so funny?" she asked, insulted at his sudden mirth.

James chuckled, "Why are you worried about your credit rating?"

"Well, yeah, I guess that's just how I was raised," she said, her mouth twitching until it became a smile. She tried to stifle the laugh that was sneaking in, then gave in to it, too. "Yeah, right, we're going 230 years into the past, and I'm worried about a credit rating that I won't even be around for!" She laughed again, then composed herself. "I think I'll just sign everything over to Billy. I don't want to do it as a will because then everything will be held up in probate courts or whatever for seven years since they won't find a body..."

Leah looked at James for verification of her last statement. He nodded and said, "They won't find our bodies unless they go back with us. No, they won't find a body, so go on."

"Well, Billy can dispose of all of my assets as he sees fit. I know he's partial to the orphanage he grew up in and well, I think they did a great job with him, so I'd like to help sponsor them, too."

Leah looked back at James for validation on her little impromptu estate plan. "What's wrong with you? Why are you frowning now?" She punched him gently in the arm. She wanted to tell him that he was mood swinging—was he on his period?—but bit back the smart aleck remark.

James's eyes shifted with the feeling that she was about to make a remark about him being an emotional woman, but rather than respond to it, he ignored it. However, maybe now he had an answer to his earlier dilemma—who would take care of his family estates? "So, you have the utmost confidence in Billy?"

"I trusted him with everything before you came along. And if you weren't here, he'd still be my number one."

James now had something else to smile about. He let his radiance shine, but stayed mum.

"Oh, happy now are you, my number one?" she chided.

"Yes, and for two reasons, but for right now, let's go see Walter. I think we're going to have to alter the pants I'm getting, and his sister may have a shift for you." He wasn't ready to tell her that Billy might have more estate monies to take care of than just hers.

ЖЖ

Walter's home was easy to find with the street address and his directions. "Just look for the one with the tallest sunflowers," he had told James.  The huge double-wide trailer was on a heavily planted corner lot, not too far from the hospital. There were sunflowers and clusters of assorted shrubby plants covering the lot, with nothing to suggest a design or plan in their layout, at least as far as James could see in the glow of the moth-haloed street light.

Walter came out to greet them. "Come on in. Hey, look at this first," he said with pride, and pointed to the first cluster of plants inside the gated yard. "See, these are the wife's little herb gardens. She put them in according to the use of the plants. Turns out that wasn't such a good idea since the creeping thyme is a small, low-growing plant, the Echinacea is a tall flower, and the horseradish is invasive. The initial plan kind of got out of control, but the wife knows which ones are which and what they're used for. She's a healer in the re-enactments and gives talks on the herbs and all that stuff. Come on in and meet her." Walter led the way, opened the screen door, and let them in.

"Colleen, this is James and Leah. He's the man who's buying my spare shirt and pants. Do you think you'll have a chance in the next few days to alter the pants for him?" Walter asked.

"Unfortunately, yes," she replied, then realized how rude she sounded. "I mean, since I can't get anyone to talk to me about publishing my book without a thousand dollars in my hand, yes, I'll have all sorts of time." Colleen lightly stroked the book on the credenza, a hand-lettered and handbound book on plants and herbs of North Carolina, her pride and masterpiece, the result of many hours of research, drawing, and coloring.

"May I?" James asked when he saw the title of the book.

Colleen handed it to him graciously, and he accepted it in the same manner. "Wow," he said softly, as he gently turned the pages. Each one was hand-lettered with watercolor-tinted line drawings of the flora of North Carolina. "Did you do this yourself?" he asked incredulously.

"Yes, I did," she said proudly. "Every bit of research from the Latin name, physical characteristics, uses, antidotes, and then the illustrations. I didn't want to get too carried away with those, but it was important to show the colors of the flowers and the leaves, too. I thought I would have found a publisher by now, but each one I called said it was of limited interest, and I would be better off to publish it myself. Of course, that would cost at least $1,000, and where could I possibly get that much money?"

"Do you have all of this scanned into a computer?" James asked, looking up briefly before poring back over the work of art and science.

"It's already formatted and camera ready for the printer. They told me how to do it. All I need is enough money for the first run. I'll own all the copies and can sell them for whatever I can get at the events or maybe to some of the garden clubs. There are lots of groups interested in buying it, but I can't sell them if I can't get them printed!"

"So, would you sell me this original for, say $2,000?"

Colleen's eyes opened almost beyond her eyebrows. "Absolutely!" she said, then suddenly started coughing. She stumbled into the kitchen and poured herself a glass of water to try and settle her cough. "Excuse me, but, are you serious?" She took a long drink then asked, "I mean, you'd do that?"

"I would if I could have this hand-illustrated copy, just like it is right now." James lifted the book to his face and sniffed it. "You've used this to press leaves or flowers in, haven't you?"

"No, but I did make the paper for the front piece. See, it's a little thicker and has violet petals embossed in it. I only did it for the title page, though. That's okay, isn't it? I mean, I can take it out if you'd like. I mean, I'd do whatever you want for $2,000!"

"No, the book is fine, but if you could see fit to take in the pair of pants your brother has for sale and have it done in, say, two days, I'd throw in a few extra bucks."

"No extra bucks needed. Walter, bring me my sewing basket and those pants. I'm going to take some measurements and make this fine…British?" she asked, raising her eyebrows. James nodded. "Make this fine 21st century British citizen into a common 18th century American."

"And I will make this fine 18th century *botanist extraordinaire* and seamstress into a 21st century publisher. Deal?" he asked, as he reached into his pocket and rolled off twenty $100 bills.

"Deal!" she said. She snatched the bills from his hand and did a little two-step money dance. "And here," she added, reaching for the book that was still in his hands, "I'll even autograph it for you."

She read as she wrote out in broad script, "For James, May all your ivies be non-poisonous. Colleen Joest. You're a life saver, James."

"No, your life was never in danger. I am, however, an investor and believe in the entrepreneurial spirit. I'm sure you'll make enough with your first printing to be able to take care of the next several printings by yourself. That is, unless a big publisher decides that there's more to this fine reference piece than just data. Your illustrations are fantastic. This is a great work of art. Thank you."

"Oh, thank you. Now, put the book down and stand up straight. I'll need a few measurements, and then you're free to go and do whatever you want."

## **38 Frustrated

*August 12, 2013, 4:00 PM*

"Sometimes it feels like it's going to take forever for August 17th to get here, and then other times, it's like we can't possibly get our shit together—I mean, our act together—in less than a week. I mean, what have we accomplished? Squat. There, that's better. See, I didn't say *shit*. Damn, I just said it, didn't I? Well, you're just going to have to believe me when I say I am trying to curb my cursing." Leah pursed her lips in reflection. "I don't think women were supposed to cuss back then."

James didn't remark on her last comment, but wanted to. He opened his mouth to address the 'what have we done so far' situation, but Leah cut him off. "Yeah, yeah, women aren't supposed to cuss now, either. Right? That's what you were thinking?"

"Well, it doesn't take a psychic to pick up on that one, does it? I mean cursing is pretty much a bad habit or laziness or…"

"Or frustration," she finished for him. "Damn, shit, hell, and well, I only say the 'f' word if I'm really, really mad. Sorry, I cut you off again, didn't I? That's mostly habit, a bad one I know, and well…I don't do it to be rude. I guess I've spent so much time around sick or injured people who either couldn't talk at all or had such a hard time speaking that I just found it more convenient to finish their sentences for them so they didn't have to strain themselves. Well, it's something like that. Impatience is part of it, too. I promise to be a good wife and keep my mouth shut unless it's appropriate, okay?"

"Honey, I don't mind if you talk. What I have to say isn't any more important than what you have to contribute. Why would you think otherwise?"

"Well, I picked up one of the Sinclaire novels this morning and scanned through it again. I'd read this one before and would like to read some—well, all of them, again—but I don't have the time. I was just refreshing my memory about what went on. One of the things Sarah," Leah dipped her head to make sure he knew who she was talking about.

He nodded back. He had read the first book in the 'Lost' series just a week ago and knew Sarah was the 20th century doctor who had found herself back in 18th century Scotland.

Leah continued, "Well, one of the frustrations Sarah had was that no one—until she met and became friends with Jody—would listen to her because she was a female. Hey," she said with an expression of surprise, as if she had just discovered the answer to why there was air, "Sarah married Jody because she pretty much had to. Kind of like you and me. They were friends, too, but she didn't plan on getting married. She really wanted to go back to her life in the 20th century. Well, at least at first, she did. I just

210

thought it was kind of strange that we're doing the same thing."

"No," James declared adamantly.

"What do you mean *no*?" she asked, feeling very insulted. She had just had an epiphany, and he was emphatically denying it.

"I mean, we don't *have* to get married. Like I told you before, I *want* to marry you, okay?" James looked at Leah's suddenly pale face and continued. "Now, I will concede that we are becoming good friends first like they did, but you know, I think Jody wanted to marry Sarah, and that greedy and selfish lawyer just happened to find a way to make it easy for him to get it accomplished. And Sarah did make a choice, remember? She chose him; she didn't take that one free-shot to go back to her 20th century lifestyle. Now, I want you to be clear on this—whether we are in the 21st century or the 18th century, I want to marry you, okay?"

Leah studied the freckles on her hands, not wanting to look into his deep brown eyes. "Uh, yeah, but I thought we were only getting married so you could protect me in the wilds of 1781."

"Yeah, well, what did you think I was going to do? Dump you back there and come back here and forget all about you? Or maybe both of us would come back here if it was too crazy or scary or whatever, and then I'd ask you for a divorce? Really?" He nudged her head up with the side of his finger so she had to look him in the eyes, "Do you think I'm a cad?"

"No," she said softly, her cheeks flushed with embarrassment. "I guess I didn't think very far ahead. I mean, not really, I mean realistically. Those *grand delusions* that we talk about, having a family and farming, and well… I want them to happen, I really do, but it just doesn't seem possible."

"Okay, here, maybe I can help you visualize it. You have a box of seeds coming today, right?" Leah nodded, her eyes closed to help with the visualization. "Now, I have a bit of experience with gardening. Believe it or not, your mother and I have that in common. Now, have you ever seen a petunia seed?" Leah shook her head. "Hmm, well how about a pumpkin seed?"

"Oh, I…" Leah began to finish his thought for him, but decided she'd better settle for a polite, "uh-huh."

"One white seed, smaller than a fingernail, can grow into a vine that spreads for meters in all directions and produces fruits over fifty kilos. Now," James lifted Leah's head and opened her eye with his thumb and index finger, "we have both a seed and fertile ground, and we are going to have a bumper crop of a marriage, okay?"

"Yes, Peter," she answered with a grin.

"Huh? Oh, well in that case," he said, suddenly getting the pun, "I'll get started a little early on the pumpkin eating." He bent over her neck and nibbled under her ear, tickling her with his week-old beard. "You're good enough to eat even without the sugar and spices…."

James pulled back from his neck-nuzzling to see her face. He could tell by the way she had scrunched her shoulders into him that she had enjoyed it. He had, too, and was finding it difficult to back away from a full-fledged pass, complete with groping and long, deep kissing. He forced himself to stop, pulled away, and patted her on the shoulder, sucking in a deep breath to rein in his compulsions.

She sat down and was evidently doing a little composing herself. Her hair wasn't messy, but she was running her fingers through it, pushing it behind her ears, twisting it into a rope like she was going to wrap it into a bun. Her next softly spoken words shocked him.

"So, do you *want* to have sex with me?" she asked gingerly, her eyes cast down. She didn't have the nerve to look at him—it was difficult enough to voice the question without looking into those beautiful, dark, long-lashed eyes. And it was more than a matter of curiosity. She really needed to know if he could enjoy having sex with her.

James put the side of his index finger under her chin, brought her face up to meet his, and looked her in the eye, "Only if you're sober."

She gulped hard. He was thinking of his ex-wife's need to be drunk before she would let him touch her. That wasn't the kind of answer she had expected. Shoot! That was about as horrid an answer as he could have given!

*Damn! He had unintentionally put her in an awkward position. His sarcastic remark hadn't answered her question, and she obviously didn't want to ask again. He had to perform damage control quickly.* James gently pushed a non-existent hair off her forehead and tried to give her an opening for mutual reassurance. "Now, if you want to see if *it* is even possible, I'd be willing to give it a trial run. I mean, how do you say in America, two consenting adults?"

Leah blinked hard twice, stunned, and mute.

*Her body was a mere foot away from his—a motionless—frozen yet warm—a breathing statue of Athena with unseeing eyes. Her silence made him uneasy. He had apparently just committed a foul with his unromantic 'sex only' pass. His foolhardy proposal of a technical, biological exercise rather than suggesting they share a passionate, caring intimacy had now become a major fumble in their game plan. Hopefully, he wouldn't lose her affections altogether.*

Leah remained mum, but wasn't going to let the subject die. She was intentionally maintaining and stretching the tension of the moment by walking away from him. She played with her smartphone on the table, spinning it around on its axis to see how long it would spin, then flipped the light switch on and off. She turned to him, allowed, "Hmm…" to escape her lips, then walked over to his bag on the floor and turned it slightly so it was aligned with the room's air conditioning unit.

*Her delayed response was eating him alive, but he wasn't brave enough to say, 'Yes, I want you; sorry I was such a jerk.' He bit his bottom lip. He thought the titillation of 'two consenting adults' would allow them to get close enough physically that she could see how it really was for him. Maybe his actions—releasing his pent up passion—could say what his words could not. He wanted her to know he was a heterosexual man and that she very much appealed to him. Hell, he wanted her in every way possible: both physically and emotionally! But he couldn't—or didn't want to—tell her flat out, 'I'm not gay; sorry you had the wrong impression about me.' If he did, he would be admitting that he knowingly deceived her, allowed her to believe he was homosexual just so he could, well...he just couldn't tell her. That would possibly—no, would most likely—ruin the trust aspect of their relationship. He doubted she would believe he had allowed the misconception to continue because he wanted to be close to her, to really get to know her as a person. That sounded lame to him, and he knew it was the truth!*

Leah opened a dresser drawer slowly, slammed it shut, then quickly turned about to face him, her decision made. "Can we cuddle first and see what *pops* up?" she asked with a sly grin. If nothing *popped up* with some serious snuggling—and she could even throw in some slightly aggressive foreplay, if necessary—then she would know he was a dud. She did want to marry him and loved him as a person. But if she was going to be with him for a *very* long time—or at least till death do us part—she wanted children and passion. She wasn't bold enough to explain that to him, but really wished she could.

"You see," he replied stoically, trying to hide the immense sense of relief he felt, "cuddling—now that's a good idea. I know for a fact that *it* is possible, but I want you to know two things."

He pulled himself up tall and addressed her as if she was the Queen of Spain and he was declaring his intent to discover America for her, "I want children, but I have to have passion, too. I care for you deeply, but if we can't be passionate in our intimacy, well, I think we'd both end up frustrated, no matter how much we *cared for* each other." He relaxed his posture, found a fistful of moxie, moved two inches away from her, his voice now casual and added, "Shoot, you might as well be a lesbian if that were the case."

"Me, a lesbian?!" Leah straightened her back, pulled back her shoulders and screeched, "Why, why..."

James reached out and quickly pulled her to him, stopping her protests with a quick, closed-mouthed kiss. Her body was rigid from lips to shoulders, and although she didn't push him away, she was unresponsive. He didn't let her posture stop him, though—he was in control now. He continued his soft yet firm smooch until he felt her mouth soften and yield to his. She was melting like milk chocolate in his mouth. His lips relaxed and parted with the mental image. He felt her respond, her tongue gently probing his. He released her arms and reached around her back, holding the air around her without clutching her to him.

The hands that had wanted to push him away, now slid around his waist, slipping down to gently hold his buttocks, cupping them, letting him know they were hers. She paused for a breath, so he did, too.

"Can we cuddle now?" he asked with a wry smile, looking deep into her eyes with confidence.

Her answer in the affirmative was a low, purring moan, as her hands possessively clutched his bottom. Her eyes shifted side to side, as if making a decision. She swallowed, found her voice, and whispered, "Just a minute."

She leaned sideways toward the table, keeping one hand on his butt cheek, and grabbed her smartphone. She used her free hand to awkwardly push the power button, then set it back down. She straightened up again and pulled her upper body away from his, but maintained contact in their nether regions. She reached into his shirt pocket for his phone. It was easy to grasp, but she decided to play, and rubbed her finger across his nipple a couple of times. "Ooh, it gets hard in a hurry," she whispered, as she removed both her hand and the phone from his pocket."

"That's not all that does," he murmured back. She held up his phone for him to power down, then set it down on the table next to hers.

"No distractions," he said, and let go of her shoulder. He took a half step back, still holding her left hand, and led her to the bed. They stood beside it, neither wanting to make the first horizontal move, and continued kissing until he was physically uncomfortable.

"Hold on a minute," he said. He turned away from her, stuck his hand down his pants, and rearranged his manhood. "I think I almost broke it," he said sheepishly.

"Do you want me to kiss it better?" Leah offered, her eyes cast down so he wouldn't see her blush. She'd never done anything like that, but wanted to try, at least with him.

James gulped. He did want her to kiss it better, to kiss him anywhere and everywhere. He was just ready to answer in the affirmative when they both heard noises outside.

"Wait right here," he said, and helped her sit on the edge of the king-sized, bedspread-covered play area that they had been sleeping on for a week. "I'll put out the sign."

James removed the 'do not disturb' sign from the doorknob, waved it at her, and smiled. He turned back to the door, opened it, and stood face to face with Clark.

"I got an important message," the eager young man said. "I hope I wasn't interrupting anything," he added, as he tried to look behind the door.

James stepped outside, blocking his view completely by holding the door open just enough that it didn't latch.

"From whom?" James asked flatly. He was glaring and didn't care if he was being rude or not.

Clark looked down at the pizza flyer in his hand with the scribbles on it. "Uh, he said to have Lord Melbourne call him right away. He said your phone didn't work, and it was important. He said his name was Detective Billy Burke. His number…"

James grabbed the green handout and turned to go inside. He paused, turned back around quickly, and said, "Thanks, I appreciate it." He reached inside his front pocket and pulled out his cash roll, peeled off a $20 bill, and handed it to him. "Buy yourself dinner," he groused, then slipped back into the room.

Leah was already off the bed and standing at the table, powering on both of the smartphones. Beep, beep; their phones chimed at the same time, signaling notifications of voice mails. She handed James his phone, then sat down in the chair. "He tried to call me, too," she said as James waited for his call to go through.

"Yes, yes, we're fine. We just turned off the phones. Now what's so important?" James asked, trying not to be surly, but making sure Billy knew he was in no mood for chit chat. "Okay, we'll be right there. Thanks, bye."

James put the phone back into his shirt pocket and said, "Get your keys. We're needed. I'll tell you about it on the way."

Leah slipped on her sandals and grabbed her purse and keys. James flashed the room key at her, letting her know he had it, then put it in his back pocket. She climbed into the little purple Prius, gasped, and popped right back out of the car. James read her mind. "I'll get some towels," he said, opened up the room again, grabbed two clean washcloths and bath towels, and tossed one of each to Leah. She had already started the car, got the windows rolled down and air conditioning turned on, and was standing outside of it with the doors opened, waiting to get some of the hot air blown out. She arranged the bath towel over the seat and gingerly sat back in. "Here," he said as he gave her the second washcloth. "I think you'll need both of these for the steering wheel and the shifter. Damn, could hell be any hotter?"

"I don't want to find out," she snorted, as she checked her mirrors, threw the car into reverse, and sped out of the parking lot.

Billy had asked them to come to the police station as soon as possible. Something must be wrong—he wasn't even supposed to be at work at this hour. The traffic was not in their favor, either. It was afternoon commuter drive time and the signals weren't synchronized. Curses were flying out of Leah's mouth at every red light. James looked over at her and tried not to smile on the outside. He could feel his glow of satisfaction on the inside, though. She was extremely frustrated sexually. He sighed. Hopefully the next time—and he promised himself that there would be a next time—they wouldn't be interrupted.

Leah drove around the police station twice, looking for a parking place. She was just about to illegally use a handicapped space when James pointed to a car backing out. She zipped in, cutting off a car that had been waiting on the other side for the same spot. As soon as the engine was off and the key out of the ignition, she was out of the car. Ignoring the coarse call of 'bitch' from the young driver she had just cut off, she sprinted across the parking lot, over the lawn, all the way up to the front door. James chased after her, not caring if they looked like a couple of nuts. At least they were a *couple* of nuts, he thought. He'd have to save the rest of that thought for later.

Billy had arranged for Dyane to escort them into the blind side of the interrogation room where he was, observing his suspect.

"Thanks for getting here so quickly," he said. "I can only hold him for an hour on this. He hasn't been charged with anything. I asked him if he'd stay as a courtesy; that I had someone coming in who wanted to speak to him. I needed to get on his good side, so I pumped him up, telling him what an asset he was. But he didn't want to be near a police station. Then I told him I could hold him as a person of interest and *make* him stay, but would prefer that he remained of his own volition. Of course, I had to explain the word 'volition' to him," Billy said, and rolled his eyes.

"Short story is—do you know him? Longer version is this guy was in Wal-Mart buying all the lighter fluid in the store and a couple of those propane torches used for soldering. It looked suspicious, but the clerk—Teresa Daily, whose husband is a cop—couldn't do or say anything. Or at least she didn't think she could. Anyway, turns out the guy wanted to buy a pack of those little cigars, too. Well, Wal-Mart policy is to card everyone for tobacco purchases. So, she carded him and wrote his name down as soon as his back was turned. She called her husband who called me at home. He had already done the database search for me, found out what car he owned, and we put out an APB on it. He was pulled over by a traffic cop and asked to come in to 'help with a civic matter,' that he wasn't being arrested, but that the department would appreciate his help as a law abiding citizen.

"Leah, I think this might be the arsonist we're looking for. I can't tell you his name, and I couldn't get the names of any accomplices out of your two assailants, but these guys are the same age and color and well..." Billy took a deep breath. "I know this is racial profiling, and you're not supposed to do it, but gangs and bad guys tend to hang with men their own age and color. And these white guys all have something in common besides age: they all have an English accent. Or Scots or Irish, I'm not sure which, but they all seem to originate from the UK."

Billy looked over at James, "No offense," he said, "I know you're one of the good guys. Anyway, I did find one of those plastic tips from a cigarillo in the ashes at Leah's apartment. You don't smoke, do you, James?"

James shook his head just as Leah offered, "He's smarter than that." James beamed at his woman bragging about him. "But," she said changing the subject, "I don't recognize him. James, come over here and see if you've ever seen him."

James walked around Billy to get a better view of the man squirming in the chair, twisting and scooting like he had an itch on his butt that he couldn't quite scratch with the bottom of the seat. Then the man turned to look at himself in the one-way mirror.

"Oh, shit," James said when he saw the man full on.

Both Leah and Billy stared at him. "What do you mean by that?" asked Billy. Leah started to echo the comment, but bit her lip. This was Billy's party and his job.

"Um, I think I bought stolen goods from him last year when I was here. On Halloween. It was an old map," he said softly, as he turned to look at Leah, "a *very* old map."

Leah turned pale and suddenly felt sick. She gulped and stumbled to the chair at the other end of the one-way mirror. She laid her forehead on the table and did slow, deep breathing. She hadn't eaten recently, but that didn't mean she couldn't puke up bile or get an attack of the dry heaves. Slow, easy breaths, and pleasant thoughts. 'You are not allowed to freak out or panic or worry about anything. James is here to take care of you.' She smiled in peace at her mantra. She lifted her head and looked at the two men who cared so much for her. "Sorry 'bout that guys. I'm fine now. Go ahead and do what you have to. I'll stay wherever you decide to put me."

James turned his attention back to the nervous man at the table. Something was wrong, and he knew what it was. "Billy, doesn't it seem odd that a man has on a woman's bracelet, or do men wear jewelry like that here?"

Billy glanced at it and said sarcastically, "Ah, he's probably a fairy," then looked over at Leah to see if she was laughing at his self-depreciating remark. She wasn't laughing, though, she was staring.

"Leah, isn't that the bracelet you were wearing when I met you at the airport?" James asked.

Billy did a double-take, and then a palm slap to the forehead. "Crap, Leah, I gave you that bracelet! How could I have missed that?" Billy nodded an 'excuse me,' then hastily left the room, reappearing seconds later next to the 'person of interest.'

James pushed in the chairs around the table, then sat down next to Leah. "Do you want to leave?" he asked. He looked up and saw the rage in

Billy's eyes as he walked over to the suspect wearing Leah's Italian charm bracelet. There was no sound coming into the room. Apparently Billy hadn't enabled the audio function when he invited them in. The visual was a bit too stimulating for either one of them, though. The punk who had been on the edge of his seat moments before, was now scooted all the way back into it, ready to climb over the arms to get away from the detective. Billy was in his face, grabbing at the bracelet, and by the lip-reading that wasn't hard to determine, asking him, "Where did you get that?"

"Let's go to the lobby," Leah said, her back turned to the viewing wall. "I don't think any good can come from me watching this. I don't need any more fodder for nightmares."

"Okay. I'll make sure they have our phone numbers, then we can leave. I know, I know, Billy has them, but just as a matter of courtesy and good form, okay? We can always come back if they call. Besides, I want to take a walk with you. I found something you might like. Can you take me to the hospital first, though?"

"Are you okay?" she asked with genuine concern. He looked fine now, but *had* looked quite stunned and shocked at seeing the man who had sold him the map last year, the day her mother disappeared.

"I'm fine. It's just, well, just trust me, okay? Let's get out of here. I'm getting a bad case of the willies."

They reached the car, and in short order were ready to take on the afternoon traffic one more time. Leah was baffled, and for more than one reason. She could usually *feel* something with James, but right now, there was emptiness. And the void was scary. "Here, my hospital is the closest. Should I pull into the emergency entrance?"

James was concentrating on mountains of stockpiled coal, the view looking deep into a long, dark mine shaft, slate-colored blackboards without any marks. Emptiness was hard to focus on, especially with Leah asking him questions. *Do not allow chalk near the board, keep everything blank.* "Oh, no; no emergency room, just make sure we're on the north side of the building, the lot closest to Church Street would be preferable—yes, this is a good place."

"Are you sure you don't want to go in?" she asked one more time as she pulled into a parking place.

She didn't wait for him to get out and open her door, but instead popped out, rushing around to his side, helping *him* exit the car. She'd pass on the good manners this time.

He shook his head quickly, thinking of acres and acres of coffee grounds. "Let's walk," he said, as she guided him away from the car.

Leah walked close to him without speaking. She had taken his hand, but after a couple of minutes, pulled it away. "It's too hot to hold hands," she said. "Just know that if it was cooler, I wouldn't let go. Where are we going?"

"Someplace I don't think you'll ever forget," he said, hoping that he wasn't giving her any clues. He wanted to surprise her.

*Black jelly beans, buckets and big buckets of ebony black jelly beans.* They were passing the school now. The sounds of unreserved happiness filled the air. Children were playing on the swings, running around the grounds, playing tag it looked like. He sighed. One of these days, he hoped to have lots and lots of children. *Oops, back to the jelly beans, coffee grounds, and blackboards without chalk marks.*

"Are you sure you know where we're going?" Leah asked, possibly for the second or third time. He hadn't heard her before—he was still trying to keep an empty mind—but she sounded more than a little irritated.

"We're almost there. Close your eyes, clear your head, and trust me, okay?" He placed his hand softly on her shoulder so he could guide her.

"Well, all right, but I already trust you or I wouldn't be here right now. Okay, eyes closed."

He watched as her face animated with wrinkles, squints, and pursed lips as she tried to figure out what he was up to. He leaned over and gave her a kiss on the side of her forehead, then spit out her hair that had stuck to his newly sprouted mustache and found its way into his mouth. "Is your mind cleared?" he asked.

She sighed and let her face relax in trust. "I'm trying," she said in exasperation. Being blind voluntarily, eyes squeezed shut, was not comfortable for her. If it had been anyone but James or Billy, she'd have told him to pack sand in his butt and leave her alone. She might as well get used to trusting him implicitly now, though. And for some reason, she wasn't able to use her transient sixth sense to figure out where they were going.

A few hundred yards and a stumble or two later, James patted her shoulder, letting her know it was time to stop. "Okay, you can open your eyes now," he said.

They were standing under a huge tree in the front of the old Buffalo Presbyterian Church. Or rather she was standing, and he was down on one knee.

"Leah Madigan, I love you dearly. We have only known each other a little over a week, but it didn't take even 24 hours for me to know you were the one I wanted to spend the rest of my life with. Will you marry me, not because it is the *right* thing to do or because it is logical for our journey, but wholly, solely, because I love you?"

Leah looked down at James, one elbow resting on his knee, trying to steady his shaking hands that were holding hers. He looked scared, but she couldn't figure out why, at least not at first. Then she realized what it was. *He was afraid she'd say no.*

219

"You stinker!" she exclaimed.

James was shocked by her reaction and didn't know what to do. He was flustered beyond words and started to stand up, feeling like an absolute fool for opening up to her and getting shot down.

Leah put her hand on his shoulder to keep him from rising. "Hey, you, stay put. I want to enjoy this a little bit longer."

James dipped down and got back into his previous position, totally confused, baffled, and quite embarrassed.

Leah looked down on him and smiled, gave a big sigh, then moved into him and embraced his head between her bosoms, squeezing and rocking him so heartily that she nearly knocked him off his knee. "Of course, I'll marry you, silly."

She let go of his head and backed away half a step, allowing him to rise to his feet. "Oh, and just for the record, I love you, too." She put out her hand to help him get his balance, and then—when she was sure he wouldn't wobble over—sneaked in for a full body hug that ended with her face looking up into his, ready to accept him, warts and all.

"But I don't have any warts, I told you that." He grabbed her under her arms, lifted her up to his level, and kissed her without holding back any visualizations of what he wanted to do with her. He wouldn't have to concentrate on math computations, gun specifications, or mountains of coal and black jelly beans any more. She was his.

"You are so romantic," she said dreamily as she readjusted her shirt that had come up with their very worthy smooch. "You know, I was getting a little, well, afraid… But I really did have faith that marrying you was the *right* thing to do, even if we hadn't, well, both *acknowledged* that we loved each other. And how did you know that I was thinking about you and warts? I didn't say anything."

"Maybe what you have is contagious," he joked. "Or maybe you've just opened up so much to me that I can *be* inside you because you'll let me."

"Or I want you to *be* inside me," she said coyly. "Come on, let's hurry back to the car so we can go home."

"Wait just a minute," he said, keeping hold of her hand despite the heat. "Do you know where we are?"

"Well, the sign says Buffalo Presbyterian Church," she answered, wondering why that was so important. "Yeah, it's an old church, and this is a nice place for a proposal; big shady tree and all…."

"And the church was built in 1756 which means if we're married here, we can go *back* and see it again next week."

"Oh, you are more romantic than I thought," she sighed, then quickly changed moods. "But I still want to go back home." She wiggled her hips and gave him an impish grin that said, "I'm more than ready whether

220

we're married or not!"

Leah grabbed his hand and started walking fast, laughing at him as he jokingly dragged his feet, as if he didn't want to go with her. "But I don't know if I wanna do *that...*" he whined.

"When I get done with you, mister, you'll wanna. I *guar-an-tee* it!"

The two of them skipped halfway back to the car, then walked the rest of the way. He knew the two of them were getting stares, but he didn't care. "I don't think I have ever felt so happy and free in my life!" he crowed. He was in love and going to get married, and she was just as happy about it as he was!

## **39 How Hard It Is

They were both quiet, but glowing with contentment for the ride home. Leah turned the air conditioner up to full blast and James didn't protest. He wanted his core body temperature cool so a good workout wouldn't get him overheated, or at least, too sweaty.

*She must be thinking along the same lines. At least, it feels like she is. Could it be that I'm sharing her thoughts? I can see her, lying on her back—as clearly as I can see her now, a warm breath away—my hands stroking her from her calves to her hips, across her belly and.... Oh, boy. I've never fantasized about that! Those are her thoughts, for sure, not mine. I'll make certain I fulfill that desire, too.*

Leah remembered to let James open the car door for her. This hunky, smart, and well-mannered man was going to marry her—be her husband for time and eternity—as soon as Bibb was back, and they could get his birth certificate. And he really, truly, deeply loved her. Life was good and getting better every day, every hour.

"My lady," he said, as he held the motel room door open for her. "Is there anything I can do for you?"

"Yes," she said with as much prim and proper British diplomacy as she could fabricate. "I would find it most desirable if you would remove your hat, kind sir. Oh, you don't have one? Then, my dear Lord James Melbourne, since you have no hat, you will instead be obligated to remove all of your other attire, one piece at a time...starting with your shirt. You see, you are in need of a thorough inspection to make sure you have all the bits and pieces required to become a worthy husband and father, in that order. Please, do proceed."

"Well, if you insist," James replied playfully with a lisp and a curtsey. He dipped his head to unfasten his top button, then looked up coyly to watch her watch him begin his striptease. But what he saw was not what he had expected or even hoped for. Leah was stone-faced. He stood up straight and got out of character, too. "Hey, what's wrong?"

"I have to know. Are you or aren't you?" she asked flatly, barely short of being cold.

Of course, he knew what she meant, but didn't want to acknowledge it. He had been dreading this conversation since the first day—no, make that since the first few hours—he had known her.

"I am me," he declared. "However you want to parse, dissect, or analyze it: I am me—no more, no less. Will that be enough for you? I hope so, because that's all there is—me."

"You know what I mean," she said, and gave him a playful evil eye.

*Well, that's a start; at least she isn't glaring at me or throwing rocks.* He shrugged his shoulders and shook his head. "Just me," he reiterated.

Leah walked over to the bed and grabbed a pillow, recalling their first night together and the pillow fight. She was sure then that he was gay. If she hadn't believed it, she wouldn't have spent the night in the same bed with him. She fluffed the pillow, turned it around and fluffed it some more, then quickly tossed it at his head. "Are you gay?" she asked, trying to bring back that playful first encounter.

James grabbed the pillow before it caught him in the head. He did a quick pirouette, tossed it back at her chest, and declared, "No." Hopefully she wouldn't blow up at his answer, but she had finally asked it of him as a direct question. His answer couldn't be any more exact or precise, either.

Leah's face looked almost like an old cel-frame animated cartoon playing in slow motion. Her expressions were transitioning from ecstasy to happy to sad to angry, all within the space of three seconds. Unfortunately, it froze at angry.

He had to say something before she did. All he could think of was, "Don't ask, don't tell. Doesn't that work both ways here in the US?"

"You lied to me!" she hissed, then threw the pillow back, trying for a slam shot to his face.

He intercepted it and held it like an ancient talking stick—he had the right to speak since he had the pillow. "I didn't lie to you, ever," he said. "You *assumed*. I never said I was gay, and heck, up until the sixth, I was still married." He kept hold of the pillow, hoping she'd calm down and accept his explanation. He puffed and snorted. He wanted to say more, but didn't know how to phrase his feelings.

"Being married doesn't mean you're a heterosexual," she said coldly, without benefit of holding the talking pillow.

"You read those trashy stories that were out three months ago, didn't you? Damn, nothing dies on the internet!" James snorted, then breathed deeply, practically panting in a vain effort to try and compose himself.

Leah reached out and grabbed the pillow from him—it was her turn to speak. "Yeah, well, gay guys get married all the time. And from what I read, that's why she divorced you—because you were gay!" This time she held the pillow tight, clutching it to her chest so he couldn't do the same snatch and grab that she had just accomplished.

"That's what who says—her, the liar and thief?" He growled in disgust as he moved in as close as he could to her, to share in the grasp of the pillow. "No, not gay. That was just her excuse to get out of the marriage. All she wanted was the money. I could have been that *Joe Stud* you spoke of, and she still would have made the same accusation. It was the only *honorable* way for the tramp to get out of the marriage contract and keep all the money. Oh, and you must not have read far enough to see the retractions that were printed later."

He let go of the pillow and turned away, anger still rumbling in his gut. He had divorced the bitch, got by without losing the Melbourne family fortune, but she was still running—no, that would be ruining—his life.

He spun on his heel, facing Leah again, not wanting the conversation to end this way. He had put her on the defensive, and that wasn't what he meant to do. He had to let her know how he really felt. He swallowed his Melbourne pride and confessed his infatuation to her.

"Do you know how hard…er, difficult, it has been for me to be around you, to not just gather you up in my arms and smother you with kisses, and…and… Ergh! I had to whack off every morning in the shower just to keep my sanity and restrain the urge to jump…um, have my way with you." He was huffing and puffing with embarrassment and shame, but she had the right to know how strong his passion was for her.

She didn't take his revelation very well, though.

She snorted back, but didn't speak. Her anger wasn't directed at him, but he probably couldn't tell that. Now she was mad at herself for believing those trashy tabloid stories rather than asking him who he really was. He was still a great guy, but he had let her believe he was gay. He had to have known that she believed he had no sexual interest in her or any other females. And that playful limp wrist and lisping act… Shoot, she even shared the same bed with him because she was sure he was gay!

They faced each other, both furious either from being deceived or having to be the deceiver. Eye to eye, they glared and huffed and snorted, like a couple of bulls vying for the toreador. Leah backed down first. Her anger melted suddenly into compassion as she realized what he had just said to her.

"You mean you…you thought about me like that in the shower. Every day?" she asked meekly, surprisingly flattered by his passion for her.

"Well, every day since I met you," he said, uncomfortable in his own skin, embarrassed at the revelation. "I didn't do it before I met you—think about you and well, you know. It would have been impossible since I didn't even know who you were."

Leah cast her eyes down and asked sheepishly, "Did you used to do it every day, thinking about someone else—anyone else—before me, I mean?"

James tilted his head, trying to figure out what she was talking about. "What?" He shook his head quickly, "No!" he replied sharply when he realized what she was asking. "No, there hasn't been anyone around to motivate me for a long time—well, ever, before you, I guess. Geez, now I find someone who really motivates me, and she thinks I'm gay and have no interest in her."

"No, that's not right. I knew you were interested in me, but I thought it was only because of my mother and your grand…uh…father and us going *back* together.

James approached her. "But now you know I love you and want to marry you because of you and only you, right?" He was now nose to nose with her and going cross-eyed as a result. He pulled back so he could focus. "Right?" he repeated.

Leah wiggled a little bit, not sure whether she wanted to move away from her newly discovered *available* man—and to smack him for letting her think he was gay—or jump his bones and not let him up for air until he begged for mercy.

"Right," she whispered softly, as she ran her hands up his shirt. "And someone owes me a strip down for an up close and very personal examination."

"I'm ready when you are, *darlin',*" he purred, "very ready."

## **40 Handfast

*August 12, 2013*

"Here, let me help," Leah said seductively, as she snuggled up to her fiancé, her fingers working the top button of his oxford shirt. "We'll start with these, and then we can work down to," she pushed her hips up to his in a very familiar, but gentle, bump and grind, "the other buttons."

James inhaled sharply. He wasn't going to correct her—these were zippered trousers and only had one button. Instead, his whole upper body gyrated, making her move with his as she teased the buttons out of the buttonholes in his light blue cotton shirt. "Hmm," he moaned in enjoyment. *This was the shirt Pierce's brother said the ladies found irresistible. The lad was sure right about that one!*

James tugged up his shirttail, pulled it out of his waistband, and purred at the feel of the cool air rushing in on his sweaty back. He stroked the side of Leah's hair, moving the thick dark tresses from her shoulder to her back with one hand, while he unbuttoned the bottom of his shirt with the other. He straightened up suddenly at the touch of her cool hands moving across his belly.

"I'm sorry, are they too cold?" Leah asked, looking up with a stifled grin. "I'm sure they'll get warmed up in a hurry."

"No, just a little shocked, I guess. I mean, I've been imagining your hands on me for so long—well, only a week—that when I felt them truly touching me, it was reality shock, if there is such a term."

She smiled at his revelation and continued exploring his torso, both of them purring at the tactile pleasuring. She moved from the dip of his navel up the centerline ridge of his smooth dark belly hairs to his chest, feeling the firmness of his sparsely furred pectorals with her thumbs, intentionally avoiding his nipples.

James resisted the urge to move her hands so she would touch him there. *Be patient, Melbourne, let her explore you the way she wants. This will be her only opportunity for a first time with you.*

Her hands slipped down his sides—no spare tire on this body, he grinned with pride—then skin-surfed around his waist to settle on his backbone, her fingertips settling in the divots on either side of one vertebrae, completing his nervous system. It felt as if she was part of him now. And soon they really would truly be joined as one...

"Yeah, well, I have a little confession," Leah whimpered playfully, as she brought her hands back around to the front of his pants. She fiddled with the button, but really wasn't ready yet. She had to tell him.

James dipped his head down to hers, tapping hairlines then backing off so he could focus. "Yesss," he drawled.

"I, um, thought about you, too, in the shower," she murmured. She

226

quickly amended her admission in a rationalizing tone, "But only the last two days. I *knew* you were gay, but I couldn't *believe* it. It's hard," she chuckled at the word—she could tell that he was currently in that condition—"well, it's difficult to explain. It was almost as if I wanted you to be straight," she coughed and choked down another giggle at the descriptive word, then forced herself to continue. "I wanted you to be mine, and believe it or not, I was wishing it so strongly that I just about believed that if you *were* gay—yes, I did have doubts later," she smiled then licked her lips, "I was wishing and hoping and, gee, I guess I was even praying, that you'd be a heterosexual man." Leah snorted at the end of her little dissertation, proud that she had been brave enough to finish her revelation.

James opened his mouth to speak then stopped. Her hand was up asking him to wait. "I take that back," she amended. "I wanted you to be *my* heterosexual man. Okay, now what were you going to say?"

"So you wished and hoped and prayed that I would be your heterosexual *lover,* but you never wished or hoped or prayed that Billy would be?"

Leah shook her head back and forth slowly. "No, it never even crossed my mind."

James was glowing with the intimacy of her touches and the promise of what was to come. He didn't think he could possibly be happier, but he was. Now it was his turn to share more about himself with her. "Well, I told you earlier that I knew in the first 24 hours of meeting you that you were for me." Leah grinned and nodded at the recollection of his bent kneed proposal in front of the church. "But what I didn't tell you was that it was really more like the first five minutes."

Leah chuckled, "And maybe I was supposed to fall in love with you, even if I didn't want to, just because you wanted me so badly? Yeah, right. Just for your information, I thought you were hot the first time I laid eyes on you." She brought up both of her hands and stroked down the sides of his face, bringing her hands to rest on the back of his neck. "But I never thought that we were in the same league. I mean, we were from different worlds—different continents, even—with all of the culture stuff that goes with it. I never considered the two of us as a possible couple. You were just a good-looking, considerate man who was *very* unavailable."

James winced at the reference to her initial certainty that he was gay. "But I am *very* available, at least to you, and," he reached up and put his hands on top of hers and gently guided them back to their previous position on his pants button, "here we are."

Rather than unbutton the pants, Leah used her grip to guide him to the bed. "Lie down," she commanded.

James obliged her and even pulled his arms out of his shirtsleeves on the way. She climbed next to him and threw one leg over to straddle him,

227

her knees near his waist. She crossed her arms in front of herself, elbows out, and grasped her sundress. She gave a little wiggle, then tossed it toward the table, hitting the back of the chair. "Two," she shouted, as she called off the points for making the imaginary basket. She faced him again, this time both hands behind her back, grasping the hooks of her bra.

James inhaled deeply, so much so that his back arched and lifted her body up, lurching her forward. "Oops, sorry," he whispered, as she put out one hand to catch herself. She brought herself back up to her man-riding position and continued her tease.

He realized that he was staring at her bra-covered breasts, then looked up into her eyes. "Down here," she said, bringing his focus back to where it had been.

His hands raised by themselves, ready to caress her breasts as soon as they were bared. Leah took his hands and set them on her white-cotton contained bosoms, a human male support system for her mammary ducts. Her eyes shifted suddenly, as if she had just remembered that she had left the car lights on. She leaned sideways and brought her leg over and away from him. She sat down beside him, crossed her arms in front of her bra, and snorted, "I hate this!" with blatant self-disgust. Her face froze into a scowl. The hot woman had suddenly become a cold granite slab.

"What?" James exclaimed. *How could this be? Was he marrying a woman who hated sex?*

"Not sex," Leah explained apologetically, answering his unspoken inference. "I'm sorry, I didn't mean to say it like that, and I probably scared the sh...the...the—I probably upset you."

James nodded. "Scared the shit out of me is the right phrase, all right." He stilled, his eyes wide with shock, and barely moved—even to breathe—waiting for her to explain.

Leah grimaced and tucked her chin down in shame. The tension was high. James didn't want to intrude on her thought process or seem impatient, but he was. He bit the inside of his bottom lip—anything he said was sure to be wrong.

"I just wanted to come to my, my husband pure and not polluted." Leah burst out crying, her sobs barely controlled, the tears free flowing.

James heard the stumble on the word husband and curled forward like he had been punched in the gut. "Whoa, whoa, whoa," he said, and sat up and gathered her into his arms. "First off, there is nothing in my head and," he tapped hers, "there should be nothing in yours that even remotely suggests that there is *anything* polluted about you, okay?"

Leah nodded and grabbed the pillow, wiping first her tears, and then her nose on the inside of the pillowcase. "And, if we were keeping count," he continued, "which, by the way, we are not—then you and I have both had two bad experiences. That doesn't change who we are, though. Unless, of course, you want to consider that we're both wiser and stronger as a result. Okay?"

Leah nodded again. A hint of a smile began to appear on her face—he was saying the right words. "But I almost made a big mistake here, and I'm glad you stopped us before we went any further."

Leah's face fell. "I'm sorry. I really do want to marry you, and I'm sure, absolutely positive, that the sex will be great and...and," Leah stopped babbling when she saw James raise his hand.

"I do believe marriage is a sacred bond, and I don't want you to think that I don't respect you and your body, because I do. And, since the hour is a little late and we didn't—or I didn't—think far enough ahead to get a license, a preacher, and our family for witnesses... Well, what I'm trying to ask is if you'll accept being married by the rite of handfast until we can be legally wed. I mean, it's a Scottish tradition and valid for a year and a day as a moral marriage—I guess that's what you'd call it. But we won't have to wait the year—hopefully, only the day."

"Wow! Yes, I mean, I think that would be wonderful. So, will you be mine? Leah asked, "forever and ever, to love and hold and cherish, in sickness, health, poverty and abundance?" She knew all about the tradition from the later 'Lost' novels and marveled at how romantic his gesture was.

"I will. And will you, Leah Madigan, be mine—forever and ever, to love and hold and cherish, in sickness, health, poverty and abundance, no matter what time era or country we're in?"

"You betcha!" Leah exclaimed, and pushed James down on his back and rolled over on top of him. "You're mine! Lock, stock, and more than ample shotgun barrel."

## **\*41 A Good Morning

"Good morning, sweetheart," James whispered as he watched Leah's eyes flutter open. He had been awake for nearly an hour, marveling at his new bride—smart, beautiful, and his for all time. She had been dreaming, pleasant ones this time, and actually woke herself with a giggle.

Leah stretched out her arms and a little quiver ran through her muscles as the blood surged in to nourish the extremities. She turned to James and placed her hand lightly over her mouth to block her morning breath. Her eyes were shining as she blinked rapidly, trying to get the moisture back in them, "Good morning, my darling, sweet, and powerful husband. Or will be husband—as soon as we get the birth certificate, license, and preacher."

James gently brought her concealing hand away and kissed it. "I *am* your husband now, at least morally. The legally bit," he sighed in resignation, "will come after we get the birth certificate from Bibb." He realized he was frowning at the thought of having to contact his newly discovered biological mother. He quickly turned his sulk into a smile. "Shower alone or together?" he asked brightly.

But Leah had seen the glower. They needed to address his attitude about her new mother-in-law right away. The shower could—would have to—wait. Instead of answering his question, she changed the subject.

"Bibb loves you, I know she does. I was in the bar with her while she waited for you to get off the plane last week. You should have seen the way she was pawing and gloating over those pictures of you." Leah shrugged with a bashful admission. "I peeked over her shoulder and saw them. You were a cute kid. And what was that sash you had on you in the one picture? You looked to be about ten years old."

"I was twelve and had just graduated from upper school." James saw the look of confusion on her face. "High school. I was a bright student," he added modestly with a slight shoulder shrug.

"With honors, right—that's why the sash?"

James nodded, then reluctantly changed the subject back to the woman who irritated him just by her existence. "But she lied to me," he snorted with exasperation.

"When did she lie to you? Didn't you plan to buy her mill? Isn't that why you came to America? Did she ever tell you that she *wasn't* your mother?" Leah was now on a roll and relentless.

"No, but...but," James stuttered.

Leah wasn't letting up, though. They had to get this relationship issue resolved now. It was sure to fester and worsen if not addressed before they met with her again.

"Did you ever think that by not telling you who she really was—about her relationship to you—that she was trying to protect you? Maybe she just wanted the two of you to meet as regular people, for you to get to know each other as individuals. Maybe she thought by hiding the fact that she was your mother, she was sparing you from being burdened with emotional attachments that you weren't ready to handle?"

James's sputtering had stopped as soon as the word *protect* was out of Leah's mouth. Now he was grinning at her.

"What?" she asked, confused about why he was suddenly so happy. James looked down his nose at her and dipped his head like he was Tramp the dog offering Lady the last meatball.

"Oh, shit. Just like you were letting me believe you were gay so we could, well, get to know and like each other on our own merits without sex—or the possibility of it—coloring our relationship."

"Give the lady a sash," he said, then placed a firm kiss on the middle of her forehead. "Shower time?" he asked hopefully.

Leah scrunched up her nose and said, "Let's work up a good sweat first," then reached down and grabbed him familiarly. "I'd hate to waste your good-morning-to-you cock salute."

"You can have every one of them for the rest of your, our, lives, darlin'. Now roll over and get on your knees. I'm feelin' a little *cocker* spaniel this morning."

"Woof, woof," Leah barked in playful reply as she rolled over. "Give me the bone, Sparky."

## **42 Lost Mama

*August 13, 2013, a little later…*

"Whoa," Leah panted, as she leaned back against the tub enclosure. "I didn't think my body could handle that many whoopees. We're going to have to go out in public, just so my little tushie can get a rest. As it is, I think I'll be walking funny."

James laughed as he answered breathlessly. "Yeah, well with that grin you're sporting, everyone will know why."

"Yeah, and with *your* grin, they'll know who caused it! Come on, let's get dressed and go out for breakfast. I've worked up a big appetite, and bagels and cream cheese won't cut it today."

Leah sighed as she walked out of the bathroom wearing nothing but the towel wrapped around her head. "This feels so good! I don't have to hurry up and get dressed. I can run around naked and air dry while I brush my teeth and hair." She bent over and shook off the towel, and ran her fingers through her hair.

"Here," James chided, as he handed her the hairbrush, "It may feel good, but just because we're married doesn't mean you get to leave here without any clothes on."

Leah turned her back on him and started brushing her hair. "That's not what I meant, and you know it," she replied, then gulped as she felt his hands on her behind. He was caressing the outside of her hips, then cupping the bottom of her butt cheeks. "Oh no, no, no, no," she giggled. "Let's eat first."

"Hmm," James grunted suggestively, then moved in closer so she could feel that he was ready again.

"Okay, I mean, not okay. Let's go to a restaurant for eggs and sausage." James wiggled his stiffness against her backside, as he nuzzled her neck. "Not that kind of sausage and huevos," she said. "Do you need to go back in the shower? I'll even turn it to straight cold for you," she offered playfully.

"Nah, I'll be fine. Down boy," he said in a thick, western cowboy accent. "This here lady needs a break. And you do, too. If you don't settle down, you'll wind up snapping off at the root!"

Leah laughed at his antics, totally at peace with herself. Everything felt so perfect. "How about going to that little cafeteria where we had our first breakfast together? That way I know I'll get enough to eat."

The two of them eyed each other, sending a visual, not really telepathic, message that this was a race to see who could get dressed first.

"I won!" Leah declared as she thrust both arms straight up in the air like she was signaling a touchdown.

"Well, that's because of the shoes. I had you beat until I had to put on socks. Let's go before they run out of food."

The rest of the short trip was made in comfortable silence, neither one of them speaking nor feeling the need to. At least, it was that way until they got close enough to see the open sign on the café's door. Leah suddenly declared, "We're going to Billy's, right now. No passing go, no collecting $200, no getting out of jail free," then made a fast, body slamming U turn in the café's parking lot.

James pulled himself back up in the seat and stared over his left shoulder at her. It looked like breakfast was going to have to wait. "All right," he said, "whatever that's supposed to mean. Are you okay?"

"I am, but I feel like there's something wrong, and I want Billy to check it out for me. He should be off work," she paused to look at the clock set in the dash, "and back home fixing his breakfast right about now." Leah finished her little dissertation on Billy's morning routine after working his midnight shift, then didn't speak, hum, or smile. She even turned off the radio, frowning at the distraction of the music.

"Okay," James said softly. Now her *something's wrong* feeling was bleeding over to him, too.

Leah squealed the tires as she pulled into her old parking space at the apartments. She jumped out of the car, leaving James and her purse and keys behind, sprinting across the grass that used to be her front yard, bounding up to Billy's front door. She knocked three quick raps, then turned the knob and pushed to go in. Her body hit with a thud as the door refused to open. "Oof," she grunted and backed away, embarrassed at her impetuousness. Unbeknownst to her, Billy had started locking his door.

James walked up behind her as if nothing had happened and knocked again, harder this time, then handed her the purse and keys.

Billy answered the door, dressed in a bath towel. "Hi, come on in," he said, and backed away from the doorway to let them enter. He could see that Leah was frowning and silent, not her usual animated and perky self.

"What's going on?" he asked James. James shrugged his shoulders and looked over at Leah, shifting his gaze sideways twice in quick succession to let him know that she was acting a bit strange.

Billy joined Leah in the kitchen as she helped herself to a cup of coffee. "Hey, honey," he said, as he took her cup and set it on the counter. He gathered her into a big bear hug. James looked over at the pair and hoped the man's towel didn't fall off. Did he ever wear clothes in his own home?

"I...I," Leah began, but was interrupted by a call from the back of the apartment.

"Can I borrow a pair of your socks, hon? I forgot to bring another pair."

The voice and the man attached to it came into the kitchen. "Oh, hi. Leah, right?" asked Peter Anthony who—James was glad to see—was

233

completely clothed, at least down to his ankles.

Leah gave a quick nod of affirmation then froze. She didn't want to let go of Billy, but realized that she had probably just barged in on a post-liaison breakfast. She looked around and saw dirty pans on the stove and two plates on the table with the remains of omelets. She started to pull away in shame at her intrusiveness, but Billy held onto her tighter, telling her with his body language that she belonged where she was and shouldn't feel awkward. James saw the little non-verbal conversation, and was glad the man had reacted to her that way. He was definitely going to leave Billy in charge of his assets when they left.

"Help yourself to socks or whatever else you need," Billy said over Leah's head. "And don't forget to pick up steaks for dinner, okay? Hey," he said, as he turned to Leah, then James, "would you like to come over tonight at about 7 for a barbeque? All you need to bring is yourself and a bathing suit. Except you, James—I have a spare for you."

James looked over at the couple in the kitchen and decided he'd start speaking for the two of them beginning now. Leah was pale and needed a man—or two—to take charge for her. "That'd be great. I'm afraid I've been monopolizing Leah's time. I think she's going through Billy withdrawal." He smiled at Leah and she smiled back, brightening up a bit, which made him feel better, too. "Should I bring beer or salad or anything?"

"Iced tea for me, remember?" Leah volunteered, referring to her new status as the wife of a British man. *Whoa, not just a British man, a British lord.*

"Yes," James said to Billy, then nodded to Peter, "I'll bring beer for us and iced tea for my lady," he gave a short bow, "Lady James Melbourne."

"Okay, that's four steaks, and James will provide the liquid refreshments. I'll see you later," Peter said, and put his hand on the doorknob to leave.

Leah turned her head away and James turned his back so the two men could have a bit of privacy for their goodbye look—or kiss, or whatever they wanted to do. As it was, they evidently settled on a *look* because the door opened and closed, and now it was just the three of them.

"Okay, honey, let's go in the living room, and you can tell me what's going on." Billy led Leah to the overstuffed gray velour couch. "You, too," he motioned for James to come sit with them. James pulled over the ottoman and took his position in the little three-way powwow.

Leah looked at James sheepishly then back to Billy.

*Oh, crap—what did he do now to offend her? No, they were cool; stop being paranoid, Melbourne. Shut up, brain, and listen to what they're saying.*

"So, if it's not too much trouble, would you see if you could find her? Her name's Bibb Stephens." Leah had been talking to Billy about Bibb, and James hadn't heard anything except the last part.

"Hey, I know who she is. She's a real firecracker, a real tough old broad. She must have been a real looker when she was younger. She's kept that old place working for I don't know how many years. Land developers have been trying to get her property and doing everything short of burning the place down to get the land. If you don't mind me asking, why do you want to know about her?" Billy was all wound up talking about the local legend and had shifted forward on the couch, allowing his knees to spread apart.

James looked over and saw more than he needed to. At least, Leah was seated next to him and didn't have the view he had. "Ahem," James cleared his throat as if to speak, caught Billy's eyes, then looked down at his own legs and brought his knees together as a suggestion that Billy do the same. Billy saw the cue and followed through.

"She's my mother," James said with heavy sigh. "And evidently, her future daughter-in-law is getting bad vibes about her. Is that right?"

"Yes, something just doesn't seem right. I called her number several times, but I always got some man giving me evasive answers about how she's out of town and won't be back for a few days; no, she doesn't have a cell phone, and he can't get her a message. Billy, I didn't know about the land grabbers after her place. This man was lying to me—I *was* calling her cell phone. Could you maybe check into her as a missing person?"

Billy nodded thoughtfully, put his hands on his knees, quickly brought them together tightly so he didn't flash James again, and stood up. He grabbed his cell phone from the kitchen counter, pushed and held one button—evidently speed dial—and walked into the bedroom, shutting the door behind him.

"Are you okay?" James asked Leah. "Why didn't you tell me?"

"It didn't seem like anything was wrong right away. It kind of sprouted up all of a sudden. It was no big deal when I called her on the phone and she wasn't there. But then, well, it just seemed wrong all at once, just before breakfast, and since we were already in the car and Billy was nearby, I figured it would be just as easy to tell him in person. I feel kind of dumb, though, busting in on him and Peter. God, what was I thinking? He has a life, and it doesn't revolve around me."

"No, that would be my life," said James. He picked up her hand and kissed it. She rolled her eyes and smiled at his gesture. "And if Billy had something urgent and had burst in on us, I wouldn't feel bad. He's kind of like the brother I never had." Leah looked down her nose at him, suggesting a correction. "Bruce was for all intents and purposes—and legally—my father, not my brother. It was only biologically that he was my brother. We were never pals, never looked at dirty books together, or put salt in the sugar shakers. Or would that be sugar in the salt shakers? Anyhow, I feel very comfortable with your friend, which is a good thing, or I'd be very jealous."

"Jealous? Of Billy? Why?"

"Because you love him."

"But he's gay!" Leah whispered loudly.

"So, that doesn't mean anything. I'm sure that you two could, you know…"

"Do it?" Leah suggested.

"Yes, *do it* if you wanted."

"But I don't *wanna*," Billy said laughingly as he entered the room, "and neither does she, but if I weren't the way God made me, I'd want her and want to *do it* with her as much as she'd let me. Now, that being said, I found Bibb. Or at least I think I found her. They have a Jane Doe at the hospital now. She just came in and... Leah, don't you want to know which hospital?"

"It's my hospital, isn't it? Come on, James, let's go." Leah already had one hand on the doorknob and was fishing for her keys in her purse with the other.

"But, but, she's in ICU and can't have visitors. Besides, they haven't verified that it's her," Billy argued.

"Well, he's next of kin, and they'll let him in if I have to lock those nurses in the chapel and bar the door. I work with them, remember? I have rights and privileges, and for all I know, I would have been her nurse if my apartment hadn't burned down. Ergh!" she screamed, finally finding her keys and rushing, not running this time, to the car.

James hollered, "I'm coming," out the door to her, and then turned back to Billy. "Thanks. Let me know the backstory on this as soon as possible. Now *I'm* getting the bad feelings, too. I think all of this is connected, if you know what I mean."

He ran after Leah at his last remark. She was already in the car and had it started, her fingers tapping out a rapid tattoo on the steering wheel, eager for him to get in so they could hit the road.

"Let's roll," he said. She slammed the shifter into reverse, squealing the tires as she left the parking lot, all fired up and for no known reason why.

ЖЖ

"Ho there, Madigan," called the tall, good-looking black male orderly, "I thought they gave you a couple weeks off to get your life back together after your apartment got torched. How's it going?"

"Good and bad—or maybe that's great and shitty—I don't know yet. I mean, the great I know about," Leah said, turning and winking at James, "and the shitty is why I'm here. Do you think I'll have any trouble getting into ICU dressed like this, or should I put on scrubs?"

"It wouldn't hurt to grab a pair and put them on over your street clothes. Are you talking about the Jane Doe? She's in pretty rough shape. Amazing. I've worked here over 8 years and never a Jane Doe. Now all of a sudden, we have two in one week. Unreal," Neal remarked with enthusiasm.

"Yeah, unreal is right," Leah replied dryly. *He's referring to mom's visit last week, a musket ball lodged in her shoulder. No one ever found out who she was... She shook her head. Not now.* "Come on, James, let's go."

"Oh, he can't go in there, you know that—only kin, doctors and nurses. Are you trying to get yourself into some kind of trouble again?"

Leah stopped in her tracks. "What do you mean, *again*?" she asked.

"Uh, oh; my bad. I wasn't supposed to say anything, but... Well, don't you think it was awfully generous of this place to give you two weeks off, paid, to recuperate from your loss? It's just about impossible to get one week off, even unpaid and for family emergencies. I think they found some inconsistencies with the Jane Doe you looked after last week; something about some stolen goods or something. But you didn't hear it from me, girlfriend. Oh, and nice catch on the man," Neal added, then bent over to Leah's ear and whispered, "He looks like a keeper."

"Thanks," she replied, "I agree. And thanks for the intel, too. Come on, James. It's time for scrubs and a mask for you, too."

Leah casually walked into the break room, as if she belonged there. Well, she did, she thought. Her conscience was clear about any wrongdoing with taking home her mother's belongings, or as far as they had been told, her *relative's* clothing and smartphone. Nurse Gata had made sure everything was done correctly—she was a stickler for paperwork.

"Oh, shit," she said softly. She never signed any release forms for the goods Nurse Gata had given her. It probably looked like she had stolen them.

"What's wrong?" James asked. She was acting spooky and extra quiet again. "And am I supposed to be in here?"

"No, you're not," she said, changing her mind about involving him. "Go ahead and wait over there by the snack machine, if you would. Ergh! Nurse Gata gave me my mother's personal belongings the day after she disappeared because I had told her that we were related. She never asked me her name, and she didn't have me sign any paperwork for it, either. I don't know if she was setting me up or not—probably not—but now she's made it look like I stole the smartphone and dress. No one cares about the dress, but... Dang! She's not going to admit she screwed up. She'd rather see me fry. Piss on her, I mean, I don't want to think about that right now. In the long run, it won't make any difference since we won't be around. But right now, I'm going to do a little reconnaissance. I need to put on some camouflage. If I *am* potentially in trouble, I'd better not compound it with having you in a restricted access area."

237

James left the room, but rather than stay put in the coin-operated food court, he decided to do a little snooping on his own. He smelled a rat, even over the prevailing aroma of cleansers and disinfectants.

Leah donned the green scrubs and put the booties on over her sandals. There wasn't any doubt in her mind about whether the Jane Doe was Bibb or not—she knew in her gut it was her. But she wanted to have a look at the chart before she went peeking through doorways to find the woman, though.

She was in luck. Or rather, God was with her right now. She had stopped believing in luck a long time ago. It was Vanessa at the nurses' station. She was bright enough, but could also be led down whichever path of thought Leah or anyone else wanted her to go. It was time for a little investigation and diversion.

"Vanessa, how's it going today? I didn't know they'd scheduled you over here. Anything interesting going on that I should know about before I take over?"

Leah was blatantly lying and knew that she would be found out soon enough. Hopefully though, she would leave with some valuable information before her ruse was discovered. It wasn't even near time for a shift change. Hmm, maybe she could say that someone called her in to take over because she or he had an appointment or had taken ill? She'd have to figure out who was already working so she could flesh out her fabrication.

"I didn't know you were back to work already," Vanessa said in a harsh whisper, as if it was a great secret. Leah shrugged her shoulders like it was no big deal. Well, it couldn't be very hush-hush if the first two people she talked to told her about her suspension within seconds of seeing her.

"Well, if you're going to be working, then you need to know about the Jane Doe in 313. She's a little old lady who came in beat to a pulp. She didn't fall down some stairs or nothin', no matter what they said. She has two black eyes and—God, this is so gross—it looks like someone burned her with cigarette, all over her arms and then her feet, too. She has a specialist in there with her right now. He's a new doctor. I've never seen him before, but... Hey, where are you goin'? I didn't get to tell you about the other little old lady. Audie?"

Audie Leah Madigan ran down the hall as fast she possibly could in her green baggies-covered sandals. She turned to look behind her and almost overshot the room. She reached out her right hand, grabbed the doorframe, and swung into the room, ready for action.

"What the hell do you think you're doing?" she barked at the suspicious man beside the bed. It was obvious that the lanky male wasn't a doctor—or any other kind of medical personnel. For one thing, his arms were filthy under the scrubs, and she could smell him eight-feet away. She also saw that she had arrived just in time to prevent him from injecting a

238

syringe into Bibb's IV.

The startled man with scraggly beard and oily hair spun around, inadvertently banging into Bibb's bed. He pushed it and her aside in fear. The bed crashed into the wall, shaking and rattling all the cords, tubes, and other paraphernalia attached to it. Bibb didn't move or make a sound with all the jarring and banging of being shoved around—and that scared Leah.

"Put it down, mister. I'm not messing around here," Leah growled, holding back the urge to yell at him. "Now, dude!" she demanded, as she neared him cautiously, trying to cut off his exit. All of a sudden, there were too many creeps in this town, and they all seemed to look the same and wind up in her face.

The greasy, angular man ran toward the doorway. Leah shifted to her left to block him, not knowing what she could actually do to stop him. She was moving by reflex—her maternal protection mode kicking in for her future mother-in-law.

The pony-tailed intruder made one more feint, then threw the syringe at Leah. She jumped aside, trying to avoid it, and unintentionally gave him the opening he needed. He shoved her against the wall, out of his way. Her neck snapped backwards and her head smacked the drywall. She rebounded and fell forward, inert, to the floor. Her assailant hopped over her, grabbed the door jamb to regain his balance, and sprinted down the hallway, looking back briefly to make sure she wasn't following him.

ЖѺЖ

James waited in the little chapel alcove across the hall, out of sight of others, but with a partial view of the room he knew held his biological mother and Leah. Suddenly, a scrub-clad man wearing dirty, untied athletic shoes ran out of the room, clutching at the wall to keep on his feet. It didn't take a genius to see he had just done something wrong and was leaving the scene in a hurry. Damn! Flash decision—should he stop the man's escape or check on his ladies. James bolted out of the vestibule before he could make a conscious choice. He moved by gut reaction and performed a flying tackle from behind, clipping his target, knocking him face forward onto the hard, tiled floor.

Thud, crack, "ugh..."

James scrambled to his feet and stood over his quarry. The mangy man, his arms outstretched like he was praying to Mecca—stunned and at least partially incapacitated by the blow—cautiously turned his face sideways. Blood dribbled from his nose as his tongue moved gingerly around his cheek. He spat out a chunk of rotted enamel and began to rise, his fingers clutching the cool, bare floor in front of him.

James planted his foot in the middle of the prone figure's back. "Freeze," he ordered.

The body responded by relaxing back into the floor, a fart escaping

239

in an almost comedic conclusion to the dramatic episode.

James was no longer alone in the hall with the assailant. Billy had arrived—dressed in more than a towel, he was glad to see—sporting a Hawaiian shirt, shorts, his badge, and a tough cop's attitude.

Billy was directing the staff to stay back while he cuffed the intruder. James didn't wait for him to finish the bracelet job; he knew his help wasn't needed. In half a heartbeat, he was in the ICU room, tending to Leah.

"Crap," he said, and pulled the syringe out of her shoulder. "What the hell is this?" Leah was unconscious and, he noticed as he looked up at the bed shoved against the wall, so was Bibb.

"A little help in here, please," he yelled through the doorway, not wanting to leave Leah to find a doctor or nurse. He didn't know how seriously she was hurt, but at least she was breathing. "I'll be right back, don't go anywhere, okay, sweetheart?" he said softly as he patted her uninjured shoulder, trying to lighten his own frightened mood with the lame joke. She was unconscious and couldn't contribute her own witty remark, so he'd say it for her.

"Help her, help them, Lord," he prayed quickly, his request for both of his ladies. He looked around the small room. He got up and went to the side of Bibb's bed and pulled it back to its original location. She had gauze bandages covering both arms, and her feet were wrapped, too. He couldn't even guess what had happened to them, but they couldn't possibly look as horrible as what he *could*. Her face was barely recognizable. He knew it was Bibb, but her nose was three times its normal size—probably broken, he thought—both of her eyes blackened and swollen to mere slits. Hmm, the dual black eyes meant the nose was most certainly broken. Yes, even though her face was red and purple and puffy, pushed out of shape, out of kilter like a lump of clay that had been tossed against the wall a couple of times, he could tell it was her. Her long silver hair was loosed over her shoulders. She had plastic tubes up her nose, but still had a regal bearing. She wasn't of noble birth, but if what Billy had recalled of the news stories was true, she had established herself as a respectable lady in this town with her actions and integrity. Not many single women could pull that off now, and especially not thirty years ago.

James didn't know much about medicine, but the little blips on the monitor were jiggling up and down, and that was a good thing. He had seen enough dramatizations of 'flat lining' to know that a calm stream of electronic lines meant bad news. "Keep bouncing," he whispered.

Help came into the room, the scrub-attired characters now poring over Leah. "Here, I pulled this out of her shoulder." He handed the syringe to the man who looked to be in charge: Dr. Savikko, his badge said.

The composed, country-doctor-looking older man took it, turned it over, and sniffed it. "That creep threw it at her," James said. "I saw her try to dodge it and thought she had. She fell when he knocked her down on his way out the door, but I think it injected something into her first. She shouldn't be unconscious from the short fall to the ground. I think she interrupted him trying to put it into Bibb's IV."

Dr. Savikko and his emerald-clad minions looked down their noses at James, asking without words, 'Who are you?'

"Hey, I was across the hall, waiting for a chance to come in and see her. That's my mother," he said, nodding toward the bed-bound patient, "Bibb Stephens." The group let out a collective sigh of relief at his valid explanation of who he was and why he was involved with the two women.

"Take this down to the lab and see what it is. Get her into a bed, stat. Get her vitals, blood work, stat, and contact her next of kin. Did I miss anything, crew?"

"I'm her next of kin. She's my fiancée," James said, not wanting to explain being handfast to the little group. "She's an orphan and we're all we have. Well, except for him," James said, nodding to acknowledge Billy who was now standing in the doorway.

"Excuse me, sir," the orderly said, as he waited for the police officer in beach clothes to step aside.

"Where are they taking her?" Billy asked for the both of them as they automatically gravitated toward each other, drawn together by their concern and love for Leah.

"She's going to the emergency room. You can wait in the waiting room," the doctor said. "Believe me, she'll get the best possible care—she's one of our own."

"Come on, James," Billy said, putting his hand on the frowning man's shoulder.

"No, you go. I'm going to stay here for a minute," James said, then paused, reflecting on the words, "and see my mother."

"Well, okay. I'll wait outside for you. It'll be a while before they let us see Leah. I'll make a few calls and see what I can find out about this for you."

"Thanks, I appreciate it."

James walked in and stood beside the middle-aged nurse now overseeing Bibb's needs. He had never seen her before, but she looked competent. At least, she was frowning and twisting the knobs on the oxygen-feed like she knew what she was doing. She smiled at James and stepped aside, making room for him to move closer to the bed.

"No more than ten minutes at a time, okay," she stated rather than asked. She moved around to the other side of the bed and looked underneath, her hands barely touching the tubes as she made sure there weren't any cuts, kinks, or breaks in her patient's lifelines.

James didn't know what to do. He had only spoken briefly to Bibb, and that hadn't ended well. He had found out that rather than the American businesswoman who had invited him to purchase her little mill, she was really his unacknowledged mother, that his grandfather was really his biological father—and that his whole familial history was fabrication, that he had been lied to his entire life.

All he knew about her personally was the little bit of history she had revealed the day they met. She loved his father, she said. Evidently enough to let him take their baby away to England for him to rear. Well, maybe she just wanted the child out of the way. A baby wasn't conducive to starting or building a business. But, looking down at this woman tenaciously holding onto life, he would rather think that this 'tough old broad' was generous, too. He knew how much his *real father* had loved him. If she knew how much he had wanted another son, then biology and tradition be damned—she'd give him one.

He brushed aside a few stray hairs from her forehead, "Thanks for giving me to him," he said softly.

Her eyes fluttered at his words. He wasn't sure, it could be the lighting, but it looked as if she was trying to smile at him.

"Hey," the nurse said, "whatever you're doing, keep it up. Her blood pressure was too low, but it's getting into the safe range now. She's your mother, right?"

"Yes, she is," James replied with pride. "She certainly is."

"Well, I get the impression that failure isn't an option for her. I can only allow you in here for a few more minutes. Hospital policy and all, you know."

"Okay, thank you."

James spent the next few allotted minutes telling his semi-comatose mother a few stories from his youth, the little anecdotes that might not have been shared by his father. "And then the wheels fell off and I skidded nose first into the rose bushes. I didn't think I'd ever get all those prickers out," he said, then laughed softly, telling her about his little escapade as a four-year-old Grand Prix racer in a little red wagon.

"It's time to leave," the nurse whispered.

He got up to leave. Nurses: so tough when needed, but also equipped with a gentleness soft enough to brush the wings of a butterfly without allowing a touch of color to be removed. Hopefully, his own iron butterfly was awake now and ready to go home. He had only known Leah for a week, but couldn't imagine life without her now.

James followed the signs to the emergency room waiting area and found Billy pacing the floor, smartphone to his ear, listening, then softly barking orders to the person on the other end of the line. "No, he does not need a doctor *or* a dentist! Just give him an ice bag and to hell with saving the tooth." He looked up and saw James and cut the call short. "That's all I'm going to say about it. No, no, on second thought, tell him I said, 'tough shit,' that he shouldn't have attacked a woman in the first place."

Billy turned off the phone and put it in his shirt pocket. "No word yet, but hey, they now have the hospital records of one Vivian Rita Stephens. And guess what? She had a baby boy right here in this very hospital just over 28 years ago. Imagine that. A little boy she named Ignatius James Melbourne."

"You mean James Ignatius Melbourne," James corrected.

"Nope, you're an Iggy, dude." Billy laughed, trying to contain his hilarity, but not succeeding. Each little snort that escaped just made James redder and angrier. Finally, Billy got himself under control. "Nah, not really; you're just another James," he said, and thumped him on the back in an affectionate manner. "I couldn't resist."

"Wait a minute," James said, stopping Billy's chortling with his seriousness. "That means I have a birth certificate, a North Carolina birth certificate, and I can marry Leah. Hey, if she's up to it, we can do it tonight! Thank you, Lord, and hallelujah!"

"Since when did you get religion?" Billy asked, shocked but happy at seeing his friend's unbridled joy.

"How would you know whether I already had it or just found it?" James asked brightly. Something deep inside him told him that everything was going to be all right, even though the doctor hadn't come out yet to speak with either of them about Leah.

"I'm a detective, remember?" Billy said, toying with him. "No, really, you just look too happy—like you just found out there really was a Santa Claus. Well, that's putting the real Big Man in the wrong class, but that glow a person gets when he first *finds out* who's really in charge, is unmistakable. And yes, I have that wonderful feeling that Leah—and Leah and you—will be fine. And don't forget who's going to be your best man. Hey, here comes someone now."

This time, it was a tall, good-looking man in crisp-pressed blue scrubs who came out to greet them. He looked like a college athlete who had used his scholarship well, was James's first impression. He glanced at Billy to make sure he saw the medic coming over to talk to them.

He saw him all right. The look on Billy's face wasn't what he expected, though. Instead of eagerness to hear the good news about their woman, there was thinly veiled disgust at the approaching doctor.

"Are you two here for Audie Madigan?" he asked, looking first at Billy with a single raised eyebrow, then at James with genuine curiosity.

Billy took over when he saw the look of confusion on James's face. Evidently he didn't know that Leah's first name was Audie. He literally pulled him close to him by the elbow, squeezing it as if to say, 'Hush, let me handle this.' James didn't argue. Billy was trustworthy and knew the people in this town and hospital better than he ever could—or would, since he was leaving in a few days.

"Yes, we're here for her. What's going on, Dr. Andrews?"

James had never seen this side of Billy, and in the one short week since he'd known him, he'd seen lots of his aspects. Billy didn't like this doctor and didn't care if he or anyone else knew it. He was barely keeping himself in check.

The doctor took a split-second to recover from Billy's look of sheer loathing, then covered his momentary shock with a holier-than-thou attitude. The young intern was condescending in his posture and hadn't been in their presence for even one minute! The egotistical medic looked down again at his paperwork, either stalling or truly trying to figure out what to say to the pair.

Billy still had hold of James by the elbow, and his grasp was tightening. James reached across, put his other hand on top of Billy's, then felt him relax. *'Whatever this jerk has been to you, he is nothing now.'*

Billy felt the non-verbal reassurance from James, and a sense of joy and security replaced the negativity. His friend was here to help him deal with the prick in super-starched blue scrubs.

Dr. Andrews cleared his throat and looked up. James didn't need anyone to tell him that Leah was okay—he had known it deep down inside even before Dr. Full-of-himself came out. Now he was here for Billy. James placed a phony smile on his face, inviting the doctor to give it his best shot.

"Audie is fine. She was knocked out temporarily from the fall. Her blood pressure was low, but we gave her a 7-Up and that seemed to help. She said she hadn't eaten since late yesterday afternoon, so as soon as she gets some breakfast in her, she'll be ready to go home. Which one of you is she with?" he asked, looking back and forth between the faces of the two men still clutching each other.

"Both of us," said James with pride. He turned to make sure that Billy was okay. Billy was very okay. He was beaming.

"Now about the other thing..." James started to ask about the syringe, but the narcissistic doctor had turned away from them, dismissing them without a word.

"Hey, I'm talking to you," James hollered as he took three fast steps to catch up with the doctor, leaving Billy standing where he was. He grabbed the doctor's arm, causing the surprised medic to turn and swing his clipboard at him.

"Whoa, there!" James said. "I just want to know about the syringe she was stabbed with. What was in it?"

Dr. Andrews huffed and snorted, either from anger or embarrassment—or both. He calmed his breathing and brought up the clipboard again. He looked over the report and replied in a cold, clinical, and heartless manner, "Sodium Thiopental; truth serum. That may be the reason she didn't recover right away after the fall. It's a barbiturate. It was not administered intravenously, so its effect on her system was hard to predict. Now, are there any more questions? I have other patients, you know."

James wanted to ask 'Why are you such a dick?' but decided it was better to just let the man go. No, he couldn't let it lie; he had to ask. "Are you a real doctor, or did you just get busted from being an assistant high school football coach, and you carry the clipboard around to make you feel special?"

James said it with a straight face, and was able to keep it that way, even though he could hear Billy laughing out loud behind him.

Billy chortled out the answer for the vain and now very red-faced man. "He's still an intern. Nobody will let him be a 'real' doctor. His people skills suck. This is his, what, sixth, hospital? Way to go, Terry! Why don't you go to the North Pole for number seven? Nobody up there will know if you're giving them the cold shoulder or not." Billy crowed his taunts and laughed until he could barely stand upright, leaning against the admitting clerk's window for support.

Terry didn't wait around to hear all of the jeers. He rudely pushed past a little old man and went into his inner sanctum, the emergency ward.

Billy calmed down as he approached James. "Let's go check on our lady," he said, as he patted him on the back, then added softly, "And thanks for the support. Before we go in, though, let me give you a little back story. That jerk is a collector. It's amazing that he hasn't died of AIDS. And no, I've never had anything to do with him. The asshole, pardon my expression, takes great joy in 'marking' his conquests. He has a signet ring that he fires up red hot with a torch then uses it to brand his one night stands on the right butt cheek. Oh, he doesn't believe in ever having the same man twice. He says the brand is both a badge of honor and to make sure he doesn't repeat himself. However, he does have vast medical knowledge, and what I said is true; his *bedside* manner is rotten. He's offended too many patients who were good friends or relatives of board members of at least a half dozen hospitals in this state."

Billy flashed his badge at the woman at the admitting desk who pushed the button and let him through. James followed right behind him, as if it was he were a part of the official investigative team, too.

And there she was. Billy came over to her right side, James to her left. "Hey, honey, are you feeling better?" Billy asked.

She turned her head from Billy to James, then back to Billy again. She snorted then scolded, "Right or left...you both have to be on the same side, or I'll get an even bigger headache from bouncing back and forth between you."

Billy jumped up and down to James's side in an exaggerated bunny hop, making everyone laugh. He brought the mood down just a notch and pointed to the bandage on her shoulder. "Now, I was told that that creep threw a syringe full of truth serum at you and that's what stuck you..." he began.

"What? That doctor never told me that! Shoot, they must have patched me up while I was asleep. I remember seeing it flying across the room, but I don't remember anything but being thrown against the wall and falling down. And, hey, that doctor—or intern or whatever he is—should be fired. Do you know what he did?" she asked angrily.

"What?" the men asked in unison, both with glares of rage skewing their faces.

Leah saw the identical looks on her men. "You look like twins. Are you two related?"

James and Billy looked at each other. "Hell, if I know," Billy said. "I was an orphan, remember? Now, what did that sorry so and so do?"

"He asked me if I had ever had sex with a doctor. I just shut my eyes. I couldn't believe what I was hearing. I mean, really, I thought I was having another bad dream or something. Then he put his hand on my forehead, and stroked the side of my face, down to my neck and collarbone. He said that once you've had a doctor, a real doctor, that no other man can compare. Doctors, after all, know all the right places to, ugh, probe. As soon as I can sit up by myself, I'm yanking these tubes out of me and filing a report on him. He'll never work in this state again!"

Leah tried to sit up by herself and started to swoon. "Ooh, I think I'd better lie back down. I'm still a little woozy." She closed her eyes and let her head plop back into the pillow, losing the battle against dizziness.

Both men turned away from Leah and toward each other, their eyes livid, their curse words stifled. James warned his friend softly, "Don't lose your job over this, Billy. You can't go killing him in cold blood. Now, let's just get Leah taken care of."

Billy grimaced, nodded, forced the corners of his mouth into a fake smile, and then turned around to face her. James, however, gave Leah a huge, relieved grin, happy that she had been spared major injury. "I was reminded of the fact that you haven't eaten for quite a while. How about if Billy waits here while I go get you some soup or a sandwich?"

"It's too hot for soup, but a tuna sandwich on whole wheat sounds good. And a pickle, a big dill pickle. That's supposed to help settle a queasy stomach. And a glass of milk, too, if you would." She paused, stuck out her bottom lip, and added, "Puh lease."

James patted her hand, "I'm on it, darlin'. Don't leave without me, okay?"

246

Leah gave a weak smile in return, then closed her eyes with fatigue. Even talking was wearing her out.

James glanced at Billy and saw that he was seething again. He put his hand on Billy's forearm and made him look up at him. "Come outside with me just a second, okay? Leah, he'll be right back."

She nodded and sighed. Hopefully, eating would give her back her strength. She had places to go, people to see, and being a patient in her own hospital was the last place she wanted to be.

"Look, Billy," James said softly, "you know how Leah is with violence. Remember how she freaked out—well, almost—when you inferred using a rubber hose on one of her assailants?"

Billy nodded and grimaced in recall. "Yeah, you're right. It would hurt her a lot more than him if I decked that asshole. Thanks. Now go get that sandwich and don't forget the pickle." Billy gave James a gentle sock to the upper arm. *Yup, Leah was getting a great guy. If I ever had a brother, I'd want him to be just like him.*

James came back in ten minutes with three tuna on whole wheat sandwiches, three boxes of milk, and one big pickle. "I hope they don't kick us out for having a picnic in here," he said, as he took two of the sandwiches out of the bag and passed them to Billy.

Billy set them on the swing-out hospital tray, then reached his hand over to James, palm spread out flat. "Don't tell me you forgot the pickle? The lady has to have her pickle. A great big, firm juicy pickle."

James opened up the sack, looked inside blankly, and hoped he and Billy were providing a little slice of entertainment for their lady. "Oh, no, I...I..."

Billy looked over. The smile was growing on Leah's face. He decided it was okay to continue with their little extemporaneous comedy skit. "Oh, I'm sorry, James, I forgot. You can't give her *the pickle* until you're married."

James hadn't expected that remark and literally started sputtering. He looked at Leah to see if she had picked up on the innuendo. Of course, she had. She was now giggling, her left hand and the IV tubing coming out of it, bouncing as she covered her mouth.

Billy continued, "Now, since you're going to be able to marry this fine young lady this evening...."

"What?" Leah asked, sitting up from her reclined position.

"Ooh, ooh," James interrupted, mimicking Leah's excited interjection, waving his hand in the air for recognition. "I was born in this hospital! I'll bet with the help of a police officer, I could get a copy of my birth certificate...today! Ooh, ooh! Does that make you as happy as it does me?" Suddenly his face dropped. "You still want to marry me, right?" he asked, just a wee bit afraid that she would say no.

"Yes, yes, hell yes!" she exclaimed, then fell back onto the upright mattress, the glow on her face assuring both men that she was positive she wanted to marry James. Tonight!

"Well, then…" Billy resumed his role in the two-man comedy skit and reached into the lunch bag to grab the obscenely large dill pickle. He looked at James, saw he had regained his composure, and asked, "Are you going to be a man or a mouse? Are you going to give the lady *the pickle* tonight on your wedding night or wait until tomorrow? Hmm?" he asked broadly.

James smirked, unable to contain his grin, and gave his reply to keep the act going. "Well, to tell you the truth…and since you asked…" He looked at Leah to make sure it was okay with her.

She knew his thoughts, grinned, and nodded gently in answer to his unspoken question.

"Since you asked," he repeated, then hung his head in mock shame, "I was a rat. I did it last night…"

James looked up, first at Leah—she was beaming—then at Billy. Any leftover sense of anger at Terry Andrews had disappeared. Billy was now whooping and knee slapping, overjoyed with word of their union.

Billy came around the bed and punched James in the shoulder, then looked back at Leah. "See, I told you he wasn't gay!" he crowed to her.

James was wide-eyed with shock at the remark. She looked back at Billy, chagrined and embarrassed at the same time. She shrugged her good shoulder and said, "Well, not really straight as a telephone pole. He, uh, has a little curve…"

*Obviously, she had been told by her best gay friend that he wasn't a homosexual, but had believed the tabloid stories instead. Ergh!*

Leah looked into James's stern face, her hazel eyes misty, ashamed that she had not believed Billy's report on him.

James relaxed his offended stance, then shook his head at her in mock scorn. Well, it all worked out just fine. He'd forgive her without her asking. He leaned forward and kissed her on the forehead.

Leah looked up, thanking him wordlessly with her smile for forgiving her. *Crunch.* She took a big bite of the crisp pickle, chewed it in exaggerated bliss, swallowed, and said, "I'll take your pickle anytime you want to give it to me, dear. You are mine to keep, care for, and cherish. Now, let's eat these sandwiches and get the flock out of here, my hero rams. I really don't like being here on my day off. And if I'm never in here again, that will be too soon. At least, I hope I don't ever have to come here to see anyone. Oh, shit! How's Bibb?" she asked, embarrassed at her forgetfulness. "I should have asked earlier."

"The nurse said she thinks she'll make it. She could see that failure wasn't an option for her. I'll be able to go in there in a little bit. Hey, eat your sandwich. I want you to get your strength back. We have lots to do before, well, before the wedding and then our camping trip."

"Are you going camping for your honeymoon?" Billy asked.

Leah took in, then let out, a long controlled breath, finishing it with a smile that nearly split her dry lips. "That's the plan. Hey, Billy, since James can't go in to see Bibb, his mother," she added with a grin, "for a while longer, could you go in and see how she's *really* doing? I promise not to eat your sandwich. I'll even let you have a bite of my...my...dill," she said coyly, and held out the waxed-paper wrapped pickle.

Billy looked at the pickle, then James, chuckled and said, "No, that's just for you, dear. But I will go check on Bibb. But how about I take a milk for the road," he said, and held out his hand.

James gave him the half-pint carton. "Talk to her. Tell her about when you were a kid, what you liked to do, hobbies. Hey, she likes old cars, too. Talk about anything, but just talk to her—no questions. I don't know where she's been in the past week, or what's happened to her, but I'm sure she'd like to be distracted from it. Don't be a cop when you visit her, okay?"

"Can do. Hopefully, I won't be using up any of *your* ten minutes. I'll be back in a bit." Billy tipped an imaginary hat and walked down the hall to the ICU, his smile from the last few minutes fading. He was going to meet the local legend, a woman he had admired from afar. Her prognosis didn't look good, but it could have been worse if they hadn't received that anonymous phone tip and rescued her.

## **43 Visiting Bibb

*August 13, 2013, 8:00 AM*
*Intensive Care Unit*

Billy had already seen the preliminary police report about the torture the Jane Doe—now identified as Bibb Stephens—had endured. He read of the physical damage in her medical report—the cigar burns on her arms and feet, the bruised and battered face, the contusions all over her body, and the raw skin around her wrists and ankles where she had been bound with duct tape. Her nose was broken, but there were no marks from either a fist or an implement to her face. She did have bruises on the back of her neck, though. Someone must have grabbed her there then slammed her head into a desk or wall. Some of the wounds were at least three days old, too. How long had she been held against her will until the anonymous tip led the narcotics crew to the cabin in the woods? She was dehydrated, probably hadn't eaten in days, and the fiends hadn't even let her squat behind a bush, much less use a toilet. She had messed her pants, and then had to sit in it for days. Yet she still survived. Anyone with less character or fortitude would have died just because she gave up. But not Bibb. Whatever information or goods they wanted, they never received, or they wouldn't have tried one more time an hour ago with the Sodium Thiopental, the truth serum.

He felt sorry for James. From what he could gather, the man had only recently found out that this woman was his mother. There was a story behind their relationship—or lack thereof—but he didn't know it. It really didn't matter. He could tell James now felt very protective of the wounded woman. Good grief, he had to be in turmoil. He didn't even know he was born in this hospital until a few moments ago. And his new-found mother was tortured for days, rescued, and then assaulted again while in the supposed security of the ICU ward of a hospital. What a jumble of major life dramas to deal with before lunch!

And Leah—where would they be now if not for her and her intuition? The Jane Doe would have stayed a Jane Doe since Bibb didn't have a criminal record or any other reason to have fingerprints in the national data base. No one had reported her as a missing person until Leah just *felt* that something was wrong. And if she hadn't come in to work to check on her future mother-in-law, Bibb would have been subjected to that truth serum or worse. Someone could have injected any number of chemicals into her IV and killed her right in her hospital bed.

But God was watching out for the spirited old lady. Billy had no doubt that He inspired Leah to check on the woman in peril. She was alive and still in ICU, but now they had her past medical records and a next of kin to give her moral support. He didn't know much about the woman other than what he had seen on the news and in the papers. She was outspoken,

250

and didn't let herself or her company get pushed around, or at least didn't respond to threats. She had started her business with nothing but a bank loan and a magnetic personality that attracted contracts that normally would have gone to bigger companies. Maybe someone associated with those bigger companies didn't like that. He'd have to remember to check on that scenario.

Before James had popped into her life, she had no acknowledged family. She was a hard-working woman who had earned the respect of others in the small business community, speaking out for the rights of the little man. She deserved an exit with dignity—at least, a retirement at the time of her own choosing—not one that was forced upon her by being incapacitated by a three day beating. Yup, a son and daughter-in-law with lots of grandchildren would be good for her. Maybe she would finally be able to enjoy a family life.

Billy flashed his badge at the nurse behind the desk and walked towards Bibb's room. No one was posted outside the door, but he did notice Officer Rourke standing next to the snack machine across the hall, watching him as he neared the room. He nodded in tacit salute, then entered.

Bibb was fully reclined with her eyes closed. He didn't know if she was asleep or had become comatose. Hopefully she was just resting. He pulled the brown one-piece molded plastic chair to the side of her bed and gently placed his left hand on her elbow, one of the few areas on her arm not bandaged or bruised.

James had said 'just talk to her,' so that's what he'd do. He never had trouble finding words, and this shouldn't be any different. Yeah, well, he already knew it would be. He wasn't here to interrogate, or to tease, kid, or make jokes. Gee, how did he come up so short in conversation skills? Duh! He was raised in an orphanage. A quick fist or a quick wit was how he survived those first seventeen years.

The gift of gab wasn't needed in the next three acts of his life, either. In the first act—three short years in Uncle Sam's army—he hadn't been asked, so didn't tell anyone much about anything. Then two years in the police academy—conversation was dissuaded there, too.

Finally, act three, he became a cop and got on the fast track to becoming a detective. He was the 'golden boy' of the Greensboro police department. He had an analytical mind, and even as a rookie had been able to solve many cases that had stumped others using the same evidence available. But it was his prime interrogation skills that helped him to quickly rise in the ranks of the department. He was good at tricking the suspects into giving up information that many times ultimately led to the coveted case-closed status.

It was all so easy except for that one slippery thief. That case had really boggled him and everyone else in the department for years.

Billy patted Bibb's arm in recall. That cold case reminded him of when he had first met Leah, Bibb's soon to be daughter-in-law. She was new to the apartment complex and didn't know how to light the barbeque grill. She hadn't known that the old black metal-framed barbeque units near the pool were just receptacles—she would have to bring her own briquettes and lighter. She felt so stupid, she said. Where she was from, the grills always had propane bottles and an electronic clicker to ignite the fire. He brought over a bag of charcoal bricks and a couple of skewers of chopped vegetables. They shared her big steak, his kabobs, and good conversation.

She was interested in his stories about police work. He mentioned his frustration with that one slippery case. She said she had read about it in the paper, but couldn't figure out why they didn't just check the mobile dry cleaning services. All of the victims involved had higher-end jobs, she said. Didn't all lawyers, bankers, and stock brokers wear suits? Well, yes, he replied; what did that have to do with it? Well, check out their dry cleaners and see if they happened to have access to the houses. If they picked up the laundry at the homes, well, then it was pretty simple. They could walk in and take whatever they wanted at whatever time, as long as the item wasn't going to be noticed as missing right away.

After that, he really enjoyed talking with her about cases that had him stumped. He even tested her a few times on cases that had already been solved. She hit all but one. When she came up with a different culprit, he went back and double-checked the file. He asked to speak with the admitted felon one more time. Well, it turned out that the man was a schizophrenic and had been—and still was—off his meds. He'd admit to anything and actually *had* kept admitting to everything. The judge looked into it and said his confession was inadmissible because of the situation. He reopened the case and found that it was the man's brother who was the guilty party. The innocent brother was admitted to the psychiatric hospital where they got him back on track, and the evil brother was now doing 15-20 years.

Billy knew to listen to Leah's gut feelings. She was always right, whether it be that the phone was going to ring and so-and-so was calling, or if the lottery ticket he had just bought was a winner or a dud. She had also kept him away from that creepy intern, Terry Andrews. He couldn't thank her enough for *that*, although he had tried. She must have been out of it this morning, or she would have recognized him. No, she had never seen him— just talked to him on the phone that one time. Well, one time was usually enough for her, thank You, Lord.

Bibb was starting to rouse. "Hi, honey, I'm here," he said. He picked up her left hand, found a spot that wasn't covered in gauze or tape, and kissed it lightly. "It's going to be okay now. Don't worry about a thing. James is here, too. He'll be in to see you in a bit. He has Leah with him, and they're going to get married. Now, you've got to get better soon, so you can be in the ceremony, too, okay?"

"Marty? Oh, Marty, thank you for coming back! I missed you so much. I...I...I have to tell you something. I don't know how long I'll be here, but I have to tell you before I die." Bibb's eyes were swollen closed, but tears were dribbling out the side.

"But you're not going to die, at least not now," Billy said urgently. He certainly didn't want to be hearing any deathbed confessions because, well, he didn't want her to die. Besides, he wasn't Marty—whoever that was.

"Please, just let me get this out," she insisted. "Marty, I made a big mistake—a huge mistake. The first time we met... Well, you know how it was. Anyhow, I got pregnant. I didn't want to tell you. You had gone back to England, and I never thought I'd see you again. I loved you, but didn't think you loved me. I certainly wasn't going to tell you that you had a love child, and that you should come take care of both of us. I wanted you, but didn't want you to have me out of guilt. I was silly enough to think that I should be enough for you."

The pain of her story was making her voice waver, but he didn't dare interrupt her. She licked her lips and continued. "Well, I didn't think I could do it by myself—getting the mill going and raising a child."

She twisted her shoulders, trying to get comfortable. She cleared her throat, her battered face still able to show the conviction she was known for. She spoke plainly now, like she was reading a story from a novel, without personal attachment.

"He was born on the Fourth of July, 1984. I had him at the mill in my little apartment upstairs. I lived alone and never let on to anyone that I was pregnant. I read everything I could about home births at the library. And, maybe you'll be proud of me for this and maybe not, but I delivered him all by myself."

Her tone changed suddenly to maternal pride, "The little boy was perfect. Well, almost perfect. He had a little port wine stain birthmark on his abdomen, just below his little umbilicus." Her finger made a little circle, like she was tracing the mark. "I cleaned him up, tied off his cord, wrapped him in a fresh pink towel—I thought I was having a girl, you see—then took him to the emergency room of the hospital in Winston-Salem. They took him and told me they'd get him to an orphanage where they were sure he'd find a good home."

She bit her lip and started to cry silently, lonely tears trailing down her cheeks, uncomforted by sobs or hiccups. "I never saw him again."

She sniffed back the pain of the loss of her son and continued. "I never thought that I would see *you* again, either. But then two months later, you called." Her face brightened in recollection. "Then you came back to visit and it was love and passion all over again. Of course, you stayed with

253

me for those six wonderful months. You were right on top of when I had my periods, too, you rascal. Well, I think you got me pregnant on purpose that time. I could have hidden the pregnancy from you, but you were so happy about the possibility that I admitted I was going to have a baby. You confided in me that you always wanted another child, that Bruce wasn't going to be able—or willing, rather—to produce an heir and so... Well, I wanted you to be happy, and if this would help insure the Melbourne dynasty, so be it. You promised to visit every year, and you did come out as often as you could, I'm sure, but... Well, I never could figure out how to bring up the subject of your first child, your first child with me. So, if I die today, at least I've told you. You have another son out there somewhere."

Billy was ashen. He had been rubbing Bibb's fingers throughout her little exposé on her wild younger life, but stopped when she mentioned the birth date. When she told of the birthmark, he grabbed the garbage can with his free hand and leaned over it. He had a Leah moment, but managed to keep the breakfast omelet and half pint of milk in him.

"Well, say something, Marty" she beseeched softly.

What could he say? "Um, I'm not Marty. Do you want to hear about my life at the orphanage in Winston-Salem, though?"

Bibb hadn't heard him. She had fallen back to sleep. He placed her hand by her side and looked long and hard into that face. He had always wondered what his mother and father looked like. Well, now he knew what his mother looked like today in the hospital. He had seen pictures of her and always admired her strength in standing up to the land developers. Hmm, he just remembered telling James that she must have been good-looking when she was younger. Even if he hadn't known that she was his mother, she had made a good impression on him.

Shit! James! He and James had the same mother. Duh! And the same father, too! Crap! He wanted to—no, had to—talk to him right now.

He gave Bibb—his mother, he reflected with pride—a long, soft kiss on the forehead, and said, "Hey, get better, Mom. I love you, okay?" He blotted her tears, then wiped away the twin wet drops that had leaked out of his own eyes, and left the room with resolve.

He saw James walking down the hallway toward him, pushing Leah in a wheelchair. Leah saw him and blurted out, "Billy, before you say anything, it's hospital policy that I leave in a wheelchair. But I don't want to leave until I can talk to Bibb, or at least see her." James started to push the chair into the room, but Billy blocked his entrance.

"Not yet, she just fell asleep. Let's go over to the chapel. I have to ask you a couple of questions," Billy swallowed hard, "James." He had wanted to say brother, but overrode the temptation.

James rolled Leah next to the oversized wood-trimmed blue vinyl chair. He sat down next to her, glad that he had on long pants. Those plastic seat coverings didn't go well with bare skin, sticking to flesh no matter how hot or cold it was.

"So what's going on, brother?" James asked with a grin. He had thought of Billy as a brother in the confrontation earlier with the obnoxious intern, and that thought was still fresh and warm in his memory.

Billy didn't want to sit down, but also didn't want to *lord* over his two friends. He blanched at the idea. He probably was an English lord by birth then, too, just like James…or even more so since he was the elder. But he was getting ahead of himself. He took a deep calming breath, but the words wouldn't form. He tried again with the same result.

"Sit down," James said. Something had obviously upset his friend. "What just happened? You look like you've just seen a ghost and… Oh, my God, Bibb is okay, isn't she?"

Billy nodded his head. "Who is Marty?" he asked, finally finding an opening for their conversation.

"My father who, until I met Bibb, I thought was my grandfather. Why?"

"Close your eyes," Billy said. James and Leah both closed their eyes. "No, just James. I don't think it makes a difference if you do or don't, Leah. Okay now, James, tell me if this sounds like someone you know. 'This is my grandson, James Ignatius Melbourne,'" Billy said, trying to mimic James's British accent.

"Wow! You sound just like Marty. I mean my father. It was getting confusing, so Leah and I just call my biological father, Marty and my biological brother, Bruce. How'd you know what he sounded like?"

"I didn't. Bibb thought that I was Marty. She just gave what she thought was a deathbed confession. Oh, shit. I mean, oh, crap, I mean…"

Leah shook her head and explained incredulously, "Billy's your brother, James. Your real—honest to goodness, same mother and father—brother. Wow is right!"

"What?" James yelped in shock. He panted a couple of times, trying to compose himself, but was lost. He apologized, "I mean, if I was going to find out that anyone was a long lost brother, I'd want it to be you, but how…how can that be?"

"Well, it appears that Marty, our father, visited North Carolina the year before you were conceived. Bibb got pregnant, gave the baby—me—up for adoption, and never said anything to anyone about it. I mean, really, anyone. She said she delivered the baby herself in her little apartment, then drove to Winston-Salem where she gave the baby to the hospital. They said they would take the baby to an orphanage where he would be adopted out. Except that there was no adoption."

"But…but," James stammered.

Billy answered the unspoken question. "What are the odds that the baby she described would have the same birthdate, arrive at the same hospital, and have the same birthmark as me, huh?" Billy pulled up his shirt and scooted his pants down enough to show the birthmark. "It doesn't take a detective to figure that one out. Are you…are you upset?" he asked—James didn't look too good.

James leaned over and set his elbows on his knees, then his head in his hands. His fingers were splayed across his face to hide any indication of the mood he was in.

"Here." Leah offered him a plastic bag-lined trash can with a couple of empty coffee cups and paper towels in the bottom. "Just in case."

"Now are you okay, Billy," she asked, peering deep into his eyes. "Do I need to take you to the emergency room?"

James gave an involuntary cough, snorting at her little joke. He shook his head in his hands then rose up, facing Billy first then Leah. "You know, I came here on a lark after a rotten marriage. I met a wonderful young woman who I knew…really I did," he said, looking deep into Leah's eyes, "knew was going to be in my life for a long time. I didn't know I would want her to be with me forever, but anyhow. Damn! I can't focus! Did I ever tell you I had ADD? No, probably not. Please, just bear with me, I'll get there. I'm a little muddled right now. But you are, too, aren't you?" he looked hard at Billy, "Brother Billy."

"You got that right. Go ahead with your story," Billy grinned, "baby brother."

Leah shook her head and smiled. Her eyes were misting, and it wasn't from any physical pain or discomfort. She was getting overwhelmed emotionally, but it felt good letting the moisture build. These were happy saline drops forming now.

"So, I'll try to make this quick," James said curtly. He took a deep breath, then started rambling again, pausing to take a quick breath between thoughts before continuing his dissertations.

"I met the girl of my dreams, found out that I had a living mother, that the South American Indian mother who I thought had died in childbirth was a myth." James was still blabbering, and now added hand gestures to enhance his story. "That my grandfather was really my father, that my father was really my globetrotting gay brother who cared for no one but himself… Well, the last part of that I already knew—he was selfish and didn't care if that was a secret or not. And then, there were the assaults, and arsons, and meeting a best friend… You see, I can't say *new best friend* since I never had a best friend, any best friend before… Anyway, my new best friend of the male persuasion, because the best friend of the female persuasion is my fiancée, another assault, and then I find out that my best male friend is really my brother. Phew!"

"So, does that mean he's going to get recognized, I mean by the

Melbourne family?" Leah asked.

"Well, Marty…Dad," he added with a grin to Billy, "is the only other Melbourne around, and well, he really isn't *around* right now. That one, dear big brother, you'll have to accept as a mystery not to be solved right away, okay?"

"Okay by me. I went from having no relatives for nearly thirty years, to having two new ones in the last thirty minutes. Shall we go check and see how *Mom* is doing?"

"Okay," James said, "just a peek for me. Leah wants to see Mom, too, and I don't want to wear her out. We're only supposed to go in one at a time, but maybe they'll allow both of us. The worst they can do is kick one of us out."

## **44 The Family Connection

*August 13, 2013, 6:00 PM*
*Billy's apartment*

James pushed his plate away from the edge of the table. He'd offer to help with the dishes later. Right now, it was quality time with his family.

"That was great steak, Billy. Where'd you learn to do such a mean barbeque?" James teased, turning on a little western accent for the occasion.

"Why, didn't you hear, little brother," Billy replied in kind, sounding like a cross between Johnny Cash and John Wayne, "I'm an expert at grilling…"

"Right, professional interrogator," Leah deadpanned. "Hey, where'd Peter go in such a hurry? I thought you two were a couple."

Billy actually blushed at her remark, and she didn't let it go unnoticed. James looked over to see what the pause in conversation was all about. Those two were usually trading quips at machine gun pace.

"Come on, now, fess up," Leah goaded. "I know it's not bad stuff, but good news. What's going on with you two?"

"Well, he had to go to a meeting for work. That's why he wouldn't drink a beer. Not that he'd get drunk on one, but he didn't want to smell of it. He's getting a promotion."

"Yeah, and what else…" Leah was trying to pull the words out because Billy was being guarded, and she really *didn't* know what was happening between the two of them.

"Are you going to need the truck to help him move in?" James asked. He could see what was going on. "I mean, it's yours to do whatever you want with. Shoot, I've got my chauffer here and won't need the truck until the night of the 16th." James looked over at Leah and winked.

She grinned in return, then sat up straight as she flashed on what James was insinuating. "Peter's moving in with you? Will this place be big enough for both of you? I mean, shoot, it's not as if you're going to need another bedroom or… Crap, I think I'll just shut up before I cram my foot in my mouth all the way up to my kneecap."

"He said he didn't have much to move because he was renting a furnished apartment. He never felt like putting down roots until he met me. I guess it was pretty much the same with us as with you two. We just knew from the very beginning that it was the right thing to do. So, what about you two? When's the big day?"

"The day after tomorrow," James and Leah said at the same time, then looked at each other and smiled.

"Why do you have to get married so soon? I mean, shoot, you already told me that you weren't waiting…" Billy looked over at both of them to make sure he wasn't being too familiar.

Leah and James both shrugged shoulders, but it was Leah who spoke up. "You'll probably think this is weird, but James insisted that we be handfasted before we, you know…"

"I think the proper words are 'consummated the relationship.' That's the way Ramona and Gregg did it in that one 'Lost' book, right? When they didn't want to wait or look for a preacher?" Billy recalled.

"You've read them?" James exclaimed.

"Well, yeah! Leah was such a nut about them that I pretty much had to, just to keep up with her and her ramblings and ravings about them. Hey, I think I have the whole series over here now. They weren't burned in the fire! You let me borrow them, and I never gave them back."

Tension started to fill the air around James and Leah as Billy started retelling his favorite events in the Lisa Sinclaire novels, commenting on Lord Julian, and how he thought that he should have gotten a partner somewhere in the stories. After a few minutes of rambling, Billy realized they weren't contributing to the conversation.

"Hey, what's wrong with you two? You look like you've seen a ghost, and I know I'm not *that* pale," Billy joked. They didn't answer. "No, really—why do you two keep looking at each other like that? Leah, I thought you liked those books."

James literally gathered himself together—sucking in air, pulling in his elbows to rearrange his body into a formidable entity—wordlessly letting Billy know that he wanted to avoid that topic of conversation. He definitely didn't want to comment on the 'Lost' novels. Hopefully, Billy would recognize his blatant avoidance of the subject as a request that they 'discuss this later.'

"All right," James said in a formal tone, pretending he hadn't heard Billy's remarks, "so Leah and I are already handfast—or is that handfasted?—and morally wed. So, if you think Mum is up to it, would you be willing to stand up for me if we got a preacher or magistrate to come to the hospital and perform a little ceremony in her room? I want to make this legal, and the sooner the better."

Billy looked back and forth between the two of them and realized that something was amiss, but that they didn't want to talk about it now. That was okay; they were all cool. They'd spill the beans when they were ready.

"All righty," he said, then began to speak *voce basso*, as if announcing a news announcer. "Wedding ceremony to be held in ICU room with long, lost mother and brother as witnesses. Assailants kept at bay by ever vigilant members of the Greensboro Police Department."

He laughed at his own silliness, then reverted to his own voice. "Sounds good to me. Leah, do you have a preacher in mind, or should I call Jake?" he asked, then looked at James to make sure he wasn't left out of the decision.

James shook his head in wonder. "Hey, I don't know anyone, but personally, I'd rather have a minister or priest than a magistrate. Leah and I can get the license first thing in the morning—that is, if you can get my birth certificate. Then we can meet back at the hospital at what…is 9:30 okay for you?"

"9:30's fine. I already have the birth certificate." Billy saw the surprised look on James's face. "Hey, I work fast when it's important. It's on the counter. Don't forget to take it when you leave."

"Jake would be great," Leah said. "Would you call him for us? But remember, it has to be a short ceremony. Even if Bibb is out of ICU, which I believe she will be by then…" Leah gave them both a grin of smug self-assuredness and saw it come right back at her. Her men knew that all would be fine with their mother, too. "Well, the rooms are small, so it'll just be the five of us, and then…" Leah looked at James and grinned, "We'll be ready for our honeymoon."

James gasped at her words. The magnitude of leaving this world hit him suddenly, leaving him woozy and shocked. He grabbed a kitchen chair and sat down. *Whoa! They were going to be gone from this realm, this time dimension, probably forever. He had just met his real mother and brother, and now he'd never get to know them…*

"Hey, dude, are you okay? I mean, you're just getting married to the most wonderful woman in the world for the rest of your life. It's not that scary now, is it?"

James looked at him, his face pale and stunned. "It's not the marriage, but the honeymoon that has me spooked. Really, look at me, can't you tell?"

Billy could see he was telling the truth. "So why is the honeymoon scaring you? Where are you two going, Mars?" he asked sarcastically.

"No, even further away than that," Leah said softly, now frightened, too.

"Ho-kay, now you're both scaring *me*," Billy said. "Where exactly *are* you going?"

"Well, where we're going isn't far…" James began, not knowing how he was going to finish.

"Can we talk about this later, Billy," Leah interjected, saving James from the awkward and phenomenal explanation. "I want James to know more about you. I mean before we go. I, um, well, let's just say that now I'm curious, too, about how all this came about."

"Well, there's not much to it," Billy explained, still a little concerned about the secretive attitude of his two friends. "There's just me. That's all there is and all there ever has been—nothing more, nothing less. Just me."

"So Bibb just dropped you off at a hospital and you were raised in an orphanage?" Leah asked rhetorically, trying to find an opening for a different topic of conversation.

Billy shrugged his shoulders in answer. She knew he had been raised as an orphan and wasn't sensitive about it. He had it better than most kids from divorced or 'let's stay together for the children' families.

Leah shifted in her seat, then asked the question that was really on her mind. "I never thought about it before just now, but how *did* you get your name?"

Billy snorted. "I asked that too when I was in kindergarten. The other kids were talking about how they were named after a grandparent or uncle or their Dad's favorite superhero. I just walked away from them and went and played with the puzzles. When I got back *home* to the orphanage, though, I asked the housemother who I was named after. Well, it turns out she had been one of the nurses at the Winston-Salem Hospital when I came in and knew all about the naming process. She was a real nice old lady, God rest her soul, and made me and every one of her *children* feel loved. Anyhow, she and a lot of the nurses were all fascinated with the movies that were made in 1939. There were lots of us named for characters from 'Gone with the Wind' and 'The Wizard of Oz.' I guess they'd been doing it for years and had just about run out of names. I got the name Billy Burke after the actress who portrayed the Good Witch of the North, Billie Burke."

"Sounds reasonable," Leah replied, then added with a chuckle, "at least that's better than Glinda."

"Or Toto or Hattie McDaniel. The boy's names had pretty much been used up by the time I came around. No, I think Billy Burke is a decent name. I don't know what I'm supposed to do now that I have an acknowledged mother and father, though."

Now it was Billy's turn to feel uncomfortable and shift positions. He looked at James and asked sincerely, "Am I supposed to change my name now?"

"Well, it wouldn't be a bad idea. I mean, we can get the blood tests done so there's no basis for dispute. Just looking at the two of us, though, I'd say we'll have a high percentage match. After that, I would like to have you officially recognized as my brother and the legitimate heir to the Melbourne title and," James cleared his throat, still a little uncomfortable with the revelation, "family fortunes."

"Fortunes, as in plural?" Billy asked, wide-eyed and slack-jawed in shock.

"Correct." James looked around as if to make sure there wasn't anyone else within hearing distance, although he knew it was just the three of them. "There's the Melbourne account that is, well, the amount is not public information, but consists of the acknowledged finances of the family.

And then there is…" James sighed. He had to tell someone if he was going to be gone. He didn't want the monies to just *disappear* because of attrition, lack of heirs, or because no one knew about them. "The Pomeroy-Hart estate, the secret funds to be used only in case of extreme hardship. I thought I was going to have to access them when it appeared that Clotilde, the woman who is now my ex-wife, was going to wipe me out in the divorce. Here, give me your cell phone and I'll Bluetooth the files with all the account numbers to you. You're the primary heir now, the eldest."

"What? That's not what I wanted! All I care about is having a real brother, mother, and father. Hey, where is our father? You never said he died, but he's obviously not in the picture right now. Do I need to do a little detective work?" he asked as he laced his fingers together and pushed them out, cracking his knuckles in preparation of a tough task.

"No!" Leah and James exclaimed at the same time.

"What?" Billy replied, stunned. The two of them were all wound up about the subject and for no apparent reason. It was a simple question, and he just got a very emotional answer. "Why not?" he argued, "I'm pretty good at that stuff. I mean, that's how I make my living."

"We…we know where he is," James said reluctantly. "It's just that he's not, um, too available at this time, and I don't know when or if he will be…"

"Ever again? Is that what you were going to say? Hey, what's going on here? It sounds like a bad horror movie." He laughed, then saw their faces fall at his remark. "Or a real good mystery novel. How does it end?"

"We don't know yet," Leah answered before thinking. "I mean… Oh, shit, James, we have to tell him. He knows we wouldn't lie to him, so it's time for a leap of faith."

"Now you're *really* starting to scare me. This isn't 'ooh dee doo dee' Twilight Zone stuff, is it? You're not going to tell me Dad's off in some other dimension, are you?" Billy was trying to be light about the whole 'where's Dad' scenario, but he was truly concerned.

"Those tracks that disappeared into nowhere after the Jane Doe disappeared, how do you explain those?" James asked, trying to put the ball in Billy's court to see how open-minded he was.

"Well, I don't, or can't, or…shit, man, that's one I should have given to Leah instead of you. She's the great mystery solver."

"You gave *him* the report? The one you said you couldn't give me? Why, why, what the…" Leah was babbling with frustration and anger at her best friend and soon to be brother-in-law. She thought he trusted her.

"Well, there really wasn't anything in it and I… Shoot, Leah, do you want to see it now?" Billy asked, unable to explain his reasons, but willing to offer the report to her as a gesture of good will.

"That's too little too late," she replied sharply. "Besides, I already know about it." She looked over at James and smiled softly. "And he knows I do, too. AND, we both know who the first Jane Doe was, is," she proclaimed with pride.

She paused, waiting to see Billy's reaction, then saw he was mildly intrigued, but really not too excited about it. Well, he was sure to have a different reaction with her next declaration.

"She was—is—my mother. And she went back to be with her other family. And I think that's where your father is, too, right now."

Billy was now paying close attention to her, his body leaned forward, his eyes waiting for her to finish the thought. But it was James's turn.

"They both went back to 1781," he stated simply. "And that's where we're going; we're going back to be with them."

Billy scowled, was mum for a whole five seconds, then sat straight up and pronounced, "Bullshit," never taking his eyes off them, waiting for the 'gotcha' he was sure would follow their explanation.

James and Leah shared a look of exasperation then identical shrugs. "Should we show him the video?" Leah asked.

"I think it's the only way, now that the letters are gone."

Billy snorted in resignation. "I think I need a drink or six." He plopped back into the overstuffed chair and resolutely put one foot then the other on the ottoman. His eyes were still focused low, not wanting to see the faces of his friends—family, he reminded himself—right away. He brought his right hand to the bridge of his nose and rubbed his eyebrows in circles with his thumb and index finger, trying to make sense, not so much out of *what* they had said, but *why* they had said it.

Leah could see what was going on in his head, even if he wasn't looking at her. "We're not messing with you, Billy. It's just…well, the direct explanation is the easiest in this case. I mean, how can I soft pedal, 'my mother went back in time and got younger and, oh, by the way, she had triplets and I think your father went back to join her.'"

"What the fu…?" Billy exclaimed, leaning forward, ready to come out of his chair.

"Hold on there, mate," James said, with his hand held up. "Leah, don't say another word." James saw her glare at him for telling her what to do, then added sweetly, "Please." Her face softened and he continued. "Let's just show him the video and then talk, okay?"

"Okay," Leah and Billy said at the same time.

They looked at each other without words, then Leah broke the tension, "Scoot over—we'll both fit," then snuggled up to Billy.

James had Dani/Evie's smartphone. He handed it to Leah, then squatted next to them and looked over her shoulder. Leah did the button pushing, taps, and swipes to find the file.

The three of them watched the little video in total silence. Neither Leah nor James even commented that the young, very pregnant woman in the little picture-show was her mother. If Billy couldn't tell, they'd explain later, but by the look on his face, he knew. He had been forewarned.

Billy's dry response surprised them. "So why do you think you can go back to be with her? And where is our father in all of this?"

"You believe us?" Leah asked incredulously.

"Well, yeah. I don't think that this is some prank you're pulling on me. It isn't, is it?" he turned to look at each of them in turn, making sure he hadn't just been punked. "I mean, 'If you eliminate the impossible, then whatever is left—no matter how improbable—must be the truth.' That's Spock from the J.J. Abram's movie version of Star Trek™, by the way."

"Sherlock Holmes said the same thing. And it's the truth, all right," James said. "And there were letters that collaborated this, but," he drew out a long breath, "they were stolen, and I think by that slimeball, Eight."

"Or his brother, Niner, but we haven't figured out where they could have stashed them." Leah turned in the seat and looked into Billy's eyes intently, her face splashed with fear. "They're still in custody, aren't they?"

Billy winced, "Well, Eight is, but Niner got bailed out. Regardless, how would you go back, and why?"

"'Why' is because I want to see my mother again. And here, James, show him the file with the map and note you got the other day."

James tapped and slid his finger across the face of his smartphone to open the file, then handed it to Billy so he could examine the documents closer.

Billy pinched and swiped his thumb and index finger over the face of the screen to enlarge the photo. "There's a forgery here," he said. "Here, look. See, right on the edge of the XX's is where someone overlapped another piece of paper. It's been cut, and you can see the juncture. If you look closely at the thickness and consistency of the pen stroke on the XX's compared to the other writing on the map, you'll see that it was a different pen used, too. I would say someone pasted another piece of paper on top of the original map, then used a felt marker to alter the location of the XX's."

Billy looked up and saw their smiling faces. "What? Did you already notice this? Gee, I thought I was doing a good job."

"Oh, you are, big brother. Neither of us had seen the alterations, but I had, well, done a little séance-type drawing, and Leah had a dream…" James nodded to Leah, giving her credit. She nodded back, proud of the discovery, "And our sixth senses told us that the XX's were in the wrong spot." James's attitude dropped like a fart in an elevator. "Oh, shit," he moaned.

Leah started to ask *what,* then gulped, "Yeah, oh, shit. Someone else knows about all of this, and I don't think they're friendlies. Do you think

264

that the MacLeods have anything to do with this?"

James groaned, "Well, maybe, but JB—James Bradford over in London—for sure. He's the one who sent me the file. Billy, can you do any of your detective work in England? I think the man who scanned and sent me the note and the map is the one who changed this around. And then these MacLeod boys, except for Clark, seem to know what's going on, too. At least, they seem to have a keen interest in Leah, and I don't think it's just for her set of keys to the pharmaceutical cabinets at the hospital."

"I'll see what I can find out. In the meantime, when and how are you two going *back*, and when were you going to tell me?" Billy was hurt, but also concerned for their safety.

"Well, I just found out that you were my brother…" James began.

Leah interrupted, "And yes, I was going to tell you, regardless of whether you thought I was a nut or not. I mean, I didn't want you to have to go through what I did when my mother disappeared. I just didn't know how or when I was going to let you know. Now, with the family thing going on between you two... Well, we wanted to tell you as soon as possible. This was the first chance we had for all of us to be alone together."

## **45 What Next?

*August 13, 2013, 7:00 PM*

"JB has been sending copies of all of my correspondences to those damned MacLeod brothers. No wonder it seems as if they're shadowing us, one step behind us."

"Except when they're one step in front of us," Leah added. "What don't they know?"

"They don't know that I have what they're looking for with me, that the treasure isn't buried or *back* with my father, but in my valise. I don't know how much of a difference that makes, though. I believe they want to go back in time, regardless. There must be something else, another reason they want access to the time portal. Right now, you and I are flying blind—they have the letters. They know more than we do about what has happened."

"No, they know more than we do about what's in the letters, but I don't think they know where to go."

"What do you mean?" James asked, flinching because he had never told her about slipping out to go and do a little redressing with the yellow ribbons at the scene of the disappearance.

"You went out and re-taped the 'crime' scene, didn't you?" she accused more than asked.

"Well, I didn't think I needed your help for that one. It was our second night together, and you were sleeping so soundly, and...ahem... I didn't think you'd mind if I borrowed your car for an hour or two..."

Leah squinted her eyes as she slowly approached James, trying not to show a definitive emotion. She was glad and proud of him at the same time. She hoped he couldn't see her true feelings, but *could* see the trumped-up emotion of anger mixed with frustration that she was trying to portray by deliberately pinching and contorting her expression. She got to within twelve inches of his guilt-wracked face before she broke character. She couldn't hold back the elation and pride at his creative deception. They would be safe because of his forethought.

"Did anyone ever tell you that you were a genius?" she asked softly as she raised herself on tip toes to be closer to his face, placing her hands on his shoulders to steady herself.

"Not lately," he admitted. "But if you're saying so, I'm flattered." He bent his head so his nose touched hers. A smile crept up one side of his face. *Who would be the first to kiss the other at this close proximity?* He felt her hands slide over his shoulders, up the sides of his neck, until they covered his ears. He closed his eyes at the warmth and security of her hands holding his head.

*Slurp!*

"What the heck!" he screeched. "What was that?" he asked, although he knew quite well what it was. She had licked his nose!

"Well, if you're going to treat me like a dog, I'll act like a dog. Now, no more secrets, okay?"

"Okay. And no more licking me like a dog," he said.

Leah grinned and lifted her eyebrows suggestively.

"Well, at least no licking me on the nose," he amended sheepishly. He didn't have to be psychic to see what she was insinuating. All of a sudden, he knew exactly what he wanted to do next. But that would have to wait for a while. They had to finish tailoring their outfits first.

ЖЖ

*August 14, 2013, 7:00 AM*

"It's Billy on the phone," said Leah. "He said it's important, and you and I should get to the hospital as soon as possible. Or rather he said *stat*, but that's what it means."

James had the room key and the bag in his hand before she finished her sentence. "What's taking you so long?" he joked. She was ready, too, and had the car keys and purse in her hand. "And I know what stat means," he said, as he opened the car door for her.

Leah looked grim as they pulled out of the driveway. His little joke had not been well accepted. He tried again. "Hey, I know you're the one who's psychic, but I *know* that Bibb is okay. She's my blood, remember?"

"Yeah, it must be something else bothering me."

Billy was waiting for them at the hospital entrance. He held up his hand to stave off any worried questions, but quickly saw that James was composed and looking back to make sure Leah was the same.

"Okay, have you guys got some visual communication going on? I mean, I know that Leah has the *sight,* but I didn't know that you did too, little brother."

"Just with her, or at least she's the only one so far. But we're still working at perfecting the silent language skills. So, what's the big news that Bibb has? Oh, and she's feeling better, I take it." James was confident that all was well, and the look on Billy's face confirmed it, even before he had asked.

"Oh, she's a spry old lady, all right. She's insistent that she tells you about a *letter*," Billy said with emphasis on the last word and a raised eyebrow. "So, do you think maybe she has the missing letters you were talking about?"

James snorted, said, "Hell, if I know," and grabbed Leah's arm just a little too brusquely. "Come on, let's go see what she has," he said flatly, his perky mood suddenly in the trash bin.

ЖЖ

267

"I have a little confession to make," Bibb said to the group, even before they had a chance to exchange hellos. "I'm sorry, that was rude. Good morning, and thank you all for…well, everything. I don't think I'd be alive without your efforts, all of you."

'You're welcomes' were tossed back and forth, then the visitors to the hospital room each grabbed a chair and sat down.

"Are you feeling better today?" Billy asked, biting back the name Mom. He knew she didn't know that he was the one who listened to her little 'deathbed' confession. He wanted to let her know he knew her secret—that *he* was her long lost son—but she had called the meeting for them to listen to her. He'd waited nearly thirty years to have a mother. He could wait a day or two more.

Bibb put up her right hand—still covered with tape and bandaging, but without the IV—and wafted away Billy's question about her physical health. "Oh, I'm fine. I'd like to get out of here, but they said they want to do more tests. Personally, I think they just want more money. I keep telling them I don't have insurance, and that I'm just a poor working woman, but they're getting downright bossy. And I thought that *I* was belligerent! But anyway, I wanted to tell you two about a letter. I don't mean to be rude, Officer Burke, but this is kind of a family matter. You do understand, don't you?"

"Well, Bibb," James started slowly, unsure of how he was going to proceed. *He quickly looked over at Leah and gave her a 'don't interrupt me; I'm going to get this done by myself' look.* "I'm sorry, I want to call you 'Mom,' but that might take a day or two, or maybe just a minute or two, but, well, please don't think I'm being rude if I use your given, or at least your familiar name, okay?"

Bibb didn't say anything, but nodded that she understood.

"Well, I want you to know that we are all family here," he said. Bibb nodded again like she was getting weary—he was repeating himself. "I don't think you really understand, *Mom*," he said sternly, eyeing her directly like a parent to a misbehaving child. "Billy, would you come here for a minute, please?"

Billy had been standing quietly by the door, ready to make a quick exit, if requested. Now he was smiling, glad to be called over—he really wanted to be involved in the family discussion.

"Would you hike up your shirt and pull down your pants a bit, and show Bibb that little, you know, *thing*?" James asked, winking at the word *thing*.

Billy couldn't resist making a joke with an opening like that. "You mean *this* little old thing?" he asked in a playful tone. He pushed down the waistband of his pants and pulled up his shirt, holding the shirttail with his chin. He showed his belly to James, grinned at him, and then did a slow turn toward Bibb, showing her his port wine stain birthmark "Oh, and do you want to know my birthday, too, *Mom*?"

Bibb went ashen at the sight of the purplish blotch and plopped back into her stack of pillows. She didn't say a word, just stared, her eyes wide with shock.

"Hey, you were the one who told me about me," Billy explained. "There was some 'ooh dee doo dee' Twilight Zone stuff going on that day. You called me Marty, then told me all about me, all the way down to my birthday, birthmark, and the hospital you took me to. You fell back into your coma or whatever before I could tell you who I was. James said I sounded just like him—Dad—except for the accent, of course. But," Billy slowed down the pace of his banter, "do I look like him?"

Bibb nodded briskly, then brought her hand up to wipe the tears that were now flooding down her face. She pulled her hand away from her nose and stuck both arms out to accept her first-born son. Billy lifted his chin, dropped his shirt back down over his partially-bared belly, and welcomed the hug. "Here," he said, and grabbed a double fistful of tissues, "blow."

Bibb accepted them and cleaned off the spatters of joy from under her eyes and nose. "But how?" she asked.

"Well, I don't know how, but I think I know why. It's because we all need each other. Now, Mom, I know a little about some of this *mysterious stuff* that's going on, maybe more than you know, maybe not, but whatever is out there, I want to be a part of. I at least want to *know* what's going on, even if I plan on staying put."

"Staying put? What...why...who..." Bibb was sputtering and looking over at James and Leah. All the pair could do was grin and shrug. "Doesn't anyone want to stay here with me?" she finally blurted out.

"Like I said, I plan on staying put. Now, you called us—them—here, so since we're all ready to listen, how about you tell us about the letter before your blood pressure goes sky high with the excitement of having a baby, I mean, having a son."

Billy stayed at Bibb's side, his hand on the top of her left arm, glowing at her proximity. She placed her right hand on top of his, patted it gently, and began.

"Your father brought the letters to me to read. I'm not sure if it was because he trusted me that much—I'd like to think so—or if it was because I was all the way over in America and had no way of 'being a nuisance' with them." She shrugged her shoulder in acknowledgement. It could have been either, but it didn't matter. He had shared them with her.

"It was a long time ago, but I remember one of the letters clearly. He read it over and over again. He wanted me to memorize it. He was afraid it was going to get lost or stolen or burned or something. He normally wasn't paranoid, but he certainly had a fear about that one letter. I told him I had a copier and could make a copy, or could even transcribe it for him and keep it in my safe, but he said no, he wanted me to memorize it. If you want to get some paper out of the desk over there—at least, I think there's some over there—you can write it down for yourself. I really don't think those bastards referred to in the letter are going to bother you two. Ready?"

James opened up the drawer of the nightstand and took out the paper and pen. "Ready," he said, his ankle crossed over his knee making a human desktop. *Ready as I'll ever be.* He looked over at Leah and saw she was content. Right now, she wasn't stressed. Either her fear had been resolved or forgotten.

Bibb shut her eyes and recited the letter.

*"The Second Letter*

*To: Lord James Melbourne*

*To be read no sooner than November 1, 2012*

*"My dear James,*

*"Hopefully you have followed the instructions that have been passed through the generations, and this epistle has not fallen into the wrong hands or been lost due to theft, fire, or disinterest. It is of the utmost importance that you help me in order to keep 'the time line continuum' as it should be.*

*"I came back to 1781 to investigate a mystery and have discovered an enigma that I know you can help resolve. If you don't—or can't—do this, you may never be born and this letter will seem like the ramblings of an insane man.*

*"I need you to come back to help me and someone who is very close to me. On October 31, 2012 you will come into possession of an ancient map. This will lead you to the information we sought about our great-uncle, Julian Hart. You will, of course, know more about him by the time you read this. I intentionally planted the seed of curiosity in you from your youth so you would follow through with this. Sorry for the manipulation, but it was a matter of the utmost value, absolutely priceless. If you can't, or won't, come back to join me, I will lose my greatest treasure.*

*"Beware of anyone named MacLeod. They seem to be everywhere there is evil. They are, and have been, the bane of our family since the 1740's. There might be good members in their clan, but I have never heard of any."*

Bibb opened her eyes and looked up. "That's why I knew he went back just recently. He was destined to be back there to write this letter from the 18th century to you. On the bottom half of the page was a post script, written in ball point pen.

*"By now you will have read the letter from your old friend. Please have her daughter, the nurse, give you detailed instructions on how to perform blood transfusions. She should be able to help you obtain the*

*supplies for same. If I have done my job right, you won't be squeamish and will be able to help save a very important life. I need you here to help me in order to ensure your future. If you haven't heard about the family secret, I'll tell you when you get here. Love, Marty"*

"And that was that," Bibb said.

"And that was enough," Leah snorted in exclamation. Her eyes widened and her voice softened, "So he doesn't expect me to go back, does he, James?"

"I don't care whether he expects you to or not. Unless you tell me you don't want to go, you're going, okay?"

Leah brightened up immediately. "Wild horses couldn't keep me away," she said, then realized the other aspect. "MacLeods! Oh, my God!"

"Yeah, right," said Billy. "That's the last name of Eight and Niner, and they've certainly been a major problem for you, Leah, and Mom."

"What do you mean?" Bibb asked. "Those, those assholes who assaulted me—are they MacLeods?"

"Yes. Atholl Grant MacLeod the Eighth and his brother, *Asshole* the Ninth, or Niner as he's called. Eight assaulted Leah, twice, and Niner is the one who sold James the map last fall when he was here. Evidently he's also the one who torched Leah's apartment the day James flew in."

James continued the story. "Just after you left, that first day at Leah's apartment when I found out *the family secret*—that you were, um, my mother, and that Marty was my father, well..." James paused for a deep breath. "Leah and I went swimming, and while we were out there, someone broke into her place and set it on fire. It didn't look like they got anything, but the story was that they were looking for her keys so they could get into the pharmaceutical cabinet where she works, here at this hospital, in order to get drugs. Except she had the keys with her, and so they didn't get anything. Instead, they just trashed and burned her apartment."

"Did you have the letters with you then, and do you have them now?" Bibb asked.

"Yes and no; I had them then—they were in my bag and I had it with us inside the pool enclosure—but now, no. Someone stole them when I was tending to the clerk at the motel and Leah was in the shower. Someone took them out of my bag, and oh, my God! Clark is a MacLeod! But I'm *sure* he didn't, or doesn't, have anything to do with this." James put his ankle down off of his knee and leaned back in the chair. *Could he be wrong about him?*

"Would you recognize his voice on the phone?" Billy asked. James nodded, but didn't say anything. He was still stunned. "Well, good, because we have a recording of the person who called in the anonymous tip that led to Bibb's, I mean Mom's, rescue. Sorry, when I think of you before I knew you were my mother, you were Bibb. Of course, you're *Mom* now, and

271

hopefully will be for a long time…"

Just then, a doctor came in with a clipboard full of papers. "Ms. Stephens, we have the results of your latest tests. Would you like me to wait to go over them with you until after your visitors leave?"

"No," she replied calmly, surprisingly at peace with herself. She was going to have at least one son with her now. "These are all family members. You can tell all of us at the same time. I'm ready, and whether they are or not, they're going to have to be."

"Oh, so you probably know what I'm going to tell you." the doctor said. Bibb shrugged as if it didn't make a difference to her. "Well, the cancer has reappeared in your liver, but there's a good chance we can take care of that with a transplant." The doctor looked at the three young people in the room, obviously assessing their potential as donors. "It looks to me like you have two sons here who, if they are willing to get a little blood work done, could possibly be donors."

Billy quickly stood up and stuck out his arm. "Where do I go and how soon can we get it done?"

Leah looked at James with shock. They were getting ready to leave and only had a small window of time. "How soon can we get all of this done? I mean the donating and all," James asked grimly.

"Well, it takes 2-3 days for the testing to be complete. The surgery requires 4-5 days in the hospital for the donor, then about 4-6 weeks of light duty. Your liver—we'd take about half of it—will regenerate quickly, as will the portion donated to your mother here. It will grow to full size in a month or less. Do you have any time constraints?" The doctor was pretty sharp and had picked up on James's uneasiness.

"Yes, I do," he admitted reluctantly.

"But I don't," Billy crowed. "Come on, let's go stick me and see if we can give Mom a bit of *moi*. The sooner the better, I'm sure."

Billy was at the doctor's side and wasn't going to be dissuaded. "I'm serious as a heart attack, or would that be a case of liver cancer? Let's move it!"

"Okay, Ms. Stephens, it looks like this is going to be easier than I thought. Our records didn't show any next of kin on your last visit…"

"Well, we're here now, aren't we?" Billy threaded his hand into the doctor's crooked elbow and waved good-bye to everyone. "See you in a little while. Love you loads!"

Bibb sat forward in the bed, her hands folded in her lap. She shook her head slowly, the incredulousness of the miracle showing in her smile. "I really didn't think I had a chance," she said to the empty spot in the room. She changed her focus to James. "I know you have to go *back*, but I wanted to see you before you left and ask you if you would please send your father back to me. I know it's selfish, but I…I want him back." Bibb broke down with her request. Cancer and death didn't scare her, but not seeing Marty again was more than she could handle.

James walked up to her and put his hand on her shoulder. "Hey, you let me have him for 28 years—I think you deserve a few, too. I'll send him back if I can. But you have to get better now. God, I hope Billy's a good match. It's not that I don't want to be there for you. Shoot, if I could just drop off a lobe of liver and leave it, I would, but that can't—won't—happen."

"James." Leah had come up next to him without being heard. The look of dread she had earlier was back. Whatever had been bothering her was manifesting itself now. "What's your blood type?"

"Shoot, I don't know. What difference does it make if I'm not going to be Mom's donor?"

"It makes a lot of difference if I'm going to have babies. I mean have healthy babies, safely…"

"He's O negative," Bibb said. "Just like his father and just like me. You see, I had the Rh factor thing going on, too. After the first one, Billy, it was real important to know. You see," she explained to James, "when a woman with Rh *negative* blood has a baby with a man who has Rh *positive* blood, and the baby inherits the father's blood type, the baby can build up antibodies in the mother's system. That means if she has another child with an Rh *positive* father, and that baby has Rh *positive* blood, the mother's immune system will attack and kill the baby. There aren't any complications if the baby has Rh negative blood. And there are no problems if both the mother and father have Rh negative blood. What's your blood type, Leah?"

"I'm O negative, too, so I guess we'll be fine. Shoot," she said, her spirit lifting quickly, "I know we'll be fine—both with the babies and with the donating. You see, we're both universal blood donors, and whoever is supposed to get that blood transfusion will have two available donors."

"Three," corrected Bibb. "Marty is O negative, too."

"Four," added Leah. "Mom is O negative, also. Well, there should be enough blood in us to take care of a major problem. I sure hope it isn't either one of them."

"Did you ever see the other letters or remember them?" James asked, changing the subject.

"I saw them, but remember very little. There was one about a Genevieve or Jenny and Scout. I…I think they're my ancestors. By the way, you're part Cherokee. That's where you get your lovely coloring and smooth body hair. You do have a nice beard, though. You got that from your father. I sure hope he comes back soon. I miss him terribly."

"Yeah, me, too," James said softly, as he patted her hand one more time, "Me, too. Thanks for keeping up with the memorization of the second letter. We're going to leave now and let you rest. Make sure Billy calls us

273

when he verifies that he's a perfect match as a donor for you. I really doubt there will be a problem, but the doctor's verification will be nice to hear, too."

## **46 A Simple Wedding

*August 15, 2013, 9:30AM*

"Well, this isn't the first wedding I've performed in a hospital room, but at least the bride and groom are both in good health. Usually the bride's in labor. Now, I don't care if you're pregnant or not, but at least you don't look like you're ready to drop a baby any time soon. It got real close there a couple of months ago…" Jake said.

"No, we don't *have* to get married, we *want* to get married," James said emphatically. "Now, Mom, are you feeling up to this? I mean, we could wait one more day."

"No, no; I'm fine," Bibb said, her grin stretched taut across her swollen face. "I don't want you two to have to wait any longer for the wedding night. I mean, you've known each other for less than two weeks, right?" James and Leah nodded. "Well, since you seem to be comfortable with the fast pace, don't let me slow it down. Now, where's my other son?"

"Right here, Mom," Billy announced as he strutted through the door. "We couldn't have this fine lady getting married without a veil and some flowers, now, could we?" Billy handed Leah a small bouquet of orange and lavender rose buds.

"Orange and purple?" James asked. "I mean, they're lovely, but orange and purple?"

Leah took the bouquet from Billy and gave him a long, hard kiss on the cheek. "Orange means passion and excitement, and lavender," she snuggled into James's shoulder, "means love at first sight. My mother knew—knows—all about roses, the varieties, hardiness and the meanings of the colors. I picked up a few things along the way."

"Here, let me," Billy said. He set the veil on the top of her head and laid the edges evenly down the side of her cheeks. "I know it's old fashioned, and you didn't have time for a proper gown, but my housemother at the orphanage gave me this for my bride when it came time for me to get married." Billy started to look uncomfortable and stammered, "Well, I mean, you need it now. It's the something old and borrowed." *Billy would explain his lifestyle to his mother later. Now was not the time for it.*

"I hate to hurry everyone, but if we're all here, I'd like to get started. My boss cuts me some slack with being a minister and all, but I told him that this was going to be a quickie wedding, and I'd only be an hour late. Good mechanickin' jobs are hard to find, and I don't want to lose this one."

"Two weddings in three days," James whispered softly to Leah. "You look just as beautiful—no, more so—than the first one."

"That's the glow from all the consummating we've been doing," Leah whispered back, then bumped shoulders with him.

James chuckled, then choked it back into a cough. "We're ready," he announced.

"Okay, do you James Ignatius Melbourne, take this woman, Audie Leah Madigan, to be your lawful wedded wife, to have and to hold, cherish and protect, in good times and bad, in sickness and in health, in prosperity and poverty, from this day forward until death do you part?"

"No," James said, and all heads turned to him, everyone's mouth hanging open. He shook his head and clarified, "I don't want till death in the vow, I want forever and ever. Death won't break us apart."

A collective sigh was heard and Jake amended, "From this day until forever and ever—death will not break you two apart."

"I do," James said with a squeak. He cleared his throat and tried again, this time his voice just a little *too* loud. "I mean, I do." He heard the stifled giggles at his erratic volume control, tried to ignore them, then added his own laughter to the chorus.

"And do you, Audie Leah Madigan, take this man, James Ignatius Melbourne, to be your lawful wedded husband, to have and to hold, cherish and support, in good times and bad, in sickness and in health, in prosperity and poverty, from this day until forever and ever—death will not break you two apart." Jake grinned as he said the new vows. He'd have to remember them for the next wedding he performed.

"Amen, I mean, I do, too," Leah fumbled, then finally said loudly and with confidence, "I do!"

"Now, if anyone here sees any reason why these two should not be married, tough stuff! They're married! The husband may now kiss his bride. Congratulations, Mr. and Mrs. Melbourne."

James and Leah shared a sweet, sincere kiss, neither one of them wanting to make a grand, public display of their affection. Everyone who knew them was aware of their feelings for each other.

"My turn," Billy crowed. "Now this is how you kiss the girl," he said, and leaned Leah backwards. He planted a hard, closed-mouth kiss on hers, rubbing his lips side to side in a comedic lampoon of an overdone wedding buss.

"Oh, stop," Bibb laughed heartily. "You're making my lip split."

"Oh, jealous now, are we?" he said. "Well, here's one for you, Mom." He brought Leah back up from her backbend, and put her hand in James's.

"Don't worry, I'll be gentle," he said softly. "But I have to warn you, I have a lot of these to make up." He gave her a sweet, delicate kiss on the mouth and whispered, "Don't ever feel bad about what you did. I have you now, and that's all that matters."

Tears were streaming from his eyes as he brought his head back up from a second, then a third soft kiss. "Weddings always make me cry," he said as an excuse.

"Me, too," said Bibb, the tears now pouring from her eyes.

"Not me," said Jake. "Now, if you'll just give me the paper to sign, I'll make my 'X' and be out of here. Don't forget to take this back to the court and have it filed, or you won't be legally married."

James put a couple of folded up bills in the preacher's hand. "Gee," Jake added, "I'm sure glad people still get married." He waved good-bye to everyone, and went out the door, into the hall. There was a pause, then everyone heard him say loudly, "Very glad!"

Billy looked askance at James and asked without words, 'how much?' James flashed five fingers at him twice indicating that he had given him $500 twice. Billy's eyes opened wide, then he nodded his head in agreement. At least the brother the Lord had given him wasn't cheap and shared his wealth. Jake could well use the $1000 for his little start-up church, and its food and jobs ministry.

"Am I too late?" the dark-haired teenager asked breathlessly as he stuck his head through the doorway. "I ran as fast as I could." But the boy looked around and could tell by the glowing faces that the ceremony was over.

"Can I help you?" asked Billy.

James turned away from gazing at his new bride and recognized the youth. "It's okay, Bret," he said. "It just makes for a more lasting memory." He opened his hand, and the young man placed a dark blue velvet box into it.

"Something blue?" Billy asked when he saw the blue ring box.

"Oh, yeah," James said. "Leah, I'm sorry this got here a little late. May I?" and reached for her left hand.

Leah blushed as she gave it to him. She hadn't even thought about a wedding ring. She was more concerned with the other aspects—the mostly horizontal ones—of being married.

James picked up her hand and kissed it, then slipped on the platinum band with the single flawless blue diamond set into it. "I hope you like it."

"Oh, yeah," she replied, with the same tone he had given Billy. "Very, oh, yeah!"

"Well, since we all have places to go or bodies to heal, I think I'll say good-bye, or in my case, good night. I'll see you all later. Congratulations, you two, and I will definitely see you for dinner, *Mom*," Billy bragged. "Gee, I don't think I'll ever tire of calling you that, *Mom*." He bent over and gave her one more kiss good-bye, then headed home to get some sleep before working the midnight shift.

Leah and James said their good-byes to Bibb, then went back to their home—the motel—and more consummating.

Bibb lay back in her bed, looked up, and said, "Thanks, Lord. This

277

is more than I could have ever hoped for—two sons, a daughter-in-law, and a new liver. Just one more thing, though, please. Watch over Marty and bring him home to me, please. Amen."

ЖѺЖ

"This is a beautiful ring," Leah said, as she lay in bed after another round of honeymoon hopping. "What kind of stone is it?"

"It's a blue diamond. And the band is platinum. I had it custom made. It took a little longer than I thought. Actually, they did pretty good considering they only had two days to design, cast, and then mount the stone. At least the diamond was already cut."

Leah was shocked, and he knew why. She knew at least something about jewelry. "I wanted the platinum so we could claim it was only silver if someone wanted to steal it. And the diamond can pass as blue topaz, or maybe even moonstone or," he exhaled, "colored cut glass. I hope we never run into anyone who would even think about stealing it, but I wanted something for you, and I already had the stone. All I needed was the setting…and the wife," he added with a grin and a quick kiss to the top of her head. "I saw Bret's father's work in one of the shops at the mall. He's quite the artist. I gave him a free hand on the design of the setting. I think it's beautiful and unique, just like you."

Leah turned the stone to the inside of her hand. "See, a poor woman's simple silver band."

"And," James took her hand and turned the stone back the way it was meant to be worn, "a ring fitting for my Leah, the stunning Lady James Melbourne."

278

## **47 Just One More Day
*August 16, 2013, 7:00 AM*

"James, I want you to listen to this and tell me if you recognize the voice."

Billy had called and hadn't said 'hi', 'hello' or 'how's it hangin', but just jumped right into his message.

"Okay, ready," James said, and stuck his finger in his other ear in order to hear the phone message better.

*"Uh, this is an emergency. I think some bad dudes have an old woman held hostage in an old cabin down south and east of town off of the road from the Piedmont Cemetery. Look for an old beige Volvo and be careful. Those dudes are crazy! Oh, and I can't tell you my name, but you can tell the lady that Superman came to her rescue, and that I'm sorry she got hurt and hope she gets better real soon. Um, good-bye."*

James waited for Billy to get back on the line. "Well, that's a no-brainer, at least for me," he said. "I mean, yes, I recognize the voice, but the man also told me who he was. Well, he would have told you, too, if you already knew him, which I do... Hello, are you there, Billy?"

"Well, who is it and do I need to arrest him?" Billy snapped.

"It's Clark, the clerk here at the motel and no! Do not arrest him. Good God, man, he saved her life and turned in his own brothers to do so. His name is Clark Kent—as in Superman—MacLeod. He's the one who got poisoned, and Leah and I followed to the hospital. I'll bet his own brother, either Eight or Niner, gave him that date rape drug so I would be distracted and he could get the letters. I'm sure Clark called as soon as he found out about her, about Mom."

"Well, I don't know about that..." Billy paused, trying not to fume too much over the phone. He wanted someone strung up by the balls for what had been done to their mother.

"Hey, he didn't have to call at all, did he? I mean, if he had kept his mouth shut, she'd probably be dead, and we wouldn't know who he was. Give the man a break. He gave us one, a real big one. How about you let me talk to him—friend to friend—and I'll see if he knows anything. If you haul him in, his brothers will figure out that he was the one who made the anonymous call, and that's why their butts are in custody now."

"Okay, but remember, you're not a cop. I'll be more than happy to come by and just sit with you—as your brother—while you talk to him." Billy halted before speaking again. "Do you know how cool that feels to say, 'as your brother'?"

James chuckled. "Yes, as a matter of fact, I do. Now, be cool. I'll call you if I need help or back up or whatever it is you call it, okay?"

"Okay, I trust you. I'll see you tomorrow then, unless you call."

279

"Wait, wait! I need the truck tonight. I'll just have Leah drive me over to pick it up. I still have a set of keys, so I won't have to bother you at work or when you're just getting up. You can have it back tomorrow," James said, wishing he could tell him 'for good'.

ЖӦЖ

*August 16, 12:00 PM*
*motel lobby*

"So Clark, where are your brothers?" James asked as he gave him the money for their last day's stay. He was prying; he knew it. But he had to know if Clark was involved in the arson, thefts, and beatings that had plagued him and his family since he came to America.

Clark shook his head in shame. "Those *Assholes* are in jail, and I hope that *Nobody* doesn't show up to bail them out again. At least this time, the bail was set so high that their good buddy, *Nobody*, decided to let them rot. I mean, sorry, you don't know them." Clark looked at James quizzically and asked, "How did you know I had brothers?"

"You mentioned something about a brother or brothers when I first checked in here, that he or they got arrested for assault or something or other." James knew full well that Clark had mentioned only one brother, not two, but wanted Clark to tell him more about the problematic pair.

"Oh, yeah. Well, I can call them *Assholes* because they're my brothers, and their first names are Atholl. Actually, it's Atholl the Eighth, or we call him Eight, and Atholl the Ninth, Niner. But I think I told you that." James nodded. He had told him his brother's names when he revealed the history of his own name.

"My father, and then my grandfather raised them and did a pretty shi..., er...crappy job of it. They have some harebrained notion about time traveling fairies out there with treasures, just waiting to be found. It's an old family legend that just won't die. At least, it won't as long as there's an Atholl around to carry the torch or grudge or whatever. It's a bunch of hooey and has caused nothing but grief. I'm glad my mother broke the cycle, at least with me. I doubt that my brothers will reproduce, so the nonsense stops here, or now."

James looked over at him with wide eyes. Clark knew the stories, but didn't believe them.

"Oh," Clark continued his explanation, "it looks like my brothers really screwed up big this time. They beat up some nice old lady and were arrested for attempted murder and a bunch of other crimes that I can't remember. It doesn't make much difference, though. Attempted murder should be enough to keep them in prison for the rest of their lives." He chuckled, "Yup, not much chance of them having any more little *Assholes* while they're in there."

"So you think they'll be convicted?" James asked, hoping to learn

280

more of what Clark knew.

Clark's eyes shifted back and forth in thought. It was obvious to James that the man was making a decision about whether to trust him or not. Clark wiped the skin between his nose and upper lip, then stared James in the eyes. "You're an honorable man, right? I mean, you bein' a lord and all. I can tell you something and you won't repeat it to anyone, exceptin' maybe your girlfriend—I can understand that."

"She's my wife now," James said, "and yes, I'll keep what you tell me in the strictest of confidence."

"Well, Eight let it slip that they had this old lady held hostage at a rundown place just outside of town." He shook his head in disbelief. "I couldn't let it go. I pumped him for details about where she was. I kind of let him think that I wanted to watch them—him and Niner—try to get more information out of her. He was actually bragging about how tough this old woman was, how they smacked her around, burned her with cigars…" Clark sighed. He shook his head again. "It was all because of that same old horseshit, I mean nonsense, about The Letters, the ones that talked about fairies that traveled through time, and their treasure: buckets and buckets of gold and jewels. But he also wanted the deed to the old lady's property. So, as soon as he told me where they were holding her and went on his way—he said he needed more duct tape, and I wouldn't give him any that was here— I called the cops and told them what was going on. Anonymously, of course. I mean, if they need me to testify, I will. All they have to do is ask for the tipster to step forward on the news, and I'll do it. I just don't want the two of them to know it was me. I mean, they *are* my brothers, but, God! If I could change that, I would. Mom would be rolling over in her grave if she knew what they did."

Clark had tears in his eyes, tears of relief. James could tell that he felt better for telling him, for telling *someone*, what had happened. "I'm sure they'll ask for the tipster to come forward if they can't get a conviction without you, him," James said.

Clark wiped his face on the shoulder of his shirt and regained his composure. "Well, has everything been to your satisfaction, sir?" he asked with a grin, the intensity of his revelation now in the past.

"Yes, it has, and I thank you. This will be our last night here. I want to ask you a favor, though. I'll pay you, too," James offered.

Clark pulled his neck back with what he had apparently felt was an insult. "You don't need to pay me for a favor," he said.

"Okay, but I would *appreciate it* if you'd let me pay you for a service."

"Oh, well, that's different" Clark grinned. "What do you need me to do?"

"I'll bring you a letter here in a little bit. I want you to take it to the police station first thing in the morning, say seven-thirty? But you have to deliver it personally to Billy Burke and no one else, okay?"

"I can do that. It's not too far from here, and no one should be checking in or out at that time. Hey, I'm sorry to see you leave. Are you two getting a house or moving somewhere close by?"

James took a deep breath to think of an answer. "We don't know yet, we really don't know. I'll be back later with the letter." He turned and walked out the door into the noonday heat. "Don't know about a house, but nearby. Hopefully," he said, "very hopefully."

Even before he knocked, Leah was pulling open the door. She gave him a quick kiss, then explained, "I got everything packed that I can think of...rather, that's on the list. All we have left is to do a little 'closure' with Billy and your Mom."

"What about your employer?"

Leah glared at him. She had never been able to talk to anyone in personnel about the misunderstanding with the 'property' that Nurse Gata had given her—her mother's dress and smartphone. All they would tell her was that it was 'still under review' and 'we'll call you when we know more.'

"Oops, sorry," James said. "I guess that's one door we can ignore. Here," he said to change the subject. He pulled an envelope out of his pants pocket. "It's just like mine. I put both of them on a piece of cotton cord. You said your mother's was on black ribbon, but I thought that seemed a bit gruesome. Or out of season, you know, black is for autumn or winter, white for spring or summer."

Leah squinted at him. "Are you sure you aren't....nah, you just have a good sense of fashion. I *know* you aren't gay, you just have good taste." James leered at her and she picked up on his visual suggestion. "Yeah, yeah, I know. You taste good, too. Ooh, ooh," she said excitedly. "Speaking of tasting good, I have to make that granola or trail mix or whatever you want to call it. I'll have time to throw it together before we meet Billy and Mom for a last supper. Do you think they'll be okay with accepting us going back? I mean, I really don't want to get together with them tonight then have them try and talk us out of it."

"Well, I doubt that Bibb, Mom, will try. She's expected this for a long time. I mean, at least since she memorized that second letter. And then there's always the fact that she *wants* us to go so we can send my father back to her." James lay back on the bed, not bothering to take off his shoes.

Leah crawled next to him and snuggled into his arms. It was chilly in the room on purpose, and his body warmth felt good on her perpetually cold hands. "I don't think Billy will interfere. He's got his plate full with the liver transplant surgeries day after tomorrow." She chuckled, "Besides, I think he wants to meet your father, too. I know he loves me enough to let me go and you, well, he loves you, too. I guess it's better to have loved and let go than to have never loved at all. Or something like that..."

James looked down and saw that Leah had fallen asleep in mid-sentence. He slipped away from her, took off his shoes, climbed back next to her and pulled the bedspread over the both of them. They were both exhausted, and his last thought before he, too, was out was that a nap would benefit them both.

## **48 The Last Supper

*August 17, 1781, 6:35 AM*
*Just outside of Greensboro*

The dinner date the night before with Billy and Bibb had gone well. Lots of tears and 'I love you's flowed. Peter was still out of town, so discussions and theories on time travel were unbridled. "Yes, I'm sure that you have to have someone or something to focus on in order to go back, at least if you go by way of The Trees. You said your mother *fell* through time, and that your car was found at the Hanging Rock Park? Well, that's one that could use some detective work, eh, son?"

Billy blushed with embarrassment and pride. "We can work on that one together, Mom. I'm going to use up as much comp and vacation time as they'll let me for our surgeries and recovery. And who knows, we might have someone else around to join us in our research," Billy announced, then looked over at James for confirmation.

"Yes, yes," James said. "I promise both of you that if I find him, I'll tell him you want him to come back—at least to you, Mom. I'll have to see how it goes with letting him know he has another son."

"Well, I'm sure you'll find the right words," Bibb soothed as she patted Billy's arm and looked at him, glowing with pride. "And I'm sure Marty will be relieved to know you've found out that he's really your father," and reached over to comfort James.

James saw the awkward struggle she was having trying to touch him—she obviously wanted or needed a hug.

"Here," he got up and knelt next her, reaching around her for a full body embrace. "Billy's been getting more hugs than me, Mommy," he whined in a childlike voice, then looked up for her reaction.

Bibb laughed then started crying at the same time, trying to speak, but overwhelmed with emotion. "Sorry, Mom," he said, "I didn't mean to upset you..."

Bibb grabbed him around the head and pulled him close to her bosom, reaching for Billy with the other arm. "I missed so much with you two," she sobbed. "If I had to do it all over again..."

"Hey, hey, hey," Billy corrected authoritatively, taking over the parent's role with his tone and attitude. "So we started the story in the middle of the book; so what? It still has a happy ending, and we're all here, right? And you're getting a dandy daughter-in-law, to boot!"

"Okay, okay, you're right. Would you excuse me a moment? I need to freshen up." She tried to sniff back her tears, and caught a few of the wayward ones with the back of her hand.

Billy escorted her to the bathroom, then settled back into the oversized and overstuffed chair, a broad smile spreading across his face.

"Ah, life is good," he said, "very good."

"Do you have a roommate?" Bibb asked, as she came out of the bathroom, "or do you just use a lot of toothbrushes?"

"Well, he's more than a roommate..." Billy started to explain, then paused.

The air was suddenly still. James and Leah recalled how Bibb had spoken of Bruce, Marty's first-born. Bruce was a selfish gay man, and she let it be known that she didn't care for him.

"More? Oh, that's wonderful!" Bibb exclaimed with sincerity. "I hope I get to meet him soon. If you picked him, he must be a winner!" Evidently it was Bruce, the person, whom she didn't care for, and his sexual orientation wasn't even a consideration.

More laughs and stories were shared as the hour for the newlywed's bedtime came and went. Leah's yawns were now so wide, her jaws hurt. She saw James nodding, his head suddenly jerking back as he awoke from a momentary slumber. She didn't want to be rude, but noticed how late it was.

"We have to leave," she said, and stood up, suddenly wide awake and alert with the realization D-time—departure time—was less than eight hours away. "We're packed, but we still need to get some sleep, and I want to take a shower and eat breakfast before we leave."

"Oh, shoot," Billy exclaimed as he looked at the clock, "and I have to go to work! Mom, are you sure you want to go back to your place? I mean, you could stay here, in my bed and, and..."

"No, I need to go back home. I have a lot to do in the morning. Well, not heavy *lot to do*," she clarified when she saw her sons look at her, both of them squinting, admonishing her with their eyes not to overdo it. "I just want to sort through some papers and pack a bag for the hospital day after tomorrow—just little stuff. And I'd really like to sleep in my poor little excuse for a bed again. It's just twin-sized, but so much more comfortable than hospital beds. And I know I won't be awakened by some robot fist clenching my arm for blood pressure checks every half hour!"

They all laughed, got up and stretched, preparing to leave. Billy made a call to the station telling them that he'd be late. "I have to take my mother home," he boasted, "then I'll be in." Yup, he had his priorities straight and wanted them to know it.

More hugs, kisses and 'I love you's were shared, then James finally announced boldly, "We *have* to go. We'll be fine, and I'm sure you both will be, too. I have no doubt that the transplant will go smoothly, and you and Mom will live happily ever after." He grimaced as he bit off the urge to add, 'and Dad, too.'

He still wasn't sure of what would happen there. Time would tell— that was for sure.

## **49 Threshhold

*August 17, 2013 daybreak*

Zero hour had arrived and Mr. and Mrs. James Melbourne left the motel, ready to embark on the greatest adventure imaginable. They rode to the site in a contented silence, both of them at peace with their decision to change their lives forever by passing through The Trees. Neither one knew how the magnetic time portal worked—that didn't matter. What was important was that they had found a way to travel back in time 230 years to be with their families.

Leah had insisted that James drive this time. He had been to The Trees before, and although she had the sixth sense thing going on with *knowing* where they were supposed to be, he had actually navigated the roads two weeks earlier and was familiar with the landmarks. Besides, she didn't feel comfortable behind the steering wheel of 'the beast.' The '64 red and white heavy duty long bed Dodge pickup truck was definitely a man's ride.

Ж Ж

"We're here," he said solemnly, as they pulled up to the windswept barren area. There were only remnants of the yellow and black 'do not cross' police tapes dangling from the two trees now. But it didn't make any difference—the trees that were marked were the wrong ones. James counted over six trees to the right to verify the location of the true portal to the past. The ground beneath it was undisturbed. He had erased Evie's slipper prints with a leafy branch two weeks ago, and no one had walked through the area since.

He looked over at the trees bedecked with strips of weather-torn yellow plastic and saw that the ground beneath them was churned and dusty, as if someone had held a ballroom dance there. It was probably the MacLeod boys investigating the *designated* hot spot, trying to unlock the secret of traveling back in time. But, then again, JB was also involved in this. He craned his neck and looked at the beaten down area again. It was quite possible that all three of them had been stomping around in the XX area shown on the old map. But it didn't make any difference: that wasn't ground zero. The map the thieves had purloined got them in the right neighborhood, but they were barking up the wrong trees.

"That's where we go through, right?" Leah asked, pointing to the space between the two old red oaks, the true pillars. "Not there," and nodded to the faux field by the two multi-trunked magnolia trees surrounded by footprints.

"Yup," he said. He leaned over and placed his warm hand over her chilly fist—she had a death grip on her hand-sewn duffle bag. "Are you

286

ready to rock and roll, darlin'?" he asked gently.

"I'd better be," she whined. "I mean," her voice gained confidence as she rewound her answer, fingering the old Greek drachma pendant he had given her the day before, the twin of his. "I *know* I'm ready. Wow! I mean, yeah!" she added with sparkle.

James stifled, sort of, a laugh as he walked around the truck to open a motor vehicle door for her one last time. It wasn't like Leah to be speechless, but she was. "Grab the bags and the water and...oh, shit!" he said, practically spitting out the last word.

"What... Oh, shit!" Leah agreed, as she used the same tone. "We'll just have to take these," she said reluctantly, and held up two one-liter plastic water bottles with pull top lids. "I am *not* walking anywhere this time of year without water. Hey, they'll be in the bags, discreet, and no one will see them. Come on, the sun is almost up."

They each took one long, last drink of water, opened their bags, pawed through them to verify the contents, and then threw in the water bottles. James locked the doors and then buried both the door lock and ignition keys behind the right rear tire. Billy had the other set of keys, but just in case something didn't go right with traveling through The Trees, the keys would be there for their ride back to town.

But they weren't going to fail. He was sure of it. But he wasn't stupid, either.

"Here, one more thing before we leave." Leah took James's hands in hers. "Lord, please bless us and keep us safe on our journey. Let our hearts and minds be open to You and what You want us to do. And please watch over all of our family...um...wherever they may be, and keep them safe and healthy. In Jesus's name, Amen."

"Amen," James said. "Well, that should cover everything." He looked around the site one last time, then bent down to kiss Leah at the same time she looked up for her good-bye kiss. "This will be the last kiss we share in the 21st century," he said. Mouth to mouth, they shared their souls, focusing on the deep love and appreciation they felt for each other, neither one distracted by the environment or task ahead of them.

"Yes," she added dreamily, coming away from the perfect buss, "and it's the last kiss I'll get for about 230 years." She reached over and put her free arm in the crook of his elbow. "Let's go."

They marched resolutely in their 18th century-style garb and 21st century shoes to the space between the two old oak trees, excited yet scared, like a couple approaching the launch pad, ready to rocket to the moon. They were committed to their decision, ready to perform the mission requested of James in the ancient letter. They inhaled deeply—as one body—closed their eyes, and walked side by side slowly, their feet testing each footfall, cautious of the litter of rocks and exposed tree roots that covered the neglected path between the two trees. They proceeded as one spirit, nervous and eager at the same time with the prospect of being 'born' into a new world. They held each other's hands so tightly that their fingers were cold from lack of circulation. Each visualized Leah's mother—the younger version, less the belly—who they had seen in the smartphone video. They traveled as a four-legged entity down the rocky path that was their birth canal into the past, both of them confident that they were passing backwards in time to be with her family.

A steady breeze—maybe real, maybe imagined—guided them, as if they were passing through a long straight tunnel with a fan at one end. James was glad it wasn't painful. He didn't know what to expect, but remembered the description of Sarah Pomeroy going through Stonehenge-type stones in the first Lisa Sinclaire book. This was nothing like that. But then again, these were ancient trees—living entities—and not mineral slabs. Maybe that made the difference.

The air was still now, so they stopped walking. Leah turned toward him, slid into his arms, and held him close. "Did anything happen?" she asked, her face snuggled close to his chest. She pulled back a few inches and looked up at him. "It didn't hurt. My stomach is in turmoil, but that's nothing new." She gave him an extra hug. "I know that in all of the *Lost* books, the characters traveled in time by going through standing stones like Stonehenge. They described it as agonizing, like being ripped apart, disorienting, and intensely painful."

James grinned. They were still thinking the same thoughts at the same time. Psychic, ironic, or merely coincidence, it didn't matter. It was a comfortable feeling to be so in tune with another person. And now she was his wife, his mate, forever and ever.

She smiled back at him and started speaking again, reflectively. "Maybe this was different because we went through a magnetic portal. I didn't feel anything but a steady wind passing over me. But then again," a frown suddenly appeared on her face, "maybe it didn't work and we gave up everything for nothing."

"Well, first of all, we don't know yet if it worked or not. I mean, trees now are pretty much like trees back then. Or maybe trees now are like trees will be where and when we just came from. We'll know for certain when we meet other people. That, I'm sure, will happen eventually…unless we got zapped back to prehistoric times."

Leah inhaled sharply at his flip comment. He saw that he had unintentionally caused her at least a little distress. "Hey, that was a joke. But, regardless, even if it *didn't* work, I still wouldn't feel like I lost everything. Or even anything. I did gain a wife—and a fine woman she is." He put the side of his index finger under her chin, brought it up, and bent down to kiss her in appreciation. "First one of the century," he said. "Now, which direction shall we take?"

Just at that moment, a cry of intense anger split the air, scattering the birds that had been hidden amongst the leaves and branches of the trees.

"That way," pointed James with his forehead. "That sounds like someone needs help." He set his bag down quickly and took out the pistol. "Just in case," he said, and stuffed it behind his back, underneath his belt. "Let's go," he added, and took off running, Leah close behind.

## ***Part Three — Finding Mama

## ***50 Too Much Fighting
*The wilds of North Carolina*
*August 17, 1781*

Captain Asshole tugged at the hem of his jacket, obsessively adjusting the dusty and ripped red coat as if he were preparing to meet the king. He twisted the kinks out of his neck to compose himself further, looked down, and his haughty smirk grew.

It had taken three sleepless days to track him down—and one more to capture and subdue his pint-sized prey—but he finally had him. He strolled around his captive twice, eyes narrowed, giving him his best intimidating glare, his upper lip curled into a silent snarl. He stopped in front of the boy—just outside of striking distance—and squatted on his heels. His prisoner was wide-awake now, naked except for his breechclout and moccasins, securely bound with strips he had made from tearing apart the boy's threadbare shirt.

Cursing and wriggling as he tried to get free, the young half-breed was well-thrashed, but not spent. The captain watched and waited while the bare-chested boy struggled up to his knees, then chuckled and kicked him, shoving him against the ant-covered sweetgum tree.

"Did you like bein' able to give that war yell? Made you feel like a real man, eh? But you're not a man, not for quite a few more years…that is, if you live that long."

*Pah-toie!* The boy spat in the face of the ragged and physically torn-up man who had kidnapped him from his father. "Yer dead meat!" he snarled.

The captain wiped the spittle from his Y-scarred cheek, then poked the boy's bare hip with the toe of his boot—not to hurt him, but to show dominance.

"Well, I never had a boy, but I might just see how it is, you know? Fresh meat, either way, might feel the same." He leaned in, his face just inches away from Wee Ian's. "But whether it feels good to me or not, one thing's for damned sure…" He snorted, ran his tongue over his stained and split upper lip, "I'll make sure it doesn't feel good to you." He pulled back and ended his lecture with a closed-fisted punch, sending the pink calico-bound lad face first into the creek bed.

Wee Ian rolled over and glared at him as he spit out pebbles and grit. "Weel, it'll be the last thing ye do. I'll make sure of that."

The sham British officer reached out, grabbed his captive by the wrist bindings, and dragged him face first out of the creek, through the coarse gravel and scrub. He flipped him over onto his back and laughed as the struggling irate man-child swore and squirmed, trying to free himself from his cloth handcuffs and shackles.

His laughter grew to a roar; this was almost perfect. The more the boy wiggled and writhed, cursed and grunted, the more aroused he became. He untied the laces on his own pants and grabbed his cock, pulling on it in anticipation of a new form of sexual diversion. He leaned forward, wary, but still hoping to get close enough to the boy to rub his dick on the nubile body, to feel his hot, young flesh beneath him. Let the boy yell—no one would hear him. Besides, the screaming and resistance was the most exciting part.

Ж ЖЖ

James and Leah ran as fast as their lungs and new shoes could take them toward the source of the shouting—someone was definitely in trouble.

The air was blue with the curses from either a young man or a woman. Some of the words were English, although strung together with a creative flourish and in a thick Scots accent. "Get your filthy hands offa me, ye mangy fox fornicator."

There was a pause—then a grunt. The livid person started anew. "That'll be the last time ye have enough cock to hold in yer hand. I'll carve it off, piece by piece, stuff the bits up yer nose, and cram yer balls down yer throat 'til ye canna breathe." Foreign words that sounded as if they would be just as colorful if translated followed the tirade. They were certainly said with as much fervor.

Suddenly, there was a loud smack, a crunching sound, and then nothing.

"That'll teach you to mind your manners." The captain had had enough foreplay. He was ready for action.

James and Leah sensed a change in the conflict. The sudden silence, an uncomfortable stillness, was frightening. When they heard the man speak again, it was worse.

"Ooh, such nice smooth skin you have there, boy. It's just as pretty as a lass's. Now, do you want it in the mouth or the ass first? Oh, you can't speak for yourself with your head cracked up like that, can you?" he mocked in a sarcastic tone. "Well, too bad," he added with a sinister laugh, "I wouldn't be giving you a choice, anyway..."

James and Leah repeatedly screamed, "Stop! Stop!" as they ran toward the man standing over the motionless, semi-nude child on the ground. Hopefully, he was only unconscious and not dead.

The man in the tattered British officer's uniform looked up at the shouts. He paused, seeing the two strangers rushing in from nowhere, shook his head in confusion, and yelled, "What the hell? Who are you?"

The pair arrived at the site of the commotion, breathless from their frantic rescue run. They gasped, frozen in momentary shock at the drama

291

they had just interrupted. Leah saw the soldier's redcoat jacket and swore softly, "Oh, shit. We're here and in a handbag."

James heard her, but didn't respond. He, too, could see that this ugly, torn-up man was from the Revolutionary War era. He didn't look like a friendly, either, with his semi-clothed posture over the unconscious boy. His nose was puffy and red, and it looked as if the end of it had been bitten off. He was also missing his left ear, the result of a recent savage wound that hadn't completely healed. It was red and infected, maroon streaks radiating away from where the ear used to be. James's legs were shaking with the knowledge that he and Leah had just journeyed back 230 years in time, and were now interrupting the rape—or near rape—of a young, adolescent male.

James ignored the uniformed man's request to answer who he was. Instead, he said with as much wind and anger as he could muster, "Get away from the boy, NOW!"

"Oh, I don't think so, *muffin*," the captain replied coolly. "You see, I have this sweet little pistol here." He whipped out a silver-toned single-shot pistol from behind his back. He turned it over in front of his face, admiring its luster while still keeping one eye on James. "Oh, and I keep it loaded, you see, just in case an idiot like you shows up and wants to spoil my fun. You wouldn't want me to waste a bullet on you or your lady friend, now, would you?" He leaned sideways, trying to see behind James to get a better look at Leah.

The captain's eyes widened with shock and recognition at seeing her. "Who *are* you?" he asked. "And how'd you get here? I thought you were dead..." He suddenly realized he was showing confusion, so covered his weakness with impudence. "You're a long way from home and all those babies, aren't you? Oh, and it looks like you got yourself a new man, too," nodding to James. "It didn't take you long to get rid of that big sissy."

Captain Asshole took a step back and stroked his empty hand across unconscious Wee Ian's bared fanny, the breechclout yanked aside. "Does this get you excited?" he asked James, ending the question with a perverted leer, his lips widening to a smile that revealed stained and rotten teeth. "There's sweet meat on the other side, too. Nice, sweet..."

James drew and aimed his revolver at the Captain, holding back his smile. *He had just been given the upper hand. The degenerate's pistol had a plug of dirt in the end of the barrel—if he pulled the trigger, it would backfire in his face. He, Leah, and the boy were safe.*

"I will admit that I've never killed a man before," James said coolly, "but I've dispatched many an animal. I think you are about two clicks below animal grade, and so it will be of no consequence to remove you from this earthly plane. Now, get away from the boy or I. Will. Kill. You." James spread out his last words for emphasis, but also to steady his hand, sighted in on the man who was less than 20 feet away.

Captain Asshole snorted in defiance, squatted down, and grabbed the boy's butt cheek.

James flashed rage and squeezed the trigger in immediate, visceral response.

*It struck him before he could bring up his pistol. He felt a sharp, quick burn—like a hot ember on exposed skin—as the bullet struck him just above the clavicle. His gasp brought no breath. His esophagus had been blown apart and he had no airway left. His eyes widened in disbelief at the sight of blood still spurting from his gullet. He wouldn't get out of this mess alive. No strength to run for cover nor wind for excuses. He was dead.*

James watched as the captain's head wobbled on the remains of his neck. Its upright support lost; the heavy skull submitted to the pull of gravity and dropped forward, pulling the lifeless body with it, collapsing atop the boy.

James quickly thrust his pistol through his belt, rushed over, and pushed the corpse off the child.

The impact of the fallen body had awakened the boy with a start. Still face down and mistaking James for his assailant, he began anew with his foul words and furious kicking.

James stumbled wordlessly as he backed away, out of range, as Leah screamed, "Leave him alone. He didn't do it."

Hearing the urgent plea from a female's voice, the boy stopped his thrashing, craned his neck around, and stared at the unknown woman who had suddenly appeared out of nowhere. She was pointing to a bloody corpse on the other side of him. He growled in recognition, then inhaled deeply, hawked up a big wad of phlegm, and spat it at the contorted face of his would-be molester, lying dead in the dirt.

A string of words flew out of his mouth, none intelligible. He paused, then stared up at the man beside him—his rescuer—the questioning look of 'Who are you and why are you here?' evident without words.

James pulled out the blade from his Leatherman multitool and held it flat in his palm to show him what he had. The boy accepted the gesture with a nod, rolled onto his back, and offered his bound ankles. James quickly sliced through the cloth. The boy scrambled upright, turned around, and nobly presented his bound wrists.

"Do you speak English?" James asked, as he cut through the twisted cotton handcuffing. Both he and Leah had heard him speak it, but it was as good a question as any to start a conversation.

Hands now free, the boy straightened out his breechclout and turned around. He looked at James, one eye narrowed in suspicion, then down at the strange pistol. His near-glare softened to a half-grin. This man was different. He could tell that he had nothing to do with those *other* men.

"I speak it well enough." He pulled back his shoulders, puffed out

293

his skinny chest, and stood as tall as his youthful body could reach. "Thank ye fer comin' to my rescue. I owe ye one. Now, I need to go find my da. This," he kicked the contorted corpse in the ribs with his moccasined foot, "pile of shite trapped him and left him with three others to...to... Weel, I dinna ken what they were gonna do, but I'm sure they meant to kill him when they were done. Now, if ye'll excuse me..." He nodded and turned, heading into the unknown to rescue his sire.

"Wait! What's your name?" asked James. "And can we help?"

He stopped and called back. "The white man calls me Wee Ian, and if ye care to follow and can bring that wee cannon of yours, I willna send ye away. They're this way. Jest follow the creek." He pointed upstream, then resumed his swift pace.

"I'm James and this is my wife, Leah," he called after the boy, not knowing if his lame introduction was heard or not.

James bent over, grabbed his bag, said "Let's go," and didn't even ask whether she wanted to be involved in this mysterious mess or not. It was the right thing to do, and if he knew it, she did, too. Sometimes it was good to have a wife who was a mind reader.

Wee Ian was young, strong, and unencumbered, so was soon far ahead of James and Leah, who were still burdened with their packs. After several minutes, James stopped to let Leah catch up. "Here, give me that," he said, reaching for her backpack. "Remember, I'm the one with the broad shoulders. Sorry, I should have taken it before we left. Are you okay?"

"Yes, but wait just half a minute." Leah reached around him and pulled the water bottle out of the side pocket of her pack, took two gulps, and offered it to him.

He took a quick swig. "No more. You'll get a cramp if you drink too much. Come on, let's go."

Leah saluted him with the bottle, letting him know that she'd keep it with her. She gathered her skirts together and bundled as much as she could in the crook of her bent right arm. "Cursed long dresses," she hissed, then took off running.

They ran without stopping or talking, James leading the way, until it became too much for Leah. She slowed to a walk—she was getting an ache in her side and didn't want to make a scene by throwing up or falling down, but still wanted to make forward progress. James turned around and noticed her clutching her side, so stopped and waited for her to catch up.

Then he heard it. Now that he wasn't running, he could hear the sounds of confrontation.

"Put it down, and no one will get hurt." The man's voice sounded as if someone was reciting a line from an old western movie. No, the voice sounded like Billy's...but the *tone* was just like a marshal calling out the bad guys in one of those old TV westerns.

James grabbed her hand and pulled her to the shelter of a large sparkleberry bush. He recognized it from Colleen's book—tall bush, low hanging branches, perfect for a temporary hideout. "Stay here," he said, and dropped both packs at her feet.

He pulled the pistol from his belt and checked the safety, making sure it was still locked. "Stay here. Get your gun, too. Take the safety off and keep an eye out. But don't shoot anyone. That was Marty talking. I'm going over there to see what's going on. Wee Ian's around here, I'm sure. I'm *positive* Marty's not one of the men who took his father. He's probably trying to help, and that's why we're supposed to be here. Are you okay? You look a little pale."

"Yeah, well, so do you. I'm fine. Now, get out there," she whispered hoarsely, "It's show-time!" Leah puckered up, blew him a kiss, and then looked beyond him to the source of the disturbance.

James bent low and did his best to move noiselessly toward the fracas. Wee Ian popped out from behind a bush, put a finger to his lips, and directed James ahead to the next vantage point.

Marty's voice boomed out, "I'm serious now. I don't want to hurt you, but I'll shoot if you don't…" He stopped his threat at the same time as the sound of an involuntary yelp pierced the air.

"Ha, ha, hah…" someone laughed menacingly.

The cruel guffaw was quickly silenced by the crack of a gunshot.

The bushes beside James rustled. He looked over and saw Wee Ian flying through them, totally disregarding stealth or discretion. He followed suit, pausing only long enough to take the safety off his gun.

When he got there, Wee Ian was already astride the man—evidently his father—a skinny, broad-shouldered white man dressed as an Indian. The boy's small hands quickly pulled the hatchet from the fallen man's neck and tossed it into the trees.

The father was a bloody mess. The man-child held his hands over the wound, trying the stop the spurting, but his efforts and the foreign words he was chanting, obviously prayers, weren't slowing the bright red flow.

Pop, pop. The sound of two black powder rifles firing struck the air. James looked toward the sound of the shots and saw two men busily cramming rods down their rifles, reloading to shoot again. He looked back. It didn't appear Wee Ian or the bloodied man in native garb had been hit. They were safe for now.

Wee Ian had said three men. The third man was dead, or nearly so, less than two feet from the boy. James's gut instinct was to call Leah from the brush to help, but he couldn't do that with two muskets loaded and ready to fire on him or anyone else helping.

"Which one do you have, Marty—the one on my right or my left?" he called out loudly, as much to frighten the two skinny musket-loading mobsters as to know which was his target.

"I got the right, you take the left. Glad you could make it here, son," Marty hollered, still in the brush and not visible. "I hope you remembered the medical kit. These two can't shoot faster or straighter than we can. The lad's father doesn't have much time…"

"I'm on it," shouted Leah, as she quickly took the initiative. She put the gun's safety back on, dropped it in her backpack, and grabbed the valise. Her hands were full—a bag in each one—so she employed them like giant baseball mitts, gathering her skirt in front of her so she didn't trip over it as she ran. "Grrr." A growl escaped her lips as she stumbled, despite her efforts.

She knelt beside the two males in breechclouts and moccasins. "Wee Ian, I'm going to see if I can fix your da. Keep doing what you're doing there while I get some cloths."

Leah pulled open her bag and grabbed one of the chamois cloths she had bought for just such a circumstance. Unlike terrycloth, these wouldn't shed into the wound, but were still small, absorbent, and reusable. She carefully slid her hand under Wee Ian's and held pressure on the wound as she made a quick assessment of the damages.

The dead assailant, shot and killed by Marty, had wielded a hatchet on her patient's neck, trying—and gratefully, failing—to separate his head from his shoulders. As she examined him, blotting away blood to find the actual site of impact, she saw that his protruding collarbone had deflected the blade. Her patient didn't have much in the way of body fat. He wasn't quite emaciated, but seemed to be built solely of hard muscle, sinew and bone, and unfortunately now, very little blood.

The bleeding had slowed down, but that might be because he had lost so much of it. The human body only had about five quarts of blood, and he had lost at least two by the looks of the mess covering his shirt and the ground around him.

Marty called out to the soldiers, trying to encourage them to make life easier for everybody. "Now, you boys saw what I can do with this gun here. How about if you two just drop your muskets, and we'll take you back to camp? The officers there told me that they'd give you a fair trial. Now put them down easy…"

Evidently they weren't interested in that offer. Leah could hear them mumbling back and forth, but couldn't understand what they were saying, nor did she try. She was concentrating on her task. She was going to have to sew up the nick in her patient's carotid vein. Fortunately, it hadn't been severed. It was a difficult repair for a surgeon with a microscope and bright overhead lights, but even more so for a recovery room nurse with only rudimentary micro-stitching skills and a pair of secondhand high-magnification glasses.

As she was guiding Wee Ian's hand back over the wound, she recognized a few of the men's words. "And I'll get the boy."

She looked up and screamed, "They're going to shoot us!" just as the renegades turned and readied their guns.

Marty and James hadn't heard the armed men's discussion, but had been following their eye and shoulder movements. They watched as the rogues turned, ready to shoot the unarmed medics in cold blood. Their muskets were halfway to their shoulders when Marty and James fired, both of them killing their targets with single shots to the chests.

Leah panted quickly three times, composed herself, and then was back to her medical dilemma. "James, if you're done there, I need some help."

He was by her side in a flash, his face set in a grim scowl, ready to work. He could reflect on taking another life later. Right now, he needed to help save one.

"Would you get me the flashlight and those goofy goggles? I'll need them for this close-up work. Get that brown bottle and a long swab, too. I'll need you to pour alcohol over my hands so I can get the needle and suture ready."

James set the magnifying apparatus on Leah's head. The headpiece looked strange, but it was what she needed: ultra-magnification goggles with a built in light. She had been able to buy it used from her dentist. She looked like a bug-eyed alien, ready to devour the bloody mess in front of her. She didn't want to scare anyone, but right now, the only one who might be frightened was the boy, and he had eyes only for his father and his wound.

"Wee Ian, put your hand right here and don't move it." He gently slid his hand under hers. She looked at him and saw that he was probably in shock. Well, at least it was a functional shock. He was her extra set of hands right now, even if they weren't sterile.

James gave her what she called her sewing kit. She took what she needed, turned towards him, and let him pour the alcohol over her hands, the hemostat, suture and needle. He opened the bottle of iodine antiseptic solution. "Take the cloth off, lad," he said, then performed a quick, but thorough swabbing of the injury site.

Leah closed her eyes in prayer then started to work. Despite the high-powered magnifying glasses, James saw her struggling to see. He retrieved the mini flashlight and squatted down at her left side, providing a small spotlight on her work area.

"Thanks," she said. "Grab a few pieces of that gauze, too. When the blood starts oozing up after a stitch or two, wipe it away *gently*. You won't be able to see what I see, so don't do anything until I tell you to."

As it turned out, there was so little blood left in the man that leakage wasn't a problem. The wound on the left side of his neck was relatively easy

297

to mend. Now what was needed was more blood in his body. Evidently that's why Marty had sent word through the ages for the IV needles and tubing.

"Are you sure you want to do this?" Leah asked James. "It's going to be awkward, and he's lost a lot of blood, more than I think you should give. But right now, any would be better than none."

"Hey! Remember? I signed up for this. Just tell me where you want me. Oh, and before you get started, I want to tank up on water."

James got a full water bottle out of the backpack. He felt conspicuous drinking out of the clear plastic container, but it was all he had. Two weeks of planning, and the one thing both of them had forgotten was a canteen. It was a good thing they had those water bottles in the truck. It would have been suicide to go out in the heat of a summer's day without water and a way to transport it. One more blessing that was unexplained. That brought it up to about 1,512, James reflected...not as if he was actually counting.

He guzzled it all down and was ready to put the bottle back into the bag when he noticed Wee Ian staring at it. "Here, do you want to look at it?" *Better to have the boy hold and examine it than suspect it was diabolical— or whatever it was the Indians believed.*

Wee Ian took it warily, twisted the cap off and on, then off again, and sniffed the opening. He frowned when he realized there had been nothing but water in it and handed it back.

"Would you do me a favor and refill it. It's the only way I have to carry water. I...um...lost my canteen."

Wee Ian nodded then headed downhill to the creek. James realized that he hadn't heard him say a word since his father had been attacked. If he didn't pull through, the boy might be an orphan. It didn't look like these two were from a tribe. It was more like they were their own tribe. Scots-speaking Indians: now that was a combination.

James looked over and saw Leah had moved aside some rocks and was using a broken tree branch to knock away the smaller pebbles, essentially sweeping a place for him to lie down.

"It would be better if you were higher than him. Gravity is a big help in pushing the blood through the tubes. The heart is a strong pump, but wasn't made to transfer fluids outside of the body and through plastic lines. Maybe we can have you lie on top of the backpacks. Oh, crap. I didn't think about this. What can we use?"

"Well, it may sound morbid, but I can stack the dead bodies, and James can lie on top of them. I can cover the men with a blanket so it won't be so messy. Hi, you must be Leah. I'm Martin Melbourne, but you can call me Marty."

"Oh," Leah shook her head, trying to separate the thought of using a stack of slain murderers to support her husband, the blood donor—and how should she greet the man who had arranged for him to help with this in the first place? She repeated, "Oh," then took a deep breath. "Or I could call you Dad. I'm your daughter-in-law now."

"You are? I sure didn't see that one coming!" Marty exclaimed. Literally taken aback, he shuffled two awkward steps in recovery, as if he had been knocked backward by a soft blow.

A split-second after regaining his composure, Marty was back into problem solving advisor mode. "Well, you two are the ones to say yeah or nay on the corpse cart. Which is it?"

"I'll help you drag them over. Glad to see you, sir." James said, and slapped his father on the back, forgoing any other conversation until later.

*What would, or should, he say to his newly discovered father? It was strange, but now that he knew Marty wasn't his grandfather, somehow the man looked different. It appears we'll have a long time to catch up. God willing. That's about number 1,513, isn't it, Lord?*

The men grabbed their kill and dragged them by the heels to the fresh swept area next to Wee Ian's father.

Leah decided she should distract herself and the boy from the Melbourne men's gruesome ministrations of shoving and tugging the corpses into position. She turned away from their construction zone, walked several feet away, and squatted down, motioning for the youth to join her at creekside. "So what's your father's name," she asked.

"Ian, Ian Kincaid," he said succinctly. "But he's also called Star Walker."

"Oh," she replied, then subconsciously held her breath. *She blinked rapidly in shock—she recognized that name. He was from the later Lost historical novels. Mom never mentioned anything about him!*

She finally remembered to breathe, glad that she was already near the ground and not standing. She was light-headed and afraid that she was going to fall over backwards. Wee Ian saw her start to swoon and rushed to her side, grasping her shoulders to keep her upright.

"Do ye need to put yer heid between yer knees?"

Leah shook her head, rocked back off of her heels, and as gracefully as she could—which wasn't much—plopped down onto her fanny. She didn't care if the dress got dirty. The fine dust would probably just brush off anyway. She leaned forward and brought her knees up to her face. "Can I have a drink of that water, please?"

Wee Ian gave her the bottle and wordlessly waited by her side to make sure she was all right. *He seems to be protecting me—quite a gentleman for being such a young person.*

James and Marty finished their body building, and then draped a horse blanket over the pile of three. They had put the two skinny ones on the ground and laid Ian's attacker, a heavyset man, on top of them.

Leah hadn't watched on purpose. It was morbid but necessary. She had to move quickly and didn't have the luxury of time for the men to build her a table, or even to scout out a sizable fallen log. Ian Kincaid needed blood, and he needed it now.

"Use what you have and be grateful," she admonished herself softly. "At least you have help." She turned to face her support crew. "I'm ready. Are you?" she asked with as much courage as she could garner.

James started settling himself onto the lumpy body of Ian's attacker. *Thank you, Lord, for the blanket. Number 1,514.* "Marty, could you come over here and make sure I don't start slipping. This is very uncomfortable and a little shaky, too."

Marty came to one side and Wee Ian, without being asked, came to the other. Leah swabbed the site on James's arm with alcohol and inserted the trocar, using a short length of surgical tape to secure it to the site. "Don't move," she said. "It's just a plug right now. I have to get him stuck, too."

Leah slapped and moved Ian's arm around, trying to get a vein to pop up.

"Can you put it in his leg?" asked Marty.

"Yes, but I'd rather not," Leah replied, frowning with concern. She exhaled sharply, squeezed her eyes shut in exasperation, and said a quick prayer.

Wee Ian had been watching and decided to take matters into his own hands. He moved over to the arm that Leah had been rather gently—or so it seemed to him—slapping to get the vein to pop up. He did a rapid fire rat-a-tat-tat drum roll with the flats of his hands, making the area scarlet red and bringing up a vein. "Like that?" he asked.

Leah grabbed the trocar and quickly inserted it on the first try. "Like that," she said. "Thanks. Now I just have to connect these guys, so your father will get a fill up—or at least a partial refill—of the blood he lost. Do you want to watch?" she asked, knowing full well the boy would not leave his father's side.

"Aye, I'll stay. Yer a good woman, and I wager a good healer, too, but I'm still his son. I'll stay to help take care of him. He hasna been doin' a verra good job of it himself, jest the noo."

The blood transfusion was slow, but without complications. As Leah removed the needles and tubes, she heard James say, "Thanks. Number 1,515."

"What's that?" she asked.

"Oh, you said something about God, and how He works in mysterious ways, and how many blessings we have, but that we never take the time to count them or thank the Lord... So, well, a few days ago, I started counting. You don't realize until you *do* pay attention, just how full life is of little miracles…every day."

"And big ones, too. I think Ian here is going to make it," she said.

ЖЖЖ

Leah continued to clean up and put away the tools of her field trauma center. After a couple of minutes, she whispered, "James, you never read beyond the first *Lost* book, or *Through the Stones* as your UK version was called, did you?"

"No, I was meaning to, but with all the other excitement, studies, and tasks we had to do in the last two weeks… No, I didn't read beyond the first one. Why?"

"Ian Kincaid here is Jody Pomeroy's nephew, his favorite nephew, if you will. Mom said in her letter that her new last name is Pomeroy-Hart. I would suspect there's a connection there. Do you mind if I ask him if he knows where the Pomeroys are when he wakes up?"

"You could do that, or you could just ask me," Marty said. "Sorry, I didn't mean to eavesdrop, but I was coming over to talk to you two about quite a few things, and that just happens to be one of them."

"Can we wait a while for any discussions?" asked James. "I feel a little sapped," and smiled at his own pun.

Marty nodded, then helped James off the platform of bodies and shoulder-bolstered him to a shady spot under the nearest tree.

It was hot, and the corpses under the blanket were starting to get ripe. Like all dead men, these three had lost their bowels at death and weren't very clean to begin with. Yes, the odor was horrific, and the bodies needed to be moved away quickly. Hopefully Marty was feeling strong. James was weak and didn't have enough strength to help.

Leah could help if needed, but right now she was feeling a little drained, too. Whether it was from the intense emotional stress of the procedures she had just performed, or from the excitement of the time travel, or from seeing firsthand four men being shot, one hacked, and a boy nearly raped… Well, she was exhausted.

Yes, she'd pass on helping with the clean-up detail. She'd stay put and help James hold up the other side of the tree. She smiled. After all, they didn't want it to fall over now, did they? She sat next to the trunk, arranged her skirts about her, and then leaned back. She reached over for her husband's hand, picked it up, and laid it on her soft, green calico skirt. Even though she wasn't holding his hand, she felt linked to him on a higher plain, their bodies and spirits joined with their pinkie-to-pinkie connection. Leah was completely at peace with herself and the world for the first time in nearly a year. Her disappearing, time traveling mother was just around the corner, figuratively speaking.

She hadn't planned on falling asleep—and didn't realize that she had—until she felt a tapping on her shoulder. She jerked away by reflex and opened her eyes to see Wee Ian's face a foot in front of hers.

"I think he needs ye," he stated without emotion, then waited for her response, eyes blank, forehead furrowed. She saw the sun was now high in the sky. She must have slept for two hours. She scrambled to her feet and was at Ian's side in the three long steps it took to get to him.

Ian was thrashing side to side, elbows flying, trying to sit up, and quite possibly undoing all of her stitches. She looked around to see who could help her restrain her hysterical patient. Marty was nowhere to be seen. She looked back and saw that James was still asleep. Awake or asleep, he couldn't help her either. She hoped she hadn't bled him too much. If she had, there was nothing she could do about it now. Nothing but pray, she scolded herself. "Lord, please heal these men and help us all in everything. In Jesus's name, amen," she prayed softly, swiftly, and sincerely.

Her tone and attitude changed quickly as she addressed her restless patient. "Hey! You! Knock it off! Lie still or you'll tear out my stitches, and then I'll be pissed!"

Her scolding him like an irate gunny sergeant seemed to work. He didn't move a muscle. Well, not exactly. He frowned as much as he could without aggravating his neck.

Leah continued in her stern voice, "Now, I'm going to give you some painkillers. You'll feel better, but that doesn't mean you can do anything. Do you promise not to move?"

"No," he replied, and remained stone-faced, his glare almost dense enough to mark a path to the sun that was now directly overhead.

"Well, then, I'm not going to ease your pain." She paused, and then snorted testily. "Why do you feel like you have to move?"

Ian remained mute, but didn't try to move.

Wee Ian came to Leah's side and held her hand. She looked down at him, and he just shook his head. Neither of them spoke and neither felt the need to. They stood there in silence, watching the grim-faced patient, until they heard a noise. Leah tensed, but Wee Ian squeezed her hand in reassurance.

It was Marty coming over the rise. His dusty tri-corner hat was black around the middle from sweat. He took it off, wiped his brow with the back of his forearm, and set it back on his head. "Well, that's done. I didn't have a shovel, so I just threw them in a heap and piled rocks on top. That should keep the stink down for a bit. The wild animals will be out to feed on them soon enough, but for now, they're downwind and out of sight. How's your patient doing, Leah?"

"Oh, he's trying for the most stubborn male of the year award. I offered him painkillers if he'd promise not to move, but he said no. It must be a macho thing about being told what to do by a woman."

"What's macho?" asked Wee Ian

"Well, that's when a man thinks he has to be tough—even when he doesn't have to be—only because he doesn't want other men to think that he's weak. It's okay to be careful when you're wounded. I mean really, if he doesn't take care of himself, or let you or me take care of him for the next few days... Well, then Marty will just have to throw his carcass on top of those other three," Leah said sarcastically.

"What other three?" Ian asked, his voice soft, but only because that was the only volume level available in his weakened condition. He couldn't have hollered angrily if he had wanted to.

"Well, there's the one who tried to take off your head with a hatchet, and then the other two who were going to shoot me because I was tending to you. Marty tossed their bodies down that way. Oh, and that asshole who kidnapped and hurt Wee Ian, well, his rotting corpse is a few miles up the road. There are only us good guys left. So, since you and everyone else here is safe, would you lie still and let me give you a painkiller?"

"Aye, I'll let ye," he whispered hoarsely, "but I'd rather have a bucket of whisky. Is there anythin' to drink?"

Wee Ian was at his side in a flash. "Here, mind yer heid, jest let me pour some in yer mouth." The son was careful, dribbling in just enough to fill his father's mouth without choking him.

Leah saw the effort it was taking and decided she needed to modify the accommodations for her prone patient. She opened her medical bag and cut off a one-foot length of the flexible tubing. "Here, let's try this," she said, and held out her hand for the bottle. She put the soft, clear plastic 'straw' into it and handed it back to Wee Ian. He frowned at the new arrangement then looked up at her.

"It's like a reed. He can suck through it. This way he can control how much he gets. But wait." She took two Percocets out of her pocket. "Open up, Ian. I want you to swallow these. Your son has the water."

Wee Ian did as he was told and held the water bottle for his father. Ian swallowed hard and almost choked, but managed to suppress his gag reflex and kept the pills down.

"I still say whisky woulda been better," he mumbled hoarsely. He squeezed his eyes shut in discomfort, settled his shoulders back into the ground, and seemed to accept his lot as an incapacitated patient.

Leah could only hope that he was really trying to rest. He was such an angry man. It appeared that it had been a long time since he had truly relaxed.

Ж ЖЖ

Wee Ian showed himself to be a clever and resourceful young man. James watched from his shady earthen bed under the tree as the bare-chested boy toiled. He had gathered leafy tree branches while he and Leah had

303

napped and was now back to his project.

No one had told him what to do, but the lad had taken it upon himself to build his father a shelter from the sun. He had gathered as many bush and tree branches as he could, then realized they needed a supporting framework. He went to the edge of the clearing and retrieved the hatchet he had thrown away in disgust after pulling it from his father's neck. He set it on the ground and rubbed dirt onto the blade, scouring the blood from it. After it was clean enough to pass his inspection, he walked toward the creek with it, head down, looking at the ground. He stopped, picked up, and then discarded several stones until he found just the right one: a fine-grained rock to use as a hone. He spit on the stone, then drew the edge of the hatchet across it in a wide semi-circle, stopping every few strokes to check the sharpness by touching it to his thumb.

When he was finally satisfied with the result, he went to the creek's edge to study the drooping tree branches overhanging the flowing water. He cut down four bowed limbs best suited for use as arches, then came back to his father, dragging the timber behind him like a proud, miniature draft horse. He assessed the site, moved a few rocks out of the way, and then began digging post holes with another piece of wood he had chosen for his shovel.

Leah watched the young man's ministrations from the shade of the healing tree. Wee Ian was determined, not angry or frustrated by his lack of tools or by the magnitude of the project. He was simply getting it done. Leah felt a hand on hers. James was awake and had also been watching the small Hercules create a temple for his wounded father.

"I'd help him if I had the strength—or thought he needed it," he said softly. "I could only hope to have a son as resourceful and devoted as he is." He patted her hand a couple more times, the taps echoing the little prayers he was sending up that he *would* be a father one day.

Marty had disappeared again, or at least was out of Leah's line of sight. She wasn't concerned. After all, he would show up when he was ready. That seemed to be his style. "Are you hungry or thirsty?" Leah asked James.

"Yes and yes. Did you bring any watermelon?" he asked, grinning.

"Yes, as a matter of fact, I did. But it'll be three months before they're ready," she said, referring to the fact that what she had were watermelon *seeds*. "Would you settle for some granola and water?"

"Actually, I'd like some of that jerky. For some reason, I have a craving for red meat. Hmm, must be I'm a little anemic..." he drolled.

"D'ya think!?" Leah replied with a laugh. She started digging into the bag, handing him the other water bottle as she searched for the beef jerky. "Wee Ian, are you hungry?"

"Aye, I could do with a bite. After I finish this, I'll catch some fish fer our dinner. I'll have to wait until the sun sets a bit, though. The fish ken not to come out when it's so hot."

"Only mad dogs and Englishmen go out in the noonday sun," James said, quoting Rudyard Kipling. "But this Englishman will pass until the sun goes down a bit. It's been a while since I went fishing. I'd like to go with you this evening, if it's all right with you."

Wee Ian shrugged his shoulders, then went back to work, trying to get his arched beams set into their foundation holes.

Leah saw that no matter how clever the boy was, he needed assistance. "May I help you? You helped me, and I'd like to return the favor."

It took her half a minute to manage her skirts so she could stand up—she'd figure out how to be graceful *and* decent later—and then went to his side. "Four hands are better than two, or something like that," she said, as an excuse to both help him and to see if her patient really was getting rest.

The arches were great, and had just the right angle, but the wisps of river grass he had been trying to use to secure the frame walls at the apex were not working. No one had any rope as far as she could see, and the only leather thongs were holding up the Ians' loincloths. As if Wee Ian were reading her mind, he looked down at his waist in a quandary.

"Wait," she said, as he started to negotiate the knot. "I think I know what we can use."

Now it was James who could see what was going on. "Do you really want to do that?" he asked softly. Leah nodded and looked in her bag.

"Here," James said, handing her the duct tape. "It was in mine. Use it well and save some for later. I might get warts."

She smiled at his joke about duct tape for wart removal. "I just need a little bit of it. Drink more water and have another piece of jerky. I think I took too much blood out of you. I am *so* sorry."

James shrugged his shoulders, grinned, and fished out the high-iron-content snack. His first mini-meal of jerky and water had helped, but he still felt he was only at 20% operating efficiency.

"I hope you don't need a building permit for that," he said, nodding at the new shelter. "It'd never pass inspection."

"Right," she drawled, and walked away, the roll of duct tape around her wrist like a fat, gray bracelet.

Wee Ian was still trying to use the lengths of grass to hold the north and south walls together at the top. "Just hold them there for a minute," Leah said, "I've got some stuff here that will work."

She shook the roll off of her wrist and used her teeth to pull the end loose. ZAAAPPP. The noise of duct tape being pulled off the roll was loud and coarse, and made Ian the elder jump. But it was an involuntary reflex. He was in a deep sleep.

"Oh, shit," Leah said softly. Hopefully he wasn't in a coma. If he was, she couldn't do anything about it except let him come out of it naturally. After she and Wee Ian got the shelter framed, she would offer him more water.

Wee Ian held the arch segments together while she wrapped the tape around the ends. One more ZAAAPPP—another length of tape torn off—and then another section of framework was secured. Now it was time to set the top beam and tie the two together.

"Do you think we need more of the tape?" she asked Wee Ian. It was his project, after all. She was just a consulting structural engineer and tape puller-offer.

"Aye, I think we'd best use more of that zap. Da will jest have to bide with the noise of it comin' off the band."

Leah tore off two more pieces—this time, one right after the other—and put them on her sleeve for easy access. She returned the roll to her wrist, and with the help of Marty—who had just appeared—the shelter frame was completed.

Wee Ian looked at the two of them in turn, said a quick, "Thanks," and returned to the next step in the project: breathing walls. He wove the brush into the twigs of the tree branches that had now become the studs and roof, creating a porous ceiling and walls. The shade factor of his creation was high, but still allowed for a cooling breeze to pass through.

"Nice work," Leah said. Wee Ian backed away to inspect his construction, looking for faults by the frown on his face. Leah interrupted his evaluation. "Can I sneak in here and offer him more water? We need to get as much as we can into him."

Wee Ian turned away and came back with the bottle of water and the plastic tubing straw. He crawled into the little hut and held the straw to his father's mouth. Leah could see that Ian wasn't drinking, or at least not sucking.

"Here, let me show you something," she said. Wee Ian scooted back out and handed her the bottle. "Look." While it was still in the water, she put one finger over the tubing, then pulled it out. She tilted her head back, opened her mouth with the straw held above it, then let her finger off the end. The water dropped all at once into her mouth. She swallowed, brought her head back up, and smiled.

"Now, don't force the water into his mouth, just dribble a few drops into it with it held high like I did. Keep your finger on the end, and just let him have a few drops at a time. He'll probably wrap his lips around it and eventually get the sucking reflex going again. If not, we'll have to do the wet washcloth trick. I'd rather use the straw, though, because we can get more fluids in him that way. When you're done, come get that snack. You've been working hard."

James was tired but awake while they worked, content to stare out at the creek, at peace with himself, and looking forward to fishing for dinner with the young man.

Leah went back to the shade of the tree and pulled the backpacks to her. She hadn't realized how hungry she was until now. She chuckled to herself as she realized that she hadn't eaten in over 230 years. A little bit of the granola would tide her over until the men caught fish for dinner.

The men—all of a sudden, she had four men in her life: three good, hard-working men and one ornery patient. Well, at least the numbers weren't reversed, and it wasn't three ornery patients and one good, hard-worker. Small blessing number 1,516.

Wee Ian came over to join them in the shade, bringing the water bottle and straw with him. "I got him to drink a bit. I think he's in the deep sleep. I dinna ken what ye call it, but he may be that way fer a few days. His body is healin' itself. I'll mind him if ye have other places to go. I sure appreciate the sewin' and gettin' more blood into him. I never saw that done." Wee Ian turned to James, obviously confused. "Does that mean he has some of yer spirit in him?"

"Well, first of all, it's called a coma. Hopefully, he's just in a deep, repairing sleep and not a deep coma. But either way, you're right—I'm sure his body is healing itself. And as far as the spirit goes, I don't know. I've been told that blood is just blood—red water that carries fuel like—well, like wood for a fire. It helps the body burn brighter, but sometimes I wonder…"

Leah cleared her throat hard—twice—to get James to stop talking. *He must be loopy from the blood loss. The boy's bewildered as it is, and he's confusing him even more.* "Would you *like* some of his spirit to be in your father?" she asked.

Wee Ian leaned over and looked at James cynically. Then he looked at Leah. "He's yer husband?" he asked.

"Yes, and a very good man. He's smart and kind and, well, practically perfect. No, I think he's a perfect man, and I'm glad he's my husband," she said, chest out with pride.

"Weel then, if it's all right with ye two, I'll hope that a bit of Mr. James's spirit got into my da. He ran out of perfect parts and pieces a long time ago. He can use all the help we can find him… What's that?" the boy said suddenly, staring at the large plastic baggie of granola he had just noticed.

"It's a mix of good foods to help you stay strong, or in your case, grow strong. Here, put out your hands, and I'll give you some."

Wee Ian reached out and accepted a fistful of the fruit/oat/chocolate-chip/nut mixture. He crossed his legs 'Indian' style, and placed the bounty on his breechclout flap. "What are these?" he asked, holding up a tan bit.

"Well, that's a cashew, a nut. There are other foods in there that I'll bet you've never seen, either. But they're all good for you. There's pineapple and coconut, oat bits, pretzels, and chocolate chips. Well, chocolate is a little bit good for you, but it tastes *real* good."

"What's this one? It looks like a wee black turd."

Leah nearly choked on her mouthful of granola. "That's the chocolate that I told you tasted so good. Go ahead and try it. If you don't like it, put the rest of them aside, and I'll eat them. They're great."

Wee Ian picked up a piece and inspected it, turned it around, sniffed it, and still wasn't sure he wanted to eat it.

"It'll melt in your hand if you hold onto it too long. Just eat it—trust me."

Wee Ian huffed in uncertainty, then put it in his mouth—he trusted her. His eyes widened and a grin of satisfaction grew to a full smile as he quickly licked the melted remains off his fingers.

"I told you so. I wouldn't lie to you," Leah said and chuckled. She didn't have a radio or television, but she was definitely being entertained.

"You wouldn't lie to me?" Wee Ian asked, suddenly somber.

"Of course not. Why, what do you want to know? Oh, your father. I'm sure he's going to be all right. If we hadn't done all the sewing and the blood transfusion, he might have died, but now he has a great chance of recovery." Leah's voice and attitude changed into head nurse mode as she stressed her most important warning, "As long as he stays still long enough for the wounds to heal."

"That's not what I meant. I figured ye were a good healer, and I'm sure ye did the best ye could. That's what healers do. But," the boy paused, looked down at the partially eaten food in his lap, then decided to ask, "Are ye my kin?"

Leah was both shocked and guarded. She had briefly thought about the Pomeroy-Hart relationship when she talked to Marty before her nap, but there didn't seem to be any way she could be related to Ian Kinkaid. "Why do you ask?"

"Not why do I ask. Are ye my kin?" he repeated, his hard stare letting her know he wanted—no, needed—her answer.

"Shoot, I don't know. I don't know your mother, and I don't think there is any way your father and I are related. So, as far as I can tell, no, we're not related. *Now* will you tell me why you think I'm your kin?"

"Yer dress and yer face. Ye look jest like Evie and yer wearin' her dress. She's my kin because her... Weel, she said to jest tell people we're kin."

"Oh, shit," Leah mumbled.

"Yeah, oh, shit," James echoed.

"Ye ken, I can hear pretty good. Why do ye say *oh, shit?*"

"Well, yes, Evie and I are kin—very, very close kin. But how are you kin to her?" Leah asked, both confused and very curious.

"Weel, since ye are her kin—and I ken ye are, jest by lookin' at yer face and seein' how kind and helpful ye are—I guess I can tell ye. Her babies are my siblings—that's the right word, I think. My da was the sperm donor."

"James..." Leah's voice squeaked.

"Come here," he said, reaching out for her, but without the strength to get up for her. "Let me hold you."

"He's my stepfather," Leah whispered, as she leaned into him. "Ian Kincaid is my stepfather?"

"No, he's not. And Wee Ian can hear you. Can't you, lad?"

"Aye, I can. Are ye a fairy, too?" he asked. "Both of ye?"

Marty walked into the scene, saving James and Leah from having to answer immediately. He looked down at Leah, glanced at James, and then winked. "What's going on here? Is everybody taking an afternoon nap? Scoot over and let me have some of that shade. What's that in your lap there, lad? Looks like you have some of what I call trail mix. What ya got in there, Leah?"

"It's granola with cashews and chocolate chips. But I guess I shouldn't have used the chocolate. It melts in your hands before you can get it into your mouth. Do you want some?" Leah's heart was beating rapid fire. The appearance of Marty and his chit-chat were only delaying the need to answer Wee Ian's question.

"Sure, how about if you just put a tad into this handkerchief." He reached into his front pocket, took out the red bandana, shook it out, and held it open to receive a little afternoon snack.

Marty sat between Wee Ian and his son and daughter-in-law, munching on his morsels, making inane comments to fill the air with words, but not information or knowledge. It got to be a waiting game after about ten minutes. Marty wouldn't move and Wee Ian didn't know if he could speak in front of the older man. It was becoming uncomfortable. James reached over and held Leah's hand, squeezing it in a request for a little visual tête-à-tête.

The glances back and forth between them confirmed that they were in accordance—Wee Ian could be told they were 'fairies.' James looked over at his father and gave him a quick eyebrow lift that said they wanted some alone time with the young man.

"Well, I guess I'll go down to the creek where it's cooler and do something creative," Marty said. "Or maybe I'll see if there're any huckleberries upstream. At least, the color of the bushes looks to be about right. Does anyone need anything before I leave? Any...ahem...well, anything?" He had almost said, 'Any dead bodies removed,' but thought better of it considering the precarious health of Ian Kincaid.

Leah heard—or sensed—the words that Marty had cut short. He seemed to be an impetuous and garrulous man, but did think at least *two* words ahead before he spoke.

"We're fine," she said, answering his request about needs. "Just don't get lost. It was a lot of trouble finding you this time. I wouldn't want to have to go through that again."

"I'll mind," he said, "and thanks for coming. We'll all sit around and catch up this evening when it's cooler. So long, for now." Marty grabbed the reins of his gray mare and walked down to the creek bed, following it upstream to the hoped for stand of wild berries.

James quietly watched his father leave. He wanted Leah close, but it was too hot to snuggle. Instead, he moved his hand next to hers, barely touching it. She tapped him back with her pinkie, letting him know that she could feel him. That small bit of tactile contact they shared was enough, though. There was no rational explanation for it, but he could practically feel her energy trickle charging into him. And right now, he needed her strength.

"Now, as to your question," Leah returned her attention to Wee Ian, "would it make a difference if we were fairies?"

Wee Ian cocked his head and thought about it for a full minute or more, and then explained. "My da said that Evie was a fairy. He said that's why he couldna stay with her. He was glad his cousin—his name's Wallace—could be there for her, though. They're probably marrit now. She's a nice lady, but still a fairy. Da said he was afraid she'd leave him and go back to her own time and her own people. He said he kent other fairies before, and they always left. Except one, and he wouldna tell me who she was. But he did say that even though she left once, she came back again, but it was a long time later. I think I ken who it is, but I dinna want to ask him. It makes him sad to talk about it."

Neither Leah nor James spoke. They could tell there was more to his story, and he was still working up to it. Finally, he asked, "It's all right to be a fairy. It's not like ye can change bein' one or anythin'…can ye?"

*Oops! Now it was time for an explanation.* "Would it be all right with you if I was a fairy…and my husband, too?"

"Aye, it's all right with me. So, I guess that means ye are, right—the both of ye?"

James felt compelled to speak for the both of them. "I never thought I'd hear myself say this, but aye, I am a fairy, and my wife, too."

Leah giggled then tried to regain her composure. James continued, "And since you believe in fairies, do you think they're bad or evil?"

"No, why would I think that?"

"Just making sure," James said, "Just making sure."

Wee Ian started picking at his granola again. "What's this one?" he asked, and held up a twisted yellow triangle.

"That's dried pineapple," Leah said, letting James regain his strength by staying mum. "It's real juicy and messy when it's fresh, so they dry it out like you do jerky or apples. I don't think you can grow it around here, though."

As soon as the words were out of her mouth, she regretted them. If it didn't grow around here, then where did she get it? Ergh! Watch what you say, woman!

But Wee Ian hadn't paid any attention to her remark. His mind was elsewhere. "Does that mean my da is part fairy now?" he asked, then took a small nibble of the pineapple ort, trying to make it last.

"Uh," James and Leah chorused softly and awkwardly at the same time, then looked at each other.

"I don't think that changes with blood," James said without much conviction.

Leah looked over at him and was glad that he hadn't expounded on the subject. This one was definitely a good topic to be left as a mystery. But either way, Wee Ian didn't seem too concerned. He was having a good time playing with his food, content that, at least for now, his father wouldn't be getting into any more trouble.

### ***51 A Second Injury

*August 17, 1781*
*Later that afternoon*

"I think he has another wound," Wee Ian said. "But I think that maybe James should help me with this one," and looked from her to the man dozing under the tree.

"What? He's not a doctor. I'm the nurse, rather healer." Leah saw the look of both embarrassment and worry on the boy's face. "Oh, my God, did they...?"

"They must have done it jest after they sold me to that Captain. He wasna missing any parts when I was with him." He huffed, then kicked a stone into the brush away from their little campsite, frustrated. "Bring yer bag if it willna bother ye to look," he said, and led the way.

Leah grabbed her backpack then paused. "James, come with me, please. I..I'm not sure I need your help in a medical sense," she stammered, "but I think I do for moral support."

She wrapped her hand around James's inner wrist, then pulled back hard to help him stand. Earlier, he had hastily whittled off side shoots from a stout stick for use as a walking cane, but she insisted he steady himself with a hand on her shoulder, too. It was only a few feet to Ian's custom-built hospital ward, but he appreciated her help.

Wee Ian waited for them, his dark eyebrows furrowed with concern. His father was modestly covered, but the bloody breechclout was untied, just lying across his loins.

Leah growled in self-loathing. Because of the urgency to repair Ian's neck wound, she had never even thought to check if he was injured anywhere else. She bit her bottom lip then squatted next to him. "Lord, give me strength and wisdom and everything else I need for this."

The words were soft, but heard by both of her assistants. "Amen," James said.

"What he said," Wee Ian added.

Leah reached for the water bottle. Wee Ian had been watching her closely, and anticipating her need, placed it in her hand. "Thanks." She poured the now lukewarm water onto the terrycloth washcloth. She pulled back the breechclout and saw that his thighs, pubic hair, and scrotum were matted with brown, clotted blood. She placed the cloth over the entire area and dribbled more water over it. She needed to soak off the dried blood and wipe the area clean to see what the damage was. She dabbed the area to make sure the wet cloth was in contact with the skin, sighed deeply in frustration, then looked up to see two pair of worried eyes staring at her.

James and Wee Ian were there for her emotionally, and would do anything asked of them, but there was nothing to do but wait and be ready when she needed help.

The only positive side of this scenario was that Ian the elder was unaware of what she was doing. What had been done to him was brutal and horrendous. But having a strange woman wipe and prod around his privates while he was awake and aware would have added humiliation and shame to the atrocity. Sometimes a coma could be a blessing.

Leah used the edge of the cloth to start the cleansing. Ian flinched when she first tugged the skin to wash it, but he never woke.

"James, hand me the goggles again, please, And Wee Ian, the water bottle…"

She irrigated the wound by exerting slight pressure on the sides of the squirt top bottle. It wasn't sterile water, but it would have to do for investigating the wound. Without asking, Wee Ian and James each grabbed one of her patient's knees and spread them out, affording her a better view of the injury.

Leah put the magnifying goggles on her face and leaned in close to see the cuts. She sighed in frustration: she was in her own shadow. She stood up and moved to let the sun flood the area to be examined. When she was able to focus, she saw that the hackers had stopped short of any permanent damage. Apparently, the bloodletting had been enough for them. Or someone or something had made them change their plan. Ugh! Or they were in a hurry to kill him. Leah shuddered at the horrible thoughts that were streaming into her head. "Stop that," she said under her breath. She wanted those images to cease and commanding them verbally to do so was the only way she could think of to do it.

"Stop what?" James whispered.

Leah looked at him, pursed her lips, and gave the slightest of head shakes. Now he could tell what she was trying to do: clear her bad thoughts. He gave a quick, soft snort to let her know he understood.

Wee Ian looked back and forth between them, scowling. He could see that they were both aware of what had happened, but he wanted to know, too. This was his father who had been hacked and knifed…and possibly more. "Stop what?" he echoed.

Leah didn't want to lie to him. He'd probably be able to tell the difference, anyhow. "Stop the evil deeds, the killing, maiming, all of…all of this senseless… Ergh!" she hissed in exasperation.

Wee Ian nodded like a bobble-headed plastic dog—he understood. "So, is he still a man?" he asked softly, his words breaking apart and losing substance as they hit the air, his whispered fear and terror as audible as a scream.

"It looks worse than it really is. I mean, his penis is still intact. It looks like they tried to castrate him, but they didn't get the job done…thank You, Lord. He has several slices to his scrotum and inner thighs, a deep stab wound in his left testicle, but they missed severing the tendons securing the testes. I need to clean it with more than just plain water, though. Wee Ian, will you bring me that other bag over there? It has more of my supplies."

Wee Ian placed the bag in her hand without comment, only giving a nod that seemed to say, 'Here ye are, ma'am,' without a noise, and then returned to his surgery-side observation post.

Leah used the sponge-tipped swab to clean the cut areas with the orange-colored antiseptic solution. She dug into the medical supply section of her bag and found the adhesive tape. "A butterfly bandage would probably be better than stitches. I mean, he isn't going to be moving around for a few days. This way, no stitches need to be removed. He can pull the tape off by himself in a week. I'm sure he'll be awake by then and be glad that he won't have to have someone else remove his sutures."

Wee Ian leaned in to get a better look at Leah's ministrations. She saw that he was interested, so moved aside for him to get a better look. "See, the plumbing is all intact and the testes—the balls—look like they're going to be fine. Although…"

Leah didn't finish her thought, and that fact wasn't lost on either James or Wee Ian. "What do ye mean 'although'?" the son asked suspiciously.

Leah glanced over at James and gave him the 'just trust me on this' look. "Well, since you know I'm a fairy, I'll tell you that there were some 'fairy deeds' I saw before I came here." She realized as soon as the words were out of her mouth, it was the wrong approach. She changed her explanation, but still fumbled with her new choice of words. "You, see… I mean… Oh, shoot. Do you know what a surgeon is?"

Wee Ian nodded. "He takes out teeth, spills yer blood into a pan, and puts leeches on ye. He's kinda like a healer, but nae as good."

"Well, yes, they usually heal with cutting, and there's blood around, but the surgeons where we're from are better than the ones around here. There's a procedure that I watched, actually assisted in…" Leah looked over and saw she was losing Wee Ian. "What I mean to say is that he may not be able to make babies again, but the…the…"

"Ye mean the cock'll work, but there willna be any more sperms?" Wee Ian asked.

"Exactly!" Leah exclaimed, then exhaled in relief. The bandaging was done and so was the explanation.

"So you've assisted in a few vasectomies?" James asked with a sly grin.

"Yes, I have," Leah answered with a modest shrug. She straightened up and added, "And that's why I would say that even though he's been stabbed in the testes and sliced in a crude attempt at castration, the ligaments are still intact. The vasa deferentia may have been severed, but men don't

314

need to have that little vessel intact. Shoot, they pay good money to have it cut! If he ever settles down and gets rid of that anger, I'm sure he'll make a good husband and be able to serve his wife well. But hopefully, he's already had all the children he wants."

"Well, he's had at least one great son. He couldn't ask for anyone smarter or more loyal, that's for sure." James looked at Wee Ian. He was sitting cross-legged in front of his father, head bowed—a young lion cub protecting his battle-scarred and ravaged elder.

The boy couldn't help but hear James. He knew he was smart enough—smarter than many boys his age—but it was nice to hear someone praise his father for having a good son. He lifted his head and smiled as sweetly as a skinny, half-naked, worried boy of eleven could. "Thanks." He swallowed hard and sniffed twice. "I'm sure he woulda appreciated hearin' it. I'll let him ken ye gave him the compliment when he wakes."

### ***52 Finally Here

The three of them returned to the shade of the tree and enjoyed an encore of their light repast in silence, no one feeling like the subjects of fairies and blood needed to be expounded upon or explained. Ian was sleeping soundly, an occasional snort coming from within his brush-walled castle. Marty came up to the little gathering, set down his handkerchief full of huckleberries next to the trail mix bag, then leaned back against the tree next to James, letting out a long, contented sigh. The world was at peace for all of them.

Well, almost all of them. Leah was happy that they had made it to their destination safely, and that Ian looked as if he was going to survive, but she was still eager to find out where her mother was. She knew it was too late in the day to head out, no matter where they were. James still needed time to recuperate, and there was Ian to consider. But, whether they were going or staying put, she still wanted—needed—to have a plan; something to look forward to, at least.

She looked over at the pensive boy and asked, "If we leave, do you think you can take care of—I mean, see to—your da's needs with Mr. Melbourne's help?"

"Oh, he can call me Marty. I'm more comfortable with that," Marty said. He gulped as he realized that he had just interrupted Wee Ian's answer. "Oops, sorry. That was rude."

Wee Ian looked at the gray-haired man from head to toe, literally. He was an older man, to be sure, but looked strong. He was nice, but just a wee bit silly. The boy nodded his head. "Aye, I can handle Da with or without *Marty's*," he stressed the name, "help. He's welcome to stay if he likes. If Da stays asleep for the healin', he willna be much trouble." He turned back to look at his comatose father, the man's mouth hanging lax, eyes squeezed tight, as if in pain. "I think he'll be asleep for another day or so. He's drinkin' water from the reed, and if I can get a squirrel, I'll make some broth." Wee Ian frowned in recollection and looked over at Leah. "Do ye happen to have a spare pot to cook in?"

"Uh, no, we don't even have one for us," James answered. *Damn, one more very important item they had forgotten. Maybe Gibsonville was nearby and they could buy one there.*

Marty piped in, "I have a pan and I'd be more than happy to share it. And I even have an onion for the stew or broth or whatever you decide to cook. Or I can cook." Marty was about to say more, then realized that he was being too chatty again. "Um, I think I'll go down by the stream and look for some watercress. Mighty tasty stuff," he said in parting, then trundled downhill toward the creek.

"Don't take too long," James called after him. "I still need to talk to

316

you."

Marty didn't turn his head, but waved his hand in acknowledgment that he had heard him. He'd have to face him soon enough.

There was an awkward silence among the remaining group, but it didn't last long. Out of the blue, Leah suddenly asked, "What happened to the horses that belonged to those bad guys?" She scrambled up from the ground and stood on tip toes, as if she could search better with the extra couple inches that that afforded. She looked beyond the trees and scrubby bushes, then turned and checked behind her in all directions, wearing a slight frown, as if she was merely searching for a mislaid coffee cup.

Wee Ian's eyes sparkled at hearing the question. He hadn't thought about that! Still seated, he looked at his immediate surroundings. He pursed his lips as he stared at his father's deep sleep, then changed focus to his new friends—the heroic but weakened James, leaning against the tree; Leah the healer doing the detective dance; and down the rise, the helpful but talkative Marty, his broad-shouldered figure disappearing into the landscape, foraging for food again. He shifted his eyes as he tried to justify his request with himself before voicing it.

Leah could see the thoughts spinning in Wee Ian's head. He had some serious decision making ahead of him—maybe she could make it easier.

"If you want to see if you can round up the horses, I'll keep an eye on your father. If you need help, I'm sure Marty would be happy to join you. I think James better stay put for a while, though."

The relieved youth stood up straight and tall to answer, addressing the couple with carefully worded solemn respect. "Ye have been most kind and helpful to me and my father in this…this mess, and if ye could see to stay by his side a wee bit longer, I'll get the horses. I only need to get the one, and then the others will follow." A grin of realization appeared on his face, and his voice brightened up. "And I'll wager there's at least one pot in the saddlebags that *used* to belong to those three." He tilted his head toward the burial mound and added, a full white-toothed smile now shining bright, "They willna be needin' their goods anymore, that's fer sure."

Ian stuck his nose in the air and turned around slowly, sniffing for the direction of the horses. He chuckled as he caught the scent, shuffled down to the creek, and stood on an oversized boulder at the edge, about thirty feet downstream from Marty.

"I'll be quick about it then," he shouted, and waved to James and Leah, then over at Marty.

The little half-naked Scot-Indian headed out to capture horses, foodstuffs, and cooking utensils, happy to be of assistance to the fairy people who had rescued him and his father.

*Marty watched the young boy tread lightly, quickly and quietly,*

317

*down to the streambed. He was both fleet and clever, a credit to his father. He looked back up the ridge and saw his son. Right now, he was weak and hardly able to stand up straight by himself, but wise—and humble—enough to use a stick as a makeshift cane to help prevent a fall. He was also generous. He had given up his safe and secure life, and all the wealth and comforts of the 21ˢᵗ century, to come follow his addlepated grandfather into the wilds of Revolutionary War era North Carolina for no other reason than he had been asked.*

*Marty sighed deeply. He wondered if James had found out yet that he was really his father, not his grandfather. He was a very bright boy— man, he corrected himself—but the paths to discovering his true heritage had been cleared of clues and hints for years.*

*There were only two people alive who knew the truth since Bruce, the acknowledged and legal father of James, was dead. Bibb had promised not to tell, and he knew that she could be trusted. He snorted. How could she even start to tell him? There was no connection between the two of them. They were on opposite sides of the Atlantic Ocean, and he couldn't think of any reason for them to meet either socially or for business. No, he had wiped away any possibility that they would haphazardly become acquainted. Unfortunately, that also meant that telling James the truth of his parentage was going to be all the harder. But he had to tell him, and tell him soon. He had lived the lie for too many years. James deserved to know that he loved him more—if that were even possible—because he was his real, biological, son.*

*And he should also know that he had another relative here besides great-uncle-many-times-over Lord Julian Hart.*

*How could he even begin to explain why he sent for him? 'Son, we needed to protect a person—your ancestor—so you will live, rather, be born.' Marty shook his head like a dog with a bug in his ear. The paradox sounded crazy to him, even inside his head, but James definitely needed to know who this ancestor was. But how in the hell was he to start the topic?*

"Just jump in with both feet like you usually do, Melbourne," he said under his breath. "No reason to start pussyfooting around now."

He gulped in a deep breath for fortitude and approached James, who was awake but prone under the shade tree. "We have to talk," Marty declared with a feigned sense of bravado.

James rose onto one elbow and said, "I agree. But I don't think I know as much as you think I do."

Marty winced and shut his eyes, but didn't say anything. He'd let James finish.

"I was only able to read the first letter in the bundle. And the map and the note about bringing the IV tools were just email copies that were sent to my phone. I never got to see the originals. If there was something on the back of them or…" He shook his head, eyes closed, apologizing without saying more.

Marty let out a deep sigh of relief and managed to utter, "Oh." He was rarely at a loss for words, but right now, he was stumped about how he could—or should—reveal their true biological relationship. He huffed again and looked over at James. His son wasn't waiting for him to reply, though. He was composing his own thoughts, getting ready to say more.

"The MacLeods were after the treasure," James said. "They broke into Leah's apartment because they thought she had it, but came out empty handed. One of them followed me to the motel and got into my valise while I was out of the room." James bit his lip, hoping he wouldn't be asked to go into detail, then sighed and continued. "That's where they found the letters, in the side pocket. Leah and I had only read the first one; we hadn't had a chance to look at the others. Eight—that is, Atholl MacLeod the 8th—poisoned his own brother as a diversion to sneak into the room to get them."

James's jaw tightened as he recalled the episode and the frustration he felt when he couldn't even dial 911. He started to say more, then stopped. Marty didn't need to know that he and Leah were sharing a room, nor that she was in the shower when that asshole broke in. He snorted, then grinned, glad that the scary story had a happy ending. "The treasure was right there in the bag the whole time, but he didn't see it." James patted the bag. "I brought it back with me."

"What do you mean 'it was right there in the bag'?" Marty asked. "What treasure would that be?"

"The jewels, of course."

Neither one of them spoke. Marty shook his head, amazed and dumbfounded. A mischievous grin grew, along a sense of irony.

"What? That was the treasure you were talking about, wasn't it?"

Marty's head still rattled back and forth. "No," he said slowly, then stopped to look James in the eye. "*You* were the treasure."

"What? I mean," he lowered his tone and volume, "what *are* you talking about?" Wee Ian was probably too far away to hear, but he still didn't want to appear to be out of control.

Marty sighed, shifted positions, and proceeded haltingly. "I got caught up in doing genealogy. I mean, the Melbourne line was already well-researched and documented to almost the beginning of time—or so it seemed. The mystery of the Hart break in the family line was fascinating, so I began investigating it. I went—rather, came here—to North Carolina because it was the last place he was known to be alive. I researched the museums and universities and churches and graveyards…" Marty stole a glance at James to see if he understood where the story was going.

"And you found nothing, so decided to go home and look at those letters to see if there was anything in them, right?" James accused more than asked.

Marty shrugged with admission of guilt and continued his story. "At first I wasn't going to, but then…well, yes—I cheated. What can I say? I went back home, debated—argued—with myself about it for nearly a year…" Marty huffed in frustration, "but I couldn't stand the temptation. I was weak and curious and bored. I read them—read them all—and then was back on the plane to North Carolina within days. There really was something in those, for me, for us. But only a small part of it related to Lord Julian.

"That second time, my friend helped me with the research. While we were working on it, we found a story—more a legend than written word—in this friend's history about an ancestor who was saved by a fairy. It wasn't Great-uncle Julian—he was in my friend's family line, too, but indirectly—but it was all so fascinating that I didn't want to stop the research.

"Yes, I got distracted." Marty rolled his eyes—James knew that it happened to him frequently, too. "The legend was about a fairy who put his blood into a warrior's father's father's body and saved his life. It never said how many generations were involved, but my friend and I did more investigating and traced it back to this time, the time when Evie was here.

"You see, Evie—the woman who had written the letters—would be considered a fairy, so I thought maybe she had something to do with this. By the way, there are tales of fairies as far back as lore goes. Fairies—that's the name they gave to people who just showed up without explanation, in strange clothes, speaking strange dialects—time travelers. Well, fairies and witches. The witches were the ones who weren't smart enough to shut up and adapt, but kept insisting…well, you get the picture."

James nodded. Yes, he got the picture. The only Lisa Sinclaire book he had read explained it well enough. And now he and Leah were here as fairies; and his father, Marty; and Leah's mother, Dani—or Evie, as she liked to be called—were, too.

"So, I think my friend's ancestor needed a blood transfusion to survive, and well, I wanted to make sure he got it, so I sent you the map and the note."

"Yes, how *did* you do that?" James asked.

"Well, I had seen the 'Back to the Future' movies where Professor Brown sent *Marty*," he winked at saying the name, "a letter because he knew where he would be on a certain date. I was sure you would be in London for your birthday, so did some creative mailing and forwarding, and yes, I even used Western Union at one point. You obviously got the letter or you wouldn't be here with the IV equipment." Marty looked pensive then added, "But I sure didn't see Leah coming. I guess everything isn't foretold or predestined."

"Yeah, well, the letter almost didn't get to me. By all rights, it should have been intercepted, but fate—no, God—was still in control. If it is meant to be, He will make sure there's a way to get it done. If I hadn't brought the IV tools, either Ian would have not been hatcheted or would have survived regardless of the transfusion...or maybe another fairy would have shown up and done the deed."

"So, it looks like Ian will live..." Marty looked around nervously, then changed the subject quickly and awkwardly. "I wonder what time the moon comes up."

"What the...?" James started to ask what was going on, but clamped off the question as soon as he realized what it was. He looked over at Leah and saw that she had figured it out at the same time. Or had read his mind, or whatever—it didn't make a difference. They both knew why Marty was uncomfortable. The truth was so close, but he wasn't ready yet to admit that there was a genetic connection between Ian and James.

*Now is as good a time as ever to let him know that I know.* James sat up straight and cleared his throat. "So I'm the treasure and Ian is my ancestor, right?" He focused on Marty, eyes narrowed, letting him know that he was on to him. "And therefore, Bibb's, too."

James and Leah giggled at the wide-eyed, slack-jawed expression on Marty's face. The old man had been found out and hadn't seen it coming.

"Leah said she was my daughter-in-law," he mumbled in recollection. "You knew?" he asked haltingly, "You know that I'm your father?"

James nodded and grinned broadly, but sobered up quickly when he remembered there was still another family member he had to talk to Marty about. "And yes, I know Bibb's my real mother," he said plainly, then shook his head to rearrange his thoughts. *Yes, I know Bibb's my mother, but you need to know that you have another son. But that subject will have to wait, or you'll never tell me why you sent for me.* "Please, continue your story."

Marty tipped his head in a tacit apology, wondered for a quick moment how James had found out, then continued. "Bibb's got a lot of Cherokee blood in her. That's where you get those high cheekbones and ruddy complexion. Anyhow, I asked her about it when I went back to visit when you were six. That was the one time I insisted Bruce stick around and spend some time with you. Anyway, Bibb and I went to the Cherokee Reservation and did research together. I'm not sure how excited she really was about researching her heritage, but she liked spending time with me. Shoot, she'd have been happy to dig through dung piles with me."

Marty's contented, glassy-eyed half-grin of recalling the conjugal times spent with Bibb evaporated when he saw James frowning, looking down his nose at him, giving him a non-verbal scolding to get on with the story.

He sputtered, "But it wasn't on paper—what we were looking for—so we went and talked to the elders. They were the ones in charge of keeping the tribe's history, but that part wasn't written; it was an oral history, a family's story not in any book. For the life of me, I can't remember the old woman's name, but she was a distant relative of Bibb's. They both had old Colonel Parks as an ancestor. He was one of the good American soldiers on the Trail of Tears." Marty noticed James was frowning at him again, so stopped rambling.

"Okay, okay, I'll try to focus. Bottom line, Bibb—and therefore, you—wouldn't be here if it weren't for the fairy who put his blood in Ian Kincaid, also known as Star Walker, because *he* was the father of Scout Kincaid who married a Janie or Junie or Genevieve Pomeroy-Hart. And *they* are your great-great-grandparents, however so many times over."

There was an awkward moment of silence. Neither James nor Leah commented on the revelation. Everyone looked at each other, and then Leah spoke up.

"Mom's name is Pomeroy-Hart, and as you know, she had triplets. Wee Ian just told us that Ian was the biological father of them, that they are his siblings. So far, the only children with Ian Kincaid's *blood* are her three and Wee Ian. And since he's now incapable of siring more children... Shoot, I'm sure those four didn't, or won't, intermarry or breed. I mean, they were, are, siblings, after all. And I'm not even sure if one of the triplets is a girl. There *is* no Scout Kincaid, and because of Ian's injury, he won't be able to sire any more children. Something is wrong with this scenario, or James wouldn't be here. I...I...I don't think we needed to come."

"Yes, we did," James said adamantly. "No matter what this story about a Scout Kincaid and a girl by the name of Pomeroy-Hart has to do with me, we are still, God willing, going to see your mother. And remember, except for that *one* relative back in Greensboro," James glanced over and winked at Leah—he'd let his father think he was referring to Bibb—"we don't have other family anywhere except for your mother and," James grinned and nodded acknowledgment, "my father."

Leah squinted her eyes and almost glared at James, backing off just enough not to be seen as mean or rude. "Oh, shit," her husband moaned softly when he realized the reason for her expression.

"Is Bibb okay?" Marty asked, the look of concern changing quickly to one of fear. Was there something wrong with that one relative back in Greensboro?

James closed his eyes, but before he could speak, Leah answered, sparing him the discomfort she knew he was feeling. "Yes and no," she replied, then quickly added, "She was attacked by Asshole MacLeod the 9th, but was recovering just fine when we left." Leah looked at Marty and saw he was biting his bottom lip, waiting for her to finish her explanation. "And no, because she has cancer—liver cancer."

"Is that a type of cancer the doctors can treat? Does she need a donor? Couldn't you help her? Is she going to be okay? Should I go back? Well, tell me!" Marty was practically—actually was—screaming by the time his questions were finished, his eyes wide in frustration with, and anger at, James for leaving Bibb when she was ill.

"Sit down, will you?" James suggested sternly, then added, "Sir." He wasn't sure how to address his father yet. Dad didn't feel right, but he didn't want to be disrespectful to him, no matter what the circumstances.

"Hmph!" Marty snorted, but sat down and was mute for about two whole seconds. "Well, spit it out, son," he grumbled, then added, "Damn, that feels good to say, knowing that you know and...well..." Marty shook his head gently, then said softly, "Go ahead, I'll try to calm down and not interrupt."

"The cancer is treatable and she has an excellent chance of recovery. As far as going back to see her, yes, I think you should. You two have spent too much time apart, and it's obvious to me," James tipped his head to Leah, "and to my wife that you both care about each other. But there's something else you need to know, and it's another reason why you should go back."

James looked up to make sure that Marty was going to be able to comprehend—or accept—what he had to say next.

"Well, get on with it! I'm listening." Marty's back was board straight, as if he slouched or relaxed in the least, his powers of hearing would be compromised.

"You see, the reason she's going to be fine is that there's another donor for her. Actually, he's a better match than I am for the liver transplant."

"Bibb m...m...married?" Marty babbled in shock. "I mean, yes, I didn't talk to her as much as I should have, but I'm sure she would have told me if she had met someone else, and they got married and had a child together. Or didn't get married," Marty rolled his eyes and continued, "and still had a child. I never saw one around last time I saw her, and that was only three years ago."

Wrinkles and scowls of fear, hurt, and pain all rolled into one horrid emotion covering Marty's face—and it looked as if it was getting ready to be swamped with saline. His eyes were brimming with tears at the lost romance, the failed relationship that was his fault because he didn't want to have an American wife.

James laid his hand on his father's leg and brought him out of his self-imposed hell. "No, she never remarried, but I have a brother. And you have another son. She got pregnant the first time you two got together. She thought she would never see you again. She didn't want you to marry her out of guilt for having a love child, so she gave him up for adoption. He's a

323

great guy and was actually Leah's best friend. He became my best friend several days before we found out that we were related, actually full-blooded brothers."

"When...who...his name?" Marty wasn't entirely speechless, but couldn't manage to put a coherent question together.

"Billy Burke was born on the fourth of July, 1984." James leaned back again and shut his eyes as he related the short biography of his brother. "He's a police detective—and a darn good one—for the Greensboro Police Department and looks a lot like me. Actually, he went to see Bibb in the hospital right after the attack by Niner. She couldn't see—her eyes were swollen shut and, well, she was in real rough shape—but she could hear just fine. When Billy spoke, she thought it was you. She thought she was telling you about your son who she had given up for adoption because she didn't believe she could rear a child by herself. Can you imagine the surprise when he found out that *he* was that child? I mean, he had the same birthmark and birth date and was dropped off at the same hospital..."

James opened his eyes to see his father's reaction to the story—and wasn't surprised. He was actually proud of him. Marty was crying, sniffing and snorting, and had resorted to wiping his runny nose on one sleeve, blotting his eyes with the other.

"Here," James said, and gave him his red handkerchief, "it looks like you donated yours to the berry basket cause."

"Oh, and here, I have a picture of the three of them I snapped just before we left." Leah handed Marty the small laminated photograph. "Bibb still looks rough, but she's going to be just fine. And I know she'd like to see you. She asked if we'd send you back. I think it might be a good idea for you to acknowledge your other son, too. He and James did blood tests for Bibb's transplant and the DNA was so close.... James wanted him to legally change his name before we came back so all was in place for inheritances and such, but Billy was hoping you'd return, and then he could get christened with you there. I mean, I know it would mean a lot to him."

James paused, then felt as if he needed to add clarification. "It's not as if he's in it for the money—he's not—but I wanted him to be a steward for the funds, even if he didn't want any of it for himself. You couldn't have asked for a better son."

Marty started to giggle. Leah and James looked at each other—they didn't see anything funny in what had just been said. Marty's giggle turned into a big belly laugh.

"No, I didn't ask for him, but according to you two, I got one. And yes, I will acknowledge him, for sure. Although," the laughing stopped suddenly, "I don't know how I'll go about explaining *you*. Hmm, see where lying gets you? You need to keep making up more lies to keep up the deception."

"Oh, don't worry about kicking Bruce out of the family lineage. If Billy is my legal uncle rather than my brother, I won't mind. I'm not going back. I guess Leah and I disappearing can just be another unsolved mystery, and one that I would prefer not be investigated. Anyone who matters to us, knows where we are, so let's just let the genealogical inaccuracy about me stay in place. I'm proud of you, whether you're my father or my grandfather. Always have been and always will be. At least, for another 230 years, anyway."

### ***53 Food Finding Foray

Wee Ian walked proudly up the creek, leading the mare by her halter, the other two horses following behind her by instinct, not rein. Capturing them had been an easy task—well, sort of—and the rewards were great. Now he had a horse for his father to ride, and Leah and James could have one, too. Hmm, the mount that had belonged to that captain might still be back at the site where he had been attacked. He shook his head. No, he didn't want to return there, even if there was a horse to be had just for the taking. He didn't want to go back there for anything. He'd rather walk barefooted for the rest of his life! His father was all that was important, and now he was safe and healing back at the camp, being watched over by the fairies.

He knew James and Leah were fairies, and the man, Marty—well, he was probably one, too. Why were there so many fairies around all of a sudden? Hmm. At least they were helpful sorts and weren't trying to hurt anyone. It was just the opposite—his father was alive because of them and their fairy healing.

The outlaws' saddlebags didn't have much in them, but was still more than he had. Well, no, not really, he argued with himself. He and his father were still breathing, and those degenerates were all dead. Each one only had a short ration of flour, oats, a bowl and a spoon, and there was but one pot between the three of them. He'd give that to James and Leah, and accept Marty's offer to stay and help cook for his father. It seemed that he wanted to stay, anyway.

Wee Ian could see their camp now. Marty was wiping his eyes and face, as if he'd been crying. He couldn't hear what was being said, but all three of them sounded cheerful. If the talkative old man was happy, then why was he crying? White men, hmph! They cried when they were happy and laughed when they were scared. He'd never understand them if he tried his whole life. But he wasn't going to try. Hopefully, he and his father would find a tribe that wouldn't mind having two more males. At least, they both were good hunters—or his father would be again after he healed.

"Hey, whatcha got there?" Leah called out when she saw Wee Ian and the three horses approaching. She glanced over at Marty and saw him swiping his face with James's red bandana, sniffling and snorting, doing his best to compose himself. She looked back at Wee Ian and saw that he had chosen not to stare at the emotional older man, but was busying himself, tying the horses to a tree.

Wee Ian pulled the single, overloaded saddlebag off the mare and stood up under it, shouldering the weight of the consolidated goods. "They dinna have much, so I put the better bits and pieces in here. There're some foodstuffs, bowls, and a pot. Ye and James can have the pot," he said, and nodded to Leah. He changed his attention to Marty. "Is yer offer to help make a broth fer my da still open?" he asked politely.

Marty sniffed one more time, then answered with more cheerfulness than the question deserved. "I'll help with anything you need, lad. I see you got the horses. If you want to go check on your da, I'll try to scare up a squirrel or some other tasty meat for his soup."

"Aye, I'd appreciate it," the boy replied with a courteous nod, then half-ran, half-skipped over to check on Ian the elder.

His father was still asleep and didn't appear feverish, but Leah had said he needed plenty of water. Using the little drops of water on the lips trick that Leah had taught him, Wee Ian managed to get him to take one long sip through the straw before he groaned and turned his face away.

Wee Ian sat back on his heels and surveyed the damages to his father's body. The neck wound hardly looked serious now that it had been cleaned and stitched. The breechclout was still stiff and stained with blood, but that was no problem. He'd take it off and clean it later, but after the others went to sleep.

It looked like his father was going to live now. Hmm. He had better not tell him that he wouldn't be able to make more babies, though. That would probably upset him, and he didn't want him to have another reason to be mad at anyone—even if they were already dead. At least all the pieces were there, and Leah said that the prick part would still work. He'd just tell him that he was fortunate not to lose his balls and would heal soon. Besides, his father didn't need any more children. What he needed—what they both needed—was a home, or at least a tribe, to call their own.

Wee Ian peered at the horizon. It wouldn't be too long before the sun would be low enough to catch fish for supper. He remembered that James wanted to go with him. He subconsciously nodded his head. Yes, he wanted to spend some time alone with the man—the fairy, he reminded himself. He had a few questions he needed answered.

ЖЖЖ

James was in the same location, now seated, propped up against the tree, shoulders bent forward, intent, focused on his project. Wee Ian stared wordlessly at the diaphanous array on his lap.

James looked up, aware that he was being watched, and explained. "I was just putting the line back on the reel. It came off and made a mess. Here, would you pick out a couple of flies that you think these fish would like?" He smiled as he handed him the little tackle box. "I've never fished here in America. I don't know if they like the same flies as English fish."

Wee Ian took the little wooden box that held the flies stuck into a roll of yellow flannel sheeting. "These," he said, and pulled out two tiny twists of black and green. "They look like mayflies."

"Great. Here, I smoothed these down while you were out after the horses." James handed him two fairly straight poles that he had knocked the branches and rough bark from, offering him his choice of fishing rods. Wee Ian took one, looked hard at the end of the pole, then at the middle section. James had screwed in little brass eyelets to run the line through.

"It's called a fly rod," James explained. "Here, I'll show you." He struggled to stand up. "On second thought, I'll show you when we get there. If you don't mind, would you carry the poles? I think I had better use this walking stick. If I don't, my wife or father will beat me with it!"

Wee Ian gave a weak smile in return, then let it grow into a full grin. He shook his head. What a difference a few hours made. This morning, he and his father were near death—or worse—and now he was fishing with a fairy, using a fairy-made rod.

"I'd be glad to carry the rods. Ye can lean on me, too, if the walking stick isna enough."

The two of them took their time getting to the pool of still water they both agreed was their best bet for getting dinner.

"Here, like this," James said, and threw a perfect cast, flicking it back and forth a few times over the water to get the attention of the fish he was sure were waiting for their fly-by dinner. It had been a long time since he had been fly fishing and was glad he hadn't tangled the line. He was used to his lightweight carbon rod, perfectly balanced, and with a foam grip. This was a crooked, roughly-finished sapling, but the fish it caught would taste just as good. "Do you want to try with this or use the other one?"

Wee Ian pursed his lips and looked back and forth, evaluating the rods, then picked up the one that hadn't been used. He put it in his right hand, found the balance point, looked over the loops with the line running through them, and fingered the roll of extra line stuck into the notch at the end of the pole. "Is this fairy string?" he asked, as he ran his finger along the top of the thin nylon line.

"Um, yes, it is. It's thin, but very strong, and hard for the fish to see. Here, let me step back and you try."

Wee Ian took the little loop of extra line out of the notch, unwound it, and held it in his left hand. He grasped the rod with his right, inching his fingers up the pole until he found the balance point again. He stood back, surveyed the area around him for low lying branches and fairies, flicked the rod a few times, and let the line play out just above the surface of the pool. He snapped it again and again, as the fish leapt out of the water, trying for the little fly tied on the end of the invisible line. Finally, one trout found the lure. Wee Ian set the line quickly, and pulled it in, grasping the line, bringing in his dinner, hand over hand.

James saw the familiarity the boy had with fly fishing. Evidently, this sport had been around for a quite a while. No, not sport—method of procuring sustenance, he reminded himself. He watched as the trout was landed with ease. Hopefully, he would be as adroit when he caught a fish.

Wee Ian looked up at him, gave him a nod of thanks, then scanned the upriver edge of the pool. He indicated with a shift of his eyes and a nod that he would head up there so James could stay where he was and fish. The new arrangement would eliminate the chance of combat fishing—lines and elbows crossing—and give them both enough casting and flicking room. The courteous and agile Wee Ian—truly a gentleman, despite his youth—had offered to take the high side.

James held back the urge to shout with victory when he caught his first fish. He didn't want to seem like a greenhorn who had never caught one before, but he *was* in a way. He had never caught an 18th century fish with 21st century line. Shoot, he hadn't caught any fish in over ten years. Yup, this was the first of many fish to be caught, he assured himself. God willing, he prayed silently.

He caught two more fish in short order. He looked up and saw Wee Ian walking toward him with a stick strung through the gills of four fish. Seven fish and four people eating solid food. It looked like a hearty meal for dinner tonight.

Wee Ian sat down next to him. "Do ye have a knife with ye? I'll do the cleanin' if ye do."

James handed him the Leatherman tool he had used to remove his bindings earlier in the day. He grunted softly as he realized how much had changed in such a short time.

"I said, is this a fairy knife?" Wee Ian asked, apparently not for the first time.

"No, actually it's American. But I guess you could also consider it a fairy knife if that makes it easier for you. Sorry, I'm a little fuddle-headed. One of these days, I'll explain it all to you if you and I meet again… Shoot, where *do* you live?"

Wee Ian shrugged his shoulders. "Right now, here," he said plainly. He was glad that James was fuddle-headed, though. Maybe he could get an unguarded answer out of him. "Leah's your wife and a healer, right?"

"Yes," James answered warily. The boy already knew it to be true.

Wee Ian, watching him carefully for his reaction, asked, "So how come she said my father was her stepfather? Does that mean that Evie is her mother?"

"Oh, shit," James exhaled in frustration.

"Why is everything 'oh, shit'?" Wee Ian asked. "Is she or isn't she?"

"She is," James said with exasperation. Sometimes he wished he could lie, but now was not a good time to start practicing.

"So my da is not her stepfather, but my two little brothers and sister are *her* brothers and sister, too," he stated, but almost asked as a question.

"So the triplets are two boys and a girl? Cool. Leah always wanted a little sister. Oh, yes, the answer is yes, but I wish you wouldn't tell anyone about it. I mean, just because something is the truth doesn't mean you have to share it with everyone."

"Aye. Evie said almost the same thing. She asked that I refer to her babies as my kin, not my sib...siblings," Wee Ian said dejectedly then brightened up. "But, can we be kin, too—or almost kin?"

"Absolutely! Come on, *cousin*, I'll show you how to open this knife, and then I'll let you clean the fish."

Tom Sawyer would be so proud of him, he thought as he pulled out the knife blade for his newly discovered brother-in-law. So proud.

### ***54 Is it all a dream?

It was late, and had been a very long day. After several 'good nights' were shared, everyone who could walk moseyed off—Wee Ian to rejoin his father, Marty to make one last inspection of the perimeter, and Leah and James back to the security of their healing tree.

The temperature had dropped quickly with the setting of the sun. Leah was chilly, even though it was still in the 70's. Her mind was totally fatigued, but her body wasn't. She snuggled close, her head under her weak husband's chin, appreciating the comfort and warmth his solidness afforded.

"I remember the first time you did that," James commented dreamily.

"Mmm, ugh," Leah replied with a sound of delight that ended with a tone of disappointment. "Yeah. In the pool, as my apartment was burning to the ground."

"Well, not to the ground, but wow—what a way to start a relationship." James paused as he realized she was sending vibes his way. "No, I disagree. It didn't start at the airport. Our relationship started there with the disaster. Before that, it was just a few words. If you hadn't shared the video with me, had just thrown it in the rubbish bin, then we never would have gone forward. You'd be back working your shift at the hospital, sharing Billy's life, not mine."

"Mmm hmmh," she repeated, this time her tone of delight ending with agreement. His warmth was beginning to make her drowsy, and she didn't want to argue the point, especially since he was mostly right. But before she lost her train of thought, she had to ask him, "Do you ever wonder if this is all a dream?"

"What? Do you mean being here?" He really didn't want to commit to a response, even though he was pretty sure that was what she meant. The doubt had crept into his consciousness, too.

"Well, yes, that, too, but also you and me together—a well-matched marriage after knowing each other for such a short time. And then there's the part with you finding out about your father, and getting a mother and the older brother that you always wanted, well…."

"Could this just be a fantasy made from all the wishes and hopes I've had for the last twenty-five plus years? Well, yes, I used to fantasize that I had a brother. Sometimes I wanted a younger brother, other times, an older one who would stand up for me when the bullies were at their worst. A mother would have been nice, too. I was reared with Bruce as my father, and I hate to say it, but I often wished that Grandpa was my real father. But I did have Grandpa's love and attention. I didn't have a mother, but my Great Aunt Mary Jane was always there for me. But how could this be a dream? I mean, the letters and your mother—they're real, right?"

"My mom's disappearance was real, that's for sure. But her getting younger, that's just too radical."

"And traveling back in time to meet fictional characters isn't?" James countered with a snort.

"Time travel has been fabled, romanticized and theorized for, what, centuries? 'Once upon a time' was the accepted way of saying 'two hundred years ago' when telling a story in the old days. You see, that was the length of time people typically time traveled in the legends. They called the people who came to them from other times 'fairies,' so the stories were called fairy tales."

Leah sat up, all drowsiness gone, excited about the new topic of conversation. "Shoot, astronomers have already named the means of transportation people will use, even though they still haven't found the ways, except in theory. They call them wormholes. That's what people used, use now, or will use in the future to transport themselves forward and backwards in time, and even travel across vast regions of space. For nearly a hundred years, modern science has been investigating...doo de doo doo..." She widened her eyes and wiggled her eyebrows as she sang the melody of the old TV series, "...'Twilight Zone' events. You can hardly watch a movie or read a book nowadays without time travel being involved somehow." She wound down and settled back into her new husband's arms, her view being stated and case won.

"Yes," James said tentatively, not sure whether he wanted to commit to her line of reasoning or not. But he felt the same way—sort of. "And flying through the air, traveling underwater, and harnessing power from the sun were all science fiction theories or fantastic dreams that have become reality in the last one hundred years or so. It seems as if we're hardwired to know that these concepts are possible, even though they haven't been proven yet. Just because we haven't seen something with our own eyes doesn't mean that our brains won't accept the idea. Our instinctive beliefs are about a hundred years ahead of current technology. I guess what you call the *hardwiring* is what makes people—scientists—push the envelope and search for what they *know* is possible. They believe the solution is out there, but man just hasn't been able to put the nine and negative five together to get four. But it looks like the ability to travel back in time has been around for ages." He sighed then added, "It's just that it hasn't been available to everyone. But, whether it's a genetic anomaly or simply some exotic knowledge that has been handed down by family or secret societies through the ages, *we* know it's possible. I'd like to think of it as a transferable gift—to be shared judiciously and not abused or used for personal gain or retribution."

"Oh," groaned Leah, "Can you imagine if someone decided to go back in time and assassinate someone? No. That's too much to fathom. Who really did kill JFK? Did the assassin sneak back to his or her own time after the shooting? Is that why the Warren Report was inconclusive?" Leah shook her head and yawned. "Nope, too much to think about, even if I wasn't so beat. Hmph. Not that it would do any good to know—who would believe it? Not many in this century, that's for sure..." she said, mumbling her last words as she scooted closer to James. "G'night, dear."

"Good night, Mrs. Melbourne." James kissed the top of his new wife's already sleeping head. "Sleep well. We have a big day ahead of us tomorrow."

### ***55 Searching for Mama

Leah popped awake at the same time she always did: 5:15 AM. But today, she didn't need to go to work, do research at the library, or go for a run. She rolled over and saw James stirring beside her. Two weeks ago, she didn't know him from Adam. Or Ian Kincaid, she chuckled to herself. And now he was her husband. 'Things happen so quickly here' came to her mind. Wasn't that Dorothy in the Wizard of Oz who said that first? Yeah, well this wasn't Kansas, but things were happening pretty fast here, too, in North Carolina.

"Are you ready to follow the yellow brick road?" James asked, as he pulled himself up into a seated position. He chuckled with satisfaction when he saw that she knew exactly what he was talking about. How did he get such a wonderful woman? Last year, he was in a miserable relationship with a conniving, thieving gold digger. And today, he was restarting his life, in a new—yet old—world, with a smart, considerate, and beautiful wife who shared the same hopes, aspirations, and insights as he did.

"Yeah, well, *if* we can find the road, and *if* it leads to my mother, then yes, I'm ready. Or will be after a...um...a little relief and some breakfast. Gee, where's a port-a-potty when you need one?" she asked.

"Right there. See? It's even green, just like the ones at the fairs and construction sites. It's just that these don't come with a seat or toilet paper." Leah snorted at his joke, and he added, "Hey, it may not have *those* amenities, but at least these bushes don't stink like those fiberglass shacks do. I'll take the loo over there," he said, nodding to a clump of scrub in the opposite direction.

Leah got up, but made a detour to look in on Ian before heading to her bathroom bushes. He was still asleep, his son curled up and dozing next to him, inside the little twig and duct tape shelter. She didn't want to disturb him by touching him to see if he had a fever, but he looked to be doing fine. She'd come back and give him a thorough examination after she took care of her own early morning needs.

She met up with Marty on the way back from the designated ladies room. He started discussing his dilemma right away, not even offering her a 'good morning' first.

"I know I said I'd stay with the boy—and I will if he wants me, needs me to—but I really want to go back. I've spent too much time away from Bibb, and now she *needs* me." The frown on his face reflected the mixed emotions churning within him, the bags under his eyes showing that he had been up all night fretting, trying to decide whether to honor his verbal commitment to the Kincaids or return to the now cancer-stricken woman who he had neglected for thirty years.

"I'll know more about Ian's condition in a few minutes and how

334

important, or necessary, a second caretaker will be," Leah said. "But first, did you happen to bring any coffee? A vanilla soy latte sounds great, but I'll settle for a cup of boiled java, grounds and all."

"I think I can set you up. Where's…oh, there he is," he said, as he spotted James, hobbling towards them, leaning on his roughly-hewn cane. "Hey, son, are you feeling better? You look better."

"Yes, I'm feeling much better, thank you. Good food, good company, and a good night's sleep—all conducive to a rapid recovery. Oh, and good family, too. I told Wee Ian yesterday that Evie was Leah's mother."

James had expected their shocked expressions. "Hey, he asked me a direct question and I answered him. He already knew, though. I'm sure he did. He just wanted confirmation. So, now I call him my little cousin, even if he is more like—no, he really is—my brother-in-law." James winked at Leah, ignored her gapped-mouthed 'huh?' and turned to his father. "Now, on another subject, you said you knew the way to the Pomeroys', right?"

"Well, yes, sort of. I was going to go with you. I'd like to meet your mother," Marty said, nodding to Leah, "but, as I was telling her," he turned back to face James, "I want to go back and see Bibb. *And* take care of her." He shook his head in shame. "Why was I so selfish?"

"Well, you could also ask, why was she so proud? I mean, she didn't—wouldn't—ask you or anyone else for help with anything. My suggestion is that both of you stop kicking yourselves in the pants for being so stubborn and start looking forward to a future together, okay?"

Marty nodded in agreement, his usual garrulous demeanor stifled by his self-imposed shame. He was locked in his own prison of sorrow and solitude, and was loathe even to look up from the ground.

"Hey," James asked suddenly, breaking the bleak silence, "How *can* you go back? I mean, isn't there some sort of time window or something? You told me precisely when to come back. Don't you have to wait for a certain moon phase or planetary alignment or something?"

"No," Marty said glumly, his terseness magnifying his despair.

"Well, then why the cryptic message to leave two weeks after my 28th birthday at sunrise?" James was drawing out the conversation on purpose. He didn't want his father to wallow in self-persecution, but he also needed an answer.

Marty shrugged his shoulders. "That's when Ian Kincaid was nearly killed, and the fairy came and put his spirit into him." Marty inhaled deeply then held his breath. He blurted out in exasperation, "But there was only one fairy in the story we heard from the Cherokee historian." He looked up, a spark of life catching fire in his eyes. "Hey, I wonder why that is? I mean, that brings up a huge subject for debate: free will and predestination." Marty was back to being his old self again—sort of. "I wonder how far forward I could go. Could I find a cure for Bibb's cancer in, what, like the 22nd century, and then come back and give it to her?"

"Whoa, whoa," James said, and held up his hand. "We aren't supposed to know everything. Leah said it best when she said there are mysteries to be solved and mysteries to be accepted. Now, Leah's free will is what brought her along with me, so that's why there are two of us. It could just as easily have been that no one came. If I had never read the letter—letters—or I did, and decided that they were just the ramblings of some old coot, and that my *real grandfather* had died out on a small sailing ship from some strange disease, drunk out of his mind on high dollar whisky..." James glared at his father—he was still slightly peeved at him for deceiving him with the fabricated tale of his own demise.

"*Or*," he continued, "it could be that because Leah is a woman, she isn't, wasn't, worthy of being mentioned in the Cherokee oral history. I mean, aren't the Indians around here and now pretty much chauvinistic? Women are to be seen, bear children, plant crops, cook, and not be heard?"

Marty grinned at the suggestion and pointed his index finger at James with the gesture of 'that's right,' then went back to the subject of finding Leah's mother.

"I think the lad or his father would be your best bets for guiding you to the Pomeroy homestead, but they can't—or shouldn't—travel yet, so we'll nix that idea. I've never been there, but I know it's due east of here. Now, if you hit the town of Gibsonville, you've gone too far. It's just a hint of a town, but someone there could probably point you in the right direction. It's not too far from there, I hear. Too bad there aren't any GPS systems around."

"Well, a good map and a compass should work. I have a good map, but I'm not exactly sure of where we are now." James pulled out his hand-drafted map. "We came through here," he pointed to the XX time portal designation, "and then we... Shoot, I didn't pay attention to which direction we ran. We just followed the screaming voice," he said in frustration. *Why didn't I pay closer attention?*

"Weel, I'm glad ye did follow the hollerin', even if it did cause ye to get turned around from where ye were heided." Wee Ian dipped his head in gratitude, then changed the subject, addressing Leah on his father's condition. "He slept fine last night. He groaned a bit, but that medicine ye gave him kept him from thrashin' about. Will ye be leavin' soon?"

Marty handed Leah his cup of cowboy coffee. She took a sip, then spit out a few grounds before replying. "I'll make sure an infection hasn't started—that's the redness and pus—and that you have extra dressings—that is, bandages—and pills, the medicine. As long as he stays put, and doesn't go wandering around the countryside for another five days or so, he should be fine. The stitches on the inside of his neck will dissolve; the ones on the

336

outside can be removed with a tool I'll leave with you. If I ever see you again—and I hope I do—you can return it to me then. Just make sure he drinks lots of fluids—that is, water or broth—eats when he can, and gets lots of rest! Oh, and the little bandage on his scrotum, er, balls… Well, probably by the time he discovers it, he can remove it. If the skin has grown together, then the bandage should be taken off. Don't let it stay on too long or the adhesive will get gummy. I guess I'll check on it while he's still sound asleep."

Leah went to the foot of the shelter and lifted the breechclout. Wee Ian must have taken it off in the middle of the night and cleaned it. It was smooth, clean, and dry, but just lying over his groin, not wrapped around properly. Such a considerate young boy, she thought. Yeah, right. Who was the child in this two-person arrangement? It seemed as if the son was taking care of the father, not the other way around. And he appeared comfortable with it, too. This must have been going on for quite a while.

Leah checked Ian's vital signs and neck wound. He was healing quickly and without complications. "Thank You, Lord," she offered, as she got to her feet.

"Let me check your vitals, too," she said to James, who was seated next to the small fire, enjoying her cup of coffee.

"I'm sure glad we're all willing to share," he said, and saluted her with the cup. She grinned and put her finger on his pulse, then lifted his sleeve to use his Rolex to check the rate. The wristwatch was a bit gaudy, but no more than the fancy pocket watches that were all over Europe and therefore, in select areas of America. They hadn't had time to convert the watchband to a fob, but it was under his sleeve and not readily visible. As soon as they found a home for themselves, it would be put away in a safe place. Gold was still gold and subject to theft from villains in any century.

"How's the father?" Marty asked, holding the pot in his hand as if he had a parrot perched on his wrist.

"He's doing fine. It's up to you and Wee Ian about whether you should stay or not. There aren't any complications, and the boy's more than capable of making sure he gets fluids in him—and anything else he needs, I'm sure. I've already given him the rundown, instructions on how to take care of him."

"We'll be fine, sir, Marty, if ye have places to go. I appreciate yer offer, though," Wee Ian said, adding a short bow of thanks.

Marty opened his mouth as if to speak, then shut it, his lips pressed together tightly as he tried to make up his mind. Should he take care of a wounded man and his son in the wilds of 18th century Revolutionary America, or go back to the cancer-stricken woman he had pretty much abandoned for the last few years—hell, thirty years—but who had hospitals and doctors to assist her. He snorted with frustration and squeezed his eyes tightly, trying to get some sort of inspiration.

"But if yer going someplace where ye willna be needin' the pan, could we use it?" Wee Ian suggested tentatively, embarrassed about asking for the pot.

"It's yours, lad!" Marty exclaimed, and put it in the boy's hand. He suddenly realized that the Kincaids could take care of each other, just like he could take care of Bibb. The *stuff* needed—whether it was a pan and a bit of extra food, or doctors and warehouses full of medicines and diagnostic equipment—made no real difference. What was needed for complete healing was to have someone by your side to love you and support you. The Ians had each other, James and Leah looked to have a great future together, and now he could go back to Bibb.

His part of insuring that his 'treasure'—his son, James—came into existence had been secured. Bibb's ancestor, Ian Kincaid, was alive because the notes handed down through the ages had ensured that he got his needed blood transfusion from 'a fairy.'

Now he could go back home to get reacquainted with Bibb and meet his middle son, Billy, the detective. He didn't know which would happen first: his new son's christening to receive the Melbourne name and acknowledging his paternity, or marriage to Bibb. Yes, he would definitely marry her, even if he had to sit on top of her to get her to agree to it. He smiled at that image. Yes, he'd sit on her all right, but as her husband, not her lover.

Marty hopped and skipped over to his saddlebags. "Here you go, lad," he called over. "I'm giving you everything I have except the horse and my canteen. Where I'm heading, I won't need any of this. I'd give you the horse, but I'll need her for a bit longer." He paused, then added jubilantly, "But if you happen to see her wandering around without me in a day or so, take her—she's yours."

Wee Ian walked over to Marty to accept the gifts. He eyed him from his dusty boots, planted firmly on the ground, up to the big, toothy grin the vibrant older man was sporting. "Are ye goin' back to fairyland?" he asked suspiciously.

Marty took a deep breath, as if he were going to give one of his long, wordy answers, then let it out and simply said, "Yes."

James walked over to the two of them, clacking his makeshift cane on the gravelly ground as he approached. "So, just like that? You're going?" he asked, trying to mask the pain in his voice. He knew that a long absence was coming, probably forever.

"Just like that," Marty crowed as he snapped his fingers, totally unaware of James's anguish. "I'm going that way," he indicated the direction they had come from the day before, "and I suggest that you go that way," he said, pointing in the opposite direction, the smile still radiant on his face.

"Leah, it's been great meeting you. I'm sure you and James will have a great life together. Make lots of grandbabies for me, okay?" Marty leaned in and gave Leah a firm kiss on the cheek, then changed his mind and pulled her close for a full body hug, ultimately picking her up off her feet and swinging her around, setting her down next to James.

"Now, son," he started in an instructional manner, then changed tones, "I am so glad I can call you 'son' now and know that you know it's the truth. I'll take care of the legalities with your brother Billy, or Uncle Billy as the corrected birth certificate will show. If he's even half the man you are, I'm sure he'll be a credit to the Melbourne name. Maybe I'll get a few grandkids out of him, too. Is he married?"

"Uh, no, but he has a very nice boyfriend," James said and grimaced.

"Huh? Oh. OH!" Marty stuttered, realizing that James had just told him that Billy was gay. "Well, they can adopt. That'll be fine by us. I doubt Bibb will care if they're ours by blood or by paper."

Marty turned away to saddle his horse. Without asking, Wee Ian had taken his canteen and run down to the creek and refilled it. "Is there anythin' else ye'll be needin'?" Wee Ian asked.

"Not here," Marty said, and mounted the horse, his smile still just as broad and bright as ever.

"Weel, then I thank ye fer all ye've done fer us. Safe travel to ye," Wee Ian handed him the filled canteen, "and if ye do come back fer a visit, I hope to see ye again,"

James walked up to his father. "Give Bibb a kiss from both of us and tell her we love her." He drew a deep breath to cover his disappointment, "Even if we never see her again. Tell her I'm sorry for being rude, too," he said and sniffed.

"Ach!" Marty snorted with disgust. "Bibb's already forgiven you, I'm sure. That is, if she ever felt like you were rude in the first place. She's the nicest person in the world. And very shortly here, she's going to be my wife!" Marty said, chest puffed out in pride.

He put his foot in the stirrup and slid into the saddle in one smooth move. "Let's go!" he called to the horse, nudging her in the flanks. He turned around and hollered, "Be safe!" and waved good-bye for the last time.

All three upright people in the camp waved back at him. "Wow. That was a short homecoming," James remarked dejectedly.

"I think that was all that was needed, though, wasn't it?" Leah asked.

"Yeah, I guess so. Who's cooking breakfast?" he said to change the subject. He didn't want Leah to see the tears in his eyes, but he knew that she knew they were there. He sniffed one of them back. It was great to have someone in his life who he didn't *have* to hide his feelings from, even if he did still try.

"Porritch can be ready soon unless ye want to try fer more fish," said Wee Ian.

James shook his head rapidly. "No, we'll be heading out just after we eat. Do you think you can help me saddle the horses, though?"

Wee Ian looked down his nose at his new brother-in-law. "No, but *I'll* saddle them fer ye," he said with a bit of mischief, then added, "Cousin."

James blushed at the joke about their relationship and his still weak condition. "Thanks. I'll let you do just that."

Ж ЖЖ

It was a quiet but comfortable breakfast. The boy cleared the dishes as the newlyweds packed their slim belongings into their two bags.

Wee Ian saddled the horses, watching Leah out of the corner of his eye as she checked over his father one last time.

She called him over. "Now, don't let him do anything for himself, save using the toilet…or whatever," she muttered in frustration. She didn't know the correct terminologies involving bathroom procedures in this era. She chuckled softly to herself when she remembered that all was forgiven with the boy because she was a fairy and unfamiliar with the nuances of language here and now.

"And remember to offer him water frequently and… What? Am I babbling?" Leah asked when she saw that Wee Ian was giving his now familiar look down his nose.

"Aye, jest a bit. I ken what to do. Ye showed me enough times, and I learn pretty fast, or so I've been told. Now *ye* remember to drink yer water. And ye may want to keep yer canteens out of sight." He winked at the bottles. "They dinna look like they belong here, if ye ken what I mean," Wee Ian said in the longest dissertation he had delivered in the 24 hours they had known each other.

"Aye, we'll mind," James replied in a Scots accent. "And make sure ye visit us at the Pomeroy's when yer in the area…Cousin."

"Aye, but dinna be lookin' fer us too soon. We need to find a new tribe before winter sets in." Wee Ian rolled his eyes like he had seen Marty and Leah do. "Or should," he amended, as he glanced back at his father under the twiggy shelter.

"You'll always be welcome at our hearth," Leah said, then snorted and added the same eye roll and grin, "if we ever get one."

Ж ЖЖ

*Later that day, at a map check and water break under still another tree…*

"You know, before I met you—before I even knew of your existence—when I met the older version of your mother, I remember

340

thinking how interesting she was, and…and… Oh shoot—open mouth, insert foot. Never mind," James mumbled, hoping that she hadn't been paying attention to him.

"What? You started the topic, now you'd better finish it, because I'm pretty sure that what *I* can imagine you were going to say is a lot worse than what *you* were going to say. Now, spit it out!"

James gulped, closed his eyes, and blurted out, "I thought how nice it would be if she had a daughter who was young enough to, well, you know, have children," then he added softly, "with me." He snorted with satisfaction at himself for being able to complete the uncomfortable revelation, then opened his eyes to see Leah glaring at him.

"What?" he asked, totally perplexed at her obviously angry attitude. He thought he had just flattered her with his disclosure that he had wanted to make babies with her.

"So you had the hots for my mother!" she accused rather than asked.

"No, no—not at all. I just thought that she was intriguing and smart, but…but," James shook his head rapidly. "No! Besides, she was too old. I just thought… Oh, crap. There's no way out of this one, is there?"

"So now that my mother has a younger body, do you think you'll want her, not me?" Leah asked with a mix of sorrow and disgust.

"No! You were, are, the only one I want, and I swear to God, you are the only woman I have *ever* loved. I knew from the first day I met you that you were," James's voice softened to a whisper, "um, mine."

Leah's hard looks were softening, but weren't yet where they should be. James sucked up courage from down behind his kidneys somewhere and continued, "But it took a few days for me to fall in love with you. It wasn't love at first sight or even instantaneous lust. But I did know you were going to be in my life for more than a few minutes as soon as I saw you salute Bibb with your coffee cup at the airport bar. Now, are we cool?"

"Yeah," Leah replied apologetically, "cool as a jumbo Slurpee. I'm sorry. I guess I have a huge case of nerves with a large side of insecurity. I just wish we were there already. I thought your map showed where Gibsonville was."

"It does, but it doesn't show where *we* are. That would involve having a GPS, and since there aren't any satellites around, we just have to hope that we meet someone with a better sense of our location than my father. I think we're farther south than what he said."

"You're wrong, but it really doesn't matter," Leah replied with a pinch of irony and a smile.

"What are you talking about? Of course, it matters!"

"No, not that. I mean, there *is* a satellite out there, and it's called the moon. But since it doesn't have any global positioning cameras or lasers or whatever generates the signals they use, it doesn't matter. Come on, if

341

you're up to it, let's put these ponies on the road and head north, *north to Alaska!*" Leah sang as she finished her moon joke.

James cleared his throat and said somberly, "No, not yet." Leah frowned, then segued into her nurse/healer persona, and started toward him. He saw the clinical look in her eye and shook his head. "Not that; I'm as fine as I can be that way. I just told you about when I first knew that you were the one for me. Now I want to know: what was your first impression of me and when did you, well, get a feeling for or about me?"

Leah sidled up to him, then turned and snuggled into his arms. The temperature was already too warm, but she needed to be close to him. She buried her nose into his chest, rubbed it back and forth a couple of times for security, then pulled back and peered into his face. "The first time I saw you, I knew who you were. Bibb had borrowed a marker from me to make a sign with your name on it. You see, I had received a weird email that morning," she paused, dipped her head and looked him right in the eye to make sure he knew she was talking about the email he had sent, "so I Googled the sender, a James Melbourne with a UK email server. His message indicated that he had met my mother the day of her disappearance."

James shrugged his shoulders and grimaced as he realized that she had had an honest motivation for checking up on him. Leah rolled her eyes and said, "So I knew from the internet who you were by name and sight. But when I saw you in person, you looked so *damned* sexy! All I could think of was what a waste. Why couldn't good-looking hunks like you be straight? Shoot, it was a good thing I thought you were gay, or I probably would have made a fool of myself. And then, when we leaned over in the bar and had that eye-to-eye moment, it was if I had a peek into our future. Not what it entailed physically, but a wisp of a warm, comfortable emotion—almost an aroma, if you know what I mean."

"Yes, I know what you mean because I felt it, too. Come on, let's go that way. The day is only going to get hotter, and our water won't last until sundown. Hopefully, we find either the Pomeroys' place or a creek before then."

### ***56 Lost in the 80's

James was disgusted with himself. He was hot, tired, hungry and weak, and felt like crying. But, besides tears being a sign of extraordinary weakness, they wouldn't help their situation. "I don't know where we are…or even how to find a reference point. I feel so useless! I spent all that time making an exact map, and then fuck up by not noticing which direction we headed when we got here!"

Leah's eyes widened at hearing him say the 'F' word. She did her best to swallow her shock, though, and stayed mum. She knew he was mad at himself, and besides, he'd let her curse without scolding if the tables were turned.

"Can't you use the moon or the stars or something to orient us?" she asked timidly, unsure whether it was a smart or a dumb question. She was directionally challenged, which was why she had made sure her car had both a compass and a navigation system in it when she bought it.

James snorted as a reply, then shook his head apologetically. "I'm sorry for cursing; I try not to. It's just that we've come so far, and I'm tired, and I feel like a complete failure. I can't find the Pomeroys' place and don't know if I could even get us back to the Ians at the creek."

"Sooo, you're saying that we're lost?" she asked, although she was pretty sure that they were.

James glanced over and gave her 'a look,' then brought out his handmade map. "It would help if it wasn't so blankety-blank-blank cloudy. See, I didn't cuss that time. All the clouds do is make the heat more miserable. Damn! Oops. Darn! It's so muggy, the sweat won't even evaporate," he said, snorting and scowling as he pulled the damp linen away from his chest.

"Yeah, well, try it with a long skirt on. Actually, though, I'm going commando, so I'm getting a bit of a breeze as long as I'm off the horse." Her eyes widened as an important thought smacked her. "Aren't we supposed to brush them or give them grass or water or something after we're done riding for the day?"

"Well, we don't have that much water left, so they'll just have to graze on green grass and hope there's enough moisture in that." James started to walk away from the tree to take care of the chore, but Leah stopped him with a glare and a palm-up gesture.

"*I'll* lead them to their supper buffet. It shouldn't be too hard to figure out how to hobble a horse like they did in the *Lost* books. When I'm done, you and I can rest over there. And, since there isn't anyone around, I'm going to take off my dress and lie down on top of it—bare-beamed and buck-naked!"

"You're wrong," James said slyly and chuckled.

"Huh?"

"*I'm* here. You said there wasn't anyone around. But if *you* don't mind being naked, I certainly don't. I'll just take off my shirt, though." He yanked it off over his head. "It's too much trouble to take off these boots, then the pants…" He sighed loudly. "Okay, I hear what you're not saying. I'll let you help. Thank you, dear; you are so considerate of the frail and infirm," he said sarcastically. She hadn't spoken a word, but she was thinking loud enough.

"Yeah, well, I'm the one who got you so frail," she said, her voice solemn with guilt. She grimaced and tried to turn it into a smile. "I'll be right back."

Leah led the horses to the greenest area, then took the short roll of rope off of each saddle. She wrapped it around one front leg, twisted it in a loop, and then tied it to the other front leg, making little rope 'hoof cuffs' to keep the horses' front legs about a foot apart. They could still take tiny steps in any direction, but certainly wouldn't be able to run.

The horses' backs twitched from the flies as they munched the sprouts of green at the base of a hillock of small boulders and big rocks, their ears flicking as if conducting a silent orchestra. They seemed content. She wasn't, though, but didn't want James to know that. She was afraid. The little bit of water they had left wouldn't last another day, and she hadn't seen any signs of a creek, a road, or civilization. She shook her head, trying to erase visions of vultures flying above, looking for a dehydrated dinner.

Her fear was replaced by a welcomed reason for spousal scolding. "Hey, you're supposed to let me do that," she hollered. James was gasping and tugging, trying to pull off his modified 'colonial-styled' cross trainer shoe. "Now lie back and chill!" she ordered, as she stomped toward him.

"Yeah, right," he drolled. "Not much chance of chillin'. With all these clouds, I don't think the temperature is going to drop much tonight. That means tomorrow's going to be even hotter and more humid." He sighed deeply and closed his eyes, a smile emerging as he recalled the chill of the car's air conditioning after he had asked Leah to marry him, the fan blasting frigid air at high speed to cool him off before going back to their first *home* to consummate their handfast marriage. "Hmm," escaped his lips as his subtle smile grew into a full sweat-prickled face grin.

Leah already had his shoes and socks off, and was working the ties on his pants when, "Hey, what's this?" she exclaimed, seeing his very firm cock. "I didn't think you had that much blood left in you."

James looked down at his exposed manhood. "Whoa!" he exclaimed, giddy and light-headed from the quick movement of lifting his head. He chuckled then lay back and looked straight up at the sky, "I can't have blood in both heads at the same time. And that's your fault. I was remembering you and the car's air conditioning…hmm."

344

"Well, hopefully it was me that caused Mr. Happy to stand up and say hi. I'd hate to rely on air conditioning to get you aroused. I'd be a very sad and deprived woman, if that were the case."

"Um, no worries there, but if you don't mind too much, I'd like to pass on the passion tonight. I think I'll need my strength tomorrow. Plus, I don't want to work up a thirst. We're running pretty short on water."

"Okay, but I'm still going to take off my clothes. An air bath is better than no bath at all. Now, turn your head," Leah said, and began unbuttoning her dress.

"Uh, no," James replied indignantly, and then laughed. "Just because I can't eat at the banquet doesn't mean that I can't appreciate the table you set."

"Okay, but no crumb snatching," she said, and slipped off the dress, revealing that all she had on was a sports bra. She shook out her mother's former dress, enjoying the quick breeze it created, and then laid it on the ground next to him. She carefully stretched out on top of it, trying to keep the fabric between her and the dry grass-covered ground.

"So that's what you were calling commando," he said, gently moving his hand across the outside of her hip where she would normally have panties.

"Hey, hey, hey," she said, picking up his hand, and putting it back at his side.

"I'm not snacking. I'm just checking out the dishes. Nice table setting, my lady."

"So which is it: Mrs. James Melbourne or Lady James Melbourne?" she asked, a little embarrassed at what seemed to be a vain question. She realized that there wasn't any pride or shame between the two of them and relaxed her attitude.

"Well, if we went back to England, then you'd be Lady James Melbourne or Lady James. But since we are *here* to see our families, and I don't want to call attention to my family title, then you'll be Mrs. Melbourne. But either way, you're *mine!*" he crowed, then grabbed a handful of flesh at her hip bone.

"That's a big ten-four!" Leah exclaimed. She moved his hand away and leaned over to kiss him on the cheek, then pulled back and looked at him to see if he knew the phrase. Obviously not, by the exaggerated frown on his face.

She explained. "That's truck driver talk from the old CB—citizens band—radio days. It's another way of saying you betcha! or boy howdy!"

"Or yes-sir-ree Bob?" James asked. He knew a little about American colloquialisms, but still had a lot to learn. He put his hand back on her hip and grinned.

"Aye," Leah replied, then sighed and patted his hand. He was

345

spunky and fun, even when they had to be platonic.

### ***57 A Scary Situation

*August 19, 1781, pre-dawn*
*Still lost*

They jerked straight up out of their deep sleep; arms flailing, legs kicking—like tangled marionettes—confused and terrified by the sudden explosion of thunder. Leah didn't know where she was, who she was, or if anyone was there with her. Her heart suddenly felt eight sizes too big, thump-thump-thumping, like a fifty-pound chipping hammer pounding against her sternum, trying to escape her chest.

James touched her arm and asked, "Are you okay?"

She batted his hand away, and grunted rudely, "Wait! Wait just a minute," as if she were directing traffic. Emotionally, she was lost, disassociated from everything, and although no longer sleepy, she wasn't fully awake either.

*Crash!* Thunder rolled over them, a simultaneous flash of million-watt white light totally illuminating the trees and ground around them. James turned around and realized what was wrong. "The horses!" he yelled. He heard them whinny again, but they were no longer under the tree just a few yards away, but were galloping, their frightened protests now indistinct—muffled by distance as they headed away.

Leah was suddenly alert—no longer foggy-headed or disoriented. She knew who she was and where she was, and at the word 'horses,' was on her feet. She ran toward the small glade and the sounds of nickering and foot stamping, but couldn't see the runaways. A bang and then a flash, and the landscape lit up again. The geldings had panicked and were running away at full speed. Another bang and flash, and she saw it. One of the horses was prancing, lifting his legs high as he danced around the hobbling rope that had come unknotted. "Shit!" she screamed.

James knew better than to run after her. He hastily dressed and waited for her return. She came back, buck-naked and beautiful, with a static-electricity charged Medusa hairstyle.

And extremely pissed.

He didn't say a word. He knew the horses must have come un-hobbled and that was why they were able to run away so quickly. And she was the one who had tied the ropes around their fetlocks.

The thunder and lightning continued, but the time interval between the flashes and the cracks grew. "One one thousand, two one thousand, three one thousand," he counted softly. "Three miles away now and headed away from us," he announced. "I'm sure we'll be fine, with or without the horses. Come on, get your clothes on. The flies will be out at sunrise and they bite. I'd offer to make coffee, but I don't want to use up the water. Will you be okay?"

Leah glared at him then softened her look. "No," she said, then changed her mind. "Maybe," she grunted. She slipped on her bra, picked up her dress, shook it out and threw it over her head, and started buttoning it. "Yeah, probably." She sniffed then started to cry softly. "Damn, it's all my fault!" she exploded with exasperation.

"No, it's the thunder's fault. And we both know who's in charge of that," James said, looking up. "Maybe the Man thought we needed another challenge. I mean really, this has been relatively easy so far. Come on, this will toughen us up."

"Yeah, what doesn't kill us will cure us…or something like that," she grumbled. "And, well, I like winning the race; it's just the running that sucks. You're right, though, I'm sure we'll be fine. At least, the clouds are moving away. Hopefully, we'll be able to see which way is east now. Come on. Let's look at the map together. I'm pretty sure I'll feel better if I have something tangible to focus on." Leah wiped her face with the back of her hand, then pulled her hair back into a bun, using her green lacquered pick to hold it in place.

"You sure are beautiful," James said. He shook his head back and forth slowly in amazement. "How did I wind up with someone so great?" He leaned in to plant a gentle kiss on her lips.

Leah, feeling insecure about her morning mouth, only gave him a token kiss in return, then pulled back. She rolled her eyes and answered with a heavy dose of sarcasm, "My mother was already taken."

She saw the immediate hurt in his eyes and backpedaled quickly. "I'm sorry. I'm lousy at making jokes. I didn't mean it. Really, I didn't. I…I…I promise never to bring it up again, okay?"

James shut his eyes and concentrated on his breathing, making sure he thought about what he was going to say before blurting out how cruel she was to say such a thing. He opened his eyes and nodded. It was better to say nothing than something wrong.

"Breakfast?" he asked, changing the subject. He picked up her backpack. "Granola or protein bar?"

"Protein bar," Leah said glumly. "The granola is too salty and will make us thirsty…thirstier." She looked up and saw the pink shades of dawn creeping into the sky. "Hey, look!" She pointed to the east. "See, things are starting to look better already."

James used his cane to steady himself as he sat down to put on his socks and shoes. He was still hurt by Leah's joke about how she thought her mother was more attractive to him than her, even though she was—or had been—an older woman. He sighed as he realized that if the misunderstood conversation had been reversed, he'd want her to forgive and forget quickly.

"Here, let me," Leah said, and squatted down to finish tying his shoes. "And I don't know why you think you did something special to get

348

me. It's me who was blessed with you." She grinned then did a double pop of her eyebrows. "And I'll show you just how much I really appreciate you when you get enough blood built up to nourish both heads at the same time."

James reached over and ran his hand down the side of her dusty, tear-stained face. "The biggest blessing is to know how much you've been blessed, and boy, don't I know it. Come on, help me to my feet. Let's walk into the sunrise and see if there's a town underneath it with someone who knows where to find the Pomeroys."

"Amen to that," Leah said, as she grabbed his elbow to help him to stand. "A double amen."

### ***58 New Folks in Town

*Gibsonville, NC*

It really wasn't much of a town—just a small tavern, a blacksmith shop, and a general store. They had only seen one person on their way in, but chose not to engage the old man and ask him directions to the Pomeroys'. They simply smiled as they passed. The town was now in sight, and he hadn't looked too friendly anyway.

"'Never speak when you can nod,' Marty used to tell me. It could be dangerous if we said the wrong thing. Of course, then there's my accent. I don't know if I can do an American accent on a consistent basis. People around here are probably still anti-British."

Leah wasn't too sure about that. A large majority of these early Americans were from England. She decided not to waste her time—and her breath—with arguing the point, though. Instead, she'd be extra cautious and do all the talking, at least with first contacts.

The tavern sign was a welcome sight. Real food, and maybe a beer, would be great. They were both thirsty and their water bottles were empty. The tree-lined creek at the far end of town was visible from where they stood, but they both wanted something closer and more substantial. As they neared the steps of the little tavern, they noticed a rough-hewn log had been set up diagonally across the door, barring entrance. "I guess that means it's closed," James huffed in disappointment.

"Do you have enough energy to get to the creek?" she asked tentatively.

She was exhausted, but he had to be even more so because of donating blood. He needed fluids and real food. He needed rest, too, but hadn't been able to get much of that on their two-day trek either. The snacks in her backpack had been enough to get them this far, but they only had one protein bar and a double fistful of granola left. If they could get food locally, they could keep the emergency stash. Hopefully, someone here knew the way to the Pomeroy homestead and it wasn't far.

"On second thought, you stay here in the shade. I'm going to check out the store. Maybe they have something that's easy to prepare, or better yet, ready to eat. I doubt they sell ready-made sandwiches and bottles of beer around here, but it sure would be nice."

James leaned back against the building with a thud, then slid to the ground. He was spent, but hated to look like a slacker, letting his woman investigate the new town while he sat and waited. "I'll be right here where you left me," he said wryly, "unless someone wants an eighty-kilo doorstop." He looked up to make sure she got the joke. She had. She bent over and kissed him on the top of the head.

"I *still* don't know what I did to deserve you, mister. A more generous man I've never met. I'll be back as soon as I can."

Ж ЖЖ

The door to the store had been left open, probably waiting for a stray cool breeze—or any breeze at all—to come through. Leah looked around. Wooden barrels and bulging cloth sacks were clustered on the floor in the corner, and glass jars of various sizes and colors sat haphazardly on the cattywumpus shelves. To the right of the door was a hand-rubbed and polished wooden display unit with a couple dozen iron pieces in it, a sharp contrast to the rest of the disorganized store. She recalled seeing some of the implements at the museum, but didn't recall what they were. She shook her head, befuddled. *Gee, I saw these only last week and still can't remember what they're used for.*

She shuddered, then inhaled deeply, shoulders back, elbows in, trying to pull herself together emotionally. There shouldn't be anything in here to be afraid of, so she'd put on her big girl pants and ignore the sudden prevalence of negative energy. As far as she could see, there was no one else in the store, but she'd check to make sure. "Hallo," she called out, her voice shaking at first, then becoming stronger. "Is anyone here? Hallo, Hallo?"

A man stomped in through the outside door, wearing a glower that made her shiver despite the heat. "What do you want?" he demanded.

Leah was taken aback by his rudeness, but didn't return the bad manners. "Do you work here?" she asked politely.

"No, I don't! What? Do I look stupid? Nobody's here, so go away," he snarled. The short, scruffy man with the week-old beard wore clothes of a decent quality, but he was filthy from the top of his tri-corn hat to his dusty shoes, their pewter buckles dangling, ready to fall off. He may have been a well-to-do man once, but appeared to have recently—very recently—either fallen on hard times or off the wagon. He didn't reek of alcohol, though, so it was probably the former.

"I just want to get some foodstuffs and maybe a couple bottles of ale. My husband and I lost our horses, and we've been walking for two days, trying to find…"

"The devil sent you, didn't he? That's why it's been hot as hell all week—he's been making it ready for you two demons. Well, we don't want any part of you. But, if you have money or barter goods to prove that you're not from the evil one, well, then we might let you pass through."-

Leah was speechless at his ravings. The man kept referring to 'we,' but was alone…unless he had a six-foot Palooka next to him that Leah couldn't see.

"What's goin' on in here?" grumbled a large-bellied man as he waddled into the store, followed by a very pale and sweaty James.

Leah immediately rushed to her husband. She pulled the handkerchief from her bodice, shook it out, and wiped the beads of sweat

351

from his brow. "You need to sit down," she said. She stood up under his shoulder and led him outside to the porch bench. Hopefully, the big man would take care of Mr. Rudeness.

"These two demons just came out of hell, meanin' to take us all back with 'em. Or even worse, they'll lead old Scratch right here to us!" the town trouble maker, Richard Short, screamed. His loud voice brought people out from the shade of trees and porches to see what was going on.

"What? Are you crazy, Dick?" the big man asked. "And why would havin' money and barter goods make them *not* from the devil? Shoot, if they had money, now that would be strange, not the other way around."

"Then why's it been so hot? Hey, Cyrus, didn't your well jest about dry up out there?" Richard Short walked away from Bill and into the crowd, waving his arms wildly, as if he were battling a swarm of wasps, trying to work the now expanding group of citizens into a frenzy.

"These two are here to make way for the devil. If we don't do somethin' about 'em now, the heat'll never stop. Right, right?" he asked one shocked man, and then another, his scraggly face inches from theirs.

"Now hold on there, fella. Don't be gettin' hasty now. They're just new folks in town, right?" Bill asked the young couple.

James put his arm around Leah's shoulder. Despite the heat, she was shaking, but it was with fear. Neither of them had anticipated hostility.

"Yes, sir," James said firmly, "we just arrived here to see family. However, we're not sure where they are. We thought they were nearby, but it appears we were mistaken. Now, if we can't get any supplies, we'd appreciate at least some water, and then we'll be on our way."

"Don't let them near the creek!" the rabble rouser screamed, "They're gonna poison it so we won't have *any* water. First they got the wells, next they'll take the creek!"

The man had gone off the deep end with his screaming and hat-waving, and was now dancing like his feet were on fire, jumping from one shocked bystander to another, blabbering about the devil, pointing at James and Leah.

"Evie?" an unfamiliar voice called out from behind them.

Leah and James turned to see who it was. A dark horse was being reined in to a halt, stirring up dust. "Evie? Evie, when did you leave?" The man was excited, standing tall in the stirrups, ready to dismount, even before coming to a full stop. "I wouldn't think you should be traveling yet. How are you feeling? Huh...hey! You're not Evie..." stammered an embarrassed Lord Julian Hart.

Before anyone else could speak, Big Bill Leuga walked up to Julian's horse. "Julian, it looks like we're havin' a bit of a problem with that confounded Dick Short fella. He thinks these two are from the devil. He wanted money or trade goods from them before he'd let them go. Sound familiar?"

Julian nodded his head in disgust, but before he could speak or reply, Leah walked forward, as if in a trance, and addressed Bill. "Where did you get those shoes?" and pointed to the dirty, but still neon green, Croc slippers on the fat man's feet.

"Oh, I did some tradin' with Miss Evie. Hey, you *do* look like her. Is she your kin?" asked Bill.

"Yes, she's her kin," James answered for her, afraid that Leah would say something intimidating or politically incorrect in her current stunned state. He looked up at the man on the horse, the man whom the fat man had called Julian. "Julian *Hart*?" he asked softly and directly, not wanting anyone else to hear.

Julian sucked in a deep breath, realized that he was acting stressed—or guilty—so let it out softly with a smile and a quick, sharp nod. "Ah, Evie will be so happy that you've arrived. Excuse me," he said, as he dismounted, "how rude of me. I'm Evie's father-in-law. You can call me Julian." Julian shot a glance over at James to tell him not to use last names right here and now. "If you would allow me, I'll escort you to, um, your kin."

"My name is James, and this is my wife, Leah. Do you happen to have some water? Mr. Short over there seems to think all the water in the creek belongs to him," James said with unveiled disgust.

Julian wordlessly untied the canteen from the back of his saddle and put the strap in James's hand. "Give me a moment, please," he said, then turned around sharply.

*The small crowd Richard 'Dick' Short had attracted was starting to dissipate, but that wasn't what Julian wanted. He wanted to make a scene, to draw everyone's attention to the problems the angry man kept creating. He had nearly caused his partner, José, to be killed earlier in the year and now was trying to wreak havoc on Evie's family, too.*

"This has got to stop right now," he said, storming up to the trouble maker, grabbing him by the shoulder to turn him around, practically yelling in the crazy man's face.

Dick kept backing away, but Julian moved forward, continuing his verbal attack. "You are being more than rude to newcomers and visitors to this area. You have attempted to extort goods from these two people who wanted nothing more than to get a drink of water from God's creek. You do not own this property. You claim anyone new to this area is from the devil. If you knew your Bible, you would know you are supposed to love your neighbor, not threaten him. Now, if you do not cease and desist, we, the good citizens of Gibsonville and the surrounding areas, will have you forcefully removed from North Carolina and returned to England where the constables will take care of you and your lies and extortion. Do I make myself clear?"

Before Dick even had a chance to reply, the crowd responded. There were cheers and 'you tell 'im's' from the gathering that had regrouped when Julian started his tirade.

Julian wasn't distracted by their presence, although he was aware of them. He was still face to face with the man who he could truly say he despised.

"Uh, all right," Richard Short squeaked out. He paused, then asked, shoulders narrowed and face low, totally intimidated, "Can I go now?"

"You can go all the way back to England or Canada or…or hell, for all I care. Just don't *ever* threaten anyone again or say that they're from the devil, or you will have to deal with me. Do you understand?" Julian's face was bright red from anger, although the heat didn't help much. He turned away from the cowering excuse for a man, paused, then turned back to face him. "Is that your wagon?" he asked sharply.

"Yes," Dick drawled, afraid of what Julian wanted.

"Good. I'll be borrowing it for a bit. That is, if you don't mind." Julian said sarcastically, looking down his nose, as he finished his thinly veiled demand, daring the man to deny him the request.

"No, no, that'll be fine," Short said softly. "We can walk home, I guess."

As Dick began walking away from the confrontation, several of the townspeople started jeering—taunting him as he tried to leave peacefully. Julian turned back on the group and eyed the offenders. "It's over for today, folks. Leave the man be. He won't be making the same mistakes." Julian looked over at the man to make sure he had safe exit, then added, "Will you, Mr. Short?"

Dick didn't say a word, but turned and nodded to Julian. He took off his hat again and gave a quick, short bow to both James and Leah. "Have a safe journey," he mumbled, then turned back to scurry into the trees, now wanting to be invisible to the crowd he had caused to gather. "Come on, Harvey," he called to the entity that no one but he could see, "let's go home."

ЖѲЖ

"So you're Evie's kin then?" asked Julian.

Leah, still shaking from nerves, managed a nod, but wasn't ready to talk yet.

"Well, you two look to have had a long walk. Would you care for a ride? It might be a bit rough, though. It would be better if we had straw to cushion the bumps, but by using his wagon, we can be at Evie's in a couple hours. It would take a lot longer if you walked." Julian noticed that James was clutching the post with one hand, the other around his wife for additional support, and frowned. "That is, if you could even make it. You

354

look a little worse for wear. Can you get into the back of the wagon by yourself, or would you like help?"

Leah helped James to the rear of the wagon, then stood back. He leaned over at the waist and pulled himself in, crawling and crabbing his way to the shade of the single plank driver's seat. He rolled over, then lay his head back in exhaustion. "This is good for me," he panted, both proud and happy that he had made the transition unassisted.

"Would you like to ride in front with me or in the back with your husband?" Julian asked, offering his hand to help her onto the bench seat, never taking his eyes from her face. "I'm sorry for staring. It's just the family resemblance is so striking. And that dress... It looks just like the one she was wearing when...when she *left* last month."

Leah ignored the last part of his observation, but did answer his question. "I'll ride in back, but do you happen to have anything to eat? As you noticed, it's been a long walk, and we're not used to the heat."

"Excuse my bad manners. I just happen to have a small lunch. I was sent to town to purchase some salt and sugar, but it appears that Mr. Gibson has left for the day. I'll need to make a stop at the Donaldson's before returning to the Pomeroy homestead. Hopefully, I can borrow those items from them. You see, Evie's father-in-law, Jody Pomeroy, was severely injured. Sarah—his wife, who happens to be a healer—said she needed the salt and sugar to make a type of tonic."

"Electrolyte solution," Leah said. "Tell me, did Jody lose a lot of blood?"

"Yes," Julian said, but didn't elaborate. He reached into his knapsack and pulled out a bundle and a bottle. "Here is some very fine ale and a sort of sandwich."

Leah yanked the plug out of the ale, took a pull from it, and then offered the drink to James. "Not too much at once now," she warned, then took back the bottle. She unwrapped the cloth covering on the sandwich. "Hey, a burrito! Here, have some," and offered it to James first.

He sniffed it. "Oh, wow! Manna from heaven," then savored a big bite of the tortilla-wrapped ham and cheese sandwich. He handed it back to Leah who took a double-sized bite herself.

She used the chewing time to figure out how much she should say to the man she recognized as Lord Julian Hart. His likeness to the portrait wasn't exact, but was close enough, taking into account the shocked look on the man's face when James had asked him his name. Yes, she was sure that the man hitching his horse to the back of the wagon was her new grandfather.

The fluids and quick calories cleared Leah's head. Now she knew what to say. "Before we take off, Julian, I want you to know that we don't need to make a stop anywhere. I have everything we need here." She patted her bag. "Don't worry about our comfort, either. Just go as fast as the horse will take us. There'll be time to take our ease after we see to Jody's needs."

"But...but," Julian stammered, "Sarah was specific about her need for the salt and sugar."

"Oh, I'm sure she was, but she didn't expect me to come today, now, did she? Trust me, please?"

"You'd be wise to trust her, Julian," James said. "And please hurry. I have a lot to ask you when we get settled."

"Speaking of settled," Julian said, "if you're settled in and ready, we'll see how fast Mr. Short's horse can pull this wagon."

"Wagons! Ho!" Leah shouted. Julian turned around and looked at her as if she were crazy. "Uh, we're ready," she amended meekly, realizing that she probably *did* appear crazy. She scooted down next to James, and held him close.

They were on their way home—to her mother.

Finally.

### ***59 A New Donor

Jenny's squeals and hollering alerted Wallace that company was coming. He set down the hoe next to the baskets filled with peppers and tomatoes at the garden gate. He could see Papa—Julian—driving someone else's wagon in at a fast clip. He was in a hurry about something. Hopefully it wasn't more bad news.

ЖЖЖ

Everyone in the family had been stressed for the last two days. It didn't appear that Father—Jody—was going to live until nightfall. The gash to the femoral artery hadn't killed him, but he had lost so much blood that his heartbeat was erratic.

Sarah had done everything she could. "I feel so helpless. All he needs is one, maybe two units of blood, then his heart would beat normally again. As it is now, he's running on almost empty. His major organs are failing. It's just a matter of time," she said, and bit her bottom lip, the sadness in her face saying what her words could not.

She looked around at everything in the room. The rustic lifestyle never bothered her before. But now, everything was irritating her. Her mood changed quickly from desperation to anger to rage. "What did we do to deserve this? We were just trying to give people a chance at freedom. We never fought from a sense of greed or hate. We only wanted to help make a country where we were free to rule ourselves. And now look. He's dying and there's not a…a blasted thing we can do about it!"

"There is something we can do," I said. "'When two or more are gathered in My name, I'll be there' the Lord said. I know we've all been praying—at least, I know I sure have—but let's all hold hands and pray together. I *do* believe in miracles, and all we have to do is ask for one."

"*All* we have to do?" Sarah screamed. "You act as if…" Sarah felt Jody's hand on her thigh. He didn't have the strength to speak, at least loud enough to be heard. He barely had enough energy to open his eyes, but managed a flutter, ending his tacit communication by squeezing his eyes tightly. He didn't want to die. Maybe she should see if the group prayer would work.

"I'll go get Wallace," I said. "I want everyone—including Jenny and the babies—here for this." *I was determined that I wouldn't disappoint her or Jody. This was going to work!*

I rushed outside and saw Wallace tending to a strange horse and wagon—at least, I had never seen them before. As he moved aside, I saw that Julian was with him and there were others, too. Well, they would either have to wait to take care of whatever business they had, or join the prayer circle, preferably the latter. I picked up my skirts and ran to the little group. We didn't have any time to spare.

"Julian, Wallace, come quick, and bring your friends, too. It's Jody. This can't wait, and I want all of us there."

Julian looked as if someone had just punched him in the stomach. He literally bent over forward and clutched his midsection. I moved in to hold him. "Julian, I want all of us there to pray for him. I will not allow...believe...whatever...that he is going to die. It can't happen, not now. We need a miracle. Come on everyone," I called out around him, not bothering to see who our visitors were. It didn't matter. Nothing mattered but Jody's healing right now.

I heard one of the babies crying, probably Wren. I picked up my skirts again and ran back to the house, wishing once again that I could wear shorts or slacks or even a shorter skirt. Fashion, bah! Why weren't women allowed to have functional clothes in this time?

It was Wren, and Sarah had picked her up and was pulling back her clout to make sure she wasn't too wet for me to hold. "Here," she said, and handed her to me. "She's dry enough, but hungry. Who's out there?"

"It's Julian and some other people. Shoot, I didn't even look to see who they were."

I unbuttoned my dress and held Wren to my breast. I closed my eyes for that initial moment when the mixed sensations of bliss and discomfort merged into that feeling with no name—the one every nursing mother knew—the joining that indicated the baby had latched on and milk was flowing, binding the two as one, ex-utero. It *was* possible to talk at that moment, but I chose not to. I always disassociated myself from the rest of the world until my body and my baby's got in sync with the feeding.

I composed myself and looked over at Jody. He was so gray. It had to be because he was out of blood. I had seen his clothes when the men brought him back. They were mottled dark brown, stiff with dried blood, and had to be cut off.

Sarah blamed herself for not going with him that day. He had told her to stay with me. I said I was fine, that Wallace was here with me, but Jody insisted Sarah stay home. It was a simple trip. He was just escorting two young recruits to their home and family.

The ambush was motivated by greed only. The men were bandits, not even fighting for a cause. They wanted the horses and anything else of value that Jody and the two young patriots had. Well, they soon found out that the men didn't have anything of worth, and only two of the three horses could be captured. No one could ride Aries but Wallace or Jody. The spirited stallion kicked one robber and bit another, and that infuriated them even more than the lack of spoils.

Jody tried to talk to them, to tell them that if they needed food, he could help. But they didn't want charity—they wanted gold and horses. And if they couldn't have Aries, then no one could. Jody stood in front of his steed, trying to keep them from goring his horse with their bayonets, begging them to leave him alone, but they were insistent.

Two of them stabbed at once. They both missed their target, and Aries escaped into the woods, unscathed. The one man probably hadn't meant to stab Jody, but the other could care less. Either way, the three robbers bolted at the sight of his gushing wound, leaving the scene immediately with nothing but the two nags and the fear that no one else would be by for them to rob.

Jody's two associates didn't know what to do. Aries had run off, and their two horses were now in the possession of the highwaymen. They started to chase the robbers, but Jody called them back—they couldn't catch them on foot.

*Jody covered the wound with his kerchief, then wrapped his belt around it. He couldn't secure it snuggly, though—the notches weren't close enough. The gash was deep, but not spurting. He knew what was going on. He had seen a good friend die from an injury just like it. He jerked on the belt again and managed to tuck the free end in, creating a haphazard knot that he hoped would last until he got home to Sarah, that horrific memory giving him a needed shot of what she called adrenaline. His only chance was to keep the belt secured, keep direct pressure on his wound, but he lost consciousness before he could tell them what to do.*

The two young soldiers hoisted him up, supporting him with their shoulders, and half-carried, half-dragged him home. They thought that getting him back to Sarah quickly was the best thing to do. Unfortunately, the jostling loosened the belt which caused more blood to be lost, weakening Jody further.

That was the day before yesterday.

"If I had been there, I could have staunched the flow. It would still be serious, but not fate...fatal. Oh, God, NO!" she screamed. She had been with Jody when he was near death before, but never felt this out of control. "How many times do we have to go through this?" she asked of no one but God.

I heard the scrambling of several people rushing toward the steps. It looked as if our company had accepted my invitation to pray for a miracle.

"Mommy! Mommy! Someone's here and she looks just like you. She's even wearing your dress!" shouted Jenny, as she burst through the door.

*I was glad I was sitting down when she entered. My daughter, Leah, had just followed Jenny through the doorway. But she and the other newcomer to the neighborhood had eyes only for Jody. I sat in the corner, bug-eyed with shock, and tried not to hyperventilate.*

"Hi, the little girl here said you were praying for a miracle. One miracle, coming up! Oh, but I'm going to need your help." Leah was addressing Sarah, but Sarah was mute—stunned and unresponsive.

*I knew what she was reacting to. Besides looking so much like me, Leah was wearing the dress she had helped me make, the one that I had on when I 'went back' to the 21st century two weeks ago. The hospital had kept my dress. I returned home to the 18th century wearing a pink terry cloth robe over two hospital-issued cotton gowns. Evidently someone had seen fit to give Leah my clothes. And probably my smartphone, too. That meant she may have—just might have—seen the little movie that Sarah, Jody, and I had accidentally recorded while I was still pregnant.*

Leah knew how to get Sarah out of her daze, and it wasn't with words. "James, hand me my bag, please," she asked.

*James Melbourne! Leah had come back through time with James Melbourne, the man I met in that Greensboro café the same day I met Master Simon, nearly a year ago. I felt as if I was in an IMAX movie theater and everything around me was larger than life. It certainly was stranger than the life I had grown up in—or even one that I had read about.*

James had eyes for no one and nothing but Leah and the situation she was trying to resolve—saving the life of Jody Pomeroy. Leah pulled out the coil of flexible tubing and the small bottle with the hollow needles in it. Sarah's eyes got huge!

Leah smiled and said, "Okay, Doc, it's showtime! Wash up. I can't do this by myself. I'm the donor."

"What?" Evidently James hadn't expected that. "But...but..." he stuttered.

I didn't know what had happened to him, but he was extremely pale and appeared to be leaning against the wall by necessity.

Leah noticed it, too. "Sit down," she said in a clinical tone. She was in attending nurse mode. "You just gave blood and need to wait a week before you give any more, 72 hours, at the least. I'm O negative, too. And if I can't give enough," she looked over and saw me sitting on the stool with the nursing baby at my breast, "I know someone else with the same blood type. Hi," she said, with a smile that would make the Mona Lisa jealous.

I uttered a weak, "Hi," in return, but didn't move, too stunned to say more.

Leah bounced back to head nurse mode. "It's a good thing he's on the floor already. Can we move that table over here, men? I need to lie down and be higher than he is for this."

Julian and Wallace picked up the table and brought it next to Jody. Now it was Sarah's turn to direct the action.

"Wallace, bring me that alcohol, and Julian, would you bring this lady something to drink? Milk would be good." She turned to Leah who was situating herself on the table. "Are you ready for this? It's been a while since I've started an IV, and I've never done a live transfusion."

"I'm not going to change my mind, so get started." Leah looked down at the gray shell of a man who was to be the recipient of her life-giving blood. "Give him all he needs. Now is the time to start praying, everyone."

Wallace walked over to me, Jenny holding onto his elbow. Julian picked up Judah from of the playpen and made his way into the crowded corner. The baby was sound asleep—I think he picked him up just to have someone to hold. Whether it was out of love, hope, or for security, it didn't matter. It was heart-warming, and a good way to bring more love into our circle.

Wallace looked over at the medical procedure getting underway, his father lying on the ground, only a faint rise of his chest showing that there was any life left in the apparent corpse. "Lord, help them, please," he prayed earnestly. "Help my father and those who are attending to him. My wife says she knows You will work a miracle if we ask, and Lord, we are all asking humbly, most humbly. In Jesus's name, Amen."

"I'm looking for a miracle, I expect the impossible, I feel the intangible, I see the invisible,"[1] I started singing a song that came from deep inside my core. I didn't remember where I had heard it and didn't know the words to sing. They just came out of my mouth, softly at first, and then with conviction. When I got to the chorus the second time, everyone who could talk in our little corner was singing, "Just believe and receive it, God will perform it today, hey, hey, hey. Just believe and receive it, God will perform it today."

It was an intimate, late-18th century gospel revival. The Spirit was with us and the dread had left. We all knew—felt all the way down to the roots of our toenails and teeth—that everything was going to be fine. At least I did, and by the smiles on Julian and Wallace's faces, they did, too. Jenny was still singing her little 'God will perform it today. Hey! Hey! Hey!' and dancing a little Indian healing dance in front of the door. Judah and Leonardo were now both wide awake, and although I knew they were 'crying,' it felt as if they, too, were rejoicing at the healing miracle.

I handed bright-eyed Wren to Wallace, and he passed me Leonardo to feed. Julian was doing a little waltz with Judah, singing softly to him, tears of pure joy spilling out of the corners of his eyes. I doubt Julian knew what the medical procedure was, but he was caught up in the spirit of hope and thanksgiving for the miracle we had all accepted.

I stood up and walked over to the table. Leah was looking down, watching Jody as the color returned to his skin. I bent over and gave her a kiss on the top of her head. She changed focus, turned her head around, and tipped it back to look up at me.

"Surprised to see me?" she asked.

---

[1] "I'm Looking for a Miracle," by The Clark Sisters

"That's a big ten-four," I replied. "Hey, how about saving a little of that juice for yourself and letting me give Jody a bit of *moi*? Sarah, about how much do you think she's given?"

Sarah pinched off the tubing in Leah's arm and said, "Enough. Here, hold this." She pressed a gauze patch to the spot where she had pulled out the IV needle. I took over applying pressure, and she clamped Jody's end of the tubing, taping it to his arm. She looked up at me and said, "He's not out of the woods yet. There's a real chance that his kidneys have failed. We could give him more blood, but I think we had better wait for a few hours. It might not make any difference."

"Sarah, I can fix the kidneys, and anything else inside that's broke," I said softly. Leah heard me and stared up at me incredulously, mouth hanging open in shock. "Leah, look at me. Don't I look a little different than last year?" I saw the men and babies were still in the corner. "Hey, everyone," I said brightly, "why don't you go out and get some fresh air? And send some of it in here, too, please."

"All right," popped up Jenny, "here it comes." She stood in the doorway, turned and sucked in air from the outside, then turned around and blew it into the house. "Is that better?" she asked.

"Yes, that's enough for now. Thank you. Would you go help your father outside? I think he has some weeds he wants you to pull." No matter what else needed to be done around our place, there were always weeds to pull. Jenny was still young and eager enough that she would do anything I asked. I appreciated it for now because I knew it wouldn't—well, probably wouldn't—last.

Wallace and Julian picked up on my request for privacy and walked outside. Judah had fallen back asleep and Wallace took Leo from me. James moved away from the wall. He had stayed apart from the group of men, me, and the children, and left Sarah and Leah to their ministrations with Jody. He didn't look too good.

"Here." I handed him the rest of the milk that Leah hadn't drunk. "When was the last time you had something to eat?"

"I ate half a sandwich wrap a couple hours ago on the way in. I'll be okay. Dani, what did you mean when you said you could fix Jody's kidneys or anything else inside of him that was broken?"

Sarah was seated on the floor, holding Jody's hand. "Yes, what did you mean? And why did he call you Dani? Is that your name?"

"Yes, but I prefer Evie," I said softly. I immediately changed the subject. "Remember that little blue bottle I told you was more precious than diamonds or gold? Well, Master Simon had given me an overdose of it, and that's what rewound my whole body chemistry, essentially making me grow younger. I was supposed to have just a few drops to mend my broken back and fractured skull, but Simon said I accidentally drank too much. It fixed

362

everything that was broken, all right, but made my body about forty years younger, and evidently acted like a fertility drug, too. We can give a little to Jody. I'm pretty sure it will seek out and repair any damaged organs. I don't know if it will make him younger at the same time, though." I turned to Sarah. "You might want to take a drop or two for yourself, just in case."

Sarah patted Jody's hand and stood up, walked to the hearth and pulled out a stone, or rather a stone façade. I had told her to put it in a safe place and she had. I didn't even know about her little secret stash spot. "Here," she said, "you do the dosing."

I took the bottle and turned it around, examining it closely for the first time. It was made from perfectly cut glass or some jewel—cobalt glass, probably. I pulled out the stopper and saw it had a glass rod attached; perfect for use as a dropper. I pushed the top back in and knelt next to Jody. He did look better, but resembled a wrecked car with a new paint job. I just hoped Master Simon's magical Fountain of Youth elixir would put his engine and transmission back in good working order. "Ready?" I asked.

Jody opened one eye and asked, "Yer not gonna stick any more needles in me, are ye?"

"No, I hadn't planned on it. Why? Do you want a few more?" I asked in jest.

"hmph," he replied weakly. "No, although I dinna think I could do anythin' to stop ye if ye did. This isna gonna give me gas, is it? I'm feelin'," he shifted his position, "a bit uncomfortable." Jody had regained lots of color, but his breathing was still shallow. He was twitching, which I took as a good sign—he was able to move unassisted.

"Here, open up," I said.

I administered three drops, then watched him. I couldn't see any difference. "You're still a big man, no matter how much blood you lost or had put back into you. Here, take two more."

There were no immediate results, and I didn't know what I was looking for. "Sarah, if he gets five, you need two, no, three. At least you can tell me what's going on. I'm pretty sure this isn't poison." Jody glared at me. That was another good sign—he could give me 'the look.'

Sarah leaned towards me, stuck out her tongue, and let me give her three drops. "What I meant to say is that Simon apparently uses this stuff all the time to stay young. Ugh, I'm glad he didn't have a larger bottle when he accidentally overdosed me. I'd hate to wind up as a baby again."

"Why not?" asked Jody. "Food brought to ye when ye squalled, no chores to do, no worries…"

"Sitting in poopy diapers, teething, going through puberty again… Uh, no thanks. Hey, you must be feeling better. You're talking and making dumb jokes again."

Sarah suddenly jumped and squealed for no apparent reason, or at least any reason that I could see. Then I saw the glimmer in Jody's eyes and his hand moved.

"Oh, like that, is it?" I asked. "Sarah, don't let him do too much too soon. I think he needs to rest for a while for the *juice* to work.

Sarah asked Jody, "Would you rather get back in our bed?" He seemed stronger already and could probably walk to it, although he'd need help.

Jody settled back into the impromptu bed on the floor. "No, I'll bide fine here. Let the lad take the bed. He looks like he's lost a lot of blood, too. Are ye ailin', lad?" he asked, his voice now stronger and very concerned.

"No and yes, or yes and no," James answered, befuddled, shaking his head slightly, as if it would help clarify his thoughts. Leah started to speak for him, but he stopped her with a glance. He continued, slowly and with determination. "No, I'm not ailin', and I have not been wounded either, but, yes, I lost a lot of blood. I lost it in the same way Leah just did, but I think I lost more. At least, she doesn't look as bad as I feel." He sighed, then looked longingly at the bed. "I think I will take you up on the offer of the bed, though."

James moved gingerly from his slumped position against the wall towards the overstuffed bed, holding onto the table and chair back on the way. He clutched the post at the head of the bed, and gently lowered himself, emitting an audible, "aww," as he laid back, his feet still on the ground.

"Don't worry about the boots," said Sarah. He lifted his feet and swung his body around, placing his slightly dusty shoes at the foot of the bed.

Leah came over and urged him to sit up a little. "Let me get the pillow under your head."

He grinned at her, remembering the pillow fights they had had. "Not this time," she whispered. She knew what he was thinking by the grin on his face. "I'll get you when you're not expecting it," she added, as she adjusted his neck and shoulders.

"Would you like a bite to eat first?" Sarah was back and had a plate with a tortilla wrapped around a thick slice of cheese.

James rolled over onto his side and precariously placed the plate on the straw-filled mattress. He sniffed it in anticipation, then took a big, oversized bite, as if he didn't get anything to eat now, he'd never get another chance at sustenance again. He chewed slowly and thoroughly, his eyes closed, alone in his little world of bliss, consuming the flour and lard wrapped chunk of enzymed cow fat.

"Don't mind him," Leah remarked, as she headed to a kitchen chair. "It's been a while since he's had much to eat, and besides the loss of blood, it's been a long walk. That and he's handled quite a few other stresses."

Leah looked longingly at the food and wondered if it would be rude to ask for something for herself. Well, if she were home with her parents back in Arizona, she'd ask. "Can I have…? Oh, thank you," she said when she saw that Sarah had prepared one for her, too. It felt like she was finally where she belonged—with home and family, a simply glorious sensation.

"How are you feeling, Sarah?" I asked, as I put my hand on her forehead. I couldn't see any physical changes in her and didn't know if I would. Jody was slumbering, a smile of peace stretched across his stubble-bearded face. "Do you have numb tongue or chills? Do you feel stronger or younger? I know I didn't feel any changes as they occurred. But then again, I had amnesia back then. I still can't figure that one out."

Sarah was only half listening to me babble about possible side effects and the memory loss that had accompanied my ingestion of the Fountain of Youth water. She looked away from her spouse who, only moments ago, was inches from death. She looked towards the three of us. "I think I'll just lie down next to my husband and take a nap with him," she said with a beatific smile on her face. "Thank you," she said, and nodded to Leah, "and thank you," she said looking at me, "for having such a wonderful, thoughtful daughter. We have lots to talk about…but, later. Now I'm getting tired, too."

### ***60 Who Are You?

Leah was glowing with happiness, but also pale. "Leah, why don't you lie down next to your husband? You look like you could use a nap, too."

She shoved the last bite of sandwich into her mouth, gave me a chipmunk-cheeked smile of gratitude, and made her way towards James, testing each step—as if she had blisters on her soles—grasping the footboard to steady herself. Once on the other side of the bed, she rolled in next to him, emitting a contented moan.

I knew she was young and in good shape, but she had also donated more than the usual one pint of blood to her new kin—her body needed recharging, too. I didn't know who had benefited from James's blood transfusion, but that story could wait. They were both going to be here for quite a while. God willing. There would be time for narratives and revelations later.

I had written the letter to James only last week—or so it seemed. I sent it with Mac Donaldson when he went to the newly renamed port of Washington. "Send it on the next ship sailing to London. Make sure the captain knows that it's for Lord Anthony Melbourne, care of Mrs. White's Chocolate House." Hopefully a British title still held some sway, and a bribe wasn't needed on this end to insure its delivery. I was certain he'd get one on the other end—or at least, I hoped he believed he would. We still didn't have any hard currency, and bribing with what little we had wouldn't impress a ship's captain.

We didn't have proper sealing wax either, so I added a dollop of some of Sarah's best beeswax, and imprinted the Pegasus side of my pendant into it. I didn't know for sure whether Julian's brother Anthony belonged to 'The Club' or not. I didn't ask Julian about it because I didn't want him involved in my plan. There might be possible repercussions for him or his family, either right away or further on down the line, generations into the future. However, I *was* sure that someone at The Club would know who Lord Anthony Melbourne was and would forward the double-sealed letter to him out of a sense of honor.

*'Please keep this in your safe at your London home with the attached note,'* I wrote on the outside letter. *'It has to do with your family. Your integrity comes with the highest recommendation. I trust my instructions will be followed. Evie Pomeroy-Hart.'*

So, apparently the letter made it—or will make it, I reminded myself. The week or two that had passed since I sent it hadn't even been long enough for the ship to leave port, much less to arrive in England. *I'll have to make sure to keep up with the letter writing, too, no matter what happens. I'll need to put substance to my good intentions so I don't ruin this whole timeline thing-a-majigger. I'll ask James and Leah later how many letters they received so I can make sure to write at least that many. I'd rather err on the side of having written too many letters than not enough. Some of them are sure to be lost over the years and over the water to England.*

*Now, the question is, when I write, do I refer to their presence here in this timeline or not?*

*That's too much to think about now. All of a sudden, I'm tired. I want to lie down, too. I think I hear that family tree calling me, telling me that I deserve a break, too—come spend some time in my shade.*

Ж ЖЖ

My little spontaneous nap was refreshing, although a bit hard on my lower spine. At least when I slept flat on my back, I was less likely to leak milk. When I relaxed and curled up on my side, the pressure of one heavy breast on top of the other was enough to start lactation. It seemed as if I was always stained, crusty, and heavily perfumed with eau de body odor. Ugh. I've never cared about riches or material goods as a rule, but a change of clothing would be nice—one outfit to wear and one to wash. Maybe we'll have a bumper corn crop this year, with a few bushels left over to barter for a bolt or two of cloth.

I was distracted from musing about an expanded wardrobe by rustling noises coming from inside the house. It sounded as if my daughter and new son-in-law were up and about. I peeked through the open doorway and saw Leah seated, bent over James, stroking his forehead, smiling with the love and devotion of a woman who was proud of her man.

"Come on outside so we don't wake Jody and Sarah. I want to get caught up with what's been going on with you two."

Leah stood back while James swung his feet over the side of the bed and carefully tested his legs before he stood, keeping one hand on the bedpost. The two moseyed to the doorway, blinking away the brightness of the afternoon sun, then helped each other sit on the porch bench, like an old married couple.

"Is that a wedding ring I see on your finger, little girl?"

"Yes, it is." James leaned over and kissed his weak but radiant bride on her rosy cheek. "She's Mrs. Melbourne. Now, what kind of place do you have here? We didn't get much of a chance to look around on the way in. The view from lying down in the back of the wagon was, ahem, limited." James craned his neck and surveyed the yard from the bench. "Looks like a nice spread, no matter which century you're in."

Leah stood up for a better view, then suddenly reached out and grasped the porch post to keep from reeling. "I'm okay, I'm okay," she blurted out when she saw the scowl of concern on her husband's face.

James plopped back down on the bench he had half-risen from, pale and breathless with fear at her near fall. "Sit back down—you're not ready to be up and about." He closed his eyes and composed himself before speaking again. "Sorry. It's just that you scared me. You don't realize how much energy there is in blood until it's gone, or rather depleted…"

The babbles of babies and tall people drifted their way, giving him the opportunity to change the subject and lighten the mood. "Hey, why don't we go lie down under that tree—with your siblings, are they?"

"Oh, and isn't that Uncle Julian next to that oversized playpen? Wow, I have at least two little brothers and, hopefully, a sister?" Leah asked.

I watched my middle-est daughter approach the house with grasshopper form and speed, bouncing all over the yard. "Jenny, would you go get that old quilt from the barn and bring it over here, please? We want to make our guests comfortable now, don't we?"

"Yes, Mommy," she chirped, then did a barefoot pirouette and sprinted to the barn. Obviously the heat didn't bother young people as much as it did adults.

"Mommy?" Leah asked, her unblinking eyes wide in shock, her legs weak again. She clutched the porch post closer, but it wasn't enough. "Uh, I think you're right. I'd better sit down before I fall down."

James rose to join her, then led her by her elbow to the base of the big tree, affording her a good view of her new siblings. He leaned his back against the trunk for support, planted his feet firmly for further stability, and helped lower her to a seated position. "There, now that's better."

"Okay, now you, too—down here," she said, patting the ground next to her. "I don't want you falling down, either."

"Yes, dear, anything you say, dear," he replied with mock sarcasm and a smile. Their journey was over, and so apparently were all the crises. They could finally relax.

She spread her skirt down and around her, tucking the fullness under her knees. "How did you get one that old?" Leah said, referring to Jenny. "You sure work fast, Mom."

"Mom? Is she your mother, too?" asked Jenny, who had just popped up beside Leah.

"Jesus, you scared me!" Leah exclaimed without thinking. She didn't know what else to add, so just played the frightened dame, fanning herself with her hand to delay an answer, hoping to appear as if she was fighting a case of the 'vapors.'

"Are you okay?" Jenny asked with an exaggerated frown of concern. Leah nodded, her lips tightly pressed together to keep from gasping in shock.

Jenny's smile returned and she repeated her question. "Okay, so is she your mother, too?" The little girl was relentless.

Leah took a deep breath then grinned ear to ear as she realized she had an answer—a truthful answer—for her little sister. "I lost my mother almost a year ago. She looked a lot like your mommy. Is it okay if I call her Mom, too? I mean, it would make me feel better if I could."

"Okay. I'm adopted. You can be adopted, too. He's my father," she said, pointing to the tall, good looking man coming up the path with a basket full of big, red tomatoes. "He can 'dopt you, too, if you want. Then you'll be my big sister!"

"Okay, I'll let your father adopt me, too," Leah said, conveniently leaving out that she didn't need to be adopted by her mother—'Mommy' already was her mother.

"Hey!" Jenny blurted out, obviously just coming to a grand conclusion. "Do you know why you're here? I do."

Leah decided to play along with her game rather than explain that she knew—or at least, had a good idea—why. "Why am I here?" she asked, totally enthralled with the girl. The little blond bubble of energy was an absolute joy.

"Because I prayed for you," Jenny said succinctly. "I prayed for a mother and father, and I got them. The little brothers and sister were just extra. I didn't know I wanted them, really—at least that many—until I saw them. Then I wanted them real bad. But I always wanted a big sister. I thought that God had given me so much after I got Mommy and Daddy and the babies that it was okay that I didn't get a big sister, but now you're here and you're my sister and we can do stuff together and you can help me with the babies and pulling weeds and we can fix each other's hair, but really..." Jenny paused for a breath after her long explanation. Now she was pondering, trying to figure out whether she should say anything else to her brand new family member. "I didn't expect you to be so big and old. Do you have a baby yet?"

"Uh, no, I just got married last week. Maybe Mom will let me help her so I can get used to babies gradually. I never had a little brother or sister before."

Leah was already enjoying her big sister role. She looked up and saw the men—Julian and the man who must be Wallace—watching their little repartee with unbridled delight. They sat down on the porch steps, a few feet awayfrom her. She caught Wallace's eye and said, "So you're my father then?"

Wallace gulped hard, shifted his eyes to me, and said, "Guilty as charged."

James corrected him, "With Leah that would be blessed beyond your grandest expectations. And I'm your son-in-law, James Melbourne."

"Melbourne?" the two men gasped in unison.

"Lord James Ignatius Melbourne, at your service," he said with a nod.

Wallace blanched at the name, and then looked over at his father, Julian. He was just as shocked as Wallace, and had spilled his cup of water in his lap, belatedly jumping up as the fluid soaked into the front of his pants.

"Excuse me for not rising," James said, "but I'm a little worse for the wear and tear of the trip and all the excitement we encountered therein. Perhaps you know of my *kin*, Anthony Melbourne of London?"

Both men looked as if they were the ones who had just donated blood. They were pale, all the way down to their hands which, he noticed, had gone limp at their sides with shock. James savored the surprised look on the men's faces. Uncle Julian in the flesh. Finally.

He continued, "You do know about the *long distance* we traveled, correct? That would be the same *distance* traveled as your wife did," he said, nodding to Wallace, "and your daughter-in-law," he nodded to Julian, "plus about one more year…um…shall we call it a measure?"

Both men were still staring, but managed to add a synchronized slow nod of understanding to their voiceless affirmation. They understood that he and Leah had just traveled from the future to be with them here in the late 18th century.

James reached into his pocket and pulled out his hemp wallet. "Julian, would you come here for a moment, please?"

Julian set his empty cup on the porch and walked the few steps to James. "Here." James put a laminated color photograph in his hand, "This reproduction of a portrait has been in my family for *years*. I never met the man—until today—but he has always been my favorite uncle."

Julian studied the photograph of the oil portrait he had sat for ten years earlier. He looked at James, then back at the photo, running the heavy plastic laminate between his thumb and forefinger, in awe of the material. He collected his wits, and replied with a wry smile, "I still don't think the man got my nose right. I don't have a bend in it like that, I'm sure." He rubbed the bridge of his nose with one hand and gave the photo back to James. "I hope I can live up to your expectations," he said, now totally composed and added with a smile, "nephew."

James took the photo, then motioned for Wallace to come look at it, too. Wallace had been eyeing their little exchange and was only slightly hesitant to look at the object of interest. He inspected the picture, glanced up at his father, then back at the representation.

"I agree and disagree," he said, then waited to make sure he had the men's attention. "Yes, I agree the nose is not a true representation of your appearance. I remember when you sat for this. Monsieur Lévesque added the bump to your nose. When I told him that you had a very nice, straight nose, he said that all good men had a bend in the nose, to portray you otherwise would be dishonoring you for eternity. However, I disagree on the other part. James is not only your nephew; he is my son, and therefore your grandson. Welcome to the family." Wallace bent over and shook James's hand heartily, then laughed softly, "son."

"Now, let me get this right about names. You're..." James wanted to make sure he didn't make a fool of himself by assuming a name. With so many stepchildren and adoptions, he almost needed a genealogical chart to get everyone's name straight.

"Wallace Joseph Pomeroy-Hart. I gave up my birth name and the hereditary title to stay here with my real family. The last name is to reflect my two fathers, Joseph—that would be Jody—Pomeroy and Julian Hart."

"And you probably know me better than I would feel comfortable with. I'm Julian Wallace Hart, but I don't live here. Our place is a few miles down the road. We passed it on the way here, but the buildings are amongst the trees and are well-hidden."

"Our?" James asked. "Are you married? I never read...er...rather, nothing was ever recorded... Oh, shit..."

"No, I am not married. I have a partner and we raise Andalusian horses and Angora goats. I never remarried after my wife died, God rest her soul."

"Sorry, I didn't mean... Oh, excuse me. I think I'll just shut up. I seem to be suffering from brain loss on top of blood loss."

Leah patted his hand, trying to reassure him that all was well, then shut her eyes again, softly 'hmm-ing' in peace.

The men all endured an awkward silence until Jenny came over to sit on Wallace's long-legged lap. She snuggled under her father's chin, and tickled him with a piece of grass. Leah looked up. She could only wonder when she had been adopted. She appeared to be about ten, and normally would have been too old for lap-sitting, but seemed to have the emotional age of a six-year-old.

"What's for dinner?" Jenny asked.

Wallace quickly snatched the grass from her and used it to return the tickles, making her squirm and giggle. "Whatever you're fixing," he said, and poked her in the ribs. "Isn't it your turn to cook?" he teased.

"Well, we could have tomato pie—that is, if we had the pie crust. Or we could have smashed tomatoes or tomato soup or..."

"Spaghetti?" Leah suggested. "Do you have any noodles, onions, and a few spices?"

"What's s'ghetti?"

I popped in, "That's a dish your sister is a master chef at creating. Yes, Leah, we have all the ingredients, although you'll have to make the pasta from scratch. Jenny, go get the big bowl and the smasher."

Jenny dashed into the house. After a minute of clanging and clashing, she returned with a huge bowl and a heavy wooden mallet with crosshatch grooves carved into the top of the head, 'the smasher.'

"Can Jenny cut up onions or should I do that?" Leah asked.

"I can do it! I can do it!" Jenny exclaimed, as she ran back into the house for the knife and onion.

"Don't run with the knife, dear," I called after her. Sometimes she was too eager!

So Jenny washed, cored, peeled, and smashed the tomatoes, and was allowed to chop onions under Leah's supervision. Wallace brought out two big iron pots and proceeded to set the outside kitchen fire ablaze. Nobody wanted to cook inside at the hearth in the summer. It was either dine on salad or sandwiches, or cook the meal outside, bringing the plates to the porch or into the small kitchen to eat.

"I'll go get the pasta dough started," I volunteered. "I always plan on making extra so I can dry the leftovers for future meals, but I never seem to be able to stay ahead of the game. Sarah's usually the cook, but I help her when I can. When you get to feeling better, you can help, too, right dear?"

"Yes, Mommy," Leah said with a radiant smile. She paused then added, "Do you have any idea how good that feels to say after so long? I mean, I know we weren't close for…um…a while, but when you were *gone,* I realized how much I missed you."

We shared a smile and a warm glow with her revelation, and it had nothing to do with the summer heat and humidity. The quiet peace between the two of us remained for quite a while, then Leah spoke up. "You know, I never thought about *where* we would live when we got here. We both—I think both James and I—were only focused on getting here. We knew we both wanted to stay, but…but…"

Wallace spoke up, "There's plenty of land here to share and even more nearby for expansion…if we ever get the money or trade goods to purchase it. There's still enough summer and autumn left that we can build a house for you two before winter sets in. Actually, my father Jody and I have started on plans for a house for Evie, the children, and me. It might be a good idea to start both at the same time. Or not. I've never built a house, although my father has built several. But not Papa—he's never built one. Oh, I guess this must be confusing to you. I've always called Julian 'Papa' and call Jody 'Father.'"

Leah and James looked at each other. James spoke for the both of them. "Leah and I did a design for a house, too. She visited a house in the desert that was cooled using natural breezes, straw insulation, and a few other tricks. We have some drawings we'd like to share. I'm sure that 'Papa' and 'Father' would like to see them, too. I don't think we'd better use those designations, though."

"Those would be better than calling them grandfather and great-great uncle. That would be difficult, or at least unwise, to explain.

Whichever feels more comfortable; I'm sure it will come naturally in short order. Come on, I know just the place for the two of you to use as temporary sleep quarters. It just needs a little rearranging. Are you up to a short walk?"

"I'll let James go with you," Leah said. "I'm going to stay and help Mom with dinner. Thank You, Lord, for Jenny giving me a way to keep calling her Mom. I don't know what I'd do if I had to call her Dani. Or Evie…or Mrs. Pomeroy-Hart or…or…or. I'd better go sit on the porch now. I think the sun is getting to me. Don't take too long, James. You're not completely up to snuff, either."

James started to escort her back to the house, but Leah put up her hand. "I can make it. Save your steps to go with Wallace." She gave him what she hoped was perceived as a big smile, but knew he could right see through it. She was happy, but she was also scared. Then again, she rationalized, she would be just as frightened starting life as a newlywed in a new town with new relatives, no matter which time era she was in.

Ж ЖЖ

The men walked to the barn in silence. James could tell that Wallace wanted to ask him something, but was either bashful or didn't know how to broach the subject. James was pretty sure he knew what it was, though, so just jumped in with the 'history' lesson.

"Danielle Madigan was her name before she came here. She went by the name Dani. She lived in the Arizona desert—far, far west of here, still part of Mexico, I think—got married, had one daughter—Audie Leah Madigan—stayed married for about twenty years, got divorced, and moved to Alaska—land of the northwest passage. Leah stayed behind in Arizona, went to school, and helped her father during his last months of terminal cancer. She graduated from college with honors as a 'healer,' took a job at a hospital in North Carolina, and was working there when her mother, Dani, came to visit her for a holiday. That was almost a year ago. While there, Dani rescued a strange little man who had been assaulted and robbed of a map. She took him to a little café—that's like a tavern—fed him, and bandaged his wounds. That's where I met her, at the café. An hour or so earlier, I had purchased 'historical documents' from a man. I thought they contained information about my great-great uncle many times over—Lord Julian Wallace Hart…"

James dipped his head at Wallace at this point to make sure he was following the story. His step-father's eyes were glazed, but he nodded back, indicating that he understood it so far.

James continued, "Well, the document I had purchased was an old map, the same one stolen from the strange man Dani was helping. That was Master Simon, by the way. For some reason, Dani…er…Evie wound up following him, or taking him, to the place where she…well…she fell out of the 21st century.

373

"Something happened there. I don't know what and don't know if she knows either. I'm sure Simon—or Master Simon, as he likes to be called—knows, but I haven't seen him around in the last two hundred years or so…"

James looked up to see if Wallace caught his little joke. By the roll of his father-in-law's eyes and quick snort, he had, but didn't care for the break in the story.

"Dani wound up here, in this time, but with a younger body and a severe case of amnesia. Well, pretty severe: from what I understand, all she recalls is that Leah is her daughter." James cleared his throat and looked at the ground, trying to hide his little lie—she also remembered the fictional story *Lost* and many of the characters in it who had become her new family.

James paused for a moment, then looked up and continued. "Well, you know the rest of the story after that better than I do. She spent ten months here—Leah and I still don't know that part of the story, by the way—was shot with a musket, then brought back to a 21st century hospital by Master Simon. There, her daughter Leah, *just happened* to be her nurse—that is, caretaker. And," James struggled to make sure he had the name right this time, "Evie unknowingly left her smartphone—which she had used while here—at the hospital. It had *information* about this era and what she looked like on it. The phone and that same stolen map *just happened* to reappear at the most fortuitous time. They gave us the information and opportunity we needed to come back here. That is, if we chose to do so."

Wallace sat down on the milking stool in the barn and pointed to the short bench next to the inside wall, offering the steadier seat to James. "So, there were too many *just happened's* to be chance—is what you're saying?"

"I don't want you to think I'm saying anything blasphemous, but I believe God wants us to be here. Now. There were just too many *coincidences* involved. Quite a few odd characters are in the mix, too, and maybe we'll get some of that figured out later. But I want you to know that Leah and I never met before two weeks ago, and now we're married. I'm *positive* the Big Man had a hand in that one. She is a wonderful woman. Just like her mother, I'm sure."

"Oh, Evie is a wonderful woman, all right." Wallace said, then was silent—too silent and for too long.

James finally spoke up. "I'm sorry, Wallace. Maybe I told you too much. Sometimes a mystery is easier to handle than a history. She loves you very much. I read the letter she sent. She chose you and this place over the daughter she had known and loved for over twenty years."

"Well, she also had the babies to come back to…," he said softly, still unsure of himself.

"Oh, do *not* doubt yourself. No woman needs that, nor do your children. She said she didn't want to be called Dani. She is *Evie*. She is very much your wife, and this time is where she wants to be. Not many people get a chance to start over again. She wasn't given the option, and from what I knew of her—the old her—she was happy with who she was as an older woman of 60."

"Sixty? Wow…"

"Yeah, wow. Do you realize what a great woman you have? And well, she's a good-looking, foxy lady, too. And besides, you're about 200 years older than she is, so don't worry about the small numbers, all right, *Dad*."

Wallace shook his head and smiled. "I didn't have any children last month, and now I have five plus a son-in-law my age. But you know, they're all great, and I wouldn't trade any one of them for all the crown jewels in Europe. I don't know what I did to deserve such a wonderful wife and family, but they are," Wallace was shaking his head again, his smile comfortable and anxious-free, "definitely a gift from God. Stay put, I'm going to move some of this old straw out of here and put in some fresh bedding for you two. It's not the best arrangement, but the privacy is great."

### ***61 Yer Not Evie

Wallace walked outside into the late afternoon sun to the water trough to wash the straw dust and leaf bits from his face and arms. It had been a quick and simple task to establish his new daughter and son-in-law's overnight accommodations—otherwise known as pitching fresh straw into a cleaned out corner of the barn. His family had increased again, and he couldn't be happier. Now he would have the chance to get acquainted with the daughter Evie had reared in her earlier life, something he never thought possible. Leah must be a wonderful, generous young woman to give up the world she knew to travel back in time to be with her mother. And she had married a distant cousin of his, to boot. He was getting two relatives in one with him.

His new son-in-law, James Melbourne from London, was also the man referred to on that fancy raised-lettered business card Evie had found in her backpack two months ago. She hadn't known the origination of the card when she discovered it. It was a mystery. Rather than fret about the enigma, she had chosen to accept it and not worry about why it was there. She called it the bumblebee. You see, she said, bumblebees could fly, but no one could explain why those fat little insects could stay aloft—much less maneuver so gracefully—with such itty bitty wings. It was a mystery and of no consequence. People got business cards all the time, or so she thought.

So, it turns out that this man—his Uncle Tony Melbourne's great-grandson many times over—and Evie—Dani, back then—were from different parts of the world and had only been visiting North Carolina when they briefly met. Had fate or predestination brought them together? He didn't know nor did he care. What he did know was that this same man was now waiting for him to finish moving hay, leaning against the split rail fence in the shade of the barn. James was still frail, but had offered to help him with the chore. Wallace knew he was just being polite—there was no way he had the strength to handle the task, he was still weak from his journey—but he had offered, and that showed good character. But still, it was such a big shock to have a son-in-law so soon. At this rate, he'd be a grandfather before he turned twenty-five!

The two of them were headed back to the shade of the 'family tree' when they heard the labored breathing. An old horse was being urged up the narrow road by its slumped-shoulder skinny rider, a young boy trotting close beside them.

Wallace knew who it was at once. His jaws clenched tight and his feet stopped, not sure whether he wanted to greet the tanned and disheveled man on the back of the old, swaybacked roan or let him fall on the hard ground and suffer the consequences. But James, as weakened as he was, didn't hesitate. He recognized him, too, and half-ran, half-stumbled up to the horse and the weakened rider.

Ian was back.

"Whoa, there, girl," James said, pulling the nag to a halt. "What are you doing, riding a horse?" he scolded, one hand on the horse's mane, the other on Ian's skinny leg for support. "You're supposed to be back where we left you, resting." He turned and asked the young, dark-haired boy wearing nothing but a breechclout and moccasins, "Wee Ian, why did you let him leave?"

"I couldna have stopped him without hurtin' him more. I even bound him up with that zap cloth Leah left me, but he was squirmin' and wigglin', tryin' so hard to get free, I figured I'd better let him loose. He was leavin', no matter if he had to walk or crawl, so I set him on the mare. I made sure I stayed alongside to protect him, thugh. Not that anyone was left what wanted to hurt him. All of them that he was mad at for that *stuff* they did are deid now. I jest wanted to protect him from fallin' off the horse or doin' somethin' else to hurt hisself ... like now!"

Wee Ian's back had been to his father as he spoke, but he dashed to his father's side as soon as he heard movement. "Dinna I tell ye to let me help ye down?" he groused. "Yer the stubbornest animal I ever did see!"

James moved in behind Wee Ian to assist in the dismount, shadowing the boy's movements, placing his big hands under the father's armpits, guiding him to the ground. Once Ian was off the horse and upright, he backed away and let the son take over as the human crutch for the walk to the house.

*Although James had donated blood to the man, he had never paid much attention to his build. He had noticed Ian was lean when he was lying on the ground next to him, during the transfusion, but hadn't realized until now that he was nearly a skeleton. Either life had been rough on him or he had been rough on life.*

"Ian Kincaid, you ignorant cur!" Leah screamed, as she came running over to the three men and the boy. "What in the *hell* do you think you're doing? You were supposed to stay down for five days."

Leah was twelfth-degree irate, but was quickly at Ian's other elbow, guiding him to the shade of the tree next to the porch. "You lie down and stay down." She turned and hollered toward the house, "Mom, would you bring me some of that milk, stat!"

Ian was bug-eyed. "Who *are* you?" he asked, ashen-faced and breathless.

"I'm your nurse, you idiot!" Leah declared, then snorted in disgust at him. She didn't think it was possible, but his eyes got bigger. She realized that he probably thought that when she said 'nurse,' she meant she was the one who had suckled him. "No, not that kind of nurse! Your...your...your *healer*. Why didn't you stay put? No, never mind. Just shut up and lie back.

377

Damn, it looks like one, maybe two, stitches came out. Have you been spitting up blood?"

Ian panted briefly, then found the strength to speak. "Weel, do ye want me to shut up or answer?"

Leah scowled at him and said, "Answer," then continued to shift his body so his shoulders were propped up securely.

"No, no blood. Who are ye? I mean, yer name?"

Leah didn't answer, just glared at him, pretending to adjust his position further, although he was already as well-situated as he could be for sitting against a tree.

"Yer not Evie then?"

"No," Leah answered flatly, and looked away, trying to avoid more conversation. She had never expected to see Ian again and hadn't thought of what she would say about who she was if she did see him.

"Stay put." She jumped up and headed for the house, stomping the dusty ground, trying to discharge her anger. She turned around at the steps and added gruffly, "And I mean it, dammit!"

Ж ЖЖ

The sudden sound of feet pounding up the stairs startled me. I had heard a commotion outside, and thought that I had heard my name, but I was in the middle of one squalling baby vying for my attention, the other happily kicking his feet in the poopy clout I was trying to change.

"Ergh," I grunted. No wonder babies usually came one at a time. I'd have to be an octopus—or would that be a sextopus?—to handle feeding and keeping three infants clean and fed. A third boob would have been handy, too.

"What's wrong?" I asked, then added, "Would you pick up your brother and hold him until I get done here, or do you want to take over the dirty diaper duty?"

Leah huffed in exasperation, then quickly calmed down. She picked up Leo and rocked him back and forth, blowing in his face to get him to stop screaming. "See, you just blow in the face of the blow hard and he shuts right up!" She was talking to the baby, but making a joke for me. As soon as she stopped blowing, he began yelling again, pounding his little fists like he was pedaling a bicycle with his hands. "Sorry dude, these are empties. You'll just have to wait for Mommy." She stood in place, rocking her body back and forth, the rhythm of her movement calming him enough that his eyes started to flutter. She brought him to her shoulder and rubbed his back.

"Blaat!" Leo had had a burp stuck, and it wasn't a dry one.

My hands were holding a baby's legs and still had poop on them, but I managed to pick up a clean clout with my teeth and offered it to Leah with a mumbled, "Here, he puked on you."

"Thanks, little brother. I love you, too." She grabbed the cloth and

378

cleaned up the regurgitated milk while I finished with Judah's de-nurtured output. The babies' poop still didn't stink, but was as messy as mustard, and impossible to get cleaned up in a hurry. No wonder so many of the mothers of this time just let their babies sit in it.

"I'm glad to see you two could calm each other down. What were you so upset about?" I asked.

"Oh, crap," she replied.

I raised my eyebrows as if to say, 'Yeah, well, there's plenty of that around with three babies.' I knew she could read my mind, at least on that one.

"I didn't get a chance to tell you. Jody's wasn't the first transfusion that I was involved with. James donated blood two days ago, just an hour or so after we got *here*."

I gave her the 'yeah, go ahead' look. She exhaled sharply, took two steps back towards the open door, and craned her neck to look out at the big tree, then came back to stand directly in front of me. "He gave blood to Ian. Ian Kincaid. And he was supposed to stay put, but instead he followed us and..."

Leah didn't get a chance to finish her story. I grabbed a rag to wipe my hands and was out the door with Judah pressed to my shoulder in two seconds. I rushed to Ian's side, squatted down beside him, looked into his eyes, and asked, "Are you all right?" I could tell if he was lying to me—or at least, I hoped I would be able to.

"Why willna anyone tell me who she is?" he asked, his breath still coming in short spurts in what I guessed was called labored breathing.

"Because you don't need to know," I answered sharply. I leaned in to within six inches of his face, glared at him, and didn't even try to contain my rage. "Why didn't you stay put like she told you to? Do you *want* to die?"

Ian tried to shrug his shoulder and let out an involuntary gasp, biting off a yelp. He had forgotten about his wounded neck. He was embarrassed about his show of weakness, so instead of answering the direct question, he asked, "Which one is that?" referring to the baby I was holding.

I was still mad at him, and he could tell. Asking me about my baby—not his, I felt like reminding him—wasn't going to calm me down, either. "What difference does it make?" I replied testily. "You'll never live long enough to see him crawl, much less walk, at the rate you're trying to kill yourself. What, do Indians think that...that...being tough and *macho* is better than sticking around to watch your...your...your *kin* grow up? Or is that just *you* being *estupido*?"

Ian cast his eyes down in shame, and then I started to feel sorry for him. "This is Judah," I said, backing down from my Spanish-spewing rage. I placed him on Ian's lap, holding onto one side of the squirming infant so he wouldn't slide off. Ian had been lean when I met him, and I doubt he had ever been fat, but now he was emaciated.

"When was the last time you ate?" I asked gently, not knowing if I was asking out of compassion or pity. Either way, he needed nourishment.

He started to shrug again, then thought better of it. Instead he let his eyes roll to the ground, then back up to face me again. "Who *is* she?" he pled.

"You have got to be the stubbornest man in the world!" I took the baby from him and sat down next to him, hard and without grace. "Why do you want to know? She was your healer and you didn't listen to her. How could it make a difference if you knew her name?"

"Weel, maybe not her name, but I ken it would make a difference if I ken *who* she is." He shut his eyes, then asked softly, his breathing still shallow, "Is she Danny?"

"I'll make you a deal. You eat some food and do as she says, and I'll tell you, all right?" I was plenty mad at him, but certainly didn't want him to die.

Ian opened his eyes, looked down that crooked nose of his at me, and without saying a word, asked me to tell him at least part of what he wanted to know. He was too tuckered out to speak, but I could see that not knowing was eating him alive.

"All right—one answer. She is 'not Dani,' okay? Now, will you at least take some broth?"

My answer seemed to make him feel better. At least he could speak again. "Do ye happen to have any of those chocolate nibs or cashews? Wee Ian gave me a few bits and that's why I thought that 'not Danny' was ye. She's kin, aye?"

"No and yes," I replied, a reluctant smile creeping in. "No, I don't have any chocolate or cashews, but I'll see if...if...the *healer* has any." I paused, then added hesitantly. "And yes, she's kin."

I put Judah in the playpen with his sister and walked into the house. Leah was standing just inside the doorway, peering at her patient with an oversized frown. I could tell she had seen and probably heard the emotional exchange.

I huffed in defeat then looked at her and rolled my eyes. "I'll fix him something to drink. Why don't you go out and sit next to him and show him Leo, or put Leo in the playpen with the other two—your choice. I know he can be hard-headed. I don't blame you for wanting to keep your distance. Well, except in a professional capacity. Don't... Well, just use your own judgment about how and when you tell him who you are. I trust you."

I watched her grimace, then take a deep, courage-gathering breath before leaving, her baby brother over her shoulder, gently patting his back to soothe him, even though he was already asleep. "Thanks. Maybe a stray breeze will come by and cool things down," she said. I doubt she knew what she was going to do or say any more than I did.

Ж ЖЖ

Jody and Sarah were still sound asleep on the floor. I wanted to check and see if there were any obvious physical changes, but decided it was more important for them to get their rest than for me to gather scientific data. What would I do with it anyhow?

What I *needed* to do was find something to feed that stubborn, pig-headed, but half-dead grouch, Ian. I realized I didn't have any broth. The leftover porridge was still good, but if he hadn't eaten anything lately, I didn't want to give him solid food. I still had some buttermilk left, though. That would have to do.

I poured a mug half-full with the clabbered milk, then had either a brainstorm or Divine inspiration. Either way, I knew what I had to do.

I set down the cup, went to the hearth, and pulled out the loose 'stone' that enshrined the little blue bottle of Master Simon's Fountain of Youth elixir. I held the bottle meditatively, rolling it back and forth between my fingers and thumb, seeking inspiration or discouragement from its physical form. Yes, using it was the right thing to do.

My hand hovered over the cup of buttermilk, the dripping rod ready to release the drops of rejuvenating and repairing potion my spirit had urged me to use. The devil's advocate side of my brain was arguing with my heart, though. Let him die. It would be easier for everyone.

No. It was *not* wrong to use this, so shut up, devil. Dosing him with the FOY water wasn't cheating death, either. Nope, it couldn't be. I didn't feel guilty. And why would the Lord allow me to have it if not to use inspired wisdom and discretion in dispensing it? If ever someone needed it—other than Jody, of course—it was Ian. He was so frail that his physical reserves were in the negative zone. But it wasn't really my decision to make and I knew it.

"Thank You, Lord, for letting this medicine be in my hands," I prayed aloud. "Guide me in its use, and when—or whether or not—I should use it. Oh, and if so, how much."

Well, after my little conference with the Lord, that wee devil shut up and there was no doubt in my mind—dose the man. I added two drops, then felt compelled to add one more. He had been through a lot of physical and mental anguish in the year that I had known him and could probably use a tune up. It wasn't me making the decision on his dosage, after all. Two drops didn't feel right, but three did. "Please, Lord, let his body use it to the best of its ability, and heal his mind, too. In Jesus's name, Amen." There, now I felt better.

I put the stopper back in the bottle and returned it to its hiding place. I felt incredibly at peace. Hopefully, Ian would, too.

381

"Hey, there," I called out in a jovial mood as I walked toward the tree. "Are you ready for your nourishment?" I saw the confused look on both Ian and Wee Ian's faces. "Hey, I'm going to start you with buttermilk. If you can tolerate this, I'll see what else I can scare up. Here." I held the cup for Ian, "you have to drink all of it or it doesn't count." He frowned at me. "I only filled it half-way, so no grumbling."

He took two sips, then leaned back against the tree and closed his eyes. Leah saw that he was having difficulty drinking. She called over, "Wee Ian, do you still have that clear reed for him to use? I guess he's still too sick to drink from a cup."

That did it. Ian opened his eyes and glared at me, telling me with the look on his face to get on with it and bring the cup to his mouth again.

I obliged him, and managed to bite my tongue, but couldn't keep the grin from spreading. It was so tempting to talk baby talk to him. 'Open wide for the airplane' or 'Here comes the choo choo.' Of course, it wouldn't have the same impact on someone from this time period. It would have taken more energy to explain airplane and choo choo to him than to find an easier way to get him to open up and eat.

As it turned out, Ian managed to drink all of his lunch, only pausing twice to get a breath. "Now keep it in you," I ordered. "And you might want to lie down for a while. You had a long ride in here, didn't you?"

"Aye, it was and yer right, I think I could do with a wee nap." Ian managed to scoot his bottom away from the tree and settle into a sleeping position without any assistance or groaning. It seemed as if the 'juice' was already working.

"You might also want to take a nap," I told Wee Ian. "You've had a long trip, too, and I'll wager a tough time trying to keep your father alive."

"Aye, there's truth in that." He rolled over, grabbed his little rucksack and fluffed it into a pillow, adjusting it under his head, "Too much truth."

I left the Ians to their *siestas* and took on another task. Dinner was going to be a three-person project. I delegated the spaghetti sauce concocting to Leah and Jenny, the prep chef. I managed to get the eggs, salt, and flour mixed into noodle dough, and by the time I had it rolled out, Jenny was standing by with her knife, ready to cut it into strips. I didn't know where the men were, but I wasn't worried about them. They were big boys and could take care of themselves. I was sure that when they smelled dinner, they would miraculously appear.

Miracles. That reminded me—it was time to check on the prime Pomeroy pair. Or not. I had heard giggles earlier and decided it was best to give them a bit of privacy. But now I needed some items from the kitchen.

"Come on, Jenny. I want you to get the cutting board and bring it outside. We'll finish cutting the s'ghetti noodles on the porch. Hopefully, the bugs and leaves won't be too bad there. Hey, where'd your sister go?" Leah had disappeared, too.

"Oh, she's taking a nap by him. See," she said, and led me to the other side of the tree.

The sun was low, the shadows long, and there was plenty of room to spread out. Ian was sleeping soundly, snorting in his deep sleep, and Leah was four feet away, Wren dozing on her chest. It was unusually quiet, but peaceful. The world was in sync.

"Can we make s'ghetti again tomorrow? I like cutting."

"We'll see, we'll see. Go stir the sauce now before it burns. I think I'll lie down for a bit, too."

I lay down on the other side of Ian, my elbow tucked into my chest, my cheek on my palm. I must have fallen asleep immediately. All I remembered was putting my hand under my face. Peace, warmth, and security—key ingredients for restful repose.

It seemed as if I had been asleep for a long time, but it must have only been moments because the sun was still up and in the same position when I was awakened by the sound of a loud and familiar voice.

"What happened out here? Are ye in charge now, lass?"

Jody had awakened and risen, and was ready to give everyone the dickens for taking a late afternoon nap.

"Grandpa, Grandpa," Jenny hollered, as she sprinted to her Jody. She collided into him, causing him to take two steps backwards with the impact. She embraced him around his hips, "Are you feelin' better? You sure look better."

"Aye, I am. I see yer mother nappin' there, but where's yer father...?" Jody suddenly recognized Ian and saw a young man and a woman he didn't recognize lying beside him. "Who's she and when did they get here," he asked, indicating the two Ian Kincaids.

"That's my big sister, and I don't know who those men are. Nobody told me yet, but I think the smaller one is the son, and the other one is the father, or maybe they're just brothers, but the big one looks a lot older than the other one, and I think the big one was sick 'cause my new big sister was hollerin' at him somethin' fierce because he didn't do what she told him to, and she was real mad and told him to lie down and..."

I had awakened when Jody spoke, and grinned as Jenny rambled her report on the afternoon's events. She was correct, and probably would have added that she now had a brother-in-law, too, but Jody cut her short.

I took the break as an opportunity to get up and check out the results of our unconventional medical procedures. "Wow, you look great! How do you feel, and how's Sarah?"

I rushed up the steps and almost collided with her. Her head down, she was running her fingers through her curly hair, trying to bring it into some sort of order. I could have sworn she was trying to suppress that undeniable post-coital grin, too. At least, that's what it looked like to me.

"Oh, I see Sarah's fine," I said softly, looking away from her and Jody.

I was embarrassed that I had recognized their very satisfied smiles. I'd have to remember to talk to her about the enhanced fertility I had as a result of my dosage. I squinted at her, looking for changes. She did look a bit younger—maybe only a few years—but I still wanted to warn her.

She strolled over to Jody and held onto his arm, looked up, and smiled at him. Her husband, her hero, was back—better than ever.

"Gee, face lift in a bottle, I see?" I said to the both of them. Sarah blushed, and Jody lifted his eyebrows in a non-verbal question of 'Am I supposed to know what that means?' I shrugged my shoulders and explained, "Sarah or I will tell you later," then looked over at the slumbering herd to change the subject.

Leah had heard our voices and started to sit up. "Oops." She had forgotten she had her two-month-old sister asleep on her chest.

"If she's dry, yank off her clout—diaper, that is—real quick. She always pees just after she wakes up. Hold her over the far edge of the bushes. But not on the bushes!"

I didn't want to wash any more clouts than I had to. Potty training was going to start very early for my kids if they were predictable in their peeing and pooping. I had designated a little 'cat box' area for quick drips and deposits. When the dirt started stinking, Wallace dug it up, tossed it in a bucket, and hauled it to the privy. We'd have to deal with the messes in the confines of a winter cabin soon enough. For now, the 'drop box' worked when I caught the babies at just the right moment.

I turned my attention back to my brother/father-in-law. "Jody, do you remember anything about what happened just before you went to sleep? Or you, Sarah—how's your memory?" I wanted to know if memory loss was a side effect, and if so, how extensive. I was the only one with a history of using the elixir and I didn't remember much. Shoot, I didn't remember anything. I had a full-blown case of amnesia.

"I think I remember everything," said Sarah. "I remember you gave me two drops of…of…anyway, two drops, and then I felt sleepy and woke up feeling great."

I looked at Jody for his answer. "I remember thinkin' I was gonna die. There was lots of prayin' and singin' and everyone seemed happy. I thought I was in heaven. The angels were singin' a song about miracles. But it couldna have been heaven because then someone was pokin' needles in me. No, not someone—that was Sarah."

Sarah smiled sheepishly, but didn't say anything. She, too, wanted to know how much he remembered.

"I think ye gave me somethin', and then I felt good enough to sleep. At least, I dinna feel like I had to stay awake so I *dinna* die." He shook his head in recall. "That is such a terrible feelin'. I dinna want to leave all of ye. But the lass, she...she... Sarah, did ye stick her with a pin, too?"

"Yes, I did, and then I stuck a tube on the end of both of the hollow needles—not pins—and she gave you enough blood to live. And then, well, Evie did something else that we don't want to talk about right now," Sarah looked over at Jenny as she spoke, "and then you and I took a nap, and then you...um...woke up and felt...um...fine, and here we are, right?"

I could tell by her nervousness that I was correct. She and Jody had a *very* nice time waking up together. Well, they deserved it. I was glad I had stayed outside!

Jody spoke out proudly. "Aye, I feel verra fine, and I'm glad to be alive. And it looks like even more of my kin have come around. Hopefully they dinna come fer my funeral and I disappointed them. When did Ian get here, and is this his lad, Wee Ian?"

"Aye, I'm Wee Ian, and ye must be my great-uncle, Jody," Wee Ian nodded in greeting. "And here comes Wallace and James. James is a fairy. Oh, I dinna ken if I was supposed to tell ye that. But he kens it."

"Well, I appreciate ye tellin' me," Jody said softly to Wee Ian. He turned and addressed Leah boldly, "And who's this fine young lady holdin' my granddaughter?"

"Oh, I'm another granddaughter. I came a *long way* to get here." Leah stressed the words and saw Jody's eyes light up in recognition of the fact that *long way* really meant *long time* journey.

"So yer Leah, eh?" Jody asked, wide-eyed and smiling.

Leah nodded and Jenny popped in, "How did you know her name, Grandpa?"

"Weel," he said, as he brought his hand to his jaw and rubbed the copper stubble, "She looks like a Leah to me. Dinna ye think so, too?"

"Yup. Leah, Pee-ah, Wee-ah," Jenny sang, and danced to her new little song. "My sister's name is Leah, Pee-ah, Wee-ah."

"Good grief," Leah said, "I thought I was done with that in kindergarten. Oh, well, at least she isn't calling me by my first name."

Jenny had heard her and stopped singing. "What's your first name? I can make a song out of that, too."

"It's Audie," James said, as he walked up to the group followed by Wallace and Julian. "Hi, I'm James Melbourne, Audie Leah's husband. I'm glad to see you're feeling better, sir."

"Not half as glad as I am to be feelin' better. And please dinna be callin' me sir. I'm not a British lord or anythin'."

Julian started laughing at his remark, then Wallace joined in. James couldn't help but chuckle, too, and then when Leah realized what they were laughing about, she began giggling, too.

"Okay, now why is that so funny?" Jody asked, pretending to be irritated.

James nodded to Wallace who nodded to Julian who answered for all of them. "Well, you see, James here is—or at least, he was a few days ago—a British lord. Looks like whenever any decent British lord gets near you, Jody Pomeroy, he decides to become an American."

"Weel, if this man is the husband of my granddaughter, then I'm glad to see that he was smart enough to come over to the American side. Ye werena a soldier, were ye?"

"No, sir," James replied, shifting his eyes, hoping that Jody would remember *when* he came from, "there was no fighting...um...near me, at least...when I left."

"Uh...oh," Jody stuttered with realization, "Sorry, I dinna mean to be gettin' personal there. Weel, somethin' smells good. Jenny, wasna it yer night to fix dinner?" he teased.

"Ooh, ooh. I mean, yes, Grandpa. Mommy, the sauce is ready, and now we need to cook the noodles. Do I need to cut anything else?"

"No, dear. You and that knife... You be careful with it, you hear. Now, go put it back inside for now. Gather all the plates and bowls you can find. We'll have some of these big strong men put together some timbers for a table. I think we'll have a Thanksgiving dinner of spaghetti and salad: a fine Scottish-American meal."

### ***62 A New Name

Wee Ian finished brushing, feeding, and watering the nag that had carried his father to Uncle Jody's. It had been a long trip for all of them. There was no doubt in his mind that his father would have headed to Uncle Jody's house, with or without his help. At first, he had hidden the horse from him and said she had strayed, that he couldn't find her. He knew his father didn't believe him, but he didn't argue. Instead, he reached into the framework of the shelter above him, and tugged and pushed at a sturdy piece of branch, working it free to use as a crutch. He ran his hand down its length, checking it for cracks or breaks, tore off the small branches protruding from it, then speared the ground, clutching at the middle of the staff, working his way up, hand over hand, struggling against gravity and his body's weakness to get up to a standing position.

"Wait! I think I ken where to find her," the son squeaked in desperation. "And I'll help ye get on her, too." He glowered, then huffed in resignation, "At least it'll be easier on ye than walking."

Before he went for the horse, though, he tried one more time to convince his father to stay, "Why canna ye jest wait fer two or three more days until yer healed?"

*Ian didn't answer his question with words, but glared in response at the suggestion. He didn't want to talk. He needed to save his breath and his strength for the trip to his uncle's house. No one else in the world—at least, in the American colonies—had cashews. It had to be Evie—or her fairy twin—who had come to help him. Could there really be two of them? Could this woman who Wee Ian had said tended to his wounds be the mysterious Danny? He had to know and was willing to die trying to find out.*

Getting his father on the horse was the easy part. Keeping him on her was the real challenge. He was still weak from his injuries and had trouble staying mounted. The wounds to his manly parts were painful to sit on, so he assumed an awkward, tilted position. Wee Ian didn't have the luxury of simply walking beside his father and the horse for the trip—he had to run from one side of the pair to the other, shoving his father back into an upright position—or catching him before he hit the ground as he slid from the old mare's bare back.

Wee Ian stumbled out of the barn and stretched his spine like an old man, one arm in the air, the other on his tender lower back. He looked up and saw his father asleep at the base of the big tree in front of the house and shook his head. His father's stubbornness had got him here alive, but there was no telling how much life was left in him. He walked over to him, dropped his rucksack, and plopped down on the ground next to the pale and winded shell of a man. Wee Ian was tired, but afraid to fall asleep. His father might not be alive when he woke up. The lad bit his bottom lip and tried not to think about what his future would be if his father died.

ЖЖЖ

I looked out and saw the Kincaid men under the tree. I told Leah to stay put. I'd take over the nursing duties and see how Ian was doing. I wanted her and James to conserve their strength.

I didn't know if my recent high energy level was because my body had finally healed or because I was so happy that I had so many family members around. But either way, I felt like a superhero. I was ready to tend to the infirm, counsel the sad, feed the hungry, and change the poopy. I could take care of everyone and everything today.

We still had at least forty-five minutes to wait until dinner was ready—a watched pot never boils and all that nonsense. While the kettle was getting up to temperature, Jenny helped me get the babies to sleep. It was one of those glorious times when all of them were down at the same time. "Are you *sure* there's nothing else you want me to do?" she begged.

"No, no, I'm fine. Why don't you go outside and play?"

"All right," she said dejectedly. She looked around and saw that there were now two people under the tree. She walked up confidently to the small one.

"Who are you?" she asked brightly of the young boy with the sad and dirty face. "I've never seen you before."

"Weel, I've never seen ye either, so we're even," he said tartly. He was concerned about what he would do if his father died, and didn't feel too friendly, especially to a girl.

I overheard the two of them as I walked up to check on my ex-husband, Ian. "I think your da is going to be fine," I told Wee Ian as I brushed the dark brown hair out of his eyes. He looked so much like his father. "I gave him some very good medicine, and I'll bet you won't even know that he'd been hurt after he wakes up. But he needs to sleep now. Why don't you and Jenny go over to the water trough and wash up? And make sure you don't get any soap in it. Use the little bucket for the soapy water, all right?"

"Yes, ma'am," he replied, and reluctantly scooted away from his father's side.

"Yes, Mommy," Jenny sang as she bounced around the tree, waiting for the young boy to get up so she could go with him.

Jenny skipped to the barn and Wee Ian trudged along behind her. He was sad and scared. Evie told him that his father would be fine, but even though she thought she was right, and he wanted to believe her, he couldn't.

Ever since he had met his father several moons ago, he looked as if he was dying a wee bit at a time. One more accident or fight, and he would be dead. And if his father died, then where would *he* go? His mother's husband made it clear that he didn't want him around their house, or even

388

their village. His grandmother was dead, which was why he was now with Star Walker. Ian Kincaid was his name when they were with the white man, he reminded himself. He liked being here with Evie, Wallace, and the bairns, but all of a sudden, there seemed to be too many people around. And now there was this obnoxious wee lass, dancing around him, blabbering all the time. Yes, if his father died, he'd like to live with his little brothers and sister, Evie, and Wallace, but he hoped the little yellow-haired girl had someplace else to go. She was already annoying him, and he hadn't even been here an hour.

"So what's your name?" she asked. "I don't know who you are except that sick man under the tree is your father, huh? My mother said he's gonna get better, so he will. She doesn't lie to me or anyone else. Do you know her?"

"Do ye ever shut up?" he asked, then dunked his head into the horse trough.

She waited until his head was out of the water. "I just shut up, but you didn't hear it because your head was underwater. Why won't you tell me your name and why do you talk funny? You sound like my Grandpa. That's my Grandpa Jody, not my Grandpa Julian. They both talk English, but they don't sound the same. My Mommy speaks English, too, but it sounds even different from them, and she's gonna teach me to read and write. Can you read and write?" Jenny paused for a breath. She looked at him, waiting for him to answer at least one of her questions.

Wee Ian turned and looked toward his father again. All of a sudden, his stomach hurt. The thought of being alone was like a dirk in his wame. He clutched his gut and walked into the barn, head down, the emotions of fear and depression battling for dominance within him.

Once his eyes adjusted, he took in his surroundings. The floor was swept, there was fresh straw laid out in the stalls and—he inhaled deeply—it smelled of leather and hay. It was also cooler in here than outside. A simple, yet glorious refuge.

"Aah," he sighed, reveling in the first sense of peace he had had in ages. The straw looked so inviting. Evie had told him he would have to let his father sleep. Well, if Da had to sleep, he'd take a nap, too. He found a shady spot, kicked the straw to make sure there weren't any varmints in it, and then lay down. He would only sleep for a wee bit. Just a few minutes for a rest, then he'd go check on his father. Evie was a good woman and Leah a good healer, but Da was his responsibility

Jenny watched the boy go into the barn. She wanted to talk to him, but he didn't look like he felt too good. She washed her face and hands, making sure she didn't get soap in the water. Her father had said it gave the horses a bellyache if they drank soapy water, so she was extra careful. She didn't want to hurt a horse, but really didn't want to make Daddy mad. She had seen him mad the day her other brothers had died, and that was real scary. She knew he would never get that mad at her, but she could also tell that he didn't like getting mad. He had cried and cried after he got angry and beat up that other man. But that might have been because her brother had just been killed. He was sad about that just like she was, even though the two of them didn't used to like each other.

Jenny sighed. Thinking about her brothers dying made her sad again. She tried not to think about them because she couldn't do anything about it. Mommy had said that when God took someone away from the earth, it was because He needed them up in heaven. And when God took her brothers, He made sure that He gave her a Mommy and Daddy, two more brothers, and a little sister, too. Jenny walked over to the barn, still sad, and looked inside. The little boy was asleep in the corner. He had been sad, too. He looked real lonely. She'd go over and hold him like her Daddy held her when she felt that way—that should make both of them feel better.

Jenny took one step onto the straw pile and Wee Ian popped up into a crouch, his dirk pulled, ready to defend himself.

"I'm sorry, I'm sorry," Jenny squealed, "I didn't mean to scare you. I just wanted to make you feel better." She wanted to say more, but remembered the boy had said she talked too much. Instead, she bit her bottom lip and stared at him, waiting to see what would happen next.

"Ye dinna scare me," he said defensively. He looked hard at her, then realized that she was the one who was frightened. At least, she wasn't blabbering. "Are ye all right, lass?" he asked. He did need to use good manners, even if she was just a girl.

*Jenny really was afraid. No one had drawn a knife on her since those bad men at the mill had threatened to cut off her clothes. Knives didn't scare her. She liked cutting with them. Men with knives scared her, though.*

The young girl stood in front of him, arms slack at her side, paralyzed, staring at his dirk. Since she hadn't say a word, she must be terrified. "I wouldna hurt ye with it," he said. "Honest."

Jenny kept staring, bug-eyed and silent. "Here, ye can touch it if ye want." He held out the knife to her, hasp first, but that didn't work. She wouldn't budge. Yes, she was a pest, but he still didn't want to get in trouble with Evie for frightening her.

Evie—she had called Evie her mommy. That must be fairy speak for mama. "Is Evie yer mother?" he asked, trying to engage her in conversation.

*Jenny smiled and nodded. She realized that if she didn't talk, then he would. It was hard not to talk, though. Hmm. She could pretend her lips were sewn shut. She clamped her jaws then squeezed her lips together— forcibly keeping them tight so she didn't start talking—and nodded again.*

"Oh," Wee Ian replied. "Does that mean the bairns are yer brothers and sister?" He knew they must be, but he was hoping she'd start talking again. He wanted to check on his father, but didn't want to leave the girl silent and alone in the barn. If she stopped talking all together, someone was sure to notice, and then he might get blamed. He didn't mind getting in trouble for deeds he had done, but he hadn't done anything to her, not really—just pulled his dirk on her when she had startled him from his nap.

*Jenny wanted to tell him all about her little brothers and sister, Wren, but pressed her lips together tighter, settling for a rapid head nodding. She liked him and hoped he stayed around. Maybe she could have a friend her own age!*

She seemed to like it when he talked about her brothers and sister. He wished he could tell her that they were his family, too—even that they were his blood family—but he had told Evie he wouldn't, that he would only refer to them as his kin. "Did ye ken that I gave Wren her name? She's my kin, too?" he said proudly, still hoping she would speak. Was it just a few minutes ago that he couldn't get her to shut up?

"You gave Wren her name? And if you're her kin, then you're my kin, too!" She couldn't contain herself or her mouth. She jumped up and grabbed him in a big bear hug.

"Watch the dirk!" he yelped, and dropped it. He pulled out of the unwelcome embrace and held her an arm's length, checking to make sure he hadn't stabbed her. "Are ye all right? Did I cut ye?"

Jenny dropped her elbows to her side, clutching one hand with the other, holding tight to the excitement of having more family, finally someone her own age. She opened her mouth to tell him all about her other sister, but suddenly recalled how he had treated her when she had talked too much. She looked at him coyly, dipped her head down, and went back into mute mode.

"Yer bleedin'!" he exclaimed, and grabbed her arm. His knife had cut her just above the elbow. "Quick, I need a cloth to stop the bleedin'. Oh, I'm so sorry. I dinna mean to hurt ye." Wee Ian found a rag hanging on a peg in the wall, shook it out, and held it on the bloody spot, applying direct pressure like Leah had told him to do for his father.

"Now will you tell me your name?" she asked, not paying any attention to her wound. It didn't hurt, and if she didn't look at it, it wouldn't bother her.

"The white man call me Wee Ian," he said, giving her the standard monotone reply he always used when asked his name. He inhaled quickly and returned to his normal voice, "Ian Kincaid is my father's name, too. He's the one who's ailin' under the tree." All of a sudden, she wasn't such a pest.

"Wee Ian? Like Wee'un, Pee'in'?" she asked. He nodded a short affirmative, but she couldn't stop herself from adding, "That's *awful!*"

He glared at her. Maybe she was a pest. A big-mouthed pest.

Jenny realized that she had made a mistake. "I mean, I can think of a better name for you, I'm sure I can." She paused, and added, "Did you really give Wren her name?"

He nodded again. He didn't feel like talking anymore.

"I *like* that name!" She felt his hand on her arm, still holding the rag to her wound. "Is it bad? I don't want to look. Blood makes me sick. Well, it does if it's mine or somebody's I care about," she added softly.

Wee Ian pulled the rag away and saw that it was just a small scratch that had bled profusely. The bleeding had already stopped. If she didn't bump it, it would be fine. "Ye'll be all right. It's naught but a scratch, but ye scarrit me. Can we go outside now? I want to go check on my da."

"Doc or Scout?" she said, then crossed her arms across her chest in a gesture of confidence.

"What?"

"Your name. Are you a Doc or a Scout? You just doctored my arm, so that's why I said Doc, but you seem like a Scout to me. I'll bet you always like to lead the way, making sure it's safe for everyone else to go ahead, right?"

"Scout. I like that. All right, ye can call me Scout," he said, smiling at getting a name that seemed to fit better than the hand-me-down name his father had also used when he was a child.

"And you can call me Jenny," she said, with a full-dimpled smile. "Come on, let's go check on your da, and I'll *try* not to talk too much. That is if you'll *try* not to stab me again," she added with a wink.

The two walked side-by-side out into the sunshine, then Jenny smacked him on the arm and said, "Tag, you're it," and ran to the big family tree. She had someone to play with, at least for a few more hours.

### ***63 You Were Wrong

Ian was awake and obviously feeling better. At least, he could sit up by himself now. He was my husband's cousin and the sire of my three babies, but also the orneriest, least-forgiving man I'd ever met. He gave me up—dropped me at Jody and Sarah's doorstep when I was pregnant—so he could go on a vengeance quest.

I turned out fine—finer than fine since I wound up marrying his cousin, Wallace—but *he* was still a wreck. I looked around. I finally had a chance to talk to him without a large audience. Wee Ian, the ever vigilant caretaker, was at his side, and it was actually better for me that he was. He needed to hear this, too. I was ready to let his father have it with both barrels.

"You lost a wife and three children because of your hate and need for revenge. Wallace let the Lord take care of vengeance, and you know what? He gained a wife, three, now four…five children and a son-in-law. What do you have to show for doing it your way? You were inches from death, and if it weren't for the goodness of…of…the lass, Leah, and her husband, you and your son would both be dead."

*I bit my tongue just before claiming Leah as my daughter. I had inferred it, but didn't feel like going into that discussion!*

Ian's head stayed low. I wasn't sure if it was shame or if he was trying to find words to refute my explanation. Either way, he wasn't ready to talk.

"And where is Rocky?" I asked. I wasn't ready to stop the conversation, and I really was curious about the huge masked-faced dog that was as much Ian's canine brother as a traveling companion. "He wasn't with you when you came last time, either—when the tax man was here."

"He's deid," Ian said flatly, humbled—or was that humiliated?—head still bowed.

Wee Ian added to the somber statement. "I dinna believe in the vengeance, but what they did to that dog was…was…" Wee Ian's eyes teared with the memory. I put my hand on his shoulder to let him know that he didn't have to recall or relate the story to me—I still understood.

"Okay, then you lost three children, a wife, and your best friend in the whole world. Do you think maybe you've learned something from it?"

"Aye, if I'm gonna be vengeful, I'd best be quick about it."

I couldn't help myself. I slapped him hard on the back of the head. "I hope you get a big headache from that, too. And you're lucky I didn't have a pot or a crappy clout in my hand when I did it. Ergh!" I stomped off in a huff before I lost control and started kicking him.

Wallace came over and sat down next to Ian. He handed him a cold stone bottle of ale. "That's not to drink," he said. "It's to put on the lump that's sure to start rising."

Ian accepted the drink with a nod, then brought it up to the tender spot, wincing as the cool hardness hit the already sore area.

Wallace settled back against the tree. "You know, Evie is a pretty even-tempered person most of the time, but you sure know how to rile her. What did you do this time?"

"Ach, she was doin' her preachin' about vengeance and God, and how ye got her and all the bairns and a few more in yer family because ye let Him," he tipped his head up to the sky, then realized how much his head was hurting. He started again, "Ye let Him take care of the vengeance. If that's true, then why did she hit me so hard?" Ian brought the bottle down, examined it casually, and then decided the cool ale would be better inside of him. He opened the bottle, took a long swig, and sighed in satisfaction.

"Well, maybe she figured God needed an extra hand right now, and she'd help Him out. I mean, you don't seem too keen on listening to reason." Wallace looked over at Ian to make sure he was listening. Ian glanced up and gave him a blank stare—he heard the words, but didn't feel like they pertained to him or this situation.

Wallace could see that he wasn't getting through to his cousin. He drew himself up and said plainly, "She's right and you're wrong. It's as simple as that. I'm with her. I'd like to see you have a happy life, but from what I've seen of you lately, I'd say you actually enjoy being miserable."

Wee Ian came up and smacked his father on the back of the head, almost in the same spot Evie had. "See, he said the same thing I did—ye like bein' miserable. Dinna ye ken yer supposed to be settin' a good example fer yer son? Do ye want me to wind up like ye: alone, hatin' and killin', always fightin' with someone about them doin' or sayin' somethin' agin ye or yer kin? I may be yer...yer son by blood, but I'd rather wind up like Cousin Wallace and Evie—with a house and a family and a dog that nobody wants to kill jest to spite me, aye?"

Ian looked over and glared at his son. "Yer not supposed to hit yer da," he said, totally ignoring what the boy had just said.

"Yeah, weel, if that's the meanest I ever get, I'll be glad," he said, and stomped off to the barn, not caring if he was stirring up dust or not.

### ***64 Gifts For You

"What's this?" asked Sarah, as she opened the master copy of the hand-illustrated book that James had invested in.

"Oh, it's the very first edition of a book on the flora of North Carolina," Leah said. "You know, helpful herbs, how to identify botanicals, process them, uses for healing, antidotes in case you get too close or ingest too much of the wrong ones. Hey, did you know that impatiens—jewelweed—helps defray the itching of poison ivy?"

James reached into his valise and took out his Smith and Wesson model 629 pistol.

"And what do ye have there, young James?" asked Jody.

"This is for, shoot, I should have brought another one. This one's mine, but I brought one for my Uncle Julian, and one for my new father-in-law."

Wallace smiled and rolled his eyes at being the father-in-law to a man nearly his age. "I'm twenty-eight," James said, answering the unspoken question. "And you, *Dad*?"

"Twenty-three," Wallace answered modestly, then quickly changed the subject. "So, what is this? I mean, I can see it's a gun, but what is this part?" He cautiously touched the revolver's swing out cylinder.

"Here, see, I can put one bullet in each hole, and then," James pointed the empty gun at the fireplace and pulled the trigger six times, "this chamber revolves after each squeeze. Each time, a fresh bullet is loaded into the firing chamber that lines up with the barrel. The hammer is activated by the double-action trigger. It hits the primer and fires the round. I can squeeze off six rounds without reloading."

"Rounds? Ye don't have to load the powder, tamp, and then add the shot?" Jody had picked up a bullet and was examining it closely. "My daughter told me about bullets. Did ye happen to bring the machine to reload—is that the right word?—reload these rounds?"

"Yes, we did," James answered. "I wanted to bring two sets, but we only had our carry-on bags. I mean, we had to pack light. I figured we could do the reloading at one place, and then, maybe, use the one reloading apparatus as a pattern to make another one. We have to make sure we save the shells, though. We only have a certain number. That and I don't want them to be found later, if you know what I mean."

"And whose is this?" I asked as I held up a Mickey and Minnie Mouse short-sleeved nightshirt. James and Leah both blushed bright red at the sight of the shirt. "Why are you two blushing? I mean, it's only a nightshirt."

"I...I just brought it to sleep in. I don't have a shift and thought this would..." Leah took it from my hand and pretended to inspect it. "Well, lookie there," she said to James and waved it at him. "Mickey has pants on. See, he's hiding behind the valentine, but you can see the bottom of his shorts right there…"

"So Mickey didn't run around without clothes…" James said, swallowing hard, as if by doing so, his red face would return to normal.

The two of them were paying too much attention to the lightweight cotton knit. I knew there was an event they were remembering but didn't care to share. Rather than make them squirm, I backed off, and changed the subject…sort of.

"Mickey and Minnie Mouse, welcome to the 18th century," I announced.

"So that's him, Michael Mouse?" Jody asked, honestly excited about the character. All four—Sarah, James, Leah, and I—nodded. "I heard about him. So that's what he looks like. Is that his wife? Or do mice marry in yer time."

"Nah, they don't marry. They do sing and dance and tell jokes, though," I said, which drew big laughs from the 20th century-born, and stares and blinks of shock from the 18th century crew.

"Cartoons are just diversions like poems and novels and music. Oh, we still have those, too, and lots of other ways to spend—or waste—time, depending on the motivation. You see, people don't have to work as hard—physically, at least—for the most part. So, the time not spent building, repairing, cooking, hunting…. Well, you get the idea, I'm sure. You have high born and aristocracy now. Well, lots of the people aren't rich—actually, most of them aren't—but they still have lots of idle time. But I digress. I want to see what else you have in your *magic* bags." I grinned at the memory of sharing my 'magic' bag, my backpack, with Sarah when I first met her. Now it was my turn to be surprised and enchanted.

"Here, these are for you," Leah said, and tossed a rolled up white cotton bundle to me. "I read that they don't have these here, so I brought enough for the both of us. Sorry, Sarah, I didn't think about bringing any for you, but we can share."

"Cool," I said, as I pulled off the thin plastic binding from the white cotton briefs. "I don't have to go commando anymore! Yee haw!" I stood up and danced with my new panties held in place over my dress. I glanced over at James and Leah who were howling with laughter, then looked at Jody and Wallace. They were both shocked at my brazenness, but then they, too, started to giggle at my unbridled delight.

"Weel, I'll take yer word fer it about their comfort. They look a might binding to me, though," Jody said, and shifted on the stool. He changed his focus back to the bag. I could tell he wanted to change the subject from scandalous underwear to anything else.

Leah had picked up on his discomfort, too. "Here, these are for the babies. I didn't know if I had all brothers or sisters or a mix. I was pretty sure, though, that there was at least one little girl. You see, I always *knew* you had a little sister in there for me somewhere."

"Whoa," I said breathlessly, "you did, didn't you? I thought you outgrew that when you were ten and I told you I...I...I had my tubes tied..."

*I was pale at the sudden memory. Leah had sparked a few minor ones with her presence, but this one was major.*

"Is there something wrong?" Wallace asked when he saw how stunned I was all of a sudden. "And what tubes did you have tied?"

*I shook my head to erase the unwelcome 21st century version of me that had suddenly appeared. I had never felt it before—the older, plump, and achy person I used to be—even when I first realized that the nurse taking care of me in the hospital last month was my daughter. Leah was who she was, my flesh and blood, and I was her mother, but I never felt old. I shuddered again.*

"Fallopian tubes," I answered with a grimace. *I was here. Now. In this body. That other person was only a memory, an odd story from a book of fairy tales.* "Woman stuff," I clarified, as I looked over at Sarah, "that got fixed last year. I'm fine or we wouldn't have these three beautiful babies, now, would we?"

I shook out the rolled-up pink fabric cylinder. 'Little Sister' was machine embroidered on the front along with hearts and butterflies. The cotton-blend gown was soft and had long sleeves. "Here," Leah said, and tossed a green roll to Wallace and a yellow one to me.

Wallace used the back of his forearm to brush off his pants, then laid out the green gown. 'Future President' was embroidered on the front. I hurriedly opened out the sunshine-colored all-purpose sleeper and saw that it said 'Grandpa's Legacy.' I handed it to Jody and smiled, but said nothing.

Jody held it up and blinked rapidly. I could see he was trying to keep tears from spilling out. "You miss him, don't you?" I asked, then immediately felt stupid.

He took a deep breath. "Aye, I do. I have other grandchildren now, and I love them all, but Benji was my first. Of course, it helped that he looked a bit like me. And he *is* my legacy, too. He's old enough now that he probably has bairns of his own."

It was uncomfortably quiet. No one knew what to say, either to continue or end the topic of conversation. Jody wiped his eyes with the insides of his wrists, then looked over at James. "I think he and his family went back to live at my family's estate at Barden Hall, or at least nearby. His father was a teacher. Did ye happen to meet him?" he asked. "I mean, I'm sure he dinna let it be known that he was from here and now, but he was sure to stand out, him bein' big and red-haired like his grandsire."

"No, sir, I'm sorry. I've never been to that part of Scotland, at least that I remember. And I've never heard of a Benji Pomeroy."

"Ach, no. His name is MacKay, after his father. Benjamin MacKay, but we called him Benji or Mac."

"Oh, shit," James mumbled. He drew in a deep breath, squeezed his eyes shut, and hoped that this was just a bad dream and really wasn't happening.

"What do you mean, 'Oh, shit'?" Sarah asked.

James opened his eyes and saw that everyone in the room was focused on him. "Before I came to America, I got a letter from a Benji MacKay in North Carolina. Oh, shit, shit, shit!" he exclaimed irrationally. He realized that this wasn't helping the tension in the room. He closed his eyes again, took a deep breath, and began to share what little he remembered.

"I wish I had a photographic memory, but crap, all I remember is the letter said something about how he needed to talk to me about Leah. I didn't know any Leah at the time, and the only people I knew in North Carolina were the ones I had met at that little café in Greensboro back in 2012..." he glanced at me, indicating that I was one of those people, whether I remembered it or not, "and a person named Bibb Stephens, a business person I was corresponding with about a property purchase nearby. Sh... Darn it. At the time, I didn't even know if Bibb was a man or a woman!"

"Yeah, right, and Bibb turned out to be your mother, and I became your wife less than two weeks later," Leah said. "Things happen so quickly here in North Carolina," she added in a perfect imitation of Judy Garland as Dorothy Gale from the Wizard of Oz.

"Don't worry about it. I'm sure he's fine," I assured both Jody and James. "And it's not as if we could go back...um...go forward...um... Well, whatever direction it would have to be, we can't go change it. Phew!"

### ***65 The Promise

"Can I see your knife?" Jenny asked.

"What?" Wee Ian replied, his voice squeaking in shock. "That's a private matter and none of yer business."

"Well, I got a knife. Do you want to see mine?"

"You canna have a knife. A girl has the other kind. Only men and boys have knives," he said.

"Oh, yeah? Then what's this?" Jenny reached into her pocket and pulled out the penknife Grandpa Jody had gifted her.

"Oh, *that* kind of knife—you mean a dirk." He had been thinking of the 'other' kind of knife. "Oh, sure, here." He unsheathed the blade he had recovered from his father's assailant's belongings and handed it to her, hilt first.

She turned the knife over in her hand, found its balance point, held it up to the sky to see if it was crooked or if the edge had nicks in it, then gave it back to him. "What kind of knife were you talking about?" she asked, her head down, concentrating on the geometric designs she was creating in the dirt with her big toe.

"Weel, like I said, it's kind of private, ye ken, the other knife." He slipped off his moccasins and decided to play in the fine, silt-y dirt, too.

"Huh?" Jenny looked up at him, nose wrinkled and mouth opened. She didn't have a clue as to what he was talking about.

He knew by her unblinking stare that she would pester him until he told her. It was better to tell her and get it over with. "Weel, the Indians refer to a man's...ye ken," he mumbled, and looked down at the front of his breechclout, "as his knife. That's why I said ye canna have a knife."

"You mean your stuff?" she asked.

"Stuff?" he echoed. He had never heard it called that.

"Yeah, stuff." She dusted off her hands and said, "Hey, if you show me your stuff, I'll show you mine. I got two hairs on my stuff now. Do you have any hair on yours? I know when you get to be a real man, you get hair down there. But you're not a real man, so you probably don't have any hair, huh?"

"Weel, I got a little," he admitted shyly.

"Can I see?"

He could tell that she was just curious, but his answer was still, "No."

"I think you're lying," she teased.

"No, I'm not," he replied adamantly, and crossed his arms. He walked away from their dirt drawing canvas and sat down next to the big chokecherry bush.

"Then what are you afraid of?" she said, then added gently, "I won't laugh."

"Why would ye laugh?"

"I don't know." She shrugged her shoulders and came over to sit down next to him—a little too close, he felt—then almost whispered, "Why won't you show me?"

"Because it's private," he said with conviction, although he didn't really know why he couldn't show her.

"Why?"

"Because it is," he declared with a tone of finality.

"Why?" Jenny didn't believe the subject was closed. Everybody had one, so why was it so personal? He should know that without her saying so.

"Because yer only supposed to show it to yer mate—ye ken, the one yer marrit to," he said with exasperation. *There, that ought to shut her up!*

"Okay, let's get married then," she said, grinning from ear to ear.

"No," he huffed, then looked around to see where he could hide. She was too close, though, and would see him wherever he went.

*He looked over and saw that his father seemed to be resting peacefully. At least, Evie was smiling at him now, even if he was asleep. He tried to recall if he had ever seen her smile at him before. If she had, she hadn't done it for very long. She looked happy, and that was a good sign.*

"I said…why can't we get married, or marrit, or however you say it? It means the same thing, right?"

He nodded and said, "Because." Evidently she had asked him at least once before. He hadn't heard her the first time, but that didn't seem to slow her down.

"Because why? Don't you like me?" she asked sadly.

He realized that he felt sorry for her. She must be an orphan because she wasn't with Wallace and Evie a few weeks ago. It wouldn't hurt him to show her a little sympathy. "Weel, yes, I like ye—sort of—but ye talk too much."

"If we get married, I promise I won't talk too much," she said, her eyes searching his to see if her pledge had made a difference.

He peered, unblinking, into her face to make sure she knew what she was saying. "Promise?" he asked, then noticed how long and soft brown her eyelashes were, perfect for setting off the sky blue of her bright, shiny eyes. She had a few freckles on her nose, too—little spots of happiness, he thought.

"I promise. You'll have to show me your stuff then because we'll be married, huh," she said, nodding her head, making sure he understood his part of the obligation.

"So if we're marrit, I'll show ye my stuff, but then ye willna talk too much, aye?"

"Uh-huh," she said quickly, trying to make her answer as short as

400

possible for him.

He was beginning to like this. She was already talking less. Maybe she *would* make a good wife. "All right. Just say that ye want me fer yer husband, then that's all there is to it." *At least, that's how he thought they did it back at his village. He wasn't sure how the white man did it, and had never really talked to his father or mother about it. But this was good enough for a girl.*

Jenny remained still—just looked at him—not saying a word. Was it working already? "But ye have to say ye want me fer yer husband first, and THEN stop talking so much."

Jenny nodded.

Scout leaned into her face and glared at her. He was beginning to get exasperated with her and wasn't going to remind her again that she had to ask him to be her husband. She didn't need to be his wife if she would stay quiet without it.

"Will you be my husband?" she asked slowly, timidly.

*She must know what a promise is. She sounded as if she was thinking about each word before saying it, not jabbering like a jay. Maybe she really will be a good woman, especially if Evie is her new mother. And she sure is pretty.* "Aye, I mean, yes," he said, then leaned forward and gave her a quick kiss on the cheek.

Jenny didn't say a word, but shook her head 'no,' and pointed to her lips. She wanted her kiss on the mouth.

Scout, the boy formerly known as Wee Ian, sighed then leaned forward and gave Jenny Pomeroy-Hart, his child-bride, a kiss on the mouth. Before he could pull away, though, she grabbed him and pressed her mouth to his, twisting and turning her head, keeping a hard pressure on his lips with hers.

"Ow! Yer teeth hurt me. Yer supposed to do it soft, like this," then showed her how gently he could touch her mouth with his. He pulled away and grinned. He just might like being marrit.

Jenny started rearranging her skirts. She pulled the green calico up and held the bundle to her chest with her chin. "See," she said, pointing to her newly discovered pubic hairs.

"Oh," is all Scout could think to say.

She dropped her skirts. Neither of them spoke. She finally looked up at him, then stared down at his crotch. He followed her gaze, shrugged his shoulders, and shifted aside his breechclout. "See," he said, and pointed to his sparse dark hairs, suddenly feeling braver. "I got more than ye do, but that's okay; ye'll get more. And yer breasts will get bigger so ye can feed bairns when I plant my seed in ye. But I think we ought to wait for that until I can build us a home of our own. Do ye think it will be all right if ye stay with yer mother and father a while longer?"

401

Jenny nodded. She wanted to be married to Scout, but didn't want to leave her new parents yet. She had been with them less than a lunar month. She knew her mother still needed her, even though she now had another daughter to help with the cooking and cleaning and babies.

"You can stay with us, too, if you'd like," she said, hoping she hadn't spoken too many words. Then she leaned in and kissed her husband again like he had showed her. She liked having a husband to kiss.

### ***66 Another Mystery

Leah stroked James's forehead with the pink terrycloth washcloth her mother had given her—a keepsake from Mom's trip to the 21st century and Leah's former place of employment, Moses H. Cone Memorial Hospital.

They were both exhausted—it had been a long day for everyone—but it was still too hot to sleep. They lay on a quilt on the floor, taking turns swiping the moist cloth across each other's face and neck. The evaporative effect was temporary, but welcome just the same. She dipped the cloth in the clay bowl, swished it around to suck up more of the cool well water, squeezed it out, and began lightly brushing it across his chest, zig-zagging down slowly to his belly button.

"Now, how is it that your Uncle Julian is related to you?" she asked, resisting the urge to flick his firm, dark nipple.

James grabbed her hand before she followed through with her impish prank. "My turn," he said. "Hand me the cloth."

Leah stood up, but held the rag tight. "Shoot, it's too hot even for this." She pulled the Mickey and Minnie Mouse nightshirt off over her head and tossed it on her pile of skirts and shoes. "I know, I know," she replied to James's unspoken admonition, "life starts early in the country. I'll wake up earlier still and throw it on again before Jody or Wallace or Julian come in. If the chickens wake them up, I'm sure they'll wake me up, too."

"It's the roosters, not the hens, who are the alarm clocks. Here, give me that cloth before it gets too warm in your hand."

Leah twirled the pink remnant from her mother's former robe in the air like a lariat, then tossed it at his head. He reflexively put his hand in front of his face and grabbed it before it made contact. "Not quite a pillow fight," he said, then dabbed it on the back of his neck, "but definitely cooler. Lie down before I change my mind and go to sleep."

Leah gracefully transitioned from standing to reclining on her back. "Lots of yoga," she said. She put her hands behind her head, presenting her entire nude torso to him. "And no fair tickling, either. I want to relax enough to sleep."

James used the corner of the washcloth like a stylus, dragging it across her collarbones then down between her breasts. "More cloth," she mumbled, eyes shut in concentration. He opened it out and, using both hands, draped it down her chest, switching it back and forth sideways to cool the underside of her still perky breasts.

She opened one eye. "I'm glad I don't have big, saggy boobs. I'd get a rash there for sure…"

James distracted her with a kiss to her tummy. He couldn't help it. She had absolutely beautiful breasts, but her belly mound seemed to be

403

calling for his attention. "How long do you think it will be before we have children?" he asked, trying not to sound too anxious.

"I don't know. I might be pregnant already and we just don't know it yet. I mean, we were sure going at it enough..."

James continued his gentle kisses, the cloth laying unemployed between her breasts. "Hey, hey, hey," Leah said. "It's too hot for that. And like I said, I might already be pregnant."

James sat upright, a scowl on his face. "If you think the only reason I want to make love to my wife is to get her with child, you are sincerely mistaken."

"Good Lord, I hope not. And the operative words in that statement are 'make love,' not have sex or carnal knowledge, or...or..." Leah looked over and saw that James was giggling like a child. "Yeah, you got me," she said, realizing that he had been joking.

"I certainly do," he said, and planted a quick kiss on her belly. "And as for Uncle Julian, his brother, my great-grandfather Anthony, was the start of my line. Or at least, the continuation of the line from the early 1700s. Uncle Julian's line stopped with his stepson, Lord Urquhart, Viscount Cavendish—that would be Wallace. It was assumed he died in the war since he simply disappeared while in His Majesty's service."

Leah reached up and stroked the sparse, dark hairs on his chest. "Bibb told me before she left that her genealogy chart, as far back as she had been able to trace it, was in the safe that the MacLeods broke into. They didn't find any money or deeds in it, so tossed everything in a trash can and set it on fire, laughing as she pled with them not to, that there were important, precious papers and family photos in there. She didn't have the family tree memorized, but said there was something about a Scout and Genevieve in the late 1700s. She also said she was pretty sure their last name was Pomeroy-Hart..."

James sighed deeply then lay back beside her. "I don't know the connection, and I forgot about asking Marty about it before he...he...left." He gulped back his feeling of abandonment, then continued. "There is a small fortune in a safe deposit box in London. Only the first-born males in the family line know about it. Hmm, I don't know if Bruce knew about it, but since he was Marty's first born from his marriage to Teighlor, he probably did. It's in Billy's care now. Anyhow, I was made aware of it at a relatively early age, probably to encourage my curiosity with the Hart part of the name. You did know that Marty manipulated me on purpose, right? Made me curious about Julian Hart and his line?"

Leah nodded, lips pressed tight so she didn't tell him to knock it off and get over it. He continued. "I wound up getting married, briefly, but not briefly enough. When that skank of the female persuasion cleaned out all she could and then tried for the rest of the family assets through the courts, I never became desperate. Shoot, even if I had been left with nothing but my skivvies, it would have been better than having *her* in my life. But I digress. I always knew that no matter how much money was gone, I still had the Pomeroy-Hart fortune."

Leah's eyebrows raised, but she remained mute. *The Pomeroy-Harts have money?*

"I know," James said and matched her eyebrow movement. "They sure don't look like they have much now. I can't be sure they're the same Pomeroy-Hart line, and that I am a long distant relative of your mother and therefore of you. No, we're not kissing cousins," he said and gave her a quick 'cousinly' kiss. "I don't know when the funds were first deposited. I didn't ask nor did I have a reason to. I don't see any Genevieves or Scouts around, either." He sighed. "I guess if it *is* this family that becomes rich, it will be a generation or more down the line. In the meantime, we'll all work hard, hopefully eat well—and keep out of musket ball range—and live long, eventually prosperous lives."

~END of AYE, I AM A FAIRY~

## Preview of *The Great Big Fairy* follows:

# The Great Big Fairy
## *1 I'm Benji: Where's Leah?

*August 17, 2013*
*Greensboro, North Carolina*
*Police Department*

Billy sighed deeply, fingering the letter the mop-haired boy had brought to him earlier. He agreed with James. The young man might be a MacLeod, but he certainly didn't resemble his brothers in anything but the overabundance of hair. The courteous young man had asked if he needed him to wait while he read the letter. Billy assured him that it wasn't necessary and even offered him a tip. 'No,' the lad had said. He was just performing a service for a very nice man, and he had already been paid. He had paused before he left.

"If I didn't know better, I'd swear that James was your brother. You sure look alike." He shook his head and let himself out of Billy's office. "Nah, couldn't be," he said to himself, as he walked out the door, "'cause James is a British lord or somethin'—some kind of royalty, I think."

Billy slipped the letter containing the contact list of who to trust and who to watch out for into the top drawer of his desk. Some of the names he recognized, others had English addresses and phone numbers. They weren't important now, but might be in the future. He'd investigate them tomorrow.

He was finally finished with his paperwork. It had been a long night. James and Leah had left only an hour and a half ago, and unless something drastic occurred—and he didn't even want to speculate on that possibility—he would never see his newfound brother or sister-in-law/best friend again. But, now he, Billy Burke the lifelong orphan, had a mother, and that was a blessing he had stopped hoping for about fifteen years ago. He also knew who his father was and, although he might never be able to meet the elusive Marty Melbourne, he could find out more about him from his mother, the sweetest woman in the world, Bibb Stephens.

There was no reason for him to delay his final task. It was time to head out of town and pick up his going-away present from James: the 'Beast,' a classic 1964 red Dodge pickup truck. He'd get one of the officers to drop him off near the site—he wouldn't have to give him an explanation. That would make the task easier, but he still wasn't ready to admit the finality of their departure. He already missed them both and actually hurt physically from their absence. The ache of emptiness went from his shoulders to his kneecaps and made it feel like his spine was an iced-up rope, just dangling down through his midsection, holding his pelvis to his

406

collarbones. He snorted. Leah would have told him that that was anatomically impossible, but that *was* how he felt.

He gathered up the piles of reports, straightened the edges by banging them just a little too hard on the top of the desk, and tugged at the drawer with more force than necessary. It felt like his left hand had four thumbs as he fumbled through the dividers. He finally found the file for the case and tossed it in like a shovelful of coal into a furnace, messing up the neat pile that he had just put it into. "That's enough of you!" he said. Hopefully, he would never hear the name Atholl MacLeod again.

"Sir, there's someone here to see you. He says it's very important," Dyane called over the intercom.

"Have Sergeant Carter take care of it, will you? I'm off shift now," he replied with exasperation. He realized it was the wrong tone, but it was better than the one he was holding back. He didn't know if he wanted to scream or laugh or cry. But he did know that work was not the place to let loose. He stood up to leave, then scanned the remaining papers still on his desk, making sure they were devoid of anything that would remind him of his time traveling family when he came back to work that evening.

"Sir," Dyane called back, "He says it's about someone named Evie and her daughter Leah, the nurse. He says you'll know who he's talking about."

Billy went weak in the knees, then everywhere else. Fortunately, his chair, strategically placed, caught him as he plopped down in a solid, controlled fall. He swallowed hard, started to speak, but only an embarrassing squeak came out. He tried again. "Send him in," he said, this time the words coming together and finding a way out of his mouth.

Dyane opened the door for the large visitor. Billy stood up and his eyes widened as they watched the man duck his head in order to enter the office. He wasn't the tallest man he had ever seen—he had met a couple of the gangly basketball players with the Hornets—but he was the biggest in terms of being a proportionately built man. Billy quickly tipped his head down when he realized he was staring. He walked around to the front of his desk and shook the hand of the huge man with auburn red hair. He glanced up again and the gentle giant grinned and whispered, "Six seven," like he was sharing a secret.

Billy pointed to the chair, offering his congenial new acquaintance a place to sit, then walked back around his desk, touching its surface as much for reassurance that he was awake as for physical support lest he fall down from shock. He sat down slowly in his seat, his head bowed down, concentrating on the desktop. He didn't think he could make the transition from standing to sitting while looking into the face of this big man.

"I didn't mean to stare," Billy apologized, as he looked up again. "It's just that you remind me of someone. All you're missing is the Scots accent." Billy couldn't help but think of the man's resemblance to Jody Pomeroy of the *Lost* novels. If James and Leah had just gone back to his time—the 18th century—could it be that Jody Pomeroy had come back here, to this time? He fought back the urge to shake his head 'no' in answer to his own unspoken question and smiled nervously.

"Weel, I guess I lost a bit of the accent since I've been back here in North Carolina. Now, that bein' said, are ye the one to talk to about Leah and Evie?"

"Who *are* you?" Billy asked incredulously before he answered the Jody look-alike's question.

"I'm sorry. I dinna introduce myself. I'm Benjamin MacKay, but ye can call me Benji."

Billy nodded his head slowly in answer to Benji's question about being familiar with Leah and Evie. He didn't even try to talk lest the sounds come out as the 'baa, baa, babble' that were coursing through his brain. He'd read all of the Lisa Sinclaire novels at least once. Benji was Jody Pomeroy's grandson and he was now sitting in front of him, all grown up. He was supposed to be a fictional character!

"Weel then, I hope it's not too late to catch a ride back with Leah. I got distracted with a couple of unsavory characters. But, it seems that ye've helped me quite a bit and have the MacLeod brothers out of my hair now. I, um, *heard* that Leah was goin' *back* to see her mother soon. I understand she knows how to, um, *travel* safely and without a lot of pain involved?" he asked rather than stated, focusing on Billy's eyes for his reaction.

Benji could see by the detective's wide-eyed and slack-jawed appearance that Billy understood what he was talking about. He waited for his reply, but the stunned police officer just sat at his desk, palms flat as if he was holding down the wooden furniture, and shook his head back and forth slowly. "You're too late," he whispered, his head still moving at the same, slow pace. "About two hours too late. They've already gone."

Benji winced, shut his eyes, and shook his head with a look of sadness and frustration. "Jest two hours…" He exhaled. "Um, do ye happen to ken how they traveled?" he asked tentatively.

Billy pinched the bridge of his nose then spread his thumb and index finger out over his eyebrows, rubbing them back and forth in a nervous manner. He wanted to delay the answer. He didn't know if this Benji, this 21st century Benji, was a good person or not. Could it be that he was in with the MacLeods? Before he could answer, he heard the cautious question.

"Are ye related to Marty Melbourne, per chance?"

Billy's head snapped to attention, the fog of indecision blown away with the hurricane force of the shocking inquiry. "Why?" was all that he could think to reply.

Benji chortled. "Weel, ye must be then or ye woulda answered 'who' or 'no.' Ye look jest like him, have his same nervous habit of pinchin' yer eyebrows, and I'll wager if ye had the English accent, ye'd sound jest like him, too. But, yer not his grandson James, are ye? I mean, yer an American and an officer of the law. He's a member of parliament and a businessman."

Billy drew a deep breath, making the snap, gut decision that this was a good man and could be trusted. "James is my brother and Marty is my father," he said. He started to say more of their relationship, but stopped. He'd let Benji talk and see how much he knew.

"Ye said 'they' went back, not jest Leah. Who went with her?" Benji asked.

"James did. He's her husband now. I don't think he would have let her go by herself. He was quite smitten with her. They only knew each other two weeks, but as soon as I saw those two together, I knew it wouldn't be too long and... Hey, how did you know Leah went back?" Billy asked, losing his original train of thought. This man was sharp and didn't miss a word.

"I read about it in a letter," Benji said plainly. He opened his mouth to say more then decided he'd wait to see if this American was going to let something slip. He wanted to know how much he knew before talking about time travel to a total stranger.

But, Billy was smart, too. He was also playing the 'show me your cards and I'll show you mine' game. "So, how do you know Marty Melbourne?" he asked with a glint in his eye, letting the big Scot know that they were playing mental poker.

Benji grinned and replied, "Ye make a livin' out of this, aye? I mean, jest any little thing a man says ye can use to find out more about a situation."

Billy pointed to the first part of the nametag on his desk. "It says detective, aye? So how do ye ken him?" he asked, mimicking Benji's accent.

"He came to our place when I was much younger. He and my father talked fer quite a while. Ye see, my father had read a letter about a James Melbourne and was tryin' to find him. He dinna ken much about him or his family, but what he kent was enough. It turns out that both men were lookin' fer each other. My father was writin' a book about, um, writin' a book that interested Lord Melbourne and the two actually took a trip here to North Carolina in the early 90's. Young James and I came with them."

Billy decided to lay out a card and see if he could gain Benji's confidence. "So was the book about," he paused then made eye contact with the large red-haired man, "about time travel?"

"What?" his new acquaintance laughed, "Do ye believe in that nonsense?"

But Billy could tell that Benji was just having fun with him. The walls were down and they were both now comfortable. "So, does this mean that you've traveled and it was painful? I mean, you mentioned Leah finding a way to travel without pain."

Benji rolled his eyes. "Ye have no idea how painful. I was only a lad, but I get the cold goose flesh jest thinkin' about it. I guess this means ye never went, um, back?"

"No, I'm sort of new to all of this. Have you had breakfast yet? I'm just getting off work and I think we have a lot to talk about."

~End of preview~

# Thanks in no particular order

I'd like to thank some of the following for their help, great products, books, songs, or general inspiration:

Elaine Boyle, for her personal insight into North Carolina, her editing skills and ability to spot the missed transitions and inconsistencies.

Thanks to Tori Sexton, a current resident of North Carolina and avid time travel fan. Tori has been proofing my stories for years and finds the faintest boo boos that others miss.

Lennon & McCartney for their songs, including 'Good Morning, Good Morning' and 'Yellow Submarine,' great songs for wake-up tunes on an alarm clock and 'She Came in Through the Bathroom Window,' just because it was so appropriate for the story.

The Clark Sisters for their inspirational hymn "I'm Looking for a Miracle," a tune so powerful that even amnesia couldn't erase it.

Carhartt Company® for making such tough work wear. My former Alaskans call them 'Carhartts' just like the rest of us up here.

Leatherman Tool Company®, makers of many different styles of multi-tools. A favorite for all of my 21$^{st}$ century characters and me.

Lamy® for producing pens so outstanding, they're referred to by brand name.

Glenturret® Distillery for creating fine whisky for over 200 years.

Levi's® jeans and shirts. Always winners and with international appeal.

Florsheim®. First class footwear of the professional class.

The Clark Sisters, for their inspirational song, 'I'm Looking for a Miracle,' so profound, an intense case of amnesia couldn't stifle it.

J.J. Abrams and Star Trek the Movie™ for Spock's quote on impossibilities and improbabilities, originally penned by Arthur Conan Doyle for the Sherlock Holmes novel, 'The Sign of Four.'

Diana Gabaldon. Several years ago, I took to heart her suggestion to write. I did and found an incredible peace. Now I wake up smiling and go to sleep the same way, my babies—my fictional family—growing and developing in my head rather than my womb. They're with me at my keyboard as I introduce them to new people, new adventures, more mysteries, and help them into and out of predicaments.

And an extra heap of thanks to Diana for penning Outlander™, the inspiration for Lisa Sinclaire's 'Lost' novel, the story Evie somehow fell into. Ms. Gabaldon's readers may notice similarities with a few of her characters and 'the fictional' people of the 'Lost' novels who my Evie character found to be real. Of course, they aren't the same people. Who knows, though? Maybe time travelers Sarah, Claire, Evie, James, and Leah were neighbors?

Rodgers & Hammerstein's 'Some Enchanted Evening' from South Pacific. ™ The song still echoes in my head, at times.

'The Way Things Work,' by David Macaulay, one of Leah's favorite books.

And of course, thanks to the most perfect man in the world, Marty Haviland, my husband. Your encouragement, faith, and patience are worth more than the Pomeroy-Hart fortune and a number one spot on the New York Times Best Seller List.

## More time traveling 'fairies' in THE FAIRIES SAGA:

**NAKED IN THE WINTER WIND** Amnesia, Abandoned, Adoptions. Read how it all begins here. A rather lengthy novel

**HA'PENNY JENNY** Learn a little bit more about the young girl who's been adopted into our time-traveling family. Novella

**DANCES NAKED** the Cherokee call him.
Marty Melbourne has his challenges and frustrations in 18th century North Carolina Cherokee country. How can—and will—he get back to the 21st century? Novel

**LITTLE BEAR AND THE LADIES** The bachelor trapper is suddenly overrun with females! 18th century novella.

**THE GREAT BIG FAIRY,** 6'7" Benji MacKay, wants to return to the 18th century and his beloved grandfather, Jody Pomeroy. Can anything— or anyone—stop him? Lengthy novel

**LITTLE DRUMMER BOY** Young Scout is on his own again, trying to make his way in a man's world. 18th century novella

**CHASING CHRISTMAS** Family dynamics change with the arrival of new family members at the small early American household. Novella

**NEVER TOO YOUNG** Scout returns after his time away from Jenny. 18th century novella

**TIME IN A LITTLE BLUE BOTTLE** An odd young couple meet in the search for the bottle of Fountain of Youth elixir. Sweet romance mash-up.

# Other books and series by Dani Haviland

## Arlie Undercover series

A Stingray Christmas

The Biggest Heart Ever

Always a Bigger Fish

How to Fix a Broken Life

## Benji the Early Years:

Pool Boy Wanted: No Experience Preferred

Luke the Unexpected

## Unaffiliated Books (not in any series)

One Arctic Summer

Be My Angel

Three Are One

The Polar Xpress

Kit Kringle: An Alaskan Tale

# FIND DANI HAVILAND:

Website: www.danihaviland.com

Amazon Author page: http://bit.ly/dhAuthor

BookBub: http://bit.ly/BBDani

Facebook: Dani Haviland Author

Twitter: @dani_haviland

email: dani@danihaviland.com

# Cast of Characters (*your easy to find page*)

**Bibb Stephens** ~ 21st century property/mill owner
**Big Bill Leuga** ~ friendly acquaintance, 18th century
**Billy** ~ Greensboro police detective, 21st century
**Captain Atholl MacLeod** ~ evil, phony Redcoat officer
**Clark** ~ motel clerk, youngest brother in 21st century MacLeod family
**Eight** ~ Atholl Grant MacLeod, the Eighth. 21st century
**Evie** ~ 20th century-born older woman, transported back to 18th century, has amnesia, now in young body due to an overdose of Fountain of Youth Water, Wallace's wife.
**Frankie** ~ 21st century waitress
**Gibson** ~ store owner, 18th century
**Ian Kincaid** ~ 18th century backwoodsman, aka Starwalker
**JB** ~ James Bradford, sly 21st century valet in London
**James Melbourne** ~ young British Lord, 21st century
**Jenny** ~ preadolescent girl, 18th century, adopted by Evie and Wallace
**Jody Pomeroy** ~ 18th century patriarch, Wallace's father
**José** ~ Spanish emigrant, 18th century
**Julian Hart** ~ British Lord, 18th century, Wallace's stepfather
**Leah** ~ 21st century daughter of Evie
**Marty Melbourne** ~ Melbourne patriarch, time traveler
**Master Simon** ~ time traveler 18th & 21st centuries
**Mrs. Donaldson** ~ 18th century homemaker
**Niner** ~ Atholl Grant MacLeod, the Ninth. 21st century
**Peter Anthony** ~ insurance adjuster, 21st century
**Ric Smith** ~ helpful 21st century postal worker, London
**Richard Short** ~ local troublemaker, 18th century
**Sarah Pomeroy** ~ Jody's wife, 20th century-born time traveler, healer, living in 18th century
**Wallace** ~ 18th century British soldier, Julian's stepson
**Wee Ian** ~ also known as Scout, about 11 years old, 18th century